# THE
# GUN
# TRIAL

# Books by Dale E. Manolakas
http://www.dalemanolakas.com

**Rogue Legal Thriller Series**
*Hollywood on Trial*
*Rogue Divorce Lawyer  A Legal Thriller*
*Rogue Lawyer to the Stars  A Legal Thriller*

**Sophia Christopoulos Legal Thriller Series**
*Lethal Lawyers  A Legal Thriller*
*The Gun Trial A Legal Thriller*

**Veronica Kennicott a Cozy Mystery Series**
*Hollywood Plays for Keeps  A Cozy Mystery*
*Death Sets Sail  A Cozy Mystery*
*Box Set of Hollywood Plays for Keeps & Death Sets Sail  Cozy Mysteries*

*http://www.DaleManolakas.com*

# THE
# GUN
# TRIAL

Dale E. Manolakas

**THE GUN TRIAL**

This book is a work of fiction. Names, characters, businesses, organizations, places, events, and incidents either are a product of the author's imagination or are used fictitiously. Any resemblance to actual persons, living or dead, events or locales is entirely coincidental. All characters appearing in this work are fictitious. Any resemblance to real persons, living or dead, is purely coincidental.

FIRST EDITION
Library of Congress Control Number: Pending
eISBN 978-1-62805-009-7 (e-publication)
ISBN   978-1-62805-010-3 (Paperback)
ISBN   978-1-62805-011-0 (Audio)

# DEDICATION

For Roy

# PREFACE

*The Gun Trial* was inspired by a real California appellate case *Jacoves* v. *United Merchandising Corp.* (1992) 9 Cal. App.4th 88, 11 Cal. Rptr.2d 468.

# PROLOGUE

## Almost Nowhere

*"American cities are like badger holes, ringed with trash . . ."*
-John Steinbeck

Bakersfield. The parched southern terminus of California's great Central Valley. Its heart beating to the regrets and sorrows of country music. Music imported with the 1930s flood of Dust Bowl migrants from Oklahoma, Arkansas, and Texas. A place redolent of Big Oil, Big Agriculture, and recurrent civic corruption. A town, not unlike so many others across the United States of America, where the Second Amendment's right to keep and bear arms is sacrosanct.
A city historically populated by gun enthusiasts, with shooting contests for kids, 4-H youth gun programs, and gun associations awarding thousands of dollars in college scholarships.

To be fair, though, Bakersfield is also prominent on more than its share of the "top ten" lists for cities—the bad ones. Worst for women and kids. Most polluted. Highest alcohol consumption. Most liver-related deaths. Highest rate of officer-involved fatalities. Lowest health care satisfaction. Worst car theft rates. Lowest credit scores. Worst for small-business employees. Worst in the state for youth homicides. A city whose residents are amongst the country's least educated and least literate.

In other words, a virtual paradise—for snakes, scorpions, and tumbleweeds.

But not for Mike Holt.

⌘

# CHAPTER 1

## The Sun, The Gun, And Other Things

*". . . from my cold dead hands."*
-Charlton Heston

Mike Holt parked his dusty blue Bronco at a strip mall on Ride Street in southwest Bakersfield. His preowned sixteenth-birthday wheels, Mike's sidekick through high school, had stayed home unused his freshman year at Yale. Reunited this summer break, Mike sat alone clutching its steering wheel—windows up, AC spitting, engine sputtering. He stared over the black, sun-cracked dashboard at Sports Gear USA, its windows popping product.

"Come on. Get out." Mike turned the engine off but ignored his own command.

With no AC, the afternoon June sun soon boiled the Bronco's innards.

"Shit." Mike wiped his forehead—sweated from the heat and his mind.

Forced out, Mike paced along a strip of shade by the windows, studying the double glass doors. The high-volume nationwide chain peddled it all: fitness equipment, bright clothes, athletic gear, and hunting supplies—including the best-priced guns and ammo in town.

"Fuck it." He shoved his trembling fingers through his dark hair and rubbed the sweat on his worn jeans.

Mike reached for the doors as two teenage girls burst out, clanging the hanging bells. Their tanned skin was barely covered by cutoffs and tube tops. Mike held the door.

Ignoring his chivalry, they darted across the sun-baked asphalt to their shiny red Toyota Tacoma.

Mike stared at the tight, white half-moons peeking out beneath their frayed cutoffs.

In their hormonal wake, the taller blonde glanced back, locking on Mike's leer—expected and enticed.

He turned away from the exposed summer flesh and his own unbridled thoughts.

* * *

In the store, Mike strolled the narrow aisles. The middle-aged manager, Arnie Davis, watched him handling pricey items and eyeing the gun cases, register, and surveillance camera.

"Excuse us, buddy." A father interrupted Mike's reach for a Cold Steel Bowie knife.

"Sure." Mike baby-stepped back, forcing the father to squeeze by, dragging his excited prepubescent son clutching his a new skateboard.

A nearby young store clerk stopped restocking hoodies.

"Can I help you there? I'm Brandon." The eager new hire pointed at the nametag pinned to his blue T-shirt with Sports Gear USA splashed chest-high in red.

"No."

Brandon asked to help Mike several times and in several ways. Ignored and defeated, he retreated to restocking.

With that, the manager, who had profiled Mike as a shoplifter, took him on.

"Need something?" Arnie eyed Mike's pockets and his lean waist tented by a wrinkled orange button-down.

They glared at each other—both silent.

Mike broke the standoff. He turned his pockets inside out. Then, he lifted his shirt, exposing nothing but his nineteen-year-old washboard abs—white from his Yale winter.

"What can we do for you?" Arnie was unapologetic and unconvinced.

"I want a shotgun." Mike lowered his shirt.

"Over there in the corner. Moss and Joe will help you."

"Whatever." Mike stuffed his pockets back in and turned.

Arnie lifted his belt, but it slid back down under the weight of his beer belly—shrink-wrapped in his blue T-shirt.

\* \* \*

In the corner, Moss Grimick and Joe Spangler, in faded tees with cracked Sports Gear logos, leaned on the long glass gun case flipping pamphlet pages. Behind them were locked racks of rifles and shotguns.

"Damn, look at the fat price of that hunt'n camp." Moss scratched his bald crown shining above the shaggy brown hair vining his ears.

"Montana's are the best." Joe's straggly graying ponytail skimmed the page.

"Hey, I'm going on break." Arnie pantomimed a smoke. "Help that guy with a shotgun."

The lean, weathered clerks sized up Mike as he approached. Then, the hard sell began.

Brandon sidled up near the cash register to listen and learn. Gun and ammo sales were where the fun was—and the real money.

\* \* \*

Twenty minutes later, Arnie came back across the parking lot with a Coke from the nearby liquor store. He passed Mike sitting in his Bronco—window cracked, revving his sputtering engine.

"Turn off the air 'til she's warmed up." Arnie blinked a chipped-tooth smile of nicotined teeth. "And wash her."

In the searing Central Valley heat wave, the men locked eyes again.

Mike revved his engine in defiance. There was a wild unsettling ferocity in his deep blue eyes. This time, Arnie broke the staredown, retreating into the store.

Mike peeled out—white smoke spewing from the exhaust, and AC mingling with the molten air.

\* \* \*

Arnie went back to the gun counter. "That kid's gone."

"We heard," Joe said.

"Somethin's off with him." Arnie slurped his Coke. "Strange look in his eyes."

"Ah, he's got a big bitch up his butt." Moss put a cigarette behind his ear for his break.

"What'd he buy?"

"Cheapest Mossberg 12-gauge and a box of shells." Joe's smirk creased his leathery face and flashed his yellow teeth. "The stupid idiot wanted to buy one."

"One what?"

"Shell," Joe said. "Dumb shit."

"Ammo by the piece." Moss sneered and returned to the pamphlet.

"That's crazy. Hell, we get loonies, but first time for that." Arnie turned and saw Brandon at the register. "What are you do'n there?"

"Noth'n."

"Get back to stocking." Arnie manned the register.

"Couldn't unload a carrying case on him neither," Joe said.

"Forget about him. Look." Moss elbowed Joe. "That Montana camp's next month. Let's close that deal on those guns in your garage. We'll go."

"Shut up, you idiot. Not here."

\* \* \*

At home, Mike sat on his unmade bed in his room surrounded with Stockdale High School keepsakes: debate plaques and trophies, pictures of girls not dated, track team photos, his senior first-place all-state medal in the quarter mile, and a copy of his class valedictorian graduation speech, framed and hung by his mother.

Mike's eyes traveled to his open closet door. His Yale duffel bag, still stuffed with freshman laundry, was where he had thrown it two weeks before along with his Yale umbrella—needed too much this past year.

He loaded his new shotgun and went into his closet. He parted the hanging clothes and sat on the floor between them. His high school varsity letterman jacket swept his shoulder.

"Stay." Mike shoved it back, resisting the pull of its memories.

As he sat, the smell of the closet repelled him—it smelled of him.

He grabbed the umbrella, slid the shotgun butt against the wall, and clamped it with his tennis shoes, cracked by Connecticut's snow. He braced it between his knees, shoved the barrel into his mouth, and let loose a primeval scream that would have brought his parents running, had they been home.

Without hesitation, as planned, the rubber tip of his umbrella pushed the trigger—hard and fast.

A blood-red shower burst over his orange button-down.

⌘

# Chapter 2

## A Clash of Colleagues

*"The business of lawyers is to talk, to interrupt one another,
and to devour each other if possible."*
-Joyce Carol Oates

"Quiet. Quiet."

Rona Krause, short but mighty, beat her knuckles at the head of a battered oak table. She fought for control over six lawyers whose debate had morphed into a war in the firm's crowded conference room.

"One at a time."

Rona, raised Beverly Hills Jewish, had founded Krause & White, a downtown Los Angeles startup, with her law school classmate and friend Derek White. Rona prided herself on their mission to help wronged, powerless plaintiffs get justice against the powerful. At least, she wanted to pride herself on that. These days, they took on almost any case that paid the bills, from collections to dog bites.

"Take your turn and stop shouting." Rona rapped harder on the table with her sore knuckles.

Not one of the lawyers obeyed—not Derek, the three senior associates, or the two first-year hires.

"We're not taking on the Holts's gun trial. And that's final." At the *other* head of the table, Derek rose to his full six feet, four inches as he slammed his fist down, silencing the fracas. "It'll bleed us dry. It's a loser. The law's against us."

"Derek, sit down," Rona said.

Rona was in charge of the Monday-morning business meetings. In fact, she was in charge of every meeting—boring, harmonious, contentious, or nuclear. Lately, the tighter the budget, the more the meetings had degenerated.

"Deep pockets or not," Derek said, "Sports Gear legally sold that guy the shotgun, and he offed himself. That's the law. Justice is great as long as there's a check attached, and there won't be here."

"There *will* be a check. A big one, if that's all you care about." Sophia Christopoulos's dark Greek eyes danced like flames. "Look, bartenders can be held liable for serving drunks. Why not gun sellers for selling to the suicidal? I found analogous cases, and we can create new law . . . better law here in California. It'll put us on the map."

"Create new law? Put us on the map? It will wipe us off. It's a time-eating loser. It'll bankrupt us," Derek, a striking, charismatic black man, thundered with finality. "No gun trial. That's it."

Sophia had come to Krause & White from Thorne & Chase—a powerful New York-based law firm and defender of corporate America worldwide. When its L.A. office closed amidst scandal, criminal indictments, and lawsuits, Rona, Sophia's law school classmate and close friend, enticed her to join Krause & White. In turn, Sophia convinced two of her Thorne & Chase friends to follow: Paul Viola, a seventh-year senior associate, and Tricia Manning, a fourth-year.

The three joined what they thought was an idealistic, plaintiff-oriented, and collegial law practice—but found it was an illusion.

"What do you mean, 'that's it'?" Sophia shouted. "That's not *it*. We get to vote."

Krause & White's altruistic bylaws gave each attorney—partner and associate alike—an equal voice and equal vote. Rona and Derek had learned too late that conventional law firm bylaws, granting only partners a voice and vote, were that way for a good reason. But hindsight was always twenty-twenty.

"Vote? Look. We have enough nonbillable bleeding-heart contingency cases on the books sucking up time. We're not taking on a loser against the gun establishment. It'll draw fire from every red-necked Constitution-waving gun crazy."

"Oh, stop with the scare tactics," Paul said.

"Scare tactics?" Derek interrupted. "Pro-gun nuts waving the Constitution and anti-gun wackos tearing it up are all looking for fodder. And we'll be it. The media will eat us alive . . . and for nothing . . . no payout. There's nothing to discuss."

"Look, Derek. I interviewed the Holts on the phone," Sophia said. "They're nice people, and I can . . ."

"Who cares if they're nice?" Derek cut Sophia off. "Sports Gear *legally* sold that kid . . . that man . . . the shotgun. He was nineteen. Who the hell has the money to gamble on making new law, especially in Bakersfield? It's a foreign country to us."

"You two stop." Rona curbed the escalation—or tried.

"What exactly are you saying here, Derek?" Tricia spoke up. "No more cases for deserving plaintiffs? Because that's not why I came to this firm."

"Not losers that are political dynamite."

"Sure, it'll be an uphill battle," Sophia said. "But we'll win, and in the process, we'll all be doing challenging and meaningful work. That's what this firm is about."

Bryce McLaughlin and Eddie Herrera, the two first-years, perked up because that was why they came to Krause & White: to fight for justice and do *real* legal work right away, not just push paper for years, the fate of too many big-firm young lawyers.

"Oh?" Derek said. "And how many nonpaying hours will that meaningful work eat up before your case is dismissed or summarily adjudicated under well-established California law?"

"Put it to a vote. I believe in this firm's democratic process and in justice." Sophia counted on the votes of her friends and the first-years. "I'm not here just to do *your* clients' corporate litigation."

"Let's vote." Tricia backed her friend because she was sick of being a drone for Derek's corporate clients too.

"Now," Sophia demanded over the bang and clang of voices taking sides.

"I'm ready. There's real money in this one. Are you guys up for it?" Paul courted Bryce and Eddie.

"Sounds interesting to me," Bryce said.

"Me too," Eddie agreed. "Will we get to take depositions?"

"Sure," Sophia said, lobbying for their votes with a carrot.

"Stop pandering, Sophia." Derek cowed Bryce and Eddie with an angry glare. "What do they know about the bottom line?"

"Don't bully them," Tricia fired back.

"Then don't lie to them. Paul, you've been at this longer than any of us. You should have more sense."

"I'm with Sophia all the way." Paul looked at this as a game changer and equalizer in the firm's internal power struggle, a way to diminish the increasing iron control of Derek and Rona. "Sophia's last contingency case brought in a chunk of change."

"That was a legal slam-dunk from the Thorne & Chase implode. She discounted our fee to land it," Derek argued. "This time, the law's against her, and I'm not discounting anything."

"There's analogous law," Sophia said. "And no discounts here. We all know Sports Gear shouldn't have sold Mike that shotgun."

"Or what, he wouldn't be dead?" Rona finally weighed in. "Where's the logic in that? I'm with Derek. The parents feel guilty. They want to play the blame game at our expense. Besides, the publicity could be bad for us."

"You're wrong," Sophia said. "It'll be great."

"Great for who?" Derek asked. "Do you even care that some of us have mothers and uncles, brothers, cousins? My people will be at risk if this case hits the news."

"This case is about *legal* gun sales, and no one in South Central *even* follows the news or the law." Sophia stopped and felt her face flush. "God, I didn't mean your relatives, Derek. I'm so sorry."

"Are you?" Derek surged to his full height again, seething with anger.

Derek came from South Central—born and bred—surrounded by illegal guns, gangs, and gun violence—violence Hollywood put on the big screen, fictionalizing and glamorizing and profiting from it. He had worked hard to shed that life and become a lawyer. He lived in the Hollywood Hills now, but his relatives didn't.

"This is not productive," Rona intervened.

"I agree . . . let's take a minute." The oldest and wisest among them at thirty-four, Paul supported Rona's condemnation of the chaos. "Derek, sit down. Please."

Derek did not sit and did not take a minute. "I'm a name partner, and this firm runs on my book of business. Your gun trial is dead, Sophia."

A vacuum of silence gripped the room. Derek's clients had become their bread and butter—thinly sliced and sparsely spread— but they regularly produced enough in fees to cover the firm's monthly nut.

Derek slowly sat, convinced he had prevailed.

* * *

Sophia, Tricia, and Paul had all learned at Thorne & Chase that big-firm power came from a lawyer's client base. They were learning now that small firms were no different. A big book of business made a lawyer mobile—that was the ultimate power, the unwritten rule— such a lawyer could jump to another firm with their business and destroy the one left behind. The three now pushing the Holt case were betting on Derek's loyalty to Rona. His book of business was too small to jump firms *and* take her along with her much smaller client roster.

"You forget my settlement got us this larger office and our great first-years." Sophia flattered Bryce and Eddie to get their vote.

"We'd be better off without either," Derek said.

The two first-years slid down in their chairs.

"Stop." Rona's eyes bored in on Derek.

Derek and Sophia both had gone too far. Bryce and Eddie sat silently—wide-eyed and surprised. The new hires had been a mistake—one born of hope—but a mistake all the same. The growth they planned hadn't materialized, but in fairness, it was too soon to cut Bryce and Eddie loose.

"Everyone, cool down." Derek's rage had blinded him from seeing what they needed—the new associates' votes. "This is tabled until the noon case review meeting Wednesday. Sophia, get a presentation together with the law fully analyzed. Then we'll vote."

"That's less than two days," Sophia protested.

"So what? A loser is a loser." Derek tore out of the room.

Sophia went to her office, Tricia and Paul following.

\* \* \*

In her office, Sophia called the Holts. Two days was very little time to prove she had a viable, profitable case.

"Tomorrow morning at nine then," Sophia said. "And can you bring all the documents you have: police reports, everything you collected?"

After some guarded discussion about the viability of Mike's case, Sophia hung up.

"They're eager," Paul said.

"No kidding. They wanted to drive down today, but I have to refine my research and home in on better case precedent. I made it clear we're still evaluating, didn't I?"

"From this end," Tricia said.

"I have a depo tomorrow in Torrance, but I can help today," Paul said.

"I can too," Tricia said.

"No. You'd have to start from square one. What you guys have to do is to make sure we keep those first-year votes."

"Consider it done," Paul said.

"And clear your calendars. Derek's not blocking this, no matter what."

"Are you sure this is the case to take a stand on?" Tricia asked. "I'd personally like more controls on gun sales, but Derek's going to make this tough. Beyond the finances, he doesn't want to be associated with anything anti-gun."

"Because of his *roots*?" Paul mocked. "Bullshit. It's all about the money with him. He's making a financial power play disguised as personal outrage."

"He's a master of subterfuge," Sophia said. "A phony."

"He weighs in on the side of easy money," Paul said. "All the time now. Not justice."

"Then we make our stand," Tricia agreed.

"If we can take this case all the way," Sophia said, "we'll have our own power and plenty of it."

⌘

# CHAPTER 3

## A Gathering of Gloom

*"A client is to me a mere unit, a factor in a problem."*
-Sir Arthur Conan Doyle

The next morning, despite the California drought, the Holts drove through a now-rare, windy October rain in the Tejon Pass over the Grapevine to L.A. They left Bakersfield early, intent on making the meeting on time, and did.

For clients, first meetings usually begin as therapy sessions, even with corporate clients. For lawyers, though, they are fact-finding missions to assess a case's viability and, more importantly, the client's ability to pay. Or, as here, to weigh the worth of a contingency fee case by balancing the ultimate settlement or judgment against the nonbillable attorney hours spent to get it.

More than a therapy session, Sophia expected a minefield because the Holts's only child had committed suicide. The Holts had already voiced their anger and outrage on the phone—especially at the four Bakersfield lawyers who had dismissively rejected their case, undoubtedly based on hometown politics.

Shortly after nine, the Holts finished the new-client intake form and followed Sophia to her office. Beth was in her late fifties and Wallace over ten years her senior, at seventy-one. Both were retired high school teachers: Beth, English; and Wallace, history.

* * *

The Holts sat anxiously on the edge of their seats in Sophia's tiny office with walls only an arm's length away. The office did not exude the feel of money like her former one at Thorne & Chase, but it did convey a sense of dedication and hard work.

After the niceties, Sophia got straight to the point.

"What are you looking for with this case?"

"Justice for Mike," Beth said.

"We know nothing can bring him back," Wallace added. "We're not . . . irrational."

"But why did they sell him that shotgun?" Beth asked.

"Like I told you on the phone," Wallace said. "They told me Mike was acting odd, that something was wrong with him. They did it for money, and someone has to tell them they're wrong. Stop it from happening again."

"Punish them," Beth said. "With your legal stuff. We don't know how."

Sophia studied the couple. They knew what they wanted in layman's language. They were sincere and lost. Sophia liked them and Sports Gear USA's deep pockets.

"Tell me about the day Mike bought the shotgun and the actual sale," Sophia said.

"If they hadn't sold him that shotgun, he'd be alive today." Beth teared up and reached for the tissues Sophia had placed on her desk. "Mike was a good boy."

"My Beth's right. Mike was a good kid. He was at Yale, you know."

"Yes."

From their telephone discussions, Sophia had learned a lot about Mike. Now, she just wanted her questions answered without extraneous emoting.

"We raised him right." Wallace looked to Sophia for validation. "You would have liked him."

"I'm sure I would have."

Because of the prior rejections, the Holts were desperate. They started spouting torrents of irrelevant facts and moral judgments. Beth, particularly, was overwrought, exponentially off the charts. From their outpourings, Sophia judiciously sifted useful facts, the hard evidence to prove the elements of her well-researched causes of action.

The Holts were riveted on Sophia as if she were a judge and executioner who could lop off the head of Sports Gear, the Goliath that had killed their son.

Of course, she couldn't. She wasn't even their attorney—not literally, figuratively, or legally. Not yet. And she never would be if they didn't settle down and answer her questions.

* * *

"He had his whole life ahead of him," Wallace said.

"I understand. But he did own a gun before, right?"

Beth turned to Wallace with red, tear-stained eyes. "I never wanted you to get him that .22 when he turned twelve."

"I'm sorry," Wallace said. "How many times do I have to say that?"

"I know. I know." But Beth didn't.

Sophia stopped the arguing. "He didn't kill himself with the .22, Beth."

"He couldn't," Wallace said. "I don't even know where that thing is buried in that junky garage after all these years."

"Beth," Sophia explained, "it only meant that Mike faced no ten-day waiting period or required safety exam. He just needed a background check."

"Only a background check? That just can't be right!" Beth shouted. "They can't sell a gun to a boy who wants to kill himself."

"Well put, Beth," Sophia said. "Exactly. Our case is *not* about Mike owning a gun years ago. It's about how Mike was acting at Sports Gear when he bought the shotgun and if it's liable."

"See. That's what we mean . . . liable," Beth parroted.

"You have to tell me all the facts about Mike's *shotgun* purchase so that we can build a good case."

"We understand." Wallace scooted his chair closer to Beth. "Settle down, Beth. See. She's on our side. She's trying."

Wallace's hand shook as he patted Beth's.

"I'm sorry." Beth flashed an embarrassed smile.

"Miss Christ . . . ta . . . palos . . ." Wallace hesitated.

"It's a mouthful. Call me Sophia. Please."

"Of course," Wallace paused. "Sophia, Mike was unhappy. Anyone could see that. His first year at Yale was just too hard on him. The snow. The ribbing about shallow Californians and coming from Hicktown."

"The snobs." Beth wept again. "They looked down on him. How could they?"

"About that day?" Sophia's impatience was mounting.

"Just a couple of more hours and we would have been home. We were shopping," Beth said. "We were having stew, his favorite, for dinner."

They sat, alone but together. Sophia endured their outbursts, thinking they certainly would be sympathetic to a jury and that Wallace was so caring to Beth.

\* \* \*

"Wallace." Sophia wanted facts, not emotion. "On the phone you said the manager and the salesmen told you about that day. What did they say?"

"Of course. Ah, I . . ." Wallace paused.

"Wallace, their statements are admissions against Sports Gear because they're its employees. Did they realize Mike was depressed or acting strangely?"

"Well, the manager said they thought Mike was acting weird and odd and off in the store and in the parking lot after. I mean, um, he said he should have known something was wrong."

"Did he actually say the words 'off' and 'I should have known something was wrong'?"

"Yes. And, oh, he said Mike asked to buy one shell."

"And what about the store clerks?"

"Like I said, they talked about the strange look in his eyes . . . that he was crazy or nuts or loony. I wrote it all down a piece of paper Beth has in that packet so I could remember."

"Good."

"But then they just walked away from me to sell a gun to a customer. That's what they do . . . sell death."

"Yes," Beth interrupted. "And look at that child who killed all the kids at that elementary school."

"Let's stay focused on your son, Beth. Wallace, this is all good, if they'll testify to what they said."

"If?" Beth asked. "They have to, don't they?"

"You mean that the store will make them lie, don't you?" Wallace asked. "Unbelievable. We were even regular customers at Sports Gear when Mike was a kid."

"Let's not worry about that now." Sophia was done. She had enough facts to finish her memo and research. "Can I have the documents you brought?"

"Yes." Beth leafed through the pile. "I gathered everything together. The police report. The 911 call notes. The autopsy report. And hospital records and bills. And Wallace's summary of what those salesmen said. And, oh, the . . ."

"Honey, just give her everything. She can read."

"She has to know what's there," Beth said.

"Don't worry, Beth. I do this for a living." Sophia took the stack. "By the way, have you been in court before, either of you? Or ever had to sue anyone?"

Wallace sat up straight.

"No, of course not. We're good people."

Wallace was so like her father, who had emigrated from a small island in Greece. He would have had the same reaction. Going to court was a badge of shame.

"Yes. I see that. I had to ask."

All lawyers are wary of suit-happy clients for credibility reasons, but also of clients new to litigation because of the time-consuming hand-holding they too often require.

"I'll call if anything else is necessary." Sophia stood. "Let me get to work. I'll figure out exactly what we have here and let you know what we can do."

"Thank you." Wallace stood and helped Beth up. "Take your time."

"I'll go over the documents and get back to you very soon."

"When?" Beth asked.

"By the end of the week." Sophia opened her door. "Thank you for coming in on such short notice."

"Thank you for seeing us." Beth started down the short hall to the reception area.

Wallace hung back. "Like I told you, those other lawyers sent back our papers with a form letter real fast. Please don't do that, for Beth's sake. Wait a week. Let her think you're actually considering taking this on."

"I am."

"I saw the look in your eyes. But that's okay. Just give Beth some time."

Wallace was perceptive. Sophia was concerned about the upside potential and Derek being ultimately right about the case.

"On your intake form, you didn't write who referred you. I don't know anyone in Bakersfield."

"Oh, we remembered you from the news about that big law firm here in L.A. The stories said you were smart. Smart and feisty. We figured you could help us if anyone could."

Sophia watched Wallace walk down the hall to find Beth. He needed a can of oil for his joints and some happy news for his heart.

*Smart and feisty. That, I am*, she thought sitting at her desk.

* * *

Sophia read Beth's packet. She liked Wallace and saw Beth as an eminently compelling plaintiff if properly handled. The Holts reminded her of her own parents, whom she hadn't called for weeks.

She set the papers aside and called her mother. Her father would be at work. He had never missed a day in his life. But her mother would be home cleaning her already immaculate small house and cooking for him as she had cooked for the three of them before Sophia escaped to college.

Escaped was the right word. Her father believed until she was a married woman, she should live at home. Thankfully, her mother backed Sophia. Her father never understood why Sophia didn't stay home with them and take classes. He never would.

"Mom?"

"Sophia! My little *koritsi*." Her mom greeted her "little girl" in broken English.

The familiar life her mother led was centered around family, food, and the Greek Orthodox Church. She was Sophia's constant when life became overwhelming, and even though they rarely discussed anything of note, Sophia happily let her mother chat away. It grounded Sophia, made her mother happy, and beat psychotherapy.

⌘

# CHAPTER 4

## The Long And Lonely Labor of The Law

*"Research is what I'm doing when I don't know what I'm doing."*
-Werner von Braun

Calm and focused, Sophia studied the police report—sparse, shoddy, and *pro forma*. It had the Sports Gear employees' names, but no references to Mike acting strange or off. That wasn't good, but it was so abbreviated that it could be discounted as incomplete. Fortunately, Wallace's notes from his talk with the salesmen and manager were thorough.

Sophia created a chronology of events on her laptop, the first step to organizing any case. She referenced and summarized every document. Her intake interview with the Holts had been predictably volatile, but she had gotten the information required.

She leaned back and smiled. Wednesday, Derek would taste defeat.

\* \* \*

Just before noon, Steve Rutger called. He was Sophia's boyfriend and a Los Angeles police detective moving up the ranks. They had met at Thorne & Chase when she was a first-year associate, and he was in charge of an investigation there. He moved in with her after less than a year of dating.

"Hi. I'm downtown," Steve said. "What about lunch? The Italian place."

"I'd like more than just lunch."

"I can arrange that."

"But . . ."

"Ah, you're a tease."

"That gun case I mentioned? I have to beef up my pitch."

"Get to work then. You can do it."

"Thanks for the vote of confidence."

"Not going well?"

"I don't know. With Derek, everything's a fight."

"You want me to come over and straighten him out man-to-man?"

"No." Sophia laughed. "You're nuts. But so was my client's son. They could have a good case if . . ."

"Hold it," Steve interrupted. "It's work. Gotta go."

"Sure." Work, detective work, was his only priority, after her—most of the time.

"You go get 'em, tiger. And my offer stands with Derek."

"Bye."

Sophia loved him, but her parents didn't. Being from the old country, the island of Chios in Greece, they distrusted all authority, particularly "poli-chee-men." When she brought Steve over for Sunday dinner, her parents were guarded and uncomfortable. In the kitchen, her mom asked her more than once why she had gone to law school and taken on all those student loans just to date a "poli-chee-man." Sophia had no answer for her mom—meaning no answer her mom would understand or accept.

\* \* \*

Sophia skipped lunch and finished integrating the Holts's information into the chronology. Afterward, she looked for additional legal support.

She immersed herself in fast, electronic legal research using the firm's flat-rate, limitless access to Westlaw's computerized legal database. Everything was done electronically at Krause & White. Even with the new offices, there was no space for either file cabinets or law books. The firm was as paperless as possible. Everything was stored on their computers, with scrupulous backups.

After several hours, Sophia could find no California case on point to hold Sports Gear liable. However, she did find well-reasoned cases from other jurisdictions that would be persuasive in a California court. Not one was on "all fours," with a factual situation identical to Mike's, but some were close. Also helpful were cases dealing with "ultrahazardous" products and liability for their sale or misuse. She would also analogize to the well-known "dram shop" laws holding bar owners liable for injuries to third parties caused by drunks who were served too many drinks.

She had enough legal authority to sue Sports Gear for wrongful death, negligence, and negligent infliction of emotional distress.

After additional nonlegal Internet research, she found that she had another negligence argument. Sports Gear, unlike many other gun sellers, had no policy or procedure in place to prevent the sale of a gun to customers like Mike whose behavior was questionable.

Finally, she would bank on the fact that Sports Gear would prefer to settle rather than risk the bad publicity an all-too-public trial would bring.

Sophia concluded the Holt case was a winner and started her memo. Derek would not derail her. This firm wasn't his, not yet.

* * *

There was a tap on Sophia's door, and it swung open. Autumn Raynes, the firm's twenty-year-old, part-time receptionist and part-time student, came in and shattered the intense tranquility of Sophia's research. Autumn always knocked but never waited to enter, bulleting monologues incessantly.

"Derek sent this copy of the monthly budget to everyone." She placed it on the desk with her bangle bracelets clanging.

Autumn's seasonal name came from her commune parents who were hippie-entranced with faux-'60s idealism—over a half-century too late. Today, she had her thin, tall body covered with fringed eclectic layers that shimmied hanging from her crop top over her always-braless breasts. Autumn ran in neutral until she skipped to fourth gear—which is where she was now.

"Thanks." *And no thanks,* Sophia thought.

The tight budget was a financial flare Derek fired over the firm when he wanted his way. Sophia ignored it and returned to her research but braced herself for Autumn's usual spew about her self-indulgent *avant-garde* lifestyle. She loved invading private office ear-space.

"I went down to the Renaissance Festival last weekend." Autumn started. "You should go. It's . . ."

About to kick her out, Sophia was saved by Autumn's reception phone ringing down the short hall. Her phone often rang at the right moment for Sophia and the wrong for Autumn.

"Oops. I'll tell you about it later."

Sophia got up and closed her door after Autumn. She had no time for her or her admittedly sometimes-interesting tales today.

Later, on the way for coffee from the matchbox-size snack room, Sophia saw that Autumn had found another ear to chew before her three o'clock shift ended. It was an eager ear attached to a lonely man—Eddie. He was camped at her always-cluttered desk learning about Autumn's fictional family tree that she had manufactured from Internet misinformation and hope. For months, the entire office had politely tolerated its unfolding and her discovery that her last name went back to the Norman Conquest and meant nobility.

Sophia recognized the obvious—Eddie wanted to endure the blather because it was so charmingly packaged.

* * *

As Sophia drafted her memo, the office slowly emptied. About six o'clock, Paul came in and sat.

"I'm back."

"It's late. Bad deponent or traffic?"

"Both. How's the project? Can I help?"

"No, you'd have to play catch-up. I'm just refining, and then I have to deal with a 1992 case, *Jacoves*."

"There's always one, isn't there?"

"Can you get here early tomorrow and do a final read? Tricia too."

"Sure thing. I'll tell her."

"Thanks." Sophia's exhausted eyes were appreciative, but she didn't have the energy even to smile.

"Don't forget, the most important thing is for you and Tricia to keep Bryce and Eddie's votes."

"Give them a depo or two and they'd vote to represent the Unabomber." Paul closed the door as he left.

Later Tricia stopped by, too. She gave Sophia a doggy-bagged half ham sandwich left over from lunch.

"Anything last minute?"

"I'm dealing."

"I talked to Paul. We'll review the memo and keep Derek from sabotaging us with the first-years. Don't stay too late."

Sophia ate the half sandwich, and it gave her an energy boost.

\* \* \*

At nine her cell chimed with a text from Steve.

"Late night for me. Chinese?"

Sophia texted back. "Late 4 me 2 Chinese :-)"

Evening had turned into night. Night became midnight, then early morning. And the memo emerged—finished and masterful.

It took her some time, but she dealt with her one problem and negated *Jacoves* as controlling law. It was a California Court of Appeal Second District case published in 1992. The appeal court had affirmed the lower court's dismissal of a complaint two parents filed against a store that had sold their son a rifle he used to commit suicide.

The opinion made no sense to Sophia. Justice Margaret Grignon had authored it and cited detailed case law—all of which supported the legal theory that gun sellers could be found negligent for some sales, arguably including one like the shotgun sale to Mike Holt. Then—as other courts across the country had subsequently noted—she ignored all of those cases and held the opposite, thus relieving the gun store of any potential liability.

Presiding Justice Herbert Ashby and Justice Roger Boren were on the three-judge panel and had signed off on the opinion. Why they had baffled Sophia.

Later opinions citing *Jacoves* did not follow its holding but instead cited the very cases discussed in *Jacoves* to support potential gun seller liability. Some judges cited the *Jacoves* holding, but only in minority dissents. The majority in those cases left open the possibility of gun seller liability if a gun buyer had exhibited questionable behavior.

In her memo, Sophia concluded *Jacoves* was an aberration, a case generally ignored or criticized—certainly not controlling law.

\* \* \*

At one-thirty in the morning, Steve texted that he was on the way home with Chinese.

Sophia was done, too. With a few good hours tomorrow—or today as it were—she would be ready. Tricia and Paul's review of her memo would give her last-minute insights or hopefully just an ego boost.

*You're going down, Derek*, she thought as she drove home.

⌘

# CHAPTER 5

## Into the Pink

*"Sex is emotion in motion."*
-Mae West

At home, Sophia threw her purse on her usual living room chair. Her one-bedroom Park La Brea tower apartment near Hancock Park seemed big until Steve moved in. They had planned to get a larger place, but somehow never got around to it.

The cartons of Chinese were on the coffee table.

"Steve?"

There was no answer. She grabbed a beer from the fridge and swallowed its cool relaxation.

In the bedroom, she heard the shower. She didn't hesitate. She took off her clothes and Pied-Pipered to the sound of water pouring over Steve's naked body.

"Hey." Sophia pulled back the pink shower curtain and stood garbed with nothing but an impish smile.

"Hey, yourself." In a millisecond Steve grabbed her waist with his soapy arms and pulled her into the warm streaming water.

In the 1950s pink and green tiled shower, Steve drew her to him. Sophia felt the power of her hold over him and pressed the softness between her hips against him. She reached up and combed her fingers through his wet thick sandy hair. Then, she ran them up Steve's pumped pectorals, over his broad shoulders, and around his neck. He was hard.

The shower ritual had a primitive power of its own every time magnified by the penetrating wetness. They submitted to the magnetic chemistry that controlled them like the centrifugal force of a tornado—raging, lightning-flashing, unpredictable. When they touched, every constraint and convention melted away in their excitement and thirst for consummation—fast, slow, experimental, or efficient. Every time was different and the same. Every time was perfect in its own right. It was something Sophia had never experienced, and, according to Steve, nor had he.

"I love you," Steve said.

He coiled his arms around the small of Sophia's back. Then, his hands dropped down. He massaged and squeezed her tight buttocks with his soapy hands. The shower hit his back and trickled between their bodies. He lifted her. She spread her thighs and embraced his waist with her legs, gripping him hard with her calves.

She was ready for him—soft and wet, open and warm. As he thrust himself into her, she moaned and squealed but only softly in the apartment's quiet early morning hours. She squeezed her thighs and gripped his thick muscular neck as she undulated, pulling him deeper and deeper into her. He held her effortlessly, opening her buttocks and stroking her anus—slow and slippery. She arched her back and presented herself to him. He pushed his middle finger into it. She whined softly and melted her open mouth into his. She came. He came.

On late nights like this, there was no time for their usual foreplay ritual, a ritual embedded with signals. A slow-savored sexual dance, from the first touch to the last sigh, each asked, gave, demanded, and commanded without a word. Each played the other's body with the artistry of a pianist, a punk rocker, a sadist. Their appetites fed on each other.

However, tonight was a straight, slippery, soapy, shower fuck—an art form of its own.

So were the Chinese, the beer, the talk of memos, murders, and mindless pleasures.

* * *

The next morning, Sophia smelled coffee—his homage to her. His offering every morning after was a mug of coffee, whited with half-and-half.

Steve brought two mugs of coffee into the bedroom, moving slowly with his signature catlike walk, smooth and powerful. She had noticed his walk from the first time she met him at Thorne & Chase. He had the stealth of a lion hunting its prey.

"Good morning, beautiful."

Steve was already dressed for work—cheap-suit detective style. Sophia hadn't yet been able to upgrade that.

"Good everything." Sophia smiled.

"Here." Steve leaned over, brushed her forehead tenderly with his lips, and handed her mug to her.

"Thanks."

Sophia felt her body react to him—her nipples hardened under the covers, and her buttocks tingled at the thought of last night's urgent, efficient shower screw. He was hers. He was rugged, tan, and stone-cold handsome.

As he withdrew his weathered, unmanicured hand, he let it sweep over her sheet-covered erect nipples. He smiled. His dark blue eyes twinkled in the morning light as they read her sensuous dark-eyed gaze.

"I can't. I'll be late." He grinned with his perfect white teeth.

"Right." Sophia drank her coffee and then licked the rim slowly with her tongue. "So will I. But . . ."

Sophia put the mug on the nightstand, licked the coffee slowly from her lips, and threw back the sheets. Her smooth, flawless Greek olive skin was silhouetted on the white sheet. She slowly spread her thighs apart, slid her hands down her torso, over her dark tufted mound, and down between her thighs into herself. She was already wet.

He kneeled at the end of the bed, grabbed her ankles, and pulled her down to him, legs spread. He threw her hands away and buried his head and fingers and tongue between her thighs—until she cried out with abandon into the morning light.

⌘

# CHAPTER 6

## The Reckoning Looms

*"Anxiety is the handmaiden of creativity."*
-T.S. Eliot

In her office Wednesday morning, Sophia gave the Holt memo a fresh read. She impressed herself. Perhaps she overstated the estimated settlement amount and likely jury award if it went to trial, but she could be forgiven some puffing.

Sophia emailed the memo to Paul and Tricia and then texted, "Emailed Holt memo. Comments? Plausible upside 5 to 8 mil. Check associate votes while I prep."

A short time later, Paul texted, "Don't change a word. A+ Confirming votes."

Tricia texted, "Great job. We have first-years."

It didn't hurt their lobbying efforts that Derek was prickly and that Rona could not rescue him from his selfish and myopic arrogance.

\* \* \*

Sophia took the memo to Peggy Fitzgerald for copying and distribution. Peggy was a five-on-one assistant, covering Sophia, the two first-years, Tricia, and Paul.

"Good morning. Busy?"

Peggy looked up over her reading glasses from under thick, outdated gray bangs that covered her worry lines and topped her sagging face. She was medium everything—weight, height, and intelligence. Her biggest assets were politeness, consistency, timeliness, and doing what she was told. She was not quick or stellar, but competent. That was enough.

"Good morning. Not too busy for you." Peggy's smile popped of crow's-feet and labial folds.

"Twelve copies? For all the attorneys by ten-thirty?" Sophia smiled. "It's for the noon meeting."

"Sure. It'll be on their desks by ten. The extras for you?"

"Yes. Thanks."

Peggy liked Sophia because she was clear, concise, always professional, and, more to the point, left Peggy alone. Truthfully, Sophia was her favorite because she asked so little of her. She was self-sufficient, unlike the other attorneys.

Peggy was sixty and old-school. She "unretired" after her husband died and she lost her home to a bad variable loan refi. She had also "unretired" her dresses from Sears with matching shoes, vinyl bags, and costume jewelry.

\* \* \*

Back in her office, Sophia shut the door and practiced her pitch. It was logical, authoritative, clear, and, moreover, presented a big financial upside.

Peggy tapped on Sophia's office door and put extra copies on her desk.

"I spell-checked it . . . perfect. The format was fine. It's distributed."

"I appreciate it."

"No problem. It's well done. Clear. A good case." Peggy never offered compliments lightly. "Anything else?"

"That's it. Thanks again."

As Peggy shut the door, she whispered, "Good luck."

Sophia smiled. If her memo resonated with Peggy, then she had expressed her legal theories clearly enough for the average person—and average is what you can expect on a jury. Her litigator's mind was always thinking ahead.

She leaned back a minute to rest her eyes. Flashes of last night's shower and this morning's precoffee pleasures interrupted her focus. She took a deep breath and seized control of her wandering gray matter with a mental slap.

A text chimed from Tricia. "Paul and I confirmed first-years."

"Thnx"

Sophia went obsessively back to Westlaw to keep looking for the needle in the haystack—one California case with the facts to match those in the Holt case.

Just before noon, Paul popped his head into Sophia's office. "Hey, it's time. You ready?"

"Almost. I just want to . . ."

"Your memo is perfect. No more research. Come on."

"So the first-years are with us?"

"Sure. I promised them depos and maybe a witness at trial. They know no first-years at big law firms even get beyond grunt work for years, so they're happy."

"A witness at trial? What have you done? They'll screw it up. I can't . . ."

"Sophia. Stop. We were first-years once. They'll do fine. Besides, we'll have them depose some extra nobodies, and we'll settle before trial anyway."

"Right. Okay. I lost it for a second. Actually, very shrewd."

"Thanks, I think so. You get focused and head down there. Now."

Sophia signed off Westlaw. She gathered her memos and her equilibrium. Sophia was nervous because she was up against Derek—interrupter, yeller, shooter-from-the-hips, and an all around non-analytical reactionary jerk. He was intellectually lazy too; she hoped lazy enough not to beat her over the head with the *Jacoves* case.

The first-years were with her, but she also wanted the dollar estimates in her memo to bring Derek around—and by extension Rona. Harmony was better than harassment.

* * *

On Sophia's way to the meeting, cases and extra memo copies in hand, her cellphone pinged. She looked down.

"Gd luck. Luv u. I got new kill."

They were both professionals who went for the jugular—Sophia as a lawyer and Steve as a homicide detective, seeking justice for the brutally silenced dead. Each new murder was to him a different three-dimensional puzzle that he relished piecing together. He had advanced to sergeant quickly because of his abilities and dedication.

Sophia juggled her papers, texted "luv u 2 thnx," and turned off her phone.

* * *

Sophia took the last seat at the conference table, next to Tricia.

The ice, drinks, and cookie platter were already on the side credenza. Peggy followed Sophia in and set a tray of sandwiches on the conference table. Autumn shadowed Peggy with bags of chips in a bowl.

"Let me help you." Eddie jumped up and chivalrously took the featherweight bowl from Autumn—like the kiss-up kid in your sixth-grade class.

"Sure." Autumn, oblivious to Eddie's attentions, left with Peggy.

"Someone's in love," Tricia whispered to Sophia.

Eddie, Eduardo Emanuel Navarro Herrera, was eight months into his first year at Krause & White along with Bryce. Eddie's heritage was Latino on his father's side and German on his mother's. He skimmed the six-foot mark. He was striking rather than handsome, with his mother's hazel eyes, his father's thick black hair, and a café latte complexion blended from both. While usually pleasant, he had a hot temper—sometimes useful, sometimes not.

"Hurry up. Let's get started." Derek sat down with his lunch. "Let's dispose of Sophia's gun case."

"We'll update our pending matters first." Rona didn't want the meeting fractionalized until old business was out of the way. "Can everyone get seated?"

As the sandwiches disappeared and chips crunched, the attorneys in charge of each case gave their respective status reports.

"Then it seems that none of our contingency cases are close to resolution." Rona looked around the table. "No settlements or trials.

So Derek's right. People, we must focus on our paying billable matters. Ratchet them up and get those hours recorded so we can bill the clients."

The air of financial desperation dominoed from Rona around the small conference table with uneasy looks and murmurs.

"Wait." Paul finished chewing. "My Zeigler contingency. After Tuesday's depo, he decided on mandatory arbitration ASAP. Couldn't handle the tension."

"That'll bring in a pittance thanks to your discounting our standard one-third down to twenty percent," Derek rejoined.

"It's discounted because it won't be a pittance. You can't fire a guy today for marrying his longtime boyfriend. It's mandatory arbitration, so it *will* settle. The money's coming in. I just have to get it scheduled."

"Good news for our coffers," Rona said. "Thank you, Paul."

"For the record," Paul added. "I recommended against the arbitration because he had a winner, but he's tired."

"You're doing the right thing." Rona stroked Paul's ethics button.

"The *honorable* Paul," Derek mocked.

"What?" Paul just stared at Derek.

"The client's wishes are always paramount." Rona deftly defused the two men.

Paul got up and grabbed another can of diet cola and a couple of chocolate chip cookies.

"Now for new matters," Rona said.

"Here I go," Sophia whispered to Tricia.

⌘

# CHAPTER 7

## Damn Those Torpedoes

*"The policy of being too cautious is the greatest risk of all."*
-Jawaharlal Nehru

Before Sophia could speak, Bryce's arm shot up elementary-school style.

"I got my first client at the Irish-American Bar Association meeting last night."

"Excellent, Bryce. What is it?" Rona asked.

"The collection of a $150,000 judgment. The lawyer who referred it to me said his firm didn't do collections."

"Congratulations," Paul said.

"What are the terms?" Derek asked.

"One-third."

"Not bad," Derek said. "Is there anything to levy on?"

"A house and some kind of business."

"Run with it," Rona said. "I assume we all agree?"

The silence was a green light. "Paul, you can show Bryce how to confirm the debtor's assets before we sign the client."

"Sure. I'll do the meeting with you this week, Bryce."

"Congrats," Eddie added, without a spark of jealousy.

"Hey, I'll take you next time, and we'll land more cases together."

"It's a deal." He stood and shook Eddie's hand across the table.

Bryce was an impressive six feet, two inches tall. He wore a suit well, even with his first-year associate stomach pouch from being glued to a desk and skipping the gym. His smooth white skin, green eyes, and red hair were an unusual and attractive mix. Those green eyes, at first, had reminded Sophia of a widely hated managing partner at Thorne & Chase. But Bryce's generous collegiality helped that memory fade. She hoped Bryce and Eddie could help bring harmony back to Krause & White.

\* \* \*

"Yes, very good. Way to go." Derek zeroed in on Sophia. "Now we can get on with it."

Sophia's kumbaya bubble burst. Derek was out for the kill.

Derek took the floor. "Sophia's memo is smoke and mirrors. Cases from other jurisdictions, disparate facts, dram shop laws, booze laws. She tried hard, but she can't get around *Jacoves*. I say vote no, now."

Derek glanced at the first-years confidently.

"What's going on?" Sophia whispered to Tricia.

"I don't know."

"Sophia, go ahead and present." Rona silenced Derek.

"A formality." Derek leaned back. "Sophia, I give you the floor. Try to keep from falling on it."

To Derek contingency cases had to be slam-dunks with strong settlement leverage. That's where the money was. Not fighting to make new law to control gun sales. Any gun case was playing with fire—gunfire—news fire—media fire—Constitutional fire—hellfire. He sat in anticipation, ready to pounce.

"You all know the facts. A boy . . ."

"A *man* . . . a nineteen-year-old *man*." Derek—pounce one.

"Yes. Anyway. It's clear this couple needs our help. The issue is whether the Holts have a case for wrongful death, negligence, and negligent infliction of emotional distress against Sports Gear USA."

"Your own memo says they don't." Derek—pounce two. "We're in California, and you cited no supporting California cases. You did the opposite. You cited *Jacoves*, the controlling California Second District Court of Appeal case that held the gun seller wasn't liable in cases like this. Let's vote."

"Derek." Sophia stayed calm. "In my memo I analyzed in detail why *Jacoves* is not controlling. A gun is an ultrahazardous object, and any seller has the highest duty of care."

"I can find case law disputing just that."

"Where is it?" Paul stared at Derek. "If you have any to show us, now's the time. No one can claim that a shotgun . . . any gun . . . is not ultrahazardous."

"Oh, come on. Guns only do what people make them do . . . like Mike offed himself. Salesmen are not mind readers." Derek—pounce three.

Sophia would not be provoked. "Sports Gear's employees acted below the standard of care when they sold a gun to an obviously unbalanced—if not discernibly suicidal—kid . . . excuse me . . . *man*. It's a strong case. Sports Gear won't want it in the news and will settle. The only questions are when and how much."

"The only question," Derek interjected, "is when it will be dismissed or summarily adjudicated under *Jacoves*. Bakersfield with its gun culture will devour your case. Where's the money in that?"

Paul weighed in. "It won't be dismissed under *Jacoves*. And it will make our firm newsworthy and high-profile if they don't settle."

"A high-profile target of every Second Amendment right-winger," Derek snapped. "I gave our financials to everyone. Things are tight here. All I see are billable hours going out the window. What sense is there in gambling on a thousand-to-one case?"

"I'm sick of your financial scare tactics, Derek," Tricia said. "Paul's arbitration coming up will generate income."

"Derek makes good points," Rona moderated. "*Jacoves* bothers me, too. And we all have to admit that it is a huge financial risk."

"That's reaching," Tricia said.

"No, it's not," Derek hammered back. "The gun interests and Sports Gear will make sure of that. Besides, in gun-toting Bakersfield, we'll never get a jury to listen, much less a fair judge. And we'll be attacked by every gunned-up gang, Second Amendment purist, and the NGA. Not just in Bakersfield, either."

"NGA?" Bryce questioned.

"The National Gun Association," Derek said. "Bryce doesn't even know the basics."

"Read our mission statement," Sophia said. "These parents deserve our help. And that's what we do. We help people. We're a plaintiffs' firm. That's why I came here. Besides, Sports Gear won't risk bad publicity. They'll settle."

Sophia spoke with impact and focus. She had been in the top ten percent of her law school class, on law review, a moot court finalist, and Am Jur'ed five classes with the highest grade in each. She also had the seasoned laserlike talent of a true litigator, the ability to skillfully mince her opponents, and overall superb legal acumen.

"That's bullshit, to use a tried-and-true legal term," Derek retorted.

"We have to be practical," Rona cautioned. "We can't fund an out-of-town trial a hundred-plus miles north."

"Against Sports Gear's deep pockets," Derek chimed in.

"Very deep pockets." Bryce was a client-getter now and felt entitled to his input. "I follow the stock market, and I can tell you, that company beats its earnings estimate every quarter and is acquiring every small sporting goods chain in the Midwest."

"Then again, a deep pocket is always good from the standpoint of a potential settlement." Rona looked to Derek.

"Come on, Rona," Derek lashed back. "Everyone with a brain knows that a deep pocket means they have tons of money and layers of lawyers to bury us."

"Sophia proved her skill at pretrial strategies when she got her last settlement," Paul said. "And that's the bottom line, isn't it? Getting a strong result and our third of the take?"

"Right," Eddie spoke up.

"Are the clients paying costs as we go?" Derek asked.

"Of course." Sophia unilaterally committed the Holts. "The father is seventy-one. I can fast-track it because of his age. They won't be able to drain us."

Derek thought a moment, balancing his own interests against the possible benefit of taking this case. He wanted money and power. This case, if lost, would drain money and, if won, would jeopardize his dominant position in the firm. It was a no-win for him. And, his righteous indignation over Sophia's insult would bolster his position.

"That's discretionary, and you'll lose." Derek could not be swayed. "It's more work for a judge to speed things up. Besides, every court appearance will be hours away. They'll break us. The good-old-boy network will see to that."

The room was quiet, all the brains in the room considering what they had heard.

"The memo was solid." Eddie broke the silence. "And if Mr. Holt is old enough, we can get the trial expedited."

"I agree," Tricia said.

"It sounds to me like there could be something big here," Eddie said.

Eddie's years of grueling study to be top ten percent at Harvard Law had left him with a thick middle. But now even his third-year law school interview suit sausaged him thanks to his since-gained poundage. His belt hung low, accommodating his increased circumference. But he was beyond smart and had chosen Krause & White, a plaintiffs' firm, to do good.

"Are you kidding, Harvard?" Derek saw the sands shift in Sophia's favor. "No one is responsible for that man killing himself, but him. Not even the irrational, guilt-ridden parents who need to blame Sports Gear."

"It's true. He could have just done it some other way," Bryce considered.

"That's a red herring and not relevant." Eddie often had to refocus Bryce when they did assignments together.

"But Bryce makes a good point, red herring or not. We'll have to be careful if it goes to a jury." Paul validated Bryce's comment to keep him on their side.

Paul liked the first-years strategizing. He knew they were salivating over the promised depositions and other challenging work. Those bargaining chips were worth their vote but would also make them part of the litigation team for better or worse. They were extra hands—but, unfortunately, grossly inexperienced ones.

"The NGA will get involved. It always does. They try their cases with media blitzes. That concerns me," Rona cautioned. "We don't have the money for a 'sound bite' publicist to make us media ready."

"Rona, what the hell?" Derek leaned forward. "Are you thinking of taking this albatross?"

"Sure she is," Paul answered. "She knows Sophia's memo is masterful and shows settlement potential."

"If the news of it doesn't creep over the Tejon pass to L.A., the city of drive-bys!" Derek shouted. "And if gun activists don't burn down the courthouse first."

"No one's burning down the courthouse," Tricia said. "And, come on, 'the city of drive-bys'? Stop dramatizing."

"The out-of-town expenses will kill us. Hours on the road . . . gas . . . hotels . . . food?" Derek said.

"I'll move to change venue to L.A.," Sophia countered Derek's attack, knowing little about such motions except that they were long shots.

"Fat chance Bakersfield would let their gun case be tried here."

"We understand your position, Derek." Paul did not disclose Derek's selfish power grab as his primary motivation.

Paul didn't care about Derek's background or his bruised ego. Derek's anger and self-interest didn't belong in this firm's financial decisions. Paul was the lightning rod as well as the rudder for this young group of attorneys who had no one else to hold down the helm. He had been on track to make partner at Thorne & Chase just before it collapsed and had been there long enough to learn the tactics and diplomacy necessary to hold a law firm together.

"Derek, we do have a democratic firm here," Rona said. "We've all had our say. Let's vote. All those for?"

Five hands popped up. Bryce's slower than the others.

"All those against."

Rona hesitated and then raised her hand in solidarity with Derek. Derek voted with his feet—right out the door.

"Sophia, you'd better pull this off," Rona said. "Derek's right. If you mismanage it, we'll have to close our doors."

She marched off to placate Derek.

\* \* \*

"We have the gun case." Sophia looked at Paul and Tricia, and their eyes reflected the gravity in Sophia's.

However, Bryce and Eddie just high-fived each other, unaware of the obstacles ahead.

"I'll get everyone copies of the Holts's documents. Welcome to the team, all of you."

Eddie and Bryce grinned ear to ear. Sophia remembered her own naive days as a bright-eyed and enthusiastic new litigator. That glow hadn't lasted long.

"Study the documents and read the cases in the memo." Sophia was actually only speaking to Bryce and Eddie—Paul and Tricia knew the dance. "Any questions tomorrow, ask Paul. Tricia and I have to go to Bakersfield to sign the clients."

⌘

# CHAPTER 8

## Something Floral This Way Comes

*"Doubt, of whatever kind, can be ended by action alone."*
-Thomas Carlyle

The next morning Sophia and Tricia were on the road early to Bakersfield, Bako, or B-town—California's country music capital or Nashville West, thanks to Merle Haggard and Buck Owens and the coined "Bakersfield Sound" refined at Trout's Bar in Oildale. Sophia drove the same 2009 white Toyota Camry she had as a teacher, during law school, and at Thorne & Chase.

The October day was bright and hot. At ten they were supposed to be at the Holts's home. The client engagement agreement was in Tricia's briefcase. The California State Bar requires that lawyers have written retainer agreements with clients for most matters and for all contingency fee cases. That is, if they know what's good for them.

Sophia and Tricia also had fieldwork to do: see the home and city where Mike lived and died; visit the Sports Gear USA store to get some admissions out of the store personnel—if the corporate hierarchy had not already silenced them. Fieldwork was always invaluable when painting a sympathetic picture of the Holts and Mike and, even more importantly, the emotional distress his death caused them.

"So how much longer do you think?" Tricia asked.

"Soon. We're on the downside of the Grapevine."

"Grapevine . . . where did that come from?"

"It stuck from the old road carved in these hills. It was twisty like a grapevine and steep and dangerous, especially for truckers. You can see a piece sometimes along the way."

"Hey, I see a piece over there."

"All I know is this highway is still dangerous, and I'm still steering clear of the trucks."

"Good." Tricia looked to the right. "Those moving mountains would pancake us."

"See that turnout right there going up on the side. It's for runaway trucks."

"Christ, is that what those things are? And there's fresh tread marks."

"Yep. The turnouts are all along this downhill stretch. Makes you think."

They drove on in silence.

"Maybe Derek was right about this case," Sophia said.

"What? Are you kidding? Why?"

"I don't know. It is a long drive, and it's causing so much infighting. And he does have a point. If it's a slow news day in L.A., our suit could become a major story, and then we'll be in the crosshairs of all those groups he rattled off."

Sophia remembered in law school when she went with Rona to Derek's father's funeral and, afterwards, to Derek's large, old childhood home in South Central. Derek's parents were churchgoing and hardworking, but his younger brother Dwight and the males on his father's side wore the Grape Street Watts Crips gang colors.

"Don't be silly. Paul's right. He'll say or do anything to maintain control of the firm and keep us under his thumb. Hey, there's a sign for Gorman. Let's stop. I have to pee."

"Where?"

"Do McDonald's." Tricia pointed. "I love their biscuits."

"Really? I never knew they sold biscuits."

"Childhood memories. I was indoctrinated early by Ronald McDonald and my parents."

They laughed.

\* \* \*

By nine-thirty Sophia and Tricia had reached Bakersfield. They drove down the 99 freeway and passed an indoor mall with Sears and Macy's bookending the retail sprawl.

"This is more civilized than I thought," Tricia said. "Is there a Bloomies somewhere?"

"Don't be a snob. There's real wealth here with the oil, agriculture, and new industry. It puts out ten percent of our oil, and we all eat its produce."

"How the hell . . ."

"Do I know this? I do my homework."

"Well, don't try and sell me on bacon, beacon, wait, don't tell me . . . Bako. I'm happy with the case, but come on. No one wants to live here. At least I don't."

"Just keep an eye on the street names for me."

"Yes, ma'am."

Sophia left the freeway and drove on the same road for miles following the Googled directions Tricia had printed out to the Holts's home and the Sports Gear store.

"Where the heck do they live?" Tricia peered out the window. "We're down to a two-laner now with no curb. I'm expecting a dirt road soon. There's nothing but fields . . . of something green."

"Look at the directions again."

"We turn left in a mile. I think."

"Come on, Tricia. Directions were your job. I'm using my GPS."

Sophia asked her smartphone for directions to the Holt's address. It directed them loud and clear: "Destination is on your left in one mile."

"Sorry, you were right."

"Apology accepted. But what I want to know is, what is all that green growing in the fields. Tomatoes? With no tomatoes? It's not corn. I know what corn looks like. Remember the movie *The Children of the Corn*?"

"And every other B horror movie. What's with corn and B movies anyway?"

"You got me."

They came to an area with old wood frame houses spread out and set back from the highway.

"Left. Left!" Tricia shouted. "Up there. See the name on the mailbox? Holt."

"There?"

"Yes. Slow down."

* * *

Sophia squeezed a left turn, just barely, onto a dirt and gravel driveway. It snaked up to the Holts's two-story wood framed house that oozed original farmhouse from the 1940s. It had a beautiful, broad covered veranda running across the front with wide stairs up the middle and two matched sets of stairs leading to the side yards.

The house was on at least an acre with an unmowed front lawn spreading across to a stand of poplar and *ficus nitida* trees. Oleanders shielded the house from the highway. Near the veranda was a lawn mower and can of fuel waiting to be used.

"Well, we didn't get to a dirt road, but here we are on gravel," Tricia snickered.

The blue wood siding and white trimmed windows of the house needed fresh coats of paint, and the large oaks in the front lawn needed pruning. All the trees did, except the deciduous ones, with their leaves yellowed from October's breath. The detached double garage was newer but styled like the home. It had replaced the old single garage and ushered in the era of the two-car family, accompanied by the storage and hoarding of useless and forgotten possessions.

The Holts's truck was parked in front of the garage along with Mike's old blue Bronco.

"Very Rockwellian." Tricia got out and grabbed her briefcase with the client retainer agreement. "We're late."

"Just ten minutes. Remember, we have to get their signatures on the engagement letter agreeing to cover our costs as we go and a five thousand dollar retainer check. Rona insisted on that to appease Derek."

"I can't say I disagree. It'll be better for the firm. And it looks like they can cough up that much."

They went up the gray painted wood steps to the expansive gray veranda. It was dotted with pots of flowers and wicker chairs with green vine cushions. Sophia knocked on the white wood-framed screen door.

* * *

When the large old oak door opened, Beth and Wallace stood together in the oversized entry. Wallace pushed open the screen door, and Beth hugged Sophia. She hugged Tricia too when Sophia introduced them. Wallace squeezed both Sophia's and Tricia's hands as he shook them robustly.

"We're sorry we're late. It is rather far out, isn't it?" Sophia felt her hand re-expand from Wallace's enthusiasm.

"Don't worry. We expect people to be late. No one can ever find it the first time," Wallace said. "Even with all that Google nonsense."

"I can't believe you're taking the case." Beth started to cry, standing at the door.

"Now, Beth. Let them sit down." Wallace marshaled the three women into the living room. "It's quite a drive."

As Sophia and Tricia entered, a floral torture chamber blasted their eyes.

Wallace directed them to two green chairs splattered with white daisies, across from the red and pink rose couch where he and Beth sat. The room was wallpapered with tiny roses in red and pink dropping vertically over parallel gold stripes. The area rug was a mishmash of green vines and red roses. Even worse were the faded curtains that dripped with light purple lilacs and white baby's breath on a salmon background. The room was one that was well used, but not worn or unkempt.

Though Beth's taste was dubious, she was a good housekeeper.

"I made you chocolate chip cookies from my grandmother's recipe. See?" Beth's tears subsided as she pointed to the coffee table. "And we have coffee. It's hot in the coffee maker."

Beth was also clearly a practiced hostess, in the homey Bakersfield tradition.

"A coffee would be nice," Sophia answered. "Tricia?"

"Same here."

Beth got the coffee from the kitchen and poured a cup for everyone. Wallace took it back with automatic deftness practiced a hundred times.

"The cream and sugar are here." Beth pointed to the obvious next to the cookies.

Both attorneys participated in the hospitality dance, but only with enthusiasm appropriate to the occasion. Sophia then balanced the somberness of the situation with the required admiration of the home. She had learned this from her parents.

"You have a lovely home." Sophia sipped the bitter coffee, preplanned and on hold for hours—then she added two spoons of sugar and more cream.

"Yes." Tricia was almost speechless from the floral craziness before her and the undrinkable coffee.

"Thank you." Beth forced a smile.

Sophia quickly got down to business. Knowing the Holts were novices in litigation, she simplified everything.

"You have to understand that there is no exact law in California making Sports Gear liable for this."

Sophia saw the Holts's shoulders and expressions sink in unison with disappointment.

"But we're willing to try to do what is called 'extending' the law of gun sales liability."

The Holts reacted like twins, akin to all couples married for decades. Their posture straightened and their faces simultaneously produced smiles—smiles with aged teeth and no apology or embarrassment for not whitening them in prime L.A. fashion.

They were marionettes, and Sophia was playing their strings explaining the ups and downs of the case. As she entertained herself, she emphasized that nothing was clear-cut. She also warned that the NGA, gun lobbies, and gun enthusiasts might find out about the lawsuit after it was filed while anti-gun factions could decide to support the Holts.

"But we're not anti-gun," Wallace protested.

"They won't care, and there's nothing you can do about free speech here in America. That goes for the pro-gun groups, too."

"Ah," Wallace said.

After all was said and done, the Holts weren't dissuaded. They signed the client engagement letter agreeing to pay the costs of the lawsuit going forward, meaning everything but the lawyers' fees. Those fees would be a third of whatever settlement or judgment the Holts got. Wallace wrote out a five thousand dollar check as an advance against costs and handed it to Sophia.

She had learned early in life from her father that there is no free lunch and enforced that judiciously on those around her.

"We'll do our best for you."

⌘

# CHAPTER 9

## The Picture of Horror

*"Man is a prisoner who has no right to open the door of his prison
and run away . . . A man should wait, and not take his own life until
God summons him."*
-Plato

After the grand signing and congratulations all around, Beth food-
pushed until Sophia and Tricia each nibbled a chocolate chip cookie.

"Mike so enjoyed my cookies."

Beth wept yet again, and Wallace comforted her with
automated precision.

"She sent them to him once a month at Yale."

"That's so loving." Tricia tried for sincerity—it wasn't easy
after having tasted the cookies.

"I'm sorry, Wallace," Sophia unceremoniously interrupted his
wife's ever-pumping tears. "Do you mind if we take pictures around
the house?"

"No. Not at all. What for?"

"Just in case."

"I hope everything is neat enough." Beth stopped her eye
spigots—letting vanity rear its housewifely head.

Sophia lowered her voice. "And Mike's room?"

Wallace left Beth on the couch, the flow of tears starting again
at the mention of Mike's room. Sophia and Tricia were ecstatic to
leave her behind as they headed up the stairs.

"Mike's room is the one straight ahead."

"Thank you," Tricia said. "You should go take care of poor
Beth."

"Yes."

* * *

Mike's room was large and full of the vestiges of his life. Through them, he screamed who he was as loudly as any unrebellious teenager could in a parental home. His whole room was a revolt against the floral nightmare dominant everywhere else in the house. He was a very accomplished high school leader with mounds of memorabilia and many awards. Mike was with his friends, smiling, protesting, partying, living, and just chilling out in photos, framed and unframed—hanging on walls and sitting on the dressers, the desk, and the wide old window sills.

"I don't see a girlfriend," Tricia said.

"Me neither. Maybe that was the problem, but now's not the time to ask."

Tricia went to the closet door and opened it. "It's still here."

"What?"

"His blood . . . it smells." Tricia stepped back and stared. "It's horrible."

Sophia joined her. There was dried blood splattered in the closet—on the clothes, his letterman jacket, and his full Yale duffel bag. The blood, dry and thick, was pooled on the floor with smeared footprints. Sophia hadn't asked Beth and Wallace what they did when they found him. She presumed that some of the footprints were theirs.

"Horrible, but we're lucky it's still here. Get pictures of all this. The footprints in the blood. Let's do it. In detail. Get pictures of his photos, too, and that framed printed whatever. Everything. Even the unmade bed. From all angles. It's from his last day alive. We can use it all."

"I will, but stop with the ghoulish enthusiasm." Tricia held her breath each time she entered the closet to take shots.

"Why are the clothes separated on this side?"

"For him. That's where he sat and wedged the butt of the shotgun across on the baseboard there. See the splatter on the wall?"

"How awful." Tricia finished the pictures.

"We'll decide what to pack up and use later. We have to know everything about him."

"I wonder where his cellphone is."

\* \* \*

Almost an hour later Wallace knocked and opened the door. "How is everything?"

Sophia and Tricia stepped out. "We're done. Did he have a cell phone?"

"Sure. The police still have it with the clothes he was wearing when, when . . ." Wallace paused to regain his composure. "They said they needed it. They took his laptop too. The MacBook Pro we bought him for a graduation present to take to Yale."

"Can you get everything for us?"

"Sure. They said they were getting the surveillance tape from the store security camera, too."

"They won't hand that over," Tricia said.

"But if they offer it, take it," Sophia said. "And I'm sorry to ask this, but . . . where is the shotgun?"

"The police said they needed it."

"They don't anymore. Get it all from them."

"I will. Should I get the umbrella that he pushed the trigger with?"

"What?" Tricia asked.

"The police found it with him and said he used it to reach the trigger."

"Get all of it." Sophia started down the hall and glanced into the pink and green tiled bathroom. It was disturbingly like hers and Steve's.

Tricia followed, taking pictures of each room off the upstairs hall and the downstairs: the pink and green bathroom; the Holts's green and floral master bedroom; the guest bedroom, which doubled as Beth's now fallow sewing room; the lace table-clothed dining room table and the dining room dense with knickknacks and floral china in the hutch. Beth moved out of the living room shots.

"Why do they need all these pictures?" Beth whispered, worried about a critique of her homemaking.

"Who knows? But they do." Wallace was passive and accepting.

Sophia and Tricia ended up in the roomy entry with the antique coat and umbrella rack. As Tricia snapped her last pictures, they edged toward the door. They were not getting trapped in the living room again with the coffee, the cookies, and Beth. They were done.

"We'll let you know when we send a demand letter to Sports Gear. If there's no settlement response, we'll do a complaint and fact-check everything with you." Sophia opened the front door. "If you have any questions, just call."

"Thank you." Beth teared up yet again.

Wallace had to peel Beth's hugs off both women.

As the screen door slammed behind them, Sophia decided she didn't like Beth—at all.

⌘

# CHAPTER 10

## Doing The Redneck Tango

*"Against stupidity the very gods themselves contend in vain."*
-Friedrich Schiller

Back at the car, Tricia took pictures of the house exterior and the grounds before they escaped up the driveway.

"Which way to the Sports Gear store?" Sophia asked at the mailbox.

"Left. Careful, there's a pickup coming, fast."

"I see it." Sophia turned after it whizzed by.

As they drove, Tricia scrolled through the pictures on her phone. "Christ almighty."

"What's wrong?"

"Come on, Sophia. What's right in that house? No wonder Mike offed himself. Walking in there was like falling down the rabbit hole into the Beth-world of flowers and foul food. The cookies? Shortening. Not an iota of butter. The chocolate chips? Imitation. Brown colored wax. I mean, who eats that junk? Generic store cookies laced with preservatives are better."

"That's harsh. She tries. The poor woman." Sophia felt guilty that she disliked Beth.

"Poor Wallace, you mean. And Mike."

"At least the cookies got rid of the stale coffee taste glued to my tongue."

Sophia and Tricia laughed.

"Talk about Podunk, USA," Tricia said. "Mike must have been freaked out after seeing how the other half lived back East."

"That's not nice."

"Come on. Talk about a buzz kill, coming home to that . . . growing up with a flower garden in the living room. Pink and green everywhere. And Beth? I wonder if she cried every time he stubbed his toe growing up. Hell, his room was the only sane place in the house."

"You've never been to my parents' house."

"It couldn't be that bad."

"Want to bet? Needlepoint flower chairs, floral rugs, curtains that sort of match, but don't. It's old Greek world meets American apple pie with a twist of the modern and splashes of gold. The Greeks love that gold."

"Oops. I put my big foot in my mouth."

"No. I thought other kids' houses were boring."

After a heartbeat of silence, Sophia laughed.

They both did.

\* \* \*

They drove on an endless ribbon of asphalt with telephone poles on one side and erector-set-like towers strung with electric lines on the other. There were scattered intermittent small homes, abandoned warehouses, a few out-of-place mini-mansions, the big-box chain store Mark Down Mart, and intersections cornered with fast food, liquor stores, and donut shops.

Sophia turned on the air conditioning. "It's roasting and it's not even summer."

Finally, they reached a crossroads with the only signal for miles after the Mark Down Mart.

"Sports Gear. It's over there." Tricia pointed. "What a dump."

The intersection had an old gas station on one corner, a liquor store and Chinese takeout place on another, with an empty lot on the third, and then Sports Gear USA in a strip mall on the fourth. Sports Gear was sandwiched between vacant stores for lease. At the end of the strip mall were a laundromat, donut shop, and dance studio sucking money from mothers with delusional dreams for their little starlet wannabes.

"No time like the present." Sophia pulled in the asphalt parking lot devoid of white lines. "Remember . . . friendly and charming.

You're looking for a rifle to go hunting with your boyfriend, and I'm looking for candid statements about Mike. Let's go."

They got out, and Tricia shot pictures with her phone of the store and the surrounding intersection.

"Hey, want Chinese for lunch?" Tricia asked.

"No way. Just looking at it, I'd rate it F."

The two walked by Sports Gear's display windows.

"They sell everything." Tricia took a few more pictures. "Look at the good prices on those tennis balls."

"Jesus, Tricia, we're not here shopping. Besides, they're probably seconds. Where do you imagine the rejects go?" Sophia whispered.

"Didn't think of that."

"Be casual, but get shots of the layout with your cell."

"Consider it done."

* * *

The hanging bells on the double glass doors clanged, and Arnie lumbered over, beaming his chipped-tooth smile. His royal blue Sports Gear T-shirt covered his beer belly preceding him.

"Can I help you, girls?"

"I wanted to look at the rifles and get some information." Sophia glanced at "Arnie" on his nametag. He was the manager on duty when Mike got the shotgun.

"Or shotguns," Tricia said.

A kid in the same T-shirt said, "There's a difference, you know."

"Get back to stocking, Brandon," Arnie ordered.

"I'm Sophia Christopoulos and . . ."

"Those men in the corner will help you." Arnie reached in his pants pocket for his cigarettes and headed out the front door.

"He'll be back," Tricia whispered.

"I know. Let's hurry. You ready?"

"Sure. I can do redneck." Tricia undid the top button of her white silk blouse and popped a silly grin.

"Perfect." Sophia did the same.

"Learned it from Jay's relatives down in Brownsville, Texas."

"I didn't know about them."

"You still don't. Jay doesn't spread it around."

"My lips are sealed. I'm going over. You get pictures first."

Sophia headed to the corner with the "Guns" sign hanging over locked racks of rifles.

Tricia hung back and twirled a cylinder display of pamphlets. She snapped pictures of the store as it kaleidoscoped, pictures of sportsmen and their dead prey—feathered and furred and scaled.

\* \* \*

"Nothing but trouble. That's what kids are." Moss leaned on the glass cases of handguns. "Jake rode his hog in Riverview Park at three this morning with his junkie high school buddies . . . shooting and hollering. The sheriff brought him to me. I told him to take him to jail or his ma's. She wanted custody. She has it."

"That was him?" Joe said. "Christ. Every light in south Oildale was on, including mine. He needs a night in jail."

"You're lucky you don't have no kids."

"Excuse me." Sophia's ears been jarred enough by the lowlife prattle.

Moss turned and grinned. "Hello, missy."

Moss and Joe stood at attention behind the glass gun cases. Sophia read their nametags and knew she had the right men.

"What can we do-you-for?" Joe smiled wide enough to show his missing premolar as he smoothed his gray hair back into his scraggly gray ponytail.

"Well, we were shopping for a gun."

"Yes." Tricia joined Sophia but couldn't force a smile. "A rifle so I can go shooting with my boyfriend."

Moss sized up the inexperienced women in their big-city clothes, turned on his best shit-kicking charm, and carnival-barked, "We got anything your little heart desires here. We got the skinny ones called rifles and the big, big ones called shotguns. And, if you don't see nothing you like, we can take a look at these here catalogs."

Moss slapped his hand down on a stack of catalogs on the counter as his eyes looked through Tricia's silk blouse to her breasts.

"We . . . I was looking for a rifle." Tricia bit the bullet and smiled at Moss, knowing she would get the better of him in the end. "Can you help me find one that's not too big for me?"

Moss unlocked the rifle rack and grabbed a lady-sized one. He invited himself around the glass case to give Tricia a shooting lesson—up very close and personal.

Sophia turned her attention to Joe.

"Hi, I'm Sophia Christopoulos."

"And what can I help you with, ma'am?" Joe's respectful use of the word "ma'am" was countered by his lascivious perusal of Sophia's assets.

"I was just wondering if I could ask you a few questions." Sophia leaned forward on the counter and displayed her own big guns.

"Sure, honey. Ask away. Like Moss said, we got it all here. And we heard it all and seen it all." Joe lowered his voice. "I see you're not hitched, so trouble with the boyfriend or the exes?"

"Not right now." Sophia slid her card on the counter. "Here's my card."

Joe squinted to focus on the card.

"You graduated law school. Wow."

"Sure." Sophia upchucked a giggle despite her revulsion.

"Here in town?"

"No, another town. I actually represent the poor parents of that nice young boy Mike who committed suicide."

"So you here about that suicide? Huh." Joe scratched his head in some confusion. "So you don't want to buy a rifle too?"

"No. She's looking for one." Sophia chose her words carefully. "I'm here because the parents are upset."

"Sure they are. But that boy was kind of a strange one."

"Strange?"

"You know, like wired wrong or something. I think . . ." Joe stopped short. "His parents should know . . . they raised him."

"Shut up, Joe. You shouldn't be talking about that." Moss unwrapped himself from around Tricia and took the rifle back behind the counter. "Remember what Arnie said."

"Arnie?" Sophia feigned a quizzical innocence.

"The manager," Moss answered.

"Oh." Sophia batted her eyes at Joe, who was definitely the less savvy of the two. "I thought you were the manager."

"Oh, what harm is there? The kid's dead," Joe argued.

"You want to get fired?"

"Naw."

"We just wanted to know a little about Mike . . . you know his last hours?" Tricia leaned on the counter and grinned with slutty charm.

"Uh." Joe swallowed hard. Tricia was a real looker. "I . . . I . . ."

"Shut up, Joe. You'll lose your job."

Sophia had learned something important. She knew Joe was the vulnerable one of the two and had thought Mike was "strange" and "wired wrong." She'd also confirmed that Sports Gear's attorneys had already taken control.

"We don't want that," Sophia said. "So just tell me then, does that camera up there work? What harm can there be in telling me that?"

"None, I guess," Joe said. "The cops took it anyway."

"So how much is this one?" Tricia wanted Moss back on her side of the counter and talking.

"That one's a deal." Moss walked back to Tricia. "I'll give you fifteen percent off if you want to go for a drink tonight."

"I'll think about it." Tricia's eyes met Sophia's—they were too late for candid remarks and were lucky to have gotten what they did because the corporate ranks had already closed.

"Let's go, Sophia. We have that appointment."

"Right. We're late."

Tricia pretended to make a phone call and got a few more pictures as she left, the doorbell jangling.

\* \* \*

"Talk about textbook mouth-breathers," Sophia said after they were back in her Camry. "I need a shower."

"Ditto."

"But we confirmed the cops have a copy of the surveillance tape, like Wallace said. And we know Joe thought Mike was 'strange' and 'wired wrong.'"

"That's something."

"Not much. They'll deny the statements, but asking the question in front of a jury is sometimes enough. Jurors can sense lies."

"Too bad corporate got to them," Tricia said. "But it's been months. It's a small town. News spreads. Everyone knows the Holts were lawyer-shopping."

"We'll take a run at them in their depositions." Sophia turned on the air conditioning in the sun-baked Camry.

"You'll get them. I know you and your depo traps. Besides, no lawyer can prepare men like that well enough, and I use the term 'men' loosely."

"You give me too much credit. We'll sic Paul on them if we can. He's really good."

"Don't forget we promised the first-years some depo action."

"Who cares? We'll set the janitor's deposition for one of them," Sophia laughed.

"And some corporate 'custodian of records,'" Tricia roared.

Sophia drove across the street to the liquor store. Tricia ran in and came out with two bottles of water and two bags of plain M&M's.

"Here." Tricia tossed one of each to Sophia. "I lived on these during the bar exam. I snuck them in the pocket of my sweatshirt. Couldn't eat them again for years."

"I see that phobia has passed."

"Of course. M&M's—who can live without them?"

Sophia ripped the bag open and ate a couple. "I've been watching Sports Gear in the rear view mirror. Don't look, but that manager Arnie has been standing there making calls and watching us."

Tricia turned around and looked. "I wonder. Is he calling the lawyers?"

"I said don't look."

Tricia turned back and drank her water.

"My guess . . . corporate. I gave Joe my card and told him who I was."

"Then forget it. You were ethical."

"You bet." Sophia headed down the two-lane road toward the I-5 freeway. "We both were. Ethically slutty."

"We're litigators. Whatever it takes."

⌘

# CHAPTER 11

## Keep on Truckin'

*"Courage is being scared to death and saddling up anyway."*
-John Wayne

Sophia and Tricia drove to the I-5 with the soft sounds of the AC, the crinkle of M&M bags, and the crush of the thin sugar M&M shells between their teeth. Fellow drivers were sparse on the outlying road lined with dusty fallow fields, tree-cloaked farmhouses, orchards, and intermittent irrigated rows of green growth. Neither of them recognized the sprouting green edibles.

They sped with an unspoken urgency to get back to a world they understood. They had lost their sense of humor about the land, the people, and the day.

Tricia turned on the radio. They searched through Valley Public Radio, Clearly Classical, Christian stations, Radio Campesino, traffic reports of no traffic, and infinite country music stations. They chose country, listening to song after song bawling about jail time, mothers, lovers, and liquor.

"What the hell is that?" Sophia studied the reflection in her rearview mirror.

Tricia looked back to see a cloud of dust rising from a dirt road intersection and a massive silver pickup bearing down on them. It was an oversized behemoth raised on blocks with monster tires.

"I don't know. You only see those things in white trash movies." Tricia turned back around.

"Or on that monster truck TV show."

"Come on you watch that?"

"No. I just flip past."

"Sure." Tricia snickered. "Squeeze to the right and slow down. They want to pass."

When Sophia angled toward the shoulder, the truck mirrored her maneuver, revving its powerful engine. It thrust forward, looming over her trunk.

Tricia looked back. "What the hell? Get away from them."

Sophia floored her old Toyota Camry and veered to the left and then the right again. The truck copied Sophia's every move, getting closer and closer and louder and louder—a hair's breadth from her bumper.

"Shit," Tricia yelled over a female country crooner crying about her daddy. "They don't want to pass. They want us."

"That manager wasn't calling corporate . . . unless that's corporate."

"Not funny. What'll we do?"

"What can we do? Ride it out."

"I'll take a video," Tricia grabbed her purse to get her cell.

"No. It will antagonize them. Get the license plate."

The truck hung back and then revved and raced up again within inches of their trunk.

"They're going to ram us!" Tricia screamed.

"They wouldn't. Would they?"

The truck dropped back, revved again, and burned rubber as it burst forward—this time tapping Sophia's bumper. Sophia's car lurched.

"How far to the five?" Tricia yelled.

"Too far. Did you get the plates?"

Tricia twisted her head around. "The frame says Oildale something . . . but the plates are dirty . . . there's dust."

"Shit. Call 911." Sophia turned off the radio.

As Tricia grabbed her cell from her purse. the truck maneuvered beside them and kept pace. The driver and passenger were prime exemplars of America's obesity epidemic squeezed into dirty blue work shirts and crowned with cowboy hats grasping their clumped hair flapping in the wind. The cab's rear window racks held two rifles and a double barreled shotgun.

Before Tricia could dial, the passenger grabbed the shotgun.

"Gun!" Tricia screamed. "Duck."

Sophia ducked as ordered. Peeking over the dashboard, she slammed on her brakes and veered across the dirt shoulder just as the shotgun blasts boomed.

Tricia screamed, and Sophia shrieked as she fought for control of her Camry sidewinding through a fallow field. Sophia clutched the steering wheel and slowed as they jolted over dirt clods and bounced into holes.

There were no more shots.

"Are they chasing us?" Sophia shouted.

Tricia looked back. "No. Damn it, stop."

Sophia hit the brake, and dust encased their car.

The truck sat in the middle of the road. It revved and heaved forward—celebrating its dominance.

Sophia and Tricia were stunned, seat-belted—but uninjured. Sophia had disconnected her airbags that caused too many deaths and injuries.

The pickup revved and then peeled out.

"Are . . . are you okay?" Sophia stammered.

"I think so. You?"

"No. I'm pissed off! What the hell?"

⌘

# CHAPTER 12

## Hasten, But Slowly

*"Organize, don't agonize."*
-Nancy Pelosi

That Wednesday afternoon back at Krause & White, the conference room was packed with a firm-wide meeting to consider the ramifications of the attack. Derek was out with clients. Otherwise, his gloating would have dominated the room.

"Let's settle down." Rona said.

"The important thing is that everyone's fine." Paul took the floor. "And the car, Sophia?"

"Just some alignment stuff."

"I don't like it," Rona said. "I see why no Bakersfield lawyers touched the case, even though it does have emotional settlement value."

"Glad you admit it has value," Paul said.

"That doesn't mean it's worth anyone's life."

"We're not hurt." Sophia wanted to take down Sports Gear more than ever.

"I was the one who panicked," Tricia said.

"They pointed a shotgun at you," Bryce said. "I don't think you overreacted."

"Neither do I," Rona agreed.

"Come on," Eddie said. "They weren't going to shoot two lawyers from L.A. How stupid would that be? They were having a good time. 'Bako' fun."

"Oildale fun," Tricia said. "Their license plate said Oildale. It's a little northeast of Bakersfield."

"Oildale. Bakersfield. It doesn't matter. That shotgun was pointed right at us," Sophia said. "If he had wanted to shoot us, he would have. He obviously fired in the air because no buckshot even hit the car."

"This is serious," Rona said. "We're a firm. A unit. We have to know we'll all be safe. You already signed the Holts?"

"Yes, they're clients," Sophia was not dropping the case. "And we're keeping them. I have a retainer check."

"They were just harassing two girls because they could. It's like elementary school," Eddie said. "We all picked on the girls."

"Not all of us," Bryce said.

"Take me next time." Eddie's speech and demeanor changed from mild suit-cloaked attorney to badass in a second. "I'll kick their *pendejo* behinds. It wouldn't be the first time."

"Right on." Roxy Harrison raised fist showing her arm with a black leather studded wristband topped by a black and red fire-breathing-dragon tattoo. "I'll go too."

Despite her outlandish dress and uninhibited manner, Roxy was a loyal, top-notch assistant for Derek and Rona and had been since the birth of Krause & White.

"Quiet, everyone." Rona rapped the table with her empty coffee mug instead of her knuckles. "Stop."

Silence fell, ordained by Rona's new mug technique. She had arrested the fervor, saved her knuckles, and put an end to Roxy's unprofessional silliness. Sophia had admired Rona since she nailed the answer to the first question the professor ever asked in civil procedure. She had made sure to get in Rona's study group.

"I talked to Derek," Rona said. "This is exactly why he fought taking this case. He's even more opposed to it now. He wants us to re-evaluate litigating it and possibly filing a motion to withdraw as counsel. I have his proxy to vote."

"No judge would grant it," Paul countered. "We have an engagement letter. There's no conflict of interest. No payment issue. We have a check. And the Holts have no other lawyer to take the case. All we can argue is one run off the road, maybe, and an errant shotgun blast. We can't even prove who did it."

"I vote to keep it," Tricia said. "We were there. We know."

"We have to trust Sophia's and Tricia's judgment," Paul said.

"I trust it." Peggy glanced up from proofing a document.

"The Holts have to stay our clients." With mounting support, Sophia fought for her case. "We're a plaintiffs' firm with a reputation to protect."

"And build," Eddie added.

"We'll fire back and file the complaint Monday," Paul said. "That'll say it all."

"It sure will." Eddie glanced at Autumn for approval. "Hit them fast and hard."

She gave him a smile.

"If we keep it, we have to send them a demand letter first," Rona said.

"They've lost their chance for that," Eddie puffed for Autumn. "They're lucky we don't drag them into court for attempted murder."

"Eddie's right," Autumn smiled.

"No, he isn't." Paul was annoyed with Eddie's *amour*. "We have no evidence against Sports Gear, its lawyers, or anyone. But that doesn't change the validity of our basic strategy here. Hit back hard. Bur first the letter."

There were more murmurs of approval. The momentum had turned against Rona. Derek might have swayed the group, but he was with his client developing an affordable housing and retail project not far from USC. The approval process meant big fees. Being from that community, Derek was the go-to lawyer for these projects because everyone assumed he cared about improving the neighborhood. To him, though, the improvements were just billable work.

"Anyone else think we should get rid of it?" Rona asked.

There was silence.

A booming voice came from reception. "UPS. I need a signature."

"Coming." Autumn squeezed toward the door. "Excuse me."

Eddie got up and moved his chair.

At the door, Autumn stopped. "I'm just part time, and I know what I just said, but on second thought, I think this is dangerous. I vote to get rid of it."

However, the majority ruled.

"Then get a complaint ready to file," Rona stood. "Sophia, prepare a *pro forma* demand letter ASAP, and I'll review it. We'll FedEx it today and give them until noon Monday to respond."

The pace would be brutal, and the complaint might have to be amended later, but Sophia had won. "Who can help on both?"

"Me?" Eddie volunteered.

Sophia was charmed with his enthusiasm. "You bet."

"Count me in," Tricia said.

"Me too." Paul knew the work cold. "A formidable front may stop these assholes."

"I'll help," Bryce volunteered.

"Sophia," Rona stopped on her way out. "Better look into that venue motion if things get worse. I've never done one."

* * *

Later that afternoon, the office resounded with Derek ranting in Rona's office about having predicted all of this—the dangers, the liability if someone at the firm got hurt, and the stupidity in representing the parents of some depressed "middle-class Ivy-League" kid offing himself when he had a full ride to Yale.

Sophia and her team ignored the fight—until Derek burst into Sophia's office. "It's just like I said. Your case is already eating up billable hours and staff time. You haven't even filed the complaint and look what happened. It's just the beginning."

"Derek, it's a good case. Sports Gear will settle quickly," Sophia said. "Easy money."

"Like hell. It's not rolling over. Every gun store owner in America and the NGA will join in. Someone's going to get hurt."

"Lower the volume, Derek." Paul was close to losing it.

"We're going for a change of venue anyway," Bryce said.

"You don't know anything." Derek turned on Bryce. "There are no legal grounds to transfer the case to a different venue at this stage, and any Bako judge will call this a non-incident with two overwrought city women getting hysterical. The power there is going to keep this with a local, gun-friendly jury. Besides, you'll never connect the dots to corporate America."

"If they try again, we will," Eddie said.

"You're as naive as Bryce. They don't care who their guns kill. They let criminal gangs, hired guns, and redneck trash do their dirty work. We're all disposable just like my brother."

"Your brother," Sophia said. "I'm sorry. I forgot."

"Of course you forgot. Who hasn't? He was a black man gunned down in South Central. It wasn't news."

Derek left.

\* \* \*

Paul got up and shut the door. "What's going on here?"

"I . . . I should have remembered," Sophia said. "Derek's older brother died in a drive-by when Derek was a kid. His brother was setting up an anti-gang outreach program. Everyone knew who did it, but no one ever came forward."

"You should have told us. It explains a lot," Bryce said.

"Like he said . . . I forgot."

"But . . . am I missing something here?" Eddie said. "Shouldn't he be supporting us?"

"It's not that simple." Sophia didn't want to explain the financials and Derek's power play couched as outrage, or that his neighborhood was riddled with illegal guns anyway. "But there was never justice for his brother."

"Then he should want justice for Mike." Eddie didn't understand.

"Let's get back to work." Paul wrote off Derek's outrage as outdated and another ploy to get rid of the Holt case. "We have a deadline."

\* \* \*

Sophia's team became a smooth-running machine with her office as its hub. She prepared a demand letter, Rona reviewed and approved it, and FedEx picked it up before five. It was bare-bones, with the briefest statement of what had happened, a claim for damages in the amount of four million dollars, and a response deadline of Monday noon.

Sophia and Paul drafted the complaint together. It wasn't complicated, but it had to have all of the necessary factual and legal allegations. Her memo was their guide. Eddie proofread and Shepardized the memo's cases again to be sure there were no new developments or anything Sophia missed. Bryce checked the Internet for stories about similar cases that had not yet reached the appellate courts or settled.

Bryce had been a paralegal at a small Westside law firm, did well on scholarship at a second-tier law school, and then came to Krause & White. His memos were often disjointed, and he couldn't analyze a case all that well. Sophia, unfortunately, had been in court on his interview day. But she had to rely on him now.

She had interviewed Eddie and approved him in a heartbeat. He was not only top ten percent at Harvard Law but had also served on the Board of Student Advisers, responsible for its moot court program. He had a legal mind that was incisive and fast. And his dedication to representing plaintiffs for the wrongs they suffered inspired him to work tirelessly.

Despite Eddie's intelligence and diligence, his Latino surname had helped him land a full scholarship at his local, academically challenged, and grade-inflated liberal arts college where he had excelled. From there, and with high LSATs, he was deservedly catapulted to Harvard Law School on scholarship. His college traded on Eddie's success story. His father's Latino-American identity and his mother's hard-nosed, practical German discipline served him well.

In the end, though, he had disappointed everyone, family and classmates alike, by becoming a plaintiffs' attorney—an idealistic, poor plaintiffs' attorney.

\* \* \*

By seven o'clock that night, Sophia and Paul had drafted a passable complaint. Normally, Sophia had the first round of discovery ready to go when she filed a lawsuit, but then normally she would have had more time.

Sophia called her team to meet. She massaged her neck as they gathered.

"Are you hurt?" Paul asked.

"I'm getting some spasms. Not to worry. How are you, Tricia?"

"Truthfully? I have a headache and could use a massage."

"What did Steve and Jay say about all this?" Paul asked.

"Steve doesn't know and never will. I told him the car's in the shop for routine maintenance."

"Tricia? Don't tell me Jay doesn't know either."

Tricia was silent.

"You guys are playing with fire. I'm a guy. I know."

Tricia rolled her eyes.

Bryce and Eddie came in. Sophia went back to business.

"Good work, everyone. Tomorrow. Here at nine. We'll proof this sucker again and have the Holts read it. Get some rest."

Sophia was left alone to call the Holts. Wallace said they'd be available all day. She heard Beth crying in the background as she hung up.

*Does she ever stop? Sophia thought.*

Sophia grabbed her things and left, also.

⌘

# CHAPTER 13

## A Dinner Free But Not Without A Price

*"Everything in this world has a hidden meaning."*
-Nikos Kazantzakis

By ten Thursday morning, Emeline Booth, Sports Gear's general counsel, had received Krause & White's demand letter. She forwarded it on to Thomas J. Jackson, IV, its lead outside attorney. His firm—Jackson, Hood & Lee, headquartered in Denver, Colorado—was Sports Gear's exclusive outside law firm.

Jackson, Hood & Lee was the leading national defense law firm for firearm litigation. Jackson, its most senior name partner, had clients ranging from the foremost gun manufacturers—including Colt, Ruger, Remington, Glock, and Smith & Wesson—to the major retail gun dealers across the country, with a particular emphasis on the Western United States. Sports Gear was one of his largest and most loyal retail clients.

The other name partners, George Hood and Patrick Lee, met with Jackson about the Krause & White demand letter behind closed doors.

"This Holt case is a direct assault on gun sales in California. It's the suicide scenario again," Jackson began.

"A repeat of that 1992 *Jacoves* case?" Hood asked.

"The facts are a bit worse for our side. But Bakersfield is a good place to draw the line again. That jury pool loves their Second Amendment rights. They'll be hostile to any more limitations on gun sales. And I think the judges will follow *Jacoves*."

"What does your client want?" Lee asked.

"Sports Gear sees this case as a slippery slope to progressively cut into their gun sale profits in California."

"A settlement with a confidentiality clause might be best," Hood said.

"Possibly, but this law firm is a startup with some good lawyers. I think they'll want to make a name for themselves." *Besides*, Jackson thought, *I want to make a bundle for us.*

"Money talks." Lee was impatient with the familiar scenario. "Does Sports Gear really want to fight?"

"Let's put it this way: They don't want their employees in California authorized to make any judgment calls with respect to gun sales. In other states once a case like this makes it on the books, the floodgates open for lawsuits and laws scrutinizing gun buyers for everything. It weakens the Second Amendment through the back door and hurts their bottom line."

"I see their point. We'll settle, or we'll crush the Holts," Lee said. "Whatever they want. But you had better get a favorable outcome with this one. California is a top gun ownership state, and all our clients have big sales there."

"I will," Jackson said. "Don't worry about that. I'll use everything in our arsenal."

"Your arsenal is your own business," Lee said. "I don't want to hear about it."

"And use your usual team," Hood cautioned. "Remember, tight lips and discretion."

\* \* \*

By Thursday afternoon, the Holts's complaint was in its final form. Then the real nightmare began for Sophia and her team.

What was supposed to be a routine review of the complaint by the Holt's was a disaster. First, they had no fax machine and didn't understand email attachments. Peggy found a Mail Boxes and More near them to receive a fax of the complaint, at twenty cents a page. By the time they picked it up, they were too tired to read it.

"I'm so sorry." Sophia wasn't sorry. She was impatient and frustrated. "You read it first thing tomorrow morning, fax it over, and I'll call about ten."

\* \* \*

On Friday morning the Holts read the complaint and faxed it back. They scribbled comments and changes on every page, even in the standard boilerplate paragraphs. Worse—they put their teacher hats on and "corrected" the spelling of standard legal terms that were foreign to their eyes.

Over the phone the two expected a course on legal theories and procedure. Sophia baby-talked them down. Beth particularly didn't like the factual allegations because they were so dry and unfeeling. Over Beth's tears and stubbornness, Sophia declined to add her paragraph praising Mike. Eventually, Beth stopped arguing, but only because Sophia agreed to include several of her adoring adjectives.

Sophia's team met at five. Everyone agreed the changes were unnecessary but harmless. The complaint was finished and ready to file Monday after Sports Gear's noon response deadline.

Sophia gave her team the rest of the weekend off. But to her, Paul's, and Tricia's surprise, the first-years insisted on continuing their work researching the change of venue motion. They went off down the hall together, conferring and excited.

"Should we tell them a change of venue motion is almost hopeless this early in a lawsuit?" Paul asked.

"No," Sophia replied. "Let's see if our young hard chargers can get creative."

"Won't matter," Tricia said. "But it's their weekend to blow if they want."

The three planned a celebration dinner Saturday night for themselves and their significant others—Tricia with Jay, Sophia with Steve, and Paul with no one at the moment. Since meeting Sophia, Paul had not had any long relationship.

They reserved a table at Beatrice's Bistro on the Third Street Promenade in Santa Monica at eight-thirty. Tables there were available because it had been open a year now. After a year, as usual, the Saturday night swarming of L.A.'s fickle restaurant-goers had moved on to the next "great" place, Mondo's in West Hollywood—celebrity-backed, celebrity-packed, and reservations-stacked—for its year in the sun.

* * *

Friday night, Sophia slept hard and exhausted. When Steve finally got home and in bed, she put her arm around him.

Saturday morning she awoke to a note on his pillow: "Had to go. See you tonight."

Steve's new dead-body investigation was all-consuming. It was his obsessive nature that made him good at solving homicides.

Sophia made her own coffee and went to a spin class. Then, having nothing else to do, she headed to the office to start organizing discovery assignments. It was her obsessive nature that enabled her to win against all odds. That was what she told herself. Often.

Paul showed up just before noon with a pizza. "I knew you'd be here."

"I knew you'd be here, too, and with food."

"Of course."

"But for the record, I wouldn't be if Steve wasn't obsessing over another body."

"A dead one, I hope."

"Funny."

Paul set a large pizza box on her desk with plenty of napkins. It was from the local Italian restaurant that Steve and Sophia liked too. He opened the lid to a steaming hot thin-crust vegetarian.

"Perfect." Sophia dug in.

Paul worked every Saturday after his attempt at gym-behavior, which always triggered his hunger button and prompted the lunch ritual. Sophia had come to expect it. Krause & White was a far cry from Thorne & Chase where meals and snacks were provided at all hours to keep the attorneys billing twenty-four seven.

On the more-than-frequent Saturdays they spent together, Paul made work fun and easier. After half the pizza was polished off, he helped with the discovery conundrum—how to assign the first-years responsibilities that could not jeopardize the case and did not require inordinate supervision. Paul and Tricia remembered their first-year mistakes and how they covered their asses—sometimes well, sometimes not.

Bryce and Eddie showed up at two.

"What are you guys doing here?" Eddie said.

"Working. Obviously," Bryce answered for them.

"And you're late." Paul gave them the leftover pizza for their intended marathon and sent them on their way.

"Cute little buggers," Sophia said.

* * *

That night Sophia and Steve arrived early at Beatrice's Bistro.

Steve immediately charmed the overtly bare-cleavaged hostess, wearing skin-tight basic black, and had their kitchen-adjacent table changed to a window-adjacent one in the front. He was a magnet for females and always used his well-honed flirtation-manipulation skills when he wanted something.

Sophia used to observe and analyze them with fascination. Now, she ignored them and just accepted the benefits.

As they retraced their steps to the forward table, the women in the room were again glancing, staring at, and enjoying Steve. He was still a lady-killer. Hardly surprising. He had mesmerized Sophia just a few short years before. She was pleased to be with him, but now not quite as pleased with the recurrent gawking ritual as she once had been.

Their new table was indeed away from the kitchen, but too near the noisy entrance. Passable, but not a huge improvement. They resigned themselves to it, as you had to when you weren't sufficiently high profile in L.A.

The rest of the group arrived at the same time as the bottles of red and white wine Steve had ordered: a 2012 Bogle Vineyards Sauvignon Blanc and an unfortunately named but surprisingly good 2009 Pennywise Pinot Noir. The wine flowed along with the cacophony of greetings, catch-ups, case chat, murder scenarios, and jokes—all of which inhibited menu selection, but led to two more bottles of the same. Why interrupt a good conversation and good wine?

The big-breasted hostess came by again, put her hand on Steve's shoulder, and whispered in his ear with her lips and her breasts, "Best table I could manage. Hope it's all right."

Steve spoke to her breasts. "It's fine. Thanks."

"I comped the desserts. Enjoy."

The hostess looked at his left hand for a ring. Of course, there was none.

"Thanks . . . ah . . ."

"Charla . . . Charla Thurston."

"Well, Charla . . . Charla Thurston. That's kind of you."

He watched her walk away. Sophia was pissed. She liked the table even less now, and she viewed the comped desserts as foreplay. Sophia wouldn't bring Steve there again, and he had better not come alone.

After the two new bottles were uncorked, they ordered. Steve was a meat and potatoes man and, predictably, got a ribeye medium rare with a baked potato. No appetizer. No vegetable. No salad. Wine took their place.

The others, well-wined and hungry, over-ordered with enthusiasm—appetizers, salads, and dinner. The appetizers came instantly and were quickly followed by the salads. Saturday night was the most profitable night for a restaurant, and table turnover was the goal, unless the table kept drinking, of course. That's where the high margins brought in the big money.

\* \* \*

"So, Tricia told me about your new case," Jay said. "It's cutting edge."

Jay and Tricia had been together for over four years. Jay was an Assistant United States Attorney who was quickly moving up the ranks in the Criminal Division. His win record was almost one-hundred percent, his social I.Q. impeccable, and his office politicking unceasing.

"It is, and we hope lucrative as well." Sophia catered to Jay because he was not happy that Tricia had rejected a big law firm salary to follow her to Krause & White.

"We're trying to extend the law to better protect potentially suicidal gun purchasers from themselves," Tricia added enthusiastically.

"Extend it to get all the guns off the streets and we'd be safer," Steve joined in.

"I can't argue with that. I've prosecuted too many crimes involving guns," Jay said.

The two law enforcers always agreed when the group got together.

"You guys have to be careful. You don't know gun nuts the way we do." Steve squeezed Sophia's tabled hand; she squeezed back.

Paul glanced at Steve's possessory hand dance.

"Don't be so sure," Paul started to tell about Thursday's Bako incident. "We got our first . . ."

"How's your rack of lamb, Paul?" Sophia's look warned him off.

"I've had better. But here's to Sophia, the repeat rainmaker." Paul raised his glass to her.

"I won't be a repeat rainmaker until we win . . . but here's to doing just that." Sophia clinked Paul's glass.

"We will." Tricia, always the cheerleader, raised her glass, and the others followed suit.

The flurry brought attention to the table, and Ben Kowrilsky caught a glimpse of Sophia from across the room. He left his espresso, dessert, and a very attractive long-legged brunette date to zigzag through the tables.

"Sophia, how are you? This is the woman who made my career," he announced to the table.

Ben wasn't exaggerating. He was the Los Angeles Times news reporter chosen by Sophia to air, in public and in detail, Thorne & Chase's unethical and criminal laundry. She respected his abilities, his honesty, and his doggedness. He charmingly hounded Sophia until they became "odd bedfellows" with a common goal—the truth.

"Ben, what a surprise. You remember everyone here, don't you?"

"Of course. How could I forget?"

There were smiles, greetings, handshakes, and lively exchanges—for a polite moment—and then Ben glanced back at his abandoned date. "Better go. Nice seeing you all."

Before leaving Ben leaned over and whispered to Sophia. "Anything newsworthy . . . be sure and give me a call. My new card."

Ben handed Sophia his card, which showed he had risen in the news world. Sophia took it but hoped she would not have to use him.

"What did he say to you?" Steve suppressed his own green-eyed monster.

"Nothing. He's looking for scoops. His next headline. He thinks that where I go, high-profile stories follow."

"He's not a bad man to have on our side," Tricia said.

Paul agreed. "If Derek is right, and gun fanatics surface, we can use him for positive press. Corporate America hits back hard when you attack it."

Jay too agreed. "I've been in that spot twice, and believe me, those people don't hold back."

"We can use him again, Sophia," Paul said.

"Are you kidding? Once he starts, there's no controlling him."

"I thought we wanted this low-key," Tricia interrupted.

"We do, but the trouble has already started." Paul drank his wine.

"What trouble?" Steve asked.

"Nothing . . . just legal maneuvering." Sophia kicked Paul under the table.

"Ow."

"What's going on, Paul?" Jay asked.

"Nothing. We don't have any trouble . . . but Sports Gear does from us."

"Just don't underestimate the gun rabble," Jay said. "When they get wind of a potential soapbox, they all jump on it. The pro. The con. They show up at the federal courthouse enough. Especially those damn mothers . . ."

"Wait. Mothers?" Tricia interrupted.

"Yes. There's Mothers Against Guns, Women Against Guns, Moms Demand Action Against Guns. You name it, and those women have organized and acronymed it."

"Don't worry, sweetie," Tricia said. "We'll be careful. Especially around those maniacal mothers."

"It's not funny," Steve said. "Last year some Texans used semi-automatics to terrorize a Mothers Against Guns march."

"Not to belabor this," Jay added, "but there's gun shows and illegal sellers, too. We deal with them, and they get nasty when you undermine their gravy train. They'll weigh in. I've seen it."

"Come on. Our fight is with gun stores and their sales to the suicidal, like Mike," Tricia said.

"Don't worry, guys." Sophia gave Tricia a look telling her to back off. "We'll watch out."

* * *

Through dinner Sophia and her friends managed to keep the Bakersfield shooting incident quiet—even with the wine flowing freely and loosening lips. But the Holt case still dominated the conversation.

"We ought to bill our time for this dinner," Tricia laughed.

"But it's a contingency case," Paul said. "So let's stop talking about it."

They moved on to football, movies, the parking shortage, and L.A.'s traffic congestion, e.g., the 20-hour expanded rush hour times.

Espressos and dessert came too soon for Paul. He was going home alone. However, they did not come soon enough for the couples. They were going home together to an after-dinner party of intimacy.

When Steve asked the waitress for the bill, she told them Ben Kowrilsky had paid it.

"He thinks you're his golden goose, Sophia." Paul took the last bite of his bread pudding smothered in orange sauce.

"We may need him," Sophia whispered.

"Sometimes there's no choice," Paul agreed. "This was great bread pudding."

"You should know." Tricia remembered their bread pudding breaks at the nearby diner when they were all at Thorne & Chase.

"Tricia's right." Sophia smiled at Tricia and Paul and her memories of the old days.

Jay interrupted the foodies. "Are you guys hiding something?"

"Of course not," Sophia lied to Jay's face.

Paul deflected Jay's probe. "Forget it. Ben's just sowing seeds. It worked out last time with Sophia . . . and might again. He likes to nose around."

Sophia got up to thank Ben for picking up the check, but his table was empty.

"That was nice of him." Sophia sat again.

"I bet he used an expense account," Steve grumbled and then added loudly, "And he didn't pay for the desserts. I got those comped from the hostess."

"Thank you, dear." Sophia kissed his cheek as she would a pouting child's.

* * *

Steve continued his grumbling all the way home. But he stopped complaining in the bedroom when Sophia undressed her Saturday night prepared-and-perfumed body under the stark ceiling light. As she hung her dress in the closet, her slender back, full buttocks, and lean legs excited him. He threw his coat and tie on the chair. He unzipped his pants and freed himself.

Steve went over and grabbed Sophia's waist from behind.

"What . . ."

"Shh . . . Shh." He leaned her forward with his chest and pinched her nipples.

Sophia moaned breathlessly.

She grabbed the clothes bar, arched her back, and presented her soft round buttocks. With no foreplay, he thrust himself into her. She was moist, open, and ready.

"You horny bitch." Steve slapped her buttocks again and again.

"That hurts," Sophia whimpered with desire.

"Good, you cunt."

Steve slapped her one more time hard and then grabbed her breasts. He squeezed and kneaded them and then twisted her nipples again until she yelped from the pain and moaned from the pleasure.

Sophia held onto the closet pole, her head on her wool suit

coats, as he pounded himself deep into her—twisting and pulling her nipples harder and harder.

She shut up and reveled in every delicious moment—wanting everything he gave her.

⌘

# CHAPTER 14

## Time and Chance

*"A lawyer with a briefcase can steal more
than a hundred men with guns."*
-Mario Puzo, "The Godfather"

Friday, just after lunch, Tony Moschella, a name partner at the law offices of Quarry, Warren & Moschella in Bakersfield, got a call from Tom Jackson.

"Hi, Tony. Tom Jackson here of Jackson, Hood & Lee in Denver. How's your afternoon going?"

Moschella knew the name and the firm's reputation.

"Good. Good. I hope you're not calling to change that."

"I guarantee not. I have a client with a lawsuit in your town, and we need a local firm involved. A man of your reputation and trial experience to act as local counsel."

Moschella had joined Quarry & Warren, the largest and oldest law firm in Bakersfield, twenty-five years earlier. He quickly became the youngest partner in the firm's history, and soon a name partner, changing the firm name to Quarry, Warren & Moschella. He had advanced at lightning speed because of his incredible drive, courtroom skills, and ability to bring in business. His niche was being Bakersfield's "go-too" litigator for companies in serious trouble because of product defects, environmental issues, and employee problems.

"It's the Holts, isn't it?" Moschella asked. "They finally got someone to take their case."

"Yes. Is that a problem?"

"Not at all. They shopped around here for a while. Did they get out-of-towners?"

"An L.A. plaintiffs' startup, Krause & White."

"Never heard of them."

"Remember the Thorne & Chase demise there? These are some of the refugees. It means they're top-quality litigators, but they're also used to big-firm support, which they don't have now."

"I'm sure we can handle them."

"Sports Gear just forwarded the Holts's demand letter. We've drafted a response rejecting it. Krause & White says they'll file Monday if Sports Gear won't pony up."

Tony was pleased to get the cold call, but naturally, as with all lawyers getting referrals, he had to ask, "Why me?"

"Two reasons. We keep tabs on lawyers in gun-friendly places like Bakersfield where our clients do business. And you're one of the top litigators in the biggest and best firm in the city with the widest social network. The other reason is that you don't have any clients in the gun industry or any ties to it, so you won't look like an industry stooge. Am I right about that?"

"You are. I don't object to guns, either. My family has lived here for generations, and I grew up around them. But I have no expertise in defending gun cases. Doesn't that bother you?"

"Not if you're willing to let us do most of the motions and other paperwork here in Denver. You'd be our 'face' in the courtroom and the go-to contact person for the local media and community. Will that work for you?"

It would. Not only for the fees, but also for the potential high-profile publicity, possibly beyond Bakersfield. It wouldn't be the first time for him.

"No problem, Tom. I'm glad to get the opportunity, and my firm will be too."

"Good. Send me your client engagement letter and I will have the general counsel of Sports Gear sign it today. I'll send that back along with a copy of the Holts's demand letter and our response. The lead is Sophia Christopoulos. Do you know her?"

"The name sounds familiar, but I can't place it right now."

"Her demand is ridiculous on its face and shows a real lack of knowledge about gun sales law. Review our draft response, and, assuming you have no issue with it, sign it and deliver it to her just before noon on Monday."

"Consider it done. Thanks for thinking of me."

\* \* \*

Saturday night at the Bakersfield Country Club, Tony was in a very good mood. Not just because he won his golf foursome that afternoon. Nor because of the dinner that night at the club with his statuesque blonde wife Lynn and her friends from the Bakersfield Junior League Board of Directors. She was a former president and its new sustainer chair. Such events were common enough in his prominent Bakersfield life.

No, he was basking in the glow of the referral he had received to represent Sports Gear against the Holts, and his new Denver connection with Tom Jackson. That could lead to many more referrals if he did a good job on the case.

\* \* \*

Moschella's path in life was foreordained. His family was synonymous with Bakersfield. For over a hundred years they owned the largest agricultural operation in the southern San Joaquin Valley. Their history was Bakersfield's history, and Moschella's was too— he had been a Bakersfield High School academic and athletic standout, a champion debater, salutatorian of his high school class, and a star shortstop on the baseball team that won the CIF Central Section title his senior year.

He spent his undergraduate years at Loyola Marymount University in L.A. because he wanted to be close to home and had a strong Roman Catholic heritage. There he was a successful debater and baseball player. However, his real focus was economics, which he came to love along with Lynn, whom he married after graduation.

They had met at Loyola, where she was drawn to his dark Italian-American looks, his six-foot-tall, well-muscled physique, and his intensity. He could not get enough of her charm, beauty, quick wit, and their shared Central Valley heritage. She had grown up in a devoutly Catholic Croatian-American family in Fresno, another Central Valley city north of Bakersfield.

He graduated magna cum laude after four happy years but was glad to go back to the Central Valley for law school. He finished first in his class at the University of the Pacific's McGeorge School of Law in Sacramento, California's capital, where so many Central Valley lawyers got their law degrees, and where he had been editor-in-chief of the law review.

After law school, his family expected him to return home to Bakersfield, and that was what he and Lynn had wanted, too.

\* \* \*

Moschella enjoyed an after-dinner grappa with his friends at the club. He was pleased with his life. Sure, he was showing some gray. He also had a bit of excess flesh from too much time in the office and in fine restaurants and not enough time in the club's exercise facility.

But he and Lynn, after so many years, still had a fond, if emotionally attenuated, partnership. To his sorrow, his Italian-American family had never fully accepted her because she was not Italian and because she couldn't have children. It was a great disappointment to both of them, also. She filled her time with charitable activities. Moschella smiled across the room at his prize, but she was busy with the "girls."

As Moschella and Lynn left the club in his 2012 Maserati Quattroporte, he knew a great weekend had already started. An even better week would follow.

⌘

# CHAPTER 15

## Black Monday

*"Suspense is worse than disappointment."*
-Robert Burns

At seven-thirty Monday morning, Moschella entered the lobby of the Stockdale Tower en route to his top floor corner office. He always arrived early, and so did Theresa Sandoval, one of his third-year associates. He held the elevator for her. He watched as she stepped in confidently, her perfectly tailored suit molded to a perfectly proportioned body.

Theresa was a vision, unusually tall, with jet-black hair, dark green eyes, and high cheekbones. She was a distraction to any male, Moschella included. Getting a Yale Law grad to join the firm was a coup for him. Not only because she was incredibly beautiful, though she was, but also because she was smart and driven. She had gone from being the daughter of a farm worker—living in field shacks from Hanford to Delano to Arvin and points between and around—to earning a scholarship to Garces Memorial High School in Bakersfield. It was the best Catholic high school in the city. She then graduated with honors from both UC Berkeley and Yale Law School. Moschella didn't know that Theresa's only motivation for coming to his firm was to be near her parents.

"Good morning, Theresa," Moschella said.

"Good morning, Mr. Moschella. Why so happy?"

"Perceptive. Frankly, a enjoyable weekend and great new case. How was your weekend?"

Ignoring his personal inquiry, Theresa said, "New case? Interesting issues? Staffed it yet?"

"Defending a new client, Sports Gear USA, from a possible wrongful death, negligence, and negligent infliction of emotional distress suit."

"Sports Gear is a major corporation. Congrats. What's it about?"

"I'm sure you saw it in the news. Remember the young man who committed suicide with the shotgun he bought from their local store here . . . Yale kid, as a matter of fact?"

"Oh. Yes, I do. He was something of a high school celebrity."

"Yes, hard to fathom why he would kill himself with a free Ivy League education at your alma mater. His whole life was ahead of him. With that pedigree, it would have been a good one."

The wheels were turning in Moschella's head. Tom Jackson had hired him to be the "face" of the defense team in Bakersfield. But Moschella was old Bakersfield. Big agriculture. A member of a family that had fought the unionization of farm workers along with the other major agricultural families in the Valley. Theresa, on the other hand, was new Bakersfield, a city increasingly Latino, as was California itself. She would be an asset on this case.

"Theresa, how's your workload? If you're interested, I think I could use your help on this one."

For Sandoval, who was ambitious, there was only one answer for any senior partner, especially one as nice as Tony Moschella. "My workload is more than manageable. I'd be glad to work on the case."

Moschella paused.

"Defending a gun seller isn't a problem for you?"

"My older brother Raul is a Marine Captain. He's done two tours in the Middle East so far. I learned about guns from him when I was very young. Guns are tools. They can be used for good or bad. This case? Not a problem."

"Great. Come to my office in an hour and we'll go over what we have so far."

Moschella pushed away some less than legal thoughts that crossed his mind whenever he encountered this gorgeous woman. He was glad he was married, Catholic to the core, and nonpredatory— unlike other male lawyers he knew.

* * *

That same Monday morning at Krause & White, Sophia watched the hours go by waiting for a response from Sports Gear. Nothing came. She continued organizing the discovery. Bryce and Eddie worked on the change of venue motion. Paul and Tricia had started preparing the motion for a priority trial setting.

At eleven-thirty, there was still no response. The gamesmanship made Sophia angrier. Now she was just itching for noon to arrive so she could e-file the complaint in Kern County Superior Court.

"Hey." Autumn was standing at the door.

"What?" Sophia steeled herself for another waste of time.

"How was your weekend?" Autumn's question was rhetorical. She immediately started recounting her pot-smoke-smothered weekend with the granola set.

"Some friends and I went up to Griffith Park at midnight Saturday. It's fun up there when there's practically no one around. The city lights with all the colors were amazing because . . ."

Sophia zeroed in on the FedEx envelope Autumn held. "Is that for me?"

Autumn handed it to Sophia. "It came in the eleven o'clock delivery."

The return address was a Bakersfield law firm whose name meant nothing to her, Quarry, Warren & Moschella. Obviously, a reply to her demand letter. Sophia was furious as she ripped it open. She had alerted Autumn that she was expecting an urgent letter. She bit her tongue as Autumn flounced out unheard and petulant.

"Dear Ms. Christopoulos: We represent Sports Gear USA. We regret the death of your clients' son, but his purchase of a shotgun from our client was in accordance with California law. Our client has no liability for his suicide, and rejects your demand for any compensation."

The letter finished with the usual reservation of all rights in the event of a lawsuit. Sophia was disappointed. Offering a nominal amount would have opened a dialogue for a quick settlement. It also would have signaled some sense of vulnerability or willingness to compromise. This did neither.

Sophia sent an email to everyone: "Received response from counsel for Sports Gear USA. Demand rejected. No counter. They sent us a message, and we're sending them a bigger one back. E-filing complaint at 12:05 p.m."

Sophia left her office and went to Peggy's desk.

"Hi, Peggy. Can you wait until exactly 12:05 p.m. and then e-file the complaint with the Metropolitan Division of the Kern County Superior Court in Bakersfield? And, when we get court confirmation and a copy with the case number, get our process server to serve it on CS Corporation here in L.A. It's Sports Gear USA's designated agent for service of process in California. But can you double-check that for me?"

As always, Peggy was happy to help Sophia.

"I hope you know what you're doing. I'm afraid for you kids."

"Don't worry. But thanks." Peggy's maternal choice of the word "kids" was endearing to Sophia.

⌘

# CHAPTER 16

## A First Amendment Ambush

*"The nicest thing is to open the newspapers*
*and not to find yourself in them."*
-George Harrison

On Tuesday morning, Wallace Holt woke early as usual and before Beth. He made their coffee and then took his usual walk down the pebble and dirt driveway to get the newspaper.

The fall air was crisp and cold, and the fall leaves from the deciduous trees crackled underfoot. He got the *Bakersfield Californian* from its labeled metal cylinder next to the mailbox. The free container was the *Californian*'s way of advertising along the rural and suburban roads of Kern County.

Wallace was part of the aging population who could not let go of the smell of newsprint every morning. At the age of three, he remembered his parents drinking coffee and reading the paper. He would sit with them and "read" the funny pages. After a while, his mother would put him on her lap and tell him what the letters in the little bubbles said. He was always delighted by hearing the words in the bubbles and by sitting in his mother's soft lap. He was also happy when he had guessed exactly what happened in the comic strips before she read them. He never told her that, because he was afraid if he did she might stop reading the little bubbles to him.

At the end of the driveway, Wallace took the paper out of its cylinder. He tore the plastic cover off and put it in his pocket as usual. He always read the headlines on the way back to the house unless it was raining. This cloudless morning he opened the newspaper.

Wallace read the headline: "Bakersfield Couple to Block Gun Sales."

Wallace stopped walking and squinted down at the story in small print. He wished he had worn his reading glasses.

He hurried as fast as he could with his arthritic hobble-trot back into the house.

"Beth. Beth. Come here." Wallace shouted up the stairs and grabbed his glasses from the entry hallstand.

"I'm here," Beth called from the kitchen. "I smelled the coffee."

"Oh." Wallace beelined into the kitchen and held the front page up for her. "Look. Look at the headline. 'Bakersfield Couple to Block Gun Sales.'"

Beth squinted and read the headline herself. "Oh my, that's us."

"We're going to stop that store from hurting any other kid." Wallace hugged Beth.

"We are."

Beth poured them each a mug of coffee. They sat at the table next to each other, and both put their glasses on. They read the article together without a word passing between them.

"Oh, no." Wallace looked at a heartbroken Beth.

She wept with good reason.

Wallace called Sophia's direct line even though it was too early for her to answer. He left a message.

"Sophia, it's Wallace. Call us. It's important."

The two finished their second mugs of coffee while they reread the article again and again. They were too upset to do their usual cover-to-cover ritual of dividing up the sections to read and then exchanging them. Instead, they got dressed and waited for Sophia's call.

* * *

"The newspaper is just plain wrong," Wallace explained to Sophia. "We aren't against gun ownership. We're not trying to stop gun sales here in Bakersfield. We just want justice for Mike. Can you see there on your computer?"

Wallace tried to listen to Sophia, but he couldn't hear her with Beth nudging and coaching him.

"Tell her the National Gun Association is quoted in there . . . tell her. And then they quote Mothers Against Guns and call us anti-gun fanatics? We're not part of them. We don't want to . . ."

"Quiet, Beth, I have to hear her." Wallace listened. "I understand, but you see the whole article is wrong. They wrote it wrong. And the NGA is in the article, but the NGA isn't in our lawsuit. Is it? Or those Brady folks?"

Beth watched Wallace with the phone to his ear. She went to pick up the other line, but too late.

"All right," Wallace mumbled. "All right. I won't forget to pick up Mike's things at the police station. I'll leave now."

Wallace slammed the phone down without another word.

"What did she say? Did we sue the National Gun Association, too?"

"No. No. Let me think."

Beth obeyed for one second and then blurted, "Well, what did she say?"

"Nothing. She went on about freedom of the press and all that goddamned Constitutional bologna."

"Wallace, the Lord's name. Shame on you."

"Sorry, dear. She's going to get the article and read it. I don't want you to worry."

"What good will that do? It's already here in black and white in our newspaper. Everyone reads it. What about our neighbors? They hunt with rifles. Everyone hunts. What about your friends in those gun clubs?" Beth teared up. "What about my church groups? What about Sunday service?"

"Just stop crying, will you? It doesn't help anything, and I can't stand it anymore. What if I cried all the time? Huh?"

"That's not nice." Beth cried harder.

Wallace ignored her. "I've got to go to get Mike's things for that damn lawyer. I'll be back." Wallace started out.

"But you haven't had breakfast." Beth turned from tears to routine.

He stopped and looked back at her. "I'm sorry, dear. I can't eat. I just . . . Look. Don't worry. It'll all be fine. I'm sorry."

"I'm sorry, too."

"Do you need anything while I'm out?"

"Bananas and some milk . . . bread maybe."

"I'll be back soon. It'll all be fine."

Wallace left in his green Chevy pickup that he kept shiny and waxed—shinier and more layered in wax since he retired. He wished he had waxed Mike's Bronco before Mike came home for his summer break. But after parking it by the side of the garage and covering it, Wallace had just forgotten about it.

* * *

All wasn't fine, as Wallace had promised. It was anything but.

Wallace began his slip down the rabbit hole of despair at the Bakersfield Police Station when he asked the duty sergeant for Mike's things. The police were through with the investigation. There was no real crime, except it is technically illegal to kill yourself in the state of California.

As Wallace waited alone in the sterile hall, he paced and then finally rested on a bench. He watched uniformed officers, criminals, detectives, and victims trailing by for over an hour.

The Bakersfield police, the "BP," were the fathers, brothers, husbands, and friends of gun owners, ranchers, farmers, hunters, gun range owners, gun club enthusiasts, and gun-loving homeowners— the protectors of their own castles. Guns had always been a part of the culture, with ranches and farms covering the county.

"I found the things." The sergeant finally returned with his captain.

"I'm sorry about your boy, Wallace." The captain shook Wallace's hand.

"Thank you."

"But what is this lawsuit I saw in the paper?" the captain asked.

"I don't know. They made a mistake. We . . ."

"What do you mean you don't know?" The sergeant shoved the box at Wallace and put the blood-splattered shotgun and umbrella both wrapped in clear plastic on top. "You filed it. Didn't you?"

"Yes. But . . ."

"See, Captain, I told you," the sergeant interrupted.

"It was a mistake. The newspaper made a mistake," Wallace tried to explain.

"What mistake? It's there in black and white. You want to stop people from protecting their own and going hunting," the sergeant argued. "You want to stop gun selling and . . ."

"Wait a minute, Sergeant, let him answer," the captain ordered.

"No. No," Wallace stammered. "I just didn't want them to sell a gun to my son."

"Well, that's selling 'em," the sergeant said.

"I guess." Wallace tried to appease the men. "But when we spoke to the lawyer, Beth and me, we told her that we . . ."

"The big L.A. lawyer, right?" The sergeant put his hand on his holstered hips.

"We couldn't get a Bakersfield lawyer."

"No kidding. They're not just out for a buck like those big city L.A. lawyers who'll do anything for money."

Wallace didn't argue his side. He didn't say a contrary word. He had learned long ago as a teenager when he was pulled over for speeding that "contempt of cop" was an actual, actionable *de facto* crime. And it had a consequence commensurate with one's words and attitude.

"What about my hunting cabin?" the sergeant went on. "What about the Guns & Beer Club? What about you? You own a gun, don't you?"

"Yes." Wallace cowered.

"Those outsiders just want to use you. If you . . ."

The captain stopped the sergeant with a gesture.

"You know, Wallace," the captain said. "Like I told you, I'm real sorry for your son, but in Bakersfield we keep the crime down because we protect our own."

"What about that surveillance tape, Cap?" The sergeant eyed it poking up from the box.

"It goes back to the store."

The sergeant took it from the top of the box. The two walked back down the hall to their offices. Wallace left remembering how nice the BP had been when Mike was first discovered. He wasn't sure about the lawsuit, but he was sure it was all Beth and he could think of doing for Mike, and they couldn't live with themselves if they did nothing.

As Wallace left with Mike's things, he thought that big-city cops might want guns off the streets. But not the BP, that was certain.

\* \* \*

Getting what Beth wanted from the grocery store was not fine either.

Wallace stopped at The Ranch Stand, the local mom and pop grocery he and Beth had frequented for years. It was close to the house, cozy, and friendly. Run by his friends Bob and Mary. No big-city chain stores with abrupt cashiers for Beth and Wallace. They liked to support Bakersfield's own. Bob and Mary had been their friends for thirty years and were active in the same church.

Wallace got the bananas, milk, bread, and a case of cold beer for himself. Lately, he had been buying more beer and more often.

The store was busy, and Bob opened a second cash register to help Mary with the checkout.

"Good morning, Bob," Wallace said. "How's it going?"

"Okay." Bob didn't look up with his usual friendly smile—a smile that earned them more business than the quality of their produce.

"Ran out of a few things," Wallace said. "Seems it's always a few things."

"Yeah." Bob kept his head down.

"Something wrong?"

That was all Bob needed to unload.

"Come on, Wallace, I read the *Californian* today and, look . . . I'm almost sold out. Bob pointed to the rack of unusually depleted newspapers. "I read about your lawsuit. And so has everyone. Bringing in that L.A. law firm to change our ways."

"Bob, we didn't. The lawyer . . . we . . ."

"I live and let live. But you want us all to pay for what your kid did. Me and Mary wouldn't be stand'n here today if I didn't have my gun to pull out when those 08ers high on coke came to rob us. They were gonna shoot us both for fun."

"Bob, I know . . . we know and . . ."

"We have a right to defend ourselves, no matter what your kid did."

Bob's wife at the other register and the locals in the checkout lines, some of them Wallace's neighbors, stared at him. There was an indistinct murmur of support.

Wallace put his head down and dropped two twenties on the counter. Bob made change. But, instead of counting it into Wallace's outreached hand, Bob slammed it on the counter. Wallace picked up the change and his groceries—unbagged.

He took the tongue-lashing, his change, his groceries tottering on his case of beer, and left.

\* \* \*

At home in the kitchen, Wallace didn't tell Beth what happened at the police station or The Ranch Stand.

"Quite a bit of beer, dear," Beth said as she put the groceries away.

"On sale."

Wallace snuck Mike's things up to his bedroom. He was so tired of Beth and her crying. He just wanted to be left alone to watch his usual afternoon movie on the commercial-free classic movie channel, but this time with beers—too early and too many.

The article and his hostile outing had already robbed him of his morning game shows.

⌘

# CHAPTER 17

## Pressing Matters

*"Power in America today is control*
*of the means of communication."*
-Theodore S. White

At her office Tuesday morning, Sophia listened to Wallace complaining on the phone as she found the *Californian* article on the Internet and read it. She understood and did everything she could to placate the Holts's outrage.

She had been pre-empted and outmaneuvered by Sports Gear. The article quoted the NGA, the Association to Preserve Gun Ownership, the Jewish Gun Rights Organization, the Second Amendment Organization, and other pro-gun groups amply and aggressively opposing the Holts's lawsuit. They characterized the Holts, Krause & White, and the lawsuit as anti-gun, anti-Constitution, and anti-Bakersfield—not as an action for responsible gun sales practices.

Clearly, staying low-profile to encourage a settlement had been a bad strategy.

The speed of the anti-Holt publicity spin was unexpected, but not the tactic—trial by press was regrettably common. Sports Gear was forewarned and prepared because the Holts had attorney shopped in Bakersfield.

But the media would not stay pro-Sports Gear for long. Sophia knew how to take control of the spin. She would counter the article and "educate" the jury pool to be sympathetic to the Holts. That was Sophia's only focus now—her own media blitz.

Sophia emailed the article to her team and called a meeting in thirty minutes in her office.

* * *

"But it's a lie. The Holts aren't anti-gun," Bryce stated the obvious.

"Can they do that?" Eddie asked. "Just lie and use people?"

"They've already done it," Tricia said

"It's the news. In all its gory glory," Paul said. "It's gospel, especially in traditional, conservative small-town America. We should have already prepared our own news release to hit back fast."

"Should have. Would have. Could have." Sophia was angry with herself.

"Look, we made a choice. Flying under the radar could have opened a settlement dialogue," Tricia said.

"And filing fast to get at them showed strength," Paul said.

"It got at them all right," Bryce said.

"The article's the proof," Eddie agreed.

"Let's focus." Paul glared at the young cubs.

"The story paints their gun culture as lily white and all-American," Tricia said. "They don't mention the black market trade, the gun trafficking, and the dirty cops who turn a blind eye."

"Cops on the take," Eddie interjected.

"Careful, Eddie," Paul said. "Talk like that could get us in real trouble."

"I could take care of all this with a visit to the Bakersfield newspaper building," Eddie suggested. "If you get my drift."

The team riveted on him.

"Just joking."

But Eduardo Emanuel Navarro Herrera wasn't joking. He was half Latino, half European-American mutt—but all L.A. barrio. The street had taught him how to fight, and his mother had instilled German-American determination in him. The name Emanuel was from his mother's side, and the name branded Eduardo as culturally blended because Emanuel was derived from German, Swedish, and English etymology. He was nobody's victim. He worked hard to keep his anger in check, but it hung there, just beneath the surface, always.

"We have to get on top of this," Paul said. "It might already be going to central news outlets and coming over the Grapevine to L.A."

There was a discordant debate amongst the group on the correct approach.

"Quiet, everyone." Sophia heard herself sounding like Rona— and stopped. "Please, we have to get a press package together. And protocol dictates a partner authorizes it. We'll use Rona."

"I have my Zeigler arbitration at ten," Paul said. "I don't know how long it will run."

"We'll handle it," Sophia replied. "You'd better prep for that and get some money in here. Go."

"I'll check my emails on breaks if you need me to review it." Paul got up and left.

"Eddie and Tricia, you two work on the news release with the real facts of the case. Be sure and respond to the false accusations against the Holts and us. Otherwise, keep it general. We don't want to reveal our strategy because at the moment we have none."

Tricia saw the first-years' eyes open wide and reassured them, "Don't worry, we will."

"Work up a few good sound bites all of us can use if we get blindsided somewhere by a reporter," Sophia added.

"Will that happen?" Bryce was excited.

"Who knows? But until we're polished and ready, 'no comment' is the only comment for all of us. Understand?" Sophia looked pointedly at Bryce and Eddie.

They nodded. Sophia and Tricia knew the drill from Thorne & Chase.

"Bryce," Sophia said. "Get copies of the NGA's and Sports Gear's news statements in the other cases so we know where they're going."

"Sure."

"Okay, everyone, get to work."

Bryce left.

"Don't forget Ben." Tricia stood.

"I haven't. Believe me. I'm calling him right now."

"Who's Ben?" Eddie asked.

"My news contact."

"Come on, Eddie." Tricia marshaled him out and shut the door.

With the media war begun, their press packet for Ben had to take priority. Sports Gear had to make an appearance in the case anyway by answering or filing a demurrer within thirty days. Sophia couldn't predict which, but she could predict the damage that would happen if Ben didn't get to work now. They had to pummel Sports Gear in the press like any big firm would.

As Sophia reached for the phone, it rang. Derek wanted Sophia down in his office.

"Damn." Sophia stood. "I don't have time for his crap."

* * *

Derek's office was big for a small firm. He and Rona had taken the two largest spaces after the conference room. He filled it with an impressive black straight-lined desk, a modern chrome table, and matching black leather chairs.

Sophia had barely seated herself across from Derek's at his desk when Rona strutted in like a short wrestler in heels—barrel-chested with stout, muscular legs. Her fluffy, short, red-hued blonde hair hid a less than attractive moon-shaped face with deep-set steel blue eyes. Her best features were her flawless skin, full lips, quick wit, and analytical prowess. She was devoid of any artistic talent and most social graces. She dressed for success with Mommy's allowance—an allowance provided to fulfill her mother's hope of marriage and grandchildren. Her mother's constant pushing and disappointment made Rona mean, forceful, effective, and efficient—all good traits in a trial lawyer, but not for attracting a man.

"So Eddie says we have a press problem now?" Derek said as Rona took the chair next to Sophia.

"The speed was a surprise." Sophia noted Eddie's indiscriminate mouth and ignorance of office politics—much like Sophia in her first year.

"Well, it wouldn't have been to me. Email us that article."

"Sure."

*In your dreams*, Sophia thought. *Like I have time for you.*

"You have a new priority," Derek said. "Publicity."

"We have to get to the jury pool now," Rona added. "Before the Bakersfield virus of half-truths spreads."

"I know," Sophia said. "I have Tricia and Eddie working on a press release and drafting sound bites for us. Bryce is researching Sports Gears other retaliatory news blitzes. And I have a contact who will run with it."

"Who?" Derek asked.

"I'll let you know if it pans out." Sophia played everything close to the vest with these two.

"If it doesn't, I have someone," Rona volunteered.

"I can call my person," Derek said.

"Thanks, but I've worked with my guy before. He's a pro."

Derek shamelessly had his feelers out to get his face in front of the camera. He had been a publicity whore from day one at Krause & White. Rona was the silent partner, unseen except in court. He intended to capitalize personally on Sophia's case.

Sophia would block any move Derek made. After being in the trenches at Thorne & Chase, she was not naive. She remembered Rona's moment of hesitation before she raised her hand to vote against taking the case. If Derek was out of the office and she muzzled Eddie, Sophia could bypass Derek for publicity approval.

Sophia would win the game of firm politics here because she had learned to play it brutally from big-firm cutthroats at their best— or, rather, their worst.

* * *

Back in her office, Sophia called Ben. She explained the case, the pre-emptive news attack, the press packet they were compiling for him along with other news releases Bryce was researching.

"Sounds big to me. Glad you called. We were a good duo last time, and I'm excited about this."

"Thank you, Ben." Sophia certainly never wanted this high-energy news shark to be on the other side of the aisle against her.

"I have this evening's broadcast to deal with. My staff will assess the *Bakersfield Californian*'s article and contact my sources at the national news service to see what has been organized by Sports Gear, the NGA, and the local yokels in Bakersfield."

"Good."

"I'll get it together. I'll meet with my executive producer, confirm a 'green light,' and be at your office tomorrow afternoon."

"I'll be here. Our receptionist leaves at three, so just come in and go to the right. You'll see my office. Be warned, it's a shoebox."

"As long as I can fit in it."

Ben's "green light" was a technicality. Ben was unstoppable and never thwarted by anyone or anything. Ben was smart, tactically gifted, and vicious. He excelled at massaging facts, pounding on sound bites, initiating attacks, and damage control—in fact, he thrived on crucifying anything and anyone—much like Sophia.

* * *

The whole team, with Paul's review via email, completed the preliminary press release, talking points, and sound bites for partner approval—or, more precisely, Rona's approval. Sophia knew Derek had a meeting out of the office tomorrow.

Sophia buried herself in getting together a list of discovery assignments.

The witness list was short as far as the sale went. But figuring out Sports Gear's corporate hierarchy for other witnesses and depositions was harder. They also had to get a document production request out to obtain everything Sports Gear had on its gun selling policies, sales and profitability of guns and ammunition at its stores, training manuals, and handbooks, other incidents like Mike's, and more.

She gave the first-years some of the easier discovery assignments, both the form and special interrogatories. Tricia took point on the complex ones—including requests for admissions, specific document requests, and requests for security tapes and electronically stored data.

*Where's Paul when I need him?* Sophia thought.

⌘

# CHAPTER 18

## And So the Race Begins

*"Litigation: A machine which you go into as a pig
and come out of as a sausage."*
-Ambrose Bierce

Wednesday morning the *Bakersfield Californian* did not let up. It hurled another thunderbolt with the banner headline "Guns Don't Commit Suicide, People Do." Worse—the local news anchors jumped on the bandwagon and protested their citizens' and every Californian's constitutional right to buy guns.

Pictures of Wallace and Beth stared out from every Bakersfield television channel. The pictures were from their church's Internet directory for members only. A "member" had provided them. Beth wept. Mike Holt's high school yearbook picture was also smeared across the television with a suicide caption. Beth wept even harder.

Wallace called Sophia again, angry at the degradation of their son, invasion of their privacy, and lies. Beth was in the background whimpering.

"We're on it. I have a meeting later with my newsperson, and we'll respin this. Don't worry."

The Holts were more than worried. They were in meltdown, and, fortunately for Sophia, they had yet to find out that the story had gone national. She didn't tell them. The only good thing, so far, was that nationwide it remained a small potato buried behind bigger potatoes. When it became a frontline news story, Ben and Sophia would be ready.

The L.A. television male-female news anchor couplings, in their charming sexualized tea-party postures, had not yet bothered to showcase the small-town spat, nor did the national television talking heads. And, fortunately, the Internet buzzed with its other usual detritus about "in-depth" spoon-fed politics, film stars' sex lives, oddly named kids, and sub-slanderous fictions.

Sophia told the Holts to stay home.

"Beth wants to skip her Bible meeting anyway after the picture thing," Wallace said. "It's cold and wet, and besides she didn't sleep well."

"Just stay home for a while unless you have to go out . . . and change your grocery store too."

"I've always gone there."

"I'm sorry, but you can't now." Sophia was incredulous that they hadn't decided that themselves.

Sophia understood the Holts's despair. Her parents were first-generation Americans and only partially acculturated. They lived within the Greek community. If they were ostracized from their small circle, it would kill them. And without her church activities, her mother would be lost.

* * *

Sophia stopped her empathetic indulgences and switched into action mode. She called a team meeting immediately to update them about the continued news coverage and to have them update her on the status of their assignments.

The first years were floundering with their interrogatories. However, dependable Tricia had finished her first draft of the document requests, which also sought physical evidence, like videos and pictures, and any of Sports Gear's computerized information and data. Tricia was using the scattergun approach hoping for a "smoking gun" to strengthen their case.

Sophia wanted the discovery done yesterday, even though they could not send anything out until ten days after they had served the complaint or Sports Gear responded, whichever came first. It had to get done and done right the first time. But only she and Tricia were there to help the first-years. Paul was still arbitrating, fighting to get money for his client, which also meant for the firm and the Holt case.

"I'll see you at noon for progress reports. Autumn will get us sandwiches . . . turkey and Swiss?" The group instinctively knew not to push their personal gastronomical preferences in this pressure cooker.

"Now, get back to your offices and work. Work fast. The onslaught has begun."

When Derek left the office, Sophia went to see Rona to get the press packet authorized. Rona, regrettably, telephone conferenced Derek in. The three ironed out the talking points, sound bites, and news release. Derek needled and yelled on the speakerphone like a baby whose personal publicity bottle had been taken away.

Sophia took the draft with their input back to her office and incorporated their trivial, ego-motivated suggestions to appease them. If Paul's arbitration didn't bring in money, these jabs would turn into body blows.

Sophia finished a complete informational file for Ben to use for his campaign, his anchor presentation, and to feed to the national news services.

* * *

At lunch, Sophia's team met in her office. Paul attended too because his arbitrator had a "thing" and gave everyone a two-hour lunch break. Paul reported the amounts they were negotiating remained high.

"You push there, and we'll keep pushing here," Sophia said. "We don't know if they will answer or demur, but the minute we can serve discovery, we will. We're getting it done for a real show of force."

"A big firm show of force," Tricia added.

"Right." Bryce was proud.

"I've been going over the local court rules in Bakersfield, too," Eddie volunteered.

"Master them," Paul said. "We're going to need one expert."

Sophia saw the fire in Eddie's eyes. She liked it. She liked him. He was a rough-cut diamond, but a diamond nonetheless. He was solid and would go the distance with them. Bryce was no Eddie, but he was another brain and pair of hands.

"Thanks, Eddie," Sophia encouraged him.

"You got it." His hazel eyes sparkled.

"Bryce, do you have those form interrogatories underway?"

"I do. I've never seen them before, and it's amazing how streamlined they are . . . sort of one-size-fits-all."

"Therein lies the rub," Tricia said. "That's why you two have to start the special interrogatories also. I'll help."

"I can too," Sophia said, "I want to . . ."

"Lunch is served." Autumn burst into the room and into Sophia's thoughts.

She put the bags of sandwiches, chips, and cookies on Sophia's desk. Paul began the grab.

"Thanks, Autumn," Sophia said. "Eat up, but let's go over . . ."

"Hey, everyone," Autumn announced. "I got a part in this semester's play. I'm a maid in the second act."

Autumn pirouetted and took a bow, oblivious to Sophia's get-the-hell-out glare.

"Congratulations," Eddie said. "I tripped the lights fantastic myself in college."

"Really?" Autumn smiled. "My new boyfriend, Stefan, says I am very good. He helps me with my lines."

Eddie had waited too long to make his move.

Autumn chattered on about her play. As usual, she ignored professional boundaries and the fact that people actually worked in their offices.

"Stefan says I have the blood of actors in my heritage."

Sophia watched Eddie bury himself in his sandwich. He would have said all that and more, but it was too late—if only by days. Timing is everything in love, and Autumn's heart was now with someone else.

Autumn swept out as she had swept in. The aftermath-of-Autumn left the room silent.

"Back to our discovery." Sophia rapped her knuckles on the table and then stopped abruptly, shocked at her Rona-like behavior. "Updates?"

The team discussed the status of the interrogatories, the document production requests, and the proposed requests for admissions. Then Paul volunteered to take the lead on noticing the depositions with Sophia. The first-years frothed at the mouth once again at the mention of depositions. Sophia delineated their discovery objectives and the theory of the case that would drive them, as any good lead litigator does, cautioning that everything could change as each battle was fought.

"Tricia," Sophia said. "I want you to evaluate what type of experts we should use."

"I've never done that before. The junior partners at Thorne & Chase usually . . ."

"No junior partners here," Sophia interjected.

"Right. Sorry. What kind of experts?"

"What do you think, Paul?" Sophia had no clue herself.

"I've never organized experts on a case before either, but it stands to reason we need an expert on suicide . . . like a clinical psychologist or psychiatrist."

"Do you have any ideas, Eddie?" Sophia needed him focused and not pining for Autumn.

"I don't know . . . a gun expert on sales and an expert on the economics of gun marketing."

"Not bad." Sophia encouraged the heartbroken young man, both for himself and for the case. "We'll keep both on our list. But we have to watch expenses. Eddie, can you start a file on articles about gun sales, guns used in suicides, that sort of thing? We can analogize. Statistics will show us where to go with this thing."

"Sure." Eddie refocused. "There might be something on gun registration and how soon after a purchase a gun is typically used in a suicide."

"And don't forget crimes," Bryce added. "Suicide is technically illegal."

"Good thinking, Bryce," Sophia said, knowing Sports Gear would have to be crazy to raise that. "We'll keep that on the back burner."

"Should we find someone who can testify about the proper level of training for people who sell guns?" Bryce asked.

"Excellent, Bryce," Tricia said. "We'll see what Sports Gear's training program and policies are first in discovery."

"When are you meeting with Ben?" Paul asked.

"This afternoon."

"Good. I have to get back to my arbitration" Paul grabbed the last chocolate chip cookie and left.

"Eddie and Bryce, you haven't met Ben so I may have you come in if there's time," Sophia said.

"I'd like that." Eddie was recovering from Autumn's boyfriend blow.

"Only if there's time." Sophia brought the overeager pup to heel.

"Tricia, can you get an email out with our assignments . . . in detail?" Sophia asked. "Autumn can check it and then distribute it."

"Yes." Tricia stood.

The meeting adjourned. The first-years grabbed the leftover chips and the extra sandwich.

Sophia considered her motley crew as they left.

*God help us*, she thought.

⌘

# CHAPTER 19

## Big Ben

*"Being a reporter seems a ticket out to the world."*
-Jacqueline Kennedy

Wednesday afternoon at three-thirty, Derek strutted into Sophia's office with Ben trailing.

"Your friend Ben is here. I gave him my take on the case."

"Oh?" *Your take*, Sophia seethed.

She should have foreseen that Derek would intercept Ben now that the case was getting notoriety. She would have to be more circumspect, even with her team. She also had to deal with Eddie and lay down the law about his indiscretions.

"Great to see you, Ben." They shook hands. "I'm sure Derek introduced himself."

"Yes."

"Thanks for bringing him down. Have a seat, Ben."

Derek sat in the other chair. "I'll sit in."

Sophia was about to object, but Ben spoke up.

"If you don't mind, Derek, my source is Sophia, and she's who I cleared with my executive producer. I'm afraid for now that's it."

"Oh?" Derek, outmaneuvered, stood but didn't leave until he made it clear to Ben who ran the show at this firm. "Sophia has been counseled by me and the other name partner. She has our *authorized* talking points. Anything further she will have to run by me."

Derek got the last word and one final diminution of Sophia before he sauntered out.

Ben shut the door. "What a piece of work. He reminds me of your Thorne & Chase managing partners. The arrogance. Weren't these guys your law school buddies?"

"Rona was, and I guess Derek by association. He was her friend. But big pond or little one, assholes abound. The law is a ruthless mistress, as well as a jealous one."

"You'd better keep your eyes open. It looks like you're in another snake pit. He's after you."

"You think?" Sophia chuckled sarcastically.

"Wait until the stakes get bigger."

"You don't know the half of it. Coffee?"

"No thanks. Too late in the day for me."

"Water?"

"I'm good. And the story's a go."

"Really?"

"Yep, my producer went up the ladder, and they all liked it. But we have to play it right . . . they want traction beyond some small-town suicide."

"Like what?"

"Don't worry, we'll have it. The NGA has already grabbed hold like a pit bull. It's a ticking time bomb for the Second Amendment right-to-bear-arms activists and all the anti-gun groups . . . from Moms Against Guns to the anti-toy-gun faction . . . I sold it as a budding national three-ring circus."

"If it doesn't settle."

"Settle? In your dreams. With a blitz like they started, there's no settlement in sight. When the gun folks come early to a party, they always stay late. My execs want teasers and a feature in the can *yesterday*. It's a dead news week, which is good for us."

"When do we do it?"

"Just be ready."

"Okay, but can we do something now about the lies coming out of Bakersfield?"

"My network won't attack an affiliate."

"So they get away with it?"

"No. When we get the truth out there, they will back down. Don't forget they've been co-opted by Sports Gear so far."

Sophia told Ben about the truck incident and what was happening to the Holts.

"You'd better watch it. Media coverage will make it more dangerous for you guys and the Holts."

"I told them to stay home."

"Good. Because we're shooting background footage and interviewing the Holts at their home with you there as soon as I can schedule it."

"That's more than I could ask for."

"I'm not saying it will run soon, but we'll be ready. I'll get a legal expert and a gun expert on tape too. But I'm going to need some help here."

"Anything. We have a press packet for you." Sophia handed it to Ben, who flipped through it.

"Looks good. And you have to pave the way with the Holts, too. Write up some interview questions for me and give them suggested answers. The older ones ramble, and editing those rambles into good sound bites is hard. Do some Q&As for your guys and draft a teaser or two for me to work with if you have time."

"We'll get it done."

"You're already good on camera, but you have to prep your team and the Holts. Coach them on camera physicality. No shifty eyes. No looking off camera. No hesitation. The Holts have to look sympathetic. One has to get weepy."

"That's no problem. The mother cries on cue like a waterfall."

Sophia's good-Greek-girl side was appalled at her callousness. She had definitely changed since she started practicing law.

"Is your whole team here to brief?"

"I'll get them."

* * *

The team sardined into Sophia's office with standing room only and shut the door.

"I think Eddie Herrera and Bryce McLaughlin are the people you haven't met. They're both sharp first-years." Sophia stretched the truth about Bryce.

Ben repeated a condensed version of his plan.

"This is exciting," Tricia said. "I'll stay tonight and get the Holt interview questions done with Sophia."

"I will too," Eddie fired.

"Count me in." Bryce would not be sidelined.

"This is housekeeping," Ben said. "I'm going to take off. Have to deal with tonight's broadcast. Nice seeing everyone and glad to meet you two."

Sophia walked Ben out. Derek was in his office on the phone, or he would have been lurking.

\* \* \*

When Sophia returned to her team, they divided up the talking points for the upcoming feature and the interviews. They had to be prepared for the out-of-town interview when Ben called. She included Eddie and Bryce. Their votes to take the case had earned them that.

The two women worked together on the pivotal Holt interviews well after the rest of the team was gone. At one-thirty in the morning, they emailed Ben the work the team had done on all the players and abbreviated points about the legal landscape as well.

On her drive home, Sophia was satisfied with the preliminaries for a feature, a summary of the law and the case for a feature, and, most importantly, the substantial interview questions with answers for the Holts and her team.

She was both wired and tired—like any good litigator in overdrive.

⌘

# CHAPTER 20

## Gas Not

*"Here we are, trapped in the amber of the moment.*
*There is no why."*
-Kurt Vonnegut

Wednesday Wallace and Beth stayed home all day as Sophia advised. After dinner, the television bombarded them with disturbing local news flashes and the local stations' derogatory teasers about Mike and their case.

Wallace turned it off, and they sat together in the living room alone with each other's impaired company. Beth read her paperback romance. She picked them up at the not-so-nearby Mark Down Mart along with cozy mysteries. Wallace watched Beth. He had always hated her selfish escape into books—ignoring him.

"The wind is really whipping around out there," Wallace said. "Do you think it's going to rain?"

"No, just blow." Beth did not take her eyes off her book.

The ensuing silence was broken only by the gusting wind through the trees.

"This is ridiculous." Wallace went to the picture window and gazed out into fall's early darkness. "What are we supposed to do? Stay locked in our house, not read the newspaper, not watch television?"

Beth looked up. "You can read your Civil War magazines."

"I've read them."

"Grab one of my paperbacks from the spare room then."

"I hate your books. Those fake people's lives bore me."

"Then watch one of your movies." Beth went back to reading.

Wallace grunted and rummaged through their ever-growing cardboard box of DVDs in the corner. "I've seen them all."

"I'll play gin rummy with you."

"I'm not a child. You don't have to fill my time with rainy-day activities. I'm going to Mark Down Mart and get some new movies."

"Don't do that. Use that thing we got . . . that box . . . that shows movies."

"Streams . . . streams movies. And you know I don't know how to use that damn thing. Mike was going to show us."

Beth's eyes welled with tears. "I know."

"I'm going." Beth's crying was the last straw.

"Don't."

"I need gas anyway."

"Then put on your coat. And don't talk to anyone."

"Fine." Wallace grabbed his favorite old jacket with its sheep's wool collar hanging on the hall coat rack.

Beth dabbed her eyes with a tissue and went back to reading.

Wallace drove up his gravel drive past the large oaks, poplars, and *ficus nitidas* whipping and howling in the wind. He wished he hadn't been too cheap to get them pruned last year. He did need gas. His reserve light was on. He would never have let that happen in their "real" life.

* * *

The two-lane road was full as Wallace headed for Mark Down Mart. It was evening errand time for people who worked all day. This particular night, they all shared the road with wind-propelled tumbleweeds and gusts of sand and dry topsoil from the fields.

Even though it was in the same direction, Wallace was glad the Mart came before the Sports Gear store. He didn't want to see the place where he had bought so many things for Mike growing up.

He remembered the basketball and hoop for Mike's tenth birthday. Mike loved shooting baskets on the driveway. He still had that hoop and ball in the detritus that filled their overstuffed, spider-infested garage. Wallace regretted taking Mike's once shiny and purring blue Bronco out of the garage when Mike left for Yale and parking his own trailered fishing boat there instead.

He regretted a lot.

\* \* \*

At Mark Down Mart, the parking lot was full of cars, trucks, abandoned shopping carts, and people racing in and out bundled against the wind. Yet, even with the high winds, tire-kicking locals hung out as usual in the far corner—leaning on their cars, sitting on the hoods, drinking beers, and partying.

People from Oildale and other Bakersfield neighborhoods miles away came to buy the Mart's cheap beer and find company there. Their pickups, motorcycles, and dirt-caked cars covered the side lot, spilling onto an adjacent vacant lot. It was a gathering place for the young, from troublemakers to the downright deviant, and also just the escapees from domestic horridness or boredom. Close by were the three cheapest-in-town gas pumps that usually had lined up cars—but the wind made the lines short this time.

On the way in, Wallace frowned at the ne'er-do-wells, bundled against the wind—smoking, toking, and drinking.

A food truck was parked near the gathering out on the curb of the road with a line of waiting customers—it was a public road, and the Mart couldn't run it off—besides the salty, fatty food led to more in-store beer sales. The truck charged exorbitant prices that more than made up for the drinkers' savings on the Mart's beer.

\* \* \*

In the store, Wallace went to the dollar bin of DVDs. He grabbed twelve movies he hadn't seen before. He figured with all this "freedom of the press" to lie, things were just going to get worse before they got better. He picked the shortest checkout line.

"Excuse us, buddy." A young man and older friend got behind Wallace. "Can we just set these up here?"

They both reached past Wallace and slid their twenty-four-pack beer cases onto the conveyor belt, pushing Wallace's DVDs forward. They smelled of sweat and were crusted with dirt from construction work.

"Sure." Wallace put gray rubber dividers between their beer and his DVDs.

At the cashier, Wallace swiped his card and asked her to ring up a twenty-dollar coupon for gas. It was a few cents cheaper if you used their coupons. Probably because people forgot to use them or lost them.

"ID and credit card." The middle-aged female cashier double-bagged Wallace's DVDs.

She looked up from the ID and said, "You're that man on TV with the suicide kid. I'm sorry about that. I have boys too. They are a handful. Suicide. It's worse than them killing someone else, isn't it?"

"I guess." As Wallace signed the magnetic screen, customers who heard zeroed in on him.

"Well, I know. I can visit my oldest in prison." The cashier was devoid of any social filters. "He's in for manslaughter. He'll come home. Yours won't."

"No, he won't." Wallace reached for his license, credit card, and coupon to escape her loud mouth.

"Hey, quit your jawing and get the line going," a baseball-capped guy yelled from the growing line.

"Just hold your horses," the cashier hollered. "Have some respect. This man's got that dead son in the news."

"You?" The older construction worker stepped in front of his buddy and stood over Wallace. "You're the guy against guns."

"No. I'm just against selling guns to . . ."

"Right. That's what he said." Another man with a packed cart and a cigarette behind his ear joined in. "Against selling guns. That's un-American."

Wallace grabbed his bag. "Give me my things."

"Sure." She threw down his ID, coupon for gas, and receipt. "You don't have to be so uppity."

\* \* \*

When Wallace got outside he had to wait for three cars to get gas—he wanted to just leave, but he was on reserve. He was enraged at being humiliated by that mother of a criminal and those other ignorant, uneducated, smelly rednecks.

As Wallace gassed up, he watched the construction guys from the store encounter join the partiers at the side of the parking lot—one sitting leaning on his truck and the other on his bike. The cigarette-eared man followed and looked over at Wallace as he lit his smoke and took long needy drags. The two construction workers absorbed the giggling young estrogen of two short-shorted gals—their long bare legs cold and covered in goose pimples got the testosterone attention they planned on.

When Wallace got in his pickup, he saw the dirty-muscled males and giggling bare-thighed females looking at him and talking. He turned away and waited impatiently at the exit before finally turning right into the speeding traffic on the main road.

⌘

# CHAPTER 21

## Besieged

*"The coward only threatens when he is safe."*
-Johann Wolfgang von Goethe

On the way home Wallace blasted the heater. He was cold from pumping the twenty dollars of gas and furious at what passed for their lives now.

He drove too fast back to his prison. He avoided looking into the oncoming headlights because Beth had read that it helped night driving. It did. Wallace's own headlights magnified the sand and dust snaking over the black asphalt. The wind was worse, and tumbleweeds bounced in clusters now across the road. His thick coats of wax protected his truck.

At the giant poplars and *ficus nitidas*, Wallace turned right into his driveway. The trucks and cars behind him sped by into a mass of red taillights braking further up.

*An accident*, he thought. *People drive like fools.*

\* \* \*

"I'm back."

Wallace set his bag of hard-earned new movies on the small table near the front door. He hung his jacket on the coat rack, glad to be home safe with Beth and his movies.

"Get something good?" Beth called.

"I hope so. Want some hot chocolate? It's cold out there."

Wallace brought them both mugs of hot chocolate with miniature marshmallows melting at the top. He got the bag of DVDs and started a star-laden action adventure movie. It was a fast-paced, loud distraction that buried the noise of the wind and, more than that, the memory of his Mark Down Mart ordeal—an ordeal that exemplified his life now, and Beth's too.

He kept the incident to himself as he escaped into his movie full of sex scenes, frenetic gunfights, and car chases.

Beth looked up from her book. "That's where this whole society gets it. Movies like that with everyone killing each other."

"Not tonight, please."

She stopped and didn't look up again.

Wallace followed the movie into a world where his problems did not exist. He was happy.

\* \* \*

During a midmovie car chase with bullets flying, there was a loud crash outside.

"What was that?" Beth looked over her book.

"Just the trash cans. I'll pick them up in the morning." Wallace sipped his now lukewarm chocolate.

"No, I hear voices." She put her book down and sat up, alert.

"It's the wind and the trash cans, we'll wait 'til . . ."

"Shh. There they are again." Beth got up and looked out the window but was faced with blackness. "I think there's someone out there."

"Don't be silly." Wallace paused his movie.

Beth went to the front door.

"Don't open that. It's too cold. Forget it. It's the wind."

Beth ignored him. She opened the front door, turned on the porch lights, pushed open the screen door, and peered beyond the light into the dark.

"Beth." Wallace went to bring Beth back in. "Shut that door. Can't we have any peace? All I want to do is enjoy . . ."

"There. There." Beth pointed into the dark in the direction of a revving engine.

From the black, a motorcycle emerged into the porch light. It shot up the left veranda steps, whipping past Beth, and thudded back down the right steps. At the same time, bottles crashed onto the veranda and flew into the living room picture window shattering it—pieces and shards covering Beth's happy floral life.

Wallace grabbed Beth. "Get in here!"

As she retreated, a bottle volleyed off the screen door and grazed Beth's forehead.

"I . . ." Beth turned, dazed, with blood running down her forehead.

As Wallace pulled her back inside the house, a pickup that had been lurking unseen turned on its headlights. It began driving in circles, digging up the lawn, with its horn blaring and headlights shooting through the dark at the trees and house. Another pickup lit up in the driveway. It disgorged female laughter and epithets as it revved and honked.

Wallace slammed the front door and locked it. But the sounds came in loud and clear through the broken picture window.

He helped Beth up the stairs to the nearest room, the guest bedroom.

The yelling, whooping, and revving still sounded in the wind, and the motorcycle pounded up and down the veranda again and again.

"Wait here." Wallace got Beth a cold, wet washcloth from the bathroom and held it on the small cut at her hairline. "How do you feel? Are you dizzy?"

"No. No . . . I'm fine, dear. Really." Beth's hands shook as she held her compress and looked up at Wallace. "This is because of the suit, isn't it?"

"Of course. Damn them." Wallace didn't tell Beth they were from the Mark Down Mart.

"We shouldn't have . . . I shouldn't have made you go to the lawyers."

"What's done is done. It was the right thing." Wallace soothed Beth with a lie.

"I'm sorry," Beth whimpered.

"Stay here." Wallace got Beth a second damp washcloth for her cut and told her to stay in the bedroom.

"Don't! Don't leave me." Beth started crying.

"Not now, Beth. Stop it. I can't hear."

Wallace headed for the stairs. He went back down, opened the front door, and held the screen door open. He peered out, but the porch light only illuminated him for them.

"Get out of here. I'm calling the cops," Wallace shouted into the windy night.

As he shouted, he remembered the police station and the hostility. So, instead, Wallace chose self-help. He grabbed two unbroken beer bottles from the entry hall and went out onto the veranda. He saw their tormentors.

"Get the hell out of here. I know who you are. I have your license plate numbers from the Mark Down Mart."

Wallace threw one beer bottle at the truck, still digging into his lawn, and shattered its windshield.

"Bull's-eye," Wallace cheered.

The truck stopped.

Wallace took aim at the motorcycle stopped on the edge of the lawn. The rider had a cigarette lit and hanging from his mouth. Wallace aimed below the helmet and hit the man's shoulder.

"Son of a bitch," the bike rider screamed and then drove toward the open door.

"Get him," the two females screamed from their pickup on the driveway. "Get both of those fucking gun haters."

Wallace turned tail, hobbling back into the house, all his joints complaining. He slammed the door and locked it.

The motorcycle tire banged the front door again and again. The old farmhouse's heavy wooden door started to split but didn't give way. Giving up, the motorcycle made one last pass, crushing the metal watering can and knocking over Beth's ceramic pots, shattering them.

Wallace remembered the shotgun splattered with Mike's blood in the box of things from the police station in Mike's room. Ignoring his pain, he hurried upstairs, pulling on the stair rail to keep going. In the hall, he stopped, hearing nothing but the wind again. They'd had their fun, it seemed.

He waited for the vandals to lick their wounds and leave. There was another crash; a few more beer bottles thrown, then revved engines. They left with noisy curses and laughter down the gravel driveway. Their tires peeled onto the main street.

Other than the wind in the trees, it was quiet once again.

* * *

Wallace returned to Beth and instinctively locked the bedroom door.

"They're gone?" Beth asked.

"I heard them leave. I'm just about sure."

"Just about?"

"I'm sure. But let's wait a minute. I hit the truck and the guy on the motorcycle with their own bottles."

"Wallace, you should have just let them go. You could have made them madder. You could have been hurt."

"I didn't . . . and I wasn't."

"You're a brave man."

"Let me have a look at that." Wallace took her compress. "It's stopped bleeding. Doesn't look bad at all."

"Thank you, dear."

They waited and listened. All they heard was the wind whipping through the trees.

But then—gunshots.

Beth screamed.

"Shh. Wait . . . it's the movie . . . the pause timed out." Wallace laughed.

Beth laughed too—the tense laughter of relief.

* * *

They sat together on the bed, and Wallace put his arm around Beth. She was still shaking but no longer crying. They listened, waiting for the movie to end. It did. Then all they heard was wind still whipping their trees. Neither of them wanted to go back down.

"The wind is worse," Wallace whispered.

"It is . . . but I don't hear those thugs."

"They did what they came to do."

"I can't believe this."

"Me either," Wallace lied. He could believe it. He did believe it. Beth just hadn't been out in town as much as he had.

"Where are the police?"

"I didn't have time to call." Wallace didn't tell her he had thought better of it.

"You should have. I'll go down and do it."

"Call from our bedroom. I'll look around downstairs."

"All right."

"I've got to get some plywood from the shed to close up the window anyway."

Beth stood, but then sunk back onto the bed.

"Are you sure you're all right?"

"Yes, I'm fine. Just give me a minute."

Wallace did.

"Do you smell that?" Beth asked.

"I can't smell anything with my allergies . . . you know that."

"Were you cooking something?"

"No."

"Look . . . look . . . under the door."

"Smoke."

"Fire!" Beth screamed. "Fire! Fire!"

⌘

# CHAPTER 22

## Keep the Home Fires Burning

*"Betrayal is the only truth that sticks."*
-Arthur Miller

Smoke undulated under the bedroom door. The wind gusting in through the shattered living room window swept it through the house.

"We have to get out of here." Wallace grabbed the door handle.

"Wallace, don't . . . don't!" Beth screamed.

"It's not hot." He opened the door.

Raging noise and smoke blasted at them. Beth's screams turned to chokes. Wallace bent his arm and covered his nose and mouth with the long sleeve of his plaid shirt. He looked down the smoke-filled hall and saw fire thrusting from the living room into the entry. Their smoke alarm with its ancient, corroded batteries was silent.

Wallace hurried back to Beth, gasping and choking through her washcloths.

"Come on." Wallace led her down the hall to the master bedroom and called 911.

"Get . . . get the fire department here," Wallace rasped. "They're burning us out!"

"Wallace." Beth pulled on his arm. "We have to go."

"I'm not staying here with you on the phone and burning to death. Are you crazy?"

Wallace threw the receiver on the bed. He looked at the window. It was too high to jump. He led them back into the hall.

"I can't breathe," Beth choked.

"The fire is in the living room. We can get out through the kitchen. Fast."

"No. No."

"Put the washcloths back up on your face there. Come on." Wallace put his shirtsleeve up again, took Beth by the hand, and dragged her toward the stairs.

"I . . . can't see."

"Hold on. Stay low on the wall."

They fought together, sightless through the smoke, Wallace choking through his shirt. Beth gasped through her washcloths, but held on strong—she was younger. Wallace slowed but did not let go of her. He got them to the stairs.

"The box." Beth choked through the washcloths and over the roar. "Evidence . . . we . . ."

Wallace only heard the word "evidence."

"No." Wallace gagged and held on to the wall. "Beth. Beth."

Beth didn't answer.

His age and allergies made him even more vulnerable to the dense smoke billowing in the hallway. He couldn't see more than a few inches.

"Beth," he whispered sliding down the wall. "Help . . . hel . . ."

Beth looked at Wallace, weak and fading. She hesitated, but then handed him one of her damp washcloths. Then she pulled loose without a word and disappeared up the hallway into the smoke to Mike's room.

Wallace was alone. He couldn't move. His breath was waning with each second. He couldn't hold the washcloth up to his face. He collapsed to the floor.

\* \* \*

When Wallace came to, he was on a stretcher, breathing with an oxygen mask, painfully, but still breathing. Dazed, Wallace heard men's voices over him.

"A can of lawn mower gas in the living room?" the paramedic asked.

"From the spread . . . thrown in . . . Molotov cocktail style," the cop said.

"This old couple? I can't believe that."

"The living room window was shattered *in*. Not from the fire. And look at the torn-up lawn."

"Jesus. Who?" the paramedic asked.

"I don't know, but this is that anti-gun couple in the news."

"Oh."

"Beth," Wallace murmured.

"Sir?" the paramedic said.

Wallace opened his eyes and turned his head. The house still stood. The flames were out, but gray smoke still oozed and was swept into the black night by the wind.

"Beth." He leaned up on the stretcher and looked for her.

"Lay back, sir."

"Beth." Wallace pulled off the mask—his throat hurt—he choked.

"Hold on." The paramedic kneeled over him.

Wallace fought against the blankets to go get Beth.

"Bea . . ." Wallace's throat locked up from the pain.

"We got her, old-timer. She's been transported. We'll get you to the hospital too." The paramedic gently laid Wallace back down.

"Old-timer" rattled through Wallace's mind.

The cop left. The other paramedic hopped out of the ambulance, and the two lifted Wallace's gurney into the ambulance.

* * *

As the ambulance sped down the road and the siren wailed, Wallace remembered. Beth had abandoned him in the fire. Tears began to stream down Wallace's face under the oxygen mask.

He cried for only the third time in his adult life—the first for his mother when she died—the second for Mike when they found him—and this third time, not for Beth or the fire or his pain. He cried for himself because, after all his years of devotion to Beth, she had deserted him. He had begged her for help, and she left him in a heap in the hall.

With each labored breath, Wallace gradually stopped crying and hatred overwhelmed him. He hated the mouth-breathing rednecks who had done this, but not for the fire. He hated them because of Beth—she had chosen her dead son and uncertain vengeance over him. He wished he had never gone to Mark Down Mart that night.

Her betrayal negated all the joys they'd had, all the heartache they had endured with dignity and love, all the intimate anger and forgiveness, all the mornings of coffee and newsprint, all the companionship, all the support, all the hope—all the years were erased. All destroyed by a single decisive moment of choice.

When the paramedics lifted him from the ambulance, Wallace lay numb, thinking of Beth turning her back on him and disappearing into the smoke. Together they could have made it out. They had always made it through everything together.

In the emergency room, the noise mercifully silenced his thoughts.

⌘

# CHAPTER 23

## Not Quite Prime Time

*"There are two kinds of people,*
*those who do the work and those who take the credit."*
-Indira Gandhi

Thursday morning in L.A. Sophia overslept. Working until 2:00 a.m. with Tricia on Ben's assignment had taken its toll.

She finally stirred from a dreamy, twilight sleep with the smell of coffee coming from the kitchen. Steve was up.

"You'd better get going, sleepy head," Steve whispered in Sophia's ear, causing exciting tingles to radiate down her neck and up her scalp. "It's nine."

"Oh, no. Why didn't you wake me?" All the pleasure of her drowsy waking and sexual thoughts imploded into reality. "I've got to get to the office."

"Coffee first." Steve, half-dressed for work, handed her usual mug.

"Thanks. Flip on the news, will you? Ben's teasers for our feature are airing today."

"Record it for me. Gotta go."

"Sure." Sophia sipped her coffee. "Mmmm . . . that's good. What is it?"

"The amaretto hazelnut. My new compulsion." Steve grabbed the remote and pushed the power button.

"Besides your lips." Steve leaned over and kissed her, a long lingering kiss.

Sophia accepted the kiss but peeked at the television. Her eyes popped out of her sockets, and she left Steve kissing the air.

"What the . . ."

Sophia grabbed the control and turned the volume up. The fire-damaged Holt home flashed on MPC television, Ben's biggest competitor. Below a caption read "Arsonists Hit Bakersfield Home."

"That's their house."

"Whose?" Steve turned to look.

"My new clients."

"The gun people?"

"The Holts."

"Jeez, did they get out?"

"I don't know."

"They say it comes in threes."

"What?"

"Bad luck."

The coverage flipped to Sophia's office building in L.A. with Derek on the steps. Five reporters from local news stations crammed their alphabeted microphones in his face. "Derek White, Partner at Krause & White" was captioned.

"Yes." Derek stood tall and gloried in the moment. "The Holts are our clients, and we are going to get to the bottom of this vandalism . . . this arson."

The word "our" blasted through Sophia's brain.

"Have the Holts been released from the hospital yet?" the reporter asked.

"Hospitalized?" Sophia looked at Steve.

"They always take old people in," Steve said. "Don't worry."

Derek coughed and cleared his throat—an old stall tactic when you had no answer. "I don't have an update . . . as for . . . ."

"Mr. White?" Another reporter saved him from his own ignorance. "Does this have anything to do with their lawsuit against Sports Gear USA?"

"I can't speculate. There is an ongoing police investigation. But this firm represents the Holts because Sports Gear should not have sold their son, Mike, the shotgun he used to commit suicide. It is our contention that they knew, or should have known, that he was distraught and suicidal at the time."

"He's using my talking points and sound bites, the bastard." Sophia was infuriated.

"Question?" a reporter called from the back. "What kind of parents were the Holts? Why did their kid do it?"

"The Holts are good people," Derek repeated Sophia's assessment of the Holts that he had ridiculed at the Monday morning business meeting.

"Then what was wrong with their son?"

"Mr. White? Mr. White?" Clarissa Chang, the MPC reporter who fought Ben for ratings, interrupted the pabulum answer Derek was formulating. "How were the Sports Gear employees supposed to know what Mike was going to do with the shotgun? Are they mind readers? Is that what your anti-gun lawsuit is about?"

"There are laws that control their sales and their conduct." Derek smiled for the camera.

The camera panned to Ben's nemesis, Chang. "We'll keep you updated on the developments here. We also invite you to listen to my special report on guns in America this evening at seven on MPC. We'll have a representative from the NGA, a Constitutional Law professor at the local Magnum Opus Dei law school, some other knowledgeable panel members, and hopefully Mr. Derek White will be able to join us as well."

"I'd be happy to." Derek's face gravitated to her camera, and his mouth sucked up to the outreached microphone.

"That was Derek White," Chang jerked the microphone back. "A partner at Krause & White, the firm that represents the Holts in their anti-gun lawsuit against Sports Gear USA. And this is Clarissa Chang signing off until tonight at seven when we will bring you an analysis and in-depth coverage of guns in America."

A commercial blared at three times the volume. Sophia turned the TV off and threw the remote on the bed.

"Son of a bitch," Sophia jumped up and headed for the shower. "I sleep in once . . . once in my life and my clients are in the hospital with their house fried . . . and that ass just stole my case."

"It does sound like it's his case."

"Ya think?" Sophia screamed from the shower. "If he plans on doing that interview tonight, he's crazy. That's my case, those are my clients, and I promised Ben the exclusive."

"You go get 'em, kiddo." Steve put on his worn polyester blue tie.

"I'm going to kill him."

"I'm sure you will." Steve finished tying his single Windsor knot.

"But first, I have to see how the Holts are and if we have a case left."

Sophia jumped out of the shower and grabbed a fresh, dry-cleaner-bagged suit from the closet and dressed. "I have to get down there and head this off."

"You will. You're the smartest girl I know. If you need me to take care of that guy, just call."

Steve put on his holstered gun and suit coat. He was so sincere and so full of platitudes when it came to her work. He had no tactical mind. He was a checker player, not a chess player. He had no complex thinking skills. In fact, sometimes she doubted he did much thinking at all, satisfied to live off his looks and good instincts for detective work. He was of no help to her when the chips were down—ever. He was more of a millstone around her neck when she was in crisis mode because he didn't understand anything but an A-to-B straight line. The black and white of humanity. He didn't see the diagonal, the zigzag, the backwash of ugly legal minds, or the underhanded maneuvers, both by opponents and colleagues. His only reality was blue through and through—everyone in blue had his back, and he had theirs.

"Hey, get your cell . . . it's ringing."

Sophia, nearly ready to leave, stopped cataloguing Steve's shortcomings. She was glad her cell rang before she lost it and told Steve exactly what she thought of his irritating simplicity, platitudes, and "go-get-'ems."

Steve would never understand—he hadn't the few times she had lost it about work before. His eyes glazed over—the only extent of his understanding was his own hurt. There was no bigger picture. She would never have his intellectual support when it counted because he had none to give. And attacking his deficiencies just harmed what they did have. And she liked what they had—most of the time.

Steve gave her a quick peck on the forehead and left.

It was Paul calling, always her savior.

* * *

"Paul, I'm glad it's you."

"Did you see Derek?"

"What an asshole. I'm gonna cut him off at the knees."

"If you don't, I will. I'll . . ."

"You're on speaker," Sophia interrupted. "But we're alone. Steve's gone."

"I don't personally care at this point."

"I get it," Sophia said. "Did you call the hospital?"

"Yes, I reached Wallace. He's being discharged with a raspy voice, but he'll recover."

"Good."

"Not so good . . . he's in meltdown and insists on dropping the suit."

"Damn it. What about Beth?"

"She's still intubated for trachea and lung smoke burns, but doing okay."

"Are you sure?"

"They said it's just a precaution for now."

"Good . . . but does she want to give up, too?"

"Hell, no. The nurse said she shook her head no so hard she had to steady her tubes. Beth saw the TV coverage saying they were bad parents and calling Mike a nut. She's really mad."

"Can we go ahead with just Beth?"

"Not really. We have to have a unified front."

"Then I'll handle it."

"But speaking of a unified front, what are we going to do about Derek?"

"Kill him."

As Sophia finished getting ready, she listened to Paul's rant about betrayal and how this was a replay of Thorne & Chase. Paul understood it all—unlike Steve.

"Look, I'm leaving now," Sophia said. "I'll see you at the office."

"I know you. Don't go off half-cocked. Come see Tricia and me first. We'll figure out a strategy against Derek."

"Okay. Fine." She hung up and put on her heels.

Sophia was counting on Paul's help as always. He was smart and strong. She should be with him, not Steve. He was the one she needed. She knew that, deep down. But Steve played her body like a fine-tuned violin. He was handsome and fun. On the other hand, her parents couldn't stand him—his cop-ness, his American ways, and how he kept touching their daughter in their own home; he even kissed her at the Sunday dinner table.

"Shit. Now's not the time. Focus." She left for the office.

⌘

# CHAPTER 24

## Back, Meet Knife

*"Ambition can creep as well as soar."*
-Edmund Burke


In her car, Sophia fielded Ben's call.

"I had an exclusive on your case. What's that Derek doing going on MPC with Chang tonight?"

"He's gone rogue."

"You've got to take care of it. My producer wants a guaranteed exclusive. You have to control your people."

"Ben, tell him we'll fix it. I need you. The other reporters are mischaracterizing our case. It's not about gun control. It's about screening sales to crazies, for lack of a better word. Did you read my press packet and the email attachments?"

"Yes, it's all good, but we have to have exclusivity."

"I was up all night working on the case and overslept. How was I to know someone would burn the Holt house down?"

"Bad luck, but Chang's after my ratings, and my producer is after me. You have to stop Derek from going on her program tonight."

"I will. I'll talk to him. Quite frankly, he knows nothing about the nuances of gun law because he doesn't care. And, even if he did, his brain can't digest it in a day."

"That doesn't seem to faze him."

"I'll give him a dose of reality when I get there."

"I'll deal with my end," Ben said. "We've set up a broadcast tonight at seven, too. Even if Derek doesn't bow out, we'll ruin

Chang's ratings and take away her audience share, you'll see. I have an idea."

"What?"

"Let me sort it out. We may shoot today. We'll talk."

"When will you know?"

"I have to arrange it," Ben said. "But from now on, there has to be one face in the media from your shop. The public are sheep and have to be led . . . carefully. Chang is already calling this an anti-gun lawsuit. If that talking point sticks, we're in trouble. It's that simple."

"We're on the same page. Later."

Driving in, she got angrier and angrier.

\* \* \*

At work, Sophia didn't stop to strategize with Paul and Tricia as she had promised. She marched straight to Derek's office in full attack mode.

Derek was leaning back in his chair with his long legs crossed on his desk. Bryce sat across from him, tilted back in a leather chair. They were both laughing.

"Good morning, Sophia." Derek grinned, self-satisfied and victorious.

"Wasn't Derek great out there?" Bryce's green eyes were proud and sparkling. "And he got a gig tonight."

Sophia riveted on Derek and ignored the guileless, naive first-year.

There was silence, a long silence, and a silence that bespoke its purpose.

"Well . . . uh . . . I've got to get back to . . . uh . . ." Bryce left.

Sophia slammed the door.

"What the hell do you think you're doing? You can't speak for my clients and me. And not on another network with another reporter. We agreed on this. My contact is Ben Kowrilsky at CBT, and I gave him my word that he had an exclusive. You knew it. Hell, you met him."

"Briefly." Derek's comment was pointed and caustic.

"You son of a . . ."

"Settle down. The reporters were out front waiting. I happened to be getting a mocha latte. What did you want me to do? Just walk by? And how long did you expect them to wait? Until you decided to saunter in late?"

"I was here until two this morning, working on *my* case."

"Sorry."

"Like hell you are." Sophia blasted. "I know about tonight. And you're not going on MPC. That's my exclusive's archrival."

"You're overreacting. I just talked to Chang on the phone. She's only doing a general panel on guns. Not about your case."

"Don't bullshit me. My case is the only reason she's even having that panel. You can go troll for clients on some other channel without talking about guns or the Holts. You're not going on her program."

Derek enjoyed the spectacle of Sophia exploding. He had locked horns with her before—about staffing, expense accounts, office equipment, and cases. In her world, people who were calm in an argument either didn't care or had already gotten exactly what they wanted—like Derek. And now he had the added bonus of making her, the wronged party, look like a screaming banshee.

"Ben and his network have an exclusive. I gave him my word."

"Your word . . . not mine. I'm not working with him," Derek baited Sophia. "You saw to that."

"Oh, so this is you getting even?"

"No. But I'm appearing on that panel. It's about guns in America and not the Holt lawsuit. But if the suit is mentioned, I can hold my own."

"Chang is Ben's rival. You can't do this."

But he could. She knew it. There was no rule of law, no ethics code, nothing to stop him but honesty and decency—in other words, *nothing*.

"Sophia, look. I want to get along with you. There's enough publicity to go around. Don't get in my way. You do your thing, and I'll do mine. We all want our face time."

Sophia was beaten, and her promise of an exclusive to Ben undermined. Rona would never interfere. Together Derek and Rona had the biggest book of business—the key metric in every law firm. Thorne & Chase's big-firm politics had trained her in that and the fine art of backstabbing. She just hadn't foreseen it here—at this level. She should have insisted on being a partner, a name partner, when she joined Krause & White with her big tort case and with Paul and Tricia, both experienced litigators. But her guard was down because Rona was her best law school buddy. Sophia had just learned the hard way—again.

When the Holt case paid off big, she would renegotiate for partnership with a quick exit in mind as a backup move. For now, the firm's support system was a necessity to win, including the first-years, as inexperienced as they were.

"I don't want you screwing things up for the Holts."

"That's arrogant. Look, I'm trying to bring in clients for the firm too. No one can fault me for that."

"Fine," Sophia shouted. "But you leave my case and the Holts out of your little client-getting pursuits."

Sophia realized she was screaming like a toddler having a temper tantrum. Her loud Greek voice was radiating through Derek's door, to everyone in the office, and down the hall if not through the whole building.

Sophia shut up and stood there, unable to move. She had lost it, logically and tactically. She had made a spectacle of herself that would forever be interpreted as her bad. She was pissed at herself. The minute she gave in to her own anger, instead of using it as litigators are trained to do, she had handed all her power over to Derek.

Derek's office door burst open. Rona, Tricia, and Paul came in.

"What's all this?" Rona demanded.

"You heard it, Rona." Tricia snapped. "Derek's screwing us. Come on, Sophia."

"Let's get out of here." Paul took Sophia's arm.

Sophia was so grateful for an honorable retreat from a lost battle that she went quickly with her friends—her true friends.

Rona stayed and closed Derek's door.

* * *

Because of her loud mouth and loss of control, Sophia did the walk of shame, escorted by Paul and Tricia, down the hall passing by the staff and first-years.

Sophia ignored Roxy, Autumn, and her boyfriend, Stefan, now a firm fixture, at Autumn's desk. The three were unpacking supplies. Stefan was over six feet tall and muscular but incongruously dressed like a hippy clone of Autumn with wrinkled clothes and untrimmed hair.

"Hey, that's a bitch, man," Stefan whispered to Autumn.

"Shh." Autumn kept her head down sorting supplies.

Sophia heard Stefan's comment and ignored it.

Roxy, who was apolitical, opened another box. Roxy valued her job and her hefty paycheck born of her longevity. She was thirty-something with an expensive, drugged-out boy toy at home who mooched everything off her. She was a punk rocker by night, superlative assistant to Derek and Rona by day. She pushed the envelope at work but did remove her nose ring and cover her body paint at the office. Still, when she moved just right, tattoos peeked from above her breasts, and her row of ear studs glared from under her multihighlighted—but no longer pastel—hair.

Sophia caught glimpses of Eddie and Bryce at their desks, busily hiding in work. She was grateful for her friends' save—and their escort back to her office.

Derek had pushed every one of Sophia's buttons and with ease. He looked good this time—not her. She remembered his tactics from law school debates, but they had never been turned against her—not back then.

\* \* \*

Tricia shut the door. "That was loud."

"Who cares?" Sophia flopped in her chair.

Paul calmed her. "Hey, you're with friends now."

"Sorry."

"You had every right to lose it. But I told you we had to figure out a strategy." Paul was ever the voice of reason.

"You were right."

"Did you talk to Ben?" Paul asked.

"Yes. He's in trouble with his producer. He has to have one public face at Krause & White—me. Derek says his panel is about guns in general in America. So I'm deleting our Holt talking points and press things from the computer."

"Sophia, stop. Think." Tricia said. "Think. Derek already saw them. He and Rona read and approved them. They have printed drafts."

Sophia was in scorched-earth mode—she wanted to burn and humiliate Derek. That was all she could think about. Her entire body screamed with frustration.

She had known betrayal and office humiliation at Thorne & Chase. But there she had endured it more easily because of the big paycheck. Here, it was harder, not only because of the smaller salary but also because it was more intimate. There was no place to hide.

⌘

# CHAPTER 25

## Stealing a March

*"Adversity leads us to think properly of our state,
and so is most beneficial to us."*
-Samuel Johnson

Slowly, the three musketeers' anger mutated into grim contemplation as they sat in Sophia's office.

Uncontrolled anger was the enemy of the righteous but easily succumbed to, especially for a Greek. When Sophia was right—and so wronged—it was almost impossible for her to maintain control, especially when her volcanic Greek heritage was always bubbling just below her litigator's veneer. Anger, too easily unleashed, betrays anyone who indulges it.

"Thorne & Chase," Paul said. "Big stakes . . . big fights. Krause & White. Little stakes . . . big fights."

"I shouldn't have brought you here with me."

"You didn't. We chose to come," Paul said. "We were friends."

"'Were'?" Sophia looked at him.

"*Are*. This is no time for joking with Wallace going bonkers. I talked to him again. He still wants out of the lawsuit."

"What's next?"

"Beth's firmly on board, but she can't talk with that thing in her throat," Tricia said.

"That might be better." Sophia couldn't put up with that woman's sniveling and Derek too.

Eddie tapped on Sophia's door and joined the meeting. "Reporting in."

Bryce sheepishly followed.

"What's up?" Sophia asked.

"Wallace is out of the hospital and home," Eddie said. "He called for help when you all were . . . uh . . . busy . . . with Derek. Autumn gave me the call."

"Did he mention dropping the suit?"

"Not to me. But he's pissed about everything. The fire, the anti-gun stuff, being called bad parents. He wanted to get a contractor."

"That's what he cares about most right now," Bryce added.

"Okay, let's see if we can help him. That's something to work with," Sophia said. "Anything else?"

"I asked him about Beth."

"And?"

"He only wanted to talk about fixing their house."

"They were lucky," Tricia said.

"In a weird way," Eddie agreed.

"Sophia, you don't have to go there. A call will do," Paul said. "You can make him feel lucky and tap into his outrage . . . whatever gets him to hang in there."

"I can try. I'll play on the bad parenting comments . . . keep him focused on the house and . . ."

Eddie interrupted.

"He said their house isn't as bad as it looks on TV . . . mostly smoke damage. But he's really irate that no Bakersfield contractor will do the repairs."

"Great for us," Sophia said. "Let's ride in with our white hats on. Suggestions?"

"No," Paul said. "Tricia?"

"Are you kidding?"

"Guys, guys. I already took care of it," Eddie interrupted.

"How?" Sophia was pleased and amazed.

"I called a friend of one of my cousins. He's a contractor in Lancaster."

"Is that near Bakersfield?" Tricia asked

"Close enough. Lancaster. It's that dust bowl in northeast L.A. County. He went out to see Wallace this morning. He's supposedly anti-gun."

"As long as he can swing a hammer, who cares?" Tricia said.

"Oh, he can, and everything else too . . . he's good. A job fell through, and he needs the money. He's doing it."

"Problem solved," Sophia said.

"Real initiative there, Eddie," Paul added.

"I got the Holts's insurance company to go out to assess the damage." Bryce wanted to atone for the Derek incident. "We may have a battle about the amount, but they're covering it. And I got the telephone company to restore service . . . I pulled the age and health and safety cards."

"Good job, Bryce." She fed his hungry young ego the compliment it craved.

Bryce relaxed. He would police his conduct with Derek and was glad Sophia had let it go. In reality, she had no choice. They had to keep maximum manpower on the case, no matter what. The case was exploding in every direction.

"I have a lot of cousins. They do everything. And they have lots of friends." Eddie grinned, upping his value with the team.

"Good," Sophia said. "And from now on, we have to coddle the Holts . . . Wallace especially. Thanks to you guys, I think we still have two plaintiffs. Let's confirm."

\* \* \*

Sophia called Beth at the hospital—primarily about the lawsuit and, secondarily, to express her sympathy.

She got through to Beth in the burn unit by playing the attorney card, as Paul had.

Beth's ventilator had been removed, but she was still on oxygen. She had not only throat and lung smoke inhalation damage but several superficial burns as well.

The nurse held the phone up to Beth's ear. Sophia chose every word she used with skill and care. She expressed outrage, wished her well, and adamantly committed the firm to getting justice for her son.

"Are you ready to keep the fight going, Beth?"

The nurse said Beth nodded yes and that tears were running down her cheeks.

"Bless you," the nurse cried along with Beth.

"Bless you for taking care of Beth." Sophia played into the nurse's caring nature and endured the two females' fountains of tears.

Personally, the female crying thing repulsed Sophia, and Beth had made a science of it. She was a sympathy-sucker. Her calculated tears clearly had kept Wallace in submission their entire marriage.

Tears or not, Sophia and her team were happy with the first call. She turned to the bigger problem—Wallace.

At home Wallace was busy with Eddie's contractor. The two had bonded. All Wallace wanted was his home back. He didn't talk about Beth, nor did he insist on canceling the suit. Sophia presumed he didn't want to fight with Beth over it.

The team high-fived each other after Sophia hung up.

"One disaster averted. Now, to tonight's broadcast usurpation."

Sophia dialed Ben.

\* \* \*

"My team's here, Ben, and you're on speaker."

"Good. What about Derek?"

"He won't cancel."

"I figured that. He loved that camera this morning. But we'll get him and Chang too. My producer is airing our special report tonight at the same time. He's going to run teasers all day and bury MPC's broadcast. No one will be tuned into it."

"I love it," Paul said. "Power plays work in your world too."

"Sure do."

"What's the special?" Sophia asked.

"You'll see. We'll pick you guys up at eleven."

"Pick us up?"

"We're all going to Bakersfield . . . the whole team . . . we're doing an interview with the Holts. I'll stream it back to the station for tonight."

"We're going to film in Bakersfield?" Sophia said. "Today?"

"You bet your life. Bring everyone. I want the public to see you guys hard at work. Mixing it up in Bako. Put the faces to the places . . . you know, the Holts, the gun store, the house, and so on. I have a van for us to work and a van for my crew and equipment. We'll brainstorm and write over the Grapevine."

Bryce and Eddie were both wide-eyed and enthused—they were included.

"We'll bring our sound bites and interview questions," Tricia said.

"Let's do it," Paul voted.

Sophia heard herself saying, "We're ready, Ben."

"Perfect. I'll go over everything on the way. When I finish doing a few preliminary teasers, I'll be over. We have to send footage out to our national affiliate before the East Coast nightly news."

"We're going national?" Sophia asked.

"You bet. We'll hit this hard. We'll get the wife in the hospital. The husband in his burned-out house. We'll blindside some cops at the station if we can. We'll try for Sports Gear's lawyers, too. It'll be sort of good old yellow journalism, Hearst-era style, but more factual, of course. Chang will be lost in the wake of our blitz."

The whole team was excited.

"How do we get out of here without Derek knowing?" Bryce asked.

"He's busy getting ready to be the media star. You think he's going to notice us?" Eddie smirked.

"This is like planning the D-Day invasion." Bryce was thrilled.

Eddie was just as enthused. "Kind of an exaggeration, but what the heck."

Sophia held her hand up to silence everyone. "So we're all set, Ben? See you at eleven."

"We'll have to be careful with Sports Gear's lawyers," Ben said. "Their firm is Bakersfield's largest and most prestigious. And that Tony Moschella is connected to everything in that town."

"Thanks, Ben. We haven't had time to check them out. Usually, it's one of the first things we do." Paul was red-faced.

"Is nothing going to break our way?" Tricia moaned.

"I broke your way," Ben replied. "You guys brainstorm ideas. Bring all your drafts. We'll shoot at the hospital, the house, Sports Gear USA, and maybe at the police station. Definitely in front of the Quarry, Warren & Moschella offices unless this Moschella guy will give us an impromptu interview. No notice for anyone. It'll leak. All of you be ready to go on camera in shirtsleeves. Remember, you're the small, idealistic firm working hard for the Holts and America."

"Good image, and true," Tricia said.

"Eleven. I'll be there. I wish it could be earlier . . . too much to do."

"We'll be around the block on the east corner, Ben," Paul interjected. "Just a precaution."

"Secrecy. Got it." Ben hung up.

Sophia told Bryce and Eddie that their only job was to keep their mouths shut until they went to the appointed corner. They understood. They wanted on camera and would do what she asked to get there. She had thrown them a bone—and silence was the price.

With Tricia's help, Sophia made copies of the press packet and Q&As she had prepared for Ben and her team. Then Sophia got her things together to go.

*Derek has buried himself,* Sophia thought. *He just doesn't know it yet.*

⌘

# CHAPTER 26

## The Early Bird Gets the Squirm

*"Get action. Seize the moment.*
*Man was never intended to become an oyster."*
-Theodore Roosevelt

Ben was waiting for them around the corner on time with his van and the crew's. As they had preplanned, Sophia's people left the office at irregular intervals.

Rona was too busy in the conference room with Derek to notice the steady, stealthy exodus. She was coaching him for his TV spot. It was nearing lunchtime, and the exits seemed natural to the staff. Only Autumn harassed the first-years about taking an early lunch.

\* \* \*

The team took off for Bakersfield in Ben's news van with CBT and its logo on the sides and top. The crew and equipment followed in a second logoed news van with a microwave dish on a telescoping mast. Bryce and Eddie were excited as they settled into their seats.

As the caravan sped over the Grapevine, Sophia and her team plotted out their strategy with Ben. They were impressed with Ben's mastery of the case and the players and also the speed with which he had created the segments for his feature. Even Sophia, who had worked with him before, had never seen what he and his people did to prepare a broadcast, especially on the fly like this.

Intermittently, Sophia got calls and text messages from Rona requesting information for Derek. She ignored them. He was on his own.

* * *

Once over the hill and in Bakersfield, they jumped from location to location—efficiently and professionally handled by Ben's cameraperson, makeup artist, and, most importantly, Ben himself.

At the Holts's fire-damaged house, they got dramatic footage and a heartwarming moment of Wallace thanking Eddie and Bryce for their help. The two were ecstatic with their short segment on camera. Tricia, Paul, and Sophia handled the hard questions afterward.

Then, Ben had Wallace come to the hospital with them for shots with Beth. Sophia's meeting with Beth was dramatic, intimate, and splattered with the ever-important and reliable flood of tears. Beth's voice, relegated to a barely audible and very hoarse whisper, was perfect. Wallace ably did his scripted and directed bit. Ben filmed the nurse insisting Beth was too frail and upset to go on. He cut filming after one last close-up of Beth's face fed with oxygen and her uncontrolled weeping.

They dropped Wallace off at home and headed downtown straight for the Bakersfield police station on Truxtun Avenue. Ben took a single cameraman into the lobby where the captain joined him and the irresistible camera lens. The captain cut the interview short and retreated back behind his wall of blue when Ben abruptly switched topics from the house fire to Mike's suicide and gun sales.

Standing alone on the public sidewalk in front, though, Ben did a scathing, well-prepared, and thoroughly researched piece on the illegal gun trade in Bakersfield. It was in the can to use whenever and however he chose. When they pulled away, a police car trailed them.

"Go the speed limit and warn the crew," Ben ordered the driver. "They can shadow us as long as they want. They can't intimidate us."

The group went to the Quarry, Warren & Moschella offices at the Stockdale Tower on California Avenue. Even at twelve stories with its terraced reflecting pool at the entrance, the building was unimpressive by L.A. standards. The building was surrounded by a flat, open parking lot and other smaller nearby office buildings. The entrances—both the front and back—were nondescript and ringed with large square concrete tree planters. Ben set up for the interview just outside the doors and between two of the planters. If Moschella didn't come out, he would do his own well-researched piece.

Unexpectedly, when Ben called Quarry, Warren & Moschella, he was put straight through to Moschella, who was more than pleased to grant him an interview.

"He knew we were coming. I'm sure the captain called him," Ben said. "You guys stay in the van."

Ben got out with his crew just as Moschella sauntered confidently out the lobby doors in a navy blue suit with a regimental red tie neatly tied in a double Windsor knot. He introduced himself to Ben and shook hands. It was the middle of the afternoon, and the few people using the building glanced over at the news cameras.

"Mr. Moschella, you and your firm are representing Sports Gear USA in the lawsuit brought by Mike Holt's parents, who believe he should never have been sold the shotgun he used to kill himself."

"Yes." Moschella proceeded with his own well-honed sound bites. "There was no way Sports Gear or its employees could have known what he was going to do with the shotgun."

"You don't usually represent gun sellers or manufacturers, do you?"

"We haven't in the past. But we are known for representing clients who are in the right. And doing so with great success. That's why we were hired for this lawsuit."

Ben realized he was volleying with a well-prepped, media-savvy attorney.

"Do you think that Krause & White being an L.A. firm will affect the trial and outcome of this case?"

"Well, Ben, this is a small town, and everyone knows everyone else around here." Moschella smiled. He did not mention Jackson, Hood & Lee and its role in the lawsuit. "But ours is a fair town with a friendly, even-handed judicial system. We're known for obeying the rule of law in Bakersfield and welcoming out-of-towners. Krause

& White's lawyers will be treated well. We believe this case is very important because the Holts are trying to interfere with the Second Amendment right of all American citizens to keep and bear arms."

"Does that mean gun merchants have the right to sell a shotgun to an obviously disturbed boy who then commits suicide with it?"

"If you were an impartial reporter, Ben, you wouldn't be parroting the Holts's complaint. You'd know that Sports Gear followed the law to the letter here. It is truly unfortunate that young Mr. Holt killed himself with the shotgun he bought. But *he* did that . . . not the shotgun . . . and not Sports Gear USA. And neither my client nor the people of Bakersfield, who have every right to buy guns, should be punished for that."

"So you believe as long as the paperwork is in order, your client and other gun sellers should be able to sell a gun to anyone, no matter how troubled they seem or how odd their behavior?"

"I never said that, nor would I, Ben. But I will say gun sellers are not omniscient, nor are they psychiatrists, and the law doesn't require them to be. That is long-settled law in California, since Justice Grignon's opinion in the *Jacoves* case in 1992. You should read it."

"And if someone commits suicide or commits murder, no problem, right?"

"I apologize. I have an appointment in a few minutes. Thanks for dropping by." Moschella reached out, shook Ben's hand, and walked back into the Stockdale Tower.

"You heard it right here. Sports Gear will sell to anyone as long as it is within the letter of the law, and that includes murderers, mass killers, and those poor souls intent on suicide."

Ben looked stonily at the camera as he concluded the segment.

Back in the van, Ben said, "He's cagey and good. I don't think we got much we can use. I'll see what the producer says about edits."

Ben called his crew driving behind to start sending footage into the station.

* * *

Their next stop was the nine-story drab modern courthouse. Its flat concrete entryway was a good staging area for Ben to summarize the Holts's case in short, dramatic, sympathetic sound bites. Only a few casual passersby took note. Ben had Sophia's team stand in front of the courthouse. He introduced each one again, not knowing the order of the segments. He then fed Sophia the hard-hitting questions they had rehearsed. She responded with calm analytical authority.

"That was terrific. Let's get to the Sports Gear store before the production lead time cuts off."

\* \* \*

They headed to Sports Gear on Ride Street. The police car was still shadowing them at a distance and most certainly reporting back to the captain.

When they arrived, Ben and his crew first shot footage of the storefront and its depressing surroundings. Brandon, the young clerk, let them inside. However, before they could do much filming, Moss Grimick and Joe Spangler yelled for Arnie, the store manager, who kicked them out the door.

Ben's crew got a good shot of Arnie yelling, "If you're not a customer, you have no business being in here, you damn L.A. news whores."

Arnie slammed the door, and Ben and his crew got some additional footage of Arnie, Moss, and Joe looking out the windows and the glass door.

Ben stood on the street in front of the store and did a short close-up piece about the store where, as Ben put it, "Mike Holt made his fateful, fatal purchase."

They then drove to the final stop on this whirlwind tour—the spot where Sophia and Tricia had been "shot at" and run off the road on their way to the I-5. Ben had the two women spin their yarn. Just as he concluded his commentary, a monster pickup sped by in the background. It couldn't have been more perfect.

They headed for the I-5 and home. Ben had plenty of material to craft a superb segment.

\* \* \*

On the way back over the Grapevine, the Bakersfield police "escort" finally stopped tracking them. Ben fed the remaining footage, including film of the cop car that had dogged them, to his editor at the station. They would put some shots together with the teasers Ben had recorded that morning to get them on the air. Ben and his producer planned the shots and their order for tonight.

"This is amazing. Is all the footage already back in L.A.?" Tricia asked.

"Sure. Being edited. And the producer is getting it together." Ben smiled. "We'll see what we can create. We got some good statements, but that Moschella was smooth and prepared."

"No wonder he was so pleased to talk to you," Bryce said.

\* \* \*

When they arrived back at the office, it was empty. They presumed Derek was on his way to the MPC studio over the Hill in the Valley.

Sophia invited her team back to her apartment for a battle-of-the-networks party. Steve was bringing Chinese for everyone at six-thirty. Eddie and Bryce committed to the beer; Tricia and Paul, the wine.

⌘

# CHAPTER 27

## Dewreckage

*"You ask anyone what their number one fear is
and it's public humiliation."*
-Mel Gibson


"**H**ey, get in here. Ben's teaser is on." Paul was already settled on Sophia's couch with his wine.

"There's you, Sophia," Paul called.

Sophia rushed in just as her picture flashed across the television screen. Then came scenes of the burned-out house and Beth crying in the hospital bed. Ben's voice-over added provocative sound bites to the dramatic and harrowing visuals.

"Turn it up," Bryce called.

"Damn, I missed it." Eddie rushed over and took a seat.

"They'll repeat it," Paul took a drink of his wine.

"Are we recording it?" Bryce sat with his beer.

Paul checked. "Yes, we got it."

"Good. We can relive it over and over again." Tricia joined the men with her wine. "Hey, Eddie, you seeing anyone?"

"No. Why?"

"Well, there's a new Assistant U.S. Attorney, Raquel . . . at my boyfriend's office. She just transferred in from Ohio . . ."

"Your boyfriend's an Assistant U.S. Attorney?" Bryce interrupted. "I'm impressed."

"Shut up, Bryce. Who is she? She works with your boyfriend?"

"She does and . . ."

"Stop stalling, Eddie. Just ask," Sophia said. "Yes, she's good looking. I've met her at drinks. She's pretty and nice . . . as nice as prosecutors can be."

Eddie laughed. "Pretty? Sure, let's do it."

"We'll double with you," Tricia suggested. "I'll get her number from Jay."

"What about me?" Bryce said.

"Don't worry." Tricia knew Bryce would be more challenging. "We'll find someone for you, too."

Paul shushed everyone. "Shh, teaser again."

Eddie watched the TV three degrees happier than he had been for a long time.

The teaser of the burned house and Beth crying in the hospital sucking oxygen was heartbreaking. At the end, the group staring at the TV cheered.

Sophia cut it short. "Let's not get ghoulish."

"I could hear you down the hall." Steve walked in with the Chinese and set it on the coffee table.

Eddie and Bryce both stood at attention when they were introduced to Steve the detective. It was amusing—first-year amusing. Sophia got some paper plates, and everyone dug in.

"Steve, do you have a split screen so we can watch Derek make a fool of himself at the same time?" Paul asked.

"No, but we can record it." Steve set it up.

The Chinese silenced the rowdy group as they waited for Ben's masterpiece.

* * *

Ben's producer had moved Ben's feature so it would start fifteen minutes before Chang's and continue through her panel discussion. The tactic worked. It captured the viewers first and kept them on CBT. Ben's real-time ratings were off the charts.

The feature started with the Sports Gear footage: the store, the aisles, and the gun corner with the cases of knives and handguns, racks of rifles and shotguns, and box after box of ammunition. Then it showed the salesmen calling for the manager and the manager throwing Ben and his crew out. Ben did his biting commentary outside the store.

Then Ben showed the interview of Sophia and her team at the courthouse—serious, hardworking, and not "big firm" in their shirtsleeves. Sophia concisely explained the gravamen of the Holts's suit.

"Great job, Sophia." Paul held his glass up to her, and the others did too.

"Thanks. But pay attention."

Then came the footage of Wallace with Bryce and Eddie, the burned Holt house, and torn-up lawn. That segued into Wallace describing the terror of the night of the attack and arson. Wallace took to the camera like a fish to water; he held up the blackened lawn fuel can that the firemen had found in his living room. He was tired, old, and sympathetic. It was perfect—even without tears, which Beth would provide in the hospital scene. The broadcast cut to commercials.

"Wow. That wasn't a small fire." Steve grabbed more rice and broccoli beef. "What do the police say?"

"Nothing," Sophia said. "Wallace couldn't identify anyone. I don't think the cops are looking that hard."

"No kidding," Paul snorted. "What did we expect?"

"Just wait, you'll see them dodging Ben's questions," Sophia said.

"You want me to get on them cop to cop?"

"No. We don't need more trouble . . . but thanks." Sophia smiled.

Sophia liked the machismo but wouldn't sidetrack their case by taking on Bakersfield's inbred, small-town power structure. However, she was reminded why she loved Steve. Part of it was his sometimes frustrating linear thinking and simple view of right and wrong.

"We have to pick our battles," Paul said. "And we don't want one with the cops there."

"Quiet." Tricia held her hand up. "Commercial's over."

* * *

As the hospital segment began, Wallace handed Beth a picture of Mike—Sophia's idea. Beth sobbed so hard that the nurse asked everyone but Wallace to leave. It couldn't have been better scripted if it were written for a movie.

"You're amazing." Steve devoured Sophia with his eyes and she, him. "I'm rooting for the old couple."

Paul kept watching the two until Eddie caught him. Eddie didn't fault Paul's obvious feelings for Sophia. He could relate.

"More wine, Paul?" Eddie topped off Paul's glass.

"Me, too." Tricia held her glass up.

The last segment was Ben interviewing Moschella. It was a heavily and artfully edited interview that presented Moschella as a powerful, connected, large-firm litigator, a lawyer who thought guns should be freely available to everyone—the negative inferences were obvious.

But that's what the news media did: tell "their" truths, which rarely involved the total picture, and usually only the juiciest, most useful fraction of it.

"Ben made Moschella look like an L.A. megafirm lawyer," Tricia said. "A Thorne & Chase clone."

"We know what that means," Sophia said.

"Yeah. The gnat versus the elephant." Bryce smiled.

"Plays well for us," Eddie said.

"Oh, it sure does." Tricia took a drink. "America loves the underdog."

"Okay. Watch," Bryce broke in. "See . . . doesn't he look shifty?"

"Shifty, but smart. That guy is savvy," Paul remarked.

"Ben was better," Sophia said.

"This time," Paul cautioned.

The special report ended with Ben's sympathetic editorializing.

"A toast to Sophia, our rainmaker." Tricia stood, and the rest followed.

"Hear, hear." Eddie felt the tribal pull.

They clanged their glasses together in an electrifying moment of triumphant solidarity.

"Let's watch Derek on the Chang show now." Bryce sat.

"Watch him sweat." Eddie sat with the others.

"I'm liking you guys more and more," Paul said.

* * *

Steve played Chang's recorded broadcast.

She highlighted Derek first, as a Krause & White name partner and attorney for the Holts. Then, she introduced Nathan Metzger, an NGA attorney; Margery Kerensky, who held an endowed chair as the Saint Gabriel Possenti Professor of Constitutional Law at the Magnum Opus Dei law school in Hawthorne; and Tony Moschella, fed in by satellite.

"Derek never said Moschella would be there," Sophia fumed.

Chang was amiable and evenhanded in her questioning about gun issues—the pros, the cons, and the controversial. She let Derek take the reins on the Holt case, emphasizing suicide and its relationship to gun sales. He was well-spoken but basically regurgitated the team's talking points and Sophia's memo that he had ridiculed.

"She's handling Derek with kid gloves," Steve said. "It looks like she's flirting with him."

Bryce observed, "There's definitely chemistry there."

"We'll see after the first commercial break," Paul said. "Her producer will be checking out Ben's feature. She'll find out you're the Holts's real mouthpiece."

"He sure will," Eddie smirked.

Paul smiled at Sophia. "A mouthpiece who looks great on camera."

"I'll say," Steve said. "That camera really likes you."

"Stop it, all of you." Sophia grabbed the remote. "I'm fast-forwarding the commercial."

When Chang's broadcast resumed, the bomb hit.

* * *

At the commercial break, Chang's producer called her into the control room.

"Just relax," Chang announced before leaving the set. "I'll be back. It's going great."

"Thanks." Derek leaned back in his chair and went over his notes.

He felt good about the first segment. He waited under the lights while the makeup artist powdered the shine off their faces. Nerves and pounding lights made even the coolest people sweat on camera. Derek straightened his tie, checked his collar, and then went back to his notes. He was doing well, and he knew it.

* * *

In the control room, Chang's producer showed her highlights of Ben's featured report with Sophia and her team. Chang realized Derek was a fraud. He wasn't the Holts's lead attorney. Ben, her prime competitor, had scooped her with his in-depth, on-site feature showcasing Sophia Christopoulos, their real lawyer.

Chang was mad as hell at Derek, but at herself, too. She had scanned the complaint her research team got from the court, but only the substance, not paying any heed to the lawyers' names. A cub-reporter mistake.

Freshly touched up, she took her seat. Derek, smug and comfortable, smiled at Chang, but she did not reciprocate. Her face was cool and professional. Period.

She abandoned the teleprompter. She didn't attack Derek herself—he was her own source, after all. That would have been career suicide. Instead, with skill and charm, she funneled other panelists down that path with leading questions.

"The love connection's over," Tricia snickered.

Chang fed Derek to the wolves with very sharp teeth. Professor Kerensky characterized the Holt case as encroaching on the Second Amendment, and Derek couldn't respond. Sophia could have because she knew the law and nuances of the relevant case holdings cold. By the end of the program, Kerensky and Metzger, the NGA attorney, were accusing Derek of being a gun control reactionary from L.A. where guns were associated with drive-bys and crimes instead of towns like Bakersfield, where guns were used for hunting and recreation. Moschella stayed above the fray with a few comments nicely phrased. He let the others do the attacking.

Chang's contribution was to paraphrase Derek unfairly and to peremptorily cut him off every time he spoke. By the end of the broadcast, Derek was inarticulate. They had destroyed him with camera shots instead of gunshots.

Chang and the panel had transformed Derek into an anti-gun fanatic.

* * *

After the broadcast, Derek confronted Chang. She had nothing to say to him. She took him into the control room and turned on Ben's broadcast. Derek stood watching it, dumbfounded and seething.

"You knew about this and made me look like a fool and against guns," Derek said.

"I didn't make you look like anything other than what you are: an unprepared impostor. You're not even part of the team handling the lawsuit."

She walked away, satisfied with her payback and hoping for good ratings in spite of—or maybe because of—Derek.

Furious and humiliated, Derek left a belittled, angry man. It never even crossed his mind that he was at fault.

* * *

At Sophia's apartment, the assembled viewers witnessed Derek's annihilation in funereal silence.

Eddie broke the blaring quiet. "Will that hurt us? Derek was just obliterated, and he's a name partner."

"It was worse than I expected," Paul said. "We let internal firm politics cloud our judgment when we weren't forthcoming with him."

"But then he might have submarined us with Ben," Tricia said. "We'll never know."

"It was bad. I had no idea she'd do this." Sophia paused and then flipped into her leadership role. "But our feature was great, and Ben will keep refocusing the issues in our favor."

"Sure." Tricia took up the baton.

"He didn't see it coming," Sophia said. "Maybe I should have warned him."

"Come on, Sophia. Warn him about what? You don't have a crystal ball," Paul interrupted the recrimination. "And you did tell him to back off. You did everything you could short of sinking us. He was the one who wouldn't listen. Remember?"

"Actually, you warned the whole office at the top of your voice," Tricia added. "Including Rona, who should have controlled him."

"Paul's right," Eddie said.

Sophia replied, "What I mean is, I should have told him that Ben was going to do a story too."

"He would have told Chang," Eddie said "Definitely not,"

"Are you kidding?" Bryce added. "He would have torpedoed our broadcast."

"I still feel bad," Sophia said.

"He brought it on himself," Eddie said.

Bryce joined in. "He did,. And he brought it on us too."

"Sounds like he made his own bed." Steve poured wine all around and then popped the cap on a bottle of Dos Equis for himself. "Let him lie in it."

"We had no choice. We have a case to win," Paul said. "Derek stuck his nose in where it didn't belong. And he tainted our case because Chang made him look like an anti-gun fanatic, an anti-Second Amendment crusader."

"Instead of being opposed to selling guns to disturbed people," Bryce added.

"Ben's broadcast should make up for that," Tricia replied. "He'll keep hammering on that."

"He has to," Paul said.

"It's sad," Tricia said. "The only reason Derek did this was to get clients, and it backfired. He doesn't believe Holt case will pay."

"I do—if he doesn't screw us again." Paul held his glass up. "It's our media night. To Sophia."

"To Sophia." The group toasted.

"Fortune cookies?" Steve emptied the bag on the coffee table. "Sophia's favorites."

The cookies were oversized and dipped in dark and white chocolate. Everyone grabbed one.

"Let's read the fortunes. Me first." Tricia cracked a white chocolate and unraveled the fortune. "'Soon two hearts will be one.'"

"What does that mean?" Paul scoffed. "You're already with Jay."

"I'm setting Eddie up with Raquel . . . remember? This is a good omen." Tricia put half in her mouth and crunched. "Mmm."

"Cool," Eddie said. "How can it go wrong if my blind date is fortune cookie'd?"

Everyone laughed.

"My turn." Steve cracked his and read the fortune. "'Time is shorter than you think.'"

Steve threw the halved cookie and fortune on the table and drank his beer.

"That's a nasty little one. Let me." Sophia broke her dark chocolate open. "'Good news is on the way.'"

"What does that mean? We already had it," Paul said. "Right there on TV."

"Simple. More good news? I call bullshit on fortune cookies." Bryce downed his cookie without reading his fortune.

Eddie grabbed a dark chocolate and snapped it open. "'Grab life and love while you can.'"

"That's the truth." Sophia leaned over and kissed Steve.

Paul watched the kiss. "This is all stupid. I have to go."

Paul's departure triggered an exodus.

Steve shut the door.

"Alone." He grabbed Sophia and parted her lips with his beer-infused tongue that collided with her sweet chocolate breath.

Sophia fought the crushing advance. "Race to the shower."

Steve ripped off his shirt and followed.

⌘

# CHAPTER 28

## Fate, Fallout, and Fatality

*"Consequences are unpitying."*
-George Eliot

Chang's unfair obliteration of Derek had consequences that were unpredictably devastating. That night L.A.'s network news, local radio, and the Internet went wild—not with the Holt case, as Ben and Sophia had wanted, but with Derek's image as an anti-gun radical. Derek's unbalanced edited and distorted statements were further edited by the NGA and sent across the Internet.

Catalyzed by Chang's panel, Ben's actual statements were lost. Carefully chosen phrases edited from Derek's interview were transformed into anti-gun arguments and un-American attacks on the Constitution. The NGA littered the media with effective pro-gun and pro-Second Amendment sound bites. They carved and hacked apart Derek's remarks to turn people against the Holts.

Sports Gear also spammed the airwaves and the Internet with edited sound bites and more anti-Holt rhetoric. Chang and her network took all the credit. They had their secondary contacts blog away, painting Derek and the Holts as anti-gun rights, anti-Second Amendment, and even anti-American.

Derek's name and face were flashed to the world along with his butchered statements. He was an instant public face for gun control advocates, and the personification of the enemy to gun enthusiasts, supporters of open-carry laws, gun show owners, and all the other forces in the country drunk on gun-love.

Derek became public relations problem number one for the Holts, their case, Sophia's team, and Ben.

* * *

Derek sat for some time in the MPC television station parking lot in his black 2005 Porsche 911 Carrera S coupe—his pride and joy—and his regret since Krause & White's revenues had started to decline while his hefty monthly payments did not. Its only redemption was that it still got him the mileage he wanted with women.

Finally, Derek headed out. He took the 134 freeway and listened silently to the dull roar of the traffic pulsing through the flat, smoggy Valley night air. His mind reran each shattering moment of the panel feeding frenzy sequentially ripping him apart.

In his rage he wished he had a gun to blow his humiliation away—but where would he point it? At his own stupidity? He screamed and beat his steering wheel with the heel of his left hand until it hurt. Then he took deep breaths to steady himself. He turned on his phone, Bluetoothed to his Porsche, to call Rona, but he didn't want to hear her placating voice.

On his way home from the Valley, he chose the route with the least congestion going east. As he transitioned the 134 onto the 101, he ignored the pings and toots signaling messages and voice mails, mostly from Rona. He skimmed his programmed radio stations—and stopped when he heard his name. Each talk show and news station he scanned was polarized, racing to degrade or extol him. His name was broadcast with half-truths edited out of context: rallying the pro-gun fundamentalists against him and the anti-Second Amendment nuts for him. He sounded like a fool.

Derek flipped to the irreverent talk show of two notorious aging L.A. attack masters, Kent and Stine. They were playing edited quips from the Chang panel, transforming Derek into a court jester—not a name partner at a law firm. They laughed; he didn't.

The NGA and Sports Gear USA had made him their patsy—their anti-gun poster child. They had anticipated Sophia might try to change the venue to L.A. Thus, they were poisoning the potential L.A. jury pool like they had Bakersfield's.

He switched the channel to the KUSC classical music station to calm himself.

Derek wished that he could have kept the Holt case out of the firm. He wished more that he had kept out of that panel discussion. He mentally kicked himself for trying to ride on Sophia's coattails to get clients. He knew that Sophia had a "white immunity" that he, as a black man who had grown up in the inner city of Los Angeles, didn't.

Law school was a reward for his brains and hard work, but it didn't wipe out his heritage. He came from South Central L.A.— black and poor. Guns, registered or not, were ingrained in the underbelly of its gangster subculture, sucking in generations of cousins, brothers, uncles, fathers, and now even the women and girls.

That once-hidden subculture was now exploited and exalted in rap, hip-hop, and movies—monetized by the elite in the entertainment industry, the "biz," the music, films, television, computer gaming, and the movers and shakers that ran L.A. However, these industry executives and producers lived far from South Central. They had homes in Beverly Hills, Brentwood, Bel Air, Encino, Toluca Lake, Malibu, or behind the large gated estates on San Vicente Boulevard in Santa Monica.

Derek had escaped South Central, but only to a modest apartment in the Hollywood Hills above L.A. And only in that limited physical sense. He would always carry South Central with him.

\* \* \*

He exited the 101 onto Sunset Boulevard going west. As he sat in the dense traffic, his phone rang with Beethoven's Fifth—a ring he had picked to distance himself from those South Central roots. It flashed Rona's name again. He ignored it and gripped the steering wheel through Hollywood proper with its tourist buses and nightlife seekers cruising with him.

Rona called again. He relented and answered.

"You saw it?" Derek turned right up towards Mulholland.

"Yes. That bitch Chang sacrificed you to cover her ass because of Kowrilsky's feature story. All she wanted was ratings."

"Chang covered her ass and put a target on mine."

"She let the other panelists do that. There was nothing you could have done."

"I tried."

"I saw."

"I made it worse by arguing."

"The way they have it edited now makes you look anti-Second Amendment for sure."

As he wound through the hills, he slowed when he came to his street corner, but still took the turn too fast, even for his high-performance Porsche. His tires screeched, and he skidded.

"What was that?" Rona asked.

"Nothing."

"Be careful. Slow down."

"Okay. Okay."

"And don't go on the Internet tonight. The NGA has its bloggers doing a number on you. They know we may try for a change of venue and are prejudicing as many potential L.A. jury members as they can."

"I made a mistake."

"We did. Sophia was the only one who knew the law well enough to take on those sharks. The firm doesn't deserve this, and neither do the Holts."

"I just wanted some face time. I'm not anti-gun. Chang's bullshit editing fucked my family and me. She might as well have put a bull's-eye on our backs."

Derek's phone showed an incoming call from his mother.

"Have to go. My mom. She's never up this late."

"Take it and . . ."

Derek dropped Rona midsentence. He knew his mother was not calling about his TV appearance because he hadn't told her about it. Something was wrong.

"Mom? Mom?"

She was sobbing at the other end.

"Mom, what's wrong?"

"Your brother . . . Dwight . . . got shot."

Derek went numb. He pulled over.

"Shot."

"Yes . . . he's . . . dead . . . he's . . ." His mother's sentence stopped in a torrent of tears.

"Oh, God. No. What happened?"

"What does it matter? He's gone . . . Dwight's dead . . . just . . ."

She sobbed.

"I'll be there, Mom."

"Be careful, dear."

Derek turned on an app that showed where the cops were concentrating and hung an illegal U-turn.

\* \* \*

Dwight, Derek's kid brother, had been killed in a shootout up the block from the family home where he stayed when he wasn't with his baby mama.

There were no witnesses—or, rather, none willing to come forward.

The old man who lived at the end of the block had heard arguing. From his window he saw young guys screaming about acting white, big lawyer, guns, Oreos, Toms, and wigger lover. Then a fight—a beatdown. The old man hid in the kitchen when the shooting started. Cars peeled out. The old man thought he saw two gangs, but he didn't know. He didn't care either. He was still alive. That was all the cops had to go on—noise and a whole lot of nothing.

Derek's mom didn't understand. But he did. She hadn't seen Chang's broadcast. She also hadn't seen and heard Derek's face associated with unfairly edited phrases in the anti-gun media blitz that followed.

Derek knew he was responsible. Dwight got shot in a fight with males disrespecting his older brother. Derek could not, would not, tell his mother that. It was Derek's burden to bear. The price for his appearance on Chang's damn TV show had been immeasurably, unfairly, and unjustifiably high.

⌘

# CHAPTER 29

## Imponderables and Immobility

*"Press on. Obstacles are seldom
the same size tomorrow as they are today."*
-The Reverend Robert H. Schuller

Dwight's murder deepened the schism at Krause & White and shattered what remained of the façade of collegiality. Derek shouldn't have blamed Sophia, but he did. He shouldn't have blamed himself, either, but he couldn't help it. He oughtn't to have blamed Chang and her panelists, but he did—despite the fact that they were merely opportunists, just as he was that night.

Ben's feature had grabbed the highest ratings of the evening news broadcasts, but the lingering impact of Chang's panel and the NGA and Sports Gear's Internet blitz pancaked any afterglow. Her MPC network obliterated the positive traction Ben had gained. MPC replayed carefully selected and edited brutal panel sound bites on the late-night news. Ben's network repeated his feature, but the public was fickle and preferred Chang's vicious dog pile to Beth's crying.

Any sympathy for the Holts that night was secondarily annihilated by the dynamic carousel of the NGA's publicity machine. So much so that Ben's attempt to rehabilitate the Holts's position with selective replays during the rest of the week was wholly ineffective.

Sophia believed most people were already sick of Beth's crying. No surprise there—so were Sophia and Wallace. Besides, every time Ben hit hard, Sports Gear USA and the NGA hit back twice as hard. Ben and his producer backed off. They decided that closer to the trial they would give the story a makeover—a high concept, less content, fresh look.

Sophia agreed. Amidst their failures, she had to believe that Ben and his producer were right. Besides, Dwight's murder was too recent, and every one of Ben's blitzes hit a raw nerve with Derek.

* * *

Time passed, Dwight's funeral came and went, but there was no justice for him. Derek's and his family's anger and grief did not wane—it festered.

While Sophia knew Derek's panel had been the catalyst for Dwight's death, she also felt responsible. How could she not? Greek guilt was no less a force than Irish guilt, especially for women. Catholicism was much like Greek Orthodoxy in that way.

Soon, mercifully, the media and public switched their attention to a destructive and deadly hurricane lashing the east coast of Mexico and southern Texas, causing dozens of deaths and millions of dollars in property damage—coverage of a real blood bath beat the verbal one.

Wallace fully recovered and restored the Holts's home thanks to the contractor Eddie had found. Beth continued to suckle from her oxygen tank after her throat and lungs had mended. She said she needed it. The doctors didn't agree, but she refused to give it up and whimpered about that too.

* * *

Because the Holts's complaint was simple and straightforward, Moschella and his client did not bother to challenge its legal sufficiency with a demurrer. They did not want to annoy the judge filing a demurrer guaranteed to fail at the outset. Instead, making a tactical decision, Sports Gear filed a simple answer denying the Holts's allegations and including the usual boilerplate affirmative defenses.

Moschella had strategic, procedurally lethal weapons to employ later in the lawsuit, and he would use all of them.

* * *

With the filing of Sports Gear's answer, the Holt lawsuit surged immediately into full-blown litigation mode. As in all lawsuits, weaponized words volleyed between both sides—in the media, in court filings, in hearings and depositions, discovery blitzes, unnecessary and necessary motions, and earned or gratuitous slights, jabs, accusations, and insults.

Physical and mental exhaustion were the inevitable concomitants.

Sophia and her team knew they were in trouble from the start when they were randomly assigned an all-purpose judge, Judge Robert Ortiz. He would handle everything: the pleadings, all law and motion matters, all discovery disputes, and ultimately, if there was one, the trial. The Holts would never have the potential opportunity to get a break by appearing before a different judge, or getting assigned another judge to try the case.

Of course, this being Bakersfield, that might not have mattered anyway.

* * *

Ortiz was not a bad judge, just a newer one who took the bench with little civil litigation experience. He had been a public defender and done criminal trials for eight years before being appointed.

He was born and bred in Fresno, Lynn Moschella's childhood home—blue-collar and lower-middle-class. His Latino father drove trucks, and his Oklahoma-born mother was a hardworking housewife. Ortiz grew up hunting and knew how to handle a rifle. He made Bakersfield his home after graduating from the California State University campus in Fresno and the University of California's Hastings College of the Law in San Francisco. He was neither for nor against guns in and of themselves. His wife, Marcy Marie, coincidentally had moved to Fresno from Oklahoma with her parents when she was a child. The two had met in college, and their four kids were comfortably part of the Bakersfield community.

Judge Ortiz just wanted his family to have as good a life or better than they had enjoyed in Fresno, which is why he had joined the Bakersfield Country Club. He and his wife had made a number of good friends there, among them Tony and Lynn Moschella.

He had presided over a number of trials in which Moschella was one of the attorneys. Judge Ortiz was impressed with Moschella's skill and preparation. Moschella had always been on the winning side in Ortiz's courtroom, in both jury and nonjury trials.

* * *

Ben had sources everywhere, and from his Bakersfield ones, he learned about the relationship between Judge Ortiz and Moschella. When he told Sophia, it added an overlay of trepidation and another analytical filter to her planned strategy.

She and her team immediately considered a motion asking Judge Ortiz to "recuse" himself—meaning take himself off the case due to the appearance of bias, prejudice, or impropriety because of his friendship with Moschella.

"Sophia, we have to put up a strong front," Eddie said. "Taking out this judge would show we're not going to be pushovers for the old-boy network. Besides, I hate it when one of my people goes all Anglo like this guy has."

Despite his mixed heritage, Eddie viewed himself as a Latino first and foremost, and proudly identified himself as such.

"I'm not sure," Sophia said. "Even though Ortiz has only been a judge for a few years, he's considered decent, and we could get worse."

"That's an understatement," Paul said. "I looked at them all. A couple of the oldies there are just drawing a paycheck until they die, another has a reputation of letting his clerk make all the decisions behind the scenes, there's a couple of closet alcoholics, and some are condemned as just lazy. We're looking at pluses and minuses with all of them."

"I'm with Sophia," Tricia added. "It's a close-knit community. I bet Moschella's friendly with every judge there. Besides, if Ortiz denied the motion, then we'd have to seek a writ, which we'd undoubtedly lose. Then, we'd be stuck with him after totally alienating him. I say we stay with him."

"Me too," Paul confirmed. "If we appear to be judge-shopping, that could hurt us with a new judge anyway and the jury pool too."

"Agreed," Bryce said. "We stay with him."

"I see there's no choice," Eddie conceded.

It was done.

* * *

They turned to the possible change of venue motion instead, which, if successful, would not only give them a new judge, but also a different—and they hoped a less tainted—jury pool. Not expecting much, Sophia still hoped Eddie and Bryce had come up with an angle to move the case to Los Angeles County, Kern County's immediate neighbor to the south.

Eddie was fast. His research skills were formidable, and he applied them with care and diligence, despite his sometimes impetuous, unseasoned approach towards the case. Bryce was a prodder but thorough. In the end, both their efforts didn't matter.

"Hate to have to say this," Eddie reported to the team. "But there's no chance in hell of getting a change of venue until jury selection. The only argument we have is that we can't get an impartial trial in Kern County. That truck incident with Sophia and Tricia isn't enough. Courts won't generally consider a transfer for local bias until it's clear that a neutral jury can't be impaneled."

"We have to wait." Bryce handed out the detailed legal memorandum confirming the conclusion.

"So we're stuck in Bakersfield," Sophia said.

"Well," Tricia said. "The bright side is, after the media hatchet job NGA and Sports Gear did here in L.A., I don't think an L.A. jury would be any better."

"Damn, Derek was right. This will be an expensive, time-eating mess," Paul said. "We want justice for the Holts, but now we need a really fat fee for ourselves more than ever."

No one disagreed.

⌘

# CHAPTER 30

## Sisyphus Is No Myth

*"Come what may, all bad fortune is to be*
*conquered by endurance."*
-Virgil

From the moment the rules allowed, Moschella waged a continuous discovery war over everything and anything: dates, times, and extensions to respond to every one of Krause & White's sets of discovery.

Sophia's team met when they finally received responses to their first round of discovery.

"What the hell," Paul said. "There are no answers to most of our interrogatories. Just boilerplate objections."

"The same with the requests for admissions," Eddie said.

"Ditto with the request to produce documents." Tricia threw the pack of papers on Sophia's desk.

"And we gave Moschella two 30-day extensions," Paul said. "What an ass."

"I have to meet and confer with him before we file our motions to compel." Sophia was angry.

"Meet and confer all you want. It'll go nowhere," Paul said.

"This is just plain obstructive," Tricia said. "They're trying to overwhelm us."

"And they are," Bryce said.

"Judge Ortiz will not like us haggling this out in his courtroom."

* * *

And Ortiz didn't.

Drives over the Grapevine to Bakersfield became a dreadful, repetitive, and draining reality for Sophia, Tricia, Paul, Bryce, and Eddie. Moschella forced hearings on things that should have been resolved by agreement between the attorneys in phone calls.

Yet Judge Ortiz never sanctioned Moschella for forcing any of the hearings, because Moschella was smart. He always did a friendly telephonic meet and confer in advance. He just never compromised on even the most minor disputes, always coming up with some superficially valid reason for his position.

After the initial flurry of paper discovery, the timing of depositions led to another prolonged struggle over priorities, dates, and locations.

\* \* \*

Derek added to the pressures by depriving Sophia of Bryce's help the first chance he got.

Forcing Bryce off the Holt case was his revenge.

Derek candy-coated it for Bryce by catering to his first-year lust for minor court appearances and substantive depositions. It was billable work, so admittedly it benefited everyone from a monetary standpoint in the short term. But losing Bryce was hard on Sophia's team. He had been one-fifth of their manpower.

\* \* \*

The remaining four met and debated whether they should move for a trial priority setting, advancing the Holts's trial date ahead of other cases in Ortiz's court. They could do that based on Wallace's age and Beth's ill health after the fire.

"We have no choice. We can't keep this up." Tricia was slumped in a chair.

"It's more pressure because things will move faster," Paul said. "But Moschella won't be able to keep multiplying pretenses to drag us over the Grapevine. The discovery and pretrial motion cutoffs will hit sooner and save us."

"I agree," Sophia said. "We're already flagging. We file for priority next week."

Moschella opposed their motion, arguing that the case had too many complex issues requiring numerous experts and witnesses. And Moschella went even further by moving to prolong the trial date because of the complexity, suspending the normal California rule that all civil cases conclude within two years of the filing of a complaint. It was a total reversal of his media campaign that the Holts's suit was frivolous and contrary to simple, clear, well-established law.

At the hearing, for once, Judge Ortiz ruled in Sophia's favor, based on the age and health of the Holts. But he pandered to Moschella in the process, complimenting him on his excellent opposition and additional motion. Ortiz announced that it was a very close call.

These comments made Sophia's team even more anxious concerning the judge's underlying bias if the case did not settle before trial.

* * *

Winning the trial priority was truly a Pyrrhic victory. The expedited trial abbreviated the Holts's suffering and meant fewer trips to "beautiful" Bakersfield for their weary lawyers. However, it also meant more work in less time and without Bryce.

Moschella's office filed every pretrial motion allowed—one after another.

Sophia's team barely got their oppositions filed, using canned law from memos in other cases and minimal facts hastily thrown together. They also missed one filing deadline, for the first time in any of their careers, but Judge Ortiz accommodated them, with a reproach. He even went to bat for them on another occasion in the interest of justice, citing obvious case precedent Sophia and her team had missed.

Krause & White lost one skirmish after another and savored its rare victories.

* * *

"How is Moschella keeping this up?" Paul asked.

"I don't know," Tricia said. "They look like pros litigating this gun case, and I looked into it. Their firm has never done one before."

"Then how does Moschella keep filing so many superb, well-researched motions and oppositions?" Sophia asked. "I mean, they do have other clients, and his firm's not that big, just Bakersfield big."

"How can they even think of all the motions they throw at us?" Eddie asked. "Let alone research the law, draft them, and get them filed?"

"There's something we're not seeing," Sophia said. "And I know I'm not paranoid, but they seem to know what we're going to do before we do it. They're always ready. I don't understand."

"Me either," Paul said. "We're not dealing with some legal titan here. I mean, Moschella got his law degree from McGeorge. Not Harvard or Stanford or UCLA. Every time I see him, he looks tan and relaxed. Like he just stepped off the golf course."

What Sophia's team didn't know was that they weren't just facing Quarry, Warren & Moschella. They were actually fighting against all the resources of the premier gun defense firm in the nation: Jackson, Hood & Lee. That firm's lawyers were preparing every one of the court filings for Moschella. All Moschella and his team had to do was read them, sign them, and argue them.

\* \* \*

Meanwhile, life for everyone at Krause & White had shifted, and not for the better. The onslaught of discovery and motions continued without letup, and so did the almost-insurmountable time pressures, frequent late-nighters, and far too many all-nighters for Sophia and her three comrades.

Sophia's relationship with Steve was not flourishing. Tricia and Jay's was actually on the rocks from all the pressure and her constant absence. Paul, however, was happy being busy and being with Sophia. Eddie was happy too because he had connected with Raquel, the new Assistant U.S. Attorney. Tricia followed through with her matchmaking despite her own relationship problems.

Autumn and her new love, Stefan, were no longer on Eddie's radar, except that Stefan continued to be a too-frequent presence in the office.

\* \* \*

After Derek buried his brother, Rona, Derek, and Bryce became a threesome. They billed the hours necessary to meet the firm's monthly overhead and didn't let Sophia or her team forget it.

The rift between Derek and Sophia worsened because Steve's unit had failed to make an arrest in Dwight's shooting. There were no witnesses, no one who would admit to having seen anything. The one old man who saw the fighting "lost" his memory, too. It didn't matter that Derek's mother was well-liked in the neighborhood or that Derek had done many legal favors for families and neighbors there. The bottom line was that his younger brother had spent his short life in bad company, going in and out of juvie and graduating from petty to serious crimes. His latest arrests for drug dealing hadn't stuck, but eventually they would have.

Dwight's criminal history was beside the point to Derek. His brother was dead—dead because of Sophia's case, not because of any gang involvement or his criminal activities. And the murderer was still running free because, as far as Derek was concerned, Sophia's detective boyfriend didn't care. Everything else was irrelevant.

\* \* \*

While Krause & White was hurting financially, it hadn't yet been forced to borrow to meet its monthly expenses. Bryce's collection action brought in some money. Paul's Zeigler arbitration netted $105,000 after costs and expenses, even though the award was $575,000. Those two amounts together with Derek's and Rona's billable matters were barely enough for the firm to hold on.

Peggy, though stalwart and experienced, was overwhelmed. She could only keep up because the court allowed e-filing of all papers now, and the lawyers had agreed to use email for most written communications. Autumn pitched in to help Peggy with the Holt case and even got a small raise for doing it.

The NGA stepped up its lobbying in all fifty states and in Washington, D.C., at the federal level. It was focused and on the offensive. The NGA was being assaulted over far more than the Holt case. However, it had the resources to keep up with everything the gun control advocates threw at them with the unending stream of mass killings, suicides, and general gun violence. Keeping the pressure on in the Holt case at the same time was a snap for the NGA.

* * *

The trial was set for September 14, and the pretrial conference for August 14, about a year after the Holts had first contacted Sophia. There would be appearances all through the hundred-degree-plus Bakersfield summer. September's trial days would not be much better, and their personal weather-misery index would remain high.

* * *

On the plus side, the Holts turned out to be surprisingly good clients. In all honesty, Sophia wished the firm had more clients like them.

Wallace immediately paid every bill for costs without question. Beth called for updates but never complained about the case. She only complained about her loneliness and health. She and Wallace had essentially become homebound to avoid unpleasantness. Sophia listened patiently, appreciating that their lives had totally changed and they were socially isolated. Wallace rarely went out and had learned to order almost everything they needed from the Internet. They spent whatever it cost. With Mike gone, why should they economize to preserve an estate no one would inherit?

Sophia accepted the "hand-holding" as a necessary part of practicing law. Beth and Wallace were far less demanding in that department than many other clients Sophia had encountered, especially at Thorne & Chase.

* * *

Neither Beth nor Wallace ever talked about the fire. The case was closed as far as the Bakersfield police were concerned—either that or, more likely, they had never bothered to investigate at all.

In truth, Sophia, Sophia's team, Beth and Wallace all believed that the Bakersfield police had but one regret and that was that Beth and Wallace had not perished in the fire. Not that they would have investigated that with much interest or diligence either.

⌘

# CHAPTER 31

## The Spy Who Wooed Her

*"A small leak will sink a great ship."*
-Benjamin Franklin

By June, four months before trial, Team Holt had commandeered the conference room as litigation central. It was the only space big enough—except that it wasn't.

Near lunchtime the first Monday in June, Autumn hummed as she dusted and straightened her habitually cluttered reception desk.

"Hey, what's with the housecleaning, Autumn?" Paul was carrying boxes of documents produced by Sports Gear to the conference room with Tricia.

"Nothing." Autumn stopped humming.

"Lunch with Stefan again?" Tricia trailed Paul with more boxes.

"Mondays and Wednesdays," Autumn preened. "Stefan's classes start late and . . ."

"Did you get the strategy memo distributed to everyone?" Tricia didn't want to hear about budding love because she had so much less with Jay at the moment.

"I will before I go to lunch," Autumn called after them. "And you have to find room for these boxes."

Tricia glanced back at the stacks near Autumn's desk. "Good luck with that."

\* \* \*

In the conference room, Tricia dropped her boxes on the table and shut the door. "That's annoying."

"What?"

"That's nesting activity if I ever saw it and just too much joy for me."

Tricia was envious. With her consuming work schedule, she and Jay had not been able to catch lunch or do dinner for months, and he had stopped asking. Tricia needed rest and sleep. She was barely hanging on. After a while, Jay didn't care about her excuses and explanations. He wanted their old relationship back.

"She's getting laid . . . regularly," Paul said.

"You always bring relationships down to the lowest common denominator."

"I'm a guy."

"I'm not. So cool it." Tricia and Jay weren't good in that department either and hadn't been for months. "Besides, sex isn't everything in a relationship."

"Sure. Sure." Paul backed off.

"Help me get this place organized."

The room was dense with file boxes six high and two deep along three of its walls. They were only a part of the latest document production from Sports Gear. Box after box had been delivered the previous Friday. They were everywhere.

"First, Moschella gave us nothing. Now he's burying us in mountains of crap," Paul said. "We'll never get through it."

"I know."

"All we need is to find some policy statement not to sell guns to questionable buyers," Paul said. "Or something that says there are no questionable buyers. How good would that be? The smoking gun. An in-house memo, handbook, pamphlet, emails, or something. Anything."

"Right. Like that's gonna happen." Tricia stared at the box fortress surrounding them.

Sports Gear had only partially computerized its operations, an anachronism in modern American business. Paul believed it was a conscious strategy to make discovery tough on anyone suing them. He wished he could find evidence to prove that as well.

Oftentimes, parties in lawsuits object strenuously to broad document requests and seek court relief to limit them. Moschella, or really Jackson, Hood & Lee, did the same. However, when the deadline for the actual document production came, they chose to dump disorganized truckloads of documents on Krause & White. They buried them in paper knowing Krause & White did not have the manpower to get through them or find any proverbial smoking gun.

As Paul transferred boxes, a tower started to collapse.

"Grab it." Tricia held back the pile while Paul caught the top box and put it on the conference table.

"Good catch."

"What difference does any of this make?" Paul sat. "This is impossible."

"Dumping it on the floor won't help."

"Nothing will. The deadline for the last document production isn't until Thursday. They could send another truckload over."

The two started digging through boxes. Even if they hadn't fast-tracked the case, they would never have been able to review what Sports Gear had produced.

"Crap, Paul. This is just like it was in the other boxes. Nothing stapled, nothing in chronological order. Not even organized by subject."

"At Thorne & Chase," Tricia said, "we would have had a commercial document scanning service put all this on a DVD and then used software searches to review them."

"So what? We can't here. We don't have the money, and neither do the Holts."

"No. I'll look at the few CD-ROMs Sports Gear gave us. I already looked at the security tape. It's really grainy."

\* \* \*

Autumn invaded Paul and Tricia's ear space by singing a song from *Camelot* at her desk.

"It's May. It's May. The month of yes you may. The lusty month where everyone goes blissfully astray . . ."

Tricia looked up, annoyed. "It's June. And Stefan better come and lead her blissfully out of here before I kill her."

"Ditto. But it's only eleven-forty."

"I can hear her plain as day. What a cheap hollow door."

The singing stopped.

Paul and Tricia heard soft giggles and the stealthy silence of tenderness.

Stefan had come early.

\* \* \*

"I can't leave yet," Autumn said.

"That's okay," Stefan said. "I just wanted to see you. I'll wait."

"I have to spell check this memo and distribute it before we go. It's for the trial."

"Really? Interesting."

"The lawyers are heavy into it now. A lot of arguing."

"Let me help. It'll be fun looking over your shoulder . . . smelling your flowery hair."

"Sure."

There was silence and then the reverberating noise of a stolen kiss.

Autumn tapped through the spell check.

"Hey, slow down. There's one."

"No there's not, silly."

"Wait . . . ah . . . you're right. Go on."

"No. You go over there. I can't concentrate with you so snuggled up. I'd have been done before, but I had to make room for all the boxes," Autumn chattered while she finished the spell check. "And the attorneys say they're useless anyway because they're willy-nilly and they can't get through it all anyway."

"Really? So they won't be able to use them?"

"Who knows? Checking the pagination and I'm done."

\* \* \*

Behind the door, Tricia whispered to Paul, "She shouldn't have let him see that memo. Suck-face friends or not. Why is all of this so 'interesting' to him?"

"I don't know. According to you, he's just trying to get laid."

"Did they meet in classes? I'm serious now . . . why all the interest in her work? Why is he always hanging around here so much?"

"I don't know. Maybe . . ."

"Be quiet. Let me listen." Tricia went to the door and cracked it open.

"Wait here." Autumn's voice floated into the war room. "I'll do the copies and distribute this."

When Autumn left, Stefan looked up and down the hall and then stepped back around Autumn's desk. He took out a flash drive and put it in Autumn's computer and downloaded documents, including the open memo.

"Paul, come here quick."

"What? I'm busy."

"Shh."

Paul walked over.

"Look."

"What?"

Tricia shut the door.

"He's downloading stuff from Autumn's computer on a flash drive."

"Are you sure?" Paul asked. "The trial strategy memo's there."

"That and everything else."

Paul went back over and cracked the door again. Stefan was looking down the hall. Paul could see the flash drive and how Stefan kept bringing up files and downloading.

"What's he doing?" Tricia pushed Paul aside. "I can't see."

"Move over . . . damn, I can't see either . . ."

"I'm ready," Autumn called from down the hall.

"He just finished another download." Paul said. "He put the flash drive in his pocket. I'm going out there

"No." Tricia shut the door. "What are you going to do, fight him for it?"

"But the memo . . . and what else did he download? Our financials? I've got to get it."

"You can't just wrestle him and grab the flash drive, and he's never going to hand them over."

"Call the cops?"

"He'll walk out, and we have no proof. I should have videoed him."

"Citizens' arrest . . . I'll . . ."

"Don't be crazy. He's huge."

"The memo itself is a week of our work." Paul looked out. "They're leaving."

"Let 'em go."

"They already did . . ." Paul opened the door and started down the hall. "We have to tell Sophia."

"She can ask Steve what we should do." Tricia followed.

"Damn it. That explains why they're always one step ahead of us."

"Espionage. Who would have thought?"

* * *

Sophia was reviewing the proposed deposition dates of the key players with Eddie. She had served depo notices for Sports Gear's key witnesses before Moschella got his notices out for the Holts. Now, Moschella was trying to reverse the order.

"Does the order really matter?" Eddie asked.

"You always want to pin the other side's witnesses down first. Get their stories on the record under oath."

"The facts are the facts, though. They don't change regardless."

Sophia just smiled at Eddie and his naiveté as a new litigator.

"Change? A little. If you find out what the other side knows or what its people will say first, your witnesses can tailor their testimony more favorably to your position."

"Don't you mean they can lie?"

"Conform is a better word."

"That's unethical."

"Depends how far you take it. Under the canons of ethics, a litigator has to take full advantage of what the law and the rules allow to assiduously represent any client. In case law, 'diligence' and 'zeal' are emphasized."

"I really have a lot to learn."

"You'll get the hang of it. One thing to remember, though. You rarely win a case with your own client's depos, but you can lose it there. Your clients must be properly prepared, or they can be blindsided. Securing deposition priority means you get to lock in the other side's testimony first. You can use it to impeach them at trial if they contradict themselves. And if you get good admissions, you can force a settlement."

"I get why we have to fight for our right to go first."

"Litigation is a three-dimensional chess game, and the learning never stops. Let's call Moschella together about the dates."

Moschella negotiated hard on the phone to get her to change her dates.

*Like hell*, Sophia thought as she listened to him. *I got the priority. You snooze. You lose.*

Sophia kept talking only because the alternative was another trip to Bakersfield with the good-old-boy judge setting the dates. She was surprised Moschella hadn't done his notices for depos first. She suspected an associate error. She was right. However, the associate who dropped the ball was not at Moschella's firm but at Jackson, Hood & Lee.

Tricia and Paul charged into Sophia's office.

"I have to go, Tony. Call me later and we'll finish this."

\* \* \*

Paul and Tricia told Sophia and Eddie about Stefan.

Outraged? Yes. Ready to mobilize? Yes. Surprised? Not so much.

Eddie launched into a furious tirade until Tricia shut him up. He wanted to punch Stefan out or, better yet, have his cousins do a beatdown.

Eddie was a troubled and troubling combination, the explosive barrio temper that was a legacy of his childhood struggling with the acute, cool legal mind he had acquired and honed at Harvard.

Sophia got Steve on speaker and told him about Stefan. Steve's comments were discouraging. They all came down to "no proof" and that Tricia was right in stopping Paul from confronting him.

"Do you want me to question the guy?" Steve asked.

"No," Sophia said. "We have to think. Don't do anything. Talk to you later."

"Fine . . . but you guys should sweep for bugs and definitely install a security camera or two."

"Yes," Tricia said. "Remember the security Thorne & Chase installed?"

"Who could forget it?" Steve replied.

"What happened?" Eddie asked.

"Never mind." Tricia stopped the digression.

"Thanks, Steve," Sophia said.

"Sure. See you tonight."

Sophia wouldn't see him tonight—while Steve was awake anyway—and she would make sure of that because he annoyed her in every way right now. She was desexualized by the pressure—he wasn't. He talked at her all the time—about himself, her, them, the future, food, or fun. He just mundaned away. It was too much for her. Or, more accurately, too *little* for her in its everyday, unimportant drivel.

Then again, just about anything not case-related was beyond her now. She was in trial-crisis mode and didn't have time to stroke Steve's ego or his anatomy. She just wasn't in the mood.

The four sat and thought.

* * *

"I have a great idea," Eddie said. "Let's plant something phony for him to take."

"Don't be silly," Tricia pooh-poohed. "We have enough real work."

"No, wait, maybe he's got something," Paul said.

"Eddie, that's exactly what I was thinking." Sophia was pleased. "Let's do it. Paul, you and Eddie draft something totally wrong but plausible that Stefan can steal. We'll screw them over."

"We can do it again and again." Tricia was on board now.

"How could we have been so stupid as to let that guy get away with this?" Eddie said.

"We're not stupid. Look at Nixon and Watergate—who would have thought?" Paul said.

"Watergate?" Eddie asked.

"No history lesson now, Eddie. Who's paying this guy for info? The NGA . . . Sports Gear . . . some network?" Sophia asked.

"This is dirty." Eddie was incredulous.

"It is," Tricia said. "But big stakes make people ruthless. My guess is the NGA, and then they pass on what they learn to Moschella, who will keep his hands clean or plausibly so."

"He'd better," Paul added. "If we get any proof that Moschella had access to our confidential internal memos, our work product, that would be gross discovery misconduct."

"And a major breach of the canons of ethics. They'll be facing disbarment, and Sports Gear could be looking at terminating sanctions," Sophia added.

"Terminating sanctions?" Eddie asked.

"If a plaintiff is sufficiently abusive or unethical, the court can dismiss a complaint or, where the misconduct is on the defense side, like Sports Gear, it can dismiss all defenses to the complaint and effectively give the plaintiff a win."

"Wow, that would be great for us here." Eddie was enthused.

"Forget about that. Not going to happen. It's so rare. Besides we're getting ahead of ourselves," Paul said. "Right now we have to put an end to Stefan's little game or use it to our advantage."

"We'll do the latter and not worry about the 'who,'" Sophia said. "From now on, input all strategic and analytical work yourselves. No more Autumn. Our computers have passwords. Turn your computers off when you leave your offices and enter the passwords every time you log on. Keep your doors locked. Use no more staff for anything . . . not even copying."

"Unless we want to plant something," Eddie interrupted.

"Right." Eddie's eagerness to spend time on dirty tricks wearied Sophia—they all had enough real work. "Our tech guy will remove our Holt documents from all computers but ours. When we're in trial in Bakersfield, we'll do emails from our private accounts and phone texts. Don't use the office email for anything. It can be accessed by everyone."

"Pain in the ass, all of this," Paul said. "But Sophia's right."

"We should get burner phones." Eddie jumped out of his chair. "They can clone ours like in the movies."

"Not right now." Sophia refrained from rolling her eyes. "But we'll sweep for bugs and maybe install a couple of security cameras. At least, we'll have proof."

"Sweep for bugs. Cool." Eddie sat down, satisfied.

"A camera? No," Tricia objected. "I don't want to be taped all day,"

"I don't care what we have to do if it will stop the leak," Paul said. "We have too many hours invested in this case. We can't afford to lose."

"This only happens in the movies." Eddie was excited.

"Not really," Paul said. "My father's New York firm had a high-profile case and spent a boatload on security. They changed their elevator access to one reception floor. They put in cameras. It was cutthroat."

"Enough. Everyone get some lunch, turn off your computers, and lock your doors. We have a long afternoon," Sophia handed Tricia money. "Tricia, can you grab me something? I have to meet with Rona and Derek about this and then patrol when Stefan drops Autumn off."

"Sure."

"Don't forget, Paul," Sophia continued. "After lunch, help Eddie draft our first decoy strategy memo to plant."

"This is wild!" Eddie left with Paul and Tricia.

*This is tiring*, Sophia thought.

\* \* \*

Sophia met with Rona and Derek behind closed doors. She got the money for a bug sweep but no cameras. They liked the decoy memos and having Sophia's team do all of its own work. Frankly, it freed staff hours for their paying clients.

With help from Rona, Derek also agreed that Bryce could spend some time again on the Holt case—now that it was sinking deeper into litigation-and-clerical quicksand, the ever-practical Derek wanted a win for the firm.

⌘

# CHAPTER 32

## Motion and Emotion

*"There is no security on this earth;*
*there is only opportunity."*
-Douglas MacArthur

Early Tuesday morning, before anyone else had arrived, Steve brought a security specialist to Krause & White for the bug sweep. He got Sophia a discounted rate.

Sophia watched the specialist and Steve interact. But for Steve's power-anointed detective's badge, they were cut from the same simple cloth.

Watching them confirmed why she didn't socialize with Steve's friends. Steve himself had dropped his guard once and said he didn't think she would fit in well either. She didn't care because she knew she didn't want to fit in well. She liked her own friends: the way they talked, the jokes they made, the complexity of their thoughts, their analysis even about the most trivial of subjects—like how tomato soup differed from tomato bisque. It was fun. The level of discourse between these two men bored her. She hid in her office and worked while they finished.

Finally, they reported back.

"Bug-free," Steve announced.

"That's wonderful."

Sophia remained seated. There was no hug for Steve. It wasn't so wonderful. She should have appreciated his effort more but didn't. She didn't care that he had gotten her a discount of a couple of bucks.

She shook the friend's hand. "Thank you for coming so quickly. Send us a bill. And don't worry about any discount."

Steve looked like she had slapped him in the face. She had devalued his friend's favor and his own efforts.

"Nah, Steve's a great friend. It'll be the friend discount. Maybe we'll have dinner sometime. A foursome with my wife."

"I'd like that." Sophia would kill herself first.

Steve recognized Sophia's social bullshit too well now.

"When her trial is done."

The debugger used that as an invitation to start questioning her about her work.

Sophia looked at Steve, and he knew to get the guy out of there.

He did.

\* \* \*

Later that afternoon, Moschella called to finish their required meet and confer about the deposition schedule. He insisted on moving Sophia's depositions of his key witnesses to dates after the Holts's.

"No. We had priority. Your store manager can change his vacation."

"He can't. Prepaid. Penalties. And he planned it before your deposition notice arrived. It's a once-in-a-decade family reunion."

Sophia had heard that lawyer preplanned-vacation-evasion tactic for reordering the dates of depos before. The only thing preplanned were the buzzwords lawyers used to fit within the language of applicable rules and case law.

"We're on a short leash here," Sophia said.

"Because of you. My client's once-in-a-decade reunion isn't going to be sacrificed to your tactics. I know Judge Ortiz will agree. He understands family."

Another trip to Bakersfield and the courthouse was looming. Moschella's favorite ploy was stonewalling because he liked forcing a member of Sophia's team to eat time appearing in Bakersfield.

Normally, judges frowned on attorneys not cooperating, but this black-robed pillar of his small community didn't see it that way. He was overburdened by Sophia's fast-tracking of the Holt case, a friend of Moschella's at the country club and in their small legal circle, and from his biography at best neutral on gun sales and gun ownership. He was a part of Bakersfield, which had its own mores regarding guns. In fact, courtesy of Ben Kowrilsky, Sophia had discovered that Judge Ortiz was noted for his light sentencing of illegal gun sellers—after all, they had to scratch out a living and kept their dealings in the outlying surrounding small towns, not in Bakersfield itself.

She began to regret not moving to recuse Ortiz. But then she reminded herself again that she could have done worse—much worse—given their survey of the other Kern County Superior Court judges.

"These are not tactics. I have old clients and one in tenuous health thanks to that close-knit, tight-lipped, guns-at-all-costs community of yours hiding an arsonist," Sophia volleyed back.

"First, that's not how I see our community. Second, the police can't arrest suspects they can't find."

"Exactly my point. They never will. I want to see the receipts for that prepaid vacation turned monumental family reunion."

"I guess we'll see what the judge says about that."

"Fine," Sophia said. "We've changed the date once for you. No more. I'm filing the motion to compel today."

"I'm available Wednesday through Friday and I'll let his clerk know."

"Wait . . ." Sophia couldn't get up there on such short notice.

"Just expediting your fast-track, Ms. Christopoulos."

"Right." Sophia hung up before she blew up.

She was cornered again. She would be driving back to Bakersfield, and she would lose the motion as she had lost so many others. Judge Ortiz's attitude was that she had asked for "fast" and that was what she was going to get. Even when, or perhaps especially when, it was to her disadvantage and that of her clients.

Sophia called the clerk as soon as she hung up, but Moschella had beaten her to it. He got Sophia's motion to compel set for Friday afternoon. The "only" time he had available. He played the Friday-afternoon card all the time because it was the worst traffic of the week for Sophia's team. The weekenders heading out of L.A. clogged the I-5 all day. The Friday-night freeway parking lots in the sprawling megalopolis were also predictably onerous coming back. It didn't matter. Sophia's traffic complaints fell on deaf ears with the judge and the clerk.

A home-court advantage was not a myth in any town, especially Bakersfield. It was a guarantee.

Sophia considered not filing the motion, but tactically she had to try. Keeping the order was only fair—as if that ever mattered in the real legal world.

\* \* \*

In the team's afternoon meeting, Sophia threw the possible depo schedule changes at them. They evaluated Moschella's underhanded tactics and what alternative trial strategies they could adopt to counteract them. They agreed the motion to compel had to be made—win, lose, or draw.

"I'll go," Paul volunteered.

"No, but thanks," Sophia said. "I should meet with the Holts soon anyway. They could use some hand-holding. The bills are getting bigger. I have to reassure them."

Eddie said, "We should forget the motion if we're going to lose anyway."

"We can't," Paul said. "Not without a fight. We have to lock in the manager's and sales clerks' statements before the Holts's. And preserve the argument on appeal, too."

"So we're going to have to fight about the others too?" Eddie asked.

"And lose." Tricia said. "He'll use fast-tracking as an excuse, again, just like with the other discovery motions we lost."

"This sucks." Eddie yawned. The intense work and his new-girlfriend-itis with Raquel had him burning the candle at both ends.

"Too many late nights?" Tricia was torn between pride at her successful matchmaking and jealousy because she and Jay had hit a rough patch that was getting rougher.

"No . . . No." Eddie perked up. "I'm fine."

Tricia was not glad anyone was fine because she wasn't. A relationship is like a shark—it moves forward, or it dies. Jay's and hers was going nowhere. She wanted to get married now—he didn't.

They had agreed not to take that step until Tricia's student loans were paid off. That agreement morphed into Jay's indefinite delay. With the demise of Thorne & Chase and Tricia's big salary, no loan payoff was in sight. He knew it, and so did Tricia.

"Paul, has Stefan gotten his hands on our phony strategy memo yet?" Tricia asked.

"No, but the next time he comes I'm going to get Autumn in my office, and he'll be alone with her computer to do it."

"Good. Then that's begun," Sophia said. "Remember our new protocols. We help each other. If we really need something, Derek begrudgingly offered us Bryce . . . but I'd avoid it because Derek's wrath isn't worth it."

Sophia continued, "Paul and I will draft the motion to compel the manager's depo. We'll electronically file it today and both e-serve and fax serve it. Anything else?"

"Do I get to take a depo or two?" Eddie asked.

"Of course," Sophia hesitated but had to keep her word. "Let me see which one."

"One?"

"Right." Seeing his disappointment, Sophia deftly finessed him.

"There's taking, and then there's defending."

"Oh, of course." Relieved, Eddie didn't want to overstep.

"We'll work it out, but not right now. Everyone should go get to work."

\* \* \*

Paul stayed behind for the motion.

"Are you sure, Sophia?"

"About what?"

"Eddie handling depos while he's worn out from his sex life?"

"Of course not, but we need him . . . and we need him happy."

"He seems happy enough to me."

"Envious?"

"Don't be an ass. I'm not envious."

"Well, I am," Sophia mused. "There's nothing like those first six months."

Paul shouldn't have been pleased with Sophia's comment, but he was. He had loved her for years. Maybe Steve was about to be history and he could do what he should have done so long ago—tell her how he felt.

"Earth to Paul."

"Let's get this motion done. I'm going with you on Friday. I haven't seen the Holts since I dropped by after the last hearing on our document request." Paul didn't care about seeing the Holts, but he craved being alone with Sophia all day. "In court, two heads are always better than one."

What Paul meant was that two hearts are better than one.

"You're on. We'll work on the argument on the drive. Who knows—with both of us preparing, we may win."

As Paul walked out, he planned to find a great restaurant for dinner in Bakersfield with Sophia. They would wait out the rush hour there—together.

⌘

# CHAPTER 33

## Defeated and Disrespected

*"I thought these grapes were ripe,*
*but I see now they are quite sour."*
-Aesop

Friday, Sophia and Paul arrived at the Bakersfield courthouse thirty minutes before the hearing Moschella had scheduled.

They checked in with Ortiz's clerk and waited in the back row of the gallery. There was a smattering of attorneys in suits there for motions—some studying the outlines of their arguments or whispering with their clients, some texting, and others just staring into space.

"Thankfully, the air conditioning is good," Sophia whispered.

"We'd be suffering if it wasn't."

In June, Bakersfield's days ran from the high eighties to the mid-nineties, sometimes leaping higher. Today was leaping.

Judge Ortiz took the bench promptly. Sophia had appeared in front of him now several times, as had Paul and Tricia. He presided in Department 5 on the second floor, which was good. If they did go to trial, the second floor was less accessible to the expected media, and Judge Ortiz's courtroom was close to the elevator and restrooms—it saved time and steps.

Moschella hadn't checked in yet, nor did he for the next hour. He had called the clerk, yet again, and made the "unavoidably detained" excuse he had used several times before. The judge didn't care. He had a full calendar of motions to hear—from restraining order requests to trial continuance motions and other discovery fights. The attorneys in the gallery, most paid by the hour, were happily billing their collective waiting time. Sophia and Paul were the ones hurting because they weren't on the clock. They bowed to reality and relaxed.

More than an hour late, Moschella and his associate finally showed up. His associate waited in the aisle while Moschella went forward to check in with the clerk. They were chummy, if not flirtatious.

"You have to start doing some of that," Sophia whispered.

"No thanks. Not with her." Paul checked out the extremely unattractive beef-on-the-hoof crowned with a mass of blondish, unkempt strawlike hair who was parked at the clerk's desk. "I don't know how he does it."

Moschella's charm had put a silly grin across the clerk's face.

"It's his job." Sophia elbowed Paul.

Moschella returned to his associate, Theresa Sandoval. He knew what he was doing putting her on the case. There was nothing accidental about any move Moschella made and Theresa was an asset he used freely. When she came to court all eyes were on her, including the judge's. This time they watched her in her Hugo Boss Vilea pencil skirt and four-inch heels clicking behind Moschella to the back row. For the finale she hiked up her skirt, sidled into her end seat, and then elegantly and theatrically crossed her legs letting them drape out into the aisle.

Sophia recognized the Hugo Boss Vilea signature skirt. It wasn't cheap. And she recognized the female tactical distraction. It wasn't uncommon—just not so uncommonly consummated.

Sophia's team had repeatedly dealt with Sandoval on the phone. She was smart. Moschella was undoubtedly dangling a few depositions under her nose too.

"There she is again," Paul whispered to Sophia. "What's a Yale Law grad doing in Bako anyway?"

"I don't know, but the testosterone level is off the charts every time she shows up. You better believe she'll be at the trial every day if we can't settle."

"You can count on that."

"I guess I'll have to use my four-inch heels, too," Sophia said.

"Sounds good to me." Paul didn't suppress the visuals in his imagination.

\* \* \*

Judge Ortiz called the Holt depo dispute at the end of the second call, the last remaining matter on his calendar. It was after four.

"That jerk Moschella always does this," Sophia whispered as they stood. "We'll never get home."

"We'll have dinner at Noriega's." Paul had no one to go home to and had counted on his wait-out-the-traffic dinner with Sophia.

They walked up the aisle, through swinging spindle gates, and passed the bar into the well where the counsel tables were. Paul put their motion on the table with attached exhibits of the actual deposition notices served by each side. In the Exhibit Table of Contents Sophia carefully listed with dates each notice in temporal sequence to show that they had noticed theirs first.

"Let's see here." Judge Ortiz flipped through the court's case file. "The trial is set for September 14. We've calendared the pretrial conference date as well. Be ready to hammer out some kind of settlement then, after you two are done with your discovery."

"Your Honor," Moschella said. "We'd be amenable to that."

"So would we, Your Honor." Sophia made sure she never looked less reasonable than Moschella.

"Noted, Ms. Christopoulos. Now your motion?"

Sophia began, "We noticed all our depositions months ago and well before the discovery cutoff as listed in the Exhibit Table of Contents and attached documents. More than that, we have already accommodated Mr. Moschella by delaying the Arnie Davis deposition once due to a family illness. Now on the eve of Mr. Davis's rescheduled deposition, and he is a key witness, we learn about a prepaid vacation to a family reunion. The very word 'prepaid' means they necessarily knew about it and never mentioned it. Also, Your Honor, if we are forced to accommodate them, then they'll be deposing my clients first. This is a disingenuous ploy, a tactic, to take the advantage from us when we were timely in our notices and have been more than fair in extending courtesies."

"Mr. Moschella?"

When Judge Ortiz looked over at Moschella, his eyes traveled further and lingered on Sandoval.

"As you see in our exhibits, the tickets were purchased a month ago. Sworn affidavits from four extended family members state the family reunion happens only every ten years. It would be unfair to Mr. Davis and more so to his three children to interfere with the reunion or to have them go without their father. As to our timely informing Ms. Christopoulos about the reunion . . . our office did so the moment we heard about it. Mr. Davis is not an attorney and clearly states under oath in his deposition that he didn't put two and two together until this week. We're doing the best we can and proceeding in complete good faith here."

"I've studied your papers." The judge spoke with authority while continuing his side-glances at Moschella's beautiful associate.

Sophia was tired of the male gawking that went on every time that woman was in court. She had learned in law school that the scales of justice were supposed to be blind—but she had learned in real life they weren't that blind. In truth, she had used that male weakness herself to gain the upper hand also.

"While I could compel Mr. Davis to attend, I choose not to," Judge Ortiz ruled. "Your motion states nothing to suggest the family illness that led to the first postponement of his deposition was not genuine. Nor that anything Mr. Moschella or Mr. Davis has said about this family reunion was prompted by this lawsuit or any gamesmanship. This whole case is derived from familial relationships, namely the suicide of Mike Holt. It would be grossly unfair were it to harm yet more familial relationships when there are other witnesses available to depose."

"But Your Honor, we have timely noticed the deposition of the defendant's key witnesses and . . ." Sophia began to argue.

"That's the court's ruling," Judge Ortiz cut Sophia off and nodded toward Moschella. "You two find a mutually agreeable date and don't let me see you back in here. From now on, I would urge plaintiffs' counsel to read applicable case law before you waste the court's time. And, Ms. Christopoulos, the next time you have a meet and confer on the phone, you not only extend the minimum courtesies but also follow the law as established. To its full extent."

The judge left the bench. Moschella whispered to his associate, leaning close in and prolonging the proximity. She didn't retreat and instead looked past him at Paul with a satisfied smile. Her motor clearly never stopped running.

Sophia's dressing-down by the court made the Greek in her rage.

"Stand down, Sophia." Paul observed the telltale fury in her eyes. "You should be pleased with one thing—they both got your name right this time."

Sophia marched out with Paul.

\* \* \*

Outside, the courthouse building mercifully shadowed the late afternoon sun. The heat was starting its slide to the typical June-night sixties. Paul and Sophia did a depressing post-mortem.

"What crap," Paul said. "We were transparently home-courted. As if they 'forgot' the date of the family reunion until now."

"Ortiz wouldn't know how to interpret the law if it rose up and bit him in the ass. He and Moschella are definitely in bed together."

"Not from the way the judge was looking at that associate," Paul poked at Sophia with his humor.

"I meant figuratively. If I could . . ."

"Careful," Paul warned. "It's them."

"Good evening." Moschella approached with Theresa.

Paul had never seen Theresa up close before. His glance became a long gaze into her deep green intelligent eyes outlined by natural long dark unmascared lashes. She was beautiful, unwrinkled, trimmed, and toned.

"How are you, Sophia? Paul?" Tony shook their hands. "I believe you've met our lead associate on the case, Theresa Sandoval."

"Yes." Paul sunk deeper into Theresa's mesmerizing eyes.

Paul was warm with his greeting and handshake. He couldn't help it. But Sophia could and did with brevity.

"She'll be calling you Monday with some proposed dates for the deposition."

Paul only response was a nod and a goofy smile.

"Good." Sophia shouldered Paul, and they left.

"Just a minute," Moschella called. "My client has an offer for you. Mind you, no admission of liability, of course. It's nuisance money."

Paul dropped his goofy smile, turned around, and lanced Moschella with sharp litigious eyes.. "Oh, so that's what Mike was, a nuisance?"

"Anyway." Moschella ignored Paul. "Sports Gear gave me a number that would be satisfactory to it before it spends any more money. Subject to confidentiality clauses, the usual stuff. You know the drill."

Sophia didn't know the entire drill, just some of it. But she danced the dance as she thought she should.

"What's your number?"

"Twenty-five thousand."

The pretty associate smiled a pretty smile.

"Are you kidding?" Paul blurted.

Sophia studied her two opponents with no tell showing her disgust. "We'll let you know after we present it to our clients."

Paul and Sophia started for his car. Thankfully, Moschella and the pencil-skirted associate were parked in the other direction. Paul was furious.

"That wouldn't even cover the Holts's costs after we take our third," Paul blurted.

"Keep it down. I know."

"You aren't really considering, it are you?"

"Of course not."

"You worried me." Paul unlocked his Mercedes from his Thorne & Chase days and opened the door for Sophia.

"Come on. Really? I can do the math. But we're required to present every settlement offer."

"Yeah. Yeah. But we're *not* recommending that they take it." Paul got in, and they headed for the Holts's house.

"No way in hell."

"Good. I'm sick of this incestuous burg and losing at every turn."

"Me too," Sophia said. "But the trial's going to be tough."

"I know. A local jury will be as tough as Ortiz. Maybe tougher."

⌘

# CHAPTER 34

## Unsettled

*"What am I doing? Tearing myself.*
*My usual occupation at most times."*
-Charles Dickens

On the way to the Holts's, Sophia and Paul learned there was also a Bakersfield Friday rush hour of sorts.

"Hey," Paul said as he drove up the Holt driveway shaded by trees. "The lawn's resodded. Looks good. And the driveway, they repebbled it."

"Yeah, Norman Rockwell America . . . not."

"Too bad it isn't."

"They might as well live on the moon. They're so isolated and embattled in their own home."

"Let's hope we can get them some vindication."

Paul pulled up, and they got out.

"It's cooler here out of town," Sophia said.

"There's no asphalt baking the air and no buildings to stop circulation."

They both enjoyed the light breeze rustling through the trees with their fresh spring growth. The trees shaded the house, the driveway, and the grass.

"Hello," Wallace called, holding the new decorative white wood screen door open. "We heard you coming down the drive. We've been waiting for you."

"Sorry," Sophia apologized. "The hearing was delayed."

"No . . . no criticism from us. No one ever realizes we have a Friday rush hour, too."

"Welcome, Sophia. Paul." Wallace shook their hands as they walked into the entry.

* * *

Inside, the rooms were freshly painted and wallpapered. The furniture was new. It was still schizophrenically floral, but there were no signs of the fire—except for Beth with her oxygen tank and a tube pinched under her nostrils.

"Good to see you, Beth. You're still on oxygen," Sophia said. "I'm so sorry."

"Hello, Beth," Paul said. "What does the doctor say?"

"I can take it off sometimes now . . . but not long enough to make you cookies." She rasped at them from her overstuffed chair with a scratchy, weak voice. "I'm sorry, kids. All we have are the chocolate chip cookies Wallace got on that Amazon store on the Internet."

"I like any cookie. May I?" Paul took one.

Sophia smiled at Paul's proclivity to both sweets and kindness.

"I'll get the coffee." Wallace headed to the kitchen.

"And a glass of water, please?" Paul chewed.

"Bring out some iced tea, too," Beth said. "I only wish I could help."

"I'll help." Sophia followed Wallace to avoid Beth's ever-imminent, ever-predictable tear eruptions.

Wallace returned with a tray holding a matching rose-patterned coffee service and Sophia with the water.

"Here." Sophia set the bottles down carefully on coasters on the Holts's new faux early American coffee table.

"Wallace, I told you to bring the iced tea for them," Beth nattered.

"No, thank you. Really," Paul protested. "Water's better."

Beth gave Wallace a disapproving glare. He ignored her.

As Wallace served the coffee, Sophia updated them on the discovery issues and decided to disclose the foiled espionage at the firm. She needed them to understand what they were up against. Both were incredulous.

"Guns are big money." Paul dumped cream in his coffee and heaping teaspoons of sugar, New York style.

"You don't have to tell us that," Wallace said. "You know they just raided an Earl-dale house, and you wouldn't believe what they found."

"Earl-dale?"

"Sorry. 'Earl-dale' is the way us old-timers pronounced Oildale," Wallace said. "Today the young folks call them '08ers.' That's the last two digits of their ZIP code—08."

"Never mind all that, Wallace. Tell them what was there," Beth said.

"One whole room . . . a bedroom . . . had steel bars on the windows, a security door, and reinforced walls. It was like a huge gun safe with hundreds of rifles, guns, ammo, and knives. The owner was a retired Earl-dale cop. When his wife called on a domestic, she made sure they saw it."

"They said she'd had enough." Beth batted her thin, droopy eyelids at Paul.

Sophia was disgusted at Beth's flirtation, especially in front of her husband. Her tears were more acceptable to Sophia.

"I don't know. I guess so. I'm not a criminal lawyer."

"We have to be going soon," Sophia short-circuited the Beth show. "But before we take off, we have to tell you we got an offer from Sports Gear."

"What?" Beth's voice came out strong and clear as she grabbed Paul's hand and held it tightly. "I can't believe it. How much?"

"Don't get excited." Sophia noted Beth had found a strong voice and a hand to grab—next would be the predictable buildup to another tearful catharsis.

This was the first time Sophia had seen Beth's avariciousness. Sophia suspected that an interest in money might have been part of her desire for "justice" when she went after Mike's evidence box in the fire.

"Wallace, why don't you go sit with Beth?" Sophia skillfully extricated Paul from the arthritic vice grip of long-decayed but still hungry femininity.

Wallace placidly obeyed. Beth grabbed his hand, and he endured it. Sophia had observed his neutrality many times since the fire. He had changed, but Sophia had enough on her plate. All she cared was that they conveyed a sympathetic public image for the trial.

"Now, don't put too much . . . in fact, don't put any stock in this offer," Sophia said as a preface. "They are dangling it to see if you are committed to staying the course through the trial, especially after the fire."

"They want you to throw in the towel." Paul grabbed another cookie.

"What is it?" Wallace abruptly dropped Beth's hand. "Will it cover what we have laid out?"

Wallace wanted nothing more than to be done with this, but not if he was going to lose money. Mike's memory no longer ruled him—covering their outlay did.

"Twenty-five thousand." Sophia watched Beth, the proverbial Oedipal mother.

"Our son is worth more than that." Beth was angry and reached out for Wallace's hand. "Right, dear?"

He ignored her.

"Jesus . . . after all this? Are they kidding?" Wallace ranted. "This damn thing ruined our life. Cost us our friends. We can't go back to our church. I'm afraid to go into a store. Our neighbors won't talk to us. We have to skip town when this trial is over . . . far away. They tried to burn us out. Beth left me to die for her precious son's memories. Do you want us to take this? Are you telling us you want out?"

"No." Sophia was shocked at Wallace's outburst, but it confirmed why he didn't dote on Beth any longer. "No, Wallace, the law requires that we bring you every settlement offer. We never thought you'd even consider it."

"That defense lawyer Moschella would love to cause a rift between us." Paul supported Sophia. "But we're with you. We can't recommend that you accept it, and we don't. However, we are also obligated to tell you that the trial is no slam-dunk."

"But we have a chance?" Beth asked. "We have a chance, right?"

"Of course," Paul said.

Moschella had achieved some of his aims with his paltry offer—to create torment, erode client confidence, and cause doubt. He had insulted the Holts and could have broken their resolve. But he had failed at that. Instead, they were both fighting angry.

Sophia and Paul talked to them for another hour to repair any rift and mistrust. They also explained that Moschella could always make a more reasonable, if not good, settlement offer later or even at the last minute "on the courthouse steps."

Wallace went to the window and stared out silently. Then he turned calmly and asked, "Do you think we should take it, Beth? I mean, we would be quite a bit out of pocket. But we could get our life back."

"What life? Mike's dead. We have no life left here, no friends. I want out of this place." Beth's voice was loud and strong. "I want a fresh start where we can enjoy the years we have left. And that takes money. More than we will have even if we sell this house."

A skilled emotional manipulator, Beth then suddenly turned to Paul and weakened her voice. "Our son is worth more than that, isn't he?"

"Of course, he is." Paul encouraged her because they needed a substantial financial return for the firm, too.

Beth's avariciousness prevailed. She wanted to play the game out, and the scent of the trial wafted deliciously between her and Paul. "He was all I . . . we had."

Beth punctuated her response with tears. Wallace ignored her. Sophia just wanted her to shut up.

"We'll do our best for you . . . both of you," Paul said.

"Not me. Not for me." Wallace glared at Beth. "This damn thing has cost us too much. Everything."

"Wallace, stop!" Beth ordered.

"No, I want out. Can I take that offer myself and get out?" Wallace asked Paul man to man as if Paul would be on his side. "What do you think, Paul? I want to call it a day. I'll take it and good riddance."

"You both have to sign, Wallace," Paul answered.

Wallace looked down, defeated. "Fine."

Beth's now-exposed hunger for money was music to Sophia's ears, and it defeated Wallace. Sophia's firm was safe because Beth would never throw in the towel for a pittance—unlike Wallace.

Beth was Sophia's new best friend.

* * *

Paul and Sophia were relieved, hungry, and exhausted when they left the Holts's. A disaster had been averted.

"I should have presented that offer differently," Sophia said. "It let us know one thing, though. Wallace is a problem. I never thought either of them would accept it."

"I saw that coming when he went to the window, but it all happened so fast." Paul drove the car up the driveway. "He wants to throw in the towel. I hope he doesn't get another chance."

"I think Beth can control him. We should have had a plan before we went in."

"Next time," Paul said. "And how about that Beth? She wants money. Justice seems to have evolved into an afterthought."

"I never trust a woman who cries to get what she wants," Sophia said. "But it's better for us now that her motivation is money . . . it'll help us get some for ourselves. Besides, I believe in the case. Why should those gun stores be able to sell a shotgun to a suicidal kid . . . or man or anyone?"

"Agreed on all counts."

"Did you catch how bitter Wallace is that Beth left him in the fire?"

"I would be too."

"He has a lot of resentment, and it's growing. We have to keep an eye on him."

"We will, but now," Paul said, "I'm taking us to the greatest dinner you'll ever have."

"Really? In Bakersfield? Where?"

"You'll see."

"I'm up for it. No L.A. rush hour tonight."

Paul smiled. *And I'm up for having you all to myself for an evening.*

⌘

# CHAPTER 35

## Bar None

*"Rubes came and rubes went."*
-Stephen King

The June evening got cooler as Paul drove back into Bakersfield proper. He followed his phone's GPS to Noriega's Hotel and Bar. It housed the famous restaurant that served traditional Basque shepherd's meals family-style. As he approached, Sophia spotted Noriega's plain white front with its signature bright lime green neon sign.

"Noriega's." Sophia was delighted.

"You've been here?"

"No. No." Sophia validated the surprise Paul wanted. "The restaurateur side of my family just always envied those Basques who made a fortune with an all-you-can-eat family-style place. No ordering and no picky eaters."

"Really? Well, we'll try it, and you can report back to them."

"Speaking of reporting back, I'll text Tricia about Ortiz's ruling."

Sophia kept her phone turned off but in her suit coat pocket in court. She turned it on and texted Tricia about the loss and then Steve that she would be late. She slipped it back in her pocket.

"Hey, there's a line into the parking lot. Did you make reservations?"

"Of course."

"Good thinking." Sophia turned and pressed her nose to her window. "Looks funky but cute and I'm starving, too."

Paul's chest swelled. He had surprised and delighted the only woman he knew who was so smart, so focused, so serious—and then could spontaneously burst with pure, uncomplicated joy.

As he single-filed into the asphalt parking lot, he realized that he had not seen this side of her lately—in fact, it had almost disappeared since she had Steve move in. Paul recalled her dig at Steve Tuesday afternoon in the office. All was not sunshine there. Tonight's return of the delighted, fun Sophia confirmed Paul's conclusions and took his feelings for her from wishful to hopeful.

He parked in the lot that was already three-quarters full. The vehicles were of every description: BMWs next to Dodge pickup trucks, Nissan Sentras, Jeeps, even a Prius or two, an assortment of SUVs, and, of course, Paul's black 2013 Mercedes C250 sedan, which he bought after tiring of his leased Jaguar.

"Hey," Sophia asked. "Is that a jai alai court?"

Between the parking lot and the hotel-restaurant, there was indeed exactly that, a court for jai alai, a sport akin to handball on steroids. And one that clearly got some real use.

"How'd you find this place?"

"Research. I admit it." Paul downplayed his planning. "You know me and my stomach. This place is hearty and good. Like our deli with my corned beef on rye and my bread pudding."

"Yes, I remember how you sucked me into your bread pudding addiction. Trying to fatten me up." Sophia looked around. "There they are."

"What?"

"Come on, Paul, the trucks . . . the gun racks."

"I'd say about thirty percent have them."

"They all look like the one that chased us."

"Do you want to leave?"

"No way . . . a few gun-toting rubes don't scare me when I'm with you."

Paul smiled. "We'll all be putting on the feed bag in there, and my Mercedes can leave them in the dust after."

\* \* \*

In Noriega's to the left an old dark wood bar with round wood stools was lined with drinkers, two or three deep, sitting and standing. A small TV hung in one corner. Old framed photos of locals shared space on the walls with interesting shots of the original owners and historic old Bakersfield. A green neon clock ticked toward dinnertime as the early birds drank. The round tables to the right were occupied, but not full.

Most customers wore casual attire—jeans, plaid, or faded blue shirts and tops, with some men in work clothes from a day's hard labor. Sophia and Paul were overdressed in suits, as were a few others who had plainly arrived from suit-worthy work. It was loud, and everyone was there to enjoy the evening, the food, and the drink.

"This will be fun," Sophia said. "But where do we eat?"

"The dining room is through those doors over there. They do a seven to nine breakfast, but there's a single seating for lunch at noon and dinner at seven. That's what all these people are waiting for . . . those doors to open."

"Organized."

"You have to be on time, or they don't let you in. I told you I researched this place. You can tell your relatives that—that is how they make money. The bar and the wait."

Sophia enjoyed the sparkle in Paul's eyes. Her friendship for him had grown through the years but never developed into anything more. As they stood there, several women checked Paul out. He was attractive, even with his glasses hiding his quick intelligent eyes. And here in Bakersfield, evidently an extra fifteen pounds didn't matter.

The outer room had a lucrative flow of liquor, glass after glass at the bar. The round tables to the right held mostly the sippers, the one-glass drinkers. The laughter and chattering rumble heralded that one and all were there to enjoy the evening together.

"No tables." Sophia scanned the room.

"Hey, take a load off," a stout beer-drinking man—coupled with an equally stout beer-drinking woman, forming an obvious nonsipping, multi-glass duo—called from a table nearby. "We got room."

"Shall we?" Sophia asked.

"I guess." Paul shrugged. "When in Rome . . ."

"Howdy," the woman interrupted. "Have a seat. You're all dressed up. Big date?"

The man winked at Paul.

Simultaneously, Sophia answered "no" and Paul "yes." The four laughed. Sophia caught a glimpse of the man's tooth-challenged smile and the woman's gingivitis.

"Just work." Sophia regretted her answer immediately.

"Shouldn't ever do the 'work conversation' in Bako, Sophia," Paul whispered as he held out her chair. "We're not popular here."

"It slipped out." Sophia sat.

"This is my wife, Ida, and I'm Charlie."

Charlie shook hands with Paul but, in true small-town, "real male" form, not Sophia. And his wife not at all. The duo reeked of cigarettes and the sharp, aroma of unshowered human.

"Paul and Sophia.," Paul shot back. "Can I get you two another beer?"

"Sure." Charlie reacted instantaneously. "A free beer always tastes better."

The couple laughed together.

"Sophia?"

"Merlot."

"I'll be back." Paul made his way to the bar.

Sophia smiled at the couple. "The room's getting crowded,"

"Always does just before seven," Charlie explained.

"I've seen you before." Ida studied Sophia's face. "You work at the bank?"

"No."

"We live north of the river but come in to make our trailer payment."

"Oh?"

Sophia recalled that "north of the river" meant Oildale—the 08ers—and regretted sitting there even more.

"I got it." Charlie squinted at Sophia. "City Hall gals dress like that."

"So do lawyers," Ida said. "She's that bitch getting rid of guns. Remember? The news?"

"I'm not getting rid of guns." Sophia wanted Paul back—right now. "The news is wrong. We are just helping out the Holts with their son's suicide."

"By get'n rid of guns, lady," Charlie bellowed. "We're not stupid,"

"You don't understand." Sophia eyed Paul.

Paul was weaving his way back from the bar through the now-denser crowd. He had two beer mugs in one hand and two wine glasses in the other—all slopping over. At the table, he set the two beers down and then the two Merlots.

"Let's go." Sophia stood and grabbed the wine glasses. "Come on, Paul."

"What?" Paul followed her, weaving towards the bar.

"Run, you chickens," Charlie yelled.

* * *

Sophia stopped near the bar. "Here's your wine."

"What the hell was that all about?" Paul took a drink.

"They recognized me from the news. I think we should leave. Now."

"Relax," Paul said. "It's over. It'll be fine. It's a big enough place. Just don't talk about work again, and people won't put two and two together. Follow my lead. Take it easy. Drink your wine. Besides, I heard two off-duty cops talking at the bar. So don't worry."

"I doubt if they'd help us."

"Drink up. It's almost seven."

Sophia watched Paul enjoying his Merlot. He was confident. She was less so, knowing how the cops had treated the Holts. But she took a long drink of her wine to settle her nerves. Paul was right. It was a big crowd, and they could get lost in it. Besides, she liked the way Paul handled things. It was just south of macho and very acceptable to a feminist.

They let their wine unwind them.

Sophia saw a glint of the devil in Paul's eyes. She had seen it before.

* * *

By the time the doors opened to the dining room, Paul and Sophia had finished their wine and were laughing about the Charlie and Ida incident. Sophia was enjoying herself and liked the way Paul made her feel. Through the years, she always had.

"Come on." Paul grabbed her hand and dove into the stampeding diners. "It's open seating."

"This is crazy." Sophia gripped Paul's hand as they funneled across the black and dark brown weathered tile through the doors.

"Family-style and fun."

There were three long end-to-end rows of tables and chairs crammed in.

"No wonder they make money," Sophia said. "What's that table out of the way over there?"

"It's for the *real* Basque people, they say. We're heading far away from Charlie and Ida. See them?"

"Yeah, go for the center row then."

"Hold on."

The table was filling in one side, so Paul snaked through a group to the other side and followed single file down the aisle. It was adult musical chairs. The line stopped, surged back, and then took baby steps back and forth in unison. When the undulating subsided, Paul grabbed two side-by-side chairs near the middle of the table. He didn't see the hostile beer couple anywhere around.

* * *

The center table ran the length of the room with red tablecloths and country-style runners down the middle. The tables on either side looked identical but were shorter. Nondescript bottles of chilled red wine, sans any identifying labels, were placed at intervals down their length.

As the tables filled Sophia and Paul found themselves elbow to elbow and back to back with purposeful strangers focused on food, drink, and a good time. There were tourists, businessmen, out-of-towners like them, blue-collar men, families of all sorts, and even a couple of the shepherds, who had once been the primary customers here, at that special table. It was a mass of humanity in all its loudness, reservedness, bombasticness, fatness, thinness, and gluttony.

Chairs shifted as people settled in. Sophia got bumper-chaired by the well-girthed man next to her.

"Move closer." Paul pulled Sophia's chair toward his and then poured them two glasses of the cold red table wine.

"To you, our rainmaker, Sophia, and a nice dinner." Paul touched Sophia's glass and resisted also toasting to her beauty and her charm. "Bottoms up. I'm driving."

"If I didn't know better, I'd think you were trying to get me tipsy."

"Just giving you a night off."

But it was more than that for Paul. It had been, literally and forever, since he met Sophia. And now, they were together, alone, having dinner with wine—with all its possibilities.

"Hey, pass the soup," the burly, ruddy-faced man next to Paul demanded. "We're here to eat. It's twenty-two bucks a pop here, and at that price, we mean to get our money's worth."

"We sure do," his stout wife in a faded "Trout's Bar" T-shirt agreed. "Pass it over."

"Sorry." Paul slid the tureen of clam chowder over.

"Your first time?" a reserved, well-spoken middle-aged woman across from Paul asked.

Sophia smiled. "Yes. How did you know?"

"You should have taken some soup before you passed it. Now you'll have to wait for the refills."

"My wife's right," a thin man in expensive country-rustic attire said. "Before you get scolded again . . . you'd better pass the beans, salad, and pickled tongue. But take some first if you don't want to be left out."

"Okay." Sophia laughed and held her nose as she passed the thin slices of pickled beef tongue to Paul.

"That's rude, lady," the well-girthed man on her right said. "I like beef tongue."

"I'm sorry."

Sophia and Paul both put beans in their bowls sans the soup, now long gone—along with the apparently very popular pickled tongue. They also forked some of the unremarkable lettuce salad onto their plates.

Paul topped off their wine glasses and handed the carafe across the table. "Wine?"

"Sure." The thin man filled his and his wife's glasses. "If the clam chowder comes back you, should try it. Sometimes a bit thin, but not tonight. Darn good."

"If it reappears, we will," Paul replied.

"I'm Lee, and this is my wife, Betty Jane. We're on our way from San Diego to San Francisco to visit our daughter. This is our fourth time here."

"Yes, we're experienced." Betty Jane smiled.

"I can see that," Sophia said.

"Lee needs a break in the drive. And we learned about Noriega's from that television show with that nice man who travels all over California . . . uh . . ."

"Huell Howser, dear."

"Yes. Thank you. Anyway, it was so good we had to come back again and again."

"Nice to meet you," Paul said. "Sophia and Paul."

"You'll be full when you leave here." Lee smiled.

"But not if you let the food go by," Betty cautioned.

The soup tureen, food platters, and bowls were passed up and down the tables until they were emptied. Then, they were refilled by the waitresses and took the tour again. There were bowls of salad, bowls of cottage cheese, and platters of French fries and green beans. The wine was endless, as was the bread and butter, and the eclectic conversation.

The noise level rose to the frenetic as each serving dish was emptied, replaced, and restarted down the lines of diners—along with the wine bottles.

⌘

# CHAPTER 36

## No Time to Basque

*"Fear makes us feel our humanity."*
-Benjamin Disraeli

Sophia and Paul tried to pace themselves, but they had not saved enough room for Noriega's main courses. By the time the huge bowls of beef stew and platters with leg of lamb, Friday's fixed menu, arrived, they were full.

"I can't eat another bite," Sophia moaned, passing the last dishes on to Paul.

"Neither can I. But I'll try."

He took a little of everything.

"That's showing the little lady." The man next to Sophia grinned with only a smattering of front teeth.

Sophia smiled back at the tooth-challenged man. She was relaxed and mellowed by the wine. She didn't even mind being "the little lady" for a few hours on the arm of a "man."

Over the cacophony of conversations, Betty Jane asked the woman with the Trout's T-shirt near Paul, "What's Trout's?"

"Honey, you don't know Trout's?" the woman's husband burst back, inebriated and unmodulated. "It's just the best bar in California."

"Where is it?" Betty Jane asked.

"It's in *Earl-dale* . . . my backyard. We're more Texas than Texas. Across the river, men are men, and women are women, and guns settle the score."

"Guns? Really?" Betty Jane laughed. "It sounds like the Wild West."

"Don't," Lee whispered to her.

It was too late.

"What are you laughing at . . . my husband?" the Oildale wife slurred from across the table. "We have our guns in our truck if you want to st . . . step outside."

"No," Lee said. "Betty Jane didn't mean anything. And we don't have guns."

"Really we don't," Betty Jane smiled. "We don't believe in them."

"Betty Jane, be quiet," Lee whispered.

"What?" The man next to Sophia slammed his hands on the table. "Are you one of those anti-gun righteous assholes from L.A. trying to push us around?"

The diners around stared, pausing in their own celebrations, debates, flirtations, and jokes but not their eating. Paul saw Charlie and Ida look over and zero in on Sophia and him. Next to them were the two cops from the bar. They looked at the fiasco and then back down at their plates.

"No, we're from San Diego." Betty Jane nudged Lee to rescue her from the red-faced, inebriated man.

"Let's not get excited," Paul interceded.

"I'm not excited." The man swiveled his bug-eyed stare to Paul. "We know our Consti . . . Constitu . . . shul . . . rights. Hey, come to think of it, you two look like L.A. people, too, in them suits. Are you?"

"No." Paul feared a replay of Sophia's bar scene with Charlie and Ida. "We're traveling through like them, and we have to leave. It's late."

Paul looked at Lee. "All four of us . . . now."

"Yes." Lee helped Betty Jane up.

The four fought their way down the narrow space between the tables lined with back-to-back chairs—each couple on their own side of the center table. Sophia wished they had sat on the end.

"Wait," a waitress yelled as they reached the end of the chair gauntlet. "There's dessert. Ice cream. And our famous Roquefort cheese plates."

"Keep moving, Sophia. I see the bar couple eyeing us. Hurry."

"No. Stop! I forgot my purse, Paul. It's on the floor by my chair."

"You keep going. Wait for me with Betty Jane and Lee in the bar."

Paul started back down the row. This time, people were angry and uncooperative.

"Watch it," one shouted.

"What the hell?" another said.

"Sorry," Paul apologized, glancing over at the cops who kept their heads down and ate. "Excuse me."

Sophia waited by the door, but Lee and Betty Jane left—without a word.

* * *

By the time Paul got back to their empty chairs, Charlie and Ida were talking to their dinner mates and pointing at Paul and then at Sophia by the door.

Paul sat down again and felt around for Sophia's purse. It wasn't there. He looked at Sophia and shrugged. She pointed down to the floor. Paul felt again. It wasn't anywhere. He couldn't leave without it. It had her driver's license with her home address, her keys, and her credit cards. Women carried their lives in their purses.

He looked at the well-girthed man seated to the right. The man grinned with his checkerboard teeth.

Paul stood and leaned over him.

"Give it over. And everything better be there or . . ." Paul glanced over at the off-duty cops down the table who had heard everything, but no help was coming from them.

"Or what?"

"*Or* . . ."

It was a staredown.

Then the big man's wife jabbed him in the ribs.

"Give it over. He's the kind that will call the cops."

The man held the purse up and dangled it. "Here's your purse, pussy."

His wife grinned and poured her man more wine.

The Oildale 08ers laughed, roaring and snorting with the same inbred drunken rhythm. Paul grabbed Sophia's purse and started working his way out again.

By then the bar couple had stirred up the crowd around them, Paul heard the words "lawyers" and "guns" heralding the uninformed hostile consensus at the end of their long table.

Supported and inebriated, Charlie stood and pointed. "That's the lawyer trying to get rid of our guns."

Charlie's table army—real men all—popped up with him. There was a blast of profanity and shouts propelling Paul's exit. But not in time. Something or someone caught his leg as he reached the end of the table. He tripped and sprawled out on the floor to hoots and calls, including "Serves you right, you pussy punk."

He got to his feet and left. He didn't look back.

\* \* \*

When Paul emerged, Sophia was hiding behind the door with her cellphone out ready to dial 911.

"Sorry." Sophia gave him a kiss on the cheek and grabbed her purse.

Her lips were electric on his cheek. "Let's go, Sophia. Charlie and Ida really revved up the crowd."

"I heard. I was about to dial 911."

"Come on." Paul grabbed her hand.

"Are you all right?"

"Some bastard tripped me at the end of our table. For a minute I thought they were going to swarm me. If they had, they would have learned that guns aren't the only reliable weapons."

"And those off-duty cops just sat there?"

"Ignoring everything." Paul was outraged.

\* \* \*

They ran out under the green neon Noriega's to the parking lot. When Sophia stumbled, Paul put his arm around her small waist, and they slowed to a walk.

"The air is so cool now." Sophia breathed deeply.

"It's desert . . . there's a big swing in temperature." Paul looked back. "No one there. I guess they'd rather eat than chase us."

At the car Sophia leaned against the passenger door and threw back her head laughing. Paul didn't laugh. He studied her dark hair, wild from the run, and her chest heaving. He admired her long neck and her smooth flawless skin. He reached for her cheek and touched it softly. Sophia stopped laughing and gazed into Paul's eyes—a gaze that invited him to her lips. Paul leaned forward but hesitated—just an instant too long.

Sophia turned and struggled with the door handle. "Hey, let's go."

Paul wanted that instant back. He wanted her facing him and kissing him. Instead, he grabbed the keys from his pocket and unlocked the car.

* * *

They raced away from Noriega's.

"That was close." Sophia laughed with nervous relief.

"Too close."

"Thanks for getting my purse."

"Had to be done. Hey, check everything out." Paul was only thinking of the nonkiss and his disappointment at the intimate moment lost.

Sophia rummaged.

"Is everything there?"

"Sort of . . . the cash is gone."

"How much?"

"Forty bucks. Who cares? We paid for his dinner."

"Not that he needed it." Paul flashed a smile.

Sophia smiled. She studied Paul as he drove and watched the road and the rearview mirror for any trouble.

"You were terrific in there." Sophia settled back in her seat for the long drive.

"Hardly."

"No. Really you were."

Paul's heart was still pounding from adrenaline and his attraction to Sophia. "It could have turned out differently."

"But it didn't."

"It must be true what they say."

"What?"

"In Earl-dale you can divorce your wife, but she'll always be your sister."

They both roared. It relieved the tension. Then, Paul peered in his rearview mirror at large and wide-set headlights speeding up behind them. He stopped laughing.

"Anyone there?" Sophia asked.

"Ah . . . yeah."

"Damn."

"Wait . . . ah . . . not now. They turned off. I think we're clear."

"None of them would leave before dessert anyway."

"I forgot to put that into my equation. Good thinking."

Paul and Sophia remained tense until they were coming down the Grapevine to a night-lit bejeweled world they understood and appreciated—the frenzied pace, traffic, glitz, and people.

Noriega's had not been the greatest dinner she had ever had, which was what Paul had promised, but she would certainly never forget it.

⌘

# CHAPTER 37

## The Pressure Cooker

*"Perseverance is the hard work you do
after you get tired of the hard work you already did."*
-Newt Gingrich

That Monday, Krause & White was not only busy but hostile and hateful.

Sophia's combat against Sports Gear was nothing compared to the infighting at this little startup. The power struggle had a trajectory that rivaled that at the now-defunct Thorne & Chase. Sophia's small-firm envy had waned along with her imagined idyllic camaraderie. Small firm or large—money ran the legal machinery. In fact, she had learned that when resources were scarce, small-firm rats clawed at each other even more brutally than large-firm rats.

\* \* \*

The Monday business meeting focused on getting money in the door to cover July costs.

"We borrowed money to meet expenses in June, people. Not much, but first time ever." Rona's sharp voice cut through the meeting room. "Even with Paul's Zeigler arbitration money, we didn't have enough for all our expenses, rent, staff salaries, associate compensation, and our insurance installment. We're on track to borrow for July now too."

"And Rona and I cut our draws. I'll just be able to pay my rent." Unlike Rona, Derek did not have a rich mother to supplement his lifestyle.

"We don't know if they'll extend the credit line for August," Rona said.

"And we can't keep borrowing to survive anyway," Derek said.

Rona looked around the table. Grim expressions met her. Sophia looked down.

"Paul," Rona said. "The Holt case can't take all your time. You have to refocus on your own billable clients and get money in."

"I'm not superhuman, guys. I'm doing what I can, and we're in the critical last stages before trial. We need a big win."

"But there has to be a firm here to win," Derek said. "Stop working that case and rev up your own matters. Sophia will just have to make do with Tricia and Eddie. We have to get some money through the door."

"You guys are the bosses."

Paul's comment was an intentional deflection. He would never abandon Sophia, but they were right. He could pull in some money. He would find the time. He had to give Sophia her chance at a win for the Holts and a win at grabbing the power position here at Krause & White.

Sophia was alarmed. "Rona? What about Bryce? I need bodies to do the work."

"Not happening," Derek said. "He has to do billable work now. Don't you see that?"

Defeated, Sophia said nothing. Bryce gave her an unhappy look. He didn't want this either. He had been enjoying his work on the Holt case and wanted to see a real jury trial and courtroom lawyering.

* * *

As the weeks passed, the firm's Monday business meetings devolved into fights between the two firm factions—the three officially left on the Holt case and Paul always on Sophia's side, against Rona and Derek. Bryce, the pawn in the middle, was increasingly weary of it all. Wednesday case review meetings were no different.

Thanks to Paul doing double duty, he was bringing in decent money from his active cases. Rona didn't have to borrow to meet the firm budget in July.

But Dwight's shooting was the elephant in the room at every meeting. Derek was enraged at himself and everyone else. It only increased with time.

Sophia had to do something.

* * *

Over what was becoming Sophia's standard late dinner with Steve, this one from the California Kabob Kitchen on 11<sup>th</sup> Street, Sophia brought up getting an arrest in Dwight's murder.

"Hold on, babe," Steve said. "I already took care of it. I am now officially assigned to lead the investigation."

"When were you going to tell me?"

"As soon as I ate a few bites of dinner. I'm hungry."

"I can't believe it." Sophia leaned over and kissed his cheek. "Thank you. Derek will be so happy. Or, less unpleased. You know Derek."

"Don't promise too much. We haven't a lot to go on. But I can work on the old man and start from there."

"You have to pull a rabbit out of the hat and solve this one for me, okay?"

* * *

Over the next weeks, Steve got more resources than any other garden-variety gang killing had ever been allocated. It didn't matter, though. There was no magical solution. Not one person from the neighborhood would help. No witness, no informant, no case. However, Derek couldn't accept that there would be no arrest. He still blamed the Holt case and Sophia for Dwight's death, and now Steve for not doing enough to find Dwight's killer or killers. All Derek cared about was that he had lost a second brother to guns.

At the end of June, Tricia and Jay had broken up but were still living together, because they had both signed the lease. Tricia retained false hope for a reunion, and Jay got only part of the freedom he urgently wanted. He had tried to break the lease and was still looking for loopholes.

In July, Eddie's love had become a relationship with Raquel. It energized him. He was virile and young and happy enough to deal with anything thrown at him with ease and skill. He had even made time to hit the gym more often and was noticeably slimmer. He adored Tricia for setting him up with the most wonderful woman in the world—a combination of love and youth that the rest of the team envied. He also worshiped Sophia for giving him so much responsibility and experience on the Holt case. He did everything that was asked of him as the team's last resort and junior member. He made up for Paul's absence on some assignments under Sophia's careful supervision.

Autumn's boyfriend, Stefan, was still a regular visitor to their offices, and now Eddie had the ongoing Machiavellian fun of feeding him misinformation. Sophia was convinced that the boyfriend was not on Moschella's payroll. Moschella was a gifted litigator who didn't need an espionage edge or the potentially criminal exposure it could bring. The only suspects left were the NGA, the media, or, possibly, Sports Gear itself. It wouldn't be the first time a client had gone behind its lawyer's back. Regardless, Sophia and her team knew that when the trial was over, if not before, poor Autumn's relationship would be too.

The office was tested for bugs one more time and deemed *permanently* safe. Sophia and her team understood that pronouncement just meant they could spend no more money for testing or other enhanced security measures.

\* \* \*

With less than three months until her first trial on September 14, Sophia was petrified. She was afraid of going to trial in front of Judge Ortiz and a jury of the good citizens of Bakersfield.

She was grateful Paul was there for her at the office as always, competent, solid and strong. She leaned on him more and more for legal and emotional support. At home, Steve was increasingly silent and confused.

Bryce was sullen billing hours on Derek's drudge work, all the while wishing he were still part of the Holt team. But he kept at it.

He knew he had to, for the sake of the firm and, ultimately, so the Holt case could keep going as well.

Ben consistently courted Sophia for inside news, inviting her to nice lunches and inappropriately intimate dinners. She canceled several because of impending deadlines and some because Steve was just plain jealous.

With the cancellations, Ben became anxious about his exclusive. Sophia placated him by updating him almost daily. She kept her annoyance to a minimum by texting him whenever possible instead of calling. Calls required her to be upbeat and pleasant, and Sophia was anything but that. Ben was poised for more features and to cover "the gun trial of the decade," as he called it with his typical newshound exaggeration.

There was a massacre in a church in North Carolina. It brought guns blaring into the headlines again and inflamed the Internet. Sophia shuddered because the shooter looked much like the people who were going to be in her Bakersfield jury pool. It seemed that every week brought another mass shooting, with the shooter either being killed by gunfire or committing suicide.

Death by gun was pervasive in the news.

Sophia's life was a medieval torture rack, her extremities being drawn out of their sockets slowly, creakingly, and agonizingly by everyone in her life. She decided that despite Steve's jealousy, she would not cancel more dinners with Ben. With the trial nearing, she needed him to educate potential jury members in her favor. News coverage was her priority after her legal work itself—not Steve.

* * *

As the September 14 trial date drew near, the discovery cutoff date loomed ever closer as well. Moschella continued playing scheduling games with the depositions, and returning to Judge Ortiz was pointless. Sophia just had to work with him, which meant letting him push her around—and she did.

She lost the priority of most of her noticed depos. But Moschella was shrewd. In a show of cooperation, he agreed that Krause & White could depose the store clerks before he deposed the Holts. However, that was only if he could depose the Holts immediately afterward. Sophia knew his tactic was to make it impossible timewise for her team to prepare adequately to take the store clerk depositions and defend the Holts, especially with Paul's double schedule.

She also knew that Moschella's seemingly magnanimous offer meant that Moschella was confident Sports Gear's clerks could and would tell a carefully engineered, Sports Gear-friendly "truth"—a "truth" Sophia was afraid she could not counter with the evidence she had assembled so far. They had only managed to review the documents in a disappointingly small number of the many boxes Sports Gear had produced. And so far, they had found no "smoking gun" or anything else of import.

⌘

# CHAPTER 38

## Swirls and Eddie

*"To be alive at all involves some risk."*
-Harold MacMillan

In Los Angeles the first week in July was hot, as was Krause & White's second Monday business meeting of the month. Its financial problems had eased, but Derek persisted in attacking Sophia with an uglier and uglier edge born of his brother's unsolved murder. Rona adjourned the meeting before things got out of hand.

The Holt case, however, was already totally out of hand. Moschella had manipulated the deposition scheduling so that they were one on top of the other. Sophia's tiny team was near panic. Paul faced critical deadlines on his own clients' cases. Eddie was picking up the slack, but the strain showed. Sophia was brain-fatigued and exhausted. Tricia came to the office habitually heartbroken and tense. Behind her closed office door, she cried—like Beth. It was hard not to hear. Sophia hated Tricia's Beth-metamorphosis.

\* \* \*

After lunch, Sophia's Monday team meeting was somber.

"Paul will be able to take the manager's depo and Gallo's back to back," Sophia announced. "But, Eddie, this Wednesday you're going to have to take the Spangler and Grimick depos."

"This Wednesday? It's too soon. I just watched the DVD on depos. I don't know how."

"No choice. You're it," Sophia answered. "Those guys are not mental giants. You can handle them."

"But they're the ones who sold Mike the shotgun. They're the whole case." Eddie's eyes flashed with a desperation that was not without foundation.

"No, they're not," Paul essentially lied to Eddie to talk him down—these were critical depos. "I'm doing the manager's depo. It's the big one. Besides, you can do it, Harvard."

Paul would have to destroy Davis, the store manager, in his depo. That might be all they would have if Eddie didn't pull it together.

Sophia saw she should follow Paul's lead. "Besides, Moschella will prep them to parrot the interrogatory responses he wrote for Sports Gear anyway. If you get something, that's a bonus. If not, I will at trial where Moschella can't stage-manage their testimony."

"Can we postpone?" Eddie wasn't buying the confidence-boosters.

"We can't because we have to get their stories locked in before Moschella gets to the Holts on Friday," Tricia explained.

Sophia's patience was gone. "You'll sink or swim like the rest of us had to the first time, Eddie."

"He'll swim," Paul obliquely reprimanded Sophia. "Eddie, we've all been through this, and you'll do just fine. The first depo is hard, but once you start, you'll be on a roll."

"Paul's right," Tricia added. "Besides, you're the only one free."

"We have no one else," Sophia said. "I have to prep the Holts for their Friday depositions, thanks to the schedule Moschella demanded. Paul has an appearance in Orange County to fight a demurrer in his case. Tricia's sifting through potential experts and setting up Skype meetings with some for Thursday. That's it."

"Goddamn it." Eddie was cursing and his temper was surfacing more often with the mounting pretrial pressures. "Can't you prepare the Holts Thursday?"

"No, I have to get the experts," Sophia said. "And the Holts have to be well-prepared if our case is to succeed, Eddie."

"Okay," Eddie said. "They say be careful what you wish for. I wanted depos. I got them."

"Don't worry." Tricia bucked up the kid. "We don't expect anything remarkable. These guys will be programmed. If you get something we can use, we'd love it, but don't worry if you don't."

"Yeah, no problem," Paul added, with no little artifice, because Eddie was an obvious basket case and had to be managed.

"You're right." Eddie wanted the cheerleading to stop. "You're all right. I'll just do my best."

"That's all we can ask." Sophia was an uptight perfectionist too, but for her, practical necessity trumped coddling the nervous first-year.

"I have the admonitions for the beginning and background questions." Tricia handed him eight pages neatly typed. "I use this every deposition I take. Ask them in order. If something's unclear, ask a couple of follow-up questions to clarify."

Eddie looked it over. "This is good."

"Last night I did this outline of the areas that you have to cover and some questions to ask." Paul handed him twenty pages, double-spaced, and then a file of documents.

"This is like a book." Eddie got nervous again.

"It's double-spaced. When you read the outline, you'll see most of your work is done."

"I'll drive us up to Bakersfield." Sophia gave him more encouragement. "I can coach you all the way up before I go to prep the Holts. We'll leave at the crack of dawn Wednesday. We'll make it by ten o'clock easy."

"What's this file of documents?" Eddie asked.

"The police reports and other exhibits I already had copied to distribute at the depo." Sophia replied.

"Everything is referenced in the outline," Paul said. 'Just read through it, and we'll meet tonight. I'll give you a crash course in formulating questions and getting the exhibits on the record."

"It's not so hard," Sophia said. "Just remember your English teacher red-inking your essays in school. No compound questions. Try to ask open-ended ones and let the witnesses ramble. They all do at some point. You'll dig up some dirt."

"And tonight you'll be burning the midnight oil with me, not your girlfriend," Paul chided Eddie, who turned red.

"We'll get Italian takeout and start at six," Paul said. "First, though, I have a reply brief to e-file and serve this afternoon for a client. And you watched the DVD, so don't worry so much."

Every lawyer in the room knew law schools gave you little practical knowledge. They just honed your brain to "think like a lawyer," which meant studying and dissecting appellate cases and statutory law.

"But maybe I should watch it again." Eddie threw them an unsteady grin.

"If you want. It's the one I used at Thorne & Chase," Sophia said.

"I did too," Paul added.

"Me too." Tricia got up. "I have to go call the experts."

"And I have to get to work," Eddie said.

Tricia and Eddie left.

\* \* \*

With Tricia and Eddie gone, Sophia and Paul sat looking at each other—exhausted, but wired. Wired from an inhuman, incessant, and foreboding adrenaline high. They knew the crash would come, and hard, when the adrenaline abandoned them.

For good litigators, that crash only happened when they no longer needed the high. Trials were like the torturous weeks before the three-day California Bar exam required to get a law license. Sophia and Paul had both cleared that hurdle. They resented that the State Bar had recently made it a two-day exam. Lawyers had to be able to endure the unendurable. Like they all had.

"He'll get it done, Sophia."

"Maybe. It really doesn't matter. We'll have a second chance to get these jokers at trial, assuming Ortiz slaps down Moschella's inevitable improper, obstructive objections. Eddie can't lose the case for us. Make it harder, but not lose it. Ill-prepared Holts would lose it for us."

"Agreed," Paul said. "Your focus has to be on prepping them. Since the house fire, they get confused."

"I think only Beth gets confused. Wallace just doesn't give a damn anymore."

"And we know why. I'd feel the same way if my wife chose her dead son's memorabilia over me in a burning house."

"Your wife wouldn't do that. You'd pick better."

Paul remembered the prelude to the kiss with Sophia outside Noriega's. He hoped she was remembering it too.

Sophia started to speak in a soft voice, uncharacteristic of her office persona. "I was thinking . . ."

Her cell interrupted.

"Hi, Steve. What's up?"

"Catch you later." Paul left imagining what else that soft voice would have said.

* * *

As the Steve noise rattled through her cell into her ear, Sophia swiveled her chair to look out the window but couldn't. Her office was too cluttered with the Holt case detritus.

She remembered Thorne & Chase and spinning her comfy leather chair around to look out the large picture window. She had worked so hard to get into that powerful firm, and it was all gone. Now, she worked equally hard at her relationship with Steve and at Krause & White—too hard—and for too little. She felt herself distancing herself from Steve. Her student loans were crushing her. The Thorne & Chase sweatshop, at least, came with a big paycheck. Her new practice, new colleagues, and new life were not what she had planned or expected. The best part of it was her friends Paul and Tricia and now Eddie the kid. She liked him too.

"What the hell," Steve snapped. "Sophia, did you hear what I said? Your friend Ben is calling my captain about an arrest in Derek's brother's murder. He's using my name. This is not cool."

"I didn't know."

"Now you do."

Sophia employed her tried-and-true use of the word "exact" to make him repeat the part she had tuned out.

"I'm sorry. What exactly happened?"

It always worked with Steve. He thought she didn't "exactly" understand because she was stupid, and so he repeated himself. He never realized she had zoned him out and didn't hang on his every word now, as she had at the onset of their relationship.

Steve repeated his complaints about Ben—*exactly*.

"You'd think your captain would want his face on the news," Sophia jabbed. "They love to torture the public with the ever evasive 'ongoing investigation' baloney."

"You'd better take this seriously and talk to Ben."

"Sorry. Just a joke." Sophia decided to behave. "I will. But can I tell him that you'll call him when something breaks?"

"Why should I?"

"Because it will keep him off your captain's back."

There was silence, and then Steve agreed.

Sophia had no idea whether he would keep his word, but she didn't care. She'd call Ben herself.

"By the way, has there been any progress at all? You do know it's getting more impossible to put up with Derek here."

"Short answer, no. Not yet. Long answer . . . no . . . and probably never will be. But the shooter is a criminal, and they always earn longer rap sheets and eventually make mistakes. We'll get him or them down the line for something. It's what modern-day 'read them their rights' justice is. Long rap sheets and arrests that lead nowhere—until they do."

"That's not a confidence builder."

"Take *your kind* out of the equation and we'd do a lot better."

"*My kind*?"

"Damned lawyers and all their Constitutional rights crap. We can arrest them, but how are we going to get them to trial? Huh? How are we going to convict them with all the attacks on us cops doing our jobs? We're accused of being anti-gay, anti-black, anti-Latino, anti-Muslim, anti-gun, anti-female, anti-male, anti . . ."

"Stop."

"No, I'm not going to stop. I'm fed up, and so are my friends. We put our lives on the line every day, and then we get ripped apart in court with lies. This morning my partner was crucified on the stand for being anti-Muslim when he is just anti-wife-beating. How do you think those men keep those women under wraps . . . literally? We'd be better off without lawyers. You guys are out of control."

Sophia was stunned.

This was the first time Steve had made such comments, or maybe just the first time she had heard them. As he ranted on and on, she rewound their relationship. She remembered his not infrequent and injudicious comments about her profession over the years. And although she avoided socializing with his friends, it became clear he didn't want her around them. He had let her think it was her choice alone. She understood why now.

The rant ended. There was a vacuum of silence at both ends.

"I'm sorry. I'm having a rough day," Steve said.

"I can tell. But every day is going to be rough for me with Derek until you get his brother's killer."

Sophia was having no part of his apology. She was beginning to agree with Derek. Cops were all donut-eaters and coffee-drinkers waiting for criminals to fall in their laps. If the criminals stayed away from the donut shops, they'd be scot-free.

She would deal with Ben the next day when she had the equilibrium to cajole and manipulate him.

"I'm sorry," Steve repeated.

"I gotta go."

Sophia wanted no part of Steve now—and maybe not tomorrow either. In her heart, she knew that he wasn't having a rough day—he was having a truthful one.

⌘

# CHAPTER 39

## Heavy Hangs A Haggard Heart

*"Here we are, trapped in the amber of the moment.*
*There is no why."*
-Kurt Vonnegut

Monday night Sophia got home late. So did Steve. In the living room, she found a peace offering of her favorite Chinese. It was on the coffee table. But she left it untouched.

In the bedroom, she put her things on the dresser next to Steve's gun and badge. He was in the shower. She did not join him.

Sophia put on a nightgown. She was trapped in their one-bedroom apartment. There was no place to get away. She didn't want to sleep next to Steve and most certainly didn't want to fuck him. She was startled at her mind's own word choice—"fuck." Her hurt and anger from this afternoon had changed everything. It was disconcerting when she decided she had used the appropriate word. He may have been making love to her, but for her, it had become a straight, very good fuck. The fuck of an uncreative, good-looking, monotonous, and apparently anti-lawyer mental midget.

The shower stopped.

Sophia made a quick exit to the living room. She grabbed a file from her briefcase about nothing and sat on the couch reading the nothing. She opened a carton of Chinese. Eating and engaging in a fake read would absolve her from his freshly showered male body, one that she didn't want.

Sophia hoped Steve would just go to bed. Then she could "fall asleep" on the couch.

"Hey, I got you your favorite." Steve came in wrapped in a towel.

"I saw," Sophia said with her mouth full. "Thanks."

"I was waiting for you. Why didn't you hop in the shower?"

"Hungry," Sophia lied.

Steve sat down next to her and ate as if the conversation that afternoon had never happened.

Sophia turned back to her nonreading. She could tell this was going to be a cathartic night—for Steve—where the main event was him making sure she still adored him. But she didn't. She was weary of his simplicity. The very simplicity that had first attracted her to him. It wasn't fair, but that's the way it was.

"Hungry and quiet," Steve smiled his winning big-teethed smile. "You're mad. I can tell."

"No. I have some work to get done."

"I said I was sorry," Steve started. "I just lost it today."

"I know. I understand."

"We'll get the guy who gunned down Derek's brother . . . eventually. Don't forget his brother was in a gang. That makes it harder. They do their own justice before we can get to them."

"He has a family, and they deserve something. We all have faith in the justice system. Without it, we're lost."

She kicked herself for engaging. All she wanted was for Steve to go to bed, without her, and for tomorrow to come.

"Right. I know. I know," Steve said. "Want some wine? White. I put it in the fridge."

After the phone call, she recognized he ran on automaton cop-thought. His life was narrow. His thoughts were narrower. He was the personification of the unthinking man's man.

"No, thanks." Sophia kept her nose in the file and flipped pages. "I've got to get this done."

Steve got a bottle of wine and two glasses.

"No, you don't. You're still pissed. I said I was sorry. Ben's your friend, so I don't want to be rude, but I will be if he makes me." Steve poured the wine and set Sophia's glass near her.

"'Sorry' doesn't make everything right. This isn't about Ben."

Sophia had no choice at this point. She was being forced into the path of Steve's plan for a guilt-relieving lover's quarrel and makeup. What he didn't know is that there would be no makeup. Not tonight.

"Don't you even remember the horrible things you said? About me?"

"They weren't about you." Steve gulped his wine. "They were just about . . . things."

"No. They were about me, my profession, my friends, our life."

"Come on."

"Do you really believe them?" Sophia didn't touch her wine.

"Some of them." Steve sat down again and topped off his glass.

"Which ones? That we'd be better off without lawyers and a return to the dark ages?"

"Don't be an ass. I didn't say anything about the dark ages."

Sophia just rolled her eyes. He couldn't even fight on point.

"I'm not an ass. You're the ass. You think lawyers are out of control? Well, what about the cop beatings? The traffic stop shootings? The unarmed people arrested for nothing, who die in prison under suspicious circumstances? Most of them minorities and women. You guys gang up on the defenseless. You kill. You cripple. You maim. And then you accuse my kind of being out of control. Try your kind."

"Sophia, I'm sorry. I am just tired of bad guys getting off. You agree with me on that. I know you do."

"And why do they get off? Bad police work. That's why."

"All right. Yes. Anything you say," Steve moved closer to Sophia. "I love you. Please. Let's forget about all this. I don't care about it. I just want us to be happy."

"No." Sophia turned to him without any anger, just sadness. "You . . . *you* just want to be happy."

"What? No, not me. Us. I want *us* to be happy. I want things the way they were. The way they have been."

"I don't know if they can be."

"I love you."

Sophia believed him, but she didn't want this kind of love. She hadn't for a long time. She admitted that to herself now. This afternoon's call was just an excuse, a catalyst, for her to distance herself emotionally. If Steve didn't know that, then he was denser than she thought.

Steve went to bed when he was finished with his apologies, his opinions, and the bottle of wine. Sophia slept on the couch.

\* \* \*

In the morning, Steve brought her coffee. He acted like nothing had happened. Sophia did too. It was the only way to neutralize him, but she didn't know what she was going to do. She couldn't run back to her parents because then they would know she had been living with him.

After Steve left, she sat with her coffee on the couch she had slept on. She studied the oxblood, shoulder-strapped briefcase her parents had given her for her new lawyer life at Krause & White. The loving gesture was so her parents—outdated. Sophia used a practical black canvas roller case, like most attorneys now.

Although her parents had yelled at her for quitting her "good" teaching job to go into debt for law school, they had slowly come around. At her law school graduation, they gave her a black and gold Mont Blanc pen, which never left her apartment. She was afraid to lose it. They expressed their pride the only way they could, given their lives spent in a workaday blue-collar world. They had the relatives over, and her mother cooked celebratory graduation mousaka, dolmates, galatoboutiko, and farina cake smothered in syrup.

Endearingly but impractically, they bought Sophia lawyer gifts they saw in old movies, like that oxblood briefcase, the same kind Spencer Tracy had in the film *Inherit the Wind* based on the Scopes Monkey Trial. They became proud of her new career. And Sophia's father bragged about her to the extended family—not that he knew anything about what she did—but he bragged anyway in his own broken Greek as the relatives loudly Greek'ed back in approval.

Breaking away from her ruminations, Sophia showered and left for the office. Another soul-grinding day lay ahead.

⌘

# CHAPTER 40

## Charged Circumlocutions

*"Work for something because it is good,*
*not just because it stands a chance to succeed."*
-Vaclav Havel

Tuesday morning at the office, Paul set aside his own preparation for his Orange County demurrer hearing to help Eddie gear up for the Spangler and Grimick depos. Eddie needed Paul's mentoring.

Sophia set aside her morning to review the materials necessary to defend the Holts's depositions. She had to have them come across as sympathetic, set up their emotional distress and damages claims, and establish that they did not know Mike was suicidal. Complicating their depos were the Holts's age-related fatigue factor, Beth's health, and Wallace's attitude. Sophia prepared probable questions and answers and a simple narrative to them focused. She also had to evaluate the list of medications they were on to see whether any might affect their lucidity.

She dared not actually show the Holts anything that Moschella and his office did not already have. He was entitled under the law to see anything the Holts had looked at to prepare for the deposition. He could also ask how long they spent with Sophia prepping. However, he could not ask what they discussed, because that was protected by the attorney-client privilege and the attorney work-product doctrine. This was not permissible at their depositions or at trial

Sophia reviewed Mike's medical files again. The Holts had to be ready for questions about Mike's mental state: his anxieties, problems academically or socially, and what they knew or didn't know. She had to be thorough, but sensitive, especially with Beth.

Sophia had her work cut out for her. Even though Mike was an adult, Sports Gear must not detract from its grossly negligent sale by making the jury believe the Holts were uncaring or negligent themselves about Mike's mental state. Moschella would try to portray them as harsh, abusive, or distant. Or as parents who willfully chose to ignore what should have been warning signs in Mike's behavior. Moschella would play on whatever guilt he could engender in them and do it pretending sympathy.

Tricia followed through with the affordable and, more importantly, knowledgeable experts. She confirmed Skype interviews for Wednesday and would pick the best for the second round of Skypes with Sophia Thursday. She interviewed ten in telephone interviews, to narrow the number down for the follow-up interviews. When that was done, Tricia helped Sophia with the Holt depos by reviewing their prior statements, creating probably questions to coach them with, and planning tactical approaches.

Steve called Sophia's cell four times that morning. She didn't answer. She wanted to disengage. She hadn't decided how much and how fast, but she knew she couldn't answer these calls.

* * *

Midmorning Autumn interrupted Sophia and Tricia. "Anything I can help with?"

"Nothing from me," Tricia said. "But Sophia, don't you have our strategy memo she could format and distribute?"

Sophia's head surfaced from the medical records.

"I do." Sophia turned to her laptop. "There. I emailed it to you."

Tricia waited until Autumn left and shut the door. "What fake nonsense is in that one?"

"Eddie did a memo with the names and resumes of bad experts we'd never use and some phony potential special jury instructions to lead them down the wrong path. But we don't have time to keep doing this. Not skillfully. We should stop it soon."

"Agreed. Unless we can think of something juicy just before trial. We don't seem to have derailed them so far anyway." Tricia scanned documents for the Holts's depos.

"We discovered Stefan too late," Sophia agreed. "But I'm sure they wasted some time chasing false leads. Eddie's setup in this memo is good. Hey, do you think Moschella planted the boyfriend here?"

"He wouldn't risk his license. It has to be NGA or that reporter Chang who crucified Derek. Maybe Sports Gear," Sophia answered. "Does it matter? Our counterattack wasn't bad."

"I hope we can safely use Peggy when we start doing trial prep. This paper dance is getting to be too much. It's hard doing it all."

"We will. She'll understand about excluding Autumn if we present it right. Paul used her to copy the exhibits for Eddie's depositions. But they're no secret anyway."

"I wish we could use Roxy, too. She's the best, and I trust her the most."

"In your dreams," Sophia said. "Derek will never let that happen, and Rona won't offend him."

At noon, Autumn flitted into Sophia's office and finished distributing the team's memo—the phony plant. "I've given everyone a copy, and Stefan and I are going to lunch. Do you want us to bring sandwiches back?"

"Maybe," Sophia said. "Where are you going?"

Sophia intentionally stalled Autumn to allow her boyfriend time to steal their new phony memo.

"The deli a couple of blocks up," Autumn said. "We love it."

Tricia smiled at Sophia, knowing what she was doing. "Do you think it would be too much trouble?"

"Not at all."

"Let's call Paul and Eddie," Sophia said. "They'll want something too."

Sophia's delays were superb and natural. Sophia played the unaware Autumn perfectly.

\* \* \*

By two that afternoon, Tricia and Sophia had finished everything for the Holts's prep, and Steve had called several more times.

"Obviously you're avoiding Steve," Tricia said. "Why?"

"I'm thinking about things."

"Things?"

"Him. It's just that he . . ." Sophia groped for words. "He's so . . . simple and he said horrible things about lawyers as if I wasn't one."

"Is that all?"

"What do you mean is that all? That's enough."

"I wish that was all that was wrong between Jay and me."

"No, you don't."

"Yes, I do. If Jay were that simple, I could handle him. And everything Steve said about lawyers is undoubtedly true."

"What?"

"Come on, you know what we say about ourselves. That's why we're at this law firm starving. Trying to do the right thing, instead of just making money. What could Steve possibly say about our profession that we haven't?"

"That's not everything." Sophia defended herself.

"Oh?"

"He's been hiding me from his friends."

"Good. You always say you can't stand them. And I couldn't, either. Besides, he likes being around us. So do I. You're damn lucky."

"I . . . I . . ." Sophia stuttered. "I never thought of it that way."

"To be fair, my advice is from a desperate woman. I'd compromise anything to get another chance with Jay."

"I know. I'm so sorry."

Sophia got up and hugged her. Tricia started to cry but stopped when her cell rang.

"No time for this." Tricia looked at her cell. "A message from the area code of one of the good experts. And he's cheap. I better call back. And I've got help Eddie. I promised to pound depo follow-up questions into his brain this afternoon."

"He's learning fast. I'll help him on the way to Bako too."

"He's going to be a terrific lawyer. He's a sponge when it comes to homing in on issues and getting the facts down."

"I think he's better than Bryce."

"He's hungrier for sure and has this sense of right and wrong that spurs him on."

"Reminds me of us years ago." Sophia smiled.

"Sort of." Tricia opened the door.

"Thanks for the advice."

"But remember the despairing source." Tricia left to find Eddie.

* * *

Sophia continued composing Holt prep questions and organizing the documents she could safely show them to minimize surprises. She worked quickly and efficiently when she was left alone.

Then, as she put everything she had organized into a large black trial case, her cell rang. Steve. Again. This time, she took Tricia's advice, reluctantly, and answered.

"Hi."

"I was wondering if you'd ever answer," Steve said. "I miss you."

"I've been in meetings." Sophia did miss the sound of his deep voice, one she associated with so many pleasures.

"I missed you last night."

"I just fell asleep reading," Sophia lied.

Actually, she didn't sleep well on the couch or without Steve's warm strong arms around her. They cuddled together every night. She was used to his hard male body near hers.

"I haven't called Ben yet," Sophia said. "But I will. Don't worry. I'll tell him to back off."

"Well, for your ears only, I've been doing some extra work on Dwight's murder, and I might have found a witness who'll talk. We'll see."

"Really?" Sophia smiled. Maybe her guy wasn't your average donut-and-coffee cop after all.

"Don't tell Ben yet. I don't want my lead to back away."

"I won't."

"Chinese again?" Steve asked.

"No, I'm Chinese'd out."

"Pasta?"

"No, it's just too hot. Let's do a big salad with chicken or shrimp."

"You're on. I know just the place. I'll be home at eight. Don't be late."

"I won't. I have to leave too early to get to Bako."

"I don't like you going there. It's dangerous. I can take the day off and go with you."

"Not this time. I'll be fine. Eddie's coming."

"Just be careful. I'll be worried until you get back here to me." Steve decided to push the envelope. "I love you."

There was a hiccup of silence at Sophia's end.

"I know," Sophia said. "I love you, too."

She wasn't sure of the words or the sentiment, but she knew she wanted to be in her own bed tonight with Steve enveloping her.

* * *

Sophia immediately called Ben's cell. His cell number was a precious commodity that he did not lightly share. Of course, she had it because her Thorne & Chase story had made his career, and he had always liked her. Now, to his benefit, trouble had found Sophia again.

"Long time no hear and no see. I miss our lunches."

"I'm sorry." She wasn't. "It's just with the close of discovery coming and then pretrial prep starting."

"So what's up? News on Dwight?" Excuses were not in Ben's vocabulary.

"No, not yet. I just wanted to confer on the Holt case . . . your coverage . . . the approach."

"Good. We should begin momentum building now. Start broad and end narrow. I've already outlined a kids-at-risk-from-guns feature series and shorts on school safety, kids with guns at school, and mass gun killings. When I have my ratings solid, I'll go into kids killed by guns in the home and then teen suicide emphasizing guns. The accidental thing . . ."

"Wait. Why all that? This isn't an anti-gun lawsuit. We have to make that clear."

"Because starting broad is how you pave the way. We have to get the masses interested. We suck them in with kids, schools, and old folks . . . the Holts are up there. I'll work on every angle. Then, we narrow and focus on your lawsuit."

"We don't want to come across as anti-gun. We only want more responsibility placed on gun sellers. That's our case."

"I know your case, but you don't know the news game. Leave it to me."

Sophia regretted skipping the last several scheduled lunches with Ben. She should have reined him in like she had during the Thorne & Chase scandal. She needed him for favorable trial publicity and for her rainmaking future at the firm, but he also needed her for the Holt and Dwight exclusives. His boundless ambition sometimes made him reckless.

"Let's have lunch Monday." Sophia had to make the time.

Ben jumped on it fast. "Noon at the Bluebonnet Café on Hill Street. It's new and great, and I can expense it."

"You played me. You said all that just to get our lunches going again, didn't you?"

Ben laughed. "You aren't the only tricky one. An object lesson on the importance of communication. That's how we felled Thorne & Chase last time, and that's what we'll do here."

Sophia forced a chuckle. "I won't disappear again."

"That includes on Dwight's investigation?"

"Yes, I promise."

Sophia hoped that Steve would have something for her by Monday and rescind her promise of secrecy. She also hoped he remembered to get a bottle of Chardonnay to go with the salads. She was looking forward once again to their routine. For whatever it meant.

⌘

# CHAPTER 41

## Holt Your Horses

*". . . the world was built to develop character,*
*and we must learn that the setbacks and grief which*
*we endure help us in our marching onward."*
-Henry Ford

Wednesday Sophia and Eddie began their early morning ride to a summer-hot Bakersfield. Since June, the heat had been mounting toward the fever heights of August. As they drove out of the city, Sophia helped Eddie practice his lines of questioning and then rehearsed the art of follow-up questions with him. Tricia had done a good job there.

Follow-up questions take the skill of a mentally agile litigator who can go wherever the deponent's answers' lead—expanding, clarifying, and squeezing out more information. These detours away from the prepared questions can be fruitful or wild goose chases that waste precious time. Judging when to abandon the quest and circle back to the original outline comes with experience.

Time constraints now make depositions harder since California joined the federal courts in setting strict time limits on them. Absent a court order, in most cases, and certainly in the Holt case, no deposition could exceed one seven-hour day. Before that change in the law, marathon depositions of major parties and witnesses were common. One deposition could last weeks, often just to harass and embarrass the deponent and, in the process, discourage litigation. The long depositions were also so costly that the party with no monetary resources would have to give up or take a bad settlement.

* * *

Climbing the multilane I-5 toward the Grapevine, truckers sped by, but cars were scarce. The commercial trucks dwindled in number as they split off on their separate route. However, the do-it-yourself moving trucks loaded and manned by the inexperienced remained; the amateurs didn't know a side rearview mirror from a hole in the ground. All they knew was that they were in huge vehicles, felt invincible, and were hurrying somewhere—everywhere.

"Damn," Eddie said. "Did you see that truck?"

"Yep, it almost creamed that SUV. That's why I steer clear of those do-it-yourself movers."

Sophia's cell rang. "Hold on."

"I am so pissed." Tricia seethed at the other end of the line.

"What happened?"

"Derek's on the warpath about our bottom line. He and Rona pulled me off our case and assigned me to billable work."

"What a jerk. He waited until I was gone. What is it?"

"A summary judgment motion. It will take me weeks. Right into our trial prep."

"Derek's just being a prick. Don't fight with him now. Wait until I get back there and Paul's done with his hearing. The three of us will handle it together."

"Agreed."

"How are the Skype meetings with the experts going?"

"Good. I like one so far, but I have a lot more to screen. How's Eddie?"

"We're prepping. You did a great job." Sophia smiled at Eddie.

"He just needs to relax. He's wound tighter than a drum," Tricia whispered. "I'll let you go. Give him another pep talk."

When they hit the Tejon Pass, Sophia and Eddie stopped at the Iron Skillet restaurant in Lebec for breakfast. That had become a regular team feeding station, just a standard diner with inconsistent industrial-strength offerings, but conveniently located. She continued to bolster Eddie's confidence and focus on his mental preparation as they ate. She emphasized how important it was to maintain his equilibrium, be cool and unflustered. And, even if he got nervous, he had to keep a façade of thick, calm armor.

After, on the downhill stretch into the Central Valley, Sophia drove at the speed limit. It was there the highway patrol filled its ticket quota with drivers who thought gravity was a defense to speeding. Her partners in moderation were the experienced and the smart.

\* \* \*

The duo got to Bakersfield in plenty of time. Sophia went up the drive and stopped in front of Moschella's modern office building with its large concrete planters of unkempt shade trees.

"I would feel better if we didn't have to use his conference room," Sophia said. "But we can't afford another space. The Holts have paid too much as it is."

"It's free. Can't beat that."

Eddie's comment reminded Sophia yet again that Eddie was a true beginner. You *can* "beat that" because you're at a disadvantage at your opponent's offices where they have control of everything, including the room's temperature, the bathroom keys, coffee, water, lighting, you name it.

"Call me if he plays any tricks on you like turning off the electricity."

"Don't worry. I can handle myself."

"I believe you can. Just don't let him get to you."

"Piece of cake." Eddie's hazel eyes glistened in the sun.

She watched the substantial young man with his large black leather trial case full of exhibits stride between the plantered trees and through the doors. Behind those striking looks, he had an agile brain that was always churning. That was its habit, and that would help him stay calm and adapt to whatever Moschella threw at him.

Sophia started out of the parking but then stopped. She considered staying and going in to help Eddie. But she couldn't. The Holts. They required serious prepping. She wished she could have done it the prior Sunday, but she and her team had too much work. Besides, since the Holts were older, it was useless to prepare them too far ahead of the actual depo. Short-term memory, especially in elders, was precisely that—short-term.

Even though it was a *fait accompli*, Sophia still was uneasy leaving this baby lawyer to do combat with Moschella, a seasoned litigator who knew every trick in the book. Her dealings with Moschella on the phone and in court hearings had shown her that. Although not unethical, he always used every available legal maneuver to get his way. He might harass and distract Eddie with unfounded, improper objections or, disingenuous and unnecessary objections to the form of the questions. That is how experienced lawyers often broke the momentum of a deposition going too well for the interrogator. It was also how some interrogators were tricked into losing their tempers, and Eddie certainly had one to lose.

As Sophia drove, she concluded, perhaps fatalistically, that Eddie was either going to be slaughtered or hold his own. With his Harvard-trained brain and her team's preparation, Sophia came down on the side of hold his own. He hadn't been raised poor in a big barrio family and scrapped his way up the ladder for nothing. He had grit, but also intelligence and the best legal training out there— Harvard.

Also, she had allocated the team's manpower the only way she could. Eddie had to face intransigent and hostile Sports Gear employees even though their testimony was going to be rehearsed and likely unshakeable by an amateur like Eddie. That was clear from Sports Gear's interrogatory responses, regardless of what the two salesmen might have said to Wallace.

The salesmen would be hard for Eddie to crack in a comfortable deposition setting with Moschella there to protect them. However, at trial she or Paul would have a second chance to make a good run at them. In a courtroom, there was an audience, a judge, a jury, and a formality that sometimes made witnesses nervous enough to tell the truth. Things could play out differently there—and often did.

\* \* \*

Sophia reached the Holts's house and drove up the always crunchy gravel drive. But this time, a chipper Wallace was not waiting to greet her. So she went up the freshly painted porch and knocked.

Several knocks and several minutes later, Wallace opened the new oak door. Inside, he greeted her curtly with a drawn face and a strained, unenthusiastic smile. His shoulders, once squared, were now stooped. He moved like molasses, escorting Sophia into the living room.

In the redone, again floral, living room, Beth was lounging on her new green floral sofa splattered with multicolored roses.

"Wallace, get the coffee."

"Yes, dear."

"I'll help," Sophia volunteered.

Wallace immediately accepted.

Sophia helped make the generic-brand instant coffee in mugs, and they both returned with the offering—a tray with the mugs, paper plates, and six Amazon-delivered crushed, cold, dense Danish pastries. Wallace carefully set the tray on the Cubbies Chicago Style Pizza box from the night before.

Sophia drank the weak, watery coffee, but skipped the Danishes dotted, or rather clotted, with thick colored goo representing fruit and then drizzled with white frosting. She had no desire to risk sugar shock or tackle the rubberized dough embalmed with preservatives. Wallace, however, ravenously wolfed down one of the red-centered Danish with squashed canned cherries peeking out below the frosting. The dry oil-based dough got stuck in his throat, and he washed it down with the black mugged liquid.

Beth didn't bake anymore. It appeared she didn't do much anymore.

Sophia spewed the proper guest verbiage about being too full for a Danish and then pulled out the medical records and documents from her large trial case.

"Let's start at the beginning. I have all the notes and other helpful things you sent. I appreciate your efforts."

"Too much work if you ask me," Wallace said.

"The truth is the truth," Beth snapped, in a raspy voice. "We have to prove Mike was a good boy."

"Sure, sure." Wallace grabbed another Danish, this one with yellow gel in the center presumably representing lemon—if it were pineapple, there would have been a smattering of yellow chunks.

* * *

The once-charming, sad, and unified-in-purpose couple Sophia had first met was gone. Their relationship had slowly eroded after the house fire, but it never been this bad. She now had plaintiffs who were a liability. Moschella, who had only seen them on TV, didn't know that yet, but he would after their depositions. He could crucify her case if the Holts were the same as today—ugly, bickering, and unsympathetic. No jury would like them. No one could. Sophia didn't.

At the deposition and trial, Sophia had a choice. She could compare the couple she had met to the couple they had changed into and blame it on Mike's suicide. But at trial that would effectively require a mini-trial within the trial, something that usually confused a jury—and confusion did not favor plaintiffs. Or, she could just make them get along even if they had to fake it.

"Now, before we start, Sports Gear has stated in their notice that they are going to videotape your depositions."

"Videotape?" Wallace blurted.

"We'll be on camera?" Beth perked up.

"Yes, the law allows it. It's not a big deal. It's very common now. It's a little camera. You'll hardly know it's there. But I do want to give you some pointers."

"I don't like this," Wallace objected. "Not one bit."

"Wallace, we have to do this for Mike. For us," Beth chastised him.

He glowered and slurped his coffee.

"Steady here," Sophia said. "It's not that difficult. Just be yourselves. Dress like you did when you were teaching. Look normal, but not too casual. Everyone is nervous, but be careful not to fidget. Just sit there and be pleasant for the camera. And don't look at me like you're asking me for an answer. No long pauses between the questions and your answers because that looks bad, like you are trying to make up a story."

"Well, all of that seems straightforward," Wallace grumbled. "We already know most of it from that guy Ben's interviews."

"Exactly," Sophia reassured him. "And I have a video on my phone so we can practice with it and make sure you're comfortable."

Wallace was mollified. Beth was raring to get on camera.

Wallace asked, "Are we going to put those folks on camera, too?"

"We can't. It's expensive. If I thought it would get us more information or help break one of them, I'd do it, but I don't. It's better to keep costs down since you're paying them upfront."

"Sounds right. This case has already been too expensive," Wallace said.

Beth glanced at him, preparing a tongue-lashing. Sophia cut her off.

"Now to the questions we expect. First, the lawyer for Sports Gear will ask you your name and general questions like your education and what medications you're on that may affect what you say."

"Wait," Beth interrupted. "That's nosy. Our medications are none of their business."

"In a way, you're right, but it's always done just to make sure the deponent is competent to answer questions."

"Deponent?"

"I'm sorry. That's you. You're the person who's going to answer the questions," Sophia explained as she looked over the couple's medication lists Tricia had gotten over the phone.

"I think we say no. I see nothing here that will affect your thinking. Do any of these make you cloudy or confused?"

"Just my lack of oxygen because of the fire *they* set."

"Now, Beth, we don't know it was them." Sophia didn't want Beth going off the reservation.

"It was their fault." Beth started to cry. "And it's their fault my church group doesn't like me. It is."

"I'll get her a glass of water." Wallace went to the kitchen and didn't come back.

Sophia was deserted and left to deal with Beth's histrionics by herself.

"Beth, we have to keep going. I have a lot to cover here. Can you? For Mike?"

"I guess. Where's Wallace with my water? He never . . ."

"I'll see." Sophia escaped too.

\* \* \*

In the kitchen Sophia found Wallace standing at the sink with the glass of water. He stared out the window into their expansive backyard surrounded by *ficus benjamina* trees. The single large oak in the middle had a weathered wood treehouse nestled in its limbs.

"That's Mike's old fort. I catch Beth standing here staring at it." Wallace turned to Sophia. "She doesn't need that oxygen. Her doctor says it's a crutch. But she won't stop. She won't listen to him or me. She won't do anything anymore."

"I'm sorry."

Sophia was sorry for Wallace, but sorrier for herself because Beth had become an uncontrollable client.

"She's not doing well," Wallace said.

"Neither are you."

"I'm just tired . . . tired of all this. Mike is dead. She's thrown herself on his grave and won't get up."

"She will. She'll get better, especially when the trial's over."

"From your mouth to God's ears." Wallace looked at Sophia with sad eyes. "You should have known her just a year ago. You would have liked being with her. She was a bundle of energy . . . always going."

"She's been through a lot. It's bound to change her."

"I suppose. She's a sensitive one. She's always cried a lot, but not like this . . . all the time. I hate it."

Sophia remembered her dear friend whose horse had thrown him and dragged him to his death, years ago now. Even though she had never lost a child, she had experienced and understood loss.

"I wish we could quit this suit, but Beth won't let us."

The words "quit this suit" horrified Sophia. She switched immediately to her best client-massaging mode.

"It's truly almost over. September is just around the corner. I think Beth will recover once she gets justice."

"Justice for what? Mike killed himself . . . the gun didn't kill him. This Moschella guy is right."

"Please . . . never say that again because it's not true. Without that shotgun, I believe Mike would be here today."

"Maybe."

Sophia panicked. Her plaintiffs were falling apart. She couldn't let them quit. The firm had invested too much. She had to rally them. That was her job.

But she was wary of going to trial now, with her clients teetering on the edge. She had to engineer a settlement, a good one. Sophia was confident that at some point there would be a decent offer for the Holts—and her firm. And when that happened, she would have them grab it.

Wallace went back to the living room with the water, and she followed.

* * *

Sophia spent a half hour telling them how important it was that they appear to be a loving, caring couple. Likeable to everyone—the press, the jury, and especially Moschella, who was looking for anything to beat them. The next hour and a half she did her best to get her two unstable and bickering clients in the right frame of mind for their depositions.

A lawyer defending a deposition wants his or her witness to give short answers that are utterly boring and yield nothing. When possible and not misleading or damaging, Beth and Wallace were under orders to reply "Yes," "No," or "I don't recall"—the holy trinity of deposition answers. Sophia would object if a question was dangerous and might cause problems. That was her judgment call, not theirs. And the objection would alert them to be careful.

She spent a lot of time on an attitude adjustment and did some videotaping. Beth was fully involved, but Wallace was distant. Sophia was worried, but not only about her case—the thought crossed her mind that suicide had a genetic component. She would call and talk to Wallace more often. She also decided that henceforth, anyone on her team who had a Bako run would have to couple it with a visit to the Holts for a pep talk.

Beth's justice and Sophia's firm's financial future lay in their hands.

* * *

Before noon, Sophia helped Wallace order another pizza from Cubbies Chicago Style Pizza on Hageman Road. The Holts wanted the Chi-Town Combo pizza for lunch and the leftovers for their dinner. Sophia did the ordering and added two ravioli dinners and two Caesar salads for them as well. Her heart really did go out to them when they weren't irritating her.

She kept working hard with them both, particularly Wallace, until the lunch delivery came.

"I'll get it." Sophia hopped up and beat Wallace to the door to pay for it—Wallace's hopping days were over.

Sophia and Wallace cleared the coffee tray and old pizza box away. The Holts dug into the fresh, hot pizza and were grateful for the pasta and salad for dinner.

Sophia didn't touch a bite and kept working with them while they ate. She went over Mike's medical history, his behavior before and after Yale, and what happened the day of the suicide. Beth didn't take that well but understood the importance of what they were doing. Wallace ate and mumbled. He kept looking at the time and glancing at the television. They both clearly had no idea Mike was suicidal. If they had, they would have done something. Thankfully, that was the truth.

During the lunch prep, Sophia's cell rang. It was Eddie on his deposition lunch break. His voice was tense, and he was talking too fast. She took the call in the kitchen.

"I can't get him to answer anything," Eddie said. "Moschella keeps objecting, and that Grimick smirks every time he does . . . then he gives one-word answers that don't answer the question."

"They're trying to get you upset. Just stay calm and follow the outline. If the objections are baseless and Grimick isn't answering for illegitimate reasons, we'll do a motion to compel. Don't worry. These guys are well-rehearsed, and if you get one decent thing out of them, it's a victory."

Sophia exaggerated to give Eddie confidence because he was losing it.

"Remember that. Have you finished with Grimick yet?"

"No, I have a little more and then Spangler."

"I'll get there as soon as soon as I can. Follow the game plan. I have a can of worms here, too."

Sophia saw the writing on the wall. As she and Paul had thought, breaking Spangler and Grimick would have to wait for the trial ritual and a Perry Mason moment or two. Such moments, alas, were few and far between and mostly to be found on TV, not in real trials. But it was evidently all they were going to have with those two.

She stayed with the Holts and continued to cajole and rehearse with them, including using the video camera until they were finally comfortable with it. They were actually laughing and engaging with each other. Sophia had done well. They were embattled and lonely, but she had brought them out of it for now.

She would get them through their depositions. However, now she had to get out of there and help Eddie. She wound up the prep session and headed out.

* * *

On the way to Moschella's office, Sophia turned up her air conditioner to max. The July afternoon was hot and still. She had not felt it in the Holts's home. It had the high ceilings of pre-air-conditioning times, was insulated by the upper story, and was shaded by mature trees. Sophia drove fast, hoping she could salvage something from Spangler's deposition because Grimick's was probably already over.

Paul called as she drove. He had won at his hearing and the demurrer to his complaint was not sustained in whole or in part on any cause of action. She was happy for his victory but also glad because they would have another non-Derek case lined up to work on if this one went south. Sophia explained that Eddie was upset and had lost control of the Grimick deposition. She was on her way to take over.

"He won't blow up, will he?"

"No," Sophia answered. "He knows how important this is. He's a first-year, not a child."

"Frustration leads to anger, and he's a young guy with a temper. You'd better get there."

"I'm driving into the parking lot now. Bye."

Fueled by Paul's remarks and her own misgivings, Sophia braced herself for what she would find.

*Damn, I should have left the minute Eddie called*, she thought.

⌘

# CHAPTER 42

## I'm A Loser

*"A quick temper will make a fool of you soon enough."*
-Bruce Lee

At the Quarry, Warren & Moschella office building, Sophia pulled into one of the many close parking places—so un-L.A. Sophia walked by a monster truck, cherry red and chromed down to the exhaust pipe, with two guns racked in its cab.

*It's one of theirs,* she thought. *Grimick's or Spangler's.*

Juggling her trial case and enduring the hot July sun, she took five snapshots with her cellphone. Then, she hurried, her dark hair flying, past the trees in square concrete planters standing as sentinels on either side the eight-foot-high-high double glass doors.

A bored, stocky lobby attendant was sitting at his hexagon desk. She rushed to the small bank of elevators and punched the up button. Then she punched it again and again.

"I know you," Moss Grimick called from a lobby bench nearby. "Running up there to save the wetback's ass, huh?"

Sophia whipped around. Intent on her mission, she hadn't noticed anyone. However, she recognized Grimick from the Sports Gear store as he stood, tall and lean, and walked over.

Sophia turned away and punched the call button again.

"Hold up, little lady." Grimick got in Sophia's face. "I got a bone to pick with you."

"Get away." Sophia's dark eyes were one step from angry, and she held her trial case tight between them.

"I ain't go'n nowhere. And I don't like you sic'ing some beaner bitch on me. I don't have to tell him or you or no one else what drugs I take."

"That's routine." Sophia stepped closer to the elevator door.

"Or if I did or didn't graduate high school. Joe and me make plenty of money on the side. That's his truck you were gawking at, and mine's even better. You can take a ride in it if you're real nice."

"In your dreams." Sophia turned face to face with Grimick's vapid, mean eyes.

He oozed of cigarettes and unclean male human, a ring of greasy brown hair adorning his oversized ears. Sophia held her ground, wishing for the elevator and an honorable retreat.

"In *your* dreams." Grimick grabbed his crotch and humped.

She looked down at Grimick's incongruously puny, weathered, and scarred hand clenched around unlaundered blue jeans. "Are we in grade school?"

"You fucking city bitch," Grimick's face turned red, and his eyes narrowed. "I make plenty. Guns have been good to me, real good. I can buy and sell your little ass."

"Back off!" Sophia yelled tactically and just loud enough to alert the husky attendant. He headed straight for them.

Grimick saw him and retreated. The elevator dinged and opened. Sophia jumped in and left Grimick and the attendant behind.

In the elevator, she steadied her shaking hands. Grimick was bigger than she had remembered. He obviously felt empowered by Eddie's inability to control him. She had seen that in deponents before, although not displayed in this specific offensive Oildale manner. However, the encounter was worth it because now she knew how Grimick and Spangler made their real money. It wasn't from their jobs at Sports Gear. The guns that had been good to Grimick were the illegal guns he and Spangler sold in Oildale, infamous for cops' look-the-other-way attitude there. She would dig into Spangler with that. Ben could also do background research and run with whatever he found.

Grimick was certainly right about one thing. He did have more disposable income than she did—but certainly didn't mean he showered on a regular basis.

* * *

Up on the eleventh floor, a stereotypical cute lobby receptionist in her tight, short skirt and four-inch heels escorted Sophia to Spangler's deposition.

As they approached the conference room, she heard Eddie yelling. She rushed in. He was alone on one side of the table. Across from him were Spangler, Moschella, Theresa Sandoval and another lawyer Sophia didn't recognize. He was pudgy with balding, unkempt reddish hair.

"It does not call for a narrative," Eddie shouted. "If your witness wants to run off at the mouth, that's his choice."

"Run off at the mouth?" Joe sat up and sneered. "I'm not running off at the mouth."

"I . . ." Eddie saw Sophia and stopped midsentence.

"Sorry I'm late, Eddie. Hello, Mr. Moschella. I told Eddie I might be a few minutes late for Mr. Spangler's deposition. I hope he started without me."

"Yes." Moschella played along with Sophia's obvious ploy to step in for Eddie. "We were just going over Mr. Spangler's educational background."

"Fine. Let's take ten. I'll confer with my associate and then proceed." Sophia took immediate control.

"You bet. Oh, by the way, you know Ms. Sandoval, but you haven't met my partner Riley O'Rourke. He's on the case too."

O'Rourke stood to shake Sophia's hand. He had a limp, damp handshake he should have kept to himself. She was not impressed. He was short and slump-shouldered under his ill-fitting, unkempt suit. Sophia recalled Tricia's description of O'Rourke from the discovery objection motion Tricia lost to him in front of Ortiz. She said his appearance was deceiving. He was smart and aggressive.

Eddie and Sophia stepped out into the hall. While Eddie was updating her, Spangler strutted by on his way to the restroom in jeans and dirty work boots, his greasy ponytail straggling down the back of his yellowed white T-shirt. He grinned at Eddie.

"Mommy taking over?" Joe's eyes drilled into Eddie's until he passed.

Eddie turned red.

"Ignore him," Sophia whispered. "I came here to support you, that's all."

"No. Just replace me. I blew it. I lost my cool. I'll never do it again. But the damage is done."

"We'll talk. It's my fault. You weren't ready."

"No, it's my fault. Moschella read me like a book and got to me. I would have done the same if I were in his place. You slice Spangler's balls off for me."

"Okay. That's a deal. This is the Eddie I recognize . . . a tactical fighter. We'll win this case, and you can rub Spangler's and Grimick's and everyone else's noses in it."

They started toward the door. Eddie stopped her.

"Be careful. They're lying. I tried to catch them. That's when the shit hit the fan."

"Good to know. And good for you. That means Moschella got to you but not until you struck first."

"Thanks. But my mistakes are on the record."

"Doesn't matter. You'll do a memo on the highlights, and we can use that at trial."

Sophia lied to Eddie. After all, unless her lies were in the depo transcript, they didn't matter.

"We'll kill Spangler." Sophia headed for the door. "I have something I just found out to shake them up. I'll lead with it."

\* \* \*

They went back into the deposition and Sophia first asked about Spangler's education, which he said was none of her business. She let that go and went straight into his job at Sports Gear, his hours, his wages, commissions, bonuses, and other compensation. With this innocuous line of questioning, Moschella relaxed and answered several texts.

"And your truck out front . . ."

"She's a nice one, huh?"

"How much did that cost?"

"A heap of cash."

"You paid cash?"

"You bet, all cash."

"How much?"

"Over $45,000, and then the customized chrome work cost a heap more," Spangler bragged.

"And how could you afford that on your earnings from Sports Gear?"

Theresa elbowed Moschella.

"Wait." Moschella stopped texting.

"Wait? What kind of objection is that?" Sophia needled. "Answer the question, Mr. Spangler. Where did the money come from?"

"Objection. Relevance. Mr. Spangler, I direct you not to answer that question."

"You know that's not a legitimate deposition objection," Sophia bluffed. "You can't instruct him not to answer for that reason."

"Objection. Invasion of his right to privacy. And on that one, I can and do instruct him not to answer."

Sophia changed the topic because that line of questioning was indeed irrelevant and did invade his privacy, which she had done on purpose. She proceeded to hammer Spangler about Mike's shotgun purchase, as well as Sports Gear's sales practices, training, and instructions to both employees and customers.

Moschella tried various tricks, but Sophia simply rephrased every question he objected to until he gave up. She was angry inside, but cool as a cucumber outside. That was something Eddie had to learn. Moschella eventually realized that her tenacity would not wane. He knew if he made her rephrase each question repeatedly the deposition would go on for the full seven hours allowed. That would take the depositions into the next day. He did not want Sophia to have the night to review Spangler's testimony and develop new lines of attack at her leisure.

Sophia got into a rhythm after the rough initial hour and pile-drove through the planned questions. She expanded the questioning when the answer was evasive or seemed pregnant with more information. Spangler tried to stay on script with the story in the police report and Sports Gear's interrogatory responses, but he was having trouble. He constantly looked at Moschella. He repeatedly responded "I don't really remember," and "I don't recall." When she went over Wallace's conversation at the store, he was hesitant and looked to Moschella for help.

Then, she asked him whether he had told her personally that Mike was "strange" and "wired wrong."

Spangler's face flushed, and he looked down at the table. "No. Uh, I don't know. I don't remember that."

Sophia dug harder.

"I'm going to have to object here as asked and answered." Moschella put an end to that line of questioning.

During the interrogation, Eddie sank further and further into his chair. His jaw was set and his eyes narrowed. He knew Moschella had humiliated him for sport. Now he was learning from an expert, and it would never happen to him again. Sophia didn't notice Eddie was seething as she intimidated Spangler and controlled Moschella. Every time Spangler made mistakes, Eddie cracked an unobtrusive smile that unnerved the unkempt sales clerk.

\* \* \*

The deposition climaxed with Spangler admitting to a criminal record, which included several misdemeanors for shooting up an abandoned farmhouse and possession of marijuana on more than one occasion. Before Moschella could stop him, he bragged about never being caught for his ongoing illegal gun selling and his current drug use. Sophia's rapid-fire questions and Spangler's own ignorant ego had him answering and volunteering before and during Moschella's objections. He revealed a secret expensive lifestyle, with his truck as the most prominent example. His ignorance and arrogance were transparent in his face, his demeanor, and his smugness about breaking the law with impunity.

Sophia sat quietly as Moschella again peacocked about relevance. She planned on pursuing every aspect of Spangler's life at trial. Credibility was the key issue with him.

After the deposition concluded, everyone headed down the hall. Spangler was fighting mad at Sophia and Eddie. She had redeemed Eddie in the deposition. In its aftermath, Eddie could not resist a dig at Spangler.

"See ya, Spangler," Eddie grinned and flipped him a mock salute.

"Dirty wetback." Spangler stood sullenly, impatient for the elevator.

The Sports Gear attorneys said cordial goodbyes to Sophia and Eddie. They ignored Spangler.

Sandoval, O'Rourke, and Moschella went back to his office. Moschella's face was a mask of calm—but it was only a mask. Spangler had proved to be a loose cannon, a dangerous deficit, and a witness with a criminal record and, worse, admitted current criminal activities and drug use.

\* \* \*

The tight-skirted receptionist didn't acknowledge Spangler's openly lewd stare at her crossed bare legs before he disappeared in the elevator. But as Eddie passed by, she gave him an inviting smile with cues he totally ignored.

In the elevator, Eddie clenched the heavy trial case hard. His knuckles were white, his eyes flashed with anger, and every muscle beneath his suit was tensed. He punched the lobby button once and hard.

"It's okay." Sophia soothed the humiliated hothead beside her. "I know how you feel."

"You don't."

Eddie glanced at Sophia and then glared straight ahead as they rode down.

"I do. I promise I do. But remember in the end we got to him. He admitted he's involved in the illegal gun trade and that he takes drugs. He's dead at trial, and they know it. We got him."

"You got him."

"We're a team."

In the silence that followed, Sophia decided to tell Eddie depo war stories on the way home. What had happened to him wasn't unique. She had to make him see that he wasn't alone. A small firm, unfortunately, doesn't have enough associates to share stories and vent over missteps. They're isolated. Sophia would have to correct that at Krause & White. If they could take on more first-years, it would help, and she would encourage Eddie and Bryce to join the Young Lawyers section of the L.A. County Bar Association for peer interaction.

On the way down, Sophia remembered her own humiliations at Thorne & Chase as a first-year and at the hands of her own colleagues. Eddie was luckier. At least he was humiliated by Moschella, an opposing lawyer in another firm.

* * *

In the lobby, Sophia saw Spangler and Grimick loitering outside smoking. They leaned on one of the concrete planters in the shade of its tree. Their own smoke cloud hovered around them in the heavy heat of the still afternoon air—Grimick's bald head gleamed with perspiration from the heat, and Spangler's grimy greasy ponytail hung limp.

Eddie and Sophia walked by the stocky attendant, who was on the phone. Eddie opened the glass double door for her, and a blast of hot afternoon air hit them.

Grimick and Spangler were lying in wait. Sophia walked between Eddie and them.

Grimick stood. "I hear Mommy saved your ass."

"She sure did, Mex." Spangler laughed.

"What did you say?" Eddie stopped and turned, his eyes spearing rage.

"Aw, the little *cholo* gonna cry?" Spangler taunted.

Eddie crossed behind Sophia, trial case in hand. He got in their faces and froze.

"Eddie." Sophia turned. "Forget it. Let's go."

He couldn't.

"Here comes *mamasita* to save you again, Pedro . . ." Spangler stood.

"No, Joe, his name's Eduardo . . ."

"And little Eduardo looks like he wants a fight . . ." Spangler took a long draw on his cigarette, stepped up to Eddie, and blew the smoke in Eddie's face.

"But don't beaners only fight in gangs?" Grimick snickered.

"Eddie." Sophia saw a few passersby stop, and she touched his arm. "We have to go."

He turned to Sophia and then back to Grimick and Spangler.

Grimick laughed.

"What are you going to do?" Spangler snarled.

"Shut your stinking mouth, you Oildale piece of trash," Eddie yelled.

"Hey, it's a Mexican jumping bean." Grimick hopped up and down.

"Eddie, let's go," Sophia whispered. "We have to go."

Rubberneckers gawked on their way into the building. One stopped at the attendant's counter and pointed at the ruckus.

"Eddie, come on, we have to get out of here."

"Are you gonna be a man or run away with the cunt?" Spangler blocked Eddie's path.

"Eddie, come on." Sophia's words were lost in his anger and the duo's assaults.

"She's not a cunt. She's a lawyer."

Grimick whispered, "A cunt lawyer."

"You scum . . . you shut up about her."

Spangler took a step forward and put his hand on his balls. "Got any of these . . . Pedro?"

Eddie's face was red from the heat and his fury. The humiliation from the depos was fresh and raw.

The stocky attendant ran out the glass door just in time to see Eddie blow up.

"You ignorant, inbred pigs," Eddie yelled and then let loose in Spanish.

Sophia caught the words *puta* and *chinga tu madre* and got the gist of Eddie's tirade. She knew some Spanish—particularly the more colorful basics.

"Hey. Hey." The attendant stood by the door. "Leave now, kid. I called the cops."

Eddie looked over, surprised.

"You people can't act like that around here. Get going," the attendant shouted.

"*You people* can't act like that, Mex," Grimick whispered at Eddie. "Not without us kicking your ass and that puta's back to L.A."

That was it. Eddie turned his back to Sophia, blocking her view, and swung his trial case at the men. It grazed Grimick's shoulder and thrust Eddie forward. Spangler grabbed Grimick, who fought for his balance as the men became intertwined. Suddenly, the full weight of the case in motion appeared to catapult Eddie out of the three comingled bodies. His head crashed into the corner of the concrete planter as he went down and then his head bounced against the sidewalk as he landed.

The few anonymous spectators vomited oohs and ahs.

"Eddie. Eddie," Sophia dropped her case and knelt down near him.

"Eddie?"

"Is he okay?" The attendant leaned over Eddie and Sophia. "He was out of control hitting him with that case."

Sophia said nothing. The attendant was right. Eddie had exploded and apparently struck the first blow—however intolerable the provocation.

* * *

By the time the emergency response paramedics arrived, the police had too. Most of the witnesses were able to flee, as they so often do, but the lobby attendant corralled two male latecomers who had heard Eddie and seen him attack Grimick. New arrivals parked in the lot and scurried past the scene with sideways glances.

The paramedics checked Eddie out. They bandaged the gash on his head and asked him a series of rote questions—to see whether he was alert. Sophia explained how hard Eddie had hit his head both on the concrete planter and the sidewalk. He was disoriented at first but then lucid and, in fact, engaging.

Eddie refused to go with the paramedics to the hospital despite Sophia's urging. The paramedics got another call. They had Eddie sign a release form and left.

Sophia stood next to Eddie, who leaned on the large tree planter. Grimick and Spangler were strutting around, tall and pumped.

Meanwhile, the cops had taken the statements of the attendant and two witnesses who were only present when Eddie had gone ballistic and not before. Then the cops took Spangler and Grimick's statements.

"Look, Eddie, your story is that your case accidentally hit Grimick when you turned to leave." Sophia could think of nothing else for him to say. "Do you hear me?"

"Sure, but . . ."

"I'll back you up."

Sophia justified her rendition because when Eddie turned he had blocked her view, and because he was her colleague. They were in second position talking to the cops and with that position came a disadvantage. They were at a disadvantage anyway, because Eddie had in fact swung that case at Grimick.

Sure enough, the cops drank the Kool-Aid the trio of witnesses had offered along with Grimick's and Spangler's versions. When they came to talk to Eddie and Sophia, they were hostile from the first question. All the witnesses said Eddie had attacked Grimick. Sophia tried to tell them about the Holt litigation and the taunting, thinking it would help. It didn't. Spangler and Grimick had already negated that approach. Sophia and Eddie had been labeled as anti-Bakersfield and the Bako way of life. Eddie was going to be arrested then and there unless she did something.

"Just one minute." Sophia grabbed at a straw. "Mr. Moschella can straighten this out."

The name Moschella stopped the police from making an immediate arrest. They stood aside and talked in the cooling, encroaching shade. Sophia called Moschella on her cell and explained the situation to him.

* * *

When Moschella walked out through the double glass doors, all eyes turned to the local man of stature man in the expensive suit. The players, each and every one, treated him with a deference that approached genuflection. The cops at first talked respectfully and then listened as he spoke. With a nod from Moschella, the lobby attendant returned to his post. Spangler and Grimick tried to talk to him, but Moschella cut them off with a curt chop of his arm and sternly lectured them in a low, reproving tone. They hung their heads, like bad dogs, and quickly and quietly left the scene.

Moschella walked back to the cops and this time the three of them chatted and laughed together.

"What's happening?" Eddie asked.

"Moschella is saving your ass."

"I'm so sorry. I feel like shit."

"You look it too."

"I just want out of this town."

"Me too."

\* \* \*

The heat of the early evening still radiated from the concrete, as Sophia and Eddie watched Moschella's parley with the cops conclude. They shook his hand and walked back to Eddie and Sophia. Moschella nodded at her. She mouthed a thank you. He disappeared back through the huge glass doors.

Moschella had held court outside his office building and dispensed justice Bako style. And for that, this time, Sophia was grateful.

\* \* \*

"You're lucky," the senior cop said to Eddie. "Grimick won't press charges, and Mr. Moschella doesn't want his gun case messed up. We're with him on that. You can go. No write-up. But kid, you'd better stay out of Bakersfield. We have you on our radar, son."

Eddie opened his mouth to speak, but Sophia spoke up first.

"Thank you, sir." Eddie needed to cool it—now.

"Yes. Thank you." His words were hollow, but Eddie got them out.

"And we're not all rednecks." The younger cop handed Eddie his trial case. "I graduated from college, and I know enough not to hit someone with something like this. This is a deadly weapon under the law, you know."

"Take your case and leave," the other cop ordered. "And don't come back."

* * *

Eddie was subdued as Sophia drove them back to L.A. He nodded off, came to with a start, and then nodded off again. They talked, but the conversation was spotty and forced. Sophia didn't share her deposition war stories. It wasn't the time.

Eddie slept over the Tejon Pass and down toward L.A. Sophia decided that was best, and continued past Valencia into the Valley. He woke up when they stopped for gas, and they decided to get a bite to eat at the Olympic Coffee Shop on San Fernando Road in Sylmar. They ordered burgers and fries.

"I slept a long time. I guess I was tired." Eddie took a big bite of his burger.

"Fighting will take it out of you, not to mention diving into a concrete planter." Sophia attempted some levity. "How's the head?"

"Ah, it hurts. I have a headache."

"I should take you to Cedars-Sinai to get it checked out."

Cedars was one of the best hospitals in L.A.

"No, I'll be fine. The paramedic said I'd have a headache. Do we have to tell anyone about this?"

"I . . . what do you think?"

"Me? It's embarrassing. The lowest point of my life. I don't know what happened. I just lost it."

"Hey, you've seen my own Greek thing, so if anyone understands, I do." Sophia smiled, and so did Eddie.

"I don't want this getting back to Raquel."

"You have to tell her something . . . I mean, she'll see your head."

"Right."

"What about the others at the firm?" Eddie asked. "I want to be the one to tell them if we have to."

"We don't have to make any decisions now. We're tired. We'll talk tomorrow at the office."

Sophia decided to put off the inevitable argument and necessary result. The other lawyers at Krause & White would indeed have to know, especially because Eddie was now effectively banned from Bakersfield.

"It's hard. Litigating." Sophia had finished her burger and squeezed out more ketchup for her fries. "You have to have a thick skin, and it doesn't develop overnight. It takes time and experience. It wasn't fair to drop you into all of this so fast."

"I should have handled it better. I'm sorry."

"You've been working too hard. You were tired. We should have had you find the experts and Tricia do the depos."

"That wouldn't have worked. I don't know anything about experts. You guys were right. We did what we had to do." Eddie shoved the last of his fries in his mouth.

"I'm going to hit the head. Then let's go." Eddie smiled, then grimaced. "'Hit the head'—bad choice of words."

Sophia laughed.

Eddie got up but then sat right back down.

"Are you okay?"

"Just dizzy for a second." He stood again, more slowly, and went to the men's room without any trouble.

\* \* \*

Nearer downtown L.A., Eddie called Raquel at the Federal Building. Sophia heard the love chatter and then the lie—half-lie. He told her he had slipped in Bakersfield after the depo and hit his head. He said he'd be late. She said she'd be later. She had to file a motion the next day.

"So you two moved in together?" Sophia asked.

"Sort of . . . uh . . . well . . . I guess it's no secret."

"Congratulations." Sophia remembered how ecstatic she and Steve were those first months, actually those first years.

She thought a minute and then called Steve to let him know she and Eddie were near home.

"Pizza? Ah, that's so sweet. But we stopped and ate. Save a piece for me for breakfast. You know I love cold pizza."

Sophia didn't mirror Steve's "I love you." But her absolution was her first-year in the car and her justification was her unresolved issues with Steve.

Under protest, Sophia dropped Eddie off at his apartment without taking him to Cedars first. But he was adamant. Raquel was still at work, and Eddie went straight to bed.

* * *

As Sophia drove home, she worried about how the incident would impact the case, the firm, and, of course, Eddie's litigation career at Krause & White. She also didn't trust Moschella not to capitalize on Eddie's arguably criminal act through the back door somehow—he was a litigator trained to win for his client, ultimately.

She called no one else—not even Paul. It was late, and she had to think through all the ramifications first.

⌘

# CHAPTER 43

## The Inartful Dodger

*"Is there any instinct more deeply implanted in the heart of man than the pride of protection, a protection which is constantly exerted for a fragile and defenceless creature?"*
-Honore de Balzac

On Thursday morning, Sophia stayed in bed drinking her Steve-brewed coffee and eating cold pizza. She didn't get up until he left. She was too tired to relate, and fortunately, he was in a hurry. The minute he shut the door she was up and out too.

"Good morning," Autumn greeted Sophia. "How did Bakersfield go?

"Great." Every word Sophia uttered would go through this little hippie like a sieve to Stefan, her spy boyfriend.

Sophia asked Peggy to call the Holts and remind them about their depositions the next morning. Sophia couldn't hold the crying machine's hands today.

"Here are your messages from yesterday, and there are a couple of voice mails I put through." Peggy handed Sophia a stack of messages.

"Thanks."

* * *

In her office, Sophia threw her messages on her desk and quickly typed up the highlights of her Spangler deposition for the team. She called Eddie's office. He didn't answer. She left him a message reminding him to do his deposition summary and that they had to talk first thing.

"Hey." Tricia leaned into Sophia's office. "Come on. The first Skype interview is in two minutes. My office."

Tricia had worked hard to set up the expert Skype interviews. She had picked five for this second round. They were piggybacked and had to start on time. or they would domino on top of each other.

Sophia and Tricia had Skyped the rest of the morning. Sophia rejected one candidate who was too focused on the fact this would be a high-profile case and another who was not quick enough when the questions came too fast. A third one was just a little too equivocal and, frankly, did not present well from an aesthetic standpoint. Unfair, maybe, but life is that way, and every trial is theater. The jury has to like the "cast," if you will, or, at a minimum, not dislike them.

By eleven-thirty, they had finished and had chosen their two best candidates. They came from the three Tricia had identified as the most promising from her screening calls. Her instincts had been dead on.

Sophia went back to her office and called Eddie's cell. It went to voice mail. She told him to get into the office. She needed his depo summary, and they had to decide how to handle what happened.

* * *

At noon, the team met and gave their updates without Eddie. They had sandwiches delivered. Eddie's sat uneaten. Sophia handed out her Spangler depo summary and a *pro forma* one she had done for Grimick based on Eddie's conversation with her. She filled everyone in on the Holt prep and their problems.

"Where the hell is Eddie?" Paul said. "We have to wade through the rest of that discovery and we need to know the details of his depo."

"He said he'd be late." Sophia deflected the focus from Eddie, assuming he needed time to regroup. "Read my summary to start. Spangler is the loose cannon. He's nervous, and his brain is fried and arrogant. He's a deficit to them. He admitted he sells illegal guns and does recreational drugs."

"Good stuff for trial," Paul replied. "If he denies it we impeach him with his depo."

"I know," Sophia said. "Grimick is probably his partner, but the only way to prove that is comparing his salary to his purchases and we don't have the manpower or the resources to get that done. Any other reports? Plans? Suggestions?"

"Sophia and I have settled on one suicide expert," Tricia said. "He's Dr. Simon Mapes, a psychiatrist who has published extensively on suicide methodology and pathology. We talked to him on Skype. He's young and enthused, and is a tenured professor at Stanford Medical School."

"And good-looking in a distinguished way that always works well with a jury." Sophia tossed a picture on the desk to Paul. "See?"

"Not bad," Paul responded. "Good for us."

"Our gun sales customs and practices expert is even better," Tricia said. "He's a hunter, a retired police chief, owned a gun shop himself, and is a lifetime NGA member. He couldn't have a better name either for a place like Bakersfield: Dirk Savage."

"You're kidding," Paul remarked. "How is a guy like that on our side?"

"He believes irresponsible gun selling practices hurt the business. He wants all gun sellers to adopt the polices sellers use in states like New Hampshire and Colorado."

Sophia added, "The ones that go beyond the laws on the books and call for special care when they spot a customer like Mike. Remember I mentioned them in my memo?"

"I do now." Paul smiled. "Great work, guys."

"What about Derek's summary judgment, Tricia?"

"It's all billable, but not doable. Not with our pretrial schedule. But he's right. He's up to the wire on the deadline for filing it."

"He'll have to hand it off to Bryce," Paul said. "Tricia can supervise. It's the only way."

"Derek won't go for that," Sophia said.

"He'll have to," Tricia said. "I . . . we have to get through as many of those documents Sports Gear produced as we can to try to find some edge to force a settlement and finish all our pretrial baloney."

"Well, in my case where I beat that demurrer yesterday, discovery will start soon," Paul said. "But that's a cakewalk. A simple contracts case. I can go through Sports Gear documents with you and Eddie. I'll draft the first round of discovery in that other case this weekend. Where the hell is Eddie?"

"I'm calling him." Tricia speed dialed him on her phone.

There was no answer. Sophia stuck her head out her door to see whether Autumn or Peggy had heard from him. They hadn't.

"This isn't like him," Tricia said.

"What's up, Sophia?" Paul asked. "Why isn't he here? You've been making excuses for him all morning."

"He's licking his wounds. But I don't know why he's not here yet."

"Sophia, what's going on?" Paul always read her like a book.

"Eddie lost his temper, and we're minus one litigator in Bakersfield."

"Minus one litigator?"

"He's been banned from Bako."

"Banned from Bako?" Tricia said. "That sounds like a bad country song title and not funny. We have pretrial appearances, more depos, meetings, massive trial prep and a trial. We . . ."

"Wait. Is that true? What the hell went on in those depositions?" Paul broke in. "What did he do? And who banned him?"

"The cops."

"The cops?" Paul shouted.

"Shh," Sophia said. "It was after the deposition."

Sophia told them about the incident. She toned it down, but the bare facts were damning enough.

"We shouldn't have given him those depositions," Tricia said.

"Nonsense." Paul was angry. "He's an adult. I did depositions in my first year against some vicious pricks, and I kept it together. There's always an asshole around. That's what we litigators are . . . consummate assholes. Assholery is an art form for us."

"Someone better get him into the office before we have to tell Rona and, speaking of assholes, Derek," Tricia said. "Eddie's making it worse by hiding out . . . if it could be any worse. I'll call Raquel."

"Be discreet," Sophia cautioned. "I'm not sure she knows the whole story."

"I don't care about discretion. Find out where he is," Paul said. "Now we're going to have to babysit him all day and then deal with Rona and Derek? We don't have time for this. And when were you going to tell us?"

Tricia called and got voice mail. She left a message.

"I'm sorry," Sophia answered. "He wanted to own up to it himself."

"We're a team," Paul said. "More than that, we're friends. You should have called us when it happened. It really affects the assignments. If he can't cover anything in Bakersfield now, we're in trouble."

"Damn it," Tricia said. "We have to figure out what it will do to the trial and everything we have to finish beforehand. We were already handicapped."

"I'm sorry. I should have called."

Sophia wanted to make it right. They were facing the titanic work surge that always strikes before any major trial. Paul, Tricia, and herself had always been the three musketeers, ever since her first interview lunch at Thorne & Chase. She had betrayed their trust.

"I'm really sorry. I don't know what I was thinking. I was concerned about Eddie and I was tired . . . just too tired last night. I planned on telling you this morning, but with the expert interviews and . . . there wasn't time. All I can do is apologize."

Sophia's phone rang. She glanced at it but let Peggy answer.

"We'll live," Tricia said. "We were too busy all morning. Besides, Eddie should be here 'fessing up himself and taking the heat. Not you."

"Tricia's right." Paul was embarrassed. He always took things too much to heart where Sophia was involved because to him she was more than just a colleague and friend. "I overreacted. He should be here to face this. You could have been hurt. You know that, don't you?"

"I didn't think of that."

"You should have," Tricia said. "This is no game."

The three sat quietly, each with their own thoughts, Paul's mainly about Sophia and her safety.

A single rap at the door broke the silence, and Peggy stuck her head in.

"I'm going to lunch. A Mr. Moschella left this message while you were Skyping." Peggy handed it to Sophia. "And I have a woman on hold now. A Raquel. She says it's urgent."

Sophia picked up her phone. She listened as the whole world changed.

Raquel was calling from Cedars, but she wasn't with Eddie. She was with Eddie's body.

⌘

# CHAPTER 44

## Chaos and Callousness

*"Yesterday is not ours to recover,*
*but tomorrow is ours to win or lose."*
-Lyndon B. Johnson

"I'm so, so sorry. Call us if we can do anything." Sophia wept.

"What's wrong? Where's Eddie?" Tricia asked.

"He's dead. Eddie's dead."

"What?" Paul was stunned. "What happened?"

"He was asleep when Raquel got home."

She wiped away her tears with her handkerchief.

"When she brought him coffee this morning, she couldn't wake him. The paramedics took him to Cedars. Raquel called his parents. He never regained consciousness."

"From that fall?" Tricia said.

"A subdural hematoma broke free." Sophia struggled to speak. "Damn Sports Gear and those mouth-breathers who work for it, and damn Moschella. He played on Eddie's inexperience."

Tricia looked to Paul. "We have to make them pay for this."

"We will."

"Damn right." Sophia wiped her eyes and took a deep breath. "I have to tell Rona and Derek."

"I'll go with you." Paul stood.

"Me, too."

"Thanks, guys. But you need to work. We're another man down. Permanently this time."

\* \* \*

Sophia shut Rona's office door and endured her anger—anger that Sophia hadn't called the day before or gotten Eddie to a hospital, and anger that he was dead.

Then she became all business.

"We don't have any exposure for Eddie or Grimick? You agree?"

"What?" Sophia was shocked. "You're talking liability for damages of some sort?"

"Yes, I am. And you'd better be thinking about that too. You were there."

The quick transition was offensive, but the partner mentality was not unexpected—self-protecting, firm-protecting, closing ranks.

"We can't be liable for Eddie," Sophia answered. "He swung the case."

"What about Grimick?"

"He wasn't hurt. The paramedics verified that. Besides, he and Spangler goaded Eddie with racial slurs and sexist insults to me. And Eddie is the one who's dead. No lawyer in his right mind would sue civilly. Not even an ambulance chaser."

"You're still beyond smart, Sophia."

"Not smart enough to control Eddie."

"I'll tell Derek. You have your trial work. And you're going to need Bryce."

"I know."

"Derek will make a lot of noise, but we have no choice."

"Thanks, Rona. I feel so guilty."

Sophia started to cry again.

"It wasn't your fault."

Rona hugged her. The friend Sophia had known in law school had re-emerged.

"There was nothing more you could have done. Believe me. Nothing. Telling us yesterday or today wouldn't have changed anything. When someone refuses medical help, that's on him."

Rona did her best to relieve Sophia of the guilt she felt. Rona was smart herself.

* * *

Rona went down to Derek's office. They spoke briefly and then called a firmwide damage control meeting in the conference room to announce Eddie's death, disclosing minimal facts. Everyone was ordered to say "no comment" given the inevitable press probe. The staff was dismissed, and Rona had the attorneys stay.

"Why the hell didn't you tell us about this yesterday?" Derek confronted Sophia the minute the door shut.

"Eddie insisted on telling you himself. He was ashamed. He needed a night."

"He needed not to attack a deponent," Derek said.

"'Attack' is a strong word."

"I think not," Derek said. "What did you tell the cops?"

"Nothing. They never interviewed me. Or Eddie. They didn't want to hear from us after Moschella handled them. But before Moschella came out, they took statements from people who obviously said they saw Eddie hit Grimick."

"Did you?"

"No, I couldn't see past Eddie, but I saw him swing that case."

"We need the police report," Derek said.

"When Moschella sent the cops packing, he told them no write-up."

"We'll see. Everything's changed now with Eddie dead. Bryce, call and see if there is one."

"Yes, sir."

Bryce jumped into action like a well-trained dog. Derek had been schooling him. Bryce's eyes were full of tears as he placed a call to the Bakersfield police on his cellphone. He and Eddie had been friends—first-years against the world.

"Sophia did her best."

Tricia came to Sophia's defense.

"That may be. Fortunately, the simple truth protects us," Rona said. "I've called our insurance rep. We need a unified front here."

"It's simple," Derek said. "If Eddie was acting outside the scope of his employment, we're not liable. Whacking Grimick was not part of his job. And neither was hitting his head in the process."

Then Sophia heard herself being as cold as Derek and Rona. "Moschella got rid of the cops because of the case. And we know

Grimick wants to stay in the shadows with his illegal gun sales and who knows what else."

"That would be my take," Paul said.

"We're in decent shape," Rona said.

Tricia was disheartened by the cold, detached analysis—but knew it was necessary.

Bryce got off his cell.

"No report yet."

"You stay on it," Derek said.

"If our rep takes a strong position, then our lives won't be eaten up by an insurance defense suit, and our insurance coverage will be secure."

"Doesn't anyone care that Eddie is dead?" Bryce interrupted.

"Yes. We all do." Rona was dry-eyed and direct. "It's horrible, but we have to balance our interests with Eddie's. And we need to protect the firm."

"What about his reputation?" Tricia asked.

"We have no choice, Tricia," Paul said. "The facts are what they are."

Tricia looked at Paul.

"*Et tu*, Brute?"

"Come on. That's not fair."

Sophia put her hand on Tricia's shoulder.

"He did swing at Grimick. There's no reason to advertise it, but it's no secret. I understand. So does Paul. We all do. That includes you. If we're sued and someone has to pay out for Eddie's earning power the rest of his life, that'll end the firm. We don't have that kind of insurance coverage."

Tricia jerked away from Sophia and stood to leave the room.

"Sit down," Rona said.

"We all need to be here."

Tricia didn't sit.

"Please?" Rona asked.

"I get it. I do." Tricia relented, reluctantly, and sat.

"It's just hard. I'm sorry, Bryce. I know you were friends."

"I just can't believe he's gone," Bryce said. "Why did he do something so stupid?"

"I don't know," Paul said.

"We'll see if a police report surfaces," Derek said.

Everyone agreed they would go with the truth, but not drag Eddie through the mud if they could help it.

"Are we done?" Tricia asked.

"Yes." Rona stood. "We're on the defensive. Sophia, you'd better call Ben. We have to get ahead of this before it goes public."

"I will."

\* \* \*

Sophia left Ben one message after another. When she took time to return Moschella's call, she got Theresa Sandoval instead. Sandoval said nothing about Eddie. Sophia presumed Moschella's firm didn't know yet, and Ben could still get a jump on the media spin if he'd call back. They had contacted her about a list of the missing discovery that she claimed Sophia and the Holts owed them. Sophia countered that she had a list of her own—but she didn't. How could Sophia's team know what was missing from all the boxes Sports Gear dumped on them? She'd throw together a fictitious list for leverage.

Sophia finally reached Ben emerging from a meeting. She told him about all the incidents in Bakersfield and then about Eddie in detail and the firm's concerns. They brainstormed and agreed on an approach sympathetic to Eddie. She gave him the phone number for Eddie's parents. They also decided that now was the time to start the pretrial blitz against Sports Gear, the NGA, the illegal gun trade around Bakersfield, and, finally, the justice system for trivializing Mike's death. Ben and Sophia were allies, as they had been through the Thorne & Chase debacle.

"Thanks," Sophia said. "I'm sorry I didn't tell you earlier about the pickup chase or the Noriega encounters."

"No holding back anymore. I'll blend them into Eddie's story. He'll look better."

"Thanks. He was a good kid."

"I have to be updated and filled in on everything if we want to win the publicity war. Tonight I'll lead with a reprise of Mike's death. The Holt fire. Dwight's murder. The Bakersfield incidents. Then the tragedy with Eddie. I'll bring up the refusal of gun sellers to self-police and why we need stronger laws. We'll put the onus on them."

"Sounds good."

"Then I'll hit on the illegal sales and gun shows."

"No. That will make things more dangerous."

"Sophia, it will make them back off. This is my job. I know how to do it."

"But it's our lives."

"Mine too. Don't worry. You promised to update me on Steve's investigation of Dwight. Anything new?"

"Yes." Sophia saw that the Ben-beast was as out of control as the rest of her case and life. But she needed him more than ever now.

"When?"

"Maybe tonight. I have to get back out there, Ben."

"Wait . . . I want your team down here for my broadcast."

"What? We're backed up beyond belief. I have two depositions to defend tomorrow."

"Just be here. We can get some real human interest out of this. And we have to go to Bakersfield tomorrow. You and I will get the Holts's faces and Mike's face out there again to show the tragedy of it all."

"This is too much right now."

"You have a dead associate. We have to spin this our way, and fast. I'll see you all here at five for makeup and final prep. I'll have q's and a's. We'll hit them hard tonight and harder tomorrow."

"Fine, fine."

"And bring that video of the sale with you."

"It's not very useful. It's a grainy mess."

"I'll make a copy, turn it into a DVD, and have my department look at it. They're pros."

"Sure. Anything you want."

Ben's take on things would be good for Sophia's case, but even better for his ratings. He was intent on milking this for all it was worth—he didn't care that she was actually and imminently facing the first jury trial of her career. He was only thinking of his career.

* * *

The rest of the day, the firm was beset by a parade of detectives, Eddie's enraged parents, his two hysterical sisters, and Steve trying to help, with Roxy screening calls and people. Peggy hid. Something like this was above her pay grade.

Predictably, Stefan dropped in for an unscheduled dinner date with Autumn. He waited, soaking everything in. When Paul saw him, he wanted to kick him out the door but instead told Autumn to leave early. They couldn't let Stefan know they had made him unless and until it served their purposes.

Steve and his fellow detectives left after concluding the Bakersfield police had jurisdiction. That meant the incident would get the same non-attention as the arson attack on the Holts's home.

It was just "too bad" and "oh so sad" that Eddie was dead. A barrio kid with determination and intellect had overcome language issues, a rough home life, and the neighborhood gangs, only to die because two pieces of human waste had ignited his anger.

But anger was a tool litigators had to learn to use with skill, or it became an enemy. Eddie had misused his tool. More to the point, that tool had taken over and misused him.

* * *

That night, Ben's broadcast was intense. He probed why guns got into the hands of the distraught, the demented, and mass killers. Sophia, Tricia, and Paul answered Ben's provocative questions with his legal department's carefully prepared answers, which proved to be reassuringly accurate. He then introduced Eddie as a part of the team *in absentia* and characterized his death as a tragedy. Ben ran footage they had of Eddie from before and told about his life and accomplishments.

He skillfully characterized Sports Gear as careless and uncaring gatekeepers to tragedies, both those in the past and those yet to come, making a profit on blood. He incorporated a recent gun tragedy in a New York office building, where a man shot and killed an innocent security guard and then himself.

Ben also nailed his teaser for the Holt broadcast the next day: grieving parents seeking justice, blended with the shock and grief that Eddie's parents were going through. Sophia had warned him the

Holts were at their limit and volatile, but he had a brilliant editor and wasn't concerned. Ben was an unstoppable locomotive charging down the tracks.

\* \* \*

At the office, Sophia called the Holts and told Wallace about the interviews to precede the depositions. He was irritated, but in the background Beth was excited and blurting out questions. Their reactions were always polar opposites these days.

Before Sophia left the office, Bryce received a fax of the Bakersfield police report. Because of Eddie's death, one had magically appeared. It was backdated. It said there were witnesses who saw Eddie attack Grimick. It did not mention any statements from Eddie or Sophia. In the end, that was good news for Krause & White and their insurance carrier.

\* \* \*

Later that night, Ben's broadcast condemned Sports Gear, the Bakersfield police, the virtually unchecked gun craziness nationwide, the lack of adequate rules for gun sellers, and nationwide mass shootings. He waved the American flag, talked of motherhood and apple pie, and lauded the four brave attorneys for the Holts—one of them a rising L.A. Latino star, now dead.

In his ambitious frenzy, Ben transformed Sophia's gun trial into a national cry for gun sales reform. This case was his vehicle to break into the national news scene. Watching it, despite her misgivings, Sophia began to think his single-mindedness might actually help after all.

\* \* \*

She was glad to go home that night. She went to sleep in Steve's arms. She was too tired to argue with him about anything. She just wanted those strong arms around her.

With no one to go home to, Paul and Tricia hit a nearby bar to mourn Eddie and drink to their new, if unfortunate, celebrity. They returned to Paul's place for a nightcap. Tricia almost ended up in his bed, but after their alcohol-infused test kiss, they stopped.

"Sorry," Paul said.

"Me too." Tricia burst out laughing and crying at the same time. "Crazy day."

"It was. Sad, chaotic, all of that." Paul looked sheepish. "We shouldn't do this. Goodnight."

"Goodnight, Paul. Thanks for the company."

Tricia spent the night on his couch.

⌘

# CHAPTER 45

## In Camera and Out

*"Boring people don't have to stay that way."*
-Hedy Lamarr

On Friday morning, Sophia met Ben with his crew at the Holts's. Ben set up the shot on the porch. Beth gravitated to the attention like a heat-seeking missile, chatting all through her long makeup session. She was animated, vibrant, and so excited her lips smiled spasmodically. Had she been a puppy, she would have peed herself.

Wallace stared disapprovingly at Beth's lonely, ugly, overt whoring for attention. Disgusted, he sat alone. He was done with her.

Sophia pitied them both now.

With the preliminaries done, Ben started with a close-up on himself. He did a stirring intro about Eddie and then the Holts's loss and villainized Sports Gear USA. Then, he panned to the Holts on the porch, Beth with her oxygen tank affixed to her as usual. She started out smiling too much, so they filmed Wallace looking grim and angry. Both did their canned q's and a's with candid believability. Beth figured out she got more camera time when she sobbed, so she did just that. Then, Sophia nailed her thirty seconds about justice, tragedy, and Eddie. Ben wrapped it up.

"Sophia, I've got to send some footage back to my editor for teasers. I'll be outside Moschella's office ASAP."

With that, Sophia marshaled the Holts into her car for their depositions.

\* \* \*

On the way to Moschella's, Sophia gave her last tactical and, of course, very ethical instructions to the Holts.

"Keep everything short. Be honest, but don't volunteer anything they don't ask. Yes and no is nice . . . like we rehearsed. If you need a break, let me know. And if I think you need a break, I'll let you know. Do you understand?"

"Yes." Wallace was curt and succinct, exactly as Sophia wanted him to be in the deposition.

"I think I do," Beth said. "I know we have to be honest most of all. Then we have to not talk too much because we could make a mistake."

"No." Beth was going to get Sophia censured by the bar for essentially telling her to lie with half-truths. "That's not what I said."

"Oh?"

Beth was unpredictable, and her only real value was in her crying, so Sophia simplified things for her in order to protect her law license.

"There are no mistakes. There is only the truth. It's simple. Tell the truth. Adding extra things would just be wasting everyone's time. Do you see? Isn't that logical?"

"I suppose so. But the truth is the truth, and the law wants the whole truth, doesn't it?"

"Of course."

Sophia gave up. She didn't want this stupid, attention-starved old woman saying that Sophia told her to lie or be evasive or break the law. If Beth damaged the case, Sophia would claim confusion and senility. She looked at Wallace in her rearview mirror. He would back her up on Beth's senility, if not insanity. He wouldn't be above humiliating her like she did to him when she chose her son's memory over him in that fire.

"Beth, just tell the goddamned truth!" Wallace yelled. "That's all she's saying. Tell the goddamned truth."

"Well. You don't have to take the Lord's name in vain." Beth beamed a satisfied smile. She had played Wallace's strings like a fine violinist and gotten the desired rise out of him.

Sophia thought that Beth must torture Wallace all day long. The quiet little old woman jabbing at him over and over again because he didn't give her enough attention—because no one could ever give her enough attention.

It was going to be a wearying day. Sophia would have to defend Beth from herself. All Beth needed to do was turn on her damned endless spout of tears. Why couldn't she see that?

* * *

At the Quarry, Warren & Moschella offices before the depos, Moschella and Theresa met and conferred with Sophia about discovery disputes. For leverage Sophia had created a fictionalized list of unproduced documents, CD-ROMs, and other computerized and noncomputerized materials to bargain with. She also had a number of Sports Gear's supplemental interrogatory responses, which were still inadequate.

"Good morning," Moschella began. "I was sorry to hear about that young associate of yours. I saw the news. He died of a brain clot?"

"Yes."

"Too bad. He looked fine when he left. I was sorry about yesterday after the deposition. There was no call for that on anyone's part."

"Well, your client's sales clerks initiated it and used racist and sexist language that would have incited anyone." Sophia made no attempt to hide her anger over Eddie's death, even if he had struck first.

"We'll have to agree to disagree on that, I suppose, but no need to make more of it. I just wanted to express my condolences. We're all very upset about it."

Sandoval had been told what had happened and did not engage, but rather looked away. The smart, attractive Latina lawyer clearly knew and was offended by what Grimick and Spangler had said. Sophia tucked that away for future reference. She would definitely find a way to use that when the time was right.

"Understood." Moschella got on with business. "What else did you think you were entitled to by way of document production from us?"

"These interrogatories need more complete answers and, of course, before the discovery cutoff." She handed them to Moschella.

"We'll look into it." Moschella took Sophia's three-page list of defective responses.

"Here," Moschella said. "We have an updated list Ms. Sandoval did. There are missing medical records for Mike for those years. The parents had to have taken him for a checkup so he could play high school sports. I think it's required."

"Possibly." Sophia was noncommittal. "I'll look into it."

"I'll need them before discovery cutoff."

"Of course. If they exist." Sophia had no intention of finding out, a fair trade for Eddie—not enough by a long shot, but something.

"Thanks."

Sophia forced herself to move on before she lost it like Eddie. She blamed Moschella for the license Grimick and Spangler had taken with him. Once garbage like that smells blood, they circle like wolves. Mangy ones. It was easy pickings for them with a hotheaded youngster who had been humiliated in the Grimick deposition.

"I want to confirm the length of the Holts's depositions. We agreed they'd be short . . . less than two hours each. I think they'll make it, but they're not doing that well since the fire."

Moschella had agreed weeks before to limit the couple's depositions. The Holts had answered Sports Gear's form interrogatories and special interrogatories in detail, unlike Moschella's client. Sophia had also had them admit every one of Moschella's requests for admissions submitted in the discovery that was not harmful or unclear. She did that to avoid subjecting them to lengthy depositions, and it had not hurt their case.

Since the advent of the Internet, everyone with fingers and a computer could get background on anyone, anyway—Mike's life had been made public on Facebook and Twitter and Instagram. Beth and Wallace, however, were Internet absentees; thus the responses Sophia's team drafted to Sports Gear USA's discovery requests were unchallengeable from that quarter.

"Two hours each is good," Moschella said. "As long as there are no interruptions or undue objections that slow me down."

Moschella needed these depositions, as any good trial lawyer would, to gauge how the Holts would come across on the stand at trial. He didn't expect to get any new information or to break the case open with their depos, but that didn't worry him. He remained confident the law was on his client's side. He would simply get the Holts committed to answers in their depositions, to avoid any surprises when he made the summary judgment motion he intended to drop on Sophia. Or, rather, signing and filing the one Tom Jackson and his firm were already preparing.

"As long as there are no improper or harassing questions, of course." Sophia flashed a humorless smile across the table.

* * *

Theresa left to retrieve the court reporter. Moschella had canceled the videographer. He had seen Wallace and Beth with her oxygen tank on the news. He didn't want those sympathetic images up on a screen at trial.

Sophia counted the cancellation of the videographer as a small victory. She would take what she could get at this juncture.

Beth was deposed first while Wallace waited in a smaller conference room with coffee and cookies almost as good as homemade, but supplied by Quarry, Warren & Moschella.

The depositions went well. Not perfectly—but well. Beth said very little but kept turning on the waterworks and needed break after break until Moschella finally gave up. Wallace was stoic and monosyllabic. Getting him to talk was like pulling teeth. He looked devastated and emotionally broken. Only Sophia knew his stoicism and brevity were born of disinterest and his desire to get on with his own life.

All in all, both were wins for Sophia. Emotional devastation was the key to the big bucks on her wrongful death, negligence, and negligent infliction of emotional distress causes of action. And both Beth and Wallace had demonstrated that beyond any doubt.

At the end of Wallace's depo, Sophia turned her phone back on. There were multiple text warnings from Ben to look out the window before they left.

\* \* \*

Sophia looked down from the eleventh floor.

"Oh, Jesus."

"What?" Moschella came over.

"The whole street is covered with news vans. Look at the reporters and the crowd."

Every news channel in Southern California was gathered outside in the sweltering July heat. The channels were acronymed in bold on the top of each van. Ben's CBT vans were near the entrance.

Swarming like ants, demonstrators covered the broad walkway into the building, the parking lot, and the walkway around the small water feature, competing for camera coverage by waving signs, chanting, and yelling at each other.

There were NGA banners, signs quoting the Second Amendment, and placards with "Stand Your Ground" on them. Opposing them was an equally large group waving banners and signs with poster-size pictures of victims of gun violence, including African-Americans shot by police with "Black Lives Matter" in big print, and slogans calling for increased gun control. There was a virtual alphabet soup of anti-gun groups.

The pro-gun demonstrators surged toward the anti-gun demonstrators shouting profanities and screaming. The anti-gun demonstrators held firm, but the Bakersfield police aggressively pushed them back, leaving the pro-gun forces in control. It was clear who had their sympathies. But for the cameras on them, Sophia believed the cops would have pummeled the anti-gun demonstrators.

"What the . . .? I didn't do this," Moschella insisted.

"Well, I certainly didn't." Sophia glared at him.

"How am I going to get the Holts out of here?"

"Theresa, see if they're at the back."

Prompted or not, Moschella certainly wouldn't have dissuaded the NGA or Sports Gear from doing their dirty work. But who alerted the anti-gun demonstrators? Sophia thought it might have been Ben's doing. His lust to move up the professional food chain made him a likely suspect to heighten the rhetoric and, therefore, the newsworthiness of the Holt case.

"They're at the back too."

"Well, besides the front and back," Moschella said, "there are fire exits on the side, but anyone can see them from the front or the back. So there's no good way out. Let me get you a police escort. They're already down there. They can get you out."

"No. No cops. They're a bunch of bastards," Wallace shouted. "They know who burnt our house . . . I know they know. They're in cahoots with those illegal gunrunners. They're dirty . . . on the take. I don't trust them and want nothing to do with them."

"Wallace, settle down. No police. Okay?"

"Okay."

Moschella now knew one of Wallace's vulnerabilities: his temper and his bitterness toward the police. He was revealing too much now after his controlled deposition. Moschella had one Wallace-button to push at trial. Sophia had to get the Holts out fast. Next, Beth could act out giving Moschella something to use on her.

"Thanks, Tony," Sophia said. "But we'll get through it."

"Your decision. I would call the BP."

* * *

As they descended in the elevator, Sophia texted Ben for help to get to her car.

Ben and his crew ran to the oversized double glass doors and encircled Sophia and the Holts as they came out. Other reporters and cameramen tried to break through. However, Ben's body armor created by his own people was effective—it shut out the rabid pro-gun demonstrators and other reporters with their cameras. Ben's human fortress was moving toward his van near the entrance for a getaway before the police even saw them.

"Stay close."

Ben and his full crew, with Sophia and the Holts enveloped, continued baby-stepping their way through the onslaught of reporters—yelling questions, pressing in with cameras and microphones. The anti-gun demonstrators were too far away to engage or protect the small engulfed group.

"Back off." Ben's most bulked-up crew guy led the way.

"Help Beth," Sophia shouted to Ben. "I'll grab Wallace."

"Close the damn ranks," Ben yelled at his crew.

They squeezed together closer. They made their way to Ben's news van, through the staccato blare of reporters' questions—loud, nasty, pointed. " . . . gun haters . . . illegal gun sale . . . gun rights . . . constitu . . . gun clubs . . right to bear arms . . . out-of-towners . . . L.A. . . . ."

Sophia, the Holts, and Ben's crew were jostled and shoved like it was Times Square on New Year's Eve. Ben swept Sophia and the Holts into his van and had one of the crew go get Sophia's car. The two CBT vehicles then moved through the crowd. The pro-gun demonstrators hit both vans with signs and fists as they drove away. The crew van was swarmed and had to stop and wait for police help. But Ben's van sped to the Holts's house—Beth crying and Wallace not caring.

"Everyone all right?" Ben shouted to the back.

The consensus was yes.

"How did this happen?" Sophia asked.

"We don't know, but my producer got wind of the organized demonstration and that all the channels were covering it."

"Who leaked the depos?"

"Don't know. I didn't. You know me and exclusives."

"I do." Sophia gave him a measured look.

"I tried to warn you."

"My phone is off in depos, but I saw your texts after. You saved us."

"Anytime. It's not like this frenzy is my first one."

After they dropped the Holts off, Ben looked gravely at Sophia. "Now the Holts are gone, you have to know that we have a bigger problem. We need to get back to L.A. fast. There's my guy with your car. Let's go. We can't wait for the crew."

*What now?* she thought.

⌘

# CHAPTER 46

## Fishing and Fissures

*"Regret is the worst human emotion."*
-William Shatner

Sophia was still shaken from the Bakersfield news slam as she and Ben started back to L.A. in her car.

"Eddie's parents and the L.A. Latino leadership have rallied to use Eddie's funeral tomorrow as a platform to protest his death. My producer says the mayor's speaking and all the politicos are piling on."

"They should. It was horrible."

"Sophia, focus. It is horrible, but it will be worse if we don't get our spin on it going. We have work to do. All the news channels have their teasers running. My producer's holding the spots for me. I have to get mine up with a good slant. Can you tell me anything new? They're saying he was attacked first."

"Like I said, the racial and sexist slurs precipitated it, but Eddie swung first."

"So there's no chance of those guys being indicted for manslaughter or anything?"

"I don't think so. Like I said, I couldn't see."

Ben and Sophia went over the fight in Bakersfield again. She wanted to help Ben more, but her hands were tied because of her firm's potential liability. And the firm came first.

\* \* \*

On the down side of the Grapevine, Paul called Sophia.

"Where the hell are you?"

"I'm almost there." Sophia told Paul about the chaos in Bakersfield.

"I'm glad Ben was there. There's total madness here. Demonstrators at City Hall demanding justice for Eddie. Now there's a group outside here, too. They want Grimick and Spangler arrested for murder."

"That won't happen. Too many eyewitnesses absolve them."

"I know. But you'd better get back here. Eddie's parents got a wrongful death lawyer, and Derek's on the warpath. He's accusing us of screwing up by giving a volatile kid like Eddie those depos."

"That jerk took Bryce away from us. What the hell were we supposed to do?"

"Just get here. You have to meet with our insurance people."

* * *

Ben and Sophia fielded calls the rest of the way. Ben's crew eventually caught up and leap-frogged ahead. Sophia decided to risk a speeding ticket herself.

"We shouldn't have been in Bakersfield," Ben said. "The Holt story is going to be overshadowed tonight. I'll have to change the hook to get an audience."

"How were we to know the whole Latino community would get involved?"

"Eddie's parents must be connected," Ben said.

"Eddie was a comer," Sophia said. "Harvard. Latino. L.A. barrio kid makes good. There were great expectations for him. By us too. But he had a temper. No denying that."

"Give me more background on this guy." Ben turned on his cellphone recorder. "Human interest stuff."

Sophia was happy to share Eddie's background, his new girlfriend, and his stellar resume. However, the more she spoke about him, the worse she felt.

"Stop recording," Sophia said. "Off the record?"

"Sure," Ben agreed. "What?"

"I'm feeling so guilty about not just taking Eddie to the ER."

"Is that it?" Ben thought he was going to get some juicy secret, some dirt. "Well, don't. He chose not to go. You said the paramedics cleared him anyway. No one knew what would happen. You asked to take him to Cedars."

"Repeatedly. I was insistent."

"And he refused. So you did the best you could. Besides, ERs are meat markets at best and death traps at worst. I covered them for years. I guarantee that even if you got him into one, he would have been released and died anyway. They're manned with residents and marginal doctors who can't see their noses in front of their faces. They follow scripted procedures and shove the patients out the door or, if they have good insurance, up to admissions. We all joked about the docs tossing a coin to decide a diagnosis."

"That's cynical."

"Maybe, but it's true. I covered poor John Ritter's death. The actor. He died of a misdiagnosis."

"But the jury found in favor of the doctors."

"They always do. That's why the carnage goes on. Doctors have the halo effect with jurors. Jurors are stupid. Each one of them deserves to be treated by the doctor they let off."

Sophia remembered the well-known television actor dying at the ER and the World War II vet and surgeon who died in his own hospital in Whittier. They misdiagnosed his cracked c-spine, dislocated and abused it, drugged him with Haldol to shut him up while they made him a quadriplegic, and killed him off with morphine twenty-two days later.

Sophia appreciated Ben's absolution but couldn't forgive herself nonetheless. He objectified everything and always saw the worst side of life. It scared her because, as a litigator, she had the same tendency. She put him back in her "arms-length" category of people. The ones you deal with when you must, but always with great care and a healthy dose of skepticism. They drove on in silence.

"You might have to call Eddie's parents and set something up for me," Ben said. "They haven't called me back."

"Come on. There's no way they'll speak to the woman who didn't get their son to the ER."

"Try. What an interview prize they would be."

Ben's unrealistic insistence irritated Sophia.

\* \* \*

Sophia and Ben molassesed through the Friday afternoon rush hour traffic into downtown. He texted and called his station to plan his show. Sophia touched base with Paul and Tricia as she drove. Then, during a lull in the frenetic activity, Steve called.

"Hi. Are you back yet?"

"No, Ben and I are still on the road."

"How did it go in wonderful old Bako?"

"Not good. You may see it on the news before I get home. I'll pick up dinner."

"Just for you," Steve said. "I'll be late. A tactical operation. Go to sleep."

"You be careful. See you in the morning."

"I love you."

"Me too." Sophia signed off.

"Does he have anything on Derek's brother yet? Do they have a suspect?"

"What?"

"Call him back."

"He had an emergency," Sophia lied.

She wished Steve had not called because Ben was like a dog gnawing a bone that wouldn't let go.

"We'll get him later. I'll check in with you. Promise." Sophia didn't want Ben calling Steve or his "big" boss again.

\* \* \*

She dropped Ben off at last. When he got out of the car, the tension went with him. She was relieved to leave Bako and Ben behind. He was useful, but she had to watch herself with him. He would do anything for a shot at being a big-time anchor on the national scene.

Sophia called Steve back.

"Any update on Derek's brother? I have to appease Ben. Can I tell him anything? Anything at all? If I don't he's going to call you and your captain."

"No worries. He already called me, and I answered."

"He's got a lot of gall."

"I told him we were making progress, but that was all I could say. He was an ass."

"He sure has become one since Thorne & Chase. Or maybe I just didn't notice back then."

"Never mind. I got rid of him. I told him I couldn't jeopardize the investigation or any of my officers. Then, he became a bigger ass."

"Just forget it. I'll deal."

"No. No. Wait. To shut him up, I did tell him that we might have a break."

"A break," Sophia said. "Is that true?"

"Yes. That's what tonight is about."

"You didn't say anything to Ben?"

"No. Police operations are confidential for a reason—safety."

"Well, be safe then."

Sophia did love Steve on some levels and felt guilty she didn't enjoy him or his company as she once had. She appreciated Steve's effort to placate Derek by taking the lead on Dwight's case and his efforts to keep Ben at bay.

"I'll leave your dinner in the fridge."

"It'll probably be breakfast for me. I love you."

"Me too." Sophia was not one-hundred percent honest, but she was still one-hundred percent hoping.

\* \* \*

At the firm, Sophia snuck into her office. She called Paul and Tricia and told them to come down with food if they had any. She was starving.

"Good thing you're back." Paul came in with Tricia trailing. "Derek talked to Eddie's parents' attorney. They're going to sue. Rona offered to help them with funeral arrangements, but they brushed her off. They're closing ranks."

"You can't blame them."

Tricia gave Sophia half of a corned beef sandwich from the local deli.

"Here . . . saved it just in case."

"Thanks. Your half sandwiches always save me." Sophia remembered the deli where Tricia and Paul had taken her for corned beef her first day at Thorne & Chase—it seemed a lifetime ago now.

"Eddie's parents just don't believe he died because he lost his balance," Tricia said. "They're sure those two mouth-breathers did something to him. Are you positive they didn't?"

"I couldn't see. But there are too many witnesses who saw it from a better angle and put the blame squarely on Eddie. Quantity counts. You know that. And the lobby guy has no reason to lie. I mean, Grimick and Spangler were real scum with their racist and sexist taunts, but Eddie took the swing and escalated it to the physical."

"How bad were the taunts?"

"Well, one could argue they were 'fighting words' if that's what you're thinking. But usually, that doesn't help. You can't respond physically to language, no matter how offensive. It's still on Eddie."

"Huh." Paul reflected.

"He was wound tighter than a drum after the depo," Sophia said. "I put him in over his head, and Moschella was merciless, but that's what a litigator is. Eddie just wasn't ready."

"We needed to bring him along slower," Tricia said.

"They're trying to label this an anti-Latino hate crime."

"But Eddie committed the crime if there was one," Paul said.

"Do you think this was planned by Moschella?" Tricia asked.

"Or . . . suggested," Paul said.

"Not by Moschella," Sophia said. "He's tough but not dirty."

"Were they coached?"

"Does that change the analysis, Paul?" Tricia asked. "The argument? Does planning to insult someone change the reality that Eddie jumped to the bait and did the physical aggression?"

"I don't know enough about criminal law to answer," Paul said. "Can just speech justify a physical response?"

"My best recollection is no," Sophia said. "Verbal provocation is not a defense to a battery charge in California."

Peggy knocked and popped her head in.

"Derek wants to meet with all the attorneys in ten minutes in the conference room. Sorry, Sophia. I had strict orders to tell him when you came in."

"Don't worry about it." Sophia's stealth had failed. "But tell him twenty minutes."

The three switched their analysis to how to best appease Derek and Rona. They wanted peace in the firm. But they had no control over Eddie's parents suing the firm or the fact that Derek's brother's killer had not been arrested. Or resolving the Holt case, either. They had no settlement leverage. Not yet. Despite their maximum efforts, they had been outmaneuvered and were clearly outmanned.

On the way down the hall to the meeting, Sophia got a text from Ben wanting an interview with Eddie's parents and asking about the break in the investigation of Dwight's death.

"Can't do and don't know. In firm meeting." Sophia texted back.

*He's like fly paper*, Sophia thought.

* * *

The firmwide meeting wasn't a meeting. It was an inquisition of Sophia. She was indicted for her bad supervision and mentoring of Eddie and her poor judgment in getting the firm to take on the Holt case.

Derek was the chief inquisitor, and Rona went along for the ride. Bryce cowered. Tricia, Paul, and Sophia just took the abuse. They had to prioritize and mollify Derek with the trial staring them in the face. Time was precious.

"Here." Derek played a video on his phone for all to see. "Look. There it is, a demonstration in front of LAPD headquarters on 1st Street. They want justice for Eddie."

"I can't help them," Sophia said. "I didn't see what happened after he swung the case."

"That's bullshit," Derek yelled.

Rona stepped in. "You didn't see enough to leave the door open to the possibility that they did something? We know the case did not hurt them. Maybe it didn't even hit them."

Sophia reran the encounter in her mind. "I'm sorry. It was hot. We were leaving. They started harassing Eddie. Eddie rushed up to them. It all happened so fast. But his back blocked my view."

"Now you say that you 'don't think so,'" Derek berated Sophia. "They don't even have your statement in the police report."

Derek threw the police report at Sophia. She read it. It pinned everything on Eddie. So did Spangler and Grimick, the lobby attendant, and the other witnesses.

"The cops left. They barely spoke to Eddie and me about what happened. They just wanted him gone."

"Well, maybe you should just call and be included in the report!" Derek shouted. "Stand up and be counted."

"It wouldn't help."

"It would if you wanted it to."

"I can't make things up, and I won't." Sophia was getting angry.

"That's enough, Derek." Rona saw Sophia would not play ball. "The decision we have to make now is about the funeral. Do we go?"

"We have to," Tricia said. "We're his colleagues."

"But should we all go?" Rona asked. "Frankly, it might be better if you don't, Sophia. The news reports are saying you sided with the Bakersfield rednecks."

"First, they were Oildalers," Sophia said. "Those people are worse than just rednecks."

Derek shouted, "You know damn well you should have taken him to the hospital! You killed him, and you and your damn case killed my brother too!"

"Settle down, Derek," Paul said. "You're wrong, and that's not productive."

Tricia refocused the discussion. "None of us will be popular at the funeral. I do know the legal community will be well-represented. My friend in the Mexican American Bar Association said all their members got an email to come and support the family."

"Will we be missed?" Paul asked.

"It will be an omission if it's noticed," Derek said. "Rona and I are going as name partners."

*Yeah, and to get your face in front of a news camera,* Sophia thought.

Bryce finally spoke. "But I'm not going. I liked Eddie. I feel bad, but the guy had a hot temper. I told him it would get him in trouble one day."

"Don't go then," Rona said. "But you don't talk to any press about him. Do you understand? Your comments don't go beyond these walls to anyone, especially about his temper. We could be in serious litigation. That goes for all of you."

Sophia worried that she had told Ben too much about Eddie. It was all Internet searchable, of course, except her feelings of guilt. She should have kept her mouth shut.

"Hold on," Paul said. "What if we limit it to the name partners? That's categorical."

"Categorical but disingenuous," Sophia said. "It was my case, my colleague, and I was with him. I have to show respect. That's what a funeral is for."

Sophia's Greek heritage, with its strong traditions about the passages in life, had come out. She couldn't stay away. She had learned that throughout her life and also at Thorne & Chase. No matter how aggressive the legal adversary, you had to show respect. And even more for a colleague and someone you were mentoring.

The meeting adjourned with no consensus. Obviously, Derek was going, to be seen in the news, and Rona was going with him. If Sophia decided to attend, Paul and Tricia said, they would go to support her. The firm was splintering more every day. She had to make the Holt case pay off, even though the odds were stacked against her.

After the meeting, Paul invited Tricia and Sophia out for a drink. They all needed one after the day they had endured. Maybe more than one. They got away from downtown, though, to minimize the chance of unwelcome encounters. Sophia's face was all over the TV and the Internet.

⌘

# CHAPTER 47

## The Benemy

*"The shifts of fortune test the reliability of friends."*
-Marcus Tullius Cicero

The three went to Father's Office, a local watering hole on Montana Avenue in Santa Monica, far from their downtown building. It was old Santa Monica, wood-paneled, cramped, and dimly lit. Aside from drinks, especially its exotic beer offerings, it served justifiably famous burgers with blue cheese and either sweet potato or regular fries. After-work singles and groups gathered there. They talked and watched the news on two big-screen televisions. It was noisy and relaxing escape.

Paul got three draft beers for them. They grabbed a table near a television, and Paul turned it to Ben's channel. No one objected. The three ate their burgers and sweet potato fries and waited to see Sophia in Bako on the ten o'clock news.

"There it is. The Holts's house with Ben," Tricia said.

They watched.

It was short. No Sophia interview. No Holt interview. But there sure was footage of Ben leading Sophia and the Holts as they ran the gauntlet outside Moschella's office building.

"Where are all the interviews?" Sophia asked.

Paul shushed her. "Listen."

Ben concluded in a full-face shot. "This reporter helped the Holts and their lawyer Sophia Christopoulos escape from the very place Eddie Herrera took his fatal fall outside the law offices of Quarry, Warren & Moschella in Bakersfield. His funeral will be tomorrow, and this reporter will be there. Mike Holt's decision to buy a shotgun and take his own life has claimed another victim. Eddie Herrera was a rising star in the Latino community here in Los Angeles. Did he need to die in Bakersfield? Was there foul play? This reporter asks the hard questions."

"Damn," Paul said. "Talk about fanning the flames."

"He might as well have just lit a stick of dynamite."

"I can't believe this. What does he mean asks the 'hard' questions?" Sophia said. "Ben's out for Ben and edited it just that way. We're already *persona non grata* in Bakersfield. What now? The Bakersfield news outlets already poisoned everyone against us, and now we have Ben broadcasting possible foul play in their lovely little city? What can we do?"

"We deal." Paul was cold and contemplative. "Ben has to get something out of this too."

"We need some tactical advantage to force a settlement." Sophia was becoming less thrilled at the prospect of her first trial in that awful backwater up north.

"Good luck with that now." Tricia got up. "I'll get the next round."

Sophia looked over at Paul for some answer, some wisdom. She had done that for years. He was smart and strong in the law and in life.

"Relax." Paul reached under the table and squeezed Sophia's hand. "We'll land on our feet . . . all of us."

They looked at each other for a long, still moment in the dimly lit bar. Sophia knew she was the reason Paul had no relationship. Tricia returned with the beers. She withdrew her hand and grabbed a beer. Paul was disappointed, but he always was. Sophia was grateful for the interruption.

Tricia was oblivious. "What about the funeral?"

"After Ben's story, Sophia has to be there. And that means us too." Paul was decisive.

"All for one and one for all." They clinked beer mugs.

"We'll meet at the office. We'll slip in with the crowd and then slip out too." Paul was back to his animated self. "Want your fries, Tricia?"

"No. I'm back on the market," Tricia said. "Take them. I have to be thin."

"You're perfect now," Paul said. "I hate those skinny . . ."

"Speak of . . ." Sophia said. "It's Ben texting. 'Watch Chang on MPC now. Steve shot—alive.'"

"What?" Paul got up and changed the channel, which no other partier was watching anyway.

"Detective Steve Rutger was shot in the line of duty tonight. He is in critical condition at Cedars-Sinai Hospital," Chang announced. "The detective was shot during an operation to apprehend the killer of Dwight White, brother of the prominent black attorney Derek White, founding partner of the firm of Krause & White. This exclusive MPC footage is from the actual shooting. It will be disturbing, and young children should leave the room."

They watched the film. It was graphic and showed Steve going down in a volley of gunfire.

"Steve!" Sophia cried.

Paul stood and threw cash on the table. "Let's go."

"It's Chang's work," Tricia said as they left. "She had her lighting and camera on Steve. She got him shot."

"How the hell did she know where to be?" Paul asked, unlocking his car.

"That bitch," Tricia said. "She got it out of someone."

"Let's just get to him." Sophia was sobbing.

\* \* \*

At Cedars, Paul slowed to drop Sophia and Tricia off while he parked. But the emergency entrance was crowded with the media. Reporters stood blabbing filler into the cameras, waiting for something to actually happen.

Paul gunned his engine and circled to the main entrance on the other side of the building.

"Get out. I'll park."

\* \* \*

Steve wasn't in the emergency room. He was already up in surgery and had lost a lot of blood. It was touch and go. Steve and his partner had led the operation to make an arrest in Dwight's murder, and a news crew got in the way—Chang's news crew.

Steve's partner, Steve's captain Emil Sheen, and his fellow officers paid their respects to Sophia. They were there not out of obligation, but out of friendship and respect for Steve. Sophia only had a passing acquaintance with a few of them.

Sophia, Paul, and Tricia waited together for hours.

Sophia was angry and desperate. Sophia committed herself to using Ben to destroy Chang. When Ben's number appeared on her cell, she answered.

"Not good, Ben, but he's in surgery. Obviously, this is the break he told you about. I guess Change got wind of it and got in the way. I'll give you updates . . . the exclusive."

She turned off her phone. Her parents were asleep, and there was no one else she wanted or needed to talk to. Her best friends were with her.

"I'm going to get that Chang," Sophia said. "I'll help Ben scoop her every chance we get."

Tricia hugged her.

"Sophia, don't go there now." Paul put his arms around the two women.

Finally, at 3:00 a.m., Steve came out of surgery but was still critical. His fellow officers slowly took their leave.

Paul and Tricia waited while Sophia went into the recovery room.

Steve was still out. She took his hand, and his eyes fluttered open.

"I love you," Sophia whispered, so wanting to believe her own words. "I love you."

Steve returned to a deep, medicated sleep.

Paul and Tricia took her home, insisting she needed to get some sleep herself.

On the way, she called Ben with a detailed report about the captain and all the officers who stood vigil and the outcome of Steve's surgery. It was the best she could do to get at Chang.

Ben thanked her and added his best wishes for Steve. She barely heard him. She was beyond numb.

Tricia stayed with Sophia that night and slept on the couch. It had been a long, hard, horrible day. And, aside from everything, the three had to go to Eddie's funeral a few hours later.

⌘

# CHAPTER 48

## Dia De Los Muertos

*"We die only once, and for such a long time."*
-Moliere

When Tricia and Sophia woke up, after too little sleep, Tricia went home and Sophia to visit Steve. They were meeting Paul at the office later to go together to the funeral.

\* \* \*

At the hospital Sophia missed Steve's mother, whom she had never met, by just a few minutes. Sophia sat by Steve's bedside determined to be as they once were—deeply in love. She swore to herself that she would get to know his mother, make friends with his friends, and mend the rift caused by the trial and the strain of Ben and Derek in their lives.

"Sophia?" Steve's eyes squinted open.

"Don't try to talk. Just rest."

He mumbled. His pain meds beeped. He slept.

"I'll be back." She kissed him on the cheek.

\* \* \*

Paul drove the trio to Eddie's funeral at his family's Catholic church, Saint Teresita on Zonal Avenue in East L.A. The new archbishop of the Diocese of Los Angeles, Cardinal Benedicto Chavez, had wanted to have the service in the grand new Cathedral of Our Lady of the Angels in the heart of downtown. Far be it from him to pass up a great PR opportunity with his prime constituency. Loyal to their friends and neighborhood, and knowing what Eddie would have wanted, his parents had declined.

"So Steve's all right then?" Paul asked as he fought the ever-worsening L.A. traffic.

"He recognized me and seemed good."

"Did you find out how Chang knew about Steve's operation?"

"No. And I'm not making any calls. When Steve recovers, he'll take care of it. They have protocols. I don't want any more trouble."

"What do you mean?" Tricia asked.

"This is not to go any further than this car."

"Tell us," Tricia said.

"You don't have to," Paul said. "Anyone with half a brain knows."

"Thanks, Paul," Tricia objected. "I don't know."

"Sorry, but it's obvious," Paul said. "Chang's source was a cop."

Sophia started to cry.

"Paul, shut up," Tricia said. "Who cares? He's alive."

Paul backed off.

* * *

Near Saint Teresita, there was a large LAPD presence and streams of people. The church had loudspeakers outside for the expected overflow. Demonstrators circled at the corner and across the street with signs demanding justice for Eddie.

Inside, there was standing room only, and that's what the three did—stand at a back wall. Sophia spotted Ben in an area set aside for the press.

"Evidently we wouldn't have been missed," Paul whispered to Sophia and Tricia.

"Don't say that," Sophia replied. "I feel guilty enough about not being with Steve."

"Should we leave?" Tricia asked.

"No, we're already here."

"There's the mayor," Paul whispered. "Talk about media whores. I swear, if a cockroach got stepped on in this city, he'd be there, making a speech."

"That's not fair," Sophia said. "He's part of the Latino community."

"Just shut up, Paul. Remember where you are," Tricia said. "Do you see Rona and Derek?"

"No." Sophia scanned the church. "And they aren't going to get in now."

The music started, and the procession came in with the casket. It was a long service. Every Latino politico and every hanger-on had to speak. The mayor droned on and on. Eddie's older brother Carlos gave the only speech that actually reflected Eddie's life. He spoke of Eddie's childhood, his desire to become a lawyer to make a difference, and his new love, Raquel. Tricia smiled because that had been her doing.

When the service was over, the three lined up and walked by the casket and the family to pay their respects. That was a mistake. Raquel pointed out Sophia to Eddie's parents.

"If looks could kill," Tricia whispered, "you'd be dead."

"I know." Sophia looked away and hid behind Paul.

"Forget them," Paul said. "They're way out of line."

Outside the church, the demonstrators had doubled in number, as had the police presence. Sophia spotted Derek and Rona. He was already in front of a camera.

From behind, Sophia felt a tap on her shoulder. It was Ben with his cameraman.

"Ben, is that thing running?"

"No, but can you give me something? Just a word? About Eddie and Steve."

"Sure. But Paul and Tricia are joining me. Okay?"

"Fine. We're going national with this."

The three stood shoulder to shoulder, united. They were a formidable trio, and each one spoke about the Holt case and Eddie's great career, so prematurely cut short. They wanted Ben's coverage to dwarf Chang's.

Then he stopped the camera and asked Sophia whether she could update everyone on Steve's condition. The camera rolled, and so did Sophia.

"Okay, cut it," Ben said.

"I want to get back to Steve, Ben. Is that enough?"

"Sure. Thanks, Sophia. Give him my best."

The crowd emptying from the church surged, and Ben beelined over to Eddie's family holding a news conference with the mayor. It was mainstream and would be a bunch of PC speak, but Ben was a good editor and had an even better one back at the station.

"Hey, we're getting good at sound bites," Tricia said as they hurried to the car.

"We've had enough practice," Paul replied.

"Too much," Sophia said.

* * *

Tricia, Paul, and Sophia went back to the office. Sophia redistributed Eddie's assignments and then left to see Steve.

The hospital was quiet. The demonstrators and media were at Eddie's funeral. When she turned the corner to his room, Captain Sheen was in the hall with a doctor, who shook his hand and left.

Sophia greeted him. "Captain Sheen, how's Steve?"

"I'm sorry." The captain's eyes were dark and angry. "There's no easy way to say this, Sophia. He died twenty minutes ago."

"But . . . this morning . . . he was fine."

Sophia's head spun. She reached for the wall. The captain took her arm to keep her from going to the floor. Tears streamed from her eyes.

"I am so sorry. The doctor said there was just too much internal damage and blood loss. We've called his mother."

Sophia felt guilty and responsible. Guilty because she had been avoiding Steve while continuing to take advantage of him. Responsible because she had asked him to help out in Dwight's murder investigation.

This was her doing.

⌘

# CHAPTER 49

## Lost and Adrift

*"What makes loneliness an anguish is not that I have no one to share my burden, but this: I have only my own burden to bear."*
-Dag Hammarskjold


Sophia woke Sunday morning in her own bed to the smell of coffee. For a second she expected Steve to walk in. But then she remembered.

She got up to find Tricia and Paul making breakfast. They had brought her home from Cedars and had not left her side. As the friends coffee'd and ate, Sophia grew tired of their solicitude. Her own feelings of guilt could not be solaced.

Paul addressed the elephant in the room. "Sophia, let's see if we can get a continuance from Judge Ortiz."

"Are you kidding? That's not happening. We're the ones who fought to get the trial advanced."

"Given what's happened now?" Tricia said.

"Forget it." Sophia drank her coffee. "We have to keep going."

Her friends didn't realize that she *could* keep going. She had not been old-fashioned, head-over-heels in love with Steve for months, if not years.

"Full throttle," Sophia insisted.

"Okay." Paul knew that the firm couldn't sustain a continuance anyway. "But not on Tuesday. Captain Sheen called. Steve's mother arranged to have Steve's funeral that morning. I guess his father's dead?"

"He is." Sophia dreaded meeting Steve's mother for the first time at her son's funeral—an incongruous end to a familial relationship that had never begun.

"We're taking you," Tricia said

"I'm so tired of all this death," Sophia said. "We aren't cops or in the military. We practice law. Our life was supposed to be one of dignity and justice and courtrooms, not murders and suicides and funerals. So let's get to the office and get at it."

Paul and Tricia looked at each other.

"Sophia, are you sure?" Tricia asked.

"I'm sure."

They drove together to the office and worked all day. Sophia was distracted but functional. She called Steve's mother to introduce herself, extend her condolences, and offer to help. None was needed. Steve's partner was there. Sophia didn't insist. As it turned out, Steve's mother didn't even know they had been living together. Sophia chose not to tell her.

* * *

Monday morning the firm business meeting was short and subdued with the two deaths crowding the room. As the meeting ended, Derek stood. He now knew that Sophia and Steve had done their best for Dwight and Steve was dead because of it.

"Sophia, I know what you're going through. The loss. And it can't be for nothing." Derek stopped, looked down, wiped tears from his eyes, and struggled to continue. "This all can't be for nothing. Your case is not just for the Holts or our firm anymore. We've got to get those gun sellers and make new law for Dwight, Steve, and Eddie. Even if we could give up the Holt case now, I wouldn't. We'll pull together. The whole firm."

Startled, Sophia looked up at him. The man speaking now, committed and generous, was not the Derek they had all come to know. The room of lawyers, and especially Sophia, were instantly energized by his offer—by a sense of mission and by hope.

"Thank you, Derek," Sophia said. "I know we can do it."

"Guns and my community have a bad relationship. This case didn't help, and it cost so many lives . . . so many sacrifices. We've got to win this, and if it ends up taking us down, there are worse ways to go."

* * *

Derek's support gave the firm the boost it needed. Sophia worked harder and more intensely than ever, partly because of Derek, but more because when her mind paused she blamed herself for Steve's death. She hadn't appreciated him enough for what he was and what he had always been to her. He had protected her at Thorne & Chase. He had loved her and had always tried to please her.

He had simply been too unpolished a gem for her. A wave of guilt swept over her.

* * *

Paul and Tricia went with Sophia to Steve's funeral the next morning at First Congregational Church on Commonwealth Avenue. There were no demonstrators, just hundreds of LAPD officers from all over, honoring one of their own fallen in the line of duty. Steve's coffin arrived at the church with a huge motorcycle honor guard.

Sophia, Tricia, and Paul sat in the first row with Steve's mother, his partner, and Captain Sheen. Although greetings were abbreviated as the pastor started the service, when Sophia looked into his mother's eyes, she saw Steve's eyes looking back at her. It hurt.

Rona, Derek, and Bryce stayed in the background. None of them knew Steve that well.

After his pastor finished extolling Steve and those like him who served to make Los Angeles a safer place, Steve's partner spoke. He only managed to say that there had never been a better detective or partner before he broke down. Captain Sheen lauded him as one of the best and brightest detectives in the department with an uncommon instinct for solving crimes and embodying the finest of what the LAPD represented. Not surprisingly, the mayor arrived late, spoke the longest, and left early.

Sophia was not asked to speak. It was an omission, but she couldn't have done it regardless. She was overwhelmed. She had asked her parents not to come. They understood. Her mother had known the relationship was on the verge of ending.

* * *

Following the service, there was a short motorcade to the historic Rosedale Cemetery not far from First Congregational. Many important figures in the growth of Los Angeles and California were buried there, along with other fallen LAPD officers. Steve had died for Los Angeles and deserved that much. It was not the most famous of Los Angeles cemeteries, but it was close, and Sophia was grateful for that. The graveside service was brief. Mrs. Rutger received an American flag from Captain Sheen, and there was a three-gun salute.

The reception, after the interment, was in the Mayflower Courtyard Gallery at First Congregational. Afterward, Steve's mother had a wake for only the immediate family, Steve's high school friends, and close officers from work at her own modest home in Sierra Madre at the foot of the northern hills surrounding L.A.

It was a long drive, and only about thirty-five people came, including Sophia, Tricia, and Paul.

"Mrs. Rutger . . ."

"Please. Call me Margaret."

"Margaret. I'm so sorry we didn't get to know each other. I asked Steve about meeting you, but something always seemed to interfere."

"I'm not surprised, dear. We didn't speak often. When Steve chose to 'play cops and robbers' instead of joining his dad's construction business, Frank wouldn't speak to him. I had to stick by Frank. Then, when Frank died last year . . . well, old habits, you know."

"Of course. You did the right thing." Sophia gave Margaret the absolution she wanted and understood now why she had never met his parents.

"Sometimes I wonder. But Steve did tell me he worshiped you and thought you were the most amazing person he had ever known. I think you were his life."

"He was mine, too." Sophia was so ashamed she wanted to sink into a hole.

It broke Sophia's heart that she had never known about any of this. Too late now. It didn't matter anymore.

She could not be dissuaded from returning to work with Paul and Tricia. She didn't want to be alone with her thoughts and regrets.

⌘

# CHAPTER 50

## Time and Chance

*"Profit is sweet, even if it comes from deception."*
-Sophocles

Sophia was up at seven. She made her own coffee, heartbroken that Steve would never again do his charming morning caffeine ritual. As she showered, she felt him and their memories wrap around her. She could not get dressed and out the front door fast enough. But even as she left, it was impossible for her to shake her associations.

\* \* \*

Sophia met with Derek and Rona when she got to the office.

"Thanks for supporting the Holt case," Sophia said. "But I just don't know how we can handle it without destroying the firm. I want Krause & White to survive . . . to thrive."

"That means a lot," Rona said.

"We all want the same thing. Success," Derek added.

"We decided Derek should be billing and bringing in new business," Rona said. "That's his strength."

"It is." Sophia was not merely stroking Derek's ego because what Rona said was true.

"Derek and I will cover each other's cases however we have to. And without Eddie, you're going to need Bryce. He's yours."

"But you'll be short-handed."

"We'll manage." Rona had worked her magic one more time. "We'll all put in more hours. I'm taking over Derek's summary judgment motion from Bryce and Tricia. If we have to borrow more money, we will. But that means our future rests on your gun trial."

"We just have to make it to the trial September 14," Sophia said. "I know it's a winner."

Sophia left Derek and Rona with that palpable lie. The Holt case was a loser unless something significant changed.

* * *

On July 14, Moschella called Sophia, and the gamesmanship escalated. He asked her to agree to continue the trial thirty days.

"No. We got a priority setting, and you've used that against me time and again. There's nothing that would justify me agreeing to that."

"My opposing counsel in another matter just got a priority setting ahead of yours. His client is seventy-five and on life support. That trumps the Holts."

"Someone else can defend that case."

"I wish that were true. It's a products liability case for the manufacture and sale of a defective heart valve against one of my oldest clients. I've tried these before. No one else here can get up to speed on the complex issues and technology in time."

"Then let someone else take the Holt case. From all those motions, it's obvious you have staffed this case with layers of lawyers, more than O'Rourke and Sandoval. We're keeping our trial date."

"We'll see. Since I knew what you'd say, I already had the clerk set a hearing tomorrow afternoon at four. I'll fax over the notice and the motion."

* * *

Sophia slammed the phone down and called a firmwide meeting.

"That's pure BS," Derek thundered. "He just wants to run up more costs and waste our attorney time."

"That's my take," Sophia said.

"It doesn't matter," Paul cautioned. "He has a good argument. Our clients aren't on life support. And you know Ortiz. Why oppose it?"

Sophia bridled. "We have to show Ortiz there's a game going on here."

"It's not a game if that plaintiff's lawyer brought the motion to advance the trial date," Tricia warned.

"Really?" Sophia said. "Don't be naïve. There's a good-old-boy club there, and Moschella's the ringleader. That plaintiff has probably been on life support for months, and conveniently thought to seek priority all of a sudden with Moschella's blessing?"

"That's a real stretch," Tricia said. "Even in Bakersfield. And that's not naïve."

"Sorry, Tricia," Sophia whispered.

"Don't worry about it. I'm as angry as you are."

"None of this matters," Derek said. "Sophia has to oppose this."

"I'll go with you tomorrow," Paul interjected.

Paul had an agenda for volunteering, and Sophia wasn't ready for the crosscurrents or to spend time alone with him.

"Thanks, Paul, but having two attorneys show up for this one would send the wrong signal to Ortiz. I want him to see that this really is a power play, Moschella's big firm trying to batter our little one. You're too valuable here."

Derek and Rona agreed.

\* \* \*

On Friday in Bakersfield, Sophia, as usual, had to wait for Moschella to appear. Then, she watched in consternation as Judge Ortiz expressed great sympathy for his two priority settings and none for Sophia, her firm, or the Holts.

After Moschella estimated his other trial would take three weeks, Ortiz moved the Holt trial to October 31, a Monday, and Halloween no less. He ordered all pretrial deadlines recalculated accordingly.

Sophia spread the news. Predictably the Holts were angry, and equally predictably her colleagues were not surprised.

Sophia waited out the rush hour at Uricchio's Trattoria on 17th Street near the courthouse. It was cheap and not crowded. She picked at her bland but huge Caesar salad until enough time passed. Then she jolted herself with a double espresso and headed home. As she left, she saw a gun shop called "Friendly Firearms" across from the restaurant. She was disgusted. She also was disgusted with her white Camry that looked tan with dirt and needed servicing.

She got back to L.A. late, tired, and depressed. She threw off her clothes and went straight to bed.

The only bright spot was that her team could use the extra time to go through more of the documents Sports Gear had dumped on them.

⌘

# CHAPTER 51

## Sandbagged

*"Always mislead, mystify and surprise
the enemy if possible."*
-Stonewall Jackson

Monday, July 17, after a heavy work weekend, the firm meeting was brief. Derek had picked up two new small housing cases for his regular clients that would generate some immediate and easy billables. Bryce, to everyone's surprise, brought in a noncontingency case for the vice president of a medium-sized entertainment startup. She wanted to sue her former employer for breach of her employment agreement and sexual harassment. She was able to pay costs and offered a decent retainer on top of that.

"I'll help you set up a meeting to get the client agreement signed and the retainer in," Derek offered.

It now looked like they might be able to weather the Holt storm despite the continuance.

* * *

When Sophia returned to her office, she had no sooner sat down than Peggy brought in the mail.

"Something big here in the Holt case." Peggy plopped down a huge pile of papers bound with a rubber band.

Sophia read the top page and then looked at the date on the delivery envelope. It was a motion for summary judgment or, in the alternative, for summary adjudication of issues.

"That snake!" Sophia yelled. "He got that continuance because he wasn't going to meet the cutoff date for making a summary judgment motion."

"What do you mean?" Peggy asked.

"I mean he had to serve it on us no later than one hundred and five days before the date the trial is set to begin. Today is exactly one hundred and five days before October 31 under the court's filing calculation rules. That continuance was no coincidence."

"That's dirty."

"Can you make three copies of this and distribute them? We've got to get on this."

"Sure."

Sophia immediately told her team as well as Derek and Rona. They shared her outrage, but it was a *fait accompli*.

\* \* \*

After Peggy got the team the copies to read and assess, they met in midafternoon to plan their opposition.

Paul was optimistic. "You know, for all the paper here, and despite their experts' declarations, what Moschella hangs his hat on is that *Jacoves* case. Without that, he has no legal argument because we do have disputed issues of fact. And your original memo destroyed the opinion that Justice Grignon authored."

"By the way, I dug up some background on *Jacoves*," Tricia said. "From county bar events I knew the clerk who drafted that opinion for Justice Grignon. I touched base with her."

"Do you have something that'll help?" Paul was intrigued.

"Sort of. The opinion is what the clerk drafted. All except for the holding."

"That makes sense," Sophia said. "Especially when you consider what subsequent cases say about it."

"Regardless, this is thorough and will take a ton of work to oppose." Paul brought them back to reality.

Of course, neither Paul nor anyone else at Krause & White knew that Moschella's firm hadn't prepared the summary judgment papers. As with all the Sports Gear filings in the Holt case, they were the behind-the-scenes work of Jackson, Hood & Lee.

"I know," Tricia said. "We have to eviscerate *Jacoves* and decide tactically how much of our case we have to reveal in the opposition to win. Do we want to tip our hand with all our experts we're going to use at trial or hold them in reserve?"

"We can't afford to hold anything back here," Sophia replied. "With Ortiz, to have any chance at all of a win, we need to hit Moschella with all we've got. We'll have to identify our experts soon anyway."

"I agree with Sophia," Paul added. "I'll take the lead on supervising the opposition."

"Good," Sophia said. "You've done more summary judgments than any of us."

"Hey, this is interesting," Bryce remarked. "The hearing is on September 26. If Moschella wasn't lying, that means he won't be able to argue the motion. He'll be in trial. Do you think that associate of his will? Would Sports Gear ever go for that?"

"Very astute," Paul said.

"I suspect dear old Tony will find some way to argue it," Sophia said. "Nothing that happens in Bakersfield surprises me anymore. Let's get going. Tricia, you prepare our expert declarations. You know where to focus. I'll work with you on them. Bryce, you update my memo and start on our points and authorities. Come to any of us with questions."

"I'll take the overall lead on this, prepare our opposing statement of disputed facts, and assemble the evidentiary exhibits," Paul said. "We have to file by September 12."

"I'll get declarations from the Holts," Sophia said. "And I'll finish up our supplemental discovery and respond to Sports Gear's final round of nonsense with all my 'free' time."

Gallows humor had become their norm.

They had to beat the summary judgment motion, or they would be left with nothing but an appeal. And, with the standards of review at the appellate court, that was nothing at all.

\* \* \*

Paul, the most seasoned litigator of them all, acutely felt the time crunch. Besides now being the lead on the summary judgment opposition, he had to simultaneously prepare for and take the last two witness depositions: the Sports Gear store's manager, Arnie Davis, a crucial one; and its assistant store clerk Brandon Gallo, likely a non-event.

The depositions were set for the following week. They would be in the morning on that Tuesday and Wednesday, again in Bakersfield and naturally at Moschella's offices.

Paul knew Davis was a strong company man. He would come in not just well-prepared but unshakeable. From the poor-quality store video, it appeared to him that neither Davis nor Gallo had been involved in the actual sale. With Davis, he would have to focus on Sports Gear's policies in general, its policies at its Bakersfield store, its training program, store sales procedures, and sales history. With Gallo, he only had to cover his brief encounter with Mike in the store aisle. There was little or nothing else.

\* \* \*

Paul drove up to Bakersfield Tuesday morning and arrived at Quarry, Warren & Moschella about fifteen minutes before the deposition. The receptionist called Theresa Sandoval.

When the elevator opened, Theresa walked toward Paul with her long black hair framing her stunning face, which was set off by red lipstick, simple gold earrings, and a thin gold chain hanging down to her deep V-necked white blouse. An elegant navy skirt snugged her hips, and her legs appeared even longer with her black Gucci heels.

"Hello, Mr. Viola." She disarmed him with a smile. "I hope your drive up was pleasant."

"It was fine. Will you be defending Mr. Davis at the deposition?"

"No, but I'll be there to assist Mr. Moschella and Mr. O'Rourke."

"Mr. O'Rourke?"

"Yes. Another partner here on the case. A full house just for you. Shall we head up to the conference room?"

As they went up the elevator, Paul remembered that Sophia had encountered O'Rourke at the Spangler deposition, and Tricia had lost a motion to him earlier in the case. They got off the same floor and went to the same conference room where Eddie and Sophia had taken the Grimick and Spangler depositions. Paul met O'Rourke, a red-nosed red-haired overweight man with squinty eyes who perfectly, and unfortunately, fit Tricia's description. Paul was not impressed.

Paul started the deposition with unyielding, perfectly formulated questions to which there could be no sustainable objections.

Too bad the answers were useless. Davis was everything Paul had feared—very well coached and unflappable. His responses were terse and noncommittal. He insisted that Sports Gear trained everyone in the proper way to sell all of its merchandise. He stated that Grimick and Spangler were veterans in selling guns as well as fully versed in all applicable laws, background search requirements, and the necessary customer safety training and waiting periods. Paul grilled him about talking to Mike in the aisle, referring to the video. Davis was dismissive. He said Mike misunderstood him when Mike showed him his pockets were empty and he hadn't shoplifted anything. After an apology everything was fine. He did acknowledge speaking to Wallace Holt but denied saying anything Wallace had claimed he had. He admitted he had said he *wished* he had known something was wrong, but that he said that out of sympathy for Wallace. He saw nothing strange or odd in Mike's behavior either in the store or outside. He denied speaking to anyone about the altercation between Eddie and Grimick besides Sports Gear's lawyers. Moschella instructed him to answer no questions about those conversations based on the attorney-client privilege.

Despite trying to get at Davis every way he could, Paul finally called the deposition early at around four. He checked into his room at the midrange Best Western on Truxtun Avenue. Then he reported to Sophia.

"Hi, Paul. What's the good news?"

"There isn't any. Davis isn't Grimick or Spangler. He was a perfectly trained monkey. I couldn't shake him. Nothing to use for our summary judgment opposition, and he won't help us if we go to trial either."

"Well, if you couldn't get anything out of him, no one here would have. At least he's committed on the record. If anything surprising turns up, he won't be able to back away from his testimony without committing perjury."

"Small consolation. Would you mind calling the Holts and giving them the recap? I'm tired, hungry, and want to do some prep for Brandon's depo tomorrow. He's still kind of an enigma to me."

"Sure. Happy to do it. Well, not exactly happy. I hope I get Wallace. Beth will just turn on the waterworks."

"Better you than me. Say, I met that O'Rourke guy who sat in on the Spangler deposition. He was with Moschella and Sandoval, but didn't say anything on the record, just whispered to Moschella several times."

"I'll have to look him up. I forgot with everything else we have going. All I know is he's on the case, but they don't put him out front much. Just an extra guy on depos and the one hearing with Tricia. Maybe he's their motions guy. Kind of creepy, though."

"More than creepy. No wonder he's not a front man. Look, I need some dinner."

"Something light, I'm sure," Sophia laughed.

"You know me too well. I found a place called the Hungry Hunter on the Internet over on the Rosedale Highway. It has good reviews for prime rib."

"Say no more. Go eat. I'll deal with the Holts."

Sophia called the Holts, and, just her luck, she got Beth. Wallace was tinkering in their garage. She endured Beth's sobbing about "her Mike" and about the stress the lawsuit was causing them. Eventually, Sophia got her off the phone. An hour of her life she would never get back.

At the Hungry Hunter, Paul realized he was exactly that—hungry. He ordered big and ate big, but just as he was about to finish with a Mountain High Mudd pie, he saw Davis being seated at the other side of the restaurant. Not wanting a repeat of the scene at Noriega's, he quickly asked for the check, left cash, and hurried out before Davis spotted him.

Back in his hotel room, Paul reviewed documents, the Sports Gear video he had on his laptop to use in the depositions, and his notes from the Davis deposition session. He turned in about midnight.

* * *

Paul woke at seven-thirty, got ready, packed up, and checked out. He headed straight for the 24<sup>th</sup> Street Café in downtown Bakersfield. The hotel manager said it served a good breakfast.

It turned out to be a funky, retro diner in a semi-industrial part of the city but was crowded anyway. He got a booth and coffee from a friendly waitress whose nametag said "Nancy Anne." The smile made up for the marginal coffee.

After his dinner protein extravaganza, and having missed dessert, he ordered the pumpkin pancakes. They were superb, and the serving was so large that even he couldn't finish it. Well-fueled, he drove the short distance to Stockdale Tower.

* * *

At Quarry, Warren & Moschella, Paul went through the same drill as he had the day before. Except this time, if possible, Theresa Sandoval looked even more beautiful with a sunburst smile and wearing a Thorne & Chase-worthy green Hugo Boss sleeveless sheath dress. It really didn't matter what she wore. In fact, Paul thought before he could stop himself, it would be better if she were wearing nothing at all.

"Good morning, Ms. Sandoval. Ready for round two?"

"I am. How about you? Get a good night's sleep?"

"Good enough."

Was he dreaming, or was she flirting with him? He decided he was just confusing desire for reality.

"Same place as yesterday?"

"Yes. Follow me."

Just then, he would have followed her off a cliff if she wanted. When they arrived, Paul was surprised to see only the court reporter and the witness, Brandon Gallo.

"Not getting a crowd today?"

"Sorry, Mr. Viola. Just me, I'm afraid."

Evidently, Gallo was not considered a pivotal witness by Moschella either. He had handed the depo over to his associate. According to all the written discovery responses, Gallo wasn't near during the sale to Mike. He was sweeping up and restocking. That's obviously why Sports Gear trusted Sandoval to defend the deposition alone.

Paul started slowly with general background questions, to put Gallo at ease and hopefully off-guard. Then he would hit him with questions about the day Mike bought the shotgun. He expected nothing but was programmed to try.

Brandon had barely graduated from Bakersfield's lower-socioeconomic-class South High School. His Rebel football career ended his freshman year there. His father was an auto mechanic with no high school diploma; his mother, a waitress at the VIP Lounge on California Avenue where she met Brandon's father, got pregnant, then married him and quit to be a housewife.

Brandon always hunted with his father, and his senior year he joined South High's Junior ROTC. He liked both the uniforms and the rifles, even if they weren't loaded. He had joined the NGA as a junior member at fourteen and was now a regular member along with all of his friends.

When he graduated, he got his job at Sports Gear thanks to his friendship with Joe Spangler that had developed during the years he had been buying ammunition and other hunting supplies there. Brandon liked working there and hoped to become a gun salesman someday.

After an hour of the mundane, Paul had lulled Sandoval into being a quiet observer, as he had planned. Then, he headed into the day Mike bought the shotgun.

"So, Mr. Gallo, you were there when Mike Holt bought the shotgun from the Sports Gear employees Mr. Grimick and Mr. Spangler, correct?"

"Objection, vague. What do you mean by 'there,' Mr. Viola?" Sandoval was paying attention after all.

After another round of objections, Paul established that Brandon was in the store, had spoken to Mike in the aisle, and that Mike acted normally when Brandon asked him if he needed any help finding anything.

Despite laborious and painful volleys of his questions and Sandoval's annoying but well-taken objections, Paul was unable to establish that Brandon was anywhere close when Mike was buying the shotgun. He said he heard and observed nothing. Brandon kept repeating that he had been busy sweeping and restocking.

Paul tried to get at him regarding his training in the sale of guns, the policies of Sports Gear USA, all the things he had tried with Davis. That went nowhere either. Brandon was a new assistant clerk who stocked and cleaned and helped customers with small items. He didn't sell guns and hadn't been given any training in gun sales.

Paul decided to keep the deposition going, as much to punish Gallo and Sandoval as anything else. It was that or drive back too early only to get stuck in the middle of the L.A. rush hour.

Finally, at six o'clock, Sandoval called a halt.

"Your seven hours are up, Mr. Viola. That's it."

"That's all I have anyway."

The only thing Paul had learned in the deposition was that the charming Ms. Sandoval was more serpent than siren. And far more dangerous than any of them had thought.

* * *

Paul had noted one potentially useful thing: Gallo had seemed shifty and hesitant. He couldn't put his finger on why. Maybe it was because he was just a kid. He wished they'd had the funds to videotape the deposition. Moschella's firm would clearly spend more time preparing him for trial, and he would never come across that way again.

Paul drove home with no stops for food and made it over the Grapevine into the tail end of the L.A. rush hour. He replayed both depositions in his mind. He had gotten nothing, and it seemed there was nothing to get.

They were in trouble. He called Sophia to tell her. Now everything rode on beating Moschella's summary judgment motion with what they had. It wouldn't be easy.

⌘

# CHAPTER 52

## Paper is Pitiless

*"Simplicity is the ultimate sophistication."*
-Clare Booth Luce

The team worked frenetically through July and August both to prepare for trial, meet the pretrial deadlines, and file the summary judgment opposition papers.

Even though Paul was adept at crafting opposing statements of disputed fact, they were time-consuming and tedious to write. The courts had ridiculous technical rules about columns, labels, spacing, how evidence was to be cited, and a thousand other things. Summary judgment motions were often long and hard to digest. The court clerks delighted in tossing papers, either moving or opposing, for the tiniest deviations from the often absurd and always-onerous formal technical paperwork rules. Anything to make things tougher for the lawyers.

Bryce was doing very well drafting the opposition brief based on Sophia's memo. She helped him locate a good Kansas case finding gun sellers liable with a fact pattern similar to Mike's. There were also several other helpful persuasive state cases, in Georgia, Wisconsin, Massachusetts, and, interestingly, in Arkansas, Texas, and Florida as well. And some from the United States Court of Appeals for the Ninth Circuit, which had jurisdiction over California.

None had an identical factual situation to Mike's. But that would have been a long shot because this was a cutting-edge, evolving area of gun law liability.

Bryce also impressed everyone, particularly Derek and Rona, by making the time to do billable work on his own clients. He wasn't as bright as Eddie had been, but he had a great work ethic, an overall drive to succeed, a belief in their firm, and a knack for getting business. He would have been an asset anywhere. It was unfortunate that it had been Eddie's death that both challenged him to excel and gave him the opportunity to do so.

During breaks, they all took turns sifting through the endless piles of Sports Gear documents and tried to make sense of all the computerized information dumped on them as well.

* * *

From the sidelines, Ben Kowrilsky continued to get out stories relating to the case. He was helped because of the ongoing national nightmare of gun violence. There were shootings and suicides on almost a daily basis.

A little close to home for Ben, a disgruntled newscaster, who had been fired from a TV station in Kentucky, killed two of the other broadcasters on live TV with a Glock 19 pistol, which had a 15-shot magazine. Then he went home and killed himself with a shotgun. Police were being gunned down with increasing frequency. And black people, often for nothing more than a glance, faced death nearly every day across America from the badged police in blue, or tan, or green.

* * *

Ben made Steve an ongoing story about a detective who cared about gun violence and ultimately became its victim. He also wrote about Derek's brothers, so different, both also victims of the scourge. Nor did he fail to remind readers about Mike Holt and the thousands of other Mike Holts out there. He always asked in his coverage whether there was anything to be done about them. And if not, why?

Sophia appreciated his news coverage and stories. They helped keep her case in the public eye.

* * *

Probably the biggest and best surprise for Sophia's team came from their experts. Focusing on the need to deal with *Jacoves*, Tricia had worked with Dr. Mapes and Dirk Savage to draft two compelling declarations in opposition to the summary judgment motion.

In his declaration Dr. Mapes described the prevalence of undiagnosed mental illness in our society. He also stated the potential suicide warning signs that people of ordinary intelligence, like gun sellers, should be able to recognize and act upon. Savage took that a step further. He cited various private gun store trade associations around the country that had adopted these warning signs in guidelines, stronger than current laws, to restrict gun sales. Sophia had read about these guidelines before. In Savage's opinion, so many retailers had adopted them that it was now the recognized custom and practice in the industry and certainly its "best practices."

With those declarations and Bryce's research, Sophia and the team crafted a truly persuasive opposition brief.

In the end, its simplicity was its greatest strength. Guns were by definition ultrahazardous products. Gun stores, by custom and practice, had heightened responsibilities in selling them, beyond background checks and waiting periods and beyond the ordinary standard of care that governed the sale of less dangerous products. Sophia's team showed that Sports Gear had failed to comply with any of those commonly accepted heightened responsibilities. Their evidence for its deficiencies in those areas came from the declaration of Wallace Holt and some of Spangler's deposition testimony. In addition, of course, Wallace's declaration and his deposition testimony created at a minimum a question of fact about his conversations with Davis, Grimick, and Spangler concerning how Mike looked and acted the day he bought the shotgun.

When September 12 came, they filed their opposition papers with pride. On September 21, five days before the hearing, they received Moschella's reply papers. They were uncharacteristically sparse and evasive. Sports Gear filed some formal objections to the declarations and evidence Paul had referenced but offered no additional evidence of its own. The Holt team was startled. But they weren't sorry. They were relieved.

*  *  *

The weekend before the hearing, all the Krause & White attorneys participated in a mock summary judgment argument, including Derek and Rona. Sophia practiced the argument. Rona acted as Ortiz. Derek, Paul, and Bryce took turns being Moschella. They incorporated the local bias Ortiz had consistently displayed and focused on the legal issues. Sophia honed her arguments until she felt Ortiz would have no option but to deny the motion and let the case go to trial on the merits.

Everyone at the firm knew the best thing they had going for them was California's historic hostility to summary judgment motions, which were viewed as a device to deny parties their ultimate "day in court," meaning a trial. The downside was that these days lazy judges, whose caseloads had grown, sometimes granted them as a way to clear their calendars of trials. When they did, parties often gave up because appeals could take years and were not guaranteed to succeed.

Fortunately, nothing Sophia's team had uncovered themselves, or with Ben Kowrilsky's help, indicated that Judge Ortiz was one of those lazy judges. Would he be fair? That was an altogether different question.

⌘

# CHAPTER 53

## Mashed Potatoes

*"Of all the causes which conspire to blind*
*Man's erring judgment, and misguide the mind,*
*What the weak head with strongest bias rules,*
*Is pride, the never-failing vice of fools."*
-Alexander Pope

The weekdays before the Holt summary judgment hearing were a crisis time at both firms with the trial prep and motions, but particularly at Quarry, Warren & Moschella. Moschella's heart valve trial was in full swing.

After his trial was over for the day, he called Sandoval and O'Rourke into his office to update them on the two critical cases he was juggling.

"I filed and served the reply papers Jackson, Hood & Lee drafted for our summary judgment motion," O'Rourke said. "They weren't very impressive, to be honest."

"We have a decision to make. Obviously, I'm in trial and can't argue it." Moschella was running on that adrenaline high fueling all attorneys in trial. "I couldn't prep enough to do it even if I could persuade the heart valve judge to give me that day off. Who will . . ."

O'Rourke interrupted, "Argue it? That's a no-brainer. Me."

"That's what I need to discuss."

"There's no discussion necessary. I did our experts' declarations, and I've been our point person on the legal issues from the beginning. Besides, I'm a partner. Sports Gear deserves no less for a hearing as important as this one."

Moschella looked at his partner with studied neutrality—and not for the first time. O'Rourke was slumped in the chair in his usual unkempt suit and, this time, with a stained tie. He was good with paper and legal analysis. Good in the back room. A grinder. Not a finder of clients, not a minder of clients, and not a great, or even very skilled, public speaker. Unfortunately, he possessed a disproportionate and highly developed ego.

"Riley, I agree," Moschella lied. "Ordinarily that would make sense. But I have talked at length with Tom Jackson about this, and, as you know, he's calling the shots. No pun intended. He wants Theresa to handle the hearing. Alone."

"What? She's a junior associate. You've got to be kidding me." He got louder and angrier. "No way did Jackson tell you that. I'll call him myself."

"Well, I can't stop you, but it would be bad for you and for the firm. If you'll calm down, I can explain."

"What is there that could possibly explain an insult like this?"

"Will you listen, Riley? Just for five minutes?"

"Why should I?" O'Rourke's face was as red as his hair and contorted, but he fought to control himself. "All right. Okay. I'll listen to your supposed rationale for something this insane."

Theresa, looking beautiful as always, stared at her feet, avoiding the fray but happy and proud. She had never seen partners go at it like this. It wasn't their firm culture as she had come to know it. She didn't care. She just didn't want to lose the chance to argue this major motion on such a high-profile case. It was a career-making opportunity for her.

"Thank you. As I said, this is straight from Jackson, not from me."

"First, that's bullshit."

"Riley, listen. Listen hard. Jackson has had one of his people present in court for almost every appearance we've made in front of Ortiz. Even I didn't know that until this past weekend."

"He's spying on us?"

Theresa jerked her head up, equally surprised.

"I wouldn't call it that. They're just very protective of their gun clients and their cases. Gun litigation is Jackson's specialty. He said they routinely monitor all of the local law firms they use. It's their call. In the end, it's his and his firm's reputation on the line. They pay the bills, or Sports Gear does through them, and they can do what the hell they want."

"That's not collegial or ethical," O'Rourke said.

"It is what it is. Anyway, they have assessments on all of us from various observers."

"What a bunch of sneaky bastards."

"Maybe. But Jackson and his firm agree we already have an inside track with Ortiz, being the local folks. They just want to gild the lily, if you will. Since I can't be there, they think their best chance is with Theresa. She's good. And, forgive me here, Theresa, but they also think Judge Ortiz has a thing for you. They want to use it."

While he was being truthful, Moschella was also trying to mollify O'Rourke and let him salvage a bit of his dignity and pride. He forgot that in doing so he was insulting Theresa.

"What, I'm supposed to flash my tits at him or something?" Theresa blew up. "What I *say* doesn't matter, how I *look* does? Winning through ogling?"

Now Moschella had two pissed-off lawyers to mollify and no time to do it.

O'Rourke scoffed, "I guess I can accept losing out to Miss Perky over there if that's all she is to them."

Theresa was seething. Sure, she used her looks. They were one of her tools. But she wasn't about to let the graveyard-worthy lump of male sitting next to her ridicule her for them.

"No, Theresa. Hardly that. Just be you. Being yourself is far more than how you look. I read the Gallo deposition. Your defense was brilliant. You got the best of Viola, a far more experienced attorney with a mega-firm background. You can hold your own in legal combat, young lady."

Theresa settled down, but O'Rourke sat stonily, unsatisfied.

"There is one other thing, and it stays in this room," Moschella lowered his voice. "Our firm hasn't generated much in fees in this case so far. Jackson's firm has kept the real work to themselves except for court appearances and depositions. If we were to lose this summary judgment motion, and of course I'm not saying we want to, the case would likely go to trial and get us a bigger payday and more publicity."

O'Rourke looked thoughtful. Sandoval was horrified.

"You want me to do my best to win, don't you?" she asked. "We have the law on our side, and if we save Sports Gear from a trial, won't that get us more business from them?"

"Yes, the law is with us, Theresa. As to more business, Sports Gear hasn't had any legal work here before, and I'm not counting on any after. Better a nice fee now than the faint hope of more later."

"You're both overlooking the real problem if we lose and go to trial," O'Rourke said, dismissing Sandoval's observations and Moschella's responses. "The Holts's lawyers will find out Spangler 'resigned' because he lied about his criminal record and his illegal gun sales when they hired him."

After his deposition, and then the incident with Eddie Herrera, Sports Gear had decided to get rid of Spangler. However, at Jackson's insistence, they let him "resign" rather than being fired, and gave him a six-months'-pay severance package in return for an ironclad confidentiality agreement. That would not stop him from getting a trial subpoena, but it would keep him away from the media and from volunteering any information before then. He was their weak link with a drug-fried, boozed-up brain.

"Riley's right, but it won't be the end of the world. We have other witnesses. So think of this as me taking some pressure off of you, Theresa. Prepare well, present well, and let the fates take care of the rest. I've got to get back to my heart valve trial."

Theresa and Riley got up and left, Sandoval excited about the honor and challenge, O'Rourke chafing at his perceived demotion.

* * *

Back at Krause & White, Sophia decided that in fairness, the whole team should attend the summary judgment hearing. The Holt case had been their lives—and deaths. This hearing would determine whether their case would remain viable or be tossed out of court with only the daunting prospects of an appeal remaining.

The entire team left at six the morning of the hearing. Paul drove. For once, the hearing was in the morning, but only because Ortiz's clerk had set it on the nine o'clock September 26 law and motion calendar. They were all surprised Moschella had not finagled the clerk into setting it at the worst traffic time for them, as usual.

Sophia's crew was silent on the drive over the Grapevine. Paul put on a classical music station simply to fill the air with something that wouldn't interfere with Sophia's mental preparation or his own. He also turned on the air as they approached Bakersfield. They had decided that Sophia and Paul would sit at the counsel table. Tricia and Bryce would sit behind the bar in the gallery with the other lawyers and witnesses in attendance on law and motion days.

At eight-thirty, they parked in the lot near the courthouse. When they got out of the car, a blast of hot air hit them. It was late September, but it was still going to be a ninety-plus-degree day. Bakersfield liked its heat and held on to it as long as it could.

There were no demonstrators or news crews around. China and Taiwan trumped lesser news stories like the Holt case. They were toying with war over the ownership of some obscure hunks of rock in the South China Sea. There were also forty wildfires raging throughout California, with over two hundred thousand acres burned and no end in sight.

The team met Beth and Wallace outside Judge Ortiz's courtroom. She was apprehensive. He was detached. The only commitment he had left was to getting back the money they had spent. If the case ended that day, given the practical realities, there would be no appeal—and probably no Krause & White.

After a little client tending, Sophia sent them to the Starbucks near the courthouse to wait for a report from her. They had made the tactical decision not to have the Holts in the courtroom for the hearing because their reactions were too unpredictable. Better to keep them away from Judge Ortiz until the trial, and from any further exposure to Sports Gear's lawyers.

* * *

The courtroom was about three-quarters full with lawyers, clients, and witnesses waiting for their cases to be called.

Sports Gear's summary judgment motion was third on the docket, behind a demurrer hearing on a lawsuit over an easement for irrigation, and a request for a permanent injunction to stop a billboard company from erecting signs over a local cemetery. Those hearings were brief. The demurrer was overruled; the injunction was granted. Sophia and her team tried to glean a few more clues about Judge Ortiz from his reactions to the arguments the lawyers made. There wasn't much to glean.

Smart lawyers paid close attention to matters heard before theirs on law and motion days, not only to see what kinds of arguments appealed to the judge but also to observe the judge's demeanor on that particular day. Judges were human, after all. Something that might work with them one day could put them off on another—depending on how things were at home, what the judge had for breakfast, or how the stock market was doing.

The waiting was over now.

⌘

# CHAPTER 54

## All Riley'd Up

*"We never know what stupidity is*
*until we have experimented on ourselves."*
-Paul Gauguin

Judge Ortiz's clerk called the Holt case. Sophia and Paul saw Sandoval go to the defense counsel table alone without Moschella. This confirmed their speculation, if not their expectation, that he wasn't doing the argument. He really was stuck in the heart valve trial. Sophia and Paul took their seats at the familiar counsel table.

Each side stated their names and appearances for the record. Sandoval stood to begin her argument just as O'Rourke raced up the aisle, through the gate to the well.

"Riley O'Rourke for Quarry, Warren & Moschella, Your Honor, representing Sports Gear USA."

His belated entrance annoyed the judge, who had been appreciating Sandoval in her striking black skirt, pearl white blouse that left little to the imagination, and onyx earrings and necklace.

"I expect attorneys to be on time, Mr. O'Rourke."

"Yes, Your Honor. I'm sorry. There was a traffic accident on my way here, or I'd have been here early."

"Very well. All of you take your seats. I have a tentative ruling." Judge Ortiz shuffled through his papers to find his tentative ruling.

"Thank you, Your Honor."

They all sat. There had been no tentative ruling on the docket sheet posted outside the courtroom.

Sandoval glanced at O'Rourke. He wasn't supposed to be there. It was not their agreed strategy as to Ortiz—to keep him focused on her arguments coming from a beautiful, alluring package.

Sandoval whispered to O'Rourke, "What are you doing here?"

"Tony only said you were going to argue the motion. He never said I shouldn't be here. I want to make sure nothing goes wrong."

Sandoval was angry. She had never liked O'Rourke or the way he leered at her on the sly. As if she would ever let a creature like him get near her.

Judge Ortiz cleared his throat. "Before me is the motion for summary judgment and/or summary adjudication of issues brought by defendant Sports Gear USA against the plaintiffs, Beth and Wallace Holt, in their action for wrongful death, negligence, and the negligent infliction of emotional distress. I have carefully reviewed the moving and opposing papers, and for the reasons set forth in the moving papers, my inclination is to grant the defendant's motion for summary adjudication on the cause of action for the negligent infliction of emotional distress, but I am prepared to hear arguments on that and on the balance of the motion."

Sophia was surprised. She had expected the tentative ruling to be against them on all counts. Something was apparently bothering Ortiz. She wasn't sure whether she should argue first or whether Ortiz wanted to hear from Sandoval first. He quickly resolved that quandary.

"Since I am undecided on the bulk of the defendant's motion, I'll hear from counsel for the moving party."

Sandoval quickly rose from her chair. "Thank you, Your Honor. If I may be heard?"

Ortiz did not hide his open pleasure at the sight before him.

"Of course, Ms. Sandoval. Please proceed."

"Your Honor, as our papers demonstrate, my client and its sales personnel followed the law to the letter. As the moving and opposition papers show, it is undisputed that Michael Holt was of legal age to buy a shotgun, that he was qualified to do so under California law, and that Mr. Grimick and Mr. Spangler followed the policies and procedures of Sports Gear and all applicable laws in making the sale. Guns are not viewed as ultrahazardous chattels in California, and gun sellers are not required to be psychiatrists in dealing with their customers. We agree with Your Honor as to the plaintiffs' cause of action for the negligent infliction of emotional distress. That fails for lack of duty. The Holts, aside from their son, had no contact with Sports Gear on the day in question, and it owed them no duty of care or otherwise."

"Well, Ms. Sandoval," Judge Ortiz interrupted. "Wouldn't you concede that even if guns are not viewed as ultrahazardous, their very nature imposes on gun sellers the very highest standard of care?"

"Of course, Your Honor. But that standard was met here as to the two remaining causes of action."

"The plaintiffs' expert Mr. Savage makes a persuasive case, particularly for the purposes of opposing the summary judgment motion, that the current custom and practice in the gun trade, or to use a popular buzz phrase, the 'best practices,' involve having suicide prevention materials on display in gun stores. And, even absent that, erring on the side of not selling a gun to someone if there is any doubt about that person's state of mind or competence."

Before Sandoval could respond, O'Rourke leaped to his feet.

"Your Honor, you aren't at liberty to consider that in California. The *Jacoves* case is dispositive. The purchaser there was confused, distraught, trembling. Justice Grignon ruled that was not enough to survive a demurrer, much less a summary judgment motion, and she and her panel at the appellate court unanimously affirmed the dismissal of the complaint."

Ortiz was annoyed at O'Rourke's unorthodox intervention. He was also displeased because he had anticipated a legal explanation by the fetching Ms. Sandoval. Instead, he was being *told* what he could and could not do by a latter-day incarnation of Ichabod Crane. A fatter version.

"Mr. O'Rourke, *Jacoves* has been cited almost entirely in support of dissents around the country and, as the plaintiffs point out in their opposing brief, it's not controlling law. It's clear to me that the holding there is at odds with the precedents cited in the opinion. Frankly, I find that difficult to reconcile. It appears the panel changed its mind without finding supportive authority . . . or just ruled the way it wanted to rule despite the authoritative cases it cited."

O'Rourke was over his head. He hadn't read the subsequent case history. His face flushed red with anger. This judge was a local boy. He was supposed to be in their corner, and this hearing was supposed to be perfunctory.

"It doesn't matter, Judge Ortiz. It's controlling law. You have no discretion."

"Mr. O'Rourke." The judge's face darkened as he icily eyed this lawyer presuming to lecture him. "Precedent does not control if it's not based on good authority or if there are numerous persuasive conflicting cases. In that situation, which is what we have here, as the judge it is up to me to decide what law to follow. As you know, summary judgments are strongly disfavored in California. Unless it is absolutely clear that there are no material issues of fact and that the moving party is entitled to judgment as a matter of law . . . *applicable, compelling, supported law* . . . my duty is to deny the motion and let the case proceed to trial."

"If you do that here, you'll be wrong, Your Honor, and you'll be reversed on appeal if we go to trial and our client loses."

O'Rourke slammed his hand on the table. O'Rourke didn't care about making more fees for the firm with a trial. He wanted to show up Moschella and win, as a lawyer, not because some sexpot got a horny judge going.

"You're verging on contempt, counsel. Watch your conduct." Judge Ortiz's anger was palpable and rising.

Sophia and Paul were fascinated. They had no idea what was happening. But they were definitely enjoying the show.

"Since you seem to have taken over the argument for Sports Gear, have you anything else to add?"

"I've said all that needs saying, Your Honor. And all that matters." With that, O'Rourke sat down.

*Well, he blew that big-time*, Sandoval thought in consternation, as she sat too.

Judge Ortiz looked over to Paul and Sophia. "Your turn, Ms. Christopoulos. That is, assuming *you'll* be speaking for the plaintiffs today."

"Thank you, Your Honor. I will be. Let me first address the undisputed fact that Sports Gear let Mike Holt take that shotgun out of its store in violation of the required ten-day waiting period in California between the purchase and delivery of all firearms."

"I'm going to stop you right there, Ms. Christopoulos. Didn't Mike Holt own a gun before he bought the shotgun from Sports Gear, a .22 rifle?"

"He did, Your Honor, but . . ."

"He also passed the required background check?"

"Yes."

"Judge Ishii of our Eastern District Federal Court in the *Silvester* case ruled that the ten-day waiting period for prior gun owners who passed background checks is unconstitutional in violation of the Second Amendment. Do you disagree?"

"No, Your Honor, but *Silvester* is on appeal to the Ninth Circuit . . ."

"Ms. Christopoulos, do you honestly expect me, a California state judge, to refuse to follow the holding of a federal judge in my own geographical area about a federal constitutional right?"

"But if he's overturned, Your Honor . . ."

"It won't have any impact on this case or sales of guns by Sports Gear or anyone else that complied with his opinion while the appeal was pending. As it is a matter of law, I do not expect to see evidence or argument about this waiting period if this case goes to trial. Am I clear?"

"Yes, Your Honor."

Sophia hastily regrouped.

"May I address the balance of Sports Gear's motion, your Honor"

"Briefly, please."

"We too believe the holding in *Jacoves* is wrong. Moreover, the cases it cites support our position, as Your Honor has noted. Beyond that, our evidence shows that Mike Holt was more obviously disturbed than the man there, who was confused, distraught and trembling when buying his shotgun. Mike did nothing normal for a gun purchaser. He wanted the cheapest shotgun, wanted to buy one round of ammunition, didn't ask anything about the use of the shotgun, declined a gun case for it, and, according to Wallace Holt, the salesmen and the manager thought Mike was 'crazy', had a strange look in his eyes, and that they should have known something was wrong. All of that is enough to create triable issues of fact, which is all we have to do to defeat the motion."

Judge Ortiz's body language told Sophia to quit while she was ahead on that issue.

"What about the negligent infliction of emotional distress cause of action, Ms. Christopoulos? Isn't Ms. Sandoval right about the law there?"

"Your Honor, we contend that gun sellers confronting someone behaving like Mike Holt do indeed owe a legal duty to third-party loved ones and others likely to be affected by the suicide of the gun purchaser. They can't assume the buyer is alone and unattached to any other human being. And given that, as Your Honor also noted, gun sellers are held to the highest standard of care in selling their products, the law should not excuse them when the profit motive trumps common sense in a gun sale."

The judge looked at Sophia and thought for a long moment. Of course, he did not mind watching the lovely Sophia either. She did not exude Sandoval's raw sexuality, but she was certainly equally mesmerizing, and he very much appreciated that she had a superlative legal mind and argued with respect and deference, unlike O'Rourke.

"Ms. Christopoulos, I have considered this in depth, and I just don't see that gun sellers owe a duty to unidentified third parties with whom they have had no contact. The case law doesn't support imposing that kind of duty, and it would effectively make them insurers, or force them to avoid selling guns in almost all circumstances. That goes too far. I'll take the motion under submission. You'll get my written ruling when it's ready."

"Thank you, Your Honor."

Judge Ortiz called the next matter. The attorneys collected their things and vacated the tables for the next attorneys.

As Sandoval slipped by O'Rourke at the table , she whispered, "You lost that for us."

"You watch your mouth. And remember your place. You're just an associate."

Sandoval ignored him and angrily stalked off down the hall. O'Rourke followed leisurely behind her, an unwarranted and undeserved smile on his face that proved how utterly obtuse and arrogant he was.

* * *

Sophia and Paul joined Tricia and Bryce as they left the courtroom. In the lobby downstairs, they passed by Sandoval, who was on her cellphone. What she was saying was inaudible, but her tone and demeanor were full of fury. O'Rourke was nowhere to be seen.

"Wow, that went way better than we expected," Bryce said once they were outside the courthouse. "Great job, Sophia. After the O'Rourke train wreck, you were the picture of poise and composure. You sure obliterated the local-lawyer halo effect."

Sophia looked at the brash young lawyer with some amusement.

"Thank you, but I think the local lawyer obliterated it himself. Moschella and his firm are going to be in hot water for this one, but, knock on wood, we need the judge's final ruling before we start celebrating."

"We know we lost the emotional distress claim," Paul interjected. "But from what he said, I think the others are solid."

"That emotional distress claim was always a long shot," Tricia said. "If we keep the negligence and wrongful death claims alive, that's all we need. Those are the key ones."

They all went down to the Starbucks where the Holts were waiting outside at a table in the ever-warming summer air. As they walked back to the courthouse parking lot and their cars, Sophia gave them an abbreviated but justifiably upbeat report. Or so she thought. After hearing that they had lost on the emotional distress claim, Beth got very upset. Sophia had made the right call not to have the Holts in the courtroom.

"You mean our distress over Mike's suicide means nothing?" Beth started to tear up, as usual.

"No, Beth, not at all," Sophia explained as they stood by their cars on the hot black asphalt. "It just means that the judge doesn't think Sports Gear has a duty to people who are not customers or have some other direct relationship with the store. If he lets our negligence and wrongful death claims go forward, your damages will still include the emotional distress and trauma Mike's suicide caused both of you."

She looked at Wallace, who stood staring in the distance. He said nothing.

All in all, it was a win, or so they guardedly hoped. It was early yet, only eleven o'clock. A good part of the workday would remain when they returned to their offices.

They said their goodbyes to the Holts, and chatted all the way back to Los Angeles. It was a good day. Paul put on a country music station this time, in an ironic tribute to Bakersfield. It heralded the problems of average folks with Merle Haggard's unique Bakersfield Sound, as well as new stars who whined of miseries they never experienced. Tricia even sang along to a couple of Taylor Swift songs. The others wisely chose to listen, not trusting their own vocal abilities.

When they got back to Krause & White, they were all enthused. They hammered away at their trial preparation. Judge Ortiz's written ruling would come to them by email. They believed their continued work was not going to be pointless. They had to keep doing it regardless. The weight of the upcoming trial was bearing down on them, and it looked like it would happen.

⌘

# CHAPTER 55

## When Irish Eyes Aren't Smiling

*"Idleness and pride tax with a heavier hand than kings and governments."*
-Benjamin Franklin

After O'Rourke blindsided her in court, Sandoval spent the rest of the day holed up in her office. She was worried, confused, and very unsure what to do. Moschella was still at his trial, and she had no one else to whom she could vent. Whatever else he might be, O'Rourke was indeed a partner, and she was an associate. She simply kept her door closed and worked on other cases to distract her from the morning's disaster.

She also started wondering whether this was the firm for her. She had returned to Bakersfield to be near her parents. She could have gotten a job with a big firm in L.A. or in San Francisco with her resume and her other attributes and for a lot more money. She could have still helped out her parents, but not seen them as much.

One thing she resolved to do when this case ended was to have a serious discussion with them. She really liked Tony Moschella—a little too much, if she were being honest. But she wasn't going to be a firm decoration or help them fill their Latino quota. She would be a real lawyer here, or she would be one somewhere else.

Theresa also swore she would never, ever work on a case with Riley O'Rourke again, partner or not. If that meant the firm would not keep her, so be it. She was confident enough to believe it needed her more than it did O'Rourke.

* * *

Moschella was in a foul mood. Theresa's angry voice mail message from the courthouse alarmed him. That evening, when he met with her, he hoped it wouldn't be as bad as she had described. It was worse. She told him exactly what happened, and his discomfiture grew as she talked.

"Why don't you work on other matters for now?"

Theresa left thinking she had misjudged her worth and was off the Sports Gear case. She hoped that was all. She had been insubordinate to a partner, even if he deserved it. Leaving a firm voluntarily was one thing. Being fired was another thing altogether.

Moschella called O'Rourke's cell and left a message to report to him right away.

\* \* \*

While waiting for O'Rourke, Moschella finished polishing his special jury instructions in his heart valve case. Special jury instructions are not the standard ones used in every case but are drafted by attorneys because of something unique in their case, and the wording has to be satisfactory to all the parties or approved by the judge.

Moschella was beginning to prepare his closing argument when he got a call from Tom Jackson.

"Tony, Tom here."

"Yes, Tom." Moschella knew the call was about today's hearing.

"I know you're at the end of another trial. But we need to talk about today."

"Sure, Tom. I was going to call you later. I assume you had an observer there?"

"Absolutely. This was a critical motion, and from what I was told, it was a disaster."

"What were you told, Tom?"

"That your firm screwed up royally, to be blunt. Or to be specific, O'Rourke barged in like an angry water buffalo and pissed off the judge. Does that about sum up it up?"

"Close enough. However, Ortiz did knock out the Holts's emotional distress claim."

"Which means nothing. The damn plaintiffs can get emotional distress damages in the back door on the other claims if they survive. What was your firm thinking?"

"It wasn't my firm, and it wasn't me. O'Rourke went to the hearing against orders."

"That only makes it worse. It means you have no control, Tony. If we weren't on the eve of trial, I'd drop you guys like a rotten apple. My client's president, and I emphasize that Sports Gear is *my* client, was apoplectic when I gave him this report. He wanted to fire you on the spot. But I told him the timing made that impossible."

Moschella tried to salvage the disaster as best he could. "Aside from his personal shortcomings, O'Rourke is an excellent lawyer. Your firm bet everything on *Jacoves,* which is a problematic case. He just followed your lead."

"It's still the leading precedent, and the judge could have been persuaded of that by the right lawyer. Then all the rest of the garbage that Christopoulos argued would have been irrelevant, and we would have won."

"I don't think . . ."

"Stop, Tony. I understand loyalty, but O'Rourke ruined us. We had all agreed to have Sandoval do the argument, since this judge seems to be controlled as much by his small brain as by the one in his head. Not to mention, that Christopoulos chick is the whole package herself. We needed our best package up there."

"I had no idea O'Rourke was going to do what he did. His intentions were good."

"Intentions be damned. I care about results. So does my client. It would have been better had no one shown up."

"You're being harsh, Tom."

"No, I'm being direct. You want harsh, Tony? I expect you to write off every minute your firm spent reviewing my firm's impeccable, and now wasted, summary judgment motion papers. And all the hours any of you spent preparing for and attending the hearing. And, if there was any doubt, O'Rourke is off the case. If you want me even to consider using you again, that is the minimum you have to do right now."

"Let me think about that." Tom had a right to be angry, but eating all the fees would be a hard thing for his firm. "You ask a lot. Ours is not that large a firm, and while the fees you're talking about aren't huge, they're not insignificant. Also, if I can't use O'Rourke, I'll have to get someone else up to speed. I can't do everything necessary at this end with just Theresa."

"You don't get to think about it. Agree now, or the case moves to another firm, time pressure or not. I'll try it myself if it comes to that, with some other local yokel sitting there for the sake of appearances. And you'll put no one else there on the case. My team will work in the shadows as it has been. If we need more people, my firm will supply them."

"Changing lawyers at the last minute wouldn't go over well with Judge Ortiz or the local media. You don't know this town. I'll do what you're asking to keep you from making a big mistake. But we'll still be the ones to try the case."

"I don't like it, but fine. You can continue to be our local faces, except for O'Rourke. No more screw-ups. We're done." Jackson abruptly terminated the call.

Moschella was furious. He didn't need this while at the crucial stage of another trial for a client more important to his future than Sports Gear. More than that, what O'Rourke had done was unprofessional and had probably lost them the motion. Sandoval might have been able to finesse *Jacoves* enough to pull the wool over Judge Ortiz's eyes or some other part of his anatomy. Either way, it certainly cost Moschella the thousands of dollars in billing that Tom was making him write off. That was the practical reality.

It was 10:00 p.m. He was exhausted from the pressures of the trial, the long days and longer nights, and now this. He wasn't going to be able to concentrate on anything more that night. He decided to deal with O'Rourke and then head for home.

But even that was denied him. He couldn't reach O'Rourke on his cell, at his office, or at his home. He left urgent messages telling him they needed to meet.

He went home agitated and unable to focus on his own ongoing trial.

* * *

Moschella couldn't reach O'Rourke because O'Rourke had made himself unavailable to everyone after the hearing, particularly Moschella. He was in a good mood and wasn't going to be brought down by that hoity-toity guy's whining. He had given Judge Ortiz what for, showed him what a real advocate could do—put him in his place. And that damn Latina associate as well. Just a pretty face. Even if she did share the judge's ethnicity, she wasn't the kind of lawyer Riley O'Rourke was. Committed. Driven. Born to excel. As his father and older brother, both cops, were in their own jobs.

After the hearing, he had decided to take the afternoon off. He went to celebrate with a big lunch at La Costa Mariscos, a great Mexican restaurant he loved on Chester Avenue not far from the courthouse. He had to grant that those people knew their food. He asked for the table always assigned to the buxom waitress he enjoyed watching. He ordered the Cadillac Margarita and took a healthy gulp.

"Great as always." He dipped a tortilla chip in the bowl of in-house hot salsa, happily scored a huge glob, and downed it before it slid off the chip. The homemade crunchy, fiery goodness always pleased him.

O'Rourke had graduated from Union University's Albany Law School, a second-rate institution near his home. He was no star but did well enough and had made a name as a student who could give his professors as good as he got.

After law school, O'Rourke fled as far away as he could from the cold of Albany, New York, where his family lived in a tight and clannish Irish-American community. They were so proud to have the first-ever lawyer in the family. O'Rourke didn't care. He left them for the sun and a town where he could be different and special—in Bakersfield at Quarry, Warren & Moschella. He had responded to an ad he had seen from them on the Internet. It was the only firm interested in him outside upstate New York. He was the stereotypical second-generation Irish kid with great fighting instincts—the hallmark of a litigator. Sadly, he never learned finesse or manipulation or jury-savvy and likeability, which were traits all great trial lawyers possessed.

Even though O'Rourke knew La Costa Mariscos's menu by heart, he leisurely reviewed the food descriptions and pictures over another Cadillac Margarita brought to him with a sweet and suggestive smile. He decided to mix things up today. He ordered Ceviche de Pescado and toyed with doubling the order, but decided he wanted something meaty too. So he got a regular and added a Carne Asada Azteca.

Afterward, he figured he would have a nice, long nap then hit a movie. He'd bill some client for the afternoon.

When he got home to his one-bedroom condo at Regency Park in the Seven Oaks section of Bakersfield, he ended up falling asleep and staying that way. He groggily woke around midnight, took a piss, poured himself three stiff rounds of Bushmills, and crashed again. But not before unsuccessfully trying to jack off to the image of that giggly waitress over a table begging for it.

* * *

When he woke the next morning at five, O'Rourke listened to the voice mail from Moschella.

"Why the hell does he want to meet?" He threw his phone on his bed. "Screw him. Screw them all. I did the right thing, and I'd do it again. Because of me . . . *me,* we got rid of that one cause of action, and Ortiz will bounce the other two based on *Jacoves.* Let's see what they say then."

He decided to leave town and see how they liked working on the Holt case without him. He packed to go take the depositions of a few meaningless third-party witnesses in Sacramento for another case. It involving unfair trade practices in the sale of some oil drilling machinery. He had assigned them to a senior associate, but he went early to the office, left the associate a note, took the materials the associate had prepared for the depositions, and headed off. He intended to be out of touch but billing the balance of the week.

After he finished the witness depositions, which were as boring as they were worthless, he drove to Reno to gamble and enjoy the nightlife—in all of its aspects. He had some comp tickets for the Peppermill Spa Resort Casino there and always paid extra to stay in the Tuscan Tower. It was a sensory overload. He deserved it.

When he returned the following Monday, he expected to be a vindicated hero with Judge Ortiz's dismissal of the entire Holt case. Life was better than good. That is, it was if you were in Riley O'Rourke's head.

⌘

# CHAPTER 56

## Summary Judgments

*"Everybody, soon or late, sits down to a banquet of consequences."*
-Robert Louis Stevenson

That Monday, October 3, Sophia opened her email before the firm business meeting.

The electronically transmitted ruling from Judge Ortiz was there. She stuck her head out of her office and called to anyone within hearing.

"It's here. The ruling."

Tricia, Paul, and Bryce shot right down. Derek came with Rona from the conference room where they were waiting for the meeting.

"Open it," Tricia said. "Hurry."

"Let's see it," Bryce said.

With everyone gathered looking at her computer screen, Sophia complied. They all read:

"On Sports Gear USA's motion for summary judgment, or in the alternative for summary adjudication of issues, the court grants the motion for summary adjudication of plaintiffs' third cause of action for the negligent infliction of emotional distress. That cause of action is dismissed. The motion is otherwise denied."

"A bare-bones ruling. No explanation. No detail. But a win," Derek said. "Congratulations."

"Yes," Rona said. "Now maybe we'll get a decent settlement offer."

"Especially after O'Rourke alienated Ortiz," Tricia said.

"He sure didn't do their firm any favors." Paul was ecstatic.

"It'll have residual resonance at the trial, too," Rona said. "It has to. Judges are like elephants. They don't forget."

"Finally, some luck," Bryce said.

"I wish I was a fly on the wall up there." Sophia laughed for the first time in too long.

\* \* \*

Moschella was in his office when his computer beeped Monday morning. He saw the ruling. Sandoval had received it as the attorney of record at the hearing and forwarded it to him.

"Damn him."

Moschella fumed as he scanned the short rendition of Judge Ortiz's ruling. He dialed O'Rourke's cell, as he had been doing for a week now. "Where the hell is he? He should be back."

Moschella had ferreted out that O'Rourke escaped to Sacramento to take depositions after the hearing fiasco. O'Rourke hadn't contacted the senior associate about the depositions or spoken to anyone else at the firm since leaving. Despite Moschella's repeated attempts to reach him, O'Rourke was out of touch.

Moschella forwarded the email to Tom Jackson and forced himself to initiate the dreaded call.

"Tom, this is Tony. I emailed you Ortiz's ruling. He granted us the summary adjudication knocking out the emotional distress claim. He denied the rest."

"As I expected. I told you this was a screwed-up mess. I don't want any excuses or justifications. My firm wrote that motion, and it was a sure winner if it hadn't gotten fucked up at your end. O'Rourke lost it for us."

"He's a great lawyer for research and drafting, Tom. And for organizing. Can we keep him for backroom work, just not let him in court?"

"Not even if you wrote off all his hours, Tony. He's dangerous. But I've been thinking about staffing this past week. It'll cost our client more, but my firm will augment your forces out there during the final preparation period and the trial. You and Ms. Sandoval will still handle things in court, though. You can rely on us for everything else."

Moschella knew what Jackson was really doing: generating more fees for his firm, and denying them to Quarry, Warren & Moschella. Still, getting ready for trial meant preparing witnesses; lining up direct and cross-examinations; and reviewing any motions *in limine*, jury instructions, trial briefs, or other paperwork Jackson and his people drafted. Add to that being in trial every day, and their own fees would be substantial if, as he expected, the trial went three weeks or longer. He had no real alternative. He'd have to tell the other partners.

"I guess I'll have to live with that, Tom. I think you're wrong not to let us use O'Rourke. I did write off the summary judgment hours like you asked, and I'll take him completely off the case. I only hope we don't regret that. He put a lot of time and thought into the case from the very beginning and is a good resource."

"I won't regret it, Tony."

"Fine," Moschella said. "Thanks for keeping us on for the trial."

"Don't thank me yet. You may wish I had fired you before this is over."

Moschella wasn't sure he disagreed. But the fees, the potential publicity, and the added business opportunities made it worthwhile, even if Jackson and Sports Gear never retained them again. It remained a win-win.

Moschella hung up and started down to O'Rourke's office. This morning he had seen his car reappear in his assigned spot. He had not forwarded the ruling to him. Instead, he had printed out a hard copy and carried it with him.

\* \* \*

Sandoval saw Moschella going down the hall past her office toward O'Rourke's. He looked grim and was carrying a single piece of paper. It was the ruling, obviously, and he was angry.

O'Rourke was in his office with the door closed. Moschella opened it without knocking, stepped inside, and slammed the door shut.

"Good morning, Riley. Except it isn't. I get now why you disappeared and answered none of my calls."

He tossed the single page with Judge Ortiz's ruling on the desk.

O'Rourke picked it up, scanned it, and then looked up at Moschella. No hint of guilt, no recognition of his monumental blunder.

"Nothing, Riley? No comment? No justification?"

"You never should have assigned this hearing to Sandoval. She's just a pretty face. If I had been there on my own . . ."

"That's *malarkey*, Riley, to get *all Irish* with you. Jackson had an observer there. He got a blow-by-blow. I got an earful. Not that I needed to hear it a second time. Theresa already met with me."

"I'm sure she did. Quite the little thing you have going there, eh?"

"You son of a bitch. Say that again and I'll come across that desk. You're an egotistical, arrogant little Irish punk. You've never brought in a client. They don't like you. Your colleagues don't like or trust you, but I've always defended you because of your tenacity and drive. You're just a paper pusher, not a front man. Not a trial lawyer. Not even a passable courtroom lawyer."

"Says you."

"No, Riley. Say the partners who have worked with you, the clients, and the results like this one."

"Huh," O'Rourke scoffed.

"Because of you, it took everything I had to keep the Sports Gear trial and at a price. We had to eat every minute, every hour, and every day billed to the summary judgment motion. Jackson ordered you off the case. Frankly, the word is out. There were a lot of Bakersfield attorneys in that courtroom and they talk. The legal community here is small, and the partners here are not happy."

"I don't believe you. I'll call Jackson myself. Wonder how he'll react when I tell him you wanted us to lose the motion. I was just doing your bidding and making sure."

His eyes glinted as he spoke, his agile if misguided brain working the angles.

Moschella was startled. He hadn't considered that O'Rourke might breach a firm confidence to dig out of his hole. Recovering, he had a ready rejoinder.

"You've threatened to call him before, Riley. Go ahead. Humiliate yourself. Trust me, he'll think you're just covering your ass. That will only make you look worse. He won't credit your attempt to smear me or the firm. He'll give you the tongue-lashing you deserve."

"But it's the truth!" O'Reilly feigned astonishment and indignation as a ploy.

"So what? Sure, the prospect of losing the motion didn't bother me because of the upside as long as we used Theresa. Because she was Jackson's choice. When you decided to override that, you took away our ability to claim we did our best within their parameters."

O'Rourke was check mated. In this instance, appearances were everything. He saw that now. But he still had to defend his actions.

"You're all jealous. All of you. I'm smarter than Sandoval, smarter than you, smarter than Jackson, and smarter than that ignoramus Ortiz. I could have won that motion, but instead you all played Ortiz's horny fiddle with that Mexican bitch."

Moschella could take no more. O'Rourke had become a total liability, not just on this case, but to him personally and the firm. O'Rourke wasn't going to change. Worse, he was personally threatening Moschella with a charge of unethical conduct.

"Enough, Riley. After you embarrass yourself by calling Jackson, if you're stupid enough to do that, I want your signed resignation from this firm on my desk by five today."

"I'm a partner. You can't fire me."

"No. I can't, but I can and I will call for an immediate vote of the partnership. We both know how that will turn out after all the partners you've crossed and refuse to work with you again. That vote will become very public in a small town like Bakersfield. Resign and another firm might take a chance on you. Get tossed out by your partners, and you'll be a pariah."

"You bastard! I'll take you on. I'll take you all on." O'Rourke jumped up with his white-knuckled fists cocked, toppling his full coffee mug across his desk.

"Do what you're thinking and you won't just be gone from this firm, Riley. You'll be enjoying the hospitality of the Kern County Jail."

O'Rourke flexed his fists, furious, paralyzed, calculating the costs. He glared at Moschella, frozen in place.

"Get out of my office. It's still mine until I decide otherwise or the firm kicks me out."

"Sure, Riley. I'll be on my way. But I meant what I said. Your resignation by five tonight. On my desk. I'm calling a partners' meeting for six. Make sure I have a reason to cancel it."

Moschella departed, leaving O'Rourke's door open.

* * *

Riley walked over and slammed the door shut. It resounded like a bullet. Then he dropped into his chair and sat at his desk, head in his hands. He watched the coffee spread across his leather blotter. He could not believe any of it. Not that dumb Latino Ortiz and his ruling. Not that chica bitch Sandoval with her long legs, flashing eyes, and firm tits getting the better of him. Not that old-money Bakersfield wop Moschella throwing his weight around in this hick town and dumping him like so much garbage.

Riley leaned back and took deep breaths. He was also a realist. Moschella would easily get a majority of the partners' votes to oust him. He had made many enemies and no friends in the firm. No friends at all. Ironically, Moschella had come closest to being one. Riley saw everyone there as a competitor, not a colleague. He had always been at war with the world.

He knew that whatever he did, and whatever he told them, his family would not understand if he was ousted from the firm. They would see him as a failure. Which, in fact, he was. It wasn't his fault. It couldn't be. The world was filled with ignorant fools, mental pygmies who didn't recognize his brilliance—his rightness.

Suddenly, Riley O'Rourke felt very tired. Very alone. Very depressed. He couldn't bring himself to resign. Nor could he face the agony of being rejected by his partners in an open vote. What he could do was what he always did in a real crisis—some serious drinking.

He left with the spilled coffee still trickling over the far end of his desk.

He thought of going to the Brimstone at the Padre Hotel, but it had too celebratory an air about it—and he wasn't celebrating. There was always the Belvedere Lounge, a seedy karaoke bar sandwiched between a car wash and a florist. He didn't need to hear the wailing of drunk wannabes in his present frame of mind.

Then he remembered he had stashed two bottles of Jameson 18-Year-Old Master Selection Blended Irish Whiskey in his bedroom closet for a special occasion. In its own macabre way, this occasion was certainly special. Besides, that's what an Irishman did: drown his sorrows in the golden nectar of the old country. And he always did his best drinking with the company he preferred most of all—himself, alone.

⌘

# CHAPTER 57

## No Rainbow, No Pot of Gold

*"It was my delusion and naivety that brought me here."*
-Lady Gaga

After giving O'Rourke his ultimatum, Moschella went straight to Sandoval's office.

The raging argument and the door slams had echoed down the hall. Theresa expected the worst as Moschella crossed her office threshold. He had told her not to work on the Sports Gear case. She was afraid he was going to tell her now to pack her things.

*Should I, could I have stopped O'Rourke?* Theresa thought. *Asked for a recess—a continuance? Protest to Ortiz? Could anyone have stopped him?*

Moschella sat looking at Theresa over the jumble of files on her desk. She had been working like mad on other matters to escape from her own self-doubts.

"Theresa, I heard from Tom Jackson this morning. I also met with Riley. There will be some changes."

"Changes?"

He paused and looked at her large, luminous eyes dominating her perfect face. She was so gorgeous. She waited, holding her breath. Moschella snapped out of his momentary reverie.

"Riley is no longer on the Holt case with us."

"Us?" Theresa repeated and started breathing again.

"Yes, but we'll need some help, and it will come from Jackson, Hood & Lee."

"Won't that be difficult?" Theresa leaped to reconfirm her value. "Aren't they in Denver?"

"Yes to both questions. Those weren't my decisions. Tom Jackson made them, and I assume he has the blessing of Sports Gear."

"I'm really sorry about the hearing and the ruling from Judge Ortiz."

Moschella left unsaid that if Sandoval had gotten the same result arguing alone, all would have been well. Too late for that now.

"Not your fault, Theresa. O'Rourke was out of line. It cost us credibility with the judge. What he did was totally inappropriate. It won't happen again since he's off the case."

"Where do we go from here?" Theresa covered well both her relief and her joy.

"I'm not sure. I'll need to confer with Jackson on our division of labor going forward. But the most immediate thing is the expert depositions. They're the last substantial remaining items of discovery left for both sides."

"Will I take them or defend some of them? All of them?" She decided to be bold.

"Honestly, I don't know. I can't see Jackson's firm handling the actual depositions unless they want to go public with their involvement. It's late in the process and totally counter to his *modus operandi*. It wouldn't surprise me if they wanted to do the prep sessions for our experts. But you or I would have to be there. We'll have to figure that out. Let me know if I throw you in over your head."

"What about the rest of the trial prep?"

"Not sure. We'll still be trying the case. Just you and me now. We've got to be ready. We're not English barristers. We can't just take the briefs and outlines someone else has worked up and try the case. We have to be comfortable with them ourselves and know the evidence and the case law inside and out."

"This will really cost Sports Gear."

"It will. Not good for them or for us, except in the immediate financial sense. But that's how it is."

Moschella got up to leave.

"I'll keep you posted."

"Thank you, Mr. Moschella. And thanks for having the confidence in me to keep me on."

"You're second chair. You've earned it. Don't let the comments about your looks or how Ortiz reacts to you make you doubt for one minute that I . . . we . . . recognize that you're already a great lawyer, in your paperwork, your depositions, and in court. And you'll only get better. Like the Holts's lawyer. Too bad she's on the other side."

Theresa resisted the urge to jump and scream and hug someone. Recognition for her legal ability mattered the most to her, and she had it. She was second chair. She was earning what Sophia Christopoulos had, and that was respect, despite the fact Sophia was every bit as attractive as Theresa. Beauty can appreciate beauty. So can beautiful brains.

"Oh," Moschella said at the door. "We've worked together long enough and will be working twenty-four seven going to trial. It's Tony from now on."

"Sure, Tony." She smiled.

Moschella left her office with a smile on his face too. Things were going to work out. He was sure of it.

Then he remembered O'Rourke. His smile disappeared.

\* \* \*

In his condo, O'Rourke grabbed a large, reasonably clean coffee mug and took to his bedroom. He retrieved his two bottles of special whiskey and set them on his nightstand. He put his pillows against the wall, sat straight legged on the bed, and turned on the television to a news channel. He poured a mug top-full.

Several hours later he switched to a classic film channel and continued downing the only reliable comfort he had ever known in this sunbaked hellhole of a town. He was on his second fifth now and drinking from the bottle.

His home phone rang. He unplugged it. His cell blared, and he turned the ringer off.

Somewhere in the middle of the second fifth, he picked up his cellphone and looked at the time. It was ten minutes after six in the evening.

It all fell in on him. He had gone too far. He had believed himself something he was to his family—a lawyer—a great one.

Now, he saw nothing ahead but bad or worse options. He hadn't resigned from the firm using Moschella's generous, honorable— though to Riley self-serving—out.

The partners were gathered at the firm specifically to vote to expel him. And why wouldn't they? Nobody had ever really warmed to him. Moschella was right about that. They tolerated him because of his keen research and paperwork legal skills and his obsessive work ethic.

He looked at his cell, thinking of catching Moschella in time to resign. He couldn't make the call. He didn't want to make it. He hated Moschella and always had underneath it all despite their pretense of friendship. He had never trusted anyone, really. He threw his cellphone at a bedroom wall, smashing it.

Groggily, he reached into his nightstand. He took out his Glock G30S that his cop brother Rowdy had recommended for home protection and self-defense. He should have been a cop like his brothers. He would have had a more satisfying outlet for his hatred of the world and all the people in it. He chambered a shell and turned off the safety. Too late. He was always too late.

"What a name for a cop, eh? Rowdy. But he's a winner. Always has been. Everybody loves him. Not me."

He remembered that clerk Spangler at Sports Gear USA when he bought the Glock. Spangler, the same lowlife who had sold that loser Mike Holt the shotgun.

"What a fuck'n fool." He shuddered. "Who was the fool? Who was the loser?"

O'Rourke stared at the Glock. He recalled the perfunctory "background check" and questions confirming he had had training or a prior gun. The idiot didn't even ask for proof.

"Just sold me the damn Gl . . . Glock. Shit," O'Rourke slurred. "Good thing he . . ."

He took a huge final swig from the Jameson bottle and mumbled, "C'mere, little darling. Come to Riley O'Rourke."

He put the barrel in this mouth and pulled the trigger. His arm jigged, shifting the barrel downward. The .45 caliber bullet shattered the top of his spinal column as it exited his neck and lodged low in the wall behind his bed.

So ended the life of Riley.

* * *

As afternoon turned to evening, Moschella had received nothing from O'Rourke. No written resignation. No email. No phone call. Not a word.

He called O'Rourke's office, cell, and home. It all went to voice mail. Five o' clock came and went. He didn't want to have to do what was coming. But he had no choice. Riley had given him none, nor had Tom Jackson.

By six, the other partners had already assembled in the firm's largest conference room on the tenth floor of the Stockdale Tower. They were talking and eating the sandwiches and fruit always provided at meetings along with various drinks and desserts.

At six-twenty, Moschella took his seat at the head of the table. Further delay was impossible.

"Everyone, I called you here today . . ."

Before he could say another word, the conference room door flew open.

It was Theresa Sandoval.

"Tony, everyone, I'm sorry to interrupt, but the receptionist just heard from the Bakersfield police. They were dispatched to Mr. O'Rourke's condo. There was a gunshot. It was . . . He's dead."

She was ashen and shaken.

The partners looked at her and then each other, stunned. No one spoke.

Moschella was stunned. But not for long. He assumed it was suicide but would have to confirm that. Damage control would be critical, not to mention maintaining firm morale.

He stood. Time to sugarcoat. He was glad he had never announced the purpose of the meeting.

"Obviously, this is terrible news. Riley O'Rourke was a brilliant lawyer, a great partner, and a friend to many of us. He will be greatly missed. I will advise everyone when I know more. A meeting would be inappropriate under the circumstances."

Moschella's speech was blatantly untrue. Everyone at the table knew that. Moschella himself would miss his resourcefulness, but not his ego or the costly mistakes. He made too many.

The partners left the conference room with varying sentiments. Moschella went over to Sandoval, who was still shaking. He resisted his strong inclination to hug her. He wouldn't risk a sexual harassment claim somewhere down the line because of intentions misunderstood, either in reality or by design. Those claims were too easy to make these days. He was nothing if not legally aware at all times.

"Theresa, I'm so sorry you were the one to get the news. Please go home. I'll deal with the police and contact Riley's family. We'll talk tomorrow."

"Okay, Tony. I will. I am so sorry. It was suicide, wasn't it?"

"We'll see."

"I just feel so bad about this."

"I do too. But Riley was troubled. Always had been. Apparently he chose a coward's way out. That's harsh, but it's reality."

Theresa nodded and left.

Moschella went back to his office and began making the many necessary, but unpleasant, calls his position in the firm required.

\* \* \*

The Bakersfield Police Department and the D.A. quickly concluded that O'Rourke had killed himself. There was no way Moschella or the firm could keep the local news media or Ben Kowrilsky from sensationalizing that fact. There was yet another death associated with the Holt case, another suicide with a gun purchased not just from the same Sports Gear store in Bakersfield, but from one of the same salesmen.

\* \* \*

Sophia saw the news reports of O'Rourke's death the day after it happened and went down to Paul's office. She had been spending more time there of late.

"Did you see that O'Rourke killed himself?"

"I sure did. Couldn't happen to a nicer guy."

"Geez, Paul. Sometimes I wonder about you."

"Me too." Paul smiled. "It's hard to imagine that self-important, imperious jerk, who braced Ortiz the way he did, killing the only god he obviously worshiped—the one he saw in the mirror."

"Funny," Sophia said. "Seriously, I think his suicide could well work in our favor at trial."

"And you criticize my attitude?"

"Think about it. A lawyer in the opposing firm representing a gun dealer committing suicide himself, like Mike Holt."

"Not to mention that he bought that gun at Sports Gear. From Spangler."

"We'll figure out a way to use this."

"It's already helped. Our whole potential Bakersfield jury pool has seen it in the news. Your friend Ben made sure of that."

"He's a real pro."

With that, Sophia went back to her office. Was there a curse of some kind on this case and everyone associated with it? She didn't choose to ponder that for long.

* * *

O'Rourke's parents had his body and his personal belongings sent to the family home in Albany. The service was held in the city's historic St. Mary's Church. The priest, Father Aloysius Cagney, had known Riley since childhood and agreed to preside. Because O'Rourke had taken his own life, the bishop of the Diocese of Albany, who was very old-school, refused to officiate or to allow the service in the mother church of the diocese, the Cathedral of the Immaculate Conception. The service was well-attended by those he grew up with, friends of the family, and the extended Irish-American community.

No one was there from Quarry, Warren & Moschella. The family made it clear they were unwelcome. Riley had confided in his father about his treatment at the firm, particularly in the last few weeks before his death. To Riley's family, their Irish son was a star. They were proud of him. They wished he had stayed there in Albany among his own people and not gone west.

The family also refused to permit the firm to hold any memorial service in Bakersfield. They knew Riley had never really been accepted there and were unwilling to allow the firm to pretend otherwise.

Moschella respected their wishes even though it was an insult to him and the firm. The news media in Bakersfield, with Ben Kowrilsky, the ever-present thorn in Moschella's side egging them on, ran unflattering stories about Moschella and the firm, complete with quotes Ben had gotten from O'Rourke's family.

The Holt case was starting to create negative publicity for Moschella and his firm—the kind not likely to generate confidence in present or prospective clients, new recruits, or their likely jury pool in the Holt case.

⌘

# CHAPTER 58

## Drama and Deluge

*"Burdens are for shoulders strong enough to carry them."*
-Scarlett O'Hara

At Krause & White, each day was a twenty-four-hour blur of work, punctuated with catnaps. Sophia and her team worked ceaselessly, assembling the materials to defend the expert depositions of Dr. Mapes and Savage. With equal diligence, they dug up everything possible they could use against the five shills Sports Gear had hired.

Paying for just their own two experts was a financial stretch for the Holts. Experts were expensive but essential in a case like this. Paying to depose the five experts Moschella's office had designated would be an even greater strain, but one they had to bear. On the positive side, preparing to take those depositions proved less difficult than Sophia's team had feared. All five had testified numerous times at trial, always on the side of the gun interests, and that would undermine their credibility to a jury. Sophia's team got the transcripts of their prior trial testimony at very low cost, in part due to the assistance from several cooperative anti-gun organizations that kept the transcripts in databases they had created.

Tricia took on two of the Sports Gear experts. One each went to Paul, Sophia, and Bryce, to his great surprise and delight. Paul would defend Dr. Mapes at his deposition, and Sophia would handle Savage.

* * *

Tricia was using work as an anesthetic now. Somewhere along the way, Jay had found himself a new girlfriend, a blonde, blue-eyed secretary who worked in the federal public defender's office. She was never tied up at nights or on the weekends—except by Jay.

Tricia was angry and depressed. Jay not only had a new bimbo to screw, but he also had moved out of the apartment they shared, leaving her to pay the entire rent even though they were both on the lease. She was too busy and distracted to go after him for his share now, but her salary at Krause & White was insufficient to sustain the burden for long. And why should she have to do that? She hadn't moved out. Jay had.

Paul was happy. He was in his element with the trial approaching, and he was spending increasing amounts of time with Sophia. Not romantic time, but he was patient. She was relying on him more than ever, and he made sure she knew she could call on him anytime, for anything—Holt-related or not. He magnified the possibilities every time she appeared in his office.

Bryce was enthused and endlessly ready for anything. His confidence was through the roof. He was getting more responsibility because he had shown he could handle it. He was cultivating business contacts. He was proving his worth in the ways lawyers always must yet often fail to do. He missed Eddie, though, more than anyone else knew. They had been contemporaries and had been forming a close friendship. He wished Eddie were there to see how he was excelling. Eddie had been the chosen one. Bryce believed that in the end, the firm would have seen that he was every bit as good or better. And that Eddie would have been pleased with Bryce's success.

To him, what Bryce did was no longer just work. It was confirmation and vindication.

* * *

At Quarry, Warren & Moschella the work was hard and disharmonious. Jackson had on his own decided to dispatch four lawyers from Jackson, Hood & Lee to Bakersfield to "help."

To Sandoval the manpower was simply overkill. To Moschella it was both a sign of disrespect and an invasion. Jackson's four were there to keep an eye on him; he was sure of that. They could have done their work in Denver, as they always had. Jackson had seized on the negative publicity from O'Rourke's suicide to convince the higher-ups at Sports Gear that having the Denver lawyers in Bakersfield was necessary and worth the expense given the stakes.

Jackson sent two junior partners, Porter Beauregard and Samuel French, both very white, very male, very Anglo-Saxon, and in their late thirties. They were distinguishable mainly in that Beauregard was of medium height and flaunted a thick mustache, black like his hair, while French was six foot three with auburn hair crew cut Marine-style.

Jackson also sent two senior associates: Ambrose Pickett, a young, grim-faced, prematurely balding and graying, short, heavyset man who was always nervous; and Rose Boyd—a plain but tall and buxom blonde in her twenties with a pronounced Southern accent— whom Jackson had just added to the team.

The Jackson, Hood & Lee group took rooms on the upper floors of the Padre Hotel. It was considered the best hotel in Bakersfield, recently remodeled with modern décor and, in its public areas, offbeat, modern-meets-traditional western highlights. The four were unimpressed both by the hotel and the city and did not hide their disdain from Moschella or Sandoval.

They walked into the Quarry, Warren & Moschella offices one Monday morning and unilaterally commandeered the nicest, though not the biggest, conference room at the firm. They took complete charge of preparing for all of the expert depositions, which were set for October 10 through 16, concluding fifteen days before trial as the rules required.

They "allowed" Tony and Theresa to review all of the background material they had gathered and do the actual prep sessions for their own five expert witnesses. However, the Denver lawyers watched those sessions via a video cam. They took the lead in brainstorming, assembling outlines, and selecting and organizing exhibits for the depositions of Dr. Mapes and Dirk Savage.

The tension between the factions was evident, and so was the Jackson crew's obvious disregard for Moschella and Sandoval. That didn't stop the three men from glancing lustfully at Sandoval, to the relief of Boyd, who was usually the object of their sexist leers and "jokes."

\* \* \*

As the date for the first expert deposition approached, the friction between the two groups reached the breaking point. Beauregard and French did not trust Moschella or Sandoval to handle all of the depositions. Or, frankly, any of them. Boyd didn't care either way. She was the token female hire at the firm and had made a mistake accepting their offer—she wondered how Sandoval liked her choice but didn't care to ask. She was trolling for a more female-friendly firm, but not in Bakersfield.

Pickett never criticized or questioned Jackson's orders. He was shy, nerdy, and alienated from the college social circuit at Davidson in South Carolina, as he had been in high school. He graduated in the top ten percent of his class at the University of Virginia's excellent law school. His academic record and energy were the reasons Jackson and his partners hired him. Jackson applauded himself for his good judgment because Pickett was determined to please in any way he could.

Moschella was exasperated. He herded everyone into the conference room for a prearranged call on speakerphone with Jackson at the Denver home office. After a good forty-five minutes of heated exchanges and personal attacks between and among the assembled, Jackson had heard enough.

"Okay, guys, and I mean particularly Porter and Sam. You know our strategy. We're not surfacing in this case. We stay under wraps unless our client and I deem otherwise. We aren't there yet."

"No," Moschella said. "Far from it."

"We'll see. Based on this meeting, Mr. Moschella and Ms. Sandoval will handle these depositions. They're clearly prepared. Tony will take the Holts's experts, and defend two of ours. Ms. Sandoval will defend the other three."

"Are we observing?" Beauregard looked at his group.

"No. What part of 'undercover' are you missing, Porter?"

"Whatever," Porter muttered, imperceptibly to Jackson.

Beauregard smoothed his mustache, and French shrugged. Beauregard had majored in partying at the University of Arkansas but did well enough on the LSATs to get admitted to Vanderbilt Law School. He was a late bloomer and made law review there. He came to the attention of Jackson because of his aggressively conservative student activism.

"I'll be blunt. None of this is critical. Our experts are battle-tested. They could do these depositions in their sleep and with no attorney present."

Moschella kept his cool despite Jackson's backhand slap. Jackson's decision was not an acknowledgment of Moschella and Sandoval's competence—far from it. He just didn't deem these depos important or challenging enough to warrant revealing his firm's involvement.

"Tony's as good a trial lawyer as any of you out there," Jackson added. "So that's it. Work together to create the optimum outcome for our client. All of you."

His gratuitous little stroke of Tony's ego hung in the air as he ended the call. It did not make up for the rest.

* * *

When they actually took place, the depositions proved uneventful and went according to script. Sophia, Paul, Tricia, and even Bryce did efficient, excellent jobs of confirming that Sports Gear's experts were all industry sycophants. That was their main objective, to weaken the credibility of their canned opinion testimony in the eyes of the jurors. That was their only substantial avenue of attack.

The Holts's experts—Dr. Simon Mapes, their psychiatric expert on suicide methodology and pathology, and Dirk Savage, the gun sales customs and practices expert—were stellar.

Dr. Mapes had testified in only three cases, and his academic articles were fair and balanced. Those factors made him believable to a jury. Moschella could make no inroads into his substantive testimony.

Savage was even better. He testified that he had been an expert witness for a number of gun stores and, at minimum, one industry trade association. He also revealed something neither Jackson nor anyone at Sports Gear had told Moschella or Sandoval. Lawyers for the NGA and Sports Gear had approached Savage about testifying as an expert for them, but only after Sophia's firm and the Holts had already retained him. Moschella was blindsided by that and had to address it with Jackson.

* * *

The expert depositions concluded the last stage of discovery before trial.

Moschella and Sandoval called Jackson to analyze the effect on the trial of the seven experts' testimony.

"Nothing remarkable there," Jackson said. "Of course, we knew they would hit hard on the angle that these guys are mouthpieces for the firearms industry. From what you're both telling me, they had nothing to undercut our experts' actual opinions or anything they were based on?"

"That's correct," Sandoval confirmed.

"But there's a problem with Savage," Moschella said. "Why didn't anyone tell me he had been approached by the NGA and our client?"

"It's not relevant," Jackson replied. "The Holts had already hired him. End of story."

"With all due respect, I have to disagree," Moschella said. "The fact our client's general counsel and an NGA lawyer contacted Savage for our side will make him particularly believable to a jury."

"I'm not worried. I've seen that backfire on plaintiffs' lawyers who tried to make much of it. Sorry, I have a client meeting."

Jackson hung up.

"Damn it," Tony said. "I can't run this case if they keep us out of the loop. Jackson and his people are withholding things from us. They're jeopardizing the case and our client. But why?"

"No idea," Theresa said.

"There can be no more missteps. There have been too many and our firm looks bad." Moschella was uneasy—a feeling that was undefined and unspecific, but definitely fueled by Jackson's attitude. "We shouldn't have to fight Krause & White and watch our backs here too."

* * *

That evening Moschella was on his way to meet his wife at the Bakersfield Country Club when Sandoval called.

"Theresa, what is it? I'm meeting friends for dinner."

"We were served with the pretrial Rule 3.9 things from Krause & White. Very minimal. No motions *in limine*. Only the case statement, witness and exhibit lists, and proposed jury instructions. Our *colleagues* took the papers and haven't given me copies."

"What a surprise. I'll take care of that tomorrow."

"Hold on, Tony. There's more. Jackson made me sign the Rule 3.9 papers to serve on Krause & White just after you left. He wouldn't let me call you. I had to sign and get them messengered, or it wouldn't have been timely. It's not what we discussed with him. It's a stack about two feet high."

"What?"

"It's huge. Krause & White's is maybe an inch or two."

"Damn. Jackson must have gone nuts with motions *in limine*. I told him that's not what we do here in Bakersfield."

"I know. I was there."

"What's done is done. We'll go over all of this stuff tomorrow."

"And we have to meet and confer with Krause & White to try to resolve any issues we can before the trial."

"Ortiz is a hard-ass on that. If we can't do that, we have to make it look like the Holts's lawyers are obstructive. Jackson obviously did this to eat up their trial prep time. It's not hard to do with a small firm. They don't have the resources."

"Judge Ortiz won't like this."

"No. He won't." Moschella's appetite was gone. So was his enthusiasm for what lay ahead.

* * *

Back at the Krause & White offices in Los Angeles the next morning, Sophia and her team were incensed. They were all sitting at the conference room table, looking at the forbidding stacks of paper just served on them: copies of the Rule 3.9 papers that had arrived by messenger from Moschella's firm just under the wire.

"I haven't read through all of this junk yet," Paul said. "But it's outrageous. Forget about the proposed jury instructions, exhibit and witness lists, and statement of the case. Those we can handle and hammer something out with these folks. But twenty-eight motions *in limine*, that's ridiculous."

Of course, no one on Sophia's team knew that Moschella had opposed all but a few of the motions *in limine*. Nor did they know they had all been prepared at Jackson's direction by the male Denver lawyers Moschella privately called the Three Blind Mice. Boyd had been charged with doing the other papers they had served on Krause & White, which were in good order and not excessive. The barrage of motions *in limine* was all part of Jackson's strategy to distract, demoralize, and overwhelm the lawyers for the Holts and the Holts themselves.

The acceptable and legal purpose of motions *in limine*, meaning "at the threshold," is to allow a party to get a trial judge to exclude in advance a piece of evidence that is inadmissible or unduly prejudicial. To object to that evidence at trial with a motion to strike after a jury has already heard the evidence is often too late, like trying to unring a bell. Abusing motions *in limine* to harass—or making a summary judgment motion disguised as a motion *in limine* but without the usual procedural safeguards—is improper and always angers judges.

"Do any of the ones you've read concern you?"

"You'd better believe it. They're trying a rerun of their summary judgment motion for one thing by knocking out relevant evidence. That's just unconscionable. It gives Ortiz another chance to dump the case, this time without O'Rourke there to insult him."

Sophia chewed her lip. "I'm not that worried about that one, Paul. Granting a pocket summary judgment motion like that on the eve of trial is a great way for a judge to get reversed. Ortiz may be a local boy, but he also strikes me as someone who doesn't want to get a reputation for getting his rulings overturned."

"I agree with Sophia," Tricia said.

"But we'll prepare careful oppositions," Sophia said. "Anything else of note?"

"No, just a lot of weird things," Paul said. "They want to bar any mention of where O'Rourke bought the Glock he used to kill himself. We should oppose that."

Tricia and Bryce agreed.

"That is intriguing. Ben already made sure that the media trumpeted that O'Rourke bought the Glock at Sports Gear and from Spangler. I'd like to get that into evidence just to tar Sports Gear and Spangler if for no other reason."

"Any others that trouble you?

"Only one. They want to disqualify Dirk Savage on the grounds of conflict of interest."

"You're not serious," Tricia said. "I missed that one. Why? Because their side also approached him? That's not a conflict. If anything, it makes him more credible."

"Of course. That's why they want him out of there. We have to fight that one with everything we've got. He's one of our best weapons."

Wearily, Sophia looked around the room. There was too much work.

"What about the rest, Paul?"

"They all have no basis in law, and Moschella is just trying to eviscerate our case. He wants to exclude references to Eddie, Steve, Dwight, gun shows, national gun suicide data, other things like that."

"We'll have to oppose every single one. We can't afford to have any fingers tied behind our backs, much less an arm or a leg. Let's divide them up and start analyzing and researching. We'll meet and confer with Moschella and basically tell him to shove it."

Everyone nodded.

"Oh, and Bryce, I hate to do this to you, but someone has to start drafting our trial brief. I'm afraid it's you."

"I'm game." Bryce relished his increasing prominence on the team and with the firm. "Do you want a fake one to feed to Stefan?"

"No," Paul said. "It's time we got rid of that weasel, but neither he or Autumn must ever know we used him."

"We'll tighten security as a cover," Sophia said. "No strangers in the office without real business."

"Good," Tricia said. "Rona can do a firmwide memo."

"Poor Autumn," Sophia said. "Do you think he really likes her and will keep dating her?"

"No way," Paul said. "That's a mismatch if I ever saw one."

Stefan was relegated to meeting Autumn for lunch outside the office. Because of Sophia's security measures, Autumn knew nothing useful to him, and soon the lunches stopped, their relationship died, and so did Autumn's formerly never-ending chatter about herself and her marvelous life.

Autumn did her job quietly now. No one ever told her why Stefan had dropped her. Even if they could have, that would have been too cruel.

\* \* \*

When Sophia and her team finally did meet and confer with Moschella and Sandoval in a phone conference a few days later to try to resolve the Rule 3.9 pretrial issues, the outcome was predictable.

It was a standoff. They were able to agree on the general case statement to be read to the jury, the witness lists, most of the exhibits but not all of them, and the form jury instructions out of BAJI and CALJIC—the basic, approved sources for jury instructions in California. They could not agree on several special jury instructions or any of the motions *in limine*. They would have to argue those to Judge Ortiz.

The judge would be irate that they had not been able to compromise on any of them—in fairness, not without reason. Paul and Sophia just hoped he would direct his anger at Moschella, who had filed all of the motions *in limine,* and not at them.

⌘

# CHAPTER 59

## No Compromise, No Retreat

*"I wasted time, and now doth time waste me."*
-William Shakespeare

At Quarry, Warren & Moschella on Monday a week before the trial, Moschella and Sandoval were working twenty-four seven and things were starting to gel. The Gang of Four, as Moschella referred to them between himself and Sandoval, were also laboring obsessively on their pretrial tasks.

Jackson, of course, micro-managed with incessant calls breaking Moschella's focus on his trial preparation.

"Hi, Tom. What's up?" Moschella's trial prep was interrupted again.

"I won't beat around the bush, Tony. Sports Gear doesn't like what's been happening. Lawyers and cops getting killed, committing suicide, having freak accidents. Even if our client's not responsible, this case has a bad odor. Its stench will linger even when we get the inevitable win."

"I can't disagree. Except on the *inevitable* win. Even here, you can't predict what a jury will do. It's always a crapshoot. You know that. There are no guarantees or sure things."

"That's why I'm calling. Sports Gear wants you to take a run at that Greek lady lawyer and do a mediation before trial. This case should go away."

"She won't fall for that trick. It's a transparent ploy to take time away from her trial prep. She'll know it."

"She may, but the Holts will jump at it."

"I don't think so. Mediation is voluntary here in Kern County. It's expensive. We can handle that, but I doubt they can."

"I get all that, Tony. But Sports Gear insists, and it's prepared to make the prospect more enticing for the Holts."

"How's that?"

"Sports Gear will pay one-hundred percent of the mediator's costs. And it will guarantee a minimum of fifty thousand to settle, assuming confidentiality as to both the offer to mediate and any settlement."

"That's double what we offered before. It could backfire. They might think their case is stronger than it is, Tom. A lot stronger."

"I'm sure you can present it in a way that doesn't suggest weakness on our part. We're on the eve of trial because we lost the summary judgment, and your damn rogue partner who blew his brains out caused that."

Tony held his temper at the callous irreverence for the dead—a life is a life despite the inconveniences it may have involved. "I advise against this. I can't emphasize how much."

"Doesn't matter, Tony. These are the client's instructions. Make the call."

* * *

In L.A. Sophia, Paul, and Tricia were organizing the exhibits for trial when the opening strains from the theme to the movie *Zorba the Greek* trilled out of Sophia's cellphone. She was surprised to see it was Moschella.

"Hello, Mr. Moschella."

"Hello. Do you have a few minutes?"

"Sure." Sophia covered her pretrial hysteria. "My colleagues are here. Can I put you on speaker?"

"No, I want to talk to you personally. It's sensitive and confidential. I think you'll find it to your clients' benefit."

"Hold on a sec." She put her phone on mute and discussed the options with Paul and Tricia.

"I don't like it," Tricia said.

"Who cares? Let him have his *confidential communication*," Paul rejoined. "It might be a settlement offer that means something this time. Sports Gear can't be happy with all the bad publicity. Three gun deaths now: a kid, a cop, one of its own lawyers. This case is not going well for them on the PR front."

"Hmmm," Tricia said. "Maybe. I don't trust them, and I sure don't trust Moschella. He's slick. Look at all those motions *in limine*."

"At this point we don't have much to lose. Let's hear him out."

"Fine. Fine." Tricia was irritated. "But I'm suspicious. Really suspicious."

"Understood."

Sophia unmuted the call.

"Okay, we're all going to hear what you have to say, not just me. What's this about?"

"Before I start, do we have an agreement that this conversation is confidential, whatever the end result?"

"You want a blank check?"

"I do. You'll see why. If we reach an understanding, you can, of course, discuss that with your clients as long as they also agree to keep it confidential."

"I suppose it can't hurt to listen."

"Thank you. Here's the deal. My client believes it would be in everyone's best interest to resolve this case before trial, even though the law is clearly in its favor."

"That isn't how Judge Ortiz saw things at the summary judgment hearing."

"That's your opinion."

"You weren't there."

"Putting that aside, my client thinks a mediator might have better luck than we did between ourselves getting this settled."

"Mediators are expensive, and your client's last offer was an insult. This strikes me as an attempt to bully our clients and waste their money on a fruitless exercise. Frankly, it's a waste of our trial prep time, too."

"I thought you might say that. So did my client. So I'm authorized to tell you that first, Sports Gear will pay for the entire cost of the mediation, not just the usual half. Second, it will advise the mediator that its opening offer is a minimum of fifty thousand dollars."

"Why not just let me take that offer to the Holts? It's twice what you offered before. Why the mediation?"

"Because, to be honest, Sports Gear and I believe a neutral mediator is in a better position to talk to both parties and convince them of the wisdom of a settlement than the lawyers are. You know that's true. And remember that's a minimum."

Sophia was concerned. Fifty thousand dollars wouldn't even cover the mounting costs of the case so far, much less result in any fees to Krause & White. Wallace was a worry, too. He still wanted out. On the other hand, the word "minimum" intrigued her. Besides, she was duty-bound to disclose this conversation to the Holts and Wallace would jump at the chance to settle. She had made a mistake agreeing to talk to Moschella in confidence. Too late now.

"I confess I'm surprised, Mr. Moschella. However, I'll take your offer of a mediation to our clients."

"Please do. We go to trial in a week. We can get a mediator fast. Lord knows there's a glut of them out there. Some are even good."

Sophia could not help laughing. "Understood. I'll be in touch."

\* \* \*

Sophia looked thoughtfully at Paul and Tricia.

"Fifty thousand is nothing," Paul said. "That puts no money in the pockets of the Holts, or in ours. They wouldn't recoup what they've already spent. And with the confidentiality requirement, they wouldn't even be able to get media vindication by showing that Sports Gear had settled with them."

"I agree with Paul," Tricia added. "This is designed to waste our time on the eve of trial with a distraction that will go nowhere and will definitely upset our clients."

"I think so too." Sophia agreed. "But we have to present this to the Holts. It's arguably a settlement offer of sorts. A gray area, but I'd be uncomfortable not telling them about it."

Paul was reflective and fiddled idly with a pen as he considered the problem.

"I have to concur," Paul finally said. "And, being a cynic, for one other reason."

"Which is?" Tricia asked.

"The judge. We all know Bakersfield is a small town, and these folks all talk to each other. Moschella would find a way to get the fact that we had refused to consider mediation to Ortiz, even though his client was prepared to be generous, as they saw it. That would not stand us in good stead with him at trial."

"You're paranoid, Paul. But I suppose given our experiences there, you have reason to be. I'm convinced. I'll call the Holts. And we'll encourage a one-day mediation, mostly for the sake of Ortiz."

"I still don't like it," Tricia grumbled.

\* \* \*

Sophia called the new number the Holts had gotten after they began receiving anonymous, repeated phone calls with threats and hang-ups.

Wallace answered.

"Hello, Wallace, this is Sophia. I need to speak to you and Beth about something. Is she home?"

"Where else would she be these days? Where would we both be?"

He was as angry and bitter as ever.

"I'm sorry, Wallace. But we're at the end now. Can you have Beth get on the line?"

"Beth. Beth. It's our lawyer, Sophia. She wants to talk to us. Pick up the other phone."

Beth was online in a second. "Hi, Sophia."

Sophia conveyed Moschella's offer to them and explained what she saw as the pros and cons. She tried not to be too negative, though she wanted to be.

Wallace, as she had anticipated, leaped at the mediation option.

Beth was reluctant. "Fifty thousand dollars for Mike? For us? That's nothing. And we've already paid more than that in expenses."

"You have, Beth. But it's double their original offer, and it's not a final one. A mediator with the right attitude could well get them to go higher. Maybe even much higher."

Beth wasn't convinced. "I see. But how often does that happen, Sophia?"

"It happens, Beth. Whether it will here is uncertain. I'm not hopeful, to be honest."

"But there's a chance, right?" Wallace asked. "That they could come up with a number we could accept and get on with our lives?"

Sophia heard the Beth tear spigot start on the other phone. "It's Mike, Wallace. We can't let his death mean nothing."

"I know, Beth. Your precious son, whose memory means more to you than I do alive."

"That's not fair, Wallace," Beth yelled angrily through her tears.

Sophia jumped in to keep things from spiraling out of control.

"Please. Both of you. We don't have to do the mediation if you don't want it, and if we go through with it, we don't have to accept a lowball offer. But there's another problem. If we don't do it and the judge finds out, then he may not like that we didn't try. I think that the safest thing would be to agree to participate, but not to expect much."

"If you think we should." Beth was defeated.

Sophia didn't think they should but felt they had no choice.

"I'm for it," Wallace said. "Especially since it won't cost us anything but time."

Sophia bridled at Wallace's words. Time was the one thing they couldn't spare at this point if they wanted to win the trial.

"I'll tell them we'll do a one-day mediation. One day is our limit. We're too close to trial."

Sophia hung up, thinking that clients were often a lawyer's toughest adversaries in a case. She called Moschella to inform him and to arrange for a mediator. She wouldn't challenge his choice since his client was paying, and he was unlikely to approve someone who would strong-arm Sports Gear into a big number in any event.

* * *

The mediation was set at Moschella's office for that Wednesday morning at ten. The team considered sending someone other than Sophia, but for client relations reasons, Sophia felt she had to go. Her brain should have stayed in L.A. getting ready for the trial.

She dragged herself to Bakersfield that morning, running on four hours of sleep after a grueling night at the office. When she got there to pick up the Holts, even in late October, the temperature was climbing. It would hit the mid-nineties before the day's end.

* * *

At the mediation, the first bad sign was that the Fresno-based mediator, Alec Hornitos, was an hour late. His excuse? He got lost. Sophia was incredulous. After all, one hick town in the Central Valley was like any other. Just head for the tallest building and you'll find the richest attorneys. Sophia had agreed to the Fresno mediator not only because he was available, but also because after some quick and dirty Internet research, he appeared to have a good reputation.

How wrong she was.

The mediation finally began just after eleven in the same conference room where Eddie and Sophia had taken the ill-fated Grimick and Spangler depositions. Sophia, Wallace, and Beth with her oxygen tank and tubing sat on one side of the table. Moschella and his always sultry-looking associate Theresa on the other. Hornitos was at the head.

The second bad sign was that no one from Sports Gear was there. Moschella announced that he had a corporate representative with authority to settle available by phone. Sophia kicked herself. She should have insisted that Sports Gear have an actual decision-maker in the room. Mediations rarely went anywhere if the clients on only one side were present. The dynamic was totally different.

Hornitos needlessly and laboriously set forth the procedures he followed, billing for every minute of course, even though he had already emailed every word to the lawyers. Moschella and Sandoval had already chalked up enough billable hours to "understand" his procedures. Sophia had done the same, but with no one to bill.

The mediation was like doing a mini-trial with a whole set of different rules before the main event—the actual jury trial.

The third bad sign was that Hornitos was a "transformative" mediator. Sophia had seen something about that on the Internet but hadn't given it much thought. Her tired mind had erred once again.

He wouldn't tell the parties what he thought their chances would be in court, which is what "evaluative" mediators do. No, he wanted the parties to be "empowered" and to recognize the needs, interests, and values of the other side. Any good "transformative" mediator apparently did the same.

To Sophia, that was a joke, much like his mediation was becoming, since one of the parties, namely Sports Gear, had no one in the room to be "transformed."

\* \* \*

The attorneys began by stating their cases. Sophia prudently took fifteen minutes. Moschella took over an hour. He was filibustering, eating away at the time she needed to prepare for the trial.

"I suggest we break for lunch now," Hornitos said after Moschella concluded. "I'll see you back at two sharp."

"Mr. Hornitos, we've barely begun." Sophia's deference had an edge to it.

"Oh, I think we've done quite well. I have a lot to work with here. See you all back after lunch."

Moschella held the door as all the actors in this charade filed out. The mediation was going to be a bigger waste of time than even Sophia had predicted. With this mediator Moschella would accomplish his goal in spades of wasting her time beyond his best expectations.

The Holts insisted on taking Sophia to Wool Growers for lunch, the other best-known Basque restaurant in Bakersfield besides Noriega's. They wanted her to experience this gem of East Bakersfield.

She had already been exposed to enough of Bakersfield's local color, but they had almost two hours to kill and she needed the Holts even-keeled. She didn't want to give Moschella and Sandoval any additional insight into them before the trial.

Moschella had almost surely been given some settlement amount acceptable to Sports Gear. The question was whether it was more than fifty thousand dollars. Sports Gear's officers were not being inconvenienced by the mediation. In all likelihood, they had forgotten there even was a mediation and wouldn't have cared if they remembered.

* * *

"Isn't it wonderful?" Beth said as they walked into Wool Growers. "You get so much good food."

"It looks marvelous." Sophia gagged at the massive amounts of food being served family-style to the customers. She couldn't chow down and take a nap in the afternoon. It wasn't Thanksgiving—it was more like "Misgiving."

Beth and Wallace started to head for the family-style banquet room, but it reminded Sophia too much of the horrible experience she and Paul had at Noriega's.

She stopped them. "We really don't have time to get involved in a big table full of people. Why don't we just eat in the dining room over there?"

Reluctantly, the Holts acquiesced. They appeared upset that they could not pig out, which one certainly could do in the banquet room, where the Wednesday entrée was roast pork loin with mashed potatoes and a million side dishes.

In what Sophia saw as a silent criticism, Wallace ordered the pork chops and Beth the very garlicky scampi—both with French fries and salads. Sophia would relegate Beth to the far side of Wallace back at the mediation. She went light with the chicken breast salad.

Beth did a monologue about her new floral decorations in her home while they ate. Sophia was polite, but Wallace glumly wolfed down his food. When the waiter brought the check, Wallace did not pick it up. To avoid a scene between Beth and Wallace, Sophia paid it herself. She would just add it to the cost bill, which hopefully Wallace would continue to pay.

As they left the restaurant, Sophia was just happy that no one had recognized them.

"I want to stop by Dewars," Beth insisted as they got in Sophia's car.

"Don't be silly, Beth," Wallace said. "No one wants that damn candy."

"I want to buy Sophia a box," Beth said. "She bought us lunch, after all, and I know she'll love it. In fact, she can take it back to her office."

Sophia drove to Dewars to humor the old woman who was continuing to feed off her son's suicide.

Beth was enjoying all the attention from the case. She had loved her son, and it was all worth it to her. Not to Wallace. He had worked hard for his retirement and the privilege of watching game shows all morning and old movies all afternoon. He was being bled dry by Beth's quest—Beth's guilt. He refused to leave the car.

In Dewars, Beth was happily in her element as she looked at all the candy and downed her free sample. Sophia declined hers after the Wool Growers chow down.

Beth bought two boxes, one of assorted chocolates and chews for Sophia, and another of Chocolate Roughnecks.

* * *

Back at the mediation, Beth passed the box of Chocolate Roughnecks around like she was with friends at her church group. The men each politely selected a piece and set it aside on a napkin. Sandoval solicitously ate one with enthusiasm. It was the kind of litigation nicety that Sophia indulged in herself when it was to her advantage.

At two sharp, Hornitos commenced the meat of the mediation. Or, more accurately, the Spam. He spent excessive time regurgitating the positions of the parties from the copious notes he had made and billed for. After getting Sophia and Moschella to acknowledge that his "summary" was accurate, he started infusing the Holts with Sports Gear's point of view. He pictured Sports Gear as a legitimate business that helped the community economically, was a good public citizen, and so on and so on. After nearly an hour of that, Sophia interrupted him.

"Mr. Hornitos, I'm sure Sports Gear would appreciate your compliments if anyone from the company was actually here. I can do the same spiel regarding the Holts and their contributions to the Bakersfield community, their church, you name it. None of that addresses the issue—the reality that the Holts have a dead son, killed by a shotgun this 'wonderful' company you are exalting sold him. Our position is Sports Gear made that sale knowing he was not in a balanced state of mind. How are anyone's needs, values, and interests going to be 'transformed' when Sports Gear is absent?"

"Ms. Christopoulos, Mr. Moschella will share with his client's representative by phone all that is happening here. We don't all need to be in the same room for 'transformative' mediation to be effective."

"I disagree, Mr. Hornitos. Why don't we see if you're right, and let Mr. Moschella make that call now? See if he can get a realistic figure. He knows what my clients think and what they need. And now they 'know' what Sports Gear thinks and what it needs, or what their lawyers do, at any rate."

"That's not how I usually work, Ms. Christopoulos. Nonetheless, Mr. Moschella, are you okay with that?"

Moschella smiled. "Of course."

He went outside, made the call, and returned in less than five minutes.

"My client will pay the Holts fifty thousand dollars to settle the case, with an appropriate confidentiality and nondisclosure clause."

Sophia exploded. "That's what you offered on the phone. You inferred it was a minimum starting point."

"It's also the ending point."

"This was a total waste of time. But then you knew that, didn't you?"

"It's a very generous offer, Ms. Christopoulos," Moschella said. "Now your clients have heard it directly from me. The room next door is available for you to discuss it with them."

"All sides have to vacate the room this round, Mr. Moschella." The mediator was bending over backward to appear impartial. He was neither impartial nor competent. "I won't caucus with any side this round."

In the adjacent room, it went as Sophia expected. Wallace wanted out, Beth didn't. In the end, Sophia persuaded Wallace that, if they took the fifty thousand dollars, it would be a win for Sports Gear. She pointed out the only thing he and Beth would have to show for Mike's death was a depleted bank account, since their portion of the money would not even cover their costs and other expenses.

When they returned to the conference room, Hornitos, Moschella, and Sandoval were already there. It was nearly five o'clock. Sophia curtly advised them that her clients rejected the "so-called" offer. She added that she believed the mediation had been arranged in bad faith and asked whether Moschella had authority to go higher.

"Ms. Christopoulos," Moschella said. "I think Sports Gear has offered a very fair settlement. There is nothing more on the table."

Hornitos and Sandoval were quiet and poker-faced. Sophia had been snookered. She was angry, and she was going to make these people, all of them, pay.

"Then see you at trial." Sophia and the Holts left.

⌘

# CHAPTER 60

## The Headless Horseman

*"Ability hits the mark where presumption
overshoots and diffidence falls short."*
-Golda Meir

October 31 was both Halloween and the first day of the trial. Sophia, Paul, Tricia, and Bryce arrived in Bakersfield very early, left their suitcases in the trunk, and went straight to the courthouse.

The Bakersfield population was preparing to go to Scream in the Dark, the more adventurous adults to Naughty Halloween at the Padre Hotel, and the less sensible parents readying their children for trick-or-treating in the uncertain neighborhoods of this economically depressed city.

Sophia with Paul and Moschella with Sandoval stood at their respective counsel tables in Judge Ortiz's court. The day of reckoning, a cool one in the low seventies for once, had arrived.

The judge addressed those assembled before him.

"Counsel, I have a lot of paper in front of me. Too much, really. This isn't an antitrust or mass tort class action case. Please tell me you've resolved all of these motions *in limine* and the other issues here so we can call in potential jurors and get this trial going."

Sophia and Tony spoke at the same time.

"Wait," Judge Ortiz held up his hand. "One at a time. Mr. Moschella, you filed twenty-eight motions *in limine*. Ms. Christopoulos filed none. Where do we stand with the twenty-eight?"

"We haven't been able to resolve any of the motions *in limine*," Moschella answered. "But we did agree on some photographs and other exhibits, and some special jury instructions, Your Honor."

"That doesn't cut it. Mr. Moschella, this is not what I expect from you."

The judge was clearly infuriated. Moschella said nothing, fearing he would just make things worse. He silently damned that unctuous, arrogant Jackson and his minions.

"We might as well get on with it. Let's take the motions *in limine* first. We'll get through all this today by four, I guarantee it . . . so best be brief."

The arguments on the unresolved motions and other issues took the rest of the day. When either attorney spoke too long, Judge Ortiz cut them off. At five, an hour after his "guarantee," he called a halt and had the attorneys agree to submit what was left on their papers with no oral argument. Naturally, the attorneys acquiesced.

"All right, everyone. It's been a very long day, one I extended past our normal closing time. I'll rule on everything as expeditiously as I can. I do have Halloween duties tonight. My clerk will contact you when my rulings are ready. Meanwhile, you're all on one-hour call from eight-thirty in the morning to five in the evening every court day." Judge Ortiz had his own way of getting even.

With that, everyone left. Every single one of them drained, the judge visibly so. For him, this case was a trick—a very dirty and unwelcome trick. It was definitely no treat.

\* \* \*

Sophia and her exhausted team headed for an early dinner at Thai Kitchen, which was touted as good, but more importantly cheap—a real consideration for them at all times now.

"What a day," Paul groaned as they took their seats in the small restaurant on Hageman Road, west of the city center.

Paul and Sophia had argued the bulk of the disputed items with Tricia and Bryce each taking some. They were weary from the strain of such a long and tedious day. Bryce had assumed the added burden of becoming their authority on the Kern County Superior Court's local rules in the wake of Eddie's demise. He had been up very late the night before to be sure they were in compliance with all of them. He could barely keep his eyes open.

"We did well," Sophia reflected. "Though who knows with Ortiz? He was less biased than I feared during the arguments, but he still defers to Moschella."

"We'll know soon enough," Tricia replied.

"Or not," Bryce interjected. "He really has a lot to deal with here, and this isn't his only case."

No one chastised Bryce for stating the obvious. He had earned the right to do that.

"At least there were no demonstrators," Tricia said.

"It's Halloween," Sophia cautioned. "They'll be back."

"I don't know. Sports Gear isn't publicizing the trial, and Ben hasn't jumped in yet either," Paul rejoined.

The server appeared, a short, pleasant young Thai woman. Sophia ordered the broccoli deluxe with chicken, Tricia the mee krob, Bryce the snow pea deluxe with pork, and Paul the pad Thai with tofu.

When the food came, they were almost too tired to eat.

"What? Lost your appetite, Paul?" Tricia teased.

"Trying to lose something else." Paul smiled. "Pounds."

Everyone laughed weakly. Their mood lightened as they enjoyed their excellent meal.

When darkness came they heard the sound of crisp gunshots in the distance. But this was Bakersfield, and it was Halloween—every city had its own way of commemorating the night of witches, goblins, and horror.

When they finished, they went to the nearby complex where they had rented two furnished two-bedroom condominium apartments for a month using Rona's mother's name and credit card. They were cheap, away from the courthouse, and unlikely to come to the attention of Sports Gear's legion of gun-crazy supporters in Bakersfield or the media. The complex had Wi-Fi, a small gym, laundry facilities, all the comforts of home—all the comforts of a Bakersfield home, that is. Bryce and Paul took one unit, and Sophia and Tricia the other.

By ten, they were all fast asleep. They were as prepared as they could be and well aware sleep would be a precious commodity after tonight for the duration of the trial.

* * *

For Tony Moschella and Theresa Sandoval, the evening went in a different direction. They returned to the firm's offices in the Stockdale Tower. Theresa slumped into a chair as Tony sat at his desk.

"Something to drink?"

"Some water, Tony. Anything stronger and I'd probably pass out on your floor."

Moschella gave her a humorless smile. He handed her a bottle of Evian water from the small refrigerator in his office. He uncapped a bottle of St. Pauli Girl beer for himself.

"I told Jackson not to do three-quarters of those motions *in limine*. It made no difference. They are killing us with Ortiz. We were hired because of our supposed local knowledge and clout."

"There won't be any clout left. They're spending our capital with the judge. He didn't even leer at me today."

They both chuckled.

"You did well though, Theresa. Especially on the motion about those suicide pictures. No thanks to Jackson's four toadies. We seem to be fighting them as much as we are Krause & White. But we are where we are."

They sat quietly for another few minutes, both staring into space.

Yawning, Moschella concluded their short debriefing. "Stay close to your phone, Theresa. Time to call it a night."

They left the office together, and parted to their respective cars, troubled by the case, their futures, and the contrary tides of practicing law.

⌘

# CHAPTER 61

## Off To The Races

*"Victory has a hundred fathers and defeat is an orphan."*
-John F. Kennedy

The next morning Sophia woke to her cellphone alarm playing Giuseppe Verdi's "Anvil Chorus." She chose that for the trial to make sure she'd wake up. She did. Emphatically. But then she turned it off and shut her eyes again.

She woke again to her cellphone ringing.

"Hello?"

"Good morning, Ms. Christopoulos. This is Judge Ortiz's clerk. He wants you in court at nine-thirty this morning. Please be prompt."

"Oh. Thank you for the call. We'll be there."

Sophia glanced at her phone. It was eight. She had fallen asleep again. She phoned the rest of her team. She hadn't expected the judge to get through everything in one night.

Moschella had gotten the same call—a few minutes before her, of course. He had, in turn, contacted Sandoval. They were both surprised Judge Ortiz had ruled so fast on the numerous motions. That did not bode well for them.

Lawyers scurried, coffee'd, ate, and packed the trial paraphernalia they'd be lugging daily to court. That was one trouble with trials. You always had so much to carry with you every day. You never knew how high the judge would make you jump or in what direction.

Huge briefcases full of evidence, pocket briefs on potential issues, legal resource materials, snacks, you name it—all were part of your daily baggage. Not to mention laptops, small portable printers, and display equipment for exhibits. At the end of each day, you had to pack it all up, return to the place you slept in for a few hours, reorganize everything, and prepare to do it all over again the next day. The physical ordeal made working out unnecessary.

* * *

The opposing lawyers converged on the courthouse at the same time. At least, Sophia's team and Sandoval did. Moschella was nowhere in sight—not that it would have been easy to see him. Unlike the previous day, there were demonstrators in front of the building beginning their pro-gun and anti-gun dance.

An article on the front page in the *Bakersfield Californian* had announced "Jury Selection in Anti-Gun Suicide Case Today," and the polar gun forces had predictably reacted. Not in the same numbers as in the past, but there were over a hundred people milling around the walkway and grass in front of the courthouse. They waved signs and shouted support for the Holts and gun control, or for the Second Amendment and killing big government.

Another front-page story also fueled the demonstrators. Two young, white, tattooed males were shot Halloween night after a brawl broke out at a biker bar in Oildale. News, of course, but not startling. Not for Oildale—or for Bakersfield.

Three news vans were at the scene. One was from CBT, Ben Kowrilsky's network. He'd seen Beth and Wallace Holt arrive before Sophia's team and had brought them to his van to "shelter" and, of course, interview them.

Sophia spotted him with her clients. She and Paul headed over.

"Ben, I didn't expect to see you here. I thought we were sidelined until the trial got going for real."

"I'd never sideline you, Sophia. I saw your clients here, and thought I should take care of them until you came."

"Thanks, Ben. I appreciate it. But we really don't have time for any interviews. The judge was emphatic about promptness."

Kowrilsky put up his hands in mock surrender. "Okay, okay. I got a few good sound bites, but I need more when you finish. Deal?"

"Deal," Sophia called.

Ben remained a professional necessity to Sophia. She needed him on her side. Neither she nor Ben ever discovered the source of the actual leak that led to Steve's death. But he did his best, and she owed him for that and everything else he had done and continued to do for her case.

\* \* \*

They went through the metal detectors and limited searches, which were what constituted security at Kern County Superior Court's Metropolitan Division. For once they were grateful those measures were in place.

Department 5 was empty except for the bailiff, a court reporter, Judge Ortiz and Sandoval. They did not see Moschella.

"Ladies and gentlemen, I wanted to get an early start today. Ms. Sandoval, where's your boss?"

"I'm sorry, Your Honor. I'm sure he's on his way."

"Call him and find out when we can expect him to grace us with his presence."

Sandoval left the courtroom to make the call. She returned and announced: "Mr. Moschella apologizes. He got a flat tire and has called AAA. He'll be here as soon as he can. He was in the process of calling the clerk when I reached him."

"What does 'as soon as he can' mean, Ms. Sandoval?"

"He couldn't give me a precise time, Your Honor. He said he'd call again when AAA arrives."

"We're in recess until then. Alert my clerk when you have something more definite."

With that, Judge Ortiz left the bench, his impatience obvious.

\* \* \*

Nearly an hour went by. Finally, Sandoval's cellphone rang. She left the courtroom, returned quickly, and told the clerk and everyone else AAA had arrived, was working, and that Moschella should be there in thirty minutes. It was obvious to her that he would never leave his Maserati Quattroporte unsupervised with AAA tow and service people under any circumstances.

Forty-five minutes later, a frazzled Moschella arrived. Judge Ortiz was on the bench, where he had been sitting impatiently for fifteen minutes.

"I'm sorry, Your Honor. Couldn't be helped. A tire blowout. A nail in the road. My apologies. I got here as fast as I could."

"Very well, Mr. Moschella. In the future, grab a cab or use Uber. Let's finish what we can before the noon break."

He looked up at the courtroom clock. It was 11:20.

"I don't have to tell all of you that these motions and your other disputes were burdensome to me. Ms. Christopoulos, Mr. Moschella, I don't appreciate your inability or, more accurately, unwillingness to compromise. I do have to say, in all fairness to you, Ms. Christopoulos, that most of the defendant's motions *in limine* were borderline at best."

Moschella started to protest.

"You've had your say, Mr. Moschella. Yesterday. And in your papers. At great length. So here are my rulings. The motion to suppress evidence of the photographs taken of the suicide scene is granted. The probative value of that evidence is far outweighed by the likely prejudice showing it to the jury would create. All of the other defense motions *in limine* are denied."

Sandoval had argued Sports Gear's only winning motion *in limine*.

"But, Your Honor," Moschella began. "Where my late partner bought the gun he used to commit suicide, their expert with his conflicts of interest . . ."

"I heard about most of that yesterday and read the rest in your motion papers, Mr. Moschella. Those are my rulings."

Moschella was nonplussed. "What about our motion to preclude evidence of negligence based on matters ruled irrelevant in *Jacoves*, Your Honor?"

"I told your late colleague Mr. O'Rourke what I thought of *Jacoves*, Mr. Moschella. You should know that. I don't take kindly to pocket summary judgment motions masquerading as motions *in limine*. No judge with a grain of salt does. You had your chance with that argument, presenting it the right way and in the right form, and I denied it then. Just as I am now."

"The special jury instructions . . ."

"I'm reserving judgment on those until the evidence comes in at trial. I'll consider them again when the time comes to instruct the jury. Not before."

Moschella was speechless and beside himself. Not because of what the judge had done. Because of Jackson and his Denver cabal. Moschella knew what the real problem was. He had not acted like a Bakersfield trial lawyer. He'd engaged in big-city tactics. Now he looked bad in front of Judge Ortiz, and he knew Jackson would never admit that he or his people had screwed up. He regretted taking this case more and more.

Sophia was pleased, beyond pleased, but careful not to show it.

"Anything else, counsel?"

"Nothing from us, Your Honor." She struggled to maintain a veneer of neutrality when she wanted to scream in victory.

"No, Your Honor." There was nothing else Moschella could say.

"In that case, I want everyone back here at one-thirty sharp to begin jury selection. I mean that, Mr. Moschella. Everyone."

"Yes, Your Honor. I understand."

He had squandered some, if not all, of his local-boy advantage with the too-numerous motions and his tardiness.

The lawyers and the Holts filed out of the courtroom. After Moschella and Sandoval went down in the elevator, Sophia's team gathered in the hallway with Beth and Wallace.

"Sophia, what just happened in there?" Beth asked.

"I would say a miracle. Moschella made a big mistake with those motions, and he paid the price. It doesn't mean we're going to win, but we're in a much better position now going into the trial."

Even Wallace, always now the reluctant plaintiff, had to smile. Seeing that, Sophia began to think that maybe things would work out after all.

\* \* \*

On the way out of the courthouse, Moschella gave Sandoval a deserved compliment for winning her motion *in limine*.

"Why don't you go get some lunch, Theresa? I have to break the news to our friends."

She thanked him, got in her car, and drove away.

Moschella was angry. Standing at his car, he called Jackson. After only one ring, Jackson answered. He had been waiting for the call.

"Hi, Tony. Well, is it over? Did we blow them away with those incredible motions *in limine*? Did we get the negligence claims knocked out in our second go-round there?"

"No, Tom, it's not over. Not even close. Judge Ortiz granted one of those twenty-eight motions you insisted we dump on him, the one barring the use of photographs of the suicide scene at trial. That's it. He denied all of the others."

"What? What do you mean? You're supposed to be in with this guy. This was a slam-dunk. This is on you."

"No, Tom." Moschella was seething. "This is all on you. I thought you understood that filing dozens of motions *in limine* was going to piss Ortiz off. That's not the Kern County way, and it's never been my way. You went ahead and even had Ms. Sandoval sign the Rule 3.9 behind my back at the last minute. So own what you did."

"Did you argue them right? I couldn't have anyone observe today, for obvious reasons, as you know. It would have exposed our involvement since there were just the two sides and their lawyers in the courtroom."

"Oh, hell, Tom. We argued for hours yesterday. The arguments Ms. Sandoval and I made in court were better than what was in your papers. But they were lost in the shuffle. It was overkill."

"My firm should have handled this case from the start. My only bad decision was hiring you as local counsel. Local you are. Counsel, not so much."

"Hey, the money's nice, but you're ruining my reputation here. If you want to fire me, go ahead. Maybe I should resign. Then Judge Ortiz will see the man behind the curtain. I can tell you how well that will go over. But it might be worth it for me and my firm."

"Shit. Wait." Jackson backed off. "Let's take a minute. I was just stunned. Blowing off steam. I'd never fire you. And you can't resign on the eve of trial. Our client wouldn't allow it, and the judge wouldn't either. It would mean a huge delay, and the plaintiffs won a priority motion to advance the trial date. We'll go with what we have. But let's strategize together. I'll fly to Bakersfield tomorrow and stay for the rest of the trial."

"You'd better watch yourself, Tom." Moschella paused. "Pointing fingers and laying blame for what is now a more problematic trial won't do either of us or Sports Gear any good."

"Understood, Tony, understood. By the way, Sports Gear is flying its senior vice president out there too, Jubal Kemper. He'll arrive today in time for the afternoon session tomorrow and stay through the trial. He's Sports Gear's face for the jury."

"When was I going to know that?"

"I have another call. Good luck with jury selection this afternoon."

Moschella didn't bother to say goodbye. Now he had to suck up to this Kemper. A man he knew nothing about.

Moschella didn't have time to go to the office. He did have time for disgust and anger, and to compose himself. He had to focus. He drove to get a sandwich and look at his jury selection notes. He had to fight for maximum advantage by selecting the right jurors.

Fortunately, he thought with some satisfaction, the trial would be nice and long, and his firm would make more money. That didn't remove the sting, the humiliation, the frustration, but it would have to do.

⌘

# CHAPTER 62

## The Culling of the Herd

*"A jury consists of twelve persons
chosen to decide who has the better lawyer."*
-Robert Frost

After the lunch break, Moschella and Sandoval met Jubal Kemper in the court lobby. He was an energetic man in his mid-fifties, with dark brown graying hair and sharp green eyes, and stood a tall six feet three inches. A retired Army colonel, Kemper had also been a Green Beret. He was in great physical shape and stood ramrod straight out of habit. He was everything Sports Gear USA wanted to project about itself—all American.

Moschella liked him, and Kemper liked Sandoval. Moschella did not enjoy having to explain the lost motions *in limine*, but Kemper seemed to understand small-town courts and their ways. He was nothing like Tom Jackson. They discussed their jury selection strategy and agreed Kemper could provide valuable input.

\* \* \*

Court came to order after lunch at one-thirty. Moschella introduced the client's representative, Jubal Kemper, for the record.

Sophia, her team, and the Holts took due notice. The way he carried himself demanded that. Corporate defendants needed a human face during a jury trial, an actual person to whom the jurors could relate, a personification of the cold corporate entity. This formidable-looking man was obviously that person for Sports Gear.

Time would tell whether the choice was a good one. On the surface, it looked to be.

Judge Ortiz had the bailiff bring in the first group of potential jurors and seat them in the chairs numbered one through forty.

The great majority of them were not happy to be there. That was normal. Jurors were paid virtually nothing for their service. They had to take time away from their jobs and families. Not to mention that they were subjected to dress codes, had to pass through security inspections, and were reprimanded if they ate or drank or chewed gum. To top it off, their reward for putting up with all this was to listen to the miseries and fighting of others.

There were always a few who loved it, of course. Retirees, government employees, people who hated their jobs, busybodies, people with nothing better to do. Trial lawyers were wary of those types. They often had agendas.

Judge Ortiz began by having all of the jurors swear an oath to answer questions about themselves truthfully. He then explained the jury selection process. The bailiff collected the questionnaires the potential jurors had completed. They had been prepared in advance for the juries, their content agreed to by the lawyers for the respective clients, including—though their participation was undisclosed—Jackson and the other Denverites.

"All right, everyone. We'll take a short recess so the lawyers and I can study your questionnaire responses. Prospective jurors, please remain in your seats. Everyone else, return at two. I want to get this jury in place today."

It troubled Sophia that Ortiz was rushing the jury selection. Was it because he was angry about all the motions *in limine*? Whatever his reason, she would have to be on guard during the *voir dire* process.

The bailiff gave Sophia's group the jury conference room. He led Moschella, Sandoval, and Kemper to a smaller room off of the main courtroom.

Sophia hesitated to leave the Holts alone at the counsel table, though they had nothing meaningful to contribute to this phase of the trial. But they were behaving—looking interested and aggrieved as instructed. It was easy for Beth, still hooked to her oxygen tank, and Wallace did his best. She did not think it would be wise or justified to leave Tricia or Bryce to babysit them. They did not want to advertise to the jurors, prospective or actual, that they had four lawyers on the case. That would give the wrong impression. Tricia and Bryce stayed in a back row where they sat with a few other casual court observers, looking as inconspicuous as possible.

The questionnaires proved helpful in winnowing the juror group. Two of the prospective jurors were over seventy and had health issues. Out. Four had criminal convictions of different kinds. Gone. One was a cousin of Grimick. Eliminated, hopefully for cause. Three had encountered gun violence in their lives. One whose father had committed suicide, one the victim of a home invasion burglary that left his sister dead, and another the brother of a police officer killed in a shootout during a drug bust in Oildale. They would be interesting. At a minimum, they could cost Sports Gear half of its six peremptory challenges, which were discretionary with the lawyers, if Moschella could not get Judge Ortiz to excuse any of them for cause.

In the interest of time and because Sophia feared too many potentially unfriendly local Bakersfield types even in standby mode, she agreed when Moschella asked her to stipulate that there need be only three alternate jurors, instead of the statutorily permitted six. It was a calculated risk on her part, but it limited gamesmanship on both sides.

\* \* \*

They all returned to the courtroom at the appointed time.

"All right, everyone," Judge Ortiz announced. "Based on these questionnaires, jurors 3, 8, 9, 17, 22, and 26 are excused. You may leave."

The jurors Judge Ortiz identified as having valid reasons not to serve wasted no time exiting the courtroom. That left twenty-nine still there.

"All right, ladies and gentlemen. The lawyers estimate that this trial could last three weeks. I'll do my best to see that it doesn't, but I note that four of you have indicated that jury service of that duration would be an extreme financial hardship for you. Would you please hand the bailiff the required letters from your employers indicating that you won't be paid for the days you take off for jury service?"

The four jurors, one young African-American female and three white males of varying ages, did so. The bailiff passed the letters up to Judge Ortiz.

"Well, these letters are in order. In fact, they look like copies of each other. Still, I have no choice under the law. Jurors 5, 11, 31 and 33, you are excused. Tell your employers the Kern County Superior Court has noted their names, and that they are not being supportive of our courts. Getting jurors who can serve is difficult, and their refusal to pay you for jury service days makes it that much harder for our justice system to function, which is so essential to this great country."

The four jurors nodded and hastily fled. The pool was down to twenty-four.

Obviously annoyed, Judge Ortiz continued, "Before I begin questioning you, I want to read a statement describing this case that the lawyers on both sides have agreed on."

"This is a lawsuit brought by the parents of a young man who killed himself with a shotgun he purchased at the Bakersfield store of defendant Sports Gear USA. His parents, the plaintiffs here, Beth and Wallace Holt, claim that the store was negligent in selling their son the shotgun and ask for damages for his wrongful death. Sports Gear USA denies it did anything wrong in selling him the shotgun, contends that it followed the law in all respects, and asks for a verdict in its favor."

During the reading, the jurors did not react. They saw they were being scrutinized by both the judge and the lawyers. The judge paused briefly and continued.

"Do any of you feel you could not fairly decide the issues in this case as I have described it to you?"

Five more prospective jurors raised their hands. Judge Ortiz sighed.

"Juror number 35?"

"Your Honor, my cousin Moss Grimick told me a lot about this case. You see, he said . . ."

Sophia and Moschella leaped up in unison. "Objection, Your Honor."

"One at a time. Mr. Moschella, what is your objection?"

"This juror is about to get into details of the case. We ask that the court excuse him for cause."

"Ms. Christopoulos, I assume you have the same objection."

"Yes, Your Honor."

"With reluctance, the court agrees. Juror number 35, you are excused. Please say nothing further and depart the courtroom."

Juror number 35 did so, appearing offended as he passed through the courtroom door.

Sophia was unhappy that Moschella had not been forced to waste one of his six peremptory challenges on Grimick's cousin, though relieved she hadn't been trapped into doing that either.

They were now down to twenty-three prospective jurors. If both sides used all of their peremptory challenges, they would have to call another panel of thirty-five prospective jurors and start the process all over again to fill the remaining spots.

The other four jurors who had raised their hands were those who had been affected by gun violence.

Judge Ortiz questioned them as a group.

"I know guns have touched each of your lives in a terrible way. But be very honest with me. Can you honestly say that having sworn an oath to be fair and impartial, you are too biased one way or the other to serve on this jury?

Facing his stare, each of the three prospective jurors reluctantly said no.

Sophia was pleased. Moschella just grimaced.

"Your Honor." Moschella rose. "Sports Gear thanks jurors 14, 19, 21, and 32 for their service and excuses them at this time."

That was the accepted way for lawyers to exercise their peremptory challenges of jurors. It was a face-saving device that fooled no one but kept things low-key and civil, which was the goal. Three of Moschella's peremptory challenges were gone, and Sophia still had all six of hers left.

Judge Ortiz wasn't smiling. "Very well, Mr. Moschella. Jurors 14, 19, 21, and 32, the court excuses you from further service. You may leave the courtroom."

Everyone saw that the three latest casualties were even less happy to be leaving than Grimick's cousin had been. The pool was down to nineteen.

It was nearing three o'clock. The judge was already irritated at the selection process, or rather the deselection process. He decided to make it move faster, fearing a second panel would have to be called in to complete a full jury with alternates.

"Okay, those remaining here. How many of you have read newspaper accounts, seen television news programming, or seen anything on the Internet about this case?"

Every single remaining prospective juror raised his or her hand.

"Has anything you have seen or heard about this case made you believe you could not fairly and impartially decide it based on the evidence that will be presented and the law on which I will instruct you? If so, raise your hand."

To his relief, not a hand went up.

"All right, counsel. I'm satisfied. Your turn for questions. We'll alternate between counsel for the plaintiffs and defendant. Ms. Christopoulos?"

"Thank you, Your Honor." Sophia looked out at the remaining potential jurors.

Profiling has an unpleasant connotation these days, but every good trial lawyer does it. She saw before her three Latino men, aged from the mid-twenties to the mid-forties; two African-American men, both around fifty; nine Caucasian men ranging from possibly the early twenties to the late fifties; two South Asian women around thirty years old; two Latinas about twenty-five; and eight Caucasian women around thirty to fifty years old. She was guardedly optimistic about the unexpectedly diverse group, but she would need to question them with care.

This questioning was when her relationship with the jury began. They not only had to find her case compelling and the Holts sympathetic, but they also had to like Sophia, and Paul too as he would be actively participating in the trial. She could offend no one.

"Ladies and gentlemen, I am Sophia Christopoulos, one of the attorneys for the plaintiffs, Beth and Wallace Holt. My colleague

Paul Viola, sitting at the counsel table with me, will be assisting me in the trial. I just have a few questions for you.

"First, are any of you members of the NGA, the National Gun Association?"

Six of the jurors raised their hands. Paul was noting their responses on the jury chart he had prepared.

"Thank you. Do any of you NGA members feel you could not give a verdict to my clients if you believed that the evidence and the law supported that result?"

They each said no. Sophia saw that two of the Caucasian men looked down when they did. Paul noted that on his chart.

"Have any of you ever shopped at the Sports Gear store here in Bakersfield?"

Three more hands went up: the two Caucasian men who had looked down and one of the Caucasian women. Paul recorded everything using abbreviations.

"Do you have a favorable or unfavorable opinion of Sports Gear USA?

One of the men said, "They're a great store. You can get any gun you want there."

The other man enthusiastically agreed.

The woman nodded along with them.

That was enough for Sophia. "Your Honor, plaintiffs excuse jurors 2, 6, and 16 and thank them for their service."

They were down to eighteen. Sophia had now used three of her peremptory challenges. She and Moschella each had three more.

She saw the woman smirk as she left the courtroom with the two men. She had been right to get rid of them. If she and Moschella used all of their remaining peremptory challenges, it could become a very long afternoon—or could put them into the following day. It was already nearly four.

"I'm going to give Mr. Moschella some time here, Ms. Christopoulos," the judge declared. "I want to get a jury seated today if at all possible."

"Well, Your Honor, I haven't finished . . ."

"I'm exercising my discretion here, Ms. Christopoulos. You've had enough time. Mr. Moschella?"

Kemper whispered to Moschella.

"Thank you, Your Honor." Moschella wasn't that impressed with the people remaining, and neither was Kemper. A little too "liberal looking" for them or for Sports Gear at any rate. Moschella figured he could alter that with some skillful questioning.

"Good afternoon, everyone. I'm Tony Moschella. Ms. Sandoval over there and I represent Sports Gear USA in this lawsuit. Sitting with us is Mr. Jubal Kemper, its senior vice president. Let me ask you all first if any of you have ever been a member of any anti-gun group, or been in a protest about guns at any time. If so, please raise your hand."

He got lucky. Two of the Latino men and one of the South Asian women raised their hands. With a few more quick questions, he learned that one of the women was in Mothers Against Guns and had been for years. The two men had protested the sale of illegal guns on several occasions because of the gang violence in their barrio neighborhoods. That was enough for him.

He intoned the formula: "Your Honor, Sports Gear USA respectfully excuses jurors 12, 18, and 29 and thanks them for their service." They were down to fifteen, and Moschella was out of peremptory challenges. Sophia was not.

"Anything further, Mr. Moschella?"

"Yes, Your Honor. Ladies and gentlemen, if the evidence shows that Sports Gear and its employees followed the law to the letter in selling Mike Holt the shotgun he later used to take his own life, would you be able to enter a verdict in its favor, given that it would have done nothing wrong and death would have been entirely the result of his independent act?"

"Objection, Your Honor." Sophia stood.

"Sustained, Ms. Christopoulos. Mr. Moschella, you know better than to try to condition prospective jurors to your view of the case. Do you have any more legitimate questions?"

"No, Your Honor. I think I have all I need." He sat down, rather pleased with what he had done despite the harsh words from the court. He had planted the seed he wanted in the minds of the prospective jurors, and that was enough.

"Ms. Christopoulos, do you have anything further?"

Sophia and Paul huddled a brief moment over the jury chart Paul had been keeping. They had identified three more jurors to challenge, based on little more than their gut instincts. In the end, sometimes, lawyers have to go with that in picking juries. It's not science. It's a guess informed by that lawyer's experience.

They were troubled. Jurors 4, 38, and 39 were two older, rugged-looking Caucasian women and a fifty-year-old Caucasian man who looked like a hunter, sportsman, or someone who had spent a lot of time outdoors. If they challenged them, the judge would have to call in a new panel.

Sophia whispered to Paul, "Should we use the rest of our peremptories?"

He whispered back, "I wouldn't. We could do a lot worse, and it will look like Moschella was trying to slant the jury his way if we don't use any more. It's a gamble either way."

Sophia rose and announced, "Plaintiffs find the jury acceptable, Your Honor."

Judge Ortiz eyed her thoughtfully. He knew she had been weighing her decision, and that she was aware of the risks.

"All right, counsel. We have fifteen remaining prospective jurors. Please indicate whether or not you pass each juror for cause as we proceed down the list in numerical order."

After they had passed all the remaining prospective jurors, Judge Ortiz announced: "We have our panel. Jurors 36, 37, and 40, you are our alternates. You will participate fully in the deliberations of the jury, and if any of the first twelve becomes unable to serve for any reason, one of you will be called upon to serve in his or her place. I want everyone tomorrow morning here in Department 5 at 8:00 a.m. sharp."

Sophia was content. By chance, all of the minorities remaining were on the actual twelve-person jury, not alternates. The alternates were two more of the older Caucasian men and a young Caucasian woman. She would have preferred having her on the actual jury. Younger women tended to be less gun-friendly. But she would take what she had. Alternates were automatically the last jurors passed by both sides, or the highest numbered remaining if all had been passed as had happened here.

Moschella was troubled. He anticipated another unpleasant exchange with Tom Jackson, which he could script in advance. Jackson wouldn't like this jury. There was no help for it, though.

Moschella had done what he could under the circumstances and just wished the two Caucasian men had been at lower numbers and weren't merely alternates.

* * *

In his office that evening, Moschella's conversation with Jackson went even worse than he had feared.

"What?" Jackson yelled when Moschella described the jury. "Too . . . how shall I put this . . . 'colorful.' Too unpredictable. And practically none of the gun enthusiasts we needed."

"Tom, Bakersfield isn't just redneck gun toters nowadays. It's actually a lot more diverse than people realize. It's nearly half Latino. We did fine well given our current demographics."

"I wasn't looking for some damn United Nations. We didn't need to rush. You could have challenged more of 'those' people to get a shot at more of our people."

"I used all of our peremptories and got rid of as many potentially unfavorable people as I could. I'm here on the front line. It's easy for you to second-guess not knowing the realities."

"Oh, I know the realities, all right. Most significantly, you being my worst call ever for this trial. In the end, it's my fault, for expecting some Bakersfield rube to handle this case the right way. I'm flying out tonight, as I told you. Let's hope you can put on witnesses and an actual case better than your performance so far."

Moschella nearly broke his office phone hanging up.

*What a pompous, racist piece of garbage*, he thought.

He sat and stared across at his office wall with his degrees and bar admission certificates so carefully framed by his wife. After his blood stopped boiling, he turned to review his opening statement, witness examinations, and exhibit lists—all prepared by Jackson's puppets, of course.

He felt like a marionette, hanging by strings in a horror puppet show. If it hadn't been the night before the start of one of his biggest trials, he would have spent it at a bar.

⌘

# CHAPTER 63

## The End of the Beginning

*"What we anticipate seldom occurs . . ."*
-Benjamin Disraeli

Sophia's team drove to the courthouse at seven-thirty the next morning. They couldn't be late under any circumstances, even if Ben caught them for that interview they had promised yesterday and didn't have time for.

What they met was utter chaos triggered by last night's news. During jury selection yesterday afternoon, a deranged young man had fired nearly forty rounds in a writing class at an Oregon community college, killing nine people and wounding many others. After a firefight with police, he committed suicide. He owned seventeen guns and had bought most of them himself. All of the purchases had been "legal."

"We should have expected this," Sophia said. "God, I hope the Holts made it into the courthouse."

"Park, Paul," Bryce said.

"We're four blocks away," Tricia objected. "We have too much to take."

"There's no getting through that mob scene," Bryce said. "We're going to have to walk around it."

"Yep." Paul pulled over and parked. "Our trial is the obvious magnet for gun demonstrations, just like Derek predicted."

"Stay close," Bryce admonished. "Sophia, you and Tricia stay between the two of us."

"Oh, we will." Tricia was nervous.

There were news trucks with satellites from at least five TV stations, circulating reporters, dozens of Bakersfield police, and hundreds of demonstrators. But this was a different crowd than they had seen before. Today, the anti-gun demonstrators outnumbered the pro-gun forces by a good four-to-one margin. The former held signs with the names of shooting and suicide victims, and the most recent incident in Oregon was highlighted with pictures of the dead on placards and banners.

As they made their way through the crowd, no one accosted them. The pro-gun demonstrators were subdued, even intimidated. Many looked out of place, hesitant, and ready to leave. Sophia saw none of the aggression, anger, and bravado that had characterized them before. The Bakersfield cops weren't going out of their way to harass the anti-gun protesters this time, either. Changing tides?

Sophia's group maneuvered through the crowd with their trial materials and finally reached the courthouse with the unexpected but much-appreciated help of two Bakersfield police officers. They fended off protesters and reporters.

Finally, after clearing security, Paul spotted Beth and Wallace, huddling off to the side, as the lobby filled. They hurried over to them. Beth was in a wheelchair and sucking oxygen from her tank.

"Is Beth able to do this, Wallace?" Sophia was concerned.

"Sure. She wouldn't miss it for the world." Wallace did not look terribly excited at the prospect. "She said she was feeling bad this morning. But you know Beth. Anyway, we're here for the duration."

The defense team was also in the milling lobby crowd. Standing with Moschella, Sandoval, and Kemper was a very irate Tom Jackson. They were all making their way toward the elevators, Moschella and Sandoval laden with boxes of evidence and laptop computers. Jackson was speaking in low tones with Kemper, a friend and client of many years.

Without saying anything, Paul raised his cellphone feigning a text and, instead, snapped a couple of quick pictures.

"What are you doing, Paul?" Sophia asked.

"There's some guy with Moschella and Kemper I don't recognize. I used my phone to photograph him. We have to figure out who he is and where he fits in. See?"

"I don't recognize him either. Do you think he's another lawyer?

"Could be," Paul said. "Don't look back. Ben just came into the lobby."

"Not him now."

As the two sets of attorneys and clients reached the elevators, Sophia lost sight of the fourth man who had been with Moschella. She couldn't see him anywhere.

"Ben's headed our way," Paul said.

"Get in the elevator. Fast."

As the doors shut, Ben caught Sophia's eye and mouthed the word, "Later."

She nodded.

The adversaries didn't acknowledge each other as they took separate elevators to the second floor. They passed a line of spectators and press waiting to enter Department 5. The lawyers and their clients went to the door, and the bailiff let them in. Each side checked in with the clerk, and then they arranged themselves and their litigation bags at their own tables.

In California Superior Courts the plaintiffs' attorneys and their clients usually sat at the right-hand table, closest to the jury. Sophia, Paul, and the Holts took seats there. Tricia and Bryce sat in the first row behind the "bar" separating the court itself from the audience.

Moschella, Sandoval, and Kemper were at the left-hand defendants' table, near the clerk and bailiff.

As the attorneys readied themselves, the bailiff let the gallery fill with people from the line waiting outside.

* * *

"All rise. The Superior Court of the State of California for Kern County, the Honorable Robert Ortiz presiding, is now in session." The bailiff's firm voice announced the beginning of the first day of the formal trial.

Judge Ortiz, sporting a freshly pressed black robe, entered the courtroom from his chambers and took the bench.

"Good morning, everyone. Please be seated. Bailiff, bring in the jury if you will."

The bailiff went to the jury room and returned, the twelve jurors and three alternates close behind him. The jurors took their places in the jury box, with the alternates in chairs adjacent to and just a few feet from where the Holts were seated at the table with Sophia and Paul.

As the jurors took their places, the people in the gallery chattered and whispered.

Sophia casually scanned the courtroom. It was packed. Not everyone who wanted to be there had succeeded. But she did see the man who had been with Moschella in the lobby sitting in the fourth row, and Ben, with other press people including Chang, his rival, clustered in the far corner of the last row. When her eyes passed by him, Ben nodded. She returned the nod. She did owe him an interview. And seeing him gave her an idea, which she tucked away for later.

Judge Ortiz looked out over his courtroom buzzing with whispers. He was readying himself for what promised to be an interesting trial, but first, he had to lay down some ground rules. He motioned to the bailiff to start.

"Quiet, everyone. There is no talking, eating, or drinking in this courtroom. If you do not obey these rules, you will be removed." The bailiff not only sounded severe, but also had the bulk, the bulletproof vest, and the gun to back up every word. He was, after all, a Kern County deputy sheriff assigned to the court.

With the courtroom now silent, Judge Ortiz began by giving the usual basic instructions to the jury and read to them once again the agreed statement of the case that the parties had provided to him.

Ortiz emphasized one instruction to the jury because of the notoriety of the case and the events surrounding it.

"Ladies and gentlemen of the jury, and I mean this in the strongest terms, as of this moment, you are not to read or watch anything about this case or the issues in it, or do any independent investigation or research of your own, in any medium or in any form. You are not to discuss it with anyone except with your fellow jurors during your deliberations. And I mean anyone. You are to decide the case based only on what is presented and admitted into evidence here in this courtroom. If I learn that any of you has violated either of those instructions, there could well be a mistrial here, and the person or persons involved will be guilty of juror misconduct and subject to potential fines, imprisonment, and a contempt citation. I am utterly serious about this."

The jurors looked uncomfortably at each other and at the judge. While Sophia appreciated how emphatic Ortiz had been, she doubted the efficacy of his instruction in the cellphone and Wi-Fi era. Nonetheless, he had given it with enough gravity that some of the jurors would undoubtedly obey.

"Ms. Christopoulos, are plaintiffs prepared to proceed?"

"Yes, Your Honor," Sophia replied, rising from her chair.

Here it was. Her opening statement in her first trial, a high-profile jury trial.

She and her team had fought through the morass of pretrial procedural hurdles Sports Gear and its lawyers had thrown at her and her little firm. They had been forced to cut corners. Derek was right. The distance to Bakersfield, their lack of financial and manpower resources, and the expense deprived them of many litigation advantages. They had never gotten through even a third of the documents Sports Gear produced.

The odds were clearly against her, but Sophia was here and ready to fight. She was first-chairing her first jury trial in a shit-kicking, conservative, dusty gun-rights small town with a colorful history, but she had a surprisingly representative jury, not an insular one. She and her team had done everything they could humanly and inhumanly do. It was time to put it all together like a racehorse, trained and bred, entering the starting gate at the Kentucky Derby.

Sophia stood and studied her opponents. They were well-dressed and well-armed with briefcases and state-of-the-art electronics, able to get case or statutory authority at the touch of a screen. They had NGA attorneys and supposedly the Constitution and God as their wingmen. So be it.

\* \* \*

"Your Honor, members of the jury," Sophia began. "As you know, I am Sophia Christopoulos. My colleague Paul Viola is here with me representing Beth and Wallace Holt, who are sitting at the counsel table with us. In this trial we are not challenging the Second

Amendment. We are not challenging the right of Americans to purchase or use any firearm. We simply want defendant Sports Gear USA to be held accountable for not following the law that you and I have to follow every day of our life. Law already well-established in many cases before this one."

Moschella stood and shouted, "Objection, Your Honor. Counsel is arguing."

"Sustained. Counsel, save such comments for your closing."

Sophia was unfazed. She continued.

"We will show that under the law a shotgun is not comparable to a frying pan, an everyday thing that we can cook with, or a cellphone, or a box of cereal. It is like a racecar, a railroad train, or a stick of dynamite. It is ultrahazardous when used the wrong way, or by someone who has no business even having it. Therefore, we believe the court will instruct you that defendant Sports Gear had a higher duty to you and me and to Mike Holt when they sold him a shotgun.

"We will establish from the testimony of Sports Gear's own employees that they knew, or should have known, not to sell that shotgun just to make a little money to Mike Holt, a boy in obvious distress. And that as a result of their negligent and irresponsible actions, he obtained the means and used the means to take his own life in the most decisive possible way.

"You will hear from expert witnesses about the marketing of guns in this country, and the profiles of mentally disturbed people that anyone, particularly those engaged in selling guns, should recognize. You will hear from Mike's mother and father, Beth Holt and Wallace Holt, sitting over there, about how devastating his death has been to them. You will hear about the emotional and financial price they both have paid, and the impact on their lives, because of their fight to get justice for their son and prevent this sort of thing from happening to other families.

"In the end, I trust you, and the Holts trust you, to weigh the evidence, come to a just decision, and render a verdict in their favor. Not a verdict against guns. A verdict supporting the use of judgment and common sense in the sale of guns. Thank you."

424 ◆ Dale E. Manolakas

The courtroom was quiet. Sophia had done no grandstanding, just addressed the jurors with simple eloquence, and they were spellbound. However, that did not last long.

"Mr. Moschella? Does the defense wish to make an opening statement?" Judge Ortiz's booming voice broke the stillness of the courtroom.

"Yes, Your Honor."

"Very well. Please proceed."

\* \* \*

"Ladies and gentlemen of the jury, I am Tony Moschella, a lawyer from right here in Bakersfield, like all of you. Together with my associate Ms. Theresa Sandoval, I am representing defendant Sports Gear USA in this trial. Sitting with us at the counsel table is Mr. Jubal Kemper, from whom you will be hearing later on. He is the senior vice president of Sports Gear USA, a former Green Beret, and a decorated veteran who has served in Iraq and Afghanistan.

"We are all horrified and distressed by Mike Holt's suicide. He was young and full of promise, a source of pride to Bakersfield, not just to his parents, and his death is a terrible waste. My client and I extend our deepest condolences and sympathy to his parents, Beth and Wallace Holt.

"Yet it is my duty to tell you that the evidence will show that Sports Gear and its store personnel did nothing wrong here. For whatever reason or reasons, Mike Holt decided to kill himself, and he just happened to use a shotgun he bought at my client's Bakersfield store. The evidence will show that he was not unfamiliar with guns, and had owned one when a young boy, purchased for him by his father, Wallace Holt.

"The evidence will also show that Sports Gear and its employees followed the law to the letter in selling Mike Holt that shotgun. Because he was a prior gun owner, there was no required waiting period, no safety exam to pass, and he cleared his background check with flying colors. You will hear from our experts that Sports Gear did everything right. Its store personnel are not psychologists or psychiatrists, and the law doesn't require or expect them to be.

"As tragic as his death was, for himself, his family, our community here in Bakersfield, in the end, he was the one who chose to end his own life. My client's employees had no way of knowing that he was going to do that the day they sold him that shotgun, a day when they sold guns to several other people as well. And, as you will also hear, if you find Sports Gear liable for this unfortunate act by Mike Holt, it will mean it will have to consider the wisdom of continuing to sell firearms in its store here in Bakersfield and everywhere, which could deprive you and other Americans of the ability to buy firearms for hunting, target shooting, or to protect you and yours. Something we all have every right to do.

"For those reasons, I will be asking you for a defense verdict at the close of the evidence."

Sophia was worried. She had been watching the jury throughout Moschella's presentation. He had not been histrionic, just quiet, dignified, straightforward. Several of the jurors were nodding along with him as he spoke. They liked him, and that went a long way with jurors. She had to make sure they liked her and the Holts even more, if possible. That would take some doing.

Judge Ortiz broke into her thoughts.

"Ms. Christopoulos, please call your first witness."

"Thank you, Your Honor." Sophia stood. "I call plaintiff Wallace Holt, the father of the deceased Mike Holt."

Sophia motioned for Wallace to proceed to the witness box and placed her witness outline on the small portable lectern her team had brought for the conference table. Naturally, the courts in Bakersfield provided no such conveniences for attorneys. Budget issues, or so they claimed.

Wallace, slow and arthritic, walked to the witness chair. He took his seat, glancing first at the judge and then the jury. His weariness and old age were apparent. That was a good image for the jury. What Sophia did not know was that below that beaten exterior, he had changed. He was primed for the battle. Not to obtain justice for Mike, his dead son, but for money. Money he'd use to escape Bakersfield, the memories, and especially Beth.

Just as the bailiff stood to administer the oath to Wallace, there was a tremendous explosion. The building shook. Everyone jumped.

Some people stood with nowhere to go; others ducked. Screams and questions flooded the air, and the jurors looked to the judge. Judge Ortiz looked to his bailiff. The man with the gun.

⌘

# CHAPTER 64

## Shadows and Dust

*"Subtlety may deceive you; integrity never does."*
-Oliver Cromwell

"Stay seated," the bailiff ordered, moving to get Judge Ortiz from the courtroom first. "I mean it. Stay in your seats until we know where to take you."

The judge stood, but before he could leave, the courtroom door burst open. Another deputy sheriff ran to the judge.

"Your Honor," he said. "If I may."

He approached Judge Ortiz and whispered as the full courtroom watched. Like most courtrooms, Department 5 had no windows to the outside world. With new knowledge, the judge sat again and nodded to the deputy sheriff. The judge's calming presence quieted the courtroom.

"No reason to panic, everyone," the deputy sheriff announced. "We're not in immediate danger. There was an explosion in an abandoned commercial truck in the parking lot behind the courthouse way out near the railroad tracks. As far as we know, no lives lost, just property damage. Officers are on the scene and investigating."

There was a surge of nervous cacophony throughout the courtroom.

Judge Ortiz called the deputy sheriff over and whispered, "Officer, what are we supposed to do here? Keep going? Evacuate? What about another explosion, bombing, whatever?"

"We don't know of any other threat, but we're dispersing the demonstrators and press out front and along Truxtun. We're evacuating the courthouse. We have to keep it calm and orderly. The bomb squad's on its way to check out the whole building. We want your bailiff to get you to your car. All judges are going home. We'll notify everyone when it's safe to return."

"Thank you." Judge Ortiz stood.

The bailiff held up his hand. "Silence, everyone. And that means get off your cell phones, now."

Judge Ortiz took over the silenced, obedient mass. "Everyone, as a precaution, you are to follow the instructions of the deputy sheriff to evacuate the courthouse. It is just a precaution. Please do so in an orderly manner."

At that, the bailiff swept the judge into his chambers and out of the courthouse.

People stood and talked, cried, and yelled questions at the deputy sheriff. Wallace went to Beth, who was, of course, sobbing and breathing hard with her oxygen tube.

"Quiet. You all have to hear my instructions. Sit back down. And put away your cell phones."

The deputy sheriff posted himself at the door—some people sat, others didn't, but the decibel level precipitously fell as they looked to the deputy sheriff.

"Sit and be quiet." All now obeyed. "We will be leaving in an orderly manner. We're on the second floor. It won't be long. All of you can take one thing with you. One item. Everything else stays."

Each person picked one item—purses for most of the women, laptops for the reporters, and for the attorneys a briefcase with their laptops stuffed in it. Sophia grabbed her oversized purse and put her laptop in it.

Ben Kowrilsky tried to get past the deputy sheriff to scoop his fellow reporters with this story, but the deputy sheriff stopped him.

"Sir, please stay where you are. They'll tell me when it's our turn to leave, and we'll do so by rows."

"But I'm press. See." Ben tried to use his press pass as a get-out-of-jail-free card like he always did, but this time, it didn't work.

"Go sit down." The deputy sheriff, buff and vested, placed his hand on his gun. "I don't want to have to say it again."

Ben complied. He had no other choice.

* * *

For a tense forty minutes, ticking by snail-like, everyone sat and waited in silence. Comrades in danger, their breaths were shallow, their ears on alert, their hearts racing, and their bodies perspiring. Finally, the deputy sheriff began the evacuation—row by row, person by person, as promised. They were all grateful not to be on a higher floor with a longer wait. No one spoke as they stepped single file toward the staircase and safety. The mood was somber, guarded, fearful. Men helped women. Women helped men. The healthier assisted the frail. Paul and Bryce took Beth down step by step, trying not to bounce her wheelchair.

Moschella caught up with Sophia.

"Do you need help with the Holts?"

"Thank you, Tony, Paul and Bryce have it." Sophia smiled. "But I appreciate the offer."

The cooperative exit down the stairs and out a side door was strangely heartwarming and eerily hushed. Even outside, where the police were sentineled, there was only the sound of people getting in their vehicles and leaving.

Sophia had Bryce drive the Holts in their car to meet the team back at their rentals. Moschella, Sandoval, Kemper, and Jackson set out for Moschella's law offices.

Moreover, for once, Ben Kowrilsky didn't pester Sophia for inside information. His network and all the others were in a heated race to cover the alleged bombing and the possibility of more to follow. He was in heaven—media heaven. He only regretted the lack of bodies and blood. That always got you a lead story. He felt cheated.

* * *

Sophia's team and the Holts gathered in Sophia and Tricia's unit. They were rattled but still had a trial in front of them. This was a reprieve in a way, one that would allow Sophia to prep Wallace more for his testimony.

"They were after us again," Beth cried. "They're going to kill us. I know it. Oh, Wallace."

She reached for Wallace, but he sat down at the table, ignoring her. Everyone did, and she stopped her act. To Sophia, Beth had become nothing but a necessary sympathetic lump sucking her oxygen and weeping to sway the jury.

"Who do you think did that?" Wallace asked.

"Not anti-gun people," Paul said. "Too violent. Has to be gun fanatics. They're sending a message."

"I'm not sure." Sophia was thoughtful.

"It's not a good move for anyone," Tricia said. "If they get caught, they're going away for a long time."

"Could be some twisted attempt to show why we need guns," Bryce said.

"I'm just glad it was at the court and not our house," Wallace said.

"It's a message that people who mess with gun rights will be targets," Tricia interjected. "No one died this time, but in a small town, it's easy to reach anyone."

"Tricia, cool it," Paul whispered.

"That fire took all the fear out of me." Wallace's face was gray and resigned. "Let them try again. I won't be intimidated. I'm in this to the end."

Beth stared at her husband. "Yes, Wallace, we're in this to the end."

"Thank you." Sophia was puzzled. The incident had somehow made Wallace more committed.

Paul looked around the group. "Now we have time to review our witness order. We're still starting with Wallace, and we'll finish with Beth, right?"

Everyone agreed.

"How about the Sports Gear guys?" Bryce questioned. "How can we have the greatest impact and stop one from influencing the others? Can't we get the judge to exclude all of their witnesses except the one testifying?"

"I don't think Ortiz would allow that, Bryce, and what difference does it make?" Sophia replied. "They can always talk to each other, and they will. They may parrot each other's testimony, but we have deposition statements to use to impeach them . . . even with a careful prep we can still get at them."

"I agree," Paul confirmed. "Given that, though, we should maximize our advantage by starting with Spangler. You really did a number on him in that deposition, Sophia. Then Grimick, who will be tough, and Davis, the manager, who will be tougher still. But we start with the weakest link."

"Good," Tricia said. "Then, our two experts, Dr. Mapes and Dirk Savage, and wrap things up with Beth."

Sophia added, "Who knows if everything will go according to plan, but I like it."

"It's a sound approach," Paul said. "Let's eat."

Sophia and her team made an early dinner in the unit for themselves and the Holts: pan-roasted salmon, boiled green beans, and microwaved baked potatoes. They had stocked up from the nearby Albertson's. No wine or other alcohol during the trial. For most trial lawyers, especially the best ones, alcohol and trials don't mix.

After dinner, Sophia and the team took advantage of the extra time to rehearse Wallace's coming testimony. They coached him on trick questions which were inescapable.

Wallace and Beth drove home in their own car and refused an offer by Bryce to escort them that night or the next morning.

Sophia's team made it an early night. Even though the court didn't call, they prudently planned on continuing with the trial in the morning.

* * *

Back at their offices, Moschella and Sandoval met with the Gang of Four and Jackson in the conference room the outliers had taken as their turf. Jubal Kemper went to an open office to make business calls for Sports Gear. His role here was the client face, tantamount to window dressing at the defense table.

Jackson started the debriefing in an incongruously upbeat mood.

"Quite an interesting day, eh? Bet that gave those plaintiffs, their lawyers, and the jurors, even that Mex judge, something to think about. Perfect timing on the first day, huh?"

The Gang of Four, all except Boyd, smirked. Boyd looked away.

"What? Perfect timing?" Moschella was alarmed. "You and your people better not have had anything to do with that bombing."

"Why, Tony." Jackson paused. "Do you think we would do anything that stupid? I mean, if we could have pulled off something like that without the risk of getting caught, maybe . . . but relax. We didn't. That doesn't mean I wouldn't love to get in touch with the people who did and give them a big 'thank you.'"

"That's out of line," Moschella glared at Jackson and thought of Jackson's NGA contacts. "I don't like it. We're not at war with the Holts, their lawyers, or the legal system. We're lawyers. Not outlaws. We're part of the system. We have to win by the rules . . . with the law, not despite it."

"Oh, of course, Tony, of course." Jackson grinned. "Don't get all hitchy there. Just funning you. And you don't have to like anything. You just have to win. Sometimes winning in court requires winning outside as well. Why do you think we've done such a media barrage here and let our friends the NGA pick up the baton?"

"The media is one thing. Terrorist acts are another. We had better agree on that. We'll fight for Sports Gear and win this case on the law and with the law. I don't need any *other* assistance."

Moschella was enraged but decided he didn't want to know any more about this. If he didn't know, he didn't have to report anything. Sandoval was worried, but this fight was senior partner to senior partner.

"Naturally we'll keep doing it your way," Jackson baited Moschella. "Like we have all along."

The gang collectively smiled at the obvious untruth along with Jackson.

Moschella was incredulous. The Denver group hadn't done anything "his" way. They had done it all "their" way. He and his firm, and in his mind Sports Gear, had suffered for it, in results and reputation.

"Since we have some time, Tony, why don't you tell us all again what *your way* will be for the trial, assuming it resumes anytime soon?"

Jackson lorded it over everyone as he spoke. He was the self-proclaimed alpha in the room, and he felt the need to remind everyone of that at every opportunity.

"Sure, Tom." Moschella could play any game Jackson wanted. "Finally, something substantive, relevant and legal we can discuss. Since we deposed them all, it's obvious what the plaintiffs' witnesses are going to say. Ms. Sandoval and I have divided them up, and we have our cross-examinations and exhibits all fully prepared."

"You mean my team from Denver here has all of that prepared, don't you, Tony?" Again, Jackson stuck in the knife.

"Ms. Sandoval and I have reviewed their work. We've amended it to reflect how things are done in this court and in our city. Having done that, we're ready to go."

Jackson snorted. "Oh, I get it. You've made sure to get in some extra billables at your end too. So tell me again about our witnesses and how you intend to present your case to this mongrel jury we have."

Moschella buried his anger, as any good litigator does. But he had to shorten this encounter, couched as a meeting, or he would go off louder than the bomb outside the courthouse that morning.

"We need to present our best front to the jury at the outset, and that will be Mr. Kemper," Moschella said. "He epitomizes patriotic America, he's very articulate, and the jury will be impressed with his sincerity and presence."

"Shouldn't you finish with him?" Jackson rebutted. "You know, save your best for last?"

"Not in my view. He doesn't have personal knowledge about anything in the case except the company itself. If we end with him, it will look to the jury like we're trying to PR them with a company bigwig because we aren't happy with what came before. That would be a mistake in my mind."

"Well, I'm dubious."

Moschella pressed on before Jackson could give him any more dictates.

"After Mr. Kemper, we'll call the store personnel in descending order. Arnie Davis the manager is solid and a great witness. Grimick is a jerk but will toe the line. Having them precede

Spangler, our weak link if you will, should help anchor Spangler, and the jury won't be listening as hard once they've heard the other two first. We can keep him short."

"Do you really need Spangler? You have the store manager and one of the clerks who sold the stupid kid the shotgun. Our client got rid of Spangler, and he'll be carrying a grudge despite the nice severance check. Why take a chance?"

Moschella bit his tongue. Jackson may have tried his fair share of cases, but he certainly didn't understand big-picture litigation strategy.

"A couple of very good reasons, Tom. First, not calling him would be an omission, and the jury would see it as such. He interacted with Mike Holt, Grimick, and Davis. If we don't call him, it will look like we're hiding something or are afraid to put him up there. Second, the Holts's lawyers have subpoenaed him. They will definitely call him, either in their own case in chief, which I would do, or as a rebuttal witness. My scenario is hypothetical and assumes the other side won't call him or the other Sports Gear people first. We can't count on that. We can't keep him off the stand, is what I'm saying."

"You mean, so long as he's available to testify, right?" Jackson said with studied nonchalance.

He was making Moschella uneasy. That uneasiness went far beyond his irritation over Jackson's intermeddling with his handling of the case. Jackson was showing his true colors—he wasn't an attorney but a fixer, a mouthpiece and errand boy for the gun mob. Moschella responded with caution, so as not to betray any alarm on his part.

"That's a given, but we have no reason to think he won't be. He rarely missed work at Sports Gear, is as healthy as someone from Oildale living that lifestyle can be, and believes in the case. At least, he did up until he was let go contrary to my recommendation. Excuse me, 'resigned.' But I think his love of guns will keep his testimony solid."

"Hmm." Jackson was unconvinced. "After Spangler, who do you call?"

"Some or all of our experts. We made the plaintiffs and their lawyers waste a lot of time and money taking their depositions. We can pick and choose among them. That's still up in the air, and you and your people will surely have valuable input there."

Moschella suppressed his condescension. He needn't have worried. Jackson and his coterie were used to being the big shots in these gun cases, and their egos ignored the sarcasm and accepted his statement as merely the truth and their due.

"So that's it? The case ends with our experts? Seems a little impersonal to me. Don't you think so, French?"

Samuel French had been eyeing Sandoval. More precisely, consuming her with his eyes. Every inch of her. French paused, to let his eyes linger a bit longer before answering.

Moschella spoke up. "We want to . . ."

French interrupted Moschella. "What do you think, Ms. Sandoval? Or do you think?"

Sandoval ignored his insult as she had been his visual assaults on her body.

"As Tony was trying to tell you, we want to conclude with Brandon Gallo," Theresa said. "He's the stocking clerk and is hoping to move up. He was there when Mike Holt bought the shotgun and gave a good deposition. He asked Mike in the aisle if he needed help. Mike didn't and appeared normal to Brandon. He stated unequivocally he knew nothing about the actual sale because he was sweeping and restocking. He will come across well and show how Sports Gear tries to employ our local young people, giving them a chance to improve their lives."

"So you *do* think. A bonus along with everything else you have to offer."

French chuckled, and so did his cronies, even Boyd for once, albeit involuntarily.

"That sounds good, now that you mention it," Jackson reflected. "Okay. I guess I can buy that game plan for now. Subject to change as I see fit."

Moschella and Sandoval left the self-important peacock and his pack of boot-lickers to themselves. They went to Moschella's office.

Jackson and his followers got Kemper and left immediately for the Padre Hotel and an expensive, alcohol-fueled dinner in its Belvedere Room. They were all in a very good mood and quite pleased with themselves.

* * *

In Moschella's office Theresa lashed out. "I can't stand it anymore."

"Hey, hey, you handled yourself well. It's just for a little longer."

"How can you take it all like that? Is this case worth your dignity and pride? Or mine? Is this what I can expect if I make partner here, to have to kowtow to people like that while they undress me with their eyes?"

Moschella admired and liked his fiery, impetuous, brilliant, and beautiful young colleague. But he had seen the world and its realities for many more years than she had.

"I hate this whole situation, especially how they treat you. As a lawyer, sometimes you have to put up with things you don't like for clients you like even less. Clearly, the 'client' here is Tom Jackson, not Sports Gear."

"But he was implying . . . no, he was stating outright that they would do anything to win . . . illegal . . . unethical . . . you name it. Did he arrange that bombing this morning? Are you okay with that?"

"Hardly. I'd never condone it. But do we really know? We have no proof, and he's such a blowhard he likes to stir the pot. Who knows who did it. Yes, he implied it. Should that ever cross from implication to fact, the law and the canons of ethics would force us to resign from the case and disclose the reason to Judge Ortiz. And we would."

"Imply . . . a very useful word, isn't it? I'm certainly learning about the practice of law and all its *implications*. More than I ever wanted to know."

"We're walking on a tightrope, and I committed us to it. If I hadn't, and it wasn't too late, I'd dump them. I can't get rid of Jackson, but I can make French leave. He's the worst and most arrogant of the four."

"Don't bother. It's not worth the trouble. He's obnoxious, crude, misogynistic, but otherwise just a harmless blowhard. I'm going home. I'll be in early tomorrow whether we hear from the court or not."

Moschella watched Theresa leave, captivating in every way as always.

*If I were younger, and unmarried, or not happily married . . .* but he shut those thoughts down, and hard. He had enough troubles without adding to them. He was not about to be like that insufferable French. He shuddered, disgusted at the thought.

⌘

# CHAPTER 65

## Slow Are the Wheels of Justice

*"Make crime pay. Become a lawyer."*
-Will Rogers

$A$s Sophia and Tricia drank their morning coffee together, they watched the local Channel 23 ABC News station coverage of the explosion. It had been a pipe bomb detonated by a cellphone. The entire courthouse had been swept, and no more bombs or other suspicious items were found. Speculation was rampant about the bomber's identity, but no one was taking credit. Sophia tried to reach Ben but failed.

At eight-thirty, Judge Ortiz's clerk called Sophia to tell her to report at ten for trial. She rang the Holts to let them know. They were already dressed and waiting. Tricia called Paul and Bryce, and the team was off in no time since they had been forced to leave nearly all their things in the courtroom.

They arrived to heightened security and a heavy cordon of police around the courthouse. New metal detectors, rivaling those at airports, awaited them. Everyone was also being thoroughly searched, instead of the ordinarily lackadaisical once-over that was the norm. The pace was glacial.

\* \* \*

When Sophia, her team, and the Holts finally got to Judge Ortiz's courtroom, it was past ten. Moschella, Sandoval, and Kemper were already there, and the courtroom was again nearly full. Ben

Kowrilsky had secured a seat in the middle this time, closer to the action.

With the parties and their counsel in place, the bailiff silenced the courtroom. Judge Ortiz entered and took the bench, and the jurors were seated.

"Ladies and gentlemen," Judge Ortiz began. "As you have probably learned from the news, the courthouse is safe. No one has come forward to claim responsibility for yesterday's bombing, and we have no reason to believe it has anything to do with this case."

"Sure," Sophia whispered under her breath to Paul.

"We ask that everyone proceed accordingly. Before we begin, though, I have to report that one of our jurors has been excused. Her mother had a heart attack last night and is in critical condition at Mercy Hospital Southwest. Our thoughts go out to her. That means juror number 36, our first alternate, is an alternate no longer. Please move to the vacant seat in the jury box, sir, if you will."

Juror number 36, a weathered-looking, graying Caucasian man, dressed in an ill-fitting suit and worn cowboy boots, swaggered up to his new "real" juror seat. He smiled as he sat and glanced over at the lawyers and their clients.

Sophia and her team were perturbed. He had "gun-friendly" written all over him. His appearance and demeanor screamed lower socioeconomic Bakersfield, close enough to being a redneck to warrant the label. She had been forced to pass him because she had nothing to use to get him excused for cause during the jury selection process. She hadn't wanted to face an entire new panel of prospective jurors, so she had not used a peremptory challenge on him. He was there for the duration, unless something happened to him, too.

"All right, everyone. Before Ms. Christopoulos resumes her case in chief with her first witness, we have some changes as a result of the new and increased security procedures. I'm going to abbreviate our daily trial schedule given the slower lines for inspections. I want everyone to have plenty of time to get in and out of the courthouse, and I'll do everything possible to make this trial efficient. We'll start our trial days at ten every morning after other courtrooms are already in session, break for lunch at noon, resume at one-thirty, and conclude at four. That should keep us out of the security 'rush hours' so to speak."

Sophia just shook her head. Short trial days did not mean more efficient ones. They meant a much longer trial and more expenses for her and her clients. But there was nothing she could do about it.

"Thank you, Your Honor," Moschella said. "That will help."

"Help you drain the rest of our coffers," Paul whispered under his breath to Sophia.

Moschella and Sandoval had gotten another advantage. They were on the clock, after all, and the longer the trial, the more their firm could bill.

* * *

Wallace resumed the stand. The bailiff swore him in.

Sophia took him through his own background, his marriage to Beth, and then had him paint a picture of their son Mike. She introduced photographs, award certificates, report cards, newspaper articles, all showing an accomplished, popular, well-adjusted young man who was a credit to his family and his city, a star student, a premier athlete, a competitor in high school, and a source of pride when he was admitted to Ivy League Yale with a scholarship.

It was her job to get the evidence to support emotional distress damages on the record and before the jury, so she could argue for that as part of the general damages element in the Holts's negligence and wrongful death claims. That part of her job she had accomplished, and Wallace came across as convincingly distraught.

When Sophia finished, she had also established for the jurors, through a sympathetic and sad Wallace, that his son was not and could not have been himself when he bought that shotgun. That he and Mike had been loyal customers of the Sports Gear store since Mike's childhood. And that Mike was sufficiently well-known in this small community that anyone should have recognized something was amiss with him that day.

It was noon. Sophia still had the most difficult part of her examination yet to go with Wallace, but he had performed far better than she had anticipated thus far.

Moschella had not objected once. Sophia's questions were all in proper form and unassailable on any other grounds. Besides, Moschella truly believed that none of what Wallace had testified about mattered under the applicable and controlling law.

"Time for our lunch break. I'll see all of you back here at two." Judge Ortiz left the bench.

\* \* \*

The Holt contingent went to the retro Woolworth's Diner on Nineteenth Street. It was close and inexpensive, and the Holts had recommended it. They ordered sandwiches, burgers, and sodas.

"You did a great job up there, Wallace," Tricia said. "And you looked so distinguished."

"It wasn't that hard," Wallace said. "I liked talking about how Mike was when he was growing up."

"You did do well, my dear." Beth took two hits from her oxygen tank.

"You'll do the same this afternoon, too." Paul finished his Coke. "You'll have to be on your toes for Moschella's questions, but Sophia will protect you when she can with objections. Just listen to them, try to get why she is objecting, and wait to answer."

Tactically, Moschella couldn't hit this old man too hard on the stand because the jury wouldn't like it. Jurors never liked seeing the weak or victims torn apart.

\* \* \*

Moschella, Sandoval, and Jackson met the Gang of Four at their local domicile, the Padre Hotel. They ate at the hotel's Brimstone restaurant, which had become their preferred lunch spot. The Gang had already ordered and were all busily eating when the other three arrived. Sandoval quickly ordered the vegetable salad, Moschella the lasagna Bolognese, and Jackson the Padre Wagyu burger with Cajun fries. Kemper was up in his hotel room. He had gotten a call from Sports Gear's president and had to handle some unrelated business matters with him over the lunch break.

Jackson didn't waste a second after they had all ordered. He launched another of his attacks on Moschella.

"Tony, why didn't you object to any of that Greek bitch's questions? You let her have old man Holt paint a tear-jerking story for the jury . . . uninterrupted. No good lawyer lets that happen."

"Tom, you can fire me anytime. I've made it clear to you that I don't care. But as I seem to have to remind you every day, this is Bakersfield. Jurors here hate objections. They think when lawyers object they are trying to hide something . . . the facts, the truth, whatever."

"Oh, bull. People are people everywhere. Our client needs to make a bigger impression than the plaintiffs in this case. So far, it isn't happening. Or, more precisely, you aren't making it happen."

Moschella wouldn't be baited.

"We have to present Sports Gear in the best possible light. Having a bunch of wrong-headed objections overruled by the judge wouldn't achieve that. Ms. Christopoulos's questions were relevant and all in perfect form. The judge would have overruled any objection I might have manufactured. I'm not going to piss off the judge or the jury with grandstanding and pointless objections."

"Maybe you just don't know what a good objection is, Tony."

"I'd be happy to have you and your little group of legal geniuses educate me, Tom. I've only tried a few hundred cases here, after all. I'm sure your vast collective experience could really teach me a thing or two."

Sandoval choked on her salad at Moschella's dripping sarcasm.

"You'd better do one hell of a job on that old geezer in your cross-examination," Jackson threatened. "That's all I have to say. We need to win this one . . . convincingly. We have to send a message that this kind of litigation won't work in California."

"Oh, because Sports Gear sells a lot of guns to people who kill themselves, and you want to discourage more lawsuits like this in the future?"

Jackson turned stone cold. "No. We want to show the few unfortunates who are somehow caught up in that situation that a lawsuit is not the way to deal with their grief, anger, and guilt."

Sandoval saw the three male gargoyles from Denver grinning again, and Rose Boyd sitting poker-faced.

Neither Sandoval nor Moschella knew that the Jackson firm had selectively pruned the documents it had forwarded to them to produce to Krause & White. They had held back, among many others, all documents related to several other claims and settlements involving Sports Gear and gun suicides. Somehow those documents had all been "overlooked."

Lunch was tense and silent from that point forward.

"We've got to get back." Moschella said.

Moschella and Sandoval left with their food half eaten.

French watched them leave. "I like that nice bit of eye candy."

Boyd was irritated. "Sam, we're here to work, not for you to indulge your immature sexual fantasies.

"You're just jealous, Rosie."

"Enough." Jackson slammed his hand down on the table.

Beauregard and Pickett concentrated on finishing their meals.

"All of you get back to work. I'm off to court to see if our local 'superstars' can show me something to justify my hiring them."

⌘

# CHAPTER 66

## Death in the Afternoon

*"There's no tragedy in life like the death of a child."*
-Dwight D. Eisenhower

Court resumed at two sharp. Wallace was back on the stand.

Sophia continued her examination, heading into the dark side of her case.

"Mr. Holt, I know this is difficult for you, but how did you learn that your son, Mike, had killed himself?"

An ashen Wallace whispered, "I found him."

"You'll have to speak louder, Mr. Holt, for the jury to hear you," Judge Ortiz said gently from the bench.

"Yes, sir." Wallace looked up at the judge. His pain was evident. He turned to the jury once again.

"Dinner was ready. We called, but he didn't come down. His car was home. Beth told me to get him."

Wallace stopped.

"What happened next?" Sophia used the trial lawyer's stock follow-up question.

"I found him. I mean his body . . . with no face . . . blood all over."

Wallace stopped again.

"I know this is hard, but where?"

Sophia couldn't have had a better witness with more emotional impact than Wallace. The jury was eating it up, and Moschella didn't break the momentum. She wouldn't have either. You can't safely intrude on true sorrow resonating from the stand. Not unless you want the jurors to hate you.

"In . . . in his closet upstairs in his bedroom, with a shotgun in his . . . what was left of his head . . . blood and you know parts everywhere."

"Do you need a break, Mr. Holt?" Judge Ortiz asked.

"No . . . no."

"Did you know your son owned a shotgun, Mr. Holt?"

"No. He never would have."

Moschella objected in a respectful and understated tone commensurate with the moment and acutely conscious of the jury. "Move to strike the last sentence, Your Honor. Opinion and speculation."

"Sustained, Mr. Moschella. Members of the jury, please ignore that last comment by Mr. Holt."

"Mr. Holt, in fact, Mike did own a shotgun. He had one that day, isn't that right?"

"Yes, of course. We found a receipt for it from Sports Gear. It was time stamped that afternoon."

"Did you have any other guns in your home at that time?"

"Not in our home. I had wrapped up all the guns and ammo we had in some old moving blankets and put them in our garage where Mike wouldn't see them. No one has touched them since. I don't even remember where they are."

"Are you opposed to people having guns in general, Mr. Holt?"

"Hardly. I hunted with my father all the time growing up. For food for our table. I owned two rifles and a shotgun. I was even a member of the NGA."

"That's the National Gun Association, correct?"

"Yes."

"What made you hide all your guns in the garage when Mike was about twelve?"

"It was Mike. He told me he hated them."

"Did he tell you why?"

"Yes."

"What did he say to you?"

"That he didn't want to hunt or kill anything. I had given him a .22 rifle for his twelfth birthday that summer, he did all the safety training and such, and we went to the Kern River area to camp and hunt some doves, quail, chukar, whatever was in season."

"What happened?"

"It was a little after dawn, still not much light. I saw a chukar . . . or what I thought was one . . . on a tree branch overhead and told him to take the shot. He wouldn't at first. Then after some coaxing, he did."

"What happened next?"

"It wasn't a chukar. It was a robin. He hit it all right. In the middle. Blew the bird in half. The bottom half of the robin landed on his shoulder."

"What was his reaction?"

"He was horrified. He screamed and slapped it away. Then he took off his shirt and threw it as far as he could. He started crying, said he hated hunting, hated the rifle, and never wanted to hunt or shoot again."

"What was your reaction?"

"I felt really bad. He was so upset. We went home, and the next day I took all of our guns and ammo and put them in the garage, as I said before."

"Did you ever again have a gun in your home?"

"No, not until Mike brought in that shotgun."

"Do you have that shotgun still?"

"Yes, I picked it up from the police station along with all of the other things they had taken from his room. I'm just keeping it until this trial is over."

"Do you want to stop Sports Gear from selling guns to people, Mr. Holt?"

"No. Never."

"Then why are you and your wife suing Sports Gear?"

"Because they sold that shotgun to my son, Mike, when they knew he was acting strangely and not right in the head. They . . ."

Moschella objected again with the solemnity the jury was feeling. "Speculation, Your Honor, and lack of foundation."

"Sustained, Mr. Moschella. The jury will disregard the last question and answer."

"Mr. Holt, did you ever speak to anyone at Sports Gear USA about the sale of the shotgun to Mike?"

"Yes, I did."

"When?"

"A couple of days after Mike died."

"Who did you talk to there?"

"Arnie Davis, the manager . . . and Moss Grimick and Joe Spangler. They sold my son that shotgun."

"Did you approach Mr. Davis or did he approach you?"

"Well, he saw me come into the store, and we knew each other. I had shopped there for years. He walked over to me."

"Who spoke first?"

"He did."

"What did he say?"

"He said how sorry he was about Mike, and that he should have known something was wrong because he thought Mike was acting strangely in the store and in the parking lot."

"Objection, hearsay, Your Honor," Moschella interposed.

"Those are admissions against interest, Your Honor, made by an authorized agent of the defendant. That's an exception to the hearsay rule."

"Yes, Ms. Christopoulos. I'm aware." Judge Ortiz gave her a condescending look. "Objection overruled."

"Did Mr. Davis use those exact words, namely, that he 'should have known something was wrong because Mike was acting strangely in the store and the parking lot'?"

"Yes, he . . ."

Moschella interjected, "Objection, asked and answered, cumulative."

"Sustained. Move on, Ms. Christopoulos."

"What did you say in response?"

"I asked him why he sold Mike the shotgun then."

"What was his answer?"

"He said he felt really guilty about it, but that he didn't sell the shotgun to Mike. His sales clerks who handle the gun sales did."

"Did he tell you who they were?"

"Yes. Moss Grimick and Joe Spangler. I knew who they were anyway. Like I said, I had shopped there for years."

"Did you speak to either of them?"

"I talked to both of them together."

"What did you say to them?"

"I asked them if they had sold Mike the shotgun, and they both said yes."

"Did they say anything else to you?"

"Objection, overly broad, calls for a narrative answer, Your Honor."

"Sustained, Mr. Moschella. Please rephrase your question, Ms. Christopoulos."

"Certainly, Your Honor. Did either of them say anything about Mike's behavior that afternoon?"

"Yes. Mr. Spangler said Mike had tried to buy one shell for the shotgun, which he thought was dumb since everyone knows you buy ammo by the box."

"Did he use the word 'dumb,' Mr. Holt?"

"Actually, he said it was 'odd.'"

"Did Mr. Grimick say anything?"

"Um, he just nodded in agreement."

"With what Mr. Spangler said?"

"Yes."

"Did Mr. Spangler say anything else?"

"Yes. He said Mike had a strange look in his eyes."

"Again, were those his exact words?"

"Yes."

"And did Mr. Grimick nod in agreement with those words as well?"

"He did."

"Anything else?"

"That he was crazy or nuts or loony."

"Anything else?"

"No."

"Have you spoken to Mr. Davis, Mr. Spangler, or Mr. Grimick since that day?"

"No. And I sure haven't gone near Sports Gear since then."

Sophia had her eye on the clock and asked further questions about Wallace's loss and his relationship with Mike. They were perfectly relevant and not repetitive. She made sure that Moschella would be unable to start his cross-examination before court adjourned.

"Thank you, Mr. Holt. No further questions at this time, Your Honor."

"You can step down, Mr. Holt," Judge Ortiz said.

It was four. Judge Ortiz recessed the court for the day, reminding the jurors not to speak to anyone about the case or read or watch anything about it

"Ten o'clock sharp tomorrow, everyone." As Judge Ortiz left the bench, the attorneys stood. The bailiff had the jurors file out.

* * *

Tricia and Bryce helped Sophia and Paul pack up.

"Wallace did great," Paul whispered.

"Couldn't have done better." Sophia smiled.

"Yeah," Bryce parroted the consensus.

"And the jury gets to sleep on that superb testimony," Tricia whispered.

"I would have never thought of that," Bryce said.

"Think of this, Bryce," Sophia whispered. "There's no way Moschella can cross-examine Wallace for the entire day without Ortiz pushing him along. So we'll get Spangler up there, tear him to shreds, and leave the jury with his negative testimony to chew on for the whole weekend."

Moschella and Theresa beat Sophia's team out of the courthouse and were mobbed by the press.

Sophia and her colleagues escorted the Holts stealthily out.

* * *

After dinner Sophia gave Ben his exclusive interview with the Holts at their home. Ben was at his best and did more for the Holts and their case than Sophia could have expected after putting him off for so many days.

Paul and Sophia prepped Wallace for Moschella's cross-examination while Tricia and Bryce worked back at the condo organizing the Spangler material.

⌘

# CHAPTER 67

## Holt On There Now

*"Fortunately, as it pertains to guns, my dad and uncle introduced me to guns the way it needs to be done, smart, slow and safe."*
-Ted Nugent

It was ten the next morning. Although it was a routine time, nothing else was routine for the litigators and their clients. No trial is ever routine. It is an intense, uncertain, terrifying journey until the verdict finally arrives. Few things in life are as draining as a trial for serious and dedicated litigators. Their days are spent struggling in court, and their nights in preparation. They are lucky to get four hours of sleep, if that.

Wallace was back on the stand. Judge Ortiz reminded him that he was still under oath, and then it was time for Moschella to make his first real trial impressions, not only on Wallace, but also on the jurors, Kemper, and Jackson the puppet master.

"Good morning, Mr. Holt. I'd like to repeat my sincere condolences to you and Mrs. Holt for the death of your son, Mike. It is something no parent should ever have to face. If you don't mind, I just need to clarify a few things in your testimony yesterday. In doing so I mean no disrespect to you or to your son's memory."

Wallace said nothing. He showed no reaction at all waiting for Moschella to begin his interrogation. Sophia's team was pleased, and Moschella could see that Wallace would be no pushover.

"You told us yesterday that until Mike was about twelve you had guns in the home, and were yourself a hunter and a member of the National Gun Association, correct?"

Sophia started to object with "asked and answered" and "compound," but Paul touched her arm to stop her. Paul was more experienced than Sophia. The jury had to trust that Wallace was not hiding anything. Sophia should object only when it really mattered. This was not one of those times. She took the hint. Besides, Wallace's testimony had to conclude quickly if they were to get Spangler on the hot seat.

"Yes." As he had in his deposition, Wallace answered concisely and without volunteering anything.

"You bought Mike a .22 when he was twelve?"

"Yes."

"Then, after the hunting trip with Mike when he was upset about killing a bird, you disposed of your guns and Mike's?"

"I hid them away in our garage, as I already testified."

"Did you also resign your membership in the National Gun Association?"

"I did."

"Isn't that because you had become opposed to people having guns?"

"No. I wasn't then. I'm not now. I've never been opposed to people having guns."

"So, people have a right to buy and own guns, in your view."

"Not everyone."

"Who not?"

"Not criminals, not people who aren't responsible or right in the head."

"Your son, Mike, wasn't a criminal, was he?"

"No."

"In fact, from your testimony yesterday, he was the model of a responsible person, wasn't he?"

"Yes, he was. But . . ."

"You've answered my question, Mr. Holt. Mike was never under the care of a psychiatrist or psychologist, was he?"

"No, but he should have been."

"Oh? So before he bought the shotgun at Sports Gear, you thought he should have been under the care of a psychiatrist or psychologist?"

Moschella looked knowingly at the jury.

"Um, no, I can't say that."

"No teacher or doctor ever told you that Mike exhibited any signs of mental illness or clinical depression, did they?"

Sophia objected this time. "Objection, compound, your Honor."

"Sustained."

Moschella was undeterred.

"Very well, did anyone ever tell you that your son, Mike, exhibited any signs of mental illness?"

"No."

"Or that, to use your words, he wasn't 'right in the head'?"

"No. Not in those words, no."

"Did anyone ever tell you that he was depressed?"

"He did, and so did my wife, Beth."

"What did he say to you?"

"That he wasn't happy at Yale and wished he had never gone there. The other students treated him like a hick because he was from Bakersfield."

"But did he say he was depressed?"

"He didn't say use that word, but I could tell he was."

"What did your wife, Beth, say to you about Mike's depression?"

"Just that. After he came home from Yale, he seemed depressed, listless, not interested in much. Just played computer games and didn't go out with any of his old high school friends."

"Yet you did not suggest to Mike that he see a psychiatrist or psychologist, did you?"

"I should have."

"Move to strike as nonresponsive, Your Honor," Moschella said.

"Agreed, Mr. Moschella. The jury will disregard Mr. Holt's last answer."

"Did you ever suggest to Mike that he see a psychiatrist or psychologist, Mr. Holt?"

"No."

"Did you ever discuss doing that with your wife Beth?"

"No."

"So before Mike bought the shotgun at Sports Gear, you saw nothing that made you think he was mentally unbalanced or irresponsible, did you?"

"I guess not."

"Are either you or your wife, Beth, credentialed in psychiatry or psychology, Mr. Holt?"

"No, we're retired teachers."

"As teachers, you were trained to look out for problem students and to recognize the signs of possible mental issues, weren't you?"

Wallace and Sophia were both caught off guard, but Sophia reacted quickly.

"Objection, Your Honor. Compound question again and lack of foundation."

"Sustained, Ms. Christopoulos."

"Okay. Did you receive training as a teacher in how to recognize possible mental issues with students?

"Some. A few sessions at teaching conferences, as I recall."

"Did that training ever cause you to identify a student with mental issues in any of your classes?"

"On one or two occasions, I recall doing that and sending them to the school counselor."

"So you felt you could tell when a student was sufficiently disturbed to warrant calling that to the attention of someone else at your school?"

"On some level. I'm not a professional in that area, though."

"But nonetheless, and with that training, you saw nothing in Mike's behavior before he bought the shotgun at Sports Gear indicating to you that he had any mental issues, did you?"

"No. No, I didn't. I wish I had."

"You spoke with the Sports Gear manager here in Bakersfield, Arnie Davis, and with the clerks who sold the shotgun to Mike, Moss Grimick and Joe Spangler, right?"

"I already said I did."

"To your knowledge, is Mr. Davis trained in psychiatry or psychology?"

"I have no idea."

"How about Mr. Grimick or Mr. Spangler?"

"Same answer."

"Do you contend they should have been better able to judge Mike's mental condition than yourself or your wife, Beth?"

"Objection—argumentative, Your Honor," Sophia interjected.

"I think that's a fair question, Ms. Christopoulos. Overruled."

"They sell guns. Guns are dangerous. They should be trained to spot questionable customers."

"How do you know they weren't?"

"I don't. But they told me that Mike was acting odd . . . the manager said 'off' . . . and had a strange look in his eyes, that should have been enough. I mean, he asked to buy one bullet, one shotgun shell."

"Do you have any information that in selling the shotgun to Mike, anyone at Sports Gear failed to comply with the law?"

Sophia pounced. "Objection, Your Honor. Calls for a legal conclusion, speculative, seeks expert opinion, invades the province of the court."

"Sustained on all grounds, Ms. Christopoulos. You know better than that, Mr. Moschella."

"My apologies, Your Honor. No disrespect intended to the court."

"Just a few more questions, Mr. Holt." Moschella continued.

"Have you any information indicating that anyone at Sports Gear USA was in any way involved in the attack on and burning of your home?"

"None that it was . . . none that it wasn't."

"But that attack frightened you, didn't it?"

"Of course."

"Do you know who did it?"

"No."

"Do the police know?"

"If they do, they haven't told us."

"You don't believe they're investigating it, do you?"

"I have no reason to believe that."

"Aren't you angry because the police aren't looking hard enough for the arsonists?"

"No."

Sophia had seen it coming. Moschella was trying to push the button Wallace revealed in the tumult after his deposition. She had warned Wallace not to say anything negative about the Bakersfield police.

"In fact, you believe the police don't care because you and your wife brought this anti-gun lawsuit, don't you?"

"Objection. Argumentative, asked and answered, Your Honor." Sophia checked herself—she was yelling.

"I'm going to have to sustain those objections as well, Mr. Moschella." Judge Ortiz was apologetic, an attitude that smacked of favoritism.

"I understand, Your Honor. No further questions for Mr. Holt at this time."

"Any redirect, Ms. Christopoulos?" Judge Ortiz inquired.

"Yes, Your Honor," Sophia replied. "Very briefly. Mr. Holt, Mr. Moschella never asked you why you actually stopped your membership in the National Gun Association. Why did you?"

"Simple. I had put our firearms away, didn't intend to use them again, so there was really no point in staying in that group."

"Did you have other friends at the time who were members of the National Gun Association?"

"Of course."

"Did you continue seeing them after you left the organization?"

"Yes, until the news reports about our lawsuit. They won't talk to me now."

"Have you ever been a member of any organization seeking to prohibit the sale of guns?"

"No."

"Or advocating greater controls over the sale of guns?"

"No."

"Don't you think there should be greater restrictions on who can buy guns?"

"No. I just don't think Sports Gear should have sold my son, Mike, that shotgun based on what those folks at the store told me about the way he was that day."

"Thank you, Mr. Holt. No further questions for now." Sophia wanted Spangler up after lunch.

"Nor for me, Your Honor," Moschella added. He had made his points and believed Beth would be easier to shake.

"It's eleven-fifty, everyone. Might as well break for lunch. Please be back at two."

The courtroom emptied. The scene as people made their way from the courthouse was eerie and had changed since the bomb. A heavy police presence kept the news vans a block away and the reporters at bay. The demonstrators were scattered in small pockets inhibiting their fervor and limiting their impact.

Wallace had to take Beth to an appointment with her doctor, who had agreed to see her during the lunch break.

That left Sophia and her team to themselves. They walked to the nearby Café Crepes for a quick and light lunch. Sophia and Tricia ordered the turkey avocado crepes, Paul the smoked salmon, and Bryce the chicken Florentine. The food was surprisingly good and improved their collective mood. They all agreed Wallace had done as well as or better than they expected, but it was hardly a win. Sophia, Paul, and Tricia reviewed the Spangler questions and avenues of potential attack. Bryce ate and listened.

They got a round of Peet's coffees for dessert and headed back. No time for anything else.

*I'll crucify that asshole Spangler*, Sophia thought as she remembered Eddie and Spangler's ugly verbal assault on him after the depositions.

⌘

# CHAPTER 68

## Star-Spanglered Banter

*"The difference between stupidity*
*and genius is that genius has its limits."*
-Albert Einstein

Sophia and her troops ran the security gauntlet and returned to the packed courtroom.

Tricia leaned forward and tapped on Sophia's and Paul's shoulders. She nodded to the right. "Look."

"What the hell?" Paul whispered as he spotted Spangler at the back of the center aisle.

Joe Spangler, thin and weathered, was in a wheelchair with a cast on his right leg, a brace on his left shoulder, bruises on his face, and a bandage on his forehead. For court, he had on a pressed white shirt instead of a Sports Gear T-shirt, and his graying ponytail was slicked back and tied in a knot at his neck.

"And Grimick wheeled him in," Bryce said.

\* \* \*

At the defense table, Theresa noticed the confab at the plaintiffs' table and turned to see what had caught their attention.

"Tony, look at Spangler . . ."

Moschella stopped studying his cross-examination outline and was shocked by what greeted him. Jackson saw Moschella's expression and scanned the courtroom. Spotting Spangler, he wasn't so much surprised as angry—red-faced angry. He furiously texted

Moschella, demanding that he get Spangler's testimony continued for health reasons.

"All rise," the bailiff boomed.

Judge Ortiz entered the courtroom, and before summoning the jury, he recognized Moschella.

"Your Honor, the defense would like to move to defer the testimony of Mr. Joe Spangler, who is in the aisle in a wheelchair, until next week. Mr. Spangler is obviously injured and in no condition to testify."

"Ms. Christopoulos, do you concur?"

Sophia, caught unaware, did not show it. She stood, stoic, thinking, not panicking. That was the hallmark of a good trial lawyer. Surprise, shocks, subterfuges are inevitable during trials. Litigators must embrace them, not just react to them. The Mandarin Chinese character for "crisis," is a combination of two other characters representing "danger" and "opportunity." That is how good litigators view any unexpected trial development—signaling danger and opportunity both.

"Moschella doesn't want him up there because he's their Achilles heel," Paul whispered to Sophia.

"I know." Sophia addressed Judge Ortiz. "No, Your Honor. I respectfully request a *voir dire* of Mr. Spangler in chambers to consider Mr. Moschella's request."

"If you insist, Ms. Christopoulos. Counselors and Mr. Spangler, join me in chambers with the court reporter."

\* \* \*

Paul and Theresa, the defense lawyers, and Spangler repaired to the judge's inner chamber. That personal sanctum is where, during trials, a judge hears motions not meant for the eyes and ears of jurors and the gallery. A sanctum judges made personal, but never cozy. Judge Ortiz did this with a subdued area rug, desert paintings, and a tall wood grandfather clock with the correct time.

Spangler was sworn in by the court reporter.

"Ms. Christopoulos, he looks pretty banged up to me," Judge Ortiz commented.

"I'm just fine, sir," Spangler spoke out of turn.

"I won't belabor this, Your Honor. Mr. Spangler, let's make this easy. What happened to you?"

"Well, I was driv'n my pride 'n' joy—my cherry red pickup—to Costco over to Rosedale Highway. Then, on Elm Street . . . about the 2900 block, these headlights behind me got real close. This huge black SUV was tailgating me. Then, pow!"

Spangler clapped his hands together hard.

"It rammed me. I gunned it, but they got alongside me and rammed me again. I got pushed into a big power line tower there. Simple as that. I was damn mad. Sorry?"

Sophia had signaled that she had a question.

"You said 'they.' Did you recognize the vehicle or anyone in it?

"Naw, they were on me in a second. One guy had a suit on, and I think the other guy did too. They raced away after knocking me around."

The fact the men were in suits confirmed what Moschella suspected. But he kept quiet. Again, what were suspicions without proof?

"Did you get the license plate number?" Sophia continued.

"Hell no. Excuse me, Your Judgeship. I didn't have no seatbelt on. I'm lucky I'm breath'n today. My primo cherry red ride was smashed. I was half in and half out the door. That's how my leg got busted and my shoulder dislocated."

"Didn't you have an airbag?"

"You kidding? We take those out. You can sell 'em for big bucks."

"What happened next?"

"Well, I guess someone called 911 because the cops come by and an ambulance. There was a nice young doc at the Emergency Medical Services. That group on Chester. He did X-rays, some other stuff, fixed me up real good."

"What did the doctor tell you was wrong with you?"

"Noth'n serious. A few cuts and bruises, dislocated shoulder, and a itty-bitty fracture on my shinbone. He called it a hairline."

Spangler rapped on his cast with his right hand. "He put this here on jes' to be safe."

"Did the doctor say you could testify today?"

"Didn't talk to him 'bout that. But he said I was good to go. So I'm here."

"Are you prepared to testify this afternoon, Mr. Spangler, or do you need time to recover?"

"Recover? Heck, no. I'm all set. But I'll do whatever this guy tells me to do." He nodded at Moschella.

The judge turned to Moschella. "Mr. Moschella, have you anything for Mr. Spangler before I rule on your motion?"

"I do, Your Honor. Mr. Spangler, it looks like you hit your head hard during that crash."

"I bumped it on the dashboard. Got a couple of bruises, like I said, but mostly it was my cheekbone here."

Spangler pointed to his cheek bandage.

"Not my head."

"Did your doctor do any tests to see if you had a concussion?"

"Oh, yeah, I almost forgot that. He did a bunch of 'em. Asked me some questions, made me follow his finger around with my eyes, did some sort of scan thing . . ."

"A CT scan?"

"Yep, that was it. Told me it showed I was just fine, no concussion, no problems in my head. I mean, not any you could see."

Spangler laughed at his joke. No one else did.

"But aren't you traumatized . . . disoriented?"

"Been in accidents before. Lots of folks speed 'round here. Drive drunk too. Not my first one. Won't be my last. I'm okay."

Moschella made one final effort.

"Did the doctor give you anything for pain, Mr. Spangler?"

"He sure did."

There it was. Moschella had what he needed.

"Are you on that pain medication at this moment, sir?"

"Yep."

"Do you recall the name of the pain medication he gave you?"

"'Course I do."

"What was it?"

"Tylenol. I took two before coming here."

Moschella froze. He had done what good litigators should never do—he had asked a question without knowing the answer first.

He had buried himself. But then, he had done that when he got in bed with Jackson.

After just an instant, Moschella regrouped and kept fighting because that is what litigators did. "Your Honor, the defense still believes Mr. Spangler must be in some degree of shock and challenges his competence to testify without adequate recovery time. I renew Sports Gear's motion to defer his testimony until Monday to give him the weekend to rest."

"I appreciate your solicitude for Mr. Spangler, Mr. Moschella. But it's plain to me that not only is he competent to testify, he wishes to do so. I don't want any more delays in this trial. Motion denied. Let's get back to the courtroom."

As Moschella left the chambers, he eyed Jackson in the gallery. He had warned Jackson that, even with all his prepping, Spangler was a wild card at best. While it was the truth, he shouldn't have told Jackson that. Moschella believed Spangler's accident was no "accident" at all. He had no hard evidence, nothing but his intuition and circumstantial evidence. He now understood far more than he wanted to about the man who had hired him.

"That damn Jackson," he muttered under his breath.

"What?" Teresa asked, overhearing him.

"Nothing. Nothing." Some things were better kept to himself.

Moschella focused on his immediate task—making sure Spangler didn't hurt his case. Even though he and Theresa had spent hours preparing him, Spangler had spent half the time clumsily flirting with her. Moschella finally had to make up an excuse to get her out of the room. Spangler had an unfocused brain softened from too many drugs and too much booze.

Moschella decided he would use the "gift" Jackson had given him. He could now play on the jury's sympathy with Spangler in a wheelchair and, if his testimony proved damaging, would argue in his closing to the jury that Spangler was not "all there" due to his injuries.

His job now was to find a way to derail Christopoulos without alienating the jurors. He'd also have to blunt the impact of any advantageous statements she squeezed out of Spangler. He had no doubt there would be some.

* * *

As Sophia emerged from Judge Ortiz's chambers, she nodded at her team and the Holts.

The jury returned. Spangler wheeled his chair next to the witness stand. He was duly sworn as a witness.

"Ms. Christopoulos, please proceed."

"Thank you, Your Honor. Mr. Spangler, to be sure the jury understands, is it true you were in a traffic accident last night?"

"Yes."

"You suffered some injuries, as we all can see."

"I did. Noth'n much. Looks worse than it is."

"Is there any reason you feel unable to testify here today?"

"No."

"Are you on any medication that would interfere with your memory or your ability to recall events?"

"Nope."

Moschella looked at Jackson, who was unreadable. He turned back. He didn't want to dwell on where his thoughts were taking him. He had his and Theresa's safety to think of, in the end. And still nothing concrete implicating Jackson or his people.

Sophia started her examination. "You work at Sports Gear here in Bakersfield, correct, Mr. Spangler?"

"Not anymore."

"You don't?"

Another surprise—a crisis, if you will. Sophia narrowed her eyes at Moschella.

"No, I resigned."

"When did you do that?"

"I dunno, few months back."

"Why did you resign?"

"Wanted to try something else."

"What is it you wanted to try?"

"Just something else."

Sophia instantly realized there was more to this story. Maybe a lot more.

"You remember when I took your deposition in this case?"

"Hard to forget that day, for sure."

"How long after that deposition did you resign from Sports Gear?"

"Don't remember."

"A week? A month? Three months?"

"Can't recall for certain."

"But after the deposition?"

"Yes."

"So it was within three months, give or take."

"I guess."

Moschella looked at Theresa with concern. Spangler was in trouble. He couldn't stay on script. He appeared evasive and untruthful.

"Were you pressured to resign by anyone at Sports Gear USA?"

"Objection, Your Honor. Relevance," Moschella interjected.

"Goes to credibility, Your Honor."

"Overruled, Mr. Moschella."

"They offered me a real nice severance check. I remember something about downsizing or whatever."

"When you say 'real nice,' how much was the severance check?"

"Objection again, Your Honor. Relevance, invasion of Mr. Spangler's privacy rights."

"Your Honor, that equally goes to credibility."

"And again overruled, Mr. Moschella."

"Six months' salary." Spangler grinned with his yellow teeth and missing premolar.

"Six months?"

Sophia paused and looked at the jurors, all working class, letting the immense size of that severance payment roll around in their minds. She didn't have to spell it out any further for them. They sensed bribery.

"Is that the normal severance payment a salesman who resigns from Sports Gear receives?"

"No idea. It's what I got." Spangler sat up proudly and smiled with his yellow teeth showing.

"Have you ever heard of any other salesman at Sports Gear USA receiving a severance payment in that amount?"

"I don't recall."

"You don't recall if anyone else got such a severance check, or you don't recall hearing that anyone else did?"

"Objection. Compound, Your Honor"

"Sustained."

"I'll rephrase, Your Honor. Do you know if anyone at Sports Gear USA ever received a severance payment in that amount?"

"No."

"Have you ever heard of anyone at Sports Gear USA receiving a severance payment in that amount?

"Nope."

"Based on your own personal knowledge, nothing more, do you know if anyone at Sports Gear USA has ever received a severance payment larger than six months' pay?"

"No."

"You've never heard of that happening either, have you?"

"Can't say as I have."

"Your Honor, objection. Asked and answered."

"Move on, Ms. Christopoulos."

"Did Sports Gear place any conditions on your getting that severance payment?"

"Objection, Your Honor. Ambiguous."

"Sustained."

Sophia had anticipated the objection.

"Did you sign any agreement with Sports Gear that had to do with your severance payment?"

Spangler swiveled his head, searching for Grimick in the gallery.

Sophia shifted her position to prevent them from making eye contact.

"I think so."

"Well, did you or didn't you?"

"Yeah, yeah, I did."

"What did that agreement concern?"

"Objection, Your Honor. Relevance. How much of this do we have to hear?"

"This goes once again to credibility, Your Honor, and I'm nearly finished."

"Overruled, Mr. Moschella. My patience is wearing thin, Ms. Christopoulos. We are getting a bit far afield here."

"Understood, Your Honor. Mr. Spangler, I repeat, what was the subject matter of that agreement you signed?"

"I think they called it a 'confidentiality agreement.'"

Spangler was still trying to catch Grimick's eye, but every time he leaned Sophia moved to block him.

"And by they, whom do you mean?"

"Mr. Moschella and Ms. Sandoval over there."

"What are you required to do under that agreement, Mr. Spangler?"

"Objection, Your Honor. First, hearsay; second, the document is the best evidence of what it contains; and third, it includes confidential trade secret information proprietary to Sports Gear USA."

"Your Honor, counsel for the plaintiffs are handicapped here. We've not seen that agreement. Mr. Moschella, Ms. Sandoval, and Mr. Spangler have. We request that you order it produced to us."

"Approach the bench," Judge Ortiz said.

"Mr. Moschella, do you have a copy of that agreement with you?"

"I don't, Your Honor."

"How quickly can you get one here?"

"I can have my office email a copy to the court immediately if that is Your Honor's order."

"It is. Make the call. We'll take a short recess. I'll review the agreement. Then I want to see all counsel in chambers. Everyone stay either in court or outside in the hallway so you can return when I'm ready."

Ortiz addressed the court.

"Fifteen-minute recess, everyone."

* * *

The jury returned to the jury room, and half of the people in gallery left the courtroom. The attorneys caucused at their tables.

Theresa called Rose Boyd, who had drafted the agreement. Boyd said she would email it immediately to Judge Ortiz's clerk and stand by in the event they needed anything else from the office.

The man Paul had surreptitiously photographed with his phone spoke briefly with Kemper, who was on his way out of the courtroom to make a phone call. Then he went forward and leaned over the rail to speak to Moschella and Sandoval.

More precisely, to berate them, albeit *sotto voce*.

"Tony, Spangler wasn't supposed to testify, and especially not today."

"What do you mean, Tom? He was under subpoena. He has to appear as long as he's physically able. I tried to get the judge to move him to Monday, but that didn't work."

"Thanks for stating the obvious. Those damn Holt lawyers better not see that agreement. They were never supposed to know about it or any of this other Spangler stuff."

"Not my fault, Tom. Yours. Spangler's separation from Sports Gear, the severance payment, the agreement *your office* drafted and that the other side is going to see unless you put some actual trade secrets in it and the judge thinks that's enough to keep it from them."

"The powers that be at Sports Gear are very displeased. This case is not heading in the right direction for us."

Moschella wanted to say, "You mean for you, Tom."

He didn't. With a confidence he did not feel, he replied, "We've barely begun. It's a long-distance run. Relax. You never know what's going to happen until the end and you have a verdict in hand. Don't forget this we're in a pro-gun city after all."

"I'm not reassured by that. My car's parked at your firm. I'll ride with you there when we're done for the day. Kemper has plans. We have to talk."

Jackson stalked out to the lobby.

\* \* \*

Sophia and her team caucused to discuss the ramifications of the Spangler payoff.

"That guy I took a picture of was over with Kemper and then Moschella again," Paul said.

"Forget about him," Tricia said. "There's a potential gold mine here."

"Any ideas about extracting the ore?" Sophia asked.

"Spangler was bought off," Bryce said.

"Duh." Tricia smiled.

"I can't believe that agreement has any trade secrets in it," Paul said.

"Sports Gear wouldn't trust that fool Spangler with any," Sophia concurred.

\* \* \*

The bailiff interrupted both groups and told them to report to Judge Ortiz's chambers. A stern-faced judge greeted them.

"Mr. Moschella, Ms. Sandoval, as I read this four-page agreement, your client was trying to purchase Mr. Spangler's silence, to the media and anyone outside Sports Gear. Indeed, he can't discuss the case or what he knows about the underlying facts or events with anyone even at Sports Gear without the consent of its attorneys and in their presence, and that includes its proprietary information, purchasing patterns, sales models, or internal financial reports. Yet I see no actual proprietary information or anything remotely classifiable as a trade secret in here. Am I missing something?"

Sophia had no idea what Moschella could say. Nothing was her guess. She enjoyed watching him nervously wriggling, a worm caught on a hook from which there was no escape.

Moschella's mind was whirling. Jackson's diatribe in the courtroom had prevented him from any legal brainstorming and any quick Internet research he or Sandoval might have done. Jackson was a continuing impediment, and his poor decisions were wearing Moschella down. He had advised against this whole Spangler fiasco. As always, Jackson did what he wanted, when he wanted.

"Mr. Moschella? We're all waiting."

Moschella got a grip on himself. He had to say something.

"Your Honor, the fact that one paragraph contains those particular categories of information is what makes it and the entire agreement a proprietary trade secret. That array of information itself, and the importance it places on it, is not something Sports Gear shares with its competitors or the world."

That might have worked with a novice judge, but while Ortiz was fairly new, he was no novice.

"Sorry, Mr. Moschella. That won't wash. My clerks have already made copies for all counsel. Ms. Christopoulos, you have five minutes to review this document, and then we'll continue with Mr. Spangler. Use my clerk's office to caucus. That's fair enough, Mr. Moschella?"

"Yes, Your Honor, but we renew our objections for the record."

"Noted."

Sophia and Paul sped through their copy. They emerged a scant three minutes later.

"Ready, Your Honor," Sophia announced.

"Nice and fast. I appreciate that. Let's resume."

* * *

Everyone returned to the courtroom at Judge Ortiz's direction.

From the bench, the judge called his court to order.

"Ms. Christopoulos, please continue."

"Your Honor, plaintiffs offer this document entitled 'Confidentiality Agreement' as Exhibit 124."

"Duly noted."

Sophia handed a clean copy of the agreement to the clerk, who gave it to Spangler. He had remained in his wheelchair next to the witness stand during the chambers conference.

"Mr. Spangler, is that document, marked as Exhibit 124, the confidentiality agreement Sports Gear asked you to sign in return for your severance payment?"

Spangler flipped through the pages and saw his signature on the fourth one. "Seems like it."

"That's your signature on page four, isn't it?"

"Yep."

"That's a yes?"

"That's what I said."

"Your Honor, plaintiffs move to have Exhibit 124 entered into evidence."

"Objection as to trade secrets and relevance, Your Honor."

"Your objections are in the record, Mr. Moschella. Exhibit 124 is received into evidence."

Sophia had the exhibit displayed on their Recordex Pull Up Screen Derek had charged on a credit card for the trial, along with a DocCamHQ bundle with an Elmo MO-1 document camera and ASK Proxima C3257-A projector. It was no longer enough to be armed with the most up-to-date law; trial lawyers had to have the technology to match because their opposing counsel surely would. The equipment would be of use to Krause & White long after this particular trial concluded.

The screen allowed everyone in the courtroom, including the press, to see the exhibits easily and clearly. Judge Ortiz's court did not have individual monitors for jurors. Better-funded courts sometimes did. For Sophia, that was a good thing in this trial. She wanted everyone in the courtroom to be able to see the exhibits.

She took Spangler through the key sections of the agreement. By the time she was finished, the jurors knew that he had been bought off by Sports Gear, and at an exorbitant price for his low-level employment.

Two key areas of testimony remained.

"Mr. Spangler, you said you recalled the day I took your deposition. Do you remember telling me that you had a criminal record before you came to work for Sports Gear USA?"

"Objection. Relevance, invasion of privacy."

"Credibility yet again, Your Honor."

"Overruled, Mr. Moschella."

"I . . . I did tell you that."

"What crimes had you committed?"

"Nothing big. Me and my friends shot up an abandoned farmhouse out by Wasco, didn't hurt anyone . . . suspended sentence and all. Couple of misdemeanors for possession of marijuana. I pleaded out . . . no jail time there neither."

"You didn't list those crimes on your employment application for Sports Gear USA, did you?"

"Heck no. None of their business what I do on my own time."

"You also told me you had made a number of illegal gun sales, both privately and at Bakersfield gun shows, right?" Spangler tried to find Grimick, but again Sophia was in the way.

"Uh, I guess I did. But gun sales shouldn't be illegal."

"Move to strike the second sentence of that answer, Your Honor. Irrelevant and lay opinion."

"Granted. The jury will disregard that statement."

"You were asked to *resign* from Sports Gear USA after it learned of your criminal history, including drugs and illegal gun sales, from that deposition, weren't you, Mr. Spangler?"

"Objection. Compound and argumentative, Your Honor."

"Withdrawn."

Sophia had made her point. She had driven home Spangler's lack of credibility to the jurors. She had blackened him in their eyes, and her last question answered itself.

She had also destroyed any sympathy the jury might have felt for him in his wheelchair with his bandages and cast. Now they saw a conniving, lying, disreputable lowlife with a criminal record, an illegal gun seller. She paused and looked at her outline. She still had to grill him about the sale of the shotgun to Mike and Sports Gear's training and policies, the admissions he had made to Wallace, and, of course, his statements to Sophia that Mike was "strange" and "wired wrong."

"Ms. Christopoulos, how much longer will you be with Mr. Spangler? It's getting late and Friday traffic can be bad."

"At least another hour or so, Your Honor, to be perfectly honest. As Your Honor will appreciate, plaintiffs only learned today much of what became the subject of his testimony this afternoon."

"Understood. Very well. It's almost four. We're adjourned until Monday morning at ten." Judge Ortiz banged his gavel on its wooden base, rose, and left the courtroom.

The attorneys stood as he did so, and then everyone dispersed.

Moschella arranged to meet Joe Spangler at his offices at ten the next morning for more prep. Grimick then wheeled Spangler out of the courtroom. They both glared at Sophia.

"I don't think they like you," Paul whispered to Sophia.

"I'll take that as a compliment from those two."

It had been a very good, startling day in the best way. Monday promised to be even better. Spangler was in trouble, and Sophia would take full advantage.

⌘

# CHAPTER 69

## Perturbations

*"A man without ethics is a wild beast loosed upon the world."*
-Albert Camus

Jackson drove back to Stockdale Tower with Moschella and Sandoval.

"Not a wonderful day, guys, not even close," Jackson jabbed his finger at them.

"I told you not to fire Spangler and have him sign that stupid agreement," Moschella growled, and then caught himself. "Putting that aside, Spangler is more like the jurors here than you understand. This is Bakersfield, not Chicago or New York."

"You keep saying that."

"For all we know, some of the jurors sell guns illegally on the side and think they have every right to do it," Theresa added.

"I've thought about this at length," Moschella continued. "I can characterize the six months' pay as helping out a long-term employee. That's generous of Sports Gear, and there's nothing wrong with asking an ex-employee not to talk to the press. It wasn't a bribe in return for his testimony or to suborn perjury, because the payoff came *after* his deposition. He was already on record under oath."

"Not a bad approach to salvage today's debacle. The jurors might even buy it. But it's Monday that will kill us. Spangler won't hold up. That bitch representing the Holts is going to get to him. I guarantee it. She'll break him when she starts getting into the day that stupid kid bought the shotgun."

Both Theresa and Tony winced at the ruthless coarseness of their "boss." He truly was a first-class slimeball.

"He'll do fine," Moschella lied, well aware that he wouldn't, no matter how many hours they spent rehearsing with him.

"No, he won't, and you know it. He's a liability. A big one."

"We'll see tomorrow when I do his last prep session. Care to join us?"

Moschella taunted Jackson, knowing full well his obsession with invisibility. He and the entire Denver gang. Moschella was learning why the hard way.

"You know what? I'll listen in. Have a speakerphone in the room when you meet with him. Conference me in."

"Whatever you want, Tom."

"Damn right," Jackson snapped, with an arrogant smile.

Theresa, in the back seat, watched and listened in horrified fascination as the two senior lawyers sparred with each other. It was ugly, petty, and alarming. If this was how top-drawer trial lawyers operated, she didn't want to be one.

When they parked at the office, Jackson held the door open for Theresa with exaggerated ceremony. He didn't bother hiding the good, long look he gave every inch of her as she emerged from the car.

*Asshole,* Theresa thought.

"Having dinner with my team at the Belvedere Room at the Padre tonight," Jackson said. " I'd invite you both, especially you, Theresa, but we're conferring with a client's reps about another matter in Sacramento. Client confidentiality trumps all. Dinner another time?"

"Of course." Moschella absorbed Jackson's self-aggrandizement with grace.

"See you tomorrow morning at nine-thirty. We'll set you up before Spangler arrives."

"See you then."

Jackson turned and made a call as he strutted to his car.

"Pickett?"

* * *

"You don't have to say anything, Theresa. I've never had to deal with anything like this before. It's really unpleasant."

"Unpleasant? I can think of better words than that to describe it."

"I'm sorry. All I can do, all we can do, is get through it."

"I understand. But never again for me. That guy and his lovely colleagues are pieces of work cut from the same uncouth, unethical cloth. Are they doing things that could cost us our licenses? I just got mine."

"I'll be sure to distance us from anything I discover. Nothing solid yet, though. I truly apologize."

Moschella didn't want to know or even speculate that Jackson was going beyond the unethical and into the criminal.

"Don't apologize. It's an education. About a lot of things."

"That's generous of you." Moschella intentionally changed the subject away from Jackson. "Plans tonight?"

"Dinner with my parents. It's been awhile. How about you?" Theresa was comfortable around him now. She liked him even more than she had before she got to second-chair the Sports Gear trial. She felt a bit sorry for him having to deal with Jackson and his troglodytes.

"Your folks are lucky to have you. I'm going with my wife to dinner tonight at the club. An event to raise funds for Catholic Charities."

"I volunteer for them, too."

"I might have guessed."

"Should I be there tomorrow for your final get-together with Spangler?"

"You bet, Theresa. You contribute a lot. And I'm more comfortable having a member of our own firm in on every discussion if it ever comes to that."

"Gotcha." She knew they were in potential trouble.

"Tomorrow, then."

* * *

Sophia's team drove back to L.A. and straight into the Friday rush hour. They didn't care. Relief from the Bakersfield stench was an imperative. Inching along in the interminable, eternal L.A. traffic was worth it just to have forty-eight all-too-brief hours in civilization.

Sophia conferenced in Rona and Derek on her cell to update them on the trial. They were pleased with the way things were going, but Derek, in particular, was incensed to hear of the Spangler deal and his illegal gun-selling.

"Guys like that bastard are a curse on my community, every community. You nail him for good on Monday, Sophia."

"Don't worry. He barely held it together today. He won't on Monday. His brain is pickled with alcohol and drugs. Don't forget, when Tricia and I went to Sports Gear that first day, he told me 'Mike was strange and wired wrong.' I'll get it out of him."

"We all need this one," Rona said. "See you tomorrow at the office."

"Thanks, guys."

Sophia turned off her cell, and she and her teammates talked disjointedly as they listened to classical KUSC on the car radio. They had all their trial prep materials for the weekend in the trunk. They agreed to take the night and morning off and meet at their offices at noon the next day.

* * *

They finally arrived at Krause & White after eight that night, to retrieve their own cars and head home. Bryce lived with his parents. Sophia, Paul, and Tricia drove to their own apartments—each unappealing and lonely, but home nonetheless.

Sophia called ahead for takeout from Arigato, a local sushi place on Wilshire Boulevard. She ate in her now Steve-less apartment. She let CNN distract her and her sake relax her as she drank the miso soup and savored the Japanese mackerel sashimi and California roll she had ordered.

Then she collapsed into her bed.

"Damn it. Why did I have to go to law school?"

Thanks to this case, that question hung over her as she drifted into troubled sleep.

⌘

# CHAPTER 70

## The Genie Pops Out of the Bottle

*"I think I'll just stay here and drink."*
-Merle Haggard

When Spangler left the courthouse Friday afternoon with Grimick, he was just plain ticked off.

"That damned accident. It fucked up my truck. Then that bitch trying to make me look bad. It made me sick watching her and that sleazy wop lawyer going at it with that dirty Mex acting like he was God up there in his black robe."

"Forget about it."

Grimick helped Spangler into his own customized truck, the one he had bragged about to Sophia the day of the Eddie incident. It was even more monstrous than Spangler's, with camouflage paint and Confederate flags on both cab doors. He put the wheelchair in the back.

"I still don't have another job, Moss," Spangler said. "And that wad of money they give me is running low."

"What'd you expect, popping all those pills and partying so much?"

"I already decided I'm not show'n up Monday unless I get paid more. That shyster lawyer better hand over another check tomorrow when I'm at his big fancy offices."

"Why not? You did damn good up there today."

"You sure, Moss? Didn't seem like that judge thought much of me."

"You did great. Don't worry about that jerk putting on airs. Or those fat-ass jurors neither. They're stupid, or they wouldn't be stuck wasting their time do'n that."

"They're idiots, ain't they?" Spangler grinned.

"Uh-huh, but not our people, and there look to be some on that jury. It's like with our friends. They get that we're all in this together. Our town. Our guns. Sports Gear paid you that money because they done you wrong firing you like that. We know it. You never went to jail for nothing.'"

"I know. Never one time. For nothing.'"

Grimick pulled up to the broken-down apartment building on Q Street in Oildale where Spangler lived now—Granite Heights. It was a marginal neighborhood at best, but all he could afford even with his payoff from Sports Gear.

Spangler made it up to his second-floor apartment on his own, groaning about the pain. Grimick carried his wheelchair. Spangler would need it to roll back into the courtroom Monday. If he went, that is.

"Appreciate all this, Moss."

Spangler unlocked the flimsy handle. His apartment was small and dark with sparse grimy furniture including an old square box TV. The dirty clothes and dishes thrown about smelled of carelessness and decay.

"No problem. I'll pick you up Monday, too, unless you tell me you're not going."

"That's real white of you, man." Spangler plopped down in his threadbare corduroy easy chair.

"See you then."

"Big plans for the weekend, Joe?"

"Don't be an asshole. Look at me. I got no wheels, neither. I'm gonna sit here, drink the beer in my fridge, order pizzas, and watch cable porn on my crap TV."

"Shit. Just remembered. I got something for you."

"Oh? A hot broad to massage my sore muscles?" Spangler grinned lasciviously.

"You wish. Something better than that cheap-ass Bud you buy in those eighteen-can boxes at the Walgreens, though."

"Hey. Nothing wrong with Bud . . . especially a lot of Bud."

"Gimme a sec."

Grimick went down to his truck and came back with a bag. He took out two bottles of Old Portrero 18$^{th}$ Century Style Whiskey. He handed them to Spangler.

"Holy shit, Moss. I love rye whiskey, but this booze here is way out of our league. Did you lift it somewhere?"

"Nah." Grimick laughed. "Would'a kept it for me if I had. When I was just puttin' your wheelchair in my truck, this delivery guy come up and handed this over. He said it was from that wop lawyer 'as a token of his appreciation' or some such shit."

"Maybe he's not so bad after all. Or wants to be sure I show up tomorrow. Beats the hell out of Bud for damn sure. Grab a couple glasses."

Grimick took a bottle over to the kitchen alcove and looked through the empty cupboards. He picked up the cleanest mug he saw from the piles of dirty dishes on the counter.

"Want some ice?"

"You bet."

"Here." Grimick handed the bottle and mug to Spangler.

"Hey, I said a couple. You're not stay'n?"

"Hell, no. Meet'n' a redhead with the biggest rack you ever saw at Trout's in a half hour. She eyeballed me at the shoot'n range. I'm get'n some tonight." Grimick pumped his hips.

"Hey, talking about get'n some . . . I mean it. I'm get'n some more money out of that lawyer tomorrow, not just some rye whiskey, or things just ain't gonna roll their way come Monday."

"I'm with you on that."

"I should put the screws on them, huh?"

"No harm ask'n. I gotta go."

"Dang. And me like this. Oh, well, got what I need here to make me forget what I'm missing."

"See you Monday early." Grimick opened the door.

"I'll bum a ride to that lawyer's office tomorrow, don't worry. And can you crack the other bottle for me, too, with my arm and all."

"Huh? Sure." Grimick was confused but cracked the second cap. "Shit, I'm gonna be late."

He raced out the door.

Spangler filled the mug to the brim from the Old Portrero bottle. He took a slow sip, then a fast gulp.

"Hoo-whee," he coughed. "What a kick. This beats what for outta Tylenol."

He poured another. It was 123 proof. All the better.

"You know what you need, Mr. Spangler? An Oxy chaser."

He had scored some from the guy downstairs.

"Won't feel no pain at all then."

He leaned forward, grabbed his stash of pills from under a dusty fake plant on the coffee table, and took out three. Then he shook out another one for good measure.

"Why the hell . . . s . . . sh . . . shouldn't I get m . . . more . . . money," he slurred. "Damn company. I deserve this and a whole lot else besides to shut my m . . . mouth."

He chugged down the pills with the Old Portrero. He had the TV going and nuked some frozen chicken nuggets and tater tots instead of spending money on a pizza. He was having a fine old time, he was. He looked at his mug with small melted ice cubes clumped at the bottom.

"Fuck ice."

Spangler reached for the still half-full bottle but missed it. He tried again and managed to catch it by the neck.

"Fuck the mug."

He raised the bottle to his mouth to take a drink but missed, pouring the Old Portrero all the way down his shirt to his crotch instead.

"Shit."

He staggered, limping, to his cramped bathroom, bottle in hand. He flipped on the light and picked up a dirty towel from where it hung askew on a rusty towel rack. He felt dizzy and had to lean on the sink.

"What . . . the . . ."

The room went black. He lost his balance and crashed into the cheap, soap-filmed glass door on his tub/shower combo. It shattered as he went through it, smashing both his head and the Old Portrero bottle against the mold-mottled shower tile wall. He fell in a twisted heap into the stained porcelain tub. Blood poured out of deep gashes in his side and neck.

Spangler lay still and limp. The blood from his cracked skull and lacerations blended with the splattered Old Portrero. His stilled and empty eyes stared open but unseeing at the twin streams flowing together toward the drain, taking his blood, his booze, and his life with them.

⌘

# CHAPTER 71

## Spattered Spangler

*"No one is so brave that he is not disturbed
by something unexpected."*
-Julius Caesar

Saturday, Sophia crawled out of bed and let a long, hot shower and then a strong coffee wake her. At ten, arriving at Krause & White, she saw Derek, Rona, and Bryce in Derek's office.

"Sophia," Derek called. "Bryce has been giving us more details on the great things you got from Spangler yesterday. Seems to be going well."

"I hope so. Hard to read the jury." Sophia stepped in.

"It always is," Rona replied. "Unless something shocking or stupid happens. Then you can read them fast."

"Nothing like that yet, though they were pissed at the huge payola Spangler got as 'severance.'"

"That was something else." Derek was supportive and actually nice. "And him showing up in that wheelchair for sympathy."

"Don't worry," Sophia said. "I'll shake Spangler's tree Monday when I take him through the day he sold the shotgun to Mike. Something will fall out. I'll get him to admit what he blurted out to me, too."

"Sounds like it from what Bryce told us," Rona said.

"You should see her in action." Bryce was first-year impressed.

"I'll crack the story they paid him to tell. His brain is mush. Simple as that. Only . . ."

"Only what?" Derek's edge was back.

"Nothing . . . it's just that they gave him that payoff to stick to the company line, but he's weak, and they know it. If I were a conspiracy theorist, I'd say that traffic accident was a setup to keep him off the stand. It bothers me that the men in the SUV were wearing suits."

"Come on. This is the twenty-first century," Rona laughed. "We don't off witnesses. Not in civil trials anyway . . . we prep them."

"Putting him in the hospital is easier than prepping him." Sophia stopped because she sounded paranoid to herself. She redirected the conversation. "How's it going here?"

"We landed a couple of small new matters this week," Rona said. "We'll be billing the weekend away."

"What are they?" Sophia asked.

"I have a buddy in the Black Business Association," Derek said. "He wants me to get his apartment buildings qualified for the Section 8 Housing Program."

"And some friends at my temple need to deal with the Coastal Commission on a development in San Clemente by the ocean." Rona smiled. "A small retainer, but enough."

"So we're above water?" Sophia asked in an optimistic tone.

"With our fingers in the dam." Derek the ball buster emerged again. "We're using credit cards."

"I get the message. We score, or Krause & White folds." Sophia deflated a little.

"Basically," Rona said.

Basically was a deflecting qualifier. Rona and Derek had a private agreement that Krause & White would never fold. They would just cut the dead weight—Sophia and her team, including Bryce, even though his salary was low compared to the others. Rona's mother's money was always there to save Rona and by extension Derek, however grudgingly it would be given.

Sophia heard the front door slam.

"The others are here. Come on, Bryce. We'd better get going."

She swiftly extricated herself from what had become another uncomfortable encounter.

\* \* \*

The team gathered in the conference room with coffee and, thanks to Paul, croissants and other assorted pastries—plain, almond, cheesy, gooey, and fruity.

"Paul, I love you." Tricia kissed him on the cheek and grabbed an almond croissant.

"There's nothing like this in Bakersfield." He grabbed an apple-filled cinnamon roll.

"Here's to Paris Pastries and sleeping in. But Ben has to get on the L.A. Times. The Holt case coverage was pabulum this morning."

"We're going to talk," Sophia assured him.

"Hope everyone's rested."

"Not enough, but a start." Bryce went for a piece of the cherry clafoutis.

"Derek and Rona landed some billable cases. We're still in business, but not by much or for very long. We have to bring this baby in big."

"We will," Paul rallied.

"Onward, then," Tricia replied with bravado.

Bryce was a fast learner and joined in the optimism. "I'm ready."

Sophia became all business. "The day of the sale is critical with Spangler on Monday. I'll break him, or at least make him look so untrustworthy the jurors will know he's lying. Then they'll believe Wallace's testimony about the admissions he got out of all of them."

"Either way, it'll do the job. What's with Moschella and that guy yelling at him, though?" Tricia asked.

"He's not on Sports Gear's website," Bryce said. "I looked."

"Good thinking," Sophia said. "Maybe not everyone's on the site. I assumed he was from Sports Gear, too. I'll text the picture to Ben. That's a distraction we can't afford."

"Lead on, then." Paul grabbed his second pastry.

"After I take Spangler through everything, including his training, etc., I'll call Grimick. He's smarter."

"You'll get him, too." Bryce was getting cocky.

His first-year boosterism was getting to Sophia. She wanted to slap him back into the reality of their flimsy case, dependent on a weeping woman with a spewing mouth, Wallace's so far uncorroborated statements, and two experts who, while good, had to measure up against Sports Gear's high-paid, powerhouse mouthpieces.

"No Brandon Gallo?" Paul ventured. "Is that a mistake?"

"Maybe, but he's on our witness list if we change our minds."

"His deposition and what Sports Gear said about him in its discovery responses were worthless," Paul acknowledged.

"Kind of a hear-no-evil, see-no-evil. If we put him up now, the jurors will think we're desperate, since he adds nothing. All he did was ask Mike if he needed help, and on the video that was only like a second. He said Mike acted normal. Not helpful for us."

"So our experts after Grimick then." Tricia pushed her honey-blonde ponytail back and took another croissant.

"Then Beth," Sophia said. "Just pray she doesn't waver or get tricked by Moschella into blowing it all. She'll need a lot of prepping."

Sophia dreaded that prep. Beth was a continuing problem. Despite her commitment to the case and her Oedipal attachment to her dead son, she remained moody and unpredictable.

"It's getting late." Sophia handed out assignments.

\* \* \*

As they were about to scatter, Sophia got a call from Moschella.

"Wait, guys, it's Moschella."

"What the hell does he want?" Paul's eyes flashed.

"Nothing good," Tricia said.

"Hello, Tony," Sophia said.

"Sorry for the Saturday call, but we have a problem."

"What problem?" Sophia didn't like cat-and-mouse games.

"Joe Spangler is dead."

"Dead?" Sophia blurted.

"Who's dead?" Bryce asked.

"Spangler's dead," Sophia announced.

"Spangler?" Tricia echoed.

"My team's here. I'm putting you on speaker."

"As you will."

"How?" Sophia held her hand up for silence. "From the accident?"

"No. We were supposed to meet with him at ten today. He didn't show. He didn't answer his phone. We called everyone we could. Finally, Ms. Sandoval and I went to his apartment. He didn't answer when and knocked. We found the manager. After an argument, he let us in. We found Spangler dead in his bathtub."

"In his bathtub?" Sophia parroted.

"He had his clothes on. It looks like he got drunk . . . really drunk . . . and somehow fell through his glass door. He apparently bled out. There was some Oxycontin and a whiskey bottle on his coffee table. Another broken whiskey bottle near the body. That's all I know."

"*Another* accident, Tony? Convenient, isn't it? He was a problem for you."

"I wouldn't say that."

"No, of course, *you* wouldn't."

"Believe me, this hurts Sports Gear more than it does the Holts," Moschella outright lied. "He was a key witness. This is a major blow to us."

Sophia and her team listened without comment. They all realized the implications. First, given Sophia's courtroom skills, Spangler was predictably going to do serious further damage to Sports Gear. Second, any intelligent person knew Spangler's death was too coincidental to be an accident—a second accident too soon after the first one.

"Is anyone investigating what happened?"

"Of course. Two detectives were at the scene and canvassed his neighbors. But everything points to an accident."

Moschella played dumb. Given all of Jackson's comments about Spangler, he had his own doubts that it was an accident. Again, though, he had no evidence suggesting otherwise, and neither did the police. The canons of ethics dictated that his primary obligation was to Sports Gear, not opining on the cause of Spangler's death.

"This was . . ." Sophia was enraged but had nothing to substantiate the accusation she was about to make.

"What can I say? I just wanted you to know."

"The trial has to go forward."

She would make sure of that because Krause & White was spending on credit cards, not cash, in Bakersfield.

"Candidly, I'd prefer a delay. But Judge Ortiz will agree with you. He's a pile-driver and won't waste his or the jury's time."

"Monday morning then." Condolences were irrelevant and would have been insincere.

Moschella hung up and spent the afternoon with Theresa considering their options and strategy. He recalled Jackson's quick exit from their offices when Spangler hadn't shown at ten. He saw no immediate need to call Jackson to tell him what Moschella suspected Jackson already knew.

\* \* \*

Sophia hung up and had her team re-evaluate the coming week.

"It *looks* like an accident?" Tricia mocked.

"That's bullshit," Paul shouted. "Someone wanted him out of the way."

"I agree." Sophia reflected. "Two 'accidents' in a row. But we have no proof they weren't."

"No," Paul said. "We never will, with the Bakersfield police 'investigating' it. Just like the Holts's arson."

"Just another Oildale druggie biting the dust," Bryce added.

"That's five dead," Tricia said.

The team sat silently thinking of Mike Holt, Sophia's Steve, Derek's brother Dwight, Moschella's partner O'Rourke, and now Spangler. What Sophia didn't know, and Moschella felt he had no obligation to tell her, was that Grimick was missing too.

"But the trial's still a go Monday," Tricia confirmed.

"Yes, and we'll oppose any delay. We literally can't afford it."

"Plus the shorter it is, the fewer the bodies." Bryce chuckled.

"That's not funny, but apparently true. From now on, watch yourselves," Sophia warned. "We go in pairs everywhere in that dusty corner of Hell."

"I don't scare easily," Tricia said.

"I don't either." Bryce put on his best "brave guy" face.

"It's not about being scared, but being safe. By twos everywhere, at all times." Paul was adamant. "Something's not right."

Sophia agreed, "I think it's time for Ben to find out who that guy is hanging around Moschella."

Sophia texted Ben the picture of the fourth person who had been speaking with Kemper and Moschella with a short message and told him about Spangler's death, too.

"We have to revise our game plan for next week." Paul said.

"We can put Grimick on the stand Monday," Bryce suggested.

"If he shows," Sophia said.

"We need to be prepared for Davis, too, and have our experts on deck just in case. Paul, are you ready for Davis and the experts you're covering?"

"No, but I will be by the time we leave for Bakersfield tomorrow. You can count on it."

"Then that's it. We'll all report here at nine tomorrow packed and ready. We'll work all day and leave for Bako at six. We'll prepare against the unknown and unknowable as much as we can because that has become the norm in this case."

"Guess that means I can't troll the Internet dating sites." Tricia gave a mock sigh.

Everyone laughed.

"Let's get going. Stay sharp, people."

Sophia went down to give the disturbing news to Rona and Derek.

⌘

# CHAPTER 72

## Tomato, Tomahto, They Both Start with Tom

*"The devil's finest trick is to persuade you that he does not exist."*
-Charles Baudelaire

When Spangler hadn't shown promptly at ten Saturday, Jackson raced out even though Moschella insisted Spangler, being Spangler, was probably just late.

Jackson had arranged a tactical meeting with his coven of lawyers at the Padre Hotel in the specialty coffee shop off the main lobby at ten-thirty. They drank their lattes and sat waiting for him at the high tables with stools to match. Junior partner Porter Beauregard demonstrated to the others how he kept his thick mustache from getting white foam on it as he drank his latte.

"Why don't you just cut that thing off?" Rose remarked with faux Southern charm.

Samuel French and Ambrose Pickett ignored both of them.

Jackson came through the lobby a few minutes early to meet them.

"I got you this mocha latte."

Pickett, ever the suck-up, handed Jackson the to-go cup.

"Spangler didn't show up for his prep," Jackson announced.

"Why not?" French asked.

"No idea. I'm sure Moschella and Sandoval will find him. Who knows with these people? He could be sleeping it off in a gutter somewhere."

Pickett shifted uncomfortably in his chair but said nothing. If Spangler was in a gutter somewhere, the alcohol that put him there was his and Jackson's doing.

"So, change of plans. I want you all working on the case for the client we met with last night. We've prepared enough for these Bakersfield yokels for now."

"Works for me," Beauregard drawled, betraying his Arkansas origins.

"Get the complaint done by tomorrow and I'll review it. Start on the first round of discovery."

Everyone stood to leave.

"Ambrose, hold up, would you?" Jackson sipped his latte.

The other three Denver attorneys were jealous that he had singled Pickett out but reluctantly headed off to their new tasks.

Pickett stood, apprehensive. A thin smile crossed Jackson's face.

"Thanks for the coffee, by the way."

"Sure." Pickett was even more anxious than usual because he believed he knew exactly why Spangler had not shown.

"Sit down."

"Yes, sir." He sat.

"Ambrose, my fine young associate, I assume you got that package delivered?"

"Yes sir, Mr. Jackson. I did exactly what you instructed."

"And that was?" Jackson stared at Pickett.

"I . . . I dressed in a T-shirt and my jeans. I told Grimick I made deliveries for Mr. Moschella and gave him a bag with the two bottles of Old Portrero for Spangler with Mr. Moschella's compliments."

"Excellent work, Ambrose. I'm glad I could count on you. You have a real future with our firm, son."

Pickett relaxed. He was there to please. That's why Jackson used him for special assignments.

"You don't think anything happened to Mr. Spangler, do you, Mr. Jackson?" Pickett asked.

"Guys like him are unreliable. Don't worry about it."

"Sure, of course. Unreliable." Pickett postured like one of the big boys.

"Thanks again for going the extra mile and for your discretion. The law isn't all books and briefs, you know."

"I understand, Mr. Jackson. I appreciate your confidence in me."

"It's because of that confidence that I want you back in Denver to be my point man there on the Sacramento case. You have to report Sunday to help that team gear up for the injunction motion we have to file, so leave tonight. If there are no flights, rent a car and take a red-eye from L.A."

"Yes, sir. I will. I'm grateful for the opportunity, sir." Pickett quickly departed, elated at his new assignment.

Jackson watched him leave with satisfaction. Pickett was a toady and would follow orders—especially the order to be discreet. Even so, getting him out of Bakersfield was essential to avoid any inadvertent disclosure of the liquor delivery.

Later that afternoon Jackson went up to the Padre's signature bar, the Prairie Fire, for a well-deserved single malt Scotch. He was entitled, he decided. With the Portrero delivery accomplished, his brainchild, there would be no additional Spangler prep session. Not today. Not ever.

* * *

Sitting at the bar at four in the afternoon with his second twenty-five-year-old Balvenie Doublewood Scotch, Jackson felt his cellphone buzz. His caller ID showed it was Moschella. He was going to enjoy this.

"Tony, any luck finding our errant witness?"

Jackson sounded genuinely concerned. He was practiced at that. Indeed, he was adept at sounding or looking like anything he needed to be at any given time.

"He's dead, Jackson. Another accident. This time in the shower. Or did you know that already?"

"Are you serious? I'm stunned. Was it due to the aftereffects of his earlier accident?"

"It was after drinking some very expensive whiskey outside his price range."

"Well, you know that severance check he got was substantial, Tony. He could afford some decent hooch."

"It was more than that, Tom." Tony moderated his belligerence.

"What do you mean?" Jackson feared the worst but exuded calm.

"There was a bag of Oxycontin on his coffee table, and the medical examiner said he had a boatload of it in his system."

"What do you expect from these yokels?"

"The police are dusting his place for prints to see if anyone else was there."

"Good idea, Tony. We don't want any suspicion of foul play here. He wasn't great on the stand yesterday, but I figured he'd be much better Monday after your prep. Can't say I'm overly sad, though. It cost a bundle to keep him quiet. There was no guarantee he wouldn't ask for more, either."

Moschella wanted nothing more to do with Jackson, who was smooth, unscrupulous, and, frankly, evil. However, he had no choice given what he knew and didn't know.

"The trial will go ahead. I talked to the lead lawyer for the Holts, and she and I both know Judge Ortiz won't stand for any more delays."

"If that's what you think is best, Tony. You're our guy on the spot." Jackson oozed confidence and calm.

"Fair enough, Tom. I'm trying to reach Grimick. He's next on their list of witnesses. I have to prep him too, and he's missing."

"You'll find him. Call me when you do. I'll listen in when you and your lovely associate meet with him, as I had intended to do with Spangler."

"Yeah." Moschella hung up.

To Jackson, the news was not unexpected but welcome. The Oxycodone just helped along what he had put in the Old Portrero—an undetectable, fast-acting designer poison so new it was unnamed. Jackson, being who he was, had a chemist he had saved from prison in his back pocket. Which is where he would stay so long as Jackson had possession of certain incriminating materials on him.

Jackson treated himself to a third Scotch and some so-so appetizers as he eyed what passed for local female talent. He planned to top off his successful day by topping his choice of feminine company that night.

*Too bad that Mex of Moschella's is such an uptight little bitch,* Jackson thought as he looked around. *Oh, well, anything will do after a few more of these.*

* * *

That evening, Moschella located a cousin of Spangler's to take care of his body and personal effects. He arduously searched for Grimick until late that night without success. Moschella's anxiety level rose along with his frustration.

No one had heard from or seen Grimick since Friday. He didn't answer his phone. Moschella checked Grimick's trailer at the Idle Hands trailer park on South Oildale Drive. Not there.

The next day he drafted Theresa to help. They spent all day Sunday searching. They both missed Mass. Good Catholics or not, their trial responsibilities took precedence. They made calls and drove to the home of every one of Grimick's friends. They rechecked his trailer and every trailer park, bar, and strip joint in Oildale.

"It's seven. I give up." Moschella was wrung out and frustrated. "He's gone underground, or he'll show up tomorrow. He could know about Spangler or not."

"He will Monday when Christopoulos puts him on the stand," Theresa cautioned.

"If he surfaces." Moschella pulled up to her car in the parking lot.

"We did our best," Theresa said. "See you tomorrow."

"We should meet here at seven-thirty before court to do some pre-emptive planning."

"Sure. Anything could happen tomorrow."

*Anything could happen tonight if I weren't married.* Moschella pushed the inappropriate sentiment out of his thoughts.

He watched Theresa get in her car. He drove home, not looking forward to Monday's surprises.

⌘

# CHAPTER 73

## Stand In And Deliver

*"In practice, every member of the audience
should feel like an understudy."*
-W.H. Auden

Sunday Sophia called the Holts with the news of Spangler's death. They both chimed a version of "good riddance." She didn't blame them. He wasn't a person worthy of much regard or regret in the human world. However, in the manic multidimensional trial universe, his death was very regret-worthy to Sophia and the case. He had been Sports Gear's most vulnerable witness.

Sophia's team spent an intense Sunday at the office designing artful alternative trial examination outlines to get the same damaging testimony from the other Sports Gear employees that she would have obtained from Spangler.

There was one bright spot. They could use his deposition transcript at trial because he was by definition an "unavailable" witness now—he was dead. The deposition had some damaging testimony, but nothing to equal his destructive self-imploding testimony on Friday and the damage Sophia would have inflicted on Monday.

Before they called Grimick to the stand, they would read portions of that transcript to the jury. They debated using Paul or Bryce to play Spangler on the witness stand. It would make the exchange more natural. They were still undecided after a long and circular discussion. At six, they left for Bakersfield.

Bryce volunteered to chauffeur. He and his Jeep Cherokee got them there in record time in the light traffic.

* * *

At eight, they hit town. They got Greek salads and kebabs at the Pita House on Mining Avenue and gathered in Sophia and Tricia's unit for a quick dinner meeting. They were tired but fought to be productive.

"Sophia, have you decided about one of us being Spangler on the witness stand?" Tricia asked.

"We don't have anyone with the properly seedy and disgusting bottom-dweller look," Sophia responded.

"Hey, I can dress like that guy. I can even make my teeth yellow and mess up my hair. See?" Bryce mistook Sophia's black humor and enthusiastically scrambled his hair to get the gig.

"Bryce, I was joking." Sophia made her decision. "You'll go up as your charming self."

"You have to be neutral and natural," Paul said. "You can't dramatize or slant the testimony one way or the other."

"I can do boring . . . maybe. I can try. It's tough for someone like me," Bryce teased.

After some further rehearsal, Bryce was ready. It would be easy. In his eagerness to be important to the team, he had already essentially memorized all of the depositions in the case, including Spangler's. For him, the performance would be like sleepwalking.

At eleven, all of them, drained by the day's exertions, staggered off for a few much-needed hours of sleep.

⌘

# CHAPTER 74

## Something Wicked

*"All you need in this life is ignorance
and confidence, and then success is sure."*
-Mark Twain

When Sophia's team arrived Monday, the courthouse was surrounded by a turbulent mass of demonstrators, media, and spectators. The police and Kern County deputy sheriffs were out in force, and portable barriers kept the crowd in check.

Spangler's death had hit the local news on Sunday and the Internet as well. The news vans had multiplied. The name "The Gun Trial," coined after all the gun deaths associated with it, had stuck—even though Spangler had died in his bathtub.

Many demonstrators postured in a sober vigil off on the grassy side of the entrance to the courthouse because of the mounting deaths connected with the case. Security was further tightened, with body scanners added to the metal detectors and individual searches.

\* \* \*

The Holts were waiting at the courtroom door for Sophia. They looked beaten down and tired, particularly Beth in her wheelchair. She led them to their plaintiffs' table. She knew someone should be driving them to court in case there was an incident with the ever-present demonstrators and media, but she lacked the manpower to hire a bodyguard-type driver, and they were too stubborn to have one anyway.

Moschella and his entourage were as yet nowhere to be seen, and it was already approaching ten. Kemper sat alone at the counsel table. Outside the courthouse, Moschella and Sandoval stood by anxiously, to see whether Grimick would show. They had given up and were about to enter the security funnel when he nonchalantly ambled up.

"Grimick." Moschella signaled him over. "Where the hell have you been? We've been trying to find you all weekend."

"Not that it's any of your business, but I met a lady friend of mine at Trout's Friday night, and we shacked up at her nice little house on Barnett Street all weekend. Didn't pop our heads out once, if you get my drift."

"What the . . ." Moschella stopped before the array of expletives on the tip of his tongue erupted.

"Hey, where's Spangler?" Grimick asked. "I went by his place and he wasn't there. I reckon you picked him up, huh?"

Before Moschella could explain, they were separated and funneled through security.

Moschella and Sandoval stopped again outside the courtroom to speak with Grimick. Moschella barely had time to tell him about Spangler's death when the bailiff appeared.

"Judge Ortiz is on the bench and said to find you. It's late, and he wants you in there. Now."

Grimick was pale and upset as he seated himself in the gallery. Spangler had been his friend. His really good friend.

"Thank you for joining us, Mr. Moschella, Ms. Sandoval. I hope it wasn't too much trouble." Judge Ortiz was angry and wielding his power. "It's after ten."

"I apologize, Your Honor," Moschella and Theresa stood at the counsel table. "But it's . . ."

"I don't want to hear it. One more time and I'm levying sanctions. Bailiff, bring in the jury, please." He did.

"Ladies and gentlemen of the jury, I trust you have followed my instructions not to discuss the case or watch news accounts concerning it. Therefore, it is my sad duty to tell you that Mr. Joseph Spangler, the witness you heard from last Friday, died of an apparent accident this weekend. His death is not to affect how you weigh his testimony, and while it's a tragedy, we know your time is valuable, and we won't delay this trial."

The jury box rumbled inaudibly and nervously with genuine surprise—all but five, whose reactions were obviously a cover because they already knew. The attorneys and surely Judge Ortiz were aware of that. But there were only two alternates left. Not one of the legal professionals, neither the judge nor any of the lawyers, challenged any of the jurors for breaking the rules and watching the news about the case. That would have meant redoing the trial over from day one. Nobody wanted that now.

Judge Ortiz moved on quickly, not allowing the attorneys to reconsider trying to get rid of any of the misbehaving jurors.

"Ms. Christopoulos, call your next witness."

"Yes, Your Honor. In view of Mr. Spangler's unfortunate and unexpected demise, we would like to conclude his testimony by reading from his deposition."

Sophia filed a certified copy of Spangler's deposition transcript with the court clerk as she spoke, and, just to be thorough, handed an extra copy to the clerk for the judge and one to Moschella as well.

"Very well, Ms. Christopoulos. I see despite the time constraints you have managed to mark the sections of the transcript you wish to read. A welcome courtesy. Will you be reading those sections to the jury yourself?"

"In part, Your Honor. I will read my questions, but I am going to ask that one of my associates, Mr. Bryce McLaughlin, who is here in the courtroom, take the stand to read Mr. Spangler's responses."

The judge had seen Bryce before, observing the motion *in limine* arguments and during the trial. The judge nodded at Bryce.

"Any objection, Mr. Moschella?"

"None, Your Honor."

He knew better than to object. This was proper procedure under the circumstances, and he didn't want the wrath of Ortiz on him again. He had to be careful.

"Mr. McLaughlin, please take the witness stand, if you would."

Bryce was wearing his best suit and tie for the occasion. A number of the women in the jury box were admiring him as he approached the witness stand. When he smiled at the jury, most smiled back, again especially the women. Sophia would take advantage of his charisma. It was certainly no worse than Moschella parading Sandoval around like a beauty contest competitor on the runway.

Sophia read her questions from the transcript to Spangler while Bryce read Spangler's answers. She established the basic facts of the sale of the shotgun to Mike, that Spangler didn't recall his conversation with Wallace Holt the way Wallace did but that he "didn't really remember." Bryce was studiedly straightforward but still managed to read Spangler's answers in a calculated way that signaled to the jury Spangler had been as evasive and uncertain in his deposition as he had been the previous Friday in court. Sophia and Bryce also read into the record Spangler's admissions and testimony that Sports Gear had given him basic training in gun and ammunition sales with a list of procedures to follow—a very short list only requiring him to get identification, age verification, run a three-minute background check, and make sure the customer satisfied the safety and waiting period requirements, if any. That was it.

Sophia tried to read the portions of his testimony where he admitted his criminal history and illegal gun sales, but Moschella objected to that as asked and answered. Judge Ortiz sustained the objection because it was a repeat of Friday's testimony.

The jurors had heard what Sophia wanted them to hear. As Bryce left the witness stand, the majority of the jurors, and both sexes, were smiling approvingly at him.

Before the judge could call a break, Sophia charged ahead.

"Your Honor, plaintiffs call Mr. Moss Grimick to the stand."

Moschella faced a dilemma. He'd had no final preparation session with Grimick, who was clearly upset about Spangler's death. Because of his tardiness, he knew if he asked for a recess, he would further alienate the jurors, who wanted to get back to their lives. Worse, Judge Ortiz would rightly assume that he had an ulterior motive. He wanted a chance to conform Grimick's testimony to the parts of Spangler's deposition just read and to coach Grimick on the "right" responses. Of course, Judge Ortiz had no idea Grimick had not been prepped at all over the weekend.

It would be a transparent tactic. Torn, Moschella elected to do nothing. The lunch break was nearing, and he would do a quick prep then on any topics Christopoulos had not yet covered with Grimick.

When Moschella made no effort to object, he heard coughing behind him. He turned to find a disapproving Jackson staring at him. Moschella ignored him and turned back to face the judge. This was his decision alone. Moschella knew Grimick's deposition had nothing in it with which to impeach any testimony he gave in court, thanks to Eddie Herrera's incompetence and short temper. Grimick just had to get through to the lunch break without giving up anything damaging.

*So be it,* Moschella thought.

Unfortunately for Moschella, Sophia's entire team spotted the Jackson interchange. They still didn't know who he was, but they had no doubt now that he was a key player on the defense side. Ben would come through for them with his identity.

* * *

Sophia studied Grimick as he sat in the witness stand dressed in jeans and a T-shirt, an angry expression on his face. He glowered at her when Sophia stood to begin questioning him.

Grimick thought, *No dummy me. Let the damn bitch do her worst.*

He blamed her and this stupid case for his friend's death.

"God, he's alienating all the jurors already," Theresa whispered to Moschella.

"I know. His friend is dead, and he blames the Holts and their lawyers for it. You can see it in his eyes."

Sophia threw softballs for a while, having him describe his very spotty educational and employment history, and confirm the training and instructions that Sports Gear had given him about gun and ammunition sales. She avoided any mention of Spangler's name or his deposition testimony in the process. Sophia had a plan and intended to execute it just before the lunch break, which Moschella would use to program this Neanderthal throwback on topics she hadn't covered.

"Mr. Grimick, were you and Mr. Spangler together at the Sports Gear store when you sold the shotgun to Mike Holt?"

"You know we were."

"That's a yes?"

"Yes."

"Was Mike acting odd or nuts or loony?"

"No odder than half our customers." He was smarter than this bitch. He'd show her.

"So half your gun customers act oddly?"

"Objection. Argumentative." Moschella was on his feet.

"Withdrawn, Your Honor." The jury had gotten the point.

"Did he have a 'strange look' in his eyes?"

"Not that I remember. Most people buying guns are pretty excited, though. Seems like he might have been too."

"Might have been, or was?"

"Dunno. Can't really recall. I sell a lot of guns and ammo to a lot of folks."

Sophia was at an impasse. Grimick's deposition that Eddie had botched left her with little ammunition to impeach these answers. She needed something and fast. She decided to risk a spur-of-the-moment inspiration.

"Mr. Grimick, would you sell a gun to someone in your store who was obviously drunk?"

"Objection, Your Honor. Relevance?"

"Goes to the selling practices and standard of care of Sports Gear and its employees, Your Honor," Sophia responded.

"Overruled. I'll be watching how far you take this, Ms. Christopoulos."

"Thank you, Your Honor." Sophia glanced pleasantly at the jurors to emphasize her victory as she had been taught at Thorne & Chase. "Please answer the question, Mr. Grimick."

"Heck no. I mean, that's just common sense."

"Common sense, you say. You use your common sense when you're deciding to sell someone a gun?"

"You bet. I'm a smart guy." Grimick smiled at one of the more attractive female jurors.

"So if someone were acting erratically, looked real nervous, maybe like they were on drugs or drunk, would your common sense let you sell that person a gun?"

"No way."

"But you're telling this court and the jury that nothing in the way Mike Holt acted that day made you think maybe he shouldn't be buying a gun?"

"Nope."

"Didn't it seem strange that he asked to buy one shell?"

"Naw. Besides, he bought a box of shells."

"The smallest?"

"Lots of customers buying a new gun just get a little bit of ammo to try it out. Ammo is expensive."

"It is, isn't it? You get a commission on all your sales of guns and ammo, don't you, Mr. Grimick?"

"I do."

"So you have an incentive to sell as many guns and as much ammunition as possible, don't you?"

"Every salesman is on commission at Sports Gear. We all try to sell as much as we can. So what?"

"And that includes you, doesn't it?"

"Sure."

Sophia considered asking about the relative profitability of his department at Sports Gear. Eddie had tried to question him about that in his deposition but got nowhere. He claimed ignorance then and would now. She was stumped. All she had was a toehold on the standard of care—common sense. She had to work with that.

She decided to take a leap, which would be over a cliff if it backfired. She had no choice.

"Mr. Grimick, when did you last speak to Joe Spangler?"

"Objection. Relevance, Your Honor."

"Your Honor, it's just a foundational question."

"I'll allow it," Judge Ortiz pronounced, partly because he was curious himself given Spangler's sudden and unexpected death.

"Do I need to repeat that question, Mr. Grimick?"

Grimick was worried. Was he the last person to see Joe alive? Was this uppity cunt going to try to pin something on him? He was guarded now, and it showed.

"Friday night."

"Where were you?"

"At his place."

"Are you referring to his apartment on Q Avenue in Oildale?"

"Yeah, I drove him home from court 'cause his truck was messed up and so was he."

"Did you discuss this lawsuit with him at all?"

"Objection. Hearsay," Moschella was frantic to get his objection in before Grimick answered since he had no idea what the answer would be.

"Withdrawn."

"Did you drop him off at his apartment Friday night?"

"I took him there and helped him up the stairs. He lives, lived, on the second floor."

"Did the two of you have a conversation in his apartment?"

"Just a short one."

"What did you say to him, and what did he say to you?"

"Objection. Hearsay, Your Honor."

"Offered for the fact of what was said, not for the truth of it, Your Honor."

"I'll have to overrule that objection, Mr. Moschella. Tread lightly, Ms. Christopoulos."

The judge didn't mean it. She could stomp all over Grimick if she wanted, because he wanted to hear the answer, too.

"Please tell us what you said to Joe and what he said to you, Mr. Grimick."

Grimick was tense. He chose his words carefully and began to speak very deliberately.

"I told him he done good in court . . . you know on Friday."

"What was his response?"

"He just . . . I dunno . . . thanked me."

"For your compliment?"

"For that, and giving him a ride and helping him to his apartment and all."

"Did he say anything else to you?"

"He told me Mr. Moschella wanted to meet with him Saturday morning so Mr. Moschella could tell him what he was supposed to say today here in court."

Moschella blanched at Grimick's inference that he was going to tell Spangler "what he was supposed to say." There was no way he could erase the statement from the minds of the jurors, but he had to prevent further damage and disrupt Sophia's line of questioning.

"Objection," Moschella said. "Hearsay, attorney-client communication, move to strike."

"Mr. Grimick is an employee of the defendant, Your Honor, and he has, by recounting that statement, waived any privilege."

"If so, it was an inadvertent waiver, Your Honor." Moschella was grasping at straws.

"Sorry, Mr. Moschella. Overruled. As you well know, the privilege belongs to the client, and as Sports Gear's employee, Mr. Grimick has waived it."

Sophia sought to press her advantage.

"Did Mr. Spangler tell you anything else Mr. Moschella said to him other than that he was to meet Mr. Moschella Saturday morning to talk about what Joe was supposed to say today here in court?"

"No, just that."

Sophia was disappointed there was nothing else, but now the jury had heard Grimick's answer twice. She wished there was more to show Moschella was orchestrating testimony, but there wasn't.

"Did you say anything else to Mr. Spangler in his apartment that evening?"

"Yes." Grimick was clearly not going to volunteer anything else after hearing Moschella objecting about what Joe had told him.

"What did you say?" Sophia would get it out of Grimick word by word if necessary.

"I told him I'd pick him up this morning to take him to court again since his truck was wrecked and he was hurt and everything."

"What was his reply?"

"He said that was real nice of me." Grimick was careful not to repeat the actual words Spangler had used—"real white of him"—in court. Only good old boys like him and Joe would understand and not take it wrong.

"Was that it? Did you leave then?"

Grimick thought furiously. He didn't know how Joe had died. He sure didn't want anyone to try to blame him or put him there when it happened. He decided he had to point the finger elsewhere to save his own skin.

"I went to my truck and brought him back a couple of bottles of booze. Then I left."

"Did you buy those for him?"

"Uh, no, I didn't buy them."

"How did you get them?"

"This guy stopped by my truck where I was parked down from the courthouse and give 'em to me in a paper bag."

"Just like that? Did he say anything to you?"

"Yes."

"What did he say?"

Grimick had to answer and didn't mind because that Moschella guy hadn't been on his side when that punk Mex lawyer had hit him with that briefcase. Screw him.

"He told me Mr. Moschella over there wanted me to give them to Joe in appreciation for his testimony Friday."

Grimick left out the part about keeping quiet about it. He didn't want to lose his job over this.

"Objection, Your Honor. Hearsay, more prejudicial than probative, move to strike." Moschella was being set up, and he knew it had to have been Jackson.

Judge Ortiz was furious. He stared at Moschella for a good thirty seconds. He had a hard time believing the testimony he had just heard. He had known Moschella for many years—both in court and out. Moschella was among the most ethical lawyers he knew. Nonetheless, he would not suppress the testimony. There was no objection he could or, more accurately, would sustain. It would remain on the record.

"Overruled, Mr. Moschella. Overruled."

Moschella knew he and his case were in trouble. He'd have to find some way to undercut Grimick now. His reputation with the judge and with his fellow lawyers in Bakersfield was worth more than Jackson and this client combined.

"Mr. Grimick," Sophia proceeded. "When you gave the two bottles of booze to Mr. Spangler, did you tell him what the man who had given them to you said?"

"Yes, what I just told you is what I told Joe."

"What was Mr. Spangler's response?"

"That maybe Mr. Moschella wasn't such a bad guy and wanted Joe friendly, I guess, when Mr. Moschella talked to Joe on Saturday about what he'd be sayin' here today. And that Joe thought he could get more money out of Mr. Moschella or he wouldn't testify the way they wanted him to."

"Objection, Your Honor. Hearsay, more prejudicial than probative, move to strike." Moschella spit the objections out, his voice rising.

"Overruled."

"By the way, Mr. Grimick, do you remember the name of the booze you gave Mr. Spangler Friday night?"

"I sure do because it costs a lot. Old Portrero 18th Century Style Whiskey."

Moschella felt sick. He had to keep it together. Theresa and Kemper were staring straight ahead. They didn't look at him. They couldn't.

"After that exchange with Mr. Spangler, did you say anything else to him, or he to you?"

"Sure."

"Please tell the court what you said and what he said."

"Joe asked if I wanted to stay and have some of that whiskey. I told him I wished I could, but that I was meeting a lady friend at Trout's."

"What happened next?"

"I left and went to Trout's, is what." Grimick wanted to make sure everyone know his friend was alive when he left.

"Was Mr. Spangler already drinking when you left, Mr. Grimick?"

"Not that I saw. He sure was about to, though."

"Did he appear to be in pain or unable to get around?"

"Nope. Didn't even need his wheelchair."

"Was that the last time you spoke to him?"

"Yeah, it was. Poor Joe." He looked down. Grimick was genuinely sad that his friend was dead.

"No further questions at this time, Your Honor."

The courtroom was quiet and still.

"Mr. Moschella? Cross?" Judge Ortiz asked.

Moschella didn't answer. He needed time to investigate and discredit Grimick's lies. He had none. He had to repair as much damage as possible and at least cast doubt on Grimick's smearing of his reputation. If he didn't question him now, Grimick might leave town or end up like Spangler.

"Mr. Moschella?"

"Yes, Your Honor."

* * *

Moschella stood and studied Grimick as he desperately thought of a way to rehabilitate his reputation and prove Grimick a liar. That was all that was important to him now.

"Mr. Grimick, did you ever hear me thank Joe Spangler for his testimony in this case on Friday?"

"Nope. Doesn't mean you didn't though."

"Move to strike the second part as nonresponsive, Your Honor."

"Motion granted. The jury will disregard the second sentence."

"Did you ever hear me thank Joe Spangler for his testimony at his deposition?"

"Nope."

"Or for his cooperation in this case in any way?"

"Can't say I did."

"Have I ever thanked you for your cooperation or testimony in this case?"

"Not for darn sure. And you didn't give me no booze neither."

Moschella sighed. "Again, move to strike the second sentence as unresponsive and lacking in foundation, Your Honor."

"Granted, Mr. Moschella. The jury will disregard the second sentence." Though tempted to smile at Grimick's comment, the judge managed to keep a straight face. What Grimick was saying wasn't really funny—not remotely so.

"Did you know Mr. Spangler had died before you came to court this morning, Mr. Grimick?"

"No. I feel real bad about that."

"Where were you from the time you left Mr. Spangler's apartment until you arrived at court this morning, Mr. Grimick?"

Grimick recounted his weekend.

"And if we called your lady friend as a witness, would she testify that you were at her place all weekend?"

"Objection. Calls for speculation, Your Honor." Sophia was enjoying this.

"Could you tell everyone the name of your lady friend then, Mr. Grimick, so we can confirm that?"

Grimick looked up at Judge Ortiz, disgusted with himself for having to be rescued by the same asshole judge who had pushed his friend around on Friday.

"Um, Your Honor, this is my private business. I don't see why my gal has to get involved in this. She done nothing. She don't know about this case or anything. I ain't never talked about it with her."

Judge Ortiz considered the issue for a moment. There was no reason to doubt Grimick's story. Still. This entire saga bothered him. Best not to leave loose ends. And Grimick was not a very appealing or trustworthy character.

"I'm afraid you'll have to answer that question, Mr. Grimick. The circumstances surrounding the death of Mr. Spangler are, at best, somewhat confusing."

"Dang. She's gonna be real mad at me for this. But if you say I gotta. Her name is Vera May Jerczy. That's spelled J-E-R-C-Z-Y, but she says it like 'Jersey.'"

"What is the address of her place where you say you spent the weekend, Mr. Grimick?"

"1919 Barnett Street, in Oildale."

"Did anyone else see the two of you there?"

"I don't know. We didn't come outside all weekend until this morning."

A rumble of laughter shot through the courtroom, but Judge Ortiz's harsh look immediately shut it down.

Moschella was about to stop, then realized he needed one more thing. "Mr. Grimick, you said a man handed you the two bottles of Old Portrero in a paper bag at your truck parked here on Friday, and then you gave them to Joe Spangler?"

"Yup."

"Did he give you his name?"

"Nope."

"Had you ever seen him before?"

"Can't say as I had."

"Do you see him in the courtroom today?"

Grimick looked around once, then again. He was really angry Moschella and that black-robed bully had brought Vera May into this thing.

"Don't see him here, no."

"Can you describe him to the court, please?"

"Objection, Your Honor. Relevance, needless delay." Sophia was objecting for effect, not because she meant it. She wanted the jurors to have the issue and the testimony firmly fixed in their minds.

"Your Honor, this goes to the credibility of this witness and, frankly, my own."

"I agree, Mr. Moschella. Overruled."

"Answer the question, Mr. Grimick."

"He was kinda short, heavy, a little bald, some gray hair, maybe thirty, looked like a lot of folks hereabouts. Nothing special."

"What was he wearing?"

"Just jeans, a T-shirt, I think, some tennis shoes. Ordinary stuff."

"Did you or he say anything else in your conversation Friday evening, beyond what you have already testified to?"

"Don't recall."

"Have you seen him since Friday night?"

"No. And when I left Joe, he was alive."

"Thank you, Mr. Grimick. No further questions."

"Nothing further from me, Your Honor," Sophia volunteered.

"You're excused, Mr. Grimick," the judge intoned.

Grimick swaggered down the center aisle out of the courtroom. He knew he would not be accused of killing his friend now. That wop lawyer might be, though.

* * *

Grimick's testimony left Moschella shell-shocked. Had he had a prep session with Grimick, he might have been forewarned. A lunch break would have helped. The morning session had gone long because Judge Ortiz did not want to interrupt the troubling testimony.

Why had Grimick lied about Moschella, and who had told him those things? Moschella turned around and looked straight at Jackson, "the fixer." Jackson stared back, his eyes still and cold.

"Everyone, it's late, I know, almost one. But I wanted to reach a natural breaking point in the testimony. So be back here at two-thirty. I still plan to conclude at four this afternoon as usual, but that will depend on how far along we are at that time."

The bailiff escorted the grateful jurors, who were restive and wanted their lunch, out of the jury box. As Judge Ortiz left the bench, the audience poured out of the courtroom with the lawyers and their clients on their heels.

It had been an astounding session. No one who had been there would likely forget it anytime soon, if ever—especially Moschella, whose reputation had been dragged through the mud by a lying redneck.

⌘

# CHAPTER 75

## Management Is An Art

*"He who is prudent and lies in wait*
*for an enemy who is not will be victorious."*
-Sun Tzu

For the lunch break, Moschella and Sandoval drove back to **Quarry, Warren & Moschella** together. Jackson had texted them to meet with him and Kemper at lunch.

"It's not true, Theresa."

"I know. But it's out there, and by tonight, it will be in the news."

There was little else to say.

When they arrived, Jackson and three of his people were waiting for them in the usual conference room. Ambrose Pickett was missing, but **Porter Beauregard** stroked his thick mustache, Samuel French sat tall, his auburn hair freshly cut, and Rose Boyd read on her iPad, disinterested and disrespected by her male colleagues.

"Tony, how in the hell could you pull a stunt like that?" Jackson asked. "Messengering Grimick booze to reward Spangler for saying the 'right' things? What were you thinking?"

"You goddamned son of a bitch!" Moschella roared. "Even in Bakersfield, we have laws against suborning perjury and witness tampering. I would never do anything like that, not just because it's illegal, but because it's stupid."

"It sure was."

"It wasn't me or anyone from my firm."

"That's rich. What are you suggesting there, Tony? My people did it? No one mentioned my name . . . our names."

"Where's Pickett? He fits the description Grimick gave in court almost perfectly."

"You'd best watch the accusations, Tony. Lots of people in this town fit that description. Ambrose is back in Denver fielding a crisis in another important case."

"Sure he is," Moschella scoffed.

"You want a scapegoat, and we're not going to be it." Jackson assumed his poker face and continued his relentless attack on Moschella's reputation and veracity. "I picked you and your firm. If this goes badly, it will fall on me as hard as or harder than it does on you."

Jackson was in too tight with Sports Gear to have any worries on that score. Still, he was hedging his bets. The fact that his little gambit had created a distracting problem in the courtroom for their case didn't bother Jackson. It was a minor setback, nothing more. It made Moschella look bad, not him or Sports Gear.

Sandoval and Kemper looked on silently at the intense and bitter exchange of accusations. Sandoval believed Jackson and his brood were behind the whiskey incident. Kemper was confused and beside himself. He was a man of honor, and the incident with Grimick and Spangler was hardly honorable. It was the opposite. He felt sordid by association. But he said nothing. He was the client representative. He would report on the trial's revelations to senior management himself this time and not rely on Jackson.

Jackson's three remaining flunkies waited for his orders or to affirm anything he wanted as backup against Moschella.

"Setting all this aside the issue is, Tony, can you continue to try this case with that cloud hanging over you?"

"Do you have a better idea, Tom? Are you ready to stop hiding and take over? Was that your plan all along?"

"No. I want what's best for our client here." Jackson looked over at Kemper but let his eyes scan Theresa's breasts.

"Good, because if I stepped away from the case now, the jury and Judge Ortiz would take it as an admission that I tried to bribe a witness and contributed to his death. That, without a doubt, would poison them against Sports Gear."

"Perhaps. Grimick really did us no great harm on the merits of the case. It's hardly ideal, but I guess you're still our guy, Tony. For now. Who are they calling next?"

Kemper said nothing. He watched, evaluating, noncommittal, not sure what to do. Moschella hadn't seemed like a witness tamperer to him.

"I don't know. But given we only have a couple of hours left today, I doubt it will be one of their experts. Probably Davis, the store manager. He's on deck at least."

"Is he ready?" Jackson asked.

"Absolutely. He's a rock. His deposition was utterly boring, the way you want them."

"If that woman calls him, will you examine him now or wait until you present the defense case?"

"Can't say," Moschella answered. "Depends on his testimony, how much time she takes, and whether his answers slip and he needs rehabilitation. I'll have to make that call on the spot."

"See that you do. I don't expect any more blindsides."

"I didn't expect this one. Trials always bring surprises, Tom. With your experience, I would have thought you knew that." Moschella's dig was not lost on anyone in the room.

"Of course," Jackson glared back at Moschella. "Let's grab a bite and get back to court. Separately."

"I wouldn't have it any other way." Moschella quickly propelled himself out of the conference room. Sandoval followed.

* * *

Sophia, the Holts, and the rest of their team had decamped to Café Crepes on Truxtun again for lunch. They were astonished by the day's events.

"I can't believe Moschella did that," Paul said after they ordered their crepes.

"I don't think he did." Sophia was deep in thought.

"Are you saying Grimick lied?"

"No. I'm saying Tony Moschella is too good a lawyer, with too sterling a reputation to uphold in this burg, ever to pull a stunt like that. He's not a lawyer who needs to tamper with witnesses, and from what I've seen, he's tough but he plays by the rules . . . with a little bending like all of us."

"Since we're all speculating here," Tricia said, "do you think Grimick was paid to make Spangler's death look like an accident? And make Moschella the fall guy?"

The food came, and the table silenced.

"Grimick's garbage for sure, but he seemed genuinely surprised and upset at Spangler's death, so I doubt it." Sophia couldn't eat. She sipped her cappuccino, still thinking.

"I can't see who would gain from that. Spangler's death certainly helps Sports Gear because you would have ripped him apart, Sophia. But implicating its lead lawyer in trying to manipulate testimony and a death, hardly. It's confusing."

Bryce was not to be left out. "How can we use that testimony to our best advantage?"

"I'm not sure we need to do much other than let it sit there in the minds of the jurors," Paul responded.

"The jury and Judge Ortiz think Moschella tried to tamper with or bribe a witness, and that's certainly good for our side." Tricia threw out her thought between bites of her chipotle chicken crepe. "I hate to say it, but the fact he died is better yet."

"What will you do next, Sophia?" Beth asked.

"Beth, let them talk. You're no lawyer." Wallace was more interested in his lunch than in anything Beth might say.

"No, she has every right to ask, Wallace." Sophia acted the peacemaker. "I'm calling Arnie Davis. He was solid for Sports Gear in his deposition, but I have some things to hit him with that weren't covered there. Nothing like what I had with Spangler, unless something else drops in my lap. I'll get what I can."

They headed back to court with time to spare.

* * *

When the trial reconvened, Sophia called Davis to the stand.

Her initial questions were *pro forma*: getting him to describe his position at Sports Gear, his educational and employment history, and his basic training in its policies and procedures. She moved quickly to lines of questioning that would help her case.

"Mr. Davis, your responsibilities as store manager include reviewing the store's financials each month, don't they?"

"You bet. Sports Gear cares about that bottom line, and so do I. We're in business to make money, after all."

"Indeed. Of all of the departments at your store here in Bakersfield, which one is the most profitable?"

"Well, it sort of changes month to month and year to year."

"You're quite sure of that?"

"I just said so."

"Your Honor, I am showing the witness what's been marked as Exhibit 73."

Sophia handed Davis the exhibit. It was one of the few things they had managed to tease out of the computerized portion of Sports Gear's document production.

"Do you recognize that document, Mr. Davis?"

Davis shifted in his chair and looked at it a long time. "Yes."

"You prepared it, didn't you?"

"Um, yes, um, I did."

"Isn't that a five-year comparison, on a monthly basis, of the profitability of the different departments at your store?"

"Yes."

"Your Honor, plaintiffs offer Exhibit 73 into evidence."

Hearing no objection from Moschella, Judge Ortiz so ordered. With that, Sophia had it projected on the Recordex Pull Up Screen the team had brought for everyone to see."

"Mr. Davis, do you see that four rows in, there is a label of 'Guns & Ammo'?"

"I see it."

"Looking at Exhibit 73, can you tell me if that refers to the department that sells guns and ammunition at your store?"

"It does."

"Now, you told me a moment ago that the most profitable department in your store changes month to month and year to year, correct?"

Davis looked around for help and found none.

"Mr. Davis, isn't that what you said?"

"Objection. Asked and answered." This time, Moschella intervened.

"Sustained."

"In fact, as Exhibit 73 shows, that isn't true, is it?"

"Well, department profits do change."

"That wasn't my question. Please point out on Exhibit 73 any month in any of the last five years, or any year in any of the last five years, when the guns and ammunition department was not the most profitable department in your store."

Davis looked at the document for a long time.

"I'm sure it's in here somewhere."

"But somehow you don't see it, do you, Mr. Davis?"

"Not just now."

"That's because selling guns and ammunition is the most profitable part of your store's business, isn't it?"

"If you say so, I guess."

"No, Mr. Davis. You say so in Exhibit 73, which you prepared."

"Objection, Your Honor, argumentative and that isn't a question."

Before the judge could say anything, Sophia held up her hand. "I'll move on, Your Honor. Is part of your compensation based on the profitability of your store, Mr. Davis?"

"Yup."

"And wasn't the most significant portion of the salaries of the late Mr. Spangler and Mr. Grimick based on commissions they were paid on sales in their guns and ammunition department?"

"Sure, same as all the other sales clerks in all the departments."

"Does that mean if they sold more, they made more, and if they sold less, they made less?"

"Again, no different from any other sales job."

"So the answer to my question is yes, Mr. Davis?"

"I guess so. I mean, yes."

"You spoke with my client Wallace Holt after his son's death, didn't you?"

"Yes."

"And you told him you were sorry for what had happened to his son?"

"Of course. Anyone would be."

"Especially in your case, because you told Mr. Holt you thought there was something wrong with Mike that day, didn't you?"

"I don't think I used those words. I don't remember."

"You told him Mike was acting strangely in the parking lot, didn't you?"

"Not sure about that."

"Are you saying you didn't, or you might have?"

"I'm saying I'm not sure."

"You said he had a strange look in his eyes, didn't you?"

"I don't recall that."

"You heard Mr. Holt testify on this stand that you said those things to him, didn't you?"

"I wasn't paying much attention."

"If he testified that you told him those things, are you saying he was lying?"

"I'm saying . . . I'm not sure what I said, but whatever I said was because I was sorry his son had killed himself."

That was the best Sophia could do. She had gotten a little more out of Davis than Paul had in his deposition, and the jury had seen that he was tentative, unsure, defensive, and trying to wiggle out of answers or not answer at all.

"No further questions, Your Honor."

Moschella decided that the jury did not need more of Arnie Davis. He had done well on Sports Gear's procedures and policies, and the training of Spangler and Grimick. All Christopoulos had accomplished was to imply to the jury that Davis was convenient with his answers and memory, and to suggest that Spangler and Grimick had personal motivations for trying to push the sales of guns and ammo. He could live with that. In closing, he would argue that all salesmen and managers received performance-based commissions and bonuses and that it meant nothing special insofar as the shotgun sale to Mike Holt was concerned.

"No questions at this time, Your Honor."

"Very well. It's four-thirty. I'll see everyone back here tomorrow morning, usual time."

⌘

# CHAPTER 76

## Evening Portents

*"Night brings our troubles to the light, rather than banishes them."*
-Lucius Annaeus Seneca

Monday evening was a replay of the lunch break at Quarry, Warren & Moschella. All of the lawyers met again in the conference room to discuss the next day's strategy. Kemper had gone back to the hotel to work and report in.

For once, there was relative agreement. Davis hadn't hurt them. If anything, his testimony was positive. Sandoval said nothing when everyone was nodding along with Jackson and Moschella. She thought Davis had lacked credibility but saw no point in disagreeing, especially with her boss.

"What's left for them?" Jackson asked.

"Their expert witnesses and Beth Holt." Moschella asserted control once more.

"Good, good. Our folks have prepared detailed cross-examination questions for their experts. Just use those outlines. Beth Holt will be easy. We don't want her on the stand any longer than necessary. Keep any cross-examination to a minimum."

Again, Moschella was being treated like a little boy who didn't know what he was doing. It infuriated him.

"I'll be reviewing those outlines tonight, Tom. To make any changes I think are necessary given this judge, this jury, and what's best for Sports Gear."

"If you make any changes, be sure to email them to me for my approval tonight, Tony."

The other Denver lawyers didn't even try to mask their grins.

"Sure, Tom. Whatever you want." Moschella resolved then and there to send the revised outlines to Jackson via a delayed email, at about three in the morning. Let him try to meddle then.

"Is our defense case set?" Jackson asked.

"We start with Jubal, as I said before, to put an impressive face to Sports Gear. Then our experts. I won't recall Grimick or Davis unless I need to. Too much risk there. We'll finish with Brandon Gallo."

"The kid? The intern or assistant clerk or stock boy or whatever? Why him? What does he add, especially as our last witness?"

Moschella sighed. "I told you before. I'm not going to repeat myself."

"He can't testify to much."

"That's the whole point."

"Why not end with our stellar experts? I know they're stellar because we've used them before and we spoon-fed you their prep. You're using all of them aren't you?"

"We're calling three of them. Five would be overkill, and frankly, the two we aren't using are cumulative of two we are using."

"We agreed you would call all five."

"No. You said you had five experts. I told you I needed to read the jury and decide who among them to call and how many. This jury is getting weary. Boring them to death with repetitive expert testimony won't help us."

"Who then?"

"The psychiatrist, the gun marketing economist, and the president of the Retail Gun Sellers of America."

"Not the NGA guy? He's excellent. And we owe them a lot."

"He's too political, too obviously biased. The president of the Retail Gun Sellers fits the factual situation in this case far better. We don't need speeches on the stand."

"What about the president of Colt? He's very impressive, and that name is synonymous not only with guns but the taming of the West."

Moschella's patience was nearly at an end.

"Two things. First, his bias is equally clear for the very reasons you stated, and it will be to the jury. Second, Colt has been in the news for a lot of negative things. Do you want the head of a company that has just gone into Chapter 11 bankruptcy up there on the stand? Christopoulos would have a field day with him."

"Colt is a big client of ours. We're handling that Chapter 11. It would be a gross insult not to call their president after we told him we would be."

"Sorry, Tom. You want to call him, be my guest. I won't."

Jackson stared down this little hick town lawyer who was crossing him yet again. Moschella was unmoved. In the end, Jackson retreated.

"Your funeral, Tony. Thanks for leaving me with a steaming pile of crap."

"Not my problem, Tom. You hired me to represent Sports Gear. Not to help you cultivate other clients."

Beauregard and French were aghast. Boyd didn't react at all. She didn't like Jackson's tactics but pretended loyalty for the time being because he had helped her advance as the token female at the firm. That did not stop her from enjoying his unsuccessful attempts to cow Moschella.

Jackson stood, and his Denver colleagues scurried to do the same.

"I'll leave you to your tasks. I'm taking my team to Wool Growers tonight for dinner. It's past six. Maybe Theresa needs a break?" Jackson smiled at her.

"Yes, join us," French added his own invitation. "Feminine company is always welcome."

"I can't, but thank you." Sandoval was repelled. No way would she be the evening entertainment and sex object for this bunch.

"We'll order in," Moschella interceded. "See you in court in the morning."

The Jackson contingent left. Moschella relaxed and ordered takeout from Moo Creamery on Truxtun: a burger for him and a salad combo for Theresa.

"We'll eat while we work," Moschella said. "We have a long slog ahead."

"I don't mind. Better than going with them. They all give me the creeps."

* * *

After sending the Holts home, Sophia and her team returned to their nondescript rented condos. They were careful, as they advised the Holts to be. Sophia varied their route coming and going. Bryce always watched to see whether they were being followed. All that had happened in this case warranted extreme caution on their part.

As had become their pattern, they gathered in the women's unit. No one wanted to go out for dinner. Too much to do, too much to think and talk about. They had soft drinks and waters in both units, so they ordered a couple of large pizzas delivered from the local Slice of Italy: one Greek with feta and spinach and one margherita. Even Paul didn't think they needed more.

Before they started to work, and while waiting for their pizzas, Sophia realized she had not turned back on her cellphone, which she kept off during the trial day. She had a flurry of text and voice mail messages from Ben Kowrilsky. She had been avoiding him because of the pressure of the trial. According to his texts, he had something urgent to discuss with her.

"Ben Kowrilsky really needs to talk to me. I'm going to call him before the pizzas come."

She made the call privately in her bedroom.

"Sophia. Jesus. I've been trying to reach you all afternoon."

"My cell was off in court."

"Ah, I get that. I have something intriguing."

"Well, spit it out. We have a lot of work to do tonight. Sorry to be short. I'm just tired."

"Understood. Here it is. That picture Paul Viola sent me from his phone of that guy who has been in court every day? Well, I know who he is."

"Who?"

"My research team identified him as Thomas Jackson, senior partner at Jackson, Hood & Lee. They're a big national law firm headquartered in Denver, and they represent most of the gun manufacturers and gun retailers in the western U.S. Maybe even the country."

"Is he consulting on my case?"

"No. He's running the whole show for the defense. My sources tell me Sports Gear is his biggest client. Lots of corporate, tax, real estate, and litigation work. He farms out trials to local firms but directs the lawsuits anonymously, with his people backstopping the local firms and doing most of the paperwork and motions. He hired Moschella. He's there every day to make sure his client is getting its money's worth."

"Wow, that explains a lot. That's how they deluged us with all those discovery motions and challenges . . . the summary judgment motion and the stack of motions *in limine*."

"No doubt. They are huge, and their *modus operandi* is to bury their opponents in motions and paperwork. You're lucky you survived."

"Thanks, Ben. I mean it. But what of it? It's legal for clients to have principal outside counsel choose local trial lawyers and work with them on cases."

"True, but this guy Jackson has been implicated in a lot of shady things. Favors to politicians, contributions to dark PACs and lobbyists, and other political things. Here's the most important part, though. After several trials in other cities, he's been investigated for buying off witnesses or having them disappear on vacations out of the country and other ways. I think Spangler's death may be part of that pattern."

"You think he arranged Spangler's death?"

"I don't know. My research people are getting information on his law firm, from their website, reviews, news stories on the Internet, blogs, you name it. I've asked some of my blogger contacts to put some provocative questions out there, especially in Denver and the surrounding area. See what bubbles up. Can't hurt."

"No, it can't. This is huge. We'll try to do some checking ourselves. Anything else?"

"Nothing except that you're doing a super job in court. Couldn't ask for better copy for my purposes."

"All in a day's work. For both of us."

"True. Take care."

As Sophia ended the call, the doorbell rang. The pizzas had arrived. Before she ate, she called Rona and left a message for her and Derek updating them on the day's events and the report from Ben. Then she took a second and called her parents. They were fine, and she said she was too. It was a stretch, a long stretch for her.

* * *

While Sophia ate, she filled the team in on what Kowrilsky had told her and his action plan.

"I knew there was something about that guy, Sophia." Paul smiled triumphantly as he took a large piece of the Greek pie.

"For now, that's all we know. Our most pressing task is what's in front of us tomorrow. The case and Moschella."

"Davis didn't come across as very confident or comfortable this afternoon. That was good." Tricia was sipping an instant espresso in between bites of her slice of pizza margherita.

"He didn't give us much either. Just the ability to argue that his salesmen had an incentive to push gun and ammo sales, even to nutty customers. If Moschella objects, Judge Ortiz might not let me argue that in closing. Nothing suggests that motivated Grimick or Spangler to sell the shotgun to Mike more than it would have to any other customer."

"There's Grimick's equivocal testimony and the Davis stats. The jury will make the connection if we just remind them." Paul took a large drink from his regular Coke.

"Maybe. Tomorrow we should finish with our case in chief, everyone. We're on schedule with our experts and then Beth, the human fountain, at the end of the day," Sophia said.

"If we don't get derailed by Moschella stretching out his cross-examinations," Bryce said.

"I'm ready, and so are our experts," Paul enthused.

"Paul, nothing in their backgrounds or resumes will come back to haunt us, will it?" Tricia asked.

"Not a thing," Paul said. "Too bad Sports Gear can't say that about some of its designated experts. Are they really going to call the guy from the NGA? Or the president of Colt? What a joke."

"No idea," Sophia said. "Moschella's a very good lawyer, not a stupid one. But now we know this Jackson guy is the one in charge, we'll find out."

"Do you need any help on your examination of Beth, Sophia?" Bryce, as usual, wanted to get involved.

"No, Bryce. She is just our face of mourning, to show the cost of Mike's death in human terms to her and Wallace. I just have to control her grandstanding. I think we can all agree that she's an attention hog and transparent about it. If I can curb that, we'll be fine."

Disappointed, Bryce nodded. Then he opened his laptop. He wanted to contribute something. He brought up the website of Jackson's firm.

"Hey guys, here's the Jackson, Hood & Lee website. I see Jackson. And look, here are all the other partners and associates. I'll print their pictures out and we can look for them. I may see if they're staying at the Padre Hotel. That's the best one in town."

"Excellent. Do it, Bryce."

They finished dinner, and Bryce and Paul went to their unit. Paul had a couple of hours of work to do, going over his question outlines and exhibits for Dr. Mapes and Dirk Savage. They had agreed he would do both of their experts, even though Sophia had defended Savage at his deposition.

Sophia needed to spend more time with Beth and took off for the Holts's house to make sure Beth was relaxed and ready. Tricia went with her—the rule of two. Before leaving, she printed out some background information Ben had emailed to her about Jubal Kemper. He had turned up some interesting tidbits she would use if Kemper took the stand.

⌘

# CHAPTER 77

## Emotional Expertise

*"The oldest and strongest emotion of mankind is fear,
and the oldest and strongest kind of fear is fear of the unknown."*
-H.P. Lovecraft

The next morning there was pandemonium at the courthouse. News vans, demonstrators, passersby snapping photos with their mobile phones, everyone shouting. The trial had become even more sensational after the previous day's events.

As Sophia and her team approached, she spotted Ben in a heated exchange with Jackson, the man Paul had photographed.

Sophia pointed. "Paul, there's your man from Jackson, Hood & Lee."

"Ben is after him," Paul said. "Jackson doesn't seem to be enjoying it. Too bad for him. Let's get inside. We can't be late."

\* \* \*

"Mr. Jackson, why are you here for this trial? What is your role in this case? Is your firm deciding Sports Gear's trial strategy and tactics?" Kowrilsky fired his questions at Jackson while his cameraman took a close-up.

"No comment." Jackson was cool as ice and backed away into the crowd.

"Is it true you're being investigated for offering favors and cash to legislators and lobbyists who oppose gun control legislation?" Ben followed.

"That's defamation. Keep it up and you'll get a lawsuit of your own."

"You don't deny that you have funneled large sums of dark money to pro-gun organizations like the NGA and PACs supporting the arms industry, do you?"

"I have nothing else to say to you."

With that, Jackson forced his way through the crowd and to the courthouse.

He arrived simultaneously with Sophia and her colleagues.

"Mr. Jackson? We haven't met. I'm Sophia Christopoulos, as you obviously know."

Jackson looked at her, startled, but just for an instant. He put his head down and went past her through to the courthouse doors. He elbowed to the head of the security line with a few mumblings of protest back in the line.

"Someone isn't having a good morning," Tricia said.

"Gee, I wonder why. Maybe being sniffed out on the Internet and splashed across the national media wasn't part of the game plan," Bryce said.

"No kidding." Paul enjoyed the moment.

This was Paul's tough day, but he wasn't nervous. He was the only one on the team who had real trial experience, and for him, it was a return to a familiar stage, and one he always enjoyed.

They found the Holts in the lobby and headed into the courtroom.

Wallace cornered Sophia. "I saw on the news some big national law firm guy with a lot of gun clients has been in court every day watching this trial. Is that true?"

"It is, Wallace. But we don't know what that means yet."

"But it shows this case is important."

"It was always important, Wallace. Mike was important. This just may mean the case has wider implications than your loss of Mike to the gun industry."

"Beth will be pleased. But will this make it harder to settle?"

"They haven't tried to settle with any reasonable amount, Wallace. You know that. They aren't even offering to cover our costs. I can't say this will change their position either way."

Wallace was downcast. "Okay. I was just hoping."

He still wanted out. Sophia couldn't let him falter until they got the brass ring. Or better yet, the diamond one.

* * *

Moschella and Sandoval met briefly with Jackson outside the courtroom.

"Guess the cat's out of the bag now, Tom, eh?" Moschella couldn't resist needling him.

"Means nothing, Tony. Lots of clients have their principal outside counsel monitor cases during trial. Hardly news."

"Whatever you say. Hope the jury doesn't get wind of this, though. They don't like seeing locals made to look bad."

"How would you look bad?"

"It suggests you don't trust us here to get the job done."

"Truthfully, at this stage, I don't. But I have no real choice, do I? You deal with any jury problems. After all, you have the same incentive I do. You don't want people thinking you're just a bit player, do you? Hardly a compelling image for developing additional business, is it?"

Moschella's rage again flamed white-hot. Through gritted teeth, he issued a quick directive. "Let's get into the courtroom before the bailiff comes out again."

With that, Moschella and Sandoval left to join Kemper at the counsel table.

* * *

When the courtroom was settled, Judge Ortiz invited the plaintiffs' counsel to continue. Paul Viola stood.

"Your Honor, plaintiffs call Dr. Simon Mapes."

Dr. Mapes made his way to the stand. He was six feet tall with sandy brown hair and an elegant tan suit to match. He had soft azure eyes that he directed to the jury from the moment he took his seat. He acted like a trial veteran, not someone who had very limited experience testifying.

Paul efficiently took Dr. Mapes through his educational and employment history. From their body language, the jurors identified with him to the extent that he had been born and raised in Stockton, another city in California's great Central Valley, graduating from the prestigious Stockton Early College Academy before getting his degree with highest honors in neurological sciences from Johns Hopkins University in Baltimore, Maryland, and his M.D. from the nation's top school for psychiatry, Harvard Medical School. He now held a tenured joint professorship at Stanford University and its medical school, in neurobiology and psychiatry.

"Dr. Mapes, do you have a particular specialization"

"Yes, the early identification and treatment of potential suicide victims."

"You have published in the field, have you not?"

"Extensively."

"I am handing you what's been marked as Exhibit 47. Is that a listing of your publications?

"It is."

"Your Honor, plaintiffs offer Exhibit 47 into evidence."

"Hearing no objection, received, counsel."

"Have you also testified in other cases involving gun suicides?"

"Three."

Paul brought those cases up first, even though none of them had led to a verdict against the gun seller. He had no choice, because if he didn't, Moschella would do so and also in the process imply he and Dr. Mapes weren't disclosing them because of their unfavorable outcomes.

"Were they jury trials?"

"One was. The other two were court trials, by stipulation of the parties."

"Where were those cases tried?"

"Two in Mississippi, and one in Utah."

"Did any of them result in a verdict holding the gun seller liable for selling a gun to the suicide victim?"

Dr. Mapes looked straight at the jury, a grim but determined look on his face.

"No. They did not."

The Holts were confused. They both looked questioningly at Sophia. She ignored them.

"Does anything make this case different from the others in which you testified?"

"Yes."

"What does?"

"Objection, Your Honor. Lack of foundation, vague, calls for a narrative answer, and compound."

"Sustained."

Paul had expected those objections.

"Dr. Mapes, we asked you to assume a hypothetical situation in this case, did we not?

"You did."

"What was that hypothetical?"

"You asked me to assume that a customer in the Sports Gear store here in Bakersfield was acting odd, had a strange look in his eyes, wanted the cheapest shotgun, asked to buy one shotgun shell, then bought the smallest amount of ammunition available, was agitated, and rushed to make the purchase."

"Were any of those circumstances present in any of the other cases in which you testified?"

"No."

"Based on the hypothetical we posed, in your professional opinion, was this customer, as described just now, exhibiting warning signs indicative of possible suicidal intent?"

"Objection, Your Honor. The hypothetical assumes facts not yet established."

"Overruled, Mr. Moschella. It's a fair representation of testimony by Mr. Holt and others whom the jury has already heard."

Moschella was chagrined. The hypothetical was a stretch, but Ortiz accepted it. That meant Judge Ortiz would not be doing Moschella any more favors. He could feel Jackson's eyes burrowing into his back as he sat down.

"You may answer, Dr. Mapes."

"He was."

"Again, in your opinion, given those warning signs, should the store clerks have sold such a customer a shotgun?"

"Most definitely not."

"Nothing further at this time, Your Honor."

Moschella rose.

"Dr. Mapes, you've only held your position at Stanford for two years, is that correct?"

"It is."

"You've also gone on record as favoring more extensive background checks on individuals seeking to purchase guns, haven't you?"

"I've made no secret of that. Though that wouldn't have made a difference here and is not the subject of my testimony."

"To your knowledge, were any of the Sports Gear employees in the store the day Mike Holt bought the shotgun trained in psychology or psychiatry?"

"I have no idea."

"And yet, you're saying they should have somehow known that Mike Holt was suicidal, or erratic, or read his mind?"

"Objection. Argumentative and compound, Your Honor."

"Withdrawn."

"Dr. Mapes, do you believe someone needs special training or qualifications to judge if a person is suicidal?"

"I'd say they most definitely need one thing."

Moschella had him.

"And that would be?"

"Common sense."

Moschella was nonplussed. He had walked right into it. That's exactly what Grimick had claimed he had—common sense—that it was what he always used in deciding whether to sell a gun to someone. Moschella couldn't risk making things worse.

"No further questions, Your Honor."

"Any redirect?"

Paul knew to quit while he was ahead.

"None, Your Honor."

"Thank you, Dr. Mapes. You are excused." Judge Ortiz was thoughtful as Dr. Mapes made his way out of the courtroom. It was already eleven.

As Moschella sat down, Kemper raised an eyebrow at him. Sandoval was impassive, in order not to betray her own perplexity at the abrupt end to Moschella's cross-examination.

* * *

Paul moved quickly, sensitive to their time constraints. "Plaintiffs call Mr. Dirk Savage as our next witness, Your Honor."

Savage was a character out of central casting as he took the witness stand. He was a slightly older version of the Marlboro Man, with graying auburn hair, short but not a crew cut, and ocean-blue eyes that took in everything. He wore intricately tooled deep brown cowboy boots with silver toes, casual but clearly expensive white pants, a light blue formal shirt, a bolo tie with a turquoise and silver clasp, and a matching white sports coat. He was a dominating presence.

Paul took Savage through his fascinating background. Lifetime hunter and NGA member. Veteran of the Seventh Air Cavalry in Vietnam. Longtime police officer, ultimately becoming chief of police in Nashville, Tennessee. Owner of Dirk's Den in Chattanooga, Tennessee, for fifteen years after that, where his inventory included a wide range of guns and ammunition. Paul carefully elicited from him that he had testified in a number of trials on behalf of gun store owners and a trade association of firearms wholesalers.

The jury was transfixed by this real American, a man who clearly knew and loved and owned guns. What was he doing testifying for the Holts?

"Your Honor, plaintiffs offer Mr. Savage as an expert on customs and best practices in the retail gun business."

Moschella wanted to object. He did not dare. Ortiz would overrule him, and the jury would take offense. Savage was qualified, and everyone in the courtroom was well aware of that.

"No objection, Your Honor."

"Very well. It's nearly noon. We'll take our lunch break and resume at one-thirty as usual." Judge Ortiz banged his gavel, rose from the bench, and left. The courtroom emptied.

⌘

# CHAPTER 78

## Savagery and Sentiment

*"There are no facts, only interpretations."*
-Friedrich Nietzsche

Back in the large conference room at Quarry, Warren & Moschella lunch was waiting, but the food went untouched during Jackson's tirade.

"Tony, you're just going through the motions now," Jackson asserted in his unmistakable accusatory tone, puffing for Kemper who sat at the end of the table. "You let that first expert's last answer stand unchallenged."

"Sometimes it's better not to draw attention to particular testimony. This was one of those occasions. To me."

"Then you let them drag out every loving detail of that cowboy's homespun heroic history. The jury likes this Savage guy. The women jurors are captivated. What the hell are you doing? Sleeping?"

Moschella had taken enough and was ready to blast Jackson. Caution and his litigator's experience warned him off.

"Using my judgment, because that's what you're paying me to do. We have extensive information on Savage, enough to undercut him this afternoon. You provided it, so I am simply going to rely on it. Besides, they have to lay out the backgrounds of their experts to qualify them. They would do that even if I tried to accept them as experts without the need for that. Every good trial lawyer wants jurors to hear their experts' credentials."

"Your judgment call and your mistake if it backfires." Another threat.

Kemper was hungry and wanted some peace. "Let's eat, Jackson. Moschella said he'll get at Savage, and he will."

The group ate silently, everyone choosing indifferently from an assortment of kabobs and salads delivered at Sandoval's direction from Flame & Skewers Restaurant nearby. True to form, she had run it first by Moschella, who had gotten Jackson's imprimatur. No detail was too small for Jackson to control when he chose to—and when he could.

\* \* \*

Sophia's team, Savage, and the Holts went to the Sandwich Company on 18th Street for lunch. It was close, decent, and cheap. They didn't discuss the case, except for general compliments to Paul and Savage on the impression they were making on the jury. Everyone was optimistic. They all expected Savage would do well in the afternoon session.

\* \* \*

Back in court again, Paul stood confidently at the counsel table as he addressed Savage.

"Mr. Savage, were you approached by anyone other than our office to testify as an expert in this case?"

"Objection, Your Honor. Relevance?" There was no valid objection Moschella could make to stop what would be very damaging testimony. He had already lost a motion *in limine* to keep Savage from testifying about his offer from Jackson's defense team.

"Goes to credibility, Your Honor. It could not be more relevant."

"Agreed, Mr. Viola. Objection overruled. Please proceed."

"I was."

"By whom?"

"Counsel for the National Gun Association and counsel for Sports Gear USA."

The jurors were simultaneously confused and nonplussed. How could both sides ask the same expert to testify? Did that mean he would say anything if someone paid him enough, or did it mean he was so good everybody wanted him?

"Did they contact you before or after our office sought your assistance?"

"After."

"If you had not agreed to serve as an expert witness for the Holts here, would you have agreed to serve as an expert for defendant Sports Gear USA?"

"No."

"Is that because you are opposed to the sale of guns in this country?"

"Hardly. I made my living selling guns for many years. And as you had me disclose, I have testified in support of a number of gun stores and a trade association of firearms wholesalers in other cases."

"Why not then?"

"I couldn't honestly testify on Sports Gear's behalf given the facts of this particular case."

"Based on your own experience, and in view of the testimony you have heard and reviewed, in your opinion, did Sports Gear's salesmen act responsibly in selling the shotgun to Mike Holt?"

"No."

"Again, based on your experience and given your expertise, in your opinion, did they exercise the ordinary care you would expect from a firearms seller in making that sale?

"They did not."

The courtroom was quiet, still, and curious.

"On what do you base those opinions, Mr. Savage?"

"A number of factors."

"Would you state them for the jury?"

"Certainly. First, according to Mr. Holt, his son, Mike, exhibited behaviors that should have been a warning sign to anyone with common sense. Particularly someone selling guns, an inherently dangerous product."

"Anything else?"

"Yes. According to Mr. Spangler, Mr. Grimick, and Mr. Davis, Mike asked no questions about the use of the gun he was buying, its care, or maintenance—nothing."

"Why does that matter?"

"It's important for a gun seller to have some idea how familiar a potential gun buyer is with guns in general and the gun that person is trying to buy in particular, both as a matter of safety and, again, simple common sense."

"Anything else?"

"Yes. None of Sports Gear's people testified that they had asked young Mr. Holt why he wanted a shotgun. Someone selling guns should always ask that question of their customers."

"Why?"

"To avoid situations like this one, to be sure the potential customer has the sense and competence to articulate a legitimate reason for wanting the gun, and to make sure they are buying the correct product."

"Anything else?"

"Yes. It appears from the testimony that Mike Holt's only concern about the shotgun he was buying was that it was the cheapest."

"Why does that matter?"

"That's often a red flag suggesting the potential buyer is either possibly suicidal or has some other illegitimate reason for wanting a gun."

"Are these just your personal opinions, Mr. Savage?"

"No. They are shared by enough other gun sellers in this country that I view them as constituting both 'best practices' and 'established custom and usage' among responsible gun sellers."

"Your Honor, may I approach the witness?"

"You may."

"Mr. Savage, I am showing you what has previously been marked as exhibit number 67. Do you recognize that document?"

"I do."

"Would you identify it for the jury?"

"It is a collection of tips firearms retailers should use to identify potentially suicidal customers, produced by the New Hampshire Firearm Safety Coalition."

"What is that organization?"

"A trade association of gun merchants in the state of New Hampshire."

"Do you know of other such organizations that have produced such tip sheets?"

"I do. In Shasta County here in California, in my home state of Tennessee, in Nevada, Arizona, Utah, Colorado—and I could go on."

"How are these tip sheets used?"

"Most often they are posted prominently in stores selling guns. Usually in more than one place, but always at all cash registers or checkout stations."

"Plaintiffs offer Exhibit 67 into evidence, Your Honor."

"Hearing no objection, so ordered."

Paul acted as if his examination was concluded, then paused. He knew the tricks you played with juries. He waited for a five count and then resumed.

"Mr. Savage, your name is an historic one. Are you related to Arthur Savage, founder of Savage Arms Company?"

"I'm his great-grandson."

"Do you derive any income directly or indirectly from Savage Arms?"

"I do. Significant dividends and appreciation from the substantial shareholdings left to me by my father when he died."

"So is it fair to say that you personally profit from the sale of guns every day?"

"It is."

"Doesn't that make your testimony here a bit hypocritical?"

"Not to me. The position that I take, and that I believe all responsible firearms sellers do, may mean less money to me. But I think everyone who sells guns in the manner I have described as 'best practices' sleeps better at night. You can't put a price on that."

Paul smiled.

"No further questions, Your Honor."

\* \* \*

Moschella stood up. He had a difficult task ahead.

"Mr. Savage, you'll concede that a majority of gun dealers in this country don't use the sort of tip sheet represented by Exhibit 67, correct?"

"True, but many of those have some version of suicide alerts or warning signs posted in their stores."

"Aren't you telling the jury that gun dealers should be mind readers, psychologists, suicide experts?"

"No."

Paul considered objecting to the compound, argumentative question. But Savage had shown he could handle himself. He let it go.

"Aren't you asking them to do something the parents, colleagues, and physicians of victims haven't done?"

"Objection. Calls for speculation, Your Honor." Paul and Savage had prepared a little show anticipating this very question.

"I'll allow it. But get focused, Mr. Moschella."

"Answer the question, please."

"I'm asking them, as are other responsible gun dealers, to use common sense and err on the side of conservatism, not cash flow, in selling an inherently dangerous product."

"That's nice in the abstract, Mr. Savage. Did you ever refuse to sell a firearm to someone when you had your own gun shop because of their behavior?"

"Offhand, on at least five occasions."

"Did that behavior or conduct compare in any way to what you have heard described in court as the actions and demeanor of Mike Holt the day he bought the shotgun?"

"It did three times. The others were different. One woman was tipsy, and the other one was a guy who evidently had smoked about a barn full of marijuana."

Some of the jurors laughed, drawing a warning glance from Judge Ortiz.

"Wouldn't you agree that deciding whether a customer is a suicide risk is difficult for a gun seller, Mr. Savage?"

"In some cases. Certainly it wasn't here with Mike Holt."

"Move to strike the second sentence as unresponsive, Your Honor."

Paul immediately responded.

"Mr. Moschella opened the barn door, Judge. A bit late to try to close it." This time, Judge Ortiz had to suppress a chuckle.

"Overruled."

Moschella did not know where to go. He decided to throw up one last challenge to try to soften the damage Savage had done.

"You say certainly not in this case. But you weren't there when Sports Gear's clerks sold the shotgun to Mike Holt, were you?"

"No."

"You don't know what he did or said, or how he acted that day, do you?"

"Only from reading the testimony of the Sports Gear people here in trial, and that of Mr. Wallace Holt."

"In other words, you're basing your opinion on secondhand reports and nothing more."

The look Savage gave Moschella was something between amusement and disgust.

"Yes. I used the same kind of information that you do—and that your own experts undoubtedly will."

Moschella was beaten. There was only one way to prevent further miscues. To stop.

"Nothing further, Your Honor."

"It's almost three. Do plaintiffs intend to call any other witnesses, Mr. Viola?"

"One more today, Your Honor, if we could."

"Very well. Let's take a ten-minute break. I'll see everyone back here no later than three-thirty."

\* \* \*

After the break, Sophia called Beth Holt to the stand. She sat in her wheelchair, with a cane for standing, and with her ever-present oxygen tank and tube. She would leave a final tragic and emotional impression on the jury. Or be a complete mess.

Beth struggled to the stand out of her wheelchair with the assistance of Wallace. She slowly stood in apparent pain, left her chair, walked across the well, and struggled up the step to the witness stand. She didn't need any acting lessons. She could have taught an advanced class at the Royal Academy of Dramatic Arts in London based on the performance she was giving.

For once, Sophia was glad for her theatrics. This needed to be Sophia's gut punch for the case.

After Beth was sworn in, Sophia began gently, using a soft voice to ensure that the jury would have to pay close attention.

"Mrs. Holt, are you currently employed?"

Beth rasped, "No. Wallace and I are both retired . . . retired teachers."

"Was Mike your only child?"

"Yes. Yes." Beth's voice was shaky, and she was already starting the waterworks.

Sophia reviewed Mike's childhood with Beth, then his academic and sports accomplishments. Her pride in him was evident.

"Did Mike ever speak to you during his year at Yale, Mrs. Holt?"

"Oh yes. At least once a week."

"Was he happy there?"

"Objection. Calls for speculation," Moschella called out from his seat.

"Sustained."

"Did Mike ever make any statements to you about his experiences at Yale?"

"Objection. Hearsay."

"Offered not for the truth but for what was said, Your Honor."

"Overruled. Proceed, Ms. Christopoulos."

"He did. More often as the year went by."

"What did he say to you in that regard?"

"That he felt isolated. That the other students treated him like a rube. Even the California students looked down on him because he was from Bakersfield."

"Was he involved in any student activities his freshman year?"

"Not really. He told me he just didn't fit in there. He said he had trouble studying because he was so unhappy."

"Did he tell you he wanted to transfer?"

"No. Mike was a fighter. He told me he was sure it would be better in his sophomore year, and that he was just homesick."

"Did he have friends here in Bakersfield?"

"Many friends. They loved my cookies and came over all the time to see Mike. Those were special times for me."

Beth struggled and took another hit from her oxygen tank.

"Did Mike see his friends here in Bakersfield during the two weeks after he returned from his freshman year at Yale and before his death?"

A rictus contorted Beth's mouth, and her tears gushed. She struggled to compose herself.

"Not that I knew or that he told me. He was withdrawn. He had been a happy boy. He wasn't like that anymore."

"I know this is hard, Mrs. Holt. Do you need a moment?"

"No. No, thank you."

"Did you talk to Mike the day he bought the shotgun."

"Of course. I made him blueberry pancakes with bacon for breakfast and a nice mug of hot chocolate. He loved his hot chocolate."

"What did you say to each other?"

"We talked about what we were going to do that day and laughed because we were all doing the same thing: going shopping."

"Did he tell you where he was going shopping?"

"He just said to get something he needed. I didn't pry."

"Did Mike say or do anything at breakfast that struck you as odd or unusual?"

"He seemed more eager about his plans than usual, is all."

"You were very devoted to your son, weren't you, Mrs. Holt?"

"He was my life." She choked, coughed, cried uncontrollably.

Sophia paused but only for a second—the unrelenting gush had the potential to repulse the jury as much as it did her.

"Did you file this lawsuit because you are anti-gun, Mrs. Holt?"

"No. Never. I was raised in Bakersfield. We had guns in our home. So did all our friends."

"Why then?"

"Because that store never should have sold Mike that shotgun. Because I don't want other mothers to have to sit where I am today. Because I don't want Mike to have died for nothing."

"How has your life changed since Mike's suicide, Mrs. Holt?"

"I'm depressed all the time. I don't care about my home, my cooking. My husband and I are distant." Beth coughed again and inhaled more oxygen.

"What about your friends? Have they been supportive?"

"Friends? What friends? Since Wallace and I started this lawsuit, everyone has shunned us. Our church. Our neighbors. People we thought were lifetime friends."

"How about the community here in Bakersfield?"

Beth looked indignant and angry, and her face reddened.

"The community treats us despicably. Wallace can't even shop or buy gas without being verbally abused. And I have this oxygen tank and wheelchair because the community tried to burn us alive in our own house."

"With reluctance, objection, Your Honor. More prejudicial than probative."

"The question and Mrs. Holt's response clearly go to damages, Your Honor. Physical and emotional."

"Agreed and overruled."

"Is there anything left of your life here in Bakersfield?"

"Nothing, nothing at all. Nothing except pain and exclusion."

Beth spoke in barely a whisper, her old, hollow eyes saying even more than her words. The jurors looked down. Embarrassed. Ashamed.

"No further questions, Your Honor."

"Mr. Moschella? Cross?" The judge was as subdued as the jurors. His grave face was a warning to Moschella, who would have to be very gentle with Beth—but cross-examine her, he must.

Moschella stood. "Mrs. Holt, as I have said repeatedly to you and your husband, my client and I are terribly sorry for your loss. But it is my duty to ask you a few additional questions. I hope you don't mind."

"No, no." She coughed and used her oxygen.

"Did Mike ever see a psychiatrist at any time before his death?"

"No. Never."

"Any psychologists?"

"No."

"He spoke to guidance counselors at his schools, did he not?"

"Yes, I remember that."

"Did any of them ever tell you that Mike had any psychological or emotional problems?"

Beth seemed offended.

"Not once. They always told us Mike was happy, well-adjusted, a leader, someone who knew what he wanted to do in school and in life."

"Now, during his time at Yale, in these conversations you had with Mike, did you ever suggest to him that he should see a mental health professional of any kind?"

"Why would I? He was just going through the adjustment of leaving home for college three thousand miles away. He was dealing with it. As a teacher, I saw newcomers in my classes go through the same thing."

"When he returned home from Yale, in your own words you noted he seemed depressed . . . not the same person he had been. Did you recommend that he talk to anyone, be it a mental health professional, minister, friend?"

"It never occurred to me to do that. Mike wasn't that kind of person. He didn't need that sort of help."

"Nothing in his words or behavior that led you to believe there was anything wrong with Mike, was there?

Too late, Beth realized where Moschella was going. And why.

"Um, no."

"You knew him better than anyone in the world, didn't you, Mrs. Holt?"

"I was his mother." Tricked into answering, Beth played her winning card and let her tears flow freely and purposefully.

Moschella had to wind up fast. It was almost four, and he was on treacherous ground.

"Just a few more questions, Mrs. Holt. Has anyone at Sports Gear interacted with you at all since Mike's death?"

"Me personally? No. Not that I am aware of."

"Have you any reason to believe that anyone from Sports Gear has told anyone to stop speaking to you or dealing with you in any way?"

"I'd have to say no."

"Do you know anything that would link anyone at Sports Gear to the attempt to burn down your home?"

"We started this lawsuit, didn't we? Who else would it be?"

"I understand your feelings, Mrs. Holt, but do you personally know of anything directly connecting anyone associated in any way with Sports Gear USA to that incident?"

Beth looked helplessly at Sophia and took another deep breath from her oxygen tank.

"No." Beth set her jaw and glared at him. "But you can't prove it wasn't them."

Moschella let her comment stand. He had made his point.

"No further questions, Your Honor."

Sophia stood. "That concludes plaintiffs' case in chief, Your Honor."

"Very well. We stand adjourned. Mr. Moschella, be prepared to commence your defense in the morning. And ladies and gentlemen of the jury, remember my admonitions to you. Do not discuss this case with anyone, and do not read or watch any news reports about it in any form, on any device. Nothing. I am very serious."

Down came the judge's gavel. With his exit, everyone else set about gathering their things and leaving. Bryce helped Beth from the witness stand.

* * *

As Sophia's team packed up their exhibits and materials, she assured Beth and Wallace that her testimony had been effective and solid.

"No. He tricked me," Beth cried. "I said the wrong things, didn't I?"

"I think I made more mistakes than you," Wallace said. "Sophia, were we okay?"

"Both of you *made* the case." Bryce patted Beth's hand, and she clamped onto his.

This lonely, alienated, and estranged couple needed company and validation—confirmation that they were worthwhile even though everything they had built and loved and invested in, including their son and their relationship, was gone.

"Can we to go to dinner with you and talk about it?" Beth pleaded.

"I'm sorry. We don't have time, even for dinner for ourselves." Sophia let her down as kindly as she could.

"Beth." Bryce employed his maturing people skills and inherent charm. "Tomorrow Moschella is going to really attack us with their experts. We need to prepare for that critical, case-threatening testimony."

"Oh, my. Their experts," Beth looked into the handsome young man's green eyes and stopped crying. "That's hard, isn't it?"

"Yes, very hard. They're really smart." Bryce baby-talked the old woman into seeing things his way.

"We'd better let them work. Come on." Wallace took Beth and slowly left the courtroom. Wallace's arthritic walk had become a near-constant hobble.

Sophia was ashamed to admit it to herself, but even absent the time pressure, she wouldn't have gone to dinner with them. She'd had more than enough of Beth—a lifetime's worth. She couldn't believe that Beth didn't realize that was true for Wallace too.

"Thank you, Bryce. You handled that unbelievably well."

"I feel bad for them."

"I do too, but not enough to jeopardize the case they hired us to win." Now Sophia was handling Bryce.

⌘

# CHAPTER 79

## Twists and Turns

*"To realize that you do not understand is a virtue;
not to realize that you do not understand is a defect."*
-Lao Tzu

The two legal teams headed to their respective headquarters. Both were nervous, but for very different reasons.

\* \* \*

Team Holt, as was their routine, picked up dinner on the way to their condos. This time from the Blue Elephant Thai restaurant on Stockdale Highway. Dinner and work followed. Their location was still undiscovered by the press or any pro-gun group.

"What do you think their strategy for witnesses will be now?" Paul grabbed a skewer of pork satay.

"Rehabilitation," Sophia said. "We already called their key people in our case in chief and did some real damage, to their credibility at least."

"Well, Spangler's dead and gone. They can't use him." Bryce had developed into an integral and full-fledged member of their team now.

"I don't see them recalling Grimick," Paul said. "They got what they needed from him, and with the Spangler situation he's become an unpredictable risk too."

"Maybe Davis?" Bryce asked.

"Both sides covered everything relevant from him. If they did bring him back to rehabilitate anything, I would pepper Moschella with 'asked and answered' objections." Sophia took a drink of diet cola.

"What about that Kemper guy?" Tricia stopped eating her shrimp with eggplant to contribute.

"If I were Moschella, I might call him last, to leave a good impression with the jury. He seems formidable and commanding, but likeable," Sophia said.

"He has no firsthand knowledge of the sale," Paul said.

"That's their problem, and he's no expert so he can't hypothesize. He can testify about procedures and training," Sophia replied. "Company policy. Ben emailed us more on his background and career."

"It was very complete," Paul said.

"Do you think they'll call all five of their designated experts now? Our two guys were strong." Bryce was soaking in the trial strategy.

"I wouldn't. Overkill. The jury will tune out." Paul shrugged. "But we're covered. We already know what they'll all say from their depositions."

"And their trial transcripts in other cases," Sophia said.

"What about Gallo?" Tricia said. "Do they need him at all? Do we? Did anything in his depo make him a good rebuttal witness, Paul?"

"No," Paul said. "Only that he acted shifty. Hesitant. But the jury will attribute that to him being a kid. Natural for him to be self-conscious. And Moschella will prep him better if they do call him."

"The jury will think he's a stretch and wonder why he's up there. He's a minnow in the ocean here. He'll just repeat his deposition testimony about his brief interactions with Mike, but that's it." Sophia yawned.

Paul finished off his third skewer of pork satay. He wasn't losing any weight during this trial, but he wasn't gaining any either. Normally, he would lose a lot from the tension and lack of sleep. He didn't care at this point.

"I forgot," Paul said. "Ben sent over the enhanced DVD copy of Mike at the store with an urgent look-see note. Everything is urgent with that megalomaniac. I'll check it again, just in case."

"Good. We can't afford to overlook anything," Sophia said.

They hadn't hit a home run with their side of the case, but the jury was sympathetic, and the Sports Gear store personnel had not come across well. The Holts, particularly Beth, had performed well enough, and their experts, Dr. Mapes and Dirk Savage, had been masterful.

"Okay then. We all know what we have to do. Let's get to it."

\* \* \*

That evening, the Sports Gear collective met, as usual, in the conference room at Quarry, Warren & Moschella. No food this time. Just coffee.

"This is it now, Tony. That tear-soaked old mother hurt us. You could have done better there. What's your plan? Let's hear something that sounds like you have one."

Moschella, with Sandoval at his side, was appalled at Jackson's confrontation for his audience—Kemper and his remaining Denver trio. It was a wasteful expenditure of Moschella's trial prep time and enervating, but he was stuck with it. Moschella categorically didn't trust any of them now, and the feeling was mutual. So be it.

"I'm satisfied," Moschella retorted. "We're homespun and pro-gun. The jurors don't know about your firm's involvement and must never know. That's the key. They're fellow Bakersfield gun enthusiasts . . . most of them anyway, and at least the two-thirds we need. We'll put up three experts and pound on the fact that we're protecting the right to buy guns. I don't foresee any more surprises. Unless you know of some."

"I don't. Jubal and I talked to Sports Gear's president, Wade Buckner, and its general counsel, Emeline Booth. They're upset about the deaths and Spangler's testimony. However, they accept that we can't switch lawyers at this point. Lucky for you."

"You mean lucky for you. You can hide, but you might still get some face time since Christopoulos knows who you are now. She could call you as a rebuttal witness." Moschella tossed the room a grim and unpleasant smile.

Moschella had hit a nerve.

Jackson slammed his fist down on the table. "She wouldn't dare. I have no relevant knowledge, and even if I did, it would be protected as attorney work product or by the attorney-client privilege. But since you mentioned that, we'd better have a pocket motion ready for the judge to preclude me if it's a possibility. We don't want the jury to know about me or my firm's involvement. Rose, that will be your job tonight. It had better be a winner."

Boyd answered in her Southern drawl, "Happy to oblige, Mr. Jackson. I'll see to it as soon as we finish here."

"No. Start now. We don't need any input from you."

"Don't worry, honey. The big boys will take care of what's important." French couldn't resist a smug comment of his own.

With that peremptory dismissal and the degrading remarks, Rose shoved her chair back and left the room, slamming the door behind her. Sandoval empathized, but Boyd had chosen to work for "Jackass" Jackson and his firm. She was stuck. The rule of thumb was that new associates had to survive a year or two in one position to be marketable enough to jump firms.

"What are we going to do as to the order of witnesses tomorrow? Stay with your original plan to begin with Jubal, or what?"

Jackson knew Moschella wasn't being totally open with him, and he hated not having complete control. But Moschella had the last say because once they walked in that courtroom, even if they had an agreement about the witnesses, all bets were off. Moschella was first chair, Sandoval second chair, and Jackson's only power was in the background.

"Original plan. The jury has seen all it needs to from Davis," Moschella said. "I'll start with Mr. Kemper here because he will be the first and only executive face they'll see from the Sports Gear family. Mr. Kemper, you've been sitting with us during the whole trial, and the jury seems to like you from what I've observed. I think they want to hear from you."

Kemper cleared his throat. "I appreciate that, Mr. Moschella. But if you want me to make the optimal impression, I don't think you should do my direct examination."

"What?" Moschella's face dropped.

"Then who?" Jackson blurted.

"Ms. Sandoval."

"She doesn't have the experience. Is this a joke?" Jackson dismissed Kemper's choice, displaying once again his low regard for female lawyers in general and Sandoval in particular.

Theresa was as startled as everyone but wasn't about to forgo this opportunity. "I'd be honored if Mr. Moschella approves."

"You can't be serious. Her looks don't give her a brain." French sat up to his full imposing height to support his boss.

"This is a mistake." Beauregard took the party line. "Just because she can strut her stuff doesn't make her the *man* for the job."

Jackson's sexist bootlickers did not get to Sandoval. She didn't react at all, and Moschella defended her abilities.

"Ms. Sandoval is a brilliant lawyer, Mr. Kemper. But I have to agree with Tom here. She's never examined a witness at a trial. You're pivotal as an emotional counter to the Holts and a symbol of Sports Gear."

"You know, Jubal, on reflection, that might be a great stroke of genius." Reversing himself, Jackson seized a prime opportunity to demean and irritate Moschella. "The lovely Ms. Sandoval and your own imposing self might have great appeal to that mongrel jury. Let's do it."

His lackeys instantly followed his lead, did a total about-face too, and nodded their approval.

Moschella was apoplectic. Jackson would rather score points on him and put Sandoval in over her head than do what was best for their client. It wasn't fair to her or to Sports Gear. Though he had to admit that the Denver team had prepared Kemper's direct examination questions. He had reviewed and revised them together with Theresa. She was smart. If she stumbled, the fault would lie squarely with Kemper and Jackson.

"Are you okay with this, Theresa?"

Theresa wanted to jump out of her seat. She didn't. Maintaining her composure, she embraced the challenge. "I welcome it, Tony. Really. I appreciate the confidence all of you have in me. You won't be sorry."

"That's decided then. So after Jubal testifies, what's next?" Jackson asserted himself once again.

"Pretty straightforward. Call our three best experts. They'll neutralize the heart of the Holts's case. We'll finish with Gallo, the young fresh innocent who loves the company."

"It's not what I would do, but this is a joint effort." Jackson was letting Moschella fall on his own sword because he saw a loss coming. "Speaking of which, are any revised proposed jury instructions and the trial brief about ready?" Jackson directed his question to Beauregard and French.

They both nodded in unison.

"Then we're done here," Jackson stood. "Except for Ms. Boyd's motion. And Ms. Sandoval will want to run through Jubal's direct with him here in the conference room."

Jackson pronounced his orders over an office and people not his own. He ordained by divine right. The divinity was the only one he recognized. Himself.

Moschella didn't bother to argue or even respond. Kemper and Sandoval stayed behind to go over Kemper's testimony.

"Come see me when you've finished here, Theresa." He was not leaving her alone in the offices with the Jackson tribe, and he let them know that.

"Sure." Theresa brought up Kemper's direct examination outline on her laptop.

Moschella quietly shut the door behind him as he followed the others out. He had weathered another meeting with lawyers who had become his untrustworthy and spiteful enemies. They were more insidious and far more troubling to him than the Holts or their counsel.

⌘

# CHAPTER 80

## Guns and Poses

*"The greatest deception men suffer is from their own opinions."*
-Leonardo da Vinci

As Sophia and Tricia packed to leave for court that morning, they heard Paul and Bryce banging on their door.

"Hey, wait a minute." Tricia hurried to open it.

Paul burst in with his laptop and Bryce behind him.

"What's up?" Sophia tucked in her blouse as she walked out of her bedroom.

"Sophia, it's that enhanced store video on the DVD Kowrilsky sent over."

Paul set up his laptop.

"We looked at it this morning."

"We should have done that last night," Bryce said.

"Why? What's on it?" Sophia asked.

"You'll never guess," Bryce said.

"Damn it. Tell us!" Tricia was tired and exasperated as she squeezed the last exhibit back into her trial case.

"Spit it out."

"Watch," Paul said, running the DVD. "Look there. Ben's people cleared up that shadowy part behind the cash register in the gun area. It shows Gallo there during the entire sale and after. He's just a couple of feet from Spangler, Grimick, and Davis."

"Oh, my God," Tricia blurted. "From there, he must have heard everything."

"He's hiding there," Sophia said.

"Why?"

"Who cares? They had him lie in his depo and for a reason," Paul said.

"You bet," Tricia said. "A case-winning reason for us, a case-losing one for them. Those damn clerks did say what Wallace testified to in his deposition and at trial."

"Brandon heard the entire sale and the conversation they had afterward," Sophia said.

"He'll have to confirm what Wallace said. His credibility will evaporate. Along with that of Spangler, Grimick, and Davis."

"Good thing we subpoenaed him," Paul said.

"Even though Sports Gear has him on its witness list, Moschella may not call him." Bryce was learning fast.

"Exactly, Bryce," Sophia encouraged him.

"Do you think they know what we have? Or that Gallo heard everything?" Tricia asked.

"I don't know," Paul said.

Bryce was troubled. "Do we have to tell their lawyers about the enhanced DVD?"

The three more senior lawyers zeroed in on him.

"Hell, no. It's theirs," Paul said. "They produced it to us."

"They could have 'inadvertently' sabotaged our copy," Tricia said. "If their original is no better, then they're stupid if they didn't enhance it themselves. Either way, tough luck."

"Cool," Bryce said.

\* \* \*

The courthouse on Thursday morning was at its most frenzied yet. The news media, formal and informal bloggers, and demonstrators alike ignored the hovering, damp Bakersfield fog. They had multiplied in number and zealousness. Media coverage had ballooned the previous night and that morning because the trial was almost over. Police confiscated the loudspeakers in every group. Food carts and T-shirt vendors had joined the streams of people marching and chanting with their signs and banners. The cacophony was media-induced and media-enriching.

Ben was in the very center of it. His profile was soaring. He was one happy reporter. Sophia had called him to thank him for the DVD and told him their plan.

Fanning the flames, there had been yet another shooting—this one in the city of San Bernardino, less than a three-hour drive from Bakersfield. Dozens of people had died and were wounded, all with legally purchased guns.

The country was a boiling cauldron of anger; mass shootings were happening nearly every day, with tens of thousands of gun suicides every year drawing far less publicity. Yet suicides accounted for sixty-five percent of all guns deaths, and suicide was the second most common cause of death for Americans between the ages of fifteen and thirty-four.

The "Gun Trial" had become the most publicized national battleground between the unyielding pro- and anti-gun advocates—one side for more restrictive gun control laws; the other the most outspoken champions of the broadest interpretation of the Second Amendment who opposed even the most minimal regulations on gun ownership.

The Holt case was testing the boundaries of what gun merchants could and could not do. That kept it pivotal, newsworthy, and a magnet for the unhinged. Everyone inside and outside the courtroom understood the stakes.

\* \* \*

Sophia's team ended up having to park in the lot attached to the Rabobank Arena on Q Street and rush to the courthouse rolling their evidence boxes, briefcases, and equipment on the cracked sidewalk. They suffered through security and reached Department 5 just in time. Sports Gear's people were in their seats, relaxed and waiting at their counsel table.

Judge Ortiz took the bench and had the jury brought in.

"Is the defense ready to proceed?"

"We are, Your Honor. Sports Gear USA calls Mr. Jubal Kemper to the stand." Theresa Sandoval stood, her Prada Nero heels highlighting her long legs.

Judge Ortiz smiled, the male jurors sat up, and the female jurors waited to see whether this stunningly lovely woman who had been at the defense table the entire trial was just eye candy, as they jealously hoped.

Theresa had chosen her professional "armor" carefully—an elegant but conservative green Albert Nippon sheath dress with a matching jacket. Her dark hair was fastened in a Mexican jade clasp worn in honor of her parents.

"Damn it," Paul whispered to Sophia. "That's one shrewd move."

"No kidding."

"Hey, where's Ben?" Paul scanned the gallery but did not see him anywhere.

"Shh." Sophia was concentrating.

Unable and unwilling to look away from Ms. Sandoval, Judge Ortiz offhandedly voiced his usual witness instruction.

"Mr. Kemper, please take the stand to be sworn in."

Kemper moved with an easy grace, clearly a man secure in himself, in superb shape, dressed in a dark blue suit and regimental tie. He might be in Bakersfield, but he was not of Bakersfield. That was apparent to everyone in the courtroom.

Together, Kemper and Sandoval were an immediate, compelling home-run hit.

Sandoval took Kemper through his all-American background: his father a WWII Pacific Theater Army veteran and steelworker at Hascro Corporation; his childhood and high school years in Wormleysburg in eastern Pennsylvania; his West Point years; his service as a Green Beret in the Army; his years at the Pentagon during which the Army had paid for him to complete law school, attending Georgetown University part time; and, finally, his employment at Sports Gear.

Sandoval kept her questions short, crisp, and in perfect form and content. Sophia could voice no valid objections The examination moved along smoothly, and the jury was intently interested in someone with such an honorable and successful personal and professional history.

"What is your current position at Sports Gear USA, Mr. Kemper?"

"I am its senior vice president at the moment."

"What are your duties and responsibilities?"

"I primarily handle public relations for the company, but I also coordinate and help supervise our legal compliance programs and litigation with our general counsel, Emeline Booth."

"In those capacities, did you have any role in creating or implementing the training protocols in place at Sports Gear at the time Mike Holt bought his shotgun from your Bakersfield store?"

"Yes, a major one. I made and make every effort to assure that our stores and their employees are thoroughly grounded in all applicable federal, state, and local laws relating to the sale of our wide range of products."

"How do you do that?"

"By requiring appropriate instruction for all employees involved in selling firearms or ammunition. We audit and spot check with unannounced inspections to be sure that is done."

"Do you know if any audit or inspection has taken place at your Bakersfield store?"

"I do. I get monthly reports of all such activity. That store, as is true of all our stores, is audited annually and randomly inspected twice a year."

"Were any training irregularities ever reported at your Bakersfield store?"

"Never once during my years at Sports Gear."

"Including with respect to the sale of guns or ammunition?"

"Yes. California has some of the strictest laws in the country regulating the sale of firearms, and we are very careful to make darn sure all of our stores and employees follow those laws to the letter."

"Was that done in the case of the sale of the shotgun to Mike Holt?"

"From everything I have seen, and from the testimony I've heard in this case, it absolutely was."

"Thank you, Mr. Kemper. No further questions at this time."

\* \* \*

Sophia looked over her notes. Kemper had come across even better than she feared. And the combination of Kemper and Sandoval had entranced the jury. It had been great theater and a brilliant tactical call by the Sports Gear forces.

She whispered to Paul, "I'm not sure about this brother thing."

"You have to use it."

"It could backfire."

"We don't have anything else. Softball it."

"Ms. Christopoulos, we're waiting." As always, Judge Ortiz was impatient to keep things moving.

"Yes, Your Honor." Sophia stood, as attractive and as competitively and professionally dressed as Sandoval in her elegant gray St. John ensemble. It was her most formidable power suit, acquired during her Thorne & Chase salad days.

"Mr. Kemper, good morning."

"Good morning." He smiled at the lethal beauty about to grill him.

"Just a few questions."

"Sure." Kemper dropped his smile—he had seen her in action.

"You say complying with the letter of the laws regulating the sale of guns and ammunition is very important to Sports Gear, is that correct?"

"It is."

Sophia paused and looked at the jury.

"You'll agree then, won't you, that complying with *just* the letter of those laws could allow people who are mentally unstable to buy firearms and ammunition?"

"I have no personal knowledge of that."

"Really?" Sophia turned back to Kemper. "But, sir, you do have knowledge, very personal knowledge, don't you?"

"Objection," Sandoval stood, not knowing where Sophia was going. "Asked and answered."

"Withdrawn. Mr. Kemper, respectfully, isn't it true that your brother bought a hunting rifle in a store much like Sports Gear's Bakersfield store and, in circumstances very similar to those of Mike Holt's, blew his brains out right after his purchase?"

Judge Ortiz and the jurors all recoiled. Paul wouldn't have said "blew his brains out." It was far from a softball, but it was dramatic.

Before Kemper could take a breath to answer, Moschella was on his feet, shouting, "Objection! Relevance, prejudice, invasion of privacy, badgering the witness, compound . . ."

He did not get to finish. Kemper interrupted his objections.

"Mr. Moschella, stop. I am more than willing to answer counsel's question."

The courtroom was silent, tense, unsure. Sophia held her breath. Had she made a grave mistake?

Kemper looked straight at the jury.

"Ms. Christopoulos is correct. My younger brother, Roger, did what she said. He was troubled. Had a lot of personal issues. But the circumstances were not similar to Mike Holt's. He saw bad things serving with the Marines in Afghanistan. More than his share. He came home and spiraled down, self-medicating, but never sharing his problems with anyone. Not even me. He didn't seem unbalanced or out of control, just sad and depressed. The gun shop clerks who sold him that hunting rifle had no way of knowing what he intended to do. To this day, I don't know that he did himself. I certainly don't blame them because he chose to take his own life."

"So you're saying his behavior in the gun shop where he bought that rifle was not like Mike Holt's then, aren't you? No odd looks, no nervousness, none of that?"

"I wasn't there for his purchase, but the police investigation into the circumstances of my brother's death indicated that nothing in his demeanor would have led the store personnel to think anything was wrong. He served his country honorably and deserves to be remembered for that."

"So it necessarily follows from your testimony that if your brother had exhibited questionable behavior during the sale then, you would blame the sales clerks, doesn't it?"

"Objection," Theresa stood. "Calls . . ."

"Withdrawn, Your Honor." The beauties were both razor sharp.

"Has Sports Gear considered implementing anything like the Tips for Dealers program that the New Hampshire firearms dealers are using, and about which you heard testimony earlier from Mr. Savage?"

"We have. We still are. But I'm leery of imposing that kind of responsibility on store clerks. Some of those judgment calls are as likely to cause a tragedy as to prevent one."

"Why do you say that?"

"Because people need guns for home protection, hunting food, sport, pleasure. If they are refused, they could buy them from an illegal seller with no screening or training. To me, that's worse. We should all have the right to buy a gun, but only so long as we comply with applicable laws and other requirements."

"And so, Sports Gear has the right to make as much money as possible . . . selling guns as many guns as possible and as much ammunition as possible to as many people as possible . . . without regard to the consequences?"

"Objection, harassing, argumentative, not even a question." Sandoval was again quick to intervene.

"Withdrawn, Your Honor."

Sophia had done what she could. She had left the jury with that final thought. Once again, making money was Sports Gear's primary concern as it is so often in life . . . and, in this case, death.

"No further questions."

Sophia returned to her seat. Paul's face was even and neutral. She avoided looking at the Holts. She did not want them to show signs of worry that the jury might see.

"Good job," Paul whispered.

For once, a compliment he gave to Sophia was at best a half-truth.

*  *  *

Moschella next called Sports Gear's first expert. After a lot of thought, he decided that it would be their authority on firearms marketing, Jeffrey Bundy. He was an assistant professor in both the economics and political science departments at the University of Missouri in Columbia.

He was less than impressive to the eye. Short, with thinning red hair, dressed in a travel-wrinkled tan suit, he looked a decade younger than his thirty-eight years and was cross-eyed.

His testimony went on for nearly an hour. The jury was visibly restive despite Moschella's efforts to keep the questions short and punchy.

He called Bundy to establish that, in his expert opinion, imposing more restrictions on legitimate gun dealers in the sale of firearms would do nothing to stop suicides or other gun violence because of the numerous other ways firearms can be bought and sold in this country. It would only cost jobs, jobs held by middle- and lower-class people like the jurors, because sales of firearms and ammunition would fall and necessitate layoffs. The jurors paid very close attention to that part of his testimony.

"No further questions at this time." Moschella was dissatisfied with himself and with Bundy because the jury was bored; the electric atmosphere Kemper and Sandoval had generated had totally disappeared.

Paul stood. Bundy was one of the experts he had deposed, and the cross-examination was his. He kept it brief but forceful to again capture the jury's attention.

"Professor Bundy, you haven't received tenure at the University of Missouri, have you?"

"No. I told you that in my deposition."

"Did you tell me then that one of the reasons is that you insist on carrying a concealed pistol with you on campus?"

"You didn't ask."

"Well, I'm asking now," Paul had cunningly and purposefully not asked this line of questioning in Bundy's deposition and saved it for the trial. "Is it?"

"It might be. I don't know."

"Missouri bans firearms on campus, doesn't it?"

"Yes."

"Have you sued the university about that ban?"

"Objection, relevance, prejudice. Where is this going, Your Honor?" Moschella was in damage control mode about this simple fact that Jackson should have disclosed to him.

"It goes to credibility and bias, Your Honor."

"I'll allow it, but watch yourself here, Mr. Viola."

"Please answer the question."

"Yes, my lawyers say it's unconstitutional."

Paul looked at the jurors. Each one of them perked up and looked incredulously at this "expert" who had his own lawsuit.

"Who are the lawyers representing you in that case?"

"Objection, relevance, prejudice. Where is this going, Your Honor?" Moschella stood.

"Dr. Bundy opened the door, Your Honor."

"I'll allow it, but watch yourself here, Mr. Viola."

"Please answer the question."

"Mr. Thomas Jackson of the Denver, Colorado, law firm of Jackson, Hood & Lee."

"Mr. Jackson's in the courtroom, isn't he?"

"Yes. He's over there." Bundy pointed to Jackson and blurted out his answer before Moschella could intercede. "In the middle of the fourth row behind the table where the Sports Gear lawyers are sitting."

Everyone looked where Bundy was pointing. Jackson sat still, his face a blank. He hadn't anticipated this, but he was a veteran of gun litigation and not easily shaken.

"That firm represents most of the major gun manufacturers and many of the largest firearms retailers in the country, doesn't it?"

"I believe so."

"They've retained you to testify on behalf of their clients who manufacture firearms or sell them on at least eight other occasions, haven't they?"

"Uh . . . they . . ."

"Is the answer 'yes,' Professor Bundy?"

"Yes."

"You're also on retainer as a consultant and adviser to the National Gun Association, aren't you?"

"I am indeed, and a lifelong member, I am proud to say."

"You've never actually been in the business of selling firearms yourself, have you, Mr. Bundy? I mean, *Professor* Bundy?"

"No."

"Or, any business for that matter?"

"I'm a college professor. That's my business."

"So your testimony here is entirely based on your academic studies of the industry, as in all of the other cases you have appeared as an 'expert'?"

"That's true."

"Before I forget, you're also a longtime member of Americans for Firearms Rights, are you not?"

"I am."

"That organization opposes all gun regulation, doesn't it?"

"Because it doesn't work."

"Again, the answer is 'yes'?"

"Yes."

"So you and that group oppose all the federal and California laws requiring licenses, background checks, waiting periods, training programs, correct?"

"Yes. The Second Amendment doesn't include any such restrictions on our right to keep and bear arms. That's why I'm suing the University of Missouri."

"I think we all understand where you're coming from. Thank you. No further questions."

Paul made sure the jury saw the contempt on his face for "Professor" Bundy as he returned to his seat.

\* \* \*

Paul had skillfully destroyed Sports Gear's first "expert." Jackson had again withheld important information from Moschella—Jackson's own lawsuit for Professor Bundy against the university. Moschella buried his anger so that he could focus. His only consolation was that, warts and all, this confirmed his rejection of the head of the NGA and the president of Colt, who would have been worse.

All Moschella could do was move forward. "No redirect, Your Honor."

He had to get Bundy off the stand. Viola's sharp questions and litigation skills had made Bundy come off as a rabid gun enthusiast and a paid hack for the gun industry, which he was. Moschella would not give him a chance to drive that home even more to the jury.

It was also lunchtime. The jury was impatient and too hungry to listen if Moschella made an effort to fine-tune Bundy's testimony to try to rehabilitate him.

Judge Ortiz announced, "Thank you. It's just after noon. Time for our lunch recess. See you all back at one-thirty. Members of the jury, remember my warnings. Keep to yourselves. Do not discuss this case with anyone, look at nothing containing any news about it. I can't emphasize that often enough."

With the horde of media and demonstrators outside, the judge had ordered the jury's lunch brought in.

⌘

# CHAPTER 81

## Interlude Intrigue

*". . . when you get overconfident,*
*that's when something snaps up and bites you."*
-Neil Armstrong

Sports Gear's team met at The Hidden Café Bar and Restaurant on O Street, northeast of the courthouse, to analyze the morning's testimony. French and Beauregard sat bookending Sandoval.

"I hear you did a good job for a novice." French stared at Sandoval's breasts under her Albert Nippon ensemble.

"Look at my face when you speak to me and your comments don't interest me.

"Ooh, she bites," Beauregard whispered.

"Ms. Sandoval, you did a decent job with Jubal," Jackson said.

"She deserves more praise than that." Kemper smiled at her across the table. "I'd say she came across as poised and seasoned."

"Thank you." Theresa was justifiably proud.

"But Bundy was a disaster, Tony." Jackson went on the attack even before their menus had arrived. "You let his lawsuit in, and you let him ID me right there in court."

"You picked him," Moschella said. "You vetted him, and you kept that lawsuit a secret. How do you expect me to defend Sports Gear with one arm tied behind my back? As far as I'm concerned, I got what I needed on the economic issues. You can thank yourself and your little helpers here for the rest."

"You let Viola manipulate him into looking like a gun freak at the end." Jackson didn't want Kemper to think it was his fault. "Without objecting."

"*His* answers did that." Moschella would not let Jackson get to him, nor would he cut him any slack. "I had no legitimate objections to make, and why draw attention to a disaster of your making, Tom? Mr. Kemper, don't worry. Our two other experts, Dr. Gein and Garry Owen, will hold up much better if there are no other surprises. Dr. Gein has great credentials and presence, and Garry's the salt of the earth. The jurors will like them and forget about Bundy."

Jackson started to speak, but stopped. He let up because Moschella wasn't yielding and was analytically correct. Jackson and his law firm cronies had picked and background-checked all of the experts. They had put together everything Moschella and Sandoval used to prepare them for their depositions and ghosted the prep sessions. They had drafted the examination questions for trial. They had participated—albeit silently and remotely, via occasional text messages to Moschella or Sandoval—in the prep sessions for their trial testimony. If Bundy had performed poorly, that was as much or more their doing as it was Moschella's.

"Are you handling the last two experts, or is Ms. Sandoval going to do that?" Kemper asked.

"I am. Dr. Gein first, to address the psychiatric issues, and before the jury is too tired because it gets a bit technical and statistical. Then, Mr. Owen, because he's folksy and colorful. A great contrast to Dr. Gein. He's knowledgeable and bombastic enough to keep the jury awake and interested. If we're lucky, we'll do closing arguments, and the case will go to the jury tomorrow. Theresa will do Gallo, our last witness, today probably or in the morning if not."

"You can do me anytime," French whispered to Theresa.

She pretended not to hear. Which just encouraged him.

\* \* \*

Going on their lunch break, Sophia's team and the Holts were celebrating Paul's humiliation of Dr. Bundy. But just as they left the courthouse, a frantic Ben Kowrilsky accosted them.

"Sophia, didn't you see my texts? Come here. Come here. This is your win."

Paul and Sophia looked at each other. They knew Ben was often given to exaggeration, but they had never seen him quite this excited.

"All of you, over here." Ben motioned to his van. "This is unbelievable."

"Ben, we have to get lunch and review the experts they might call. They may all be toadies for the gun industry, but they can hurt us," Sophia protested.

"No, you don't. I mean it," he insisted.

"Okay," Paul said. "By the way, we owe you for that DVD. It will really help."

"It was amazing." Ben smiled. "But look at this."

"This better be good," Tricia grumbled. "I'm starving."

When they all squeezed into the oversized the van, they found two of Ben's colleagues there, both busy on computers.

"First, I'd like to introduce Takara Pulitzer, one of my chief bloggers and a real social media expert."

"Hello." Takara was a petite, attractive young Japanese-American woman in a Goth getup with a tattoo on her left hand in kanji script and a silver nose ring.

During the greeting, Paul studied her tattoo.

Takara explained, "It means 'bite me' in Japanese."

He laughed out loud.

"That's Takara's way of thumbing her nose at people who see her last name and think she got her job because her dad's a Pulitzer. He's not one of *those* Pulitzers, as it happens," Ben said.

"She's creative and brilliant, a summa cum laude from USC in their Arts, Technology and the Business of Innovation program," he explained. "And this is Kalino Johar, hacker extraordinaire. He wanted to work in media. We grabbed him when he graduated from Cal Tech with a 4.0 in computer science. His dad's a math professor at UCLA, from India. Mom's an independent IT consultant from Maui. They met at MIT. Brains are the standard in that family."

"Aloha, everyone." Kalino, about five foot ten, with dark hair, eyes, and skin, in his early twenties, nodded, never taking his eyes off his laptop screen.

"Kalino, Takara, you've seen everyone here in the news." Ben rapidly introduced the Holt group. It was good that the CBT van was huge. There were seats for everyone.

"Okay, Ben, what gives?" Sophia was intrigued.

"You remember I told you I had bloggers put out some feelers about Jackson and his Denver law firm?"

"I do."

"We hit the mother lode this morning."

"Meaning what?"

"Takara was tweeted by a guy using the handle "Whistletime," saying he had some sensitive information about them. She tweeted back that she was with CBT and would be very interested in anything he had to tell us."

"And?"

"In brief, Takara, Kalino, and I had a long conference call with him this morning. That's why I wasn't in court. It was incredible."

"We're listening."

"His name is Joshua Dreyfus. He was the assistant IT manager for Jackson, Hood & Lee until about two weeks ago. He's setting up as an independent consultant now."

"Did they fire him, did he leave, what?" Paul asked, looking to assess Dreyfus's bona fides.

"He quit because of what he accidentally discovered there."

"Which was?" Paul asked.

"The firm spies on other law firms regularly—electronically and with human plants. They bribe witnesses and engage in lots of other underhanded tactics. They did it to you guys."

"How?" Sophia asked.

"Here's how. First off, Jackson himself personally found and hired Stefan Arnold, the boyfriend of that gal Autumn in your office, to spy on you and your firm and get everything he could about the case."

"Holy shit," Bryce said.

"We thought the NGA or maybe Sports Gear had done that, not another law firm," Tricia said.

"He could permanently lose his license to practice and be disbarred. And he damn well should be, the bastard." Tricia was outraged along with everyone else.

"Wait," Sophia whispered to Ben. "How does this Dreyfus guy know all of this? Is he a plant? Could this be a trap or a time waster? They've hit us with enough of those already."

Ben shook his head. "Relax, Sophia. I checked him out every way imaginable. He stumbled across a hidden file in the firm's main server that showed payments to Arnold for nearly a year. Two thousand dollars a month. Good money for a community college student, huh?"

"Does he have copies of what he found?" Bryce asked.

"You bet. There's more."

"More?" Bryce was astounded.

"In the same file, he found expense reimbursement requests from Tom Jackson. One was for two bottles of expensive Old Portrero."

"That's the whiskey Grimick claimed the guy gave him from Moschella." Paul was astounded. "Spangler died while he was drinking that."

"Yes. The receipt came from a place called Sandrini's on Eye Street in . . . guess where . . . Bakersfield. Arnold has a copy of that too. Jackson's secretary listed the expense as 'client entertainment.'"

"Why would anyone be so stupid as to turn that in on an expense report?" Tricia asked.

"Because he's an idiot," Bryce said.

"Or goofed. Or thinks he's invulnerable," Sophia said.

"Can I ask a question?" Beth raised her hand halfway.

"No." Wallace shut her down, for which Sophia was grateful. "We're going to sit over here and let them do their jobs."

"So Jackson had someone serve as an intermediary who delivered the booze to Grimick and tried to make it look like Moschella was the source. Odd."

Sophia was frightened by the implications. "Grimick described the delivery person in court. Did your research identify anyone resembling that description, Ben?"

"I'm not done. Be patient. There was another receipt for the rental and repair of a black SUV. Didn't Spangler say that was the kind of car that hit him?"

"Those two accidents . . ." Sophia started to reply.

"Weren't." Tricia finished her thought.

"One last thing. Dreyfus also has a copy of a memorandum Jackson wrote to three other attorneys working on the case directing them not to produce and, in fact, to destroy all documents relating to other claims against Sports Gear USA involving guns that never made it to court, and regarding payoffs made to gun sellers for not adopting gun selling codes like the New Hampshire tip sheet you brought up at trial."

"What? We didn't know to ask about payoffs, but the other documents we directly demanded in our document request," Paul said.

"Who were the three other attorneys shown on the memo?"

Ben looked at the notes on his iPad2.

"Samuel French, Porter Beauregard, and Ambrose Pickett. About the messenger Jackson used, Sophia, Pickett matches the description Grimick gave in his testimony."

Their brains were churning furiously at these astounding revelations.

Sophia had to confirm one thing before they continued.

"Were Tony Moschella or Theresa Sandoval named in the memo or involved in any of this?"

"Not that I see here."

"Did Dreyfus have anything proving that Sports Gear told Jackson to take any of those steps or knew what he had done?"

"No. I asked him. He said he hadn't found anything linking Sports Gear to any of it, except that Sports Gear plainly benefited from all of it. And he searched because once he realized what was going on, he had to protect himself in case they came after him for disclosing this information."

"We have unethical conduct in violation of the canons of ethics, witness tampering, theft, invasion of privacy, discovery abuse, and possible assault and battery, if not attempted or actual murder given the SUV incident and that booze Spangler drank," Sophia said.

"The question is, can we use any of it, should we, and if so, how and when?" Paul asked.

"Let me stop you," Ben said. "We're hitting the airwaves, the Internet, and print media all at once with everything here this evening."

"Whoa, whoa." Paul had to slow this down. "You guys have the First Amendment to protect you. You don't have to name your source. But once this gets out, what's going to happen to Dreyfus? He may well have violated some confidentiality agreement he signed. He could face a lawsuit or criminal prosecution. Does he know that?"

"He has his own lawyer. A very good one from the Law Center to Prevent Firearm Violence," Ben said. "This is evidence of criminal conduct, and he can't be prosecuted for disclosing it. If he's sued civilly, he'll win and can countersue for being forced into unknowing participation in an illegal enterprise or being subjected to a hostile work environment."

"I see that. Two more questions." Sophia barely had time to digest all of this new information. "Is Dreyfus willing to give us a declaration confirming what he told you? Which will mean disclosing his name, what he learned, and how?

"I think so. His lawyer thought you might want to bring this to the attention of Judge Ortiz. They're willing to talk to you about that."

"Good. I'm not sure how we do it. If we make a motion for a mistrial, it will mean a new trial. I don't see how our firm can afford that, or the Holts either."

Beth and Wallace both nodded.

"We can't, no way," Wallace said.

"Wait. Idea. How about this?" Tricia signaled with her hand. "Ben, if you and your people could hold off on the story until tomorrow morning, we will have finished cross-examining their last witnesses, and the case will be with the jury. Then, while they're deliberating, we can ask Judge Ortiz for a chambers conference and make a motion for a mistrial based on disqualifying all the lawyers for Sports Gear. While that's pending, I bet we can force a real settlement out of them."

"We can do more." Paul, ever aggressive, had another avenue of attack. "We move for terminating sanctions and to have Sports Gear found liable as a matter of law before the jury is charged. Then, the jury's only decision is how much Beth and Wallace get in damages."

"They're rare," Sophia said.

"Terminating sanctions? I thought you told me they were only available for discovery abuses," Bryce interjected.

"We clearly have those here. And the other things Ben has found are so egregious we could get them," Tricia said.

"The judge can dismiss a plaintiff's complaint, or he can dismiss all of a defendant's defenses to a complaint. Here Sports Gear would effectively lose all its defenses and be liable."

"Regardless, if Ben agrees, while we're in court this afternoon, Tricia and Bryce can get with Dreyfus and his lawyer, see what sort of declaration he will give us, and start working up both motions to present to Judge Ortiz tomorrow."

Sophia saw Ben's eyes deflating.

"We need until the court's in session tomorrow, Ben. Less than a day. Ten a.m. tops."

"Damn it. How can you ask that, Sophia? I won't be scooped." He was adamant.

"Come on, Ben. Has Dreyfus contacted anyone else?" Sophia asked.

"You never know. He told me he hasn't." Ben looked at Sophia's pleading eyes. "Tell you what. It's a deal if you don't tell Rona and Derek until we break the story. Derek's screwed us before."

"Agreed."

Sophia turned to her group.

"Not one word to anyone outside this van, other than Dreyfus and his lawyer."

They all nodded. They knew what this meant for their case and the firm's revenues.

"Okay, Sophia. I'm going to trust you to keep this under wraps until 9:30 a.m. tomorrow. Then it hits everywhere. Don't make me regret it."

"You won't."

\* \* \*

The lunch break was nearly over. It was time to return to court.

"Paul and I have to get back. Tricia and Bryce, you know what you need to do. Be smart, be logical, get everything you can from

572 ◆ Dale E. Manolakas

Dreyfus and find legal authority to support whatever motions are available. Work with Ben. Paul and I will pound them in court as hard as possible. Thanks, Ben."

"Go for it, Sophia."

They were all energized and could taste victory, one way or another.

Beth thumped Sophia on the shoulder.

"Is this good?"

"Yes, very good."

Sophia didn't have the time to feed her ego.

"Oh, Wallace, it's good." Beth put her head on his shoulder. "Good for us and our Mike."

Wallace stiffened. He hated her. Beth, oblivious, didn't notice.

Paul and Sophia headed back to Judge Ortiz's courtroom through the crowds with Beth in her wheelchair and Wallace hobbling. Ben's crew helped them get into the security line.

⌘

# CHAPTER 82

## It's All In How You Say It

*"Opinions are like assholes; everybody has one."*
-"Dirty Harry" Callahan, aka Clint Eastwood


"**Y**our Honor, the defense calls Dr. Charles Gein to the stand."

"Dr. Gein, please come up to be sworn."

Moschella felt far better about this witness. Dr. Gein was in his mid-fifties, with graying hair and gray eyes behind his silver wire-rimmed glasses. He looked professional and authoritative in his dark gray Ralph Lauren suit with a maroon tie and highly shined black wingtip Oxfords.

The jury paid close attention as Moschella led Gein through his background: a valedictorian at the prestigious Adlai E. Stevenson High School in Lincolnshire, Illinois; a Yale summa cum laude graduate in three years with a double major in psychology and biochemistry; a Johns Hopkins Medical School degree; a psychiatric internship and a residency at equally impressive institutions; and now physician in chief of the Resnick Neuropsychiatric Hospital at the University of California, Los Angeles, as well as the Alfred E. Neuman distinguished professor in the Department of Psychiatry and Biobehavioral Sciences at UCLA's Geffen School of Medicine.

His resume and list of academic publications were both far more formidable than those of Dr. Mapes, the Holts's expert psychiatrist. Half of Dr. Gein's publications dealt directly with identifying suicidal tendencies in people and preventing suicides.

Sophia and Paul were outgunned, and she had no idea whether she could really hurt him on cross. There were no guarantees at trial. Then again, given what Ben had told them, did it really matter? After the presentation of his credentials, Sophia had to accept him as a qualified expert.

"Dr. Gein," Moschella asked. "Is it fair to say that your practice and research primarily focuses on issues relating to suicide, its warning signs, its prevention, and the treatment of suicidal patients?"

"For nearly twenty years now, yes."

"Have you reviewed the evidence and testimony in this case about the day Mike Holt purchased a shotgun from my client's Bakersfield store?"

"I have."

"Have you also reviewed the testimony and exhibits pertaining to his suicide later that day in which he used that shotgun?"

"Yes."

"Based on that review, in your opinion, was the conduct of Mike Holt in the store that day sufficient to indicate to anyone there that he was mentally unstable?"

"No, it was not."

"Or that he was suicidal or a suicide risk?"

"Again, no."

"Having reviewed the testimony and exhibits to which I have referred, in your professional opinion, did Mr. Grimick, Mr. Spangler, or Mr. Davis have any reason not to sell the shotgun to Mike Holt that day?"

"None whatsoever."

"Thank you, Dr. Gein. No further questions at this time."

* * *

Rising from her chair, Sophia reorganized her outline papers discreetly. She would truncate her cross-examination of Dr. Gein because he was too strong. At best, she might wing him, but she couldn't fatally injure his testimony.

She began by having him confirm some routine statistics. Namely, that suicide is one of the top five causes of death in the U.S., more than half of suicides are with guns, and eighty-five percent of suicides attempted with guns succeed. More than that, of the roughly thirty thousand gun deaths in the U.S. annually in recent years, over twenty thousand, or two-thirds were suicides, not homicides. The jurors were surprised by the data, despite the matter-of-fact tone of Dr. Gein's responses.

Through the statistical barrage, Moschella sat torpid in his chair. He knew none of the data went to whether Sports Gear was liable for Mike Holt's suicide. If she wanted to waste her time that way, he didn't care.

"In your own practice, have you ever been able to identify potentially suicidal patients?"

"Many times."

"Did you manage to prevent them from committing suicide?"

"In all but eight cases, yes."

"How many of those eight cases ended up being gun suicides?"

Gein shifted a bit uncomfortably in the witness chair and looked at Moschella.

"All of them, I believe. But most had made several previous attempts using other means."

"Suicide attempts not using guns are seldom successful, are they?"

The expression on Gein's face was intense and wary.

"Far less so than with guns. Yes."

"Did you ever try to find out how your failures acquired their guns?"

"Objection. Argumentative, harassing." Moschella objected only out of habit because the cross-examination wasn't doing Sophia any good.

"Sustained."

"I'll rephrase. Did you ever try to find out how any of those eight patients who committed suicide with a gun obtained the weapon they used?"

"No. That was none of my concern. I could no longer be of any help to them. Obviously."

"Obviously. None of your concern." Sophia lifted her eyebrows and looked at the jury, making sure neither the judge nor the defense table saw her emphasis.

"Did any of those patients' friends or relatives ever tell you about how their lost loved ones acquired their guns?"

"I don't recall."

"You don't recall, or you just didn't care? Because, once again, that would have been *none of your concern*, correct?"

"Objection. Argumentative, harassing, irrelevant, Your Honor."

"Sustained. Wrap this up, Ms. Christopoulos."

Gein smiled, not noticing that some of the jurors were eyeing him with distaste.

"Isn't apparent anxiety or agitation in a person one of the strongest signs of potential suicide?"

"I wouldn't say that."

"But it is one sign, correct?"

"It can be."

"Wouldn't odd behavior, a strange look in someone's eyes, from someone buying a gun be a warning sign?"

"That's difficult to say. From all the evidence I reviewed, I saw nothing in Mike Holt's conduct that appeared to be a warning sign, just someone nervous, perhaps, about buying a gun. Nothing inherently suggesting potential suicide."

"Move to strike everything after the first sentence as nonresponsive, Your Honor."

Before Moschella could speak, the judge responded.

"Overruled, Ms. Christopoulos. You gave him the opening. You can't complain about what he did with it."

Regrouping, Sophia decided to venture just a few additional questions.

"As to what you just volunteered about Mike Holt, that was in your opinion, correct?"

"In my opinion, yes. However, I should also add that in the opinion of most of us in the field, there is no real way to screen for potential suicide. Certainly not by a couple of store clerks untrained in psychiatry or psychology."

Sophia dropped that line of questioning. Gein was too adroit. She had to end her examination, and fast.

"You reviewed the testimony and exhibit concerning the Tips for Dealers adopted by the New Hampshire Firearm Safety Coalition, did you not?"

"I did."

"Wouldn't you agree that having something like that at the counter or cash register of a store selling firearms would help prevent sales of guns to potential suicide victims?"

"Actually, no."

"Why is that?"

"In my opinion, posting such a tip sheet is just as likely to cause potential suicide victims to mask their behavior, might well cement their decision to commit suicide, and could motivate them to seek a gun elsewhere."

"So you don't think gun sellers should ask people acting like Mike Holt if they are having suicidal thoughts?"

"Of course not. That would be insulting."

"Dozens of nonprofit organizations, hospitals, medical groups and hotlines all over the world ask people at risk that very question, don't they?"

"Certainly. But I hardly think that's a routine question anyone should be asked when they are out shopping."

"Even for an ultrahazardous product like a gun?"

"Even for that."

Sophia had one last play.

"Dr. Gein, do you own a gun?"

"No."

"Why not?"

"I have a wife and children. I don't want a lethal weapon in my home."

"So it's fine for other people to put lives at risk, including their own, by buying and owning guns, but not you, and not your family?"

"People have the right to do a lot of things I wouldn't. That doesn't make it wrong. For them."

Sophia had done little except to make Gein seem callous toward suicide victims. In view of what she had learned over the lunch break, that would suffice if the case didn't settle and went to the jury only on damages.

"No further questions, Your Honor."

"No redirect, Your Honor." Moschella was elated. Gein had done real damage to the Holts's case. He had no idea that a ticking bomb was about to explode on him and Sports Gear.

\* \* \*

Moschella quickly called his final expert. It was almost three, and he wanted both experts' testimony to be fresh in the minds of the jurors when court adjourned for the day.

"The defense calls Mr. Garry Owen to the stand, Your Honor."

There was tittering in the audience and smiles from a few jurors.

Owen was a heavyset, fortyish, balding male. He wore a rumpled, tan, casual suit with an off-white dress shirt and sported a bolo tie with a silver clasp bearing an enameled American flag and worn cowboy boots. After he had shuffled to the stand, he was sworn in and spelled his name for the record.

"Mr. Owen, your first name is spelled with a double *R*. Why?"

"Well, sir, my father was a sergeant with the 1st Battalion, 7th Air Cavalry Brigade in Vietnam, at the battle of Ia Drang and others. It called itself the 'Garryowen Brigade,' after the regimental song adopted when General George Armstrong Custer commanded the unit. My father named me for that."

"That was the same unit in which Mr. Dirk Savage, one of the plaintiffs' experts, served if I recall correctly."

Sophia objected. "Is there a question, or is Mr. Moschella just testifying, Your Honor?"

"What's the question, Mr. Moschella?"

"I just thought it was interesting. I'll move on, Your Honor."

"Mr. Owen, what is your current occupation?

"I am the proud owner of three Garryowen stores selling fishing and hunting equipment and firearms for hunting, target shooting, and home defense in Waco . . . in the great state of Texas. Worked in the business ever since graduating from Baylor with my business administration degree. Took it over when my daddy passed about fifteen years ago."

"A family business then?"

"Yes, sir."

"In connection with that family business, do you presently hold a position with any trade association in your industry?"

"I do. I'm president of the Retail Gun Sellers of America."

Moschella asked that Owen be deemed a qualified expert. Christopoulos didn't object.

"What is the purpose of the Retail Gun Sellers of America, if you please?"

"We lobby to help preserve the rights of all Americans to purchase and own firearms. Also to make them affordable, so all Americans can have one, not just the government and rich people."

"Is that a paid position?"

"Yes. I get a per diem for when we have meetings and twenty-five thousand dollars a year for my work."

"Does your organization distribute tip sheets to its members regarding warning signs of potentially suicidal customers?"

"We don't."

"Do you post any signs or have any brochures in any of your own stores listing any such warning signs or otherwise cautioning your store personnel about sales to particular types of potential customers?"

"No."

"Why not?"

"Neither federal nor Texas law requires that. But my stores follow all the laws about gun sales, and all of our people are thoroughly trained on how to do that."

"Does it bother you that some of your customers might buy guns to commit suicide?"

"Heavens, yes. Now before you ask, and I know you will, I'm sure there have been some, given how many years I've been in the business, though I can't say I recall any sitting here today."

"Then why don't you issue guidelines to your stores or the members of your organization about warning signs for potentially suicidal customers?"

"For one thing, I'm told even the psychiatrists don't agree on what those signs are. What does a store clerk know? Why should a clerk interfere with the rights of Americans to buy and own firearms based on someone's mood that day? That's just not how a business should operate."

The jurors liked that answer. Owen was doing his job. Doing it well.

"Wouldn't just using common sense when selling guns to people help stop sales to potential suicide victims?"

Moschella started to wonder why no one on the Holt side was objecting to this line of questioning.

"Of course."

"Can you explain what you mean?"

"No one in his right mind would sell a firearm to a loony talking about killing other people or himself. That's against the law and God's word."

"Have you reviewed the testimony in this case relating to the events that took place in the Sports Gear store here in Bakersfield the day Mike Holt bought the shotgun?"

"I have."

"Based on that review, in your opinion, did the store clerks do anything improper by selling the shotgun to young Mr. Holt?"

"Objection. Calls for a legal opinion." Sophia rose as she objected.

"Mr. Owen is here as an expert witness, Your Honor," Moschella argued. "His opinion is what he is here to give."

"Overruled. You asked Mr. Savage, your roughly comparable expert, the same basic question. I allowed it then, and I'll allow it now."

"Mr. Owen?"

"They did not."

"Based on your review of the testimony and your knowledge of the retail firearm industry, in your opinion, was the sale of the shotgun by Sports Gear to Mike Holt consistent with the customs and practices of that industry?"

"It was. And with common sense."

Paul and Sophia watched the jury being won over. But for the intelligence Ben Kowrilsky had provided them, they would have been a lot more concerned.

"Because I know plaintiffs' counsel will ask, would you personally have sold a shotgun to Mike Holt based on what you saw in the testimony regarding his behavior and demeanor in the Sports Gear store that day?"

"Absolutely."

"No further questions at this time, Your Honor."

* * *

Sophia stood, armed with new material about Owen, also supplied by Ben. She had to do enough to avoid making Moschella suspicious or letting the jury think she was somehow giving up.

"You testified that you didn't recall any customers who bought guns at your stores in Waco who committed suicide, correct?"

"Yes, ma'am."

"Your Honor, plaintiffs would offer into evidence marked collectively as Exhibit 89 a compilation of seven articles from the Waco Tribune-Herald and the weekly Hometown News, also published in Waco."

"No objection, Your Honor."

Moschella knew what Sophia was about to do. He didn't care. It wouldn't help her case much, if at all.

"Mr. Owen, please take a moment to review Exhibit 89," Sophia continued. "I would ask the clerk to hand copies to the jurors, with the court's approval."

"That's fine, Ms. Christopoulos," Judge Ortiz said. "I assume I get one too?"

Sophia was unflappable. "Of course, Your Honor."

"Mr. Owen, those seven articles describe a total of eleven suicides, involving people of various ages, sexes, races, and ethnic groups. Gun suicides. Committed with guns they bought at one of your three Garryowen stores. Do you dispute the accuracy of that number?"

"I have no reason to doubt it."

"That doesn't bother you, does it?"

"Of course it does. Terribly. But what can we do about that? We're just average people. My store clerks and me don't have crystal balls. A lot more of our gun customers haven't committed suicide than have."

Sophia watched the jury. They were buying into his ordinary people answer.

"If you had screened them, is it possible some or all of those eleven people would still be alive?"

Before Moschella could object on the basis of speculation, Owen answered.

"They would have just used a knife, a rope, pills, poison, whatever. I mean, if they wanted to kill themselves and all."

Sophia saw she was losing the jury even more with Owen.

"Is Sports Gear USA a member of the Retail Gun Sellers of America?"

"Of course."

"It pays one hundred thousand dollars a year in dues, which go to in part to fund your twenty-five-thousand-dollar compensation, doesn't it?"

"Sure, but all the dues help pay for that, ma'am."

Sophia couldn't shake his simple down-home logic. Many of the jurors were seeing themselves in him. She had to gamble.

"Tell, me Mr. Owen, has any individual or organization ever paid you or the Retail Gun Sellers of America not to endorse and, in fact, to lobby against required codes or tip sheets of the sort used in places like New Hampshire and Colorado?"

"Objection. Irrelevant, more prejudicial than probative, compound, outside the scope of Mr. Owen's opinion testimony."

Moschella had no idea where this was coming from, but it set off his litigator's alarm bells.

"Your Honor, it goes to the very heart of his opinion and his credibility, and it's at the core of this lawsuit as well."

"I have to agree with Ms. Christopoulos here, Mr. Moschella. Objections overruled."

The objections had given Owen just enough time to decide to lie. He had been paid ten thousand dollars in cash each year of his presidency, just like his predecessors, to do exactly what this damn banshee was asking, but there was no way she could prove it.

"Absolutely not."

"You're under oath, Mr. Owen, remember that, and subject to the penalties of perjury. Do you understand?"

"I do, ma'am."

"Care to search your memory a bit harder?"

"No, I would never do that. That's up to all the store owners themselves."

Sophia had hit a wall. She had no proof. At least none she wanted to reveal just yet. Owen had called what had been a bluff on her part.

"Do you know of anyone else ever receiving such payments for that purpose?"

"No, ma'am."

"Do you receive any money or gifts or other compensation over and above your per diem and the twenty-five thousand dollars you get for being president?"

"No, ma'am."

"How much money did you personally make from your business, the Garryowen stores you own in Waco, Texas, last year, Mr. Owen?"

"My business is low margin. I took home about forty thousand dollars after all my expenses."

"So ten thousand dollars would mean a lot to you, wouldn't it?"

"Not really, ma'am. My wife and I have a real good life. We live within our means. You can do that in Waco. We're not greedy."

"Your Honor, I have to object and move to strike, on relevance grounds, for lack of foundation and because, as I understand the implication of the question, asked and answered, and harassing the witness. There is no evidence of any bribery, if that's what Ms. Christopoulos is suggesting. I move to strike those questions and his answers."

"Sustained. Motion to strike granted. The jury will disregard the last two questions about Mr. Owen's business and his answers. Ms. Christopoulos, I will not have witnesses badgered in my court."

The jury was on Owen's side, and so was Judge Ortiz. Sophia would have to bank on the other new developments, or this could all end badly for her and the Holts.

"I think I'm done here, Your Honor. No further questions."

Sophia, Paul, and the Holts maintained their composure. Moschella had, without knowing it, insulated his client from the disastrous testimony Owen could have given. Owen's credibility as an expert on customs and practices in the retail firearms business, and his own personal integrity were intact even though he had lied. He had cast further doubt on the legitimacy of the Holts's case.

It was four. Judge Ortiz declared the court in recess until ten the next morning—Friday.

"I couldn't get at them," Sophia said.

"You did enough," Paul said. "After we hit them with Gallo tomorrow and our motions, their minor triumphs with their last two experts won't matter."

"I should have been stronger."

"People lie," Tricia said. "And the jury thought twenty-five thousand was a lot."

"But they accepted it. They accept *him* as apple-pie America."

"Hey, Sophia," Bryce said. "So Moschella scored a few points with two of his experts. So what? It wasn't enough. Our experts were better."

Bryce's more senior colleagues did not disabuse him of his perceptions in front of the Holts. Time enough to give him that lesson later.

"Gallo tomorrow." Paul eyed the Sports Gear entourage strutting out the door.

"And a whole lot more besides." Sophia led her team out of the courthouse with the nervous, lagging Holts.

⌘

# CHAPTER 83

## The Deluded Arrogance of Evil

*"Time shall unfold what pleated cunning hide:*
*Who cover faults at last shame them derides."*
-William Shakespeare, *King Lear*

To call the atmosphere at Quarry, Warren & Moschella ebullient would not begin to describe it. The entire contingent gathered in the Jackson-usurped conference room to celebrate the day and to anticipate the next day's climax, and the end of the trial if there were no Holt rebuttal witnesses.

"That was masterful, Tony." Kemper, looking like the prophet Jeremiah, was glad he could congratulate Moschella. "You outdid yourself today."

"Yes, the changes we made last night really worked." Jackson claimed credit as always.

His subordinates, French, Beauregard and Boyd, supported their boss.

"Yes," French said. "It takes all hands to win a case."

"Great day," Beauregard gushed. "We did a superior job on those experts."

Boyd offered a weak smile, but that was all. The self-congratulatory puffery was too much for her.

Moschella and Sandoval had arranged themselves conspicuously on either side of Kemper, distancing themselves from Jackson and his mini-clones.

"But what was all that about the ten thousand this guy was accused of taking?" Kemper asked. "Where did they come up with that?"

"Hell if I know," Jackson dissembled.

In reality, Jackson knew all too well. Pickett, under his direct orders, regularly and routinely greased a lot of palms, including Owen's, at a standard payola rate of ten thousand dollars a year.

"They want to win dirty, I guess."

"What do you think, Tony?"

"Who knows?" He stared accusingly at Jackson.

Moschella had come to believe the man capable of just about anything. All Moschella wanted was an end to this snake-pit case and to get the Jackson group and their shady operation out of Bakersfield and his life. To acknowledge knowing anything Jackson might have done behind his back would open a Pandora's box of unethical, illegal, and possibly criminal acts that could ensnare him, Sandoval, and their firm as well. It was a standoff.

"Our psychiatrist was a marvelous witness." Sandoval stepped in to protect Moschella from himself. "He delivered on the key issue—whether the clerks at the store saw anything in Mike Holt's behavior that should have led them to refuse to sell him that shotgun. And Owen made it clear that America's firearms dealers can't judge the stability of gun customers in circumstances like Mike Holt's. We couldn't have asked for more."

"Poor Tony had to wing it a bit there, but we know he did his best." Jackson never let pass an opportunity to belittle Moschella in ways overt or subtle. "The jury bought everything our experts were selling. The only way the Holts get a verdict now is jury nullification, and that won't happen."

"We have to get to the goal line, though," Moschella said. "One more witness."

"I agree," Kemper said. "Let's get at it."

Moschella led the balance of the meeting.

"Brandon Gallo is on deck for tomorrow morning, our last witness. Ms. Sandoval very capably defended him at his deposition, and he trusts her. She'll handle his direct examination, absent any dissent. He's in the lobby waiting for a final run-through with her."

"I don't like ending with him, and I'll say it one last time," Jackson complained. "She'd better not screw up. But your call, your funeral if she does."

French let his eyes drift lasciviously over Sandoval's inviting body. He thought, *I'd love to put you over your a desk and screw you up . . . big-time.*

She ignored French's now constant and always salacious eyeballing. But she decided her role in the case now permitted her at least one dig.

"Mr. Jackson, I assume that you and your little foursome, including Pickett in Denver or wherever you've stashed him, have finished the trial brief and revised special jury instructions? Gallo's testimony will be short, and then we'll do closing arguments, barring any rebuttal. That means the jury will be charged and will start deliberating tomorrow."

"Oh, we're way ahead of you. We've prepared the closing argument too. Great pieces of work, if I do say so myself. Don't trouble your little cute head about any of that."

"To quote someone else, your call, your funeral," Theresa retorted.

Kemper observed the interplay. He approved of this sharp, beautiful woman's refusal to let Jackson intimidate her.

"We'll break to revise and finish up everything." Jackson was dismissive of Sandoval as she took her leave. His crew ignored her, except for French, whose lingering, probing eyes followed her out the door.

Moschella and Kemper went with Sandoval, leaving the conference room to the Denverites.

* * *

On the way to Moschella's office, Kemper suggested calling Buckner and Booth.

"We should," Moschella agreed. "Theresa, would you please tell Brandon we'll be a few minutes?"

"Will do, Tony."

She found Gallo reading a copy of *Field and Stream* in their lobby and relayed the message.

"No problem." He smiled and returned to a page advertising fishing rods.

Moschella had gotten coffee for all three of them.

"Tony, this is all very difficult. I think both of you have done a superb job under horrible conditions and with your hands tied . . . that O'Rourke tragedy notwithstanding."

"Thanks, Mr. Kemper. We appreciate it." Theresa truly did.

"Please, Theresa, if I may, and Tony too. It's Jubal from now on. I have a more serious question, and I need a straight answer. We did remarkably well today. But you're Bakersfield people and know the jury better than I do or anyone from outside could. Are we at risk of losing? Should we make a real settlement offer to the Holts?"

Moschella didn't answer right away. He had to be honest, even if it wasn't in his best interest, short or long term.

"It depends, Jubal. I think we have a minimum of two-thirds of the jurors with us at the moment. Our experts were beyond good, and the jury liked you before seeing and hearing from them."

"Do you agree, Theresa?"

Theresa was flattered to be asked, but wary of overstepping her bounds given her inexperience.

"I have to defer to Tony, Jubal. He's one of the best trial lawyers in California, not just here in Bakersfield. But since you asked, I agree. We should win barring something unforeseen tomorrow. I've been studying the jurors' reactions. We've got the like factor on our side. You grabbed them. And they'll warm to Brandon tomorrow."

"Well put, Theresa," Moschella said.

"Tomorrow is important, though. We'll re-evaluate then. That's how trials are."

"That's what I needed to hear. Jackson doesn't know the politics at Sports Gear. I won't go further. I would appreciate the use of one of your conference rooms to call Wade and Emeline."

"With pleasure, Jubal. Take the one at the opposite end of the hall. You'll have complete privacy. Theresa has her final session with Gallo, and I'll be here if either of you need me."

\* \* \*

A flurry of activity ensued. Kemper conferenced with Buckner and Booth and gave them a detailed report. After a thorough analysis with Booth, their in-house legal counsel, they all decided not to make a settlement offer and to play out the case until it went to the jury. They would re-evaluate settlement later if anything seemed to warrant doing so. Otherwise, they would wait for a jury verdict. Kemper reported that decision to Moschella and Jackson. Then Kemper went back to the Padre Hotel.

Jackson called his partner George Hood at the firm's home office to gloat about the day's events, emphasizing his own pivotal role. He always took credit for everything possible, warranted or not, and his inflated stories were usually entertaining. He made other calls to various clients and friends, bragging, schmoozing, amusing, and diverting, but never boring the ears on the other end.

All was well in his mind and his world. Yes. It was *his* world.

* * *

Except that all was not well. Jackson had sent the other Denver lawyers back to the Padre Hotel after they all finished reviewing, revising, and checking the last documents they would be filing with the court, particularly the special jury instructions. Boyd and Beauregard were happy to get out of offices they had come to hate. But not French. He had other plans.

Sandoval efficiently handled her final meeting with Gallo. She and Tony had agreed that its main purpose was to put him at ease. It took less than an hour. He was relaxed, smiling, and ready to do a repeat of his deposition. That was all they wanted. He would be a very sympathetic and appealing final witness for Sports Gear—this all-American, all-Bakersfield, deferential, and eager-to-please young man.

* * *

After Gallo left, Sandoval went through her inbox and then packed up her things. As she finished, she started to dictate a memo on her iPhone, a reminder to herself about a line of questioning for Gallo the next morning.

"Theresa."

She turned to find French standing in front of her office door. He had shut it behind him.

"What do you want?"

"The same thing you do."

He smiled and walked toward her.

"Get out of here."

"Why?"

"Get out of my way."

She charged forward. French blocked her and forced her back. He put his arms around her and grabbed her buttock.

"Mmm. A thong and a damn tight ass, Sandoval. It needs to be handled by someone who knows what to do with it."

Sandoval yelled, "What the hell? Get your goddamned hands off of me, you disgusting piece of filth!"

French pulled her to him and kissed her.

"Settle down." He pushed her back up against her desk. "I'm not going to hurt you. Unless you like it that way. Do you, baby? Huh?"

"Let me go."

Theresa dropped everything, including her phone, and fought him.

"Come on, you nasty little hot tamale. Let's have a little fun. It's our last chance." He shoved her back onto her desk.

"No. Let me go."

Theresa screamed for help and, using all her strength, finally broke loose. She slid away from the desk and backed up. He played with her, blocking her starts to the door. Then she charged straight at him and smashed her knee into his nuts with a force driven by thoughts of thousands of years of abused women raging in her mind. She was not going to be counted among them.

French fell to the ground, doubled over in pain.

Sandoval grabbed her phone and purse from the floor and rolled her trial case past the ball of felled and moaning male flesh. She clicked off the recording feature she had been using on her phone to do her Gallo memo and put the phone in her pocket.

She yanked her door open to find Moschella standing there. He had heard the struggle and shouts and had come running from his office.

"Theresa, are you all right?"

"I'm okay."

Her body was shaking all over, but she fought back the unwanted tears of anger and outrage. She would show no weakness.

"What happened?" Moschella saw French doubled over on the ground. That was all he needed to see to know the answer to that question.

"Are you hurt?"

"No." She looked over at French straightening himself out.

"What's going on here?"

Jackson, who had been about to leave when he heard loud noises, arrived at Sandoval's office just as French struggled to his feet and leaned on her desk.

"That bitch kneed me in the nuts for fun," French said, with his teeth clenched in pain.

"What a load of crap," Moschella said. "You tried to rape her."

"That's bull," French shouted.

"Sounds to me like a misunderstanding," Jackson said. "You know, mixed signals, he said/she said. No harm done."

"What do you mean no harm done? She hurt me. She kneed me. I should call the police. I should sue."

Sandoval's mind cleared, and her tears receded.

"Please do. I'll have you prosecuted for attempted rape and let you enjoy prison, pretty boy. There were no signals, mixed or otherwise. You're low-class trash, and that includes your Mr. Jackass here." She got in Jackson's face. "You retained us. Your firm is looking at a sexual harassment claim worth millions. You're both dicks. Tiny little dicks at that."

Theresa remembered the memo she was recording and hoped her phone had picked up the encounter.

"Don't even think of calling the police, French," Jackson said. "As to you, *Ms.* Sandoval, you can't parade around like you do and not expect men to respond. As I said, just mixed signals. Come on."

"Like hell." Defiant and indignant, Sandoval played the recording on her phone. It had indeed recorded everything.

Jackson and French blanched.

"Please, Theresa," French said. "Please. I . . . I didn't mean anything."

"Say 'pretty please,' you miserable swine." She marched out the door.

"This isn't over, you two," Moschella said. "The only thing that's saving you now is that we have a trial to finish tomorrow. I'm escorting Theresa to her car. You two get your things and get the hell out of here. Don't come back."

Moschella ran after Sandoval and apologized all the way down the elevator and out the lobby doors.

"I had no idea what these people were like when I took this case, Theresa. Certainly no reason to suspect they were capable of anything like this. It's been misery for a year. They're done."

"It's the end for me," Sandoval said, her upper lip quivering.

"The firm and I will support you, whatever you decide to do." Moschella prayed it would all just fade away.

"I'm going to save that recording on twenty flash drives and in the Cloud."

They reached Theresa's car, and she impulsively hugged Moschella. "Thank you."

It was difficult for him not to respond to this beautiful woman's body against his, but he stood, wooden, until she let go. There had been enough sexual grief for one night.

"Can you drive?"

"I can."

As he watched her car leave the parking lot, he hoped she'd forget about French and not make trouble. There was no way his firm would *not* be included in any suit she might file. Technically, it had to be named.

This blasted case had brought him enough trouble to last a lifetime and beyond.

\* \* \*

The minute Theresa was home in her apartment, she downloaded the audio from her phone on her laptop. She backed that up, put it on five flash drives she had sitting in her desk drawer, and made sure it was in her Cloud storage as well. She quickly downed a Stella Artois from her fridge and uncapped another one. She started shaking and crying uncontrollably. Her nerves started to settle down with her second beer.

As she got ready for bed, she debated whether making French pay was worth her family knowing about the incident—her mother, father, and older brother, especially her father and brother. They were proud Mexican-American men, and they would want justice—their kind of justice, man-to-man with guns or knives or clubs. She didn't need that, and neither did they.

She had to forget French. Thankfully, he'd only manhandled her. The memory brought back her fury and disgust. She went to bed, set the alarm on her phone, and took two mild sleep aids to relax.

Those worthless excuses for men would not rob her of her final opportunity to shine tomorrow in court.

⌘

# CHAPTER 84

## The Hammer Rises, The Anvil Waits

*"Let your plans be dark and impenetrable as night,
and when you move, fall like a thunderbolt."*
-Sun Tzu

Thursday evening, while leaving the courthouse, Sophia took pity on the Holts and invited them for dinner at their rented condo. The team was getting Japanese from Ninja Sushi on Calloway Drive. Beth and Wallace, while welcoming the invitation, said they'd bring their own dinners. They had never tried that that "Jap food" and didn't intend to start now.

Bryce and Tricia were cranking away when Paul and Sophia appeared with their meals. They gathered around the coffee table and filled each other in as they ate.

The Holts had stopped at Chick-Fil-A on Stockdale Highway. They crowded in at the table.

"Thank you for having us," Beth said.

"Of course. You should know what's going on." Sophia smiled.

Wallace and Beth dug into their sandwiches and waffle fries.

"I thought the day went well," Beth said.

Sophia and Paul let her comment pass.

"We found great law doing research for the motions." Tricia bit into her rainbow roll.

"Joshua Dreyfus and his lawyer gave us more than Ben had told us in our conference calls," Bryce said.

"We have his declaration drafted, and it's out to them for signature."

"So they're really ready to go public?" Paul downed a deep-fried soft shell crab with some green tea.

"They sure are." Tricia was excited, and it showed.

She explained that Dreyfus and his attorney had worked with them all that afternoon to craft a declaration and gather exhibits to go with it. They were overnighting the declaration back to them in Bakersfield, signed with all exhibits attached. The messenger service guaranteed delivery at their condo at seven the next morning.

"I don't understand any of that, but it sounds amazing," Beth said.

Wallace devoted himself to his sandwich.

"Dreyfus will be available at his lawyer's office with a notary public tomorrow at noon our time and will stay until we advise him otherwise," Bryce noted. "Just in case Judge Ortiz wants him to testify by Skype or insists that Sports Gear have the opportunity to question him. It's a show of strength on our part."

Sophia ate the calamari tempura, which satisfied her Greek-food yearnings. "Tell us about the law you found, Tricia."

"Bryce should. He did most of the research while I drafted the declaration and sorted the exhibits."

"We really appreciate all this," Beth said.

"I just want this over." Wallace dismissively stuffed waffle fries in his mouth.

"Honey, watch your manners," Beth said.

He responded by cramming more fries in his mouth.

"Go on, Bryce." Sophia had no more patience for the even more rapidly degenerating Holt relationship.

"It has several prongs," Bryce began. "Our principal argument will be for a terminating sanction, asking that Judge Ortiz grant us a default judgment and send the case to the jury just to decide the amount of damages to award."

"Wait," Paul said. "Aren't terminating sanctions only available where clients participated in or knew about the misconduct of their lawyers?"

"It's broader than that in some circumstances. Many jurisdictions have granted terminating sanctions using an agency theory. They actually held clients accountable for their lawyers' actions whether they knew about them or not . . . especially where what was involved was attorney misconduct during a trial."

"What if the misconduct is by outside counsel like Jackson, who isn't part of the trial team for Sports Gear? And what if the misconduct consists of intentional torts, not negligence?" Paul grilled Bryce because this aspect was critical.

"The key question is defining 'part of the trial.' According to my research, Jackson is 'part of the trial team' under the law. However, the dispositive factor is that an innocent opposing party and its lawyers, that's the Holts and us, shouldn't suffer for the bad acts of lawyers controlling the case on the other side, and that's Jackson *and* Moschella. The courts granting terminating sanctions are clear on that in our jurisdiction."

"You have strong authority for that?"

Tricia jumped in to confirm what Bryce was saying. "A ton. Even if Sports Gear can find some contrary case law, Judge Ortiz won't care after he sees the Dreyfus declaration."

"I get that you guys are convinced about this one." Paul was still dubious. "But let's suppose the judge isn't willing to punish Sports Gear for the sins of its lawyers. Nothing Kowrilsky or Dreyfus gave us implicates Sports Gear in any way that I can see."

Tricia was prepared. "That's what the agency theory is for, Paul. If Ortiz won't buy that theory, then we're left with the second prong of our argument. We ask him to hold Jackson and the other Denver lawyers in contempt and to issue severe monetary and other sanctions against them. And, of course, to disqualify them from representing Sports Gear in any capacity. Then settlement is more likely than a retrial."

"Jackson and his firm haven't technically appeared in our case," Paul cautioned.

"We're arguing they made a *de facto* appearance by doing the lion's share of work undercover, if you will," Tricia said. "The Dreyfus declaration includes exhibits showing that the Denver lawyers did all the paperwork for Sports Gear on this case. Those ridiculous motions *in limine*, Sports Gear's written discovery, its responses to our written discovery, gathering its documents, finding and hiring its experts, and drafting the summary judgment motion. Everything except showing their faces at depositions or in court."

"Still . . ."

"Trust me," Tricia said. "If Jackson's in that courtroom tomorrow, Ortiz won't hesitate for one second to exercise jurisdiction over him with the Dreyfus declaration and the exhibits backing it up in front of him. Jackson's looking at disbarment or possibly a criminal indictment. Ortiz's reputation for running a clean courtroom is solid. He'll do what needs to be done."

"Paul, they've done a terrific job." Sophia was elated. "Tricia's correct. Ortiz is a no-nonsense judge when it comes to respecting the court and the legal process. But, Tricia, are we going after Moschella and Sandoval, too?"

"We have nothing to tie them to any of this. That's another reason for Ortiz to assert jurisdiction over Jackson and his people. Given the old boy network, we'll try to leave Moschella and Sandoval out of it. Plus, the old divide and conquer. They won't want to get lumped together with Jackson and his people and will abandon them posthaste. You can count on that."

"You've nailed this," Paul said.

Bryce looked around the table. "There's one more prong, and we need to agree on it. We've included an alternative motion for a mistrial to demonstrate our resolution. It could give Ortiz an easy way out, but it has to be there."

"I agree," Paul said.

"Must we do that?" Wallace said. "We don't have the money."

"We can sell the house," Beth said.

"Like hell!" Wallace yelled.

"Wait a minute, both of you. It's just a power play, to show our resolve. We're not retrying the case." Sophia took charge.

"The real point of this multifaceted motion is to make things complicated enough that Judge Ortiz will take it under submission. Once he does, Sports Gear will have to make a legitimate settlement offer, one good enough that we can recommend that you accept it. With all the new revelations, they'll want out of this case. The alternative is a huge downside risk Sports Gear can't afford to run."

"I get it. I like that." It was apparent Wallace had indeed been listening while he ate.

"I think I do." Beth was lost but agreed nonetheless.

"Here's the scenario I anticipate," Tricia continued. "They put on Gallo tomorrow, and Paul nails him with the video on cross or in rebuttal if they don't call him. Then, before the lunch break, we ask the judge for an in-chambers conference to bring some grave matters to his attention."

"Okay, I'm with you so far." Paul stopped eating the Korean bulgoki he loved.

"Now this is our big play. We present our motion and serve it on Moschella," Tricia said.

"If Ortiz rules in our favor immediately, then we win. He's more likely to take it under submission and let them file some kind of response. We hope in a limited time frame."

"We'll be hitting him with a lot of issues," Sophia said.

"Don't forget," Bryce responded, "Ben will have made all this public by the time the judge gets our motion. That will devastate Sports Gear nationwide. Besides, after the jury sees the enhanced video on the DVD, they'll be for us. Moschella will come up with a big settlement offer . . . fast. What Jackson did is sanctionable, license-threatening, criminal. It will be really bad for everyone on the defense side if it turns out Moschella and Sandoval had a hand in any of it or knew about any of it." Bryce was excited and proud of his work.

"It all sounds good." Paul was satisfied. "Remember, above all, we want a settlement. Even with terminating sanctions and a jury damages award, they could use the lengthy appeal process as a weapon to keep us all from getting the money for years."

He was thoughtful for a moment, mentally tying up any loose ends. "I doubt they'll call any more of their experts before Gallo. Why bother? They left a good impression with the last two. But if they do, I'm ready for them."

"We have to go," Wallace interrupted. "My brain hurts from all this legal mumbo-jumbo."

"Wallace, wait." Sophia stopped him. "Don't forget, we're meeting Ben and his crew in the Bakersfield Marriott's lobby tomorrow so we can all get into the courthouse together. There'll be a huge mob."

"I'm not stupid. I remember." Wallace abruptly shambled out, nearer his dream of dumping Beth and vacating Bakersfield.

Beth followed, apologizing for him and thanking everyone for all the hard work.

"Damn," Paul said. "He's barely keeping it together."

"Well, it's about to end and with a fat check," Tricia said. "He'll continue keeping it together if he knows what's good for him."

The team gave the moving papers and witness outlines a final proofread and review.

"This is really something." Paul finished his review.

"I wish it was tomorrow . . . tonight."

"Me too," Sophia said. "I'm not going to get any sleep."

⌘

# CHAPTER 85

## A Gallo Is A Very Fine Whine

*"Justice has nothing to do with what goes on in a courtroom;
justice is what comes out of a courtroom."*
-Clarence Darrow

On Friday morning, Sophia and her team were up with their trial cases packed before seven. The special messenger arrived on schedule, as promised. Tricia and Bryce immediately took off for the Stockdale Highway FedEx store on the way to the courthouse to make and assemble enough copies of the papers they were going to file for the defendants and the court. Timing would be tight.

Sophia and Paul took a minute to check out on the TV what they would encounter at the courthouse that day. The media, demonstrators, and police were already there in large numbers.

"Damn," Paul said. "Things are really stirred up with the trial ending. Have a look."

Sophia did and pointed. "There's a banner saying 'Guns Kill People and Ethics Too,' and a woman wearing a placard reading "My Gun Is The Only Reason I'm Alive To Be Here Today."

"There are huge signs with pictures of the San Bernardino victims."

"Then there's that one." Sophia grinned sardonically. "'Kill All the Lawyers.' The two sides agree on something, at least. Let's get out of here."

\* \* \*

On the way, Sophia's cell sounded with the *Zorba the Greek* theme, which she had reset to replenish her Greek fire.

"It's Derek and Rona," Sophia said.

"You have to answer it."

"Hi, Derek. Rona on with you?"

"Yes, Sophia, we're both here. What the hell's going on? And why didn't you report in last night?"

"We were busy all preparing motions for today. No time."

"What motions? We need to talk." Derek had his own directives. "We saw the news reports. Yesterday was bad for us in court. You have to request a continuance to regroup over the weekend."

"Derek. Stop. We have it covered, but I can't fill you in now. We have to get past the mob and to the courtroom with the Holts on time."

"That's it? That's all you're going to give us? You have to go?"

Rona was livid. "You can't stonewall us. We're out of money. We're entitled to a say in this."

"Just watch Ben's broadcast about to air at ten. We'll be in court, but watch it. You'll understand then."

"We're not waiting to get updated on the news!" Rona yelled.

"Damn you, we have to be kept in the loop." Derek was irate.

"I literally have no time. You'll have to take my word."

Sophia hung up. The *Zorba* theme started up again—Derek. She put the phone on vibrate. He and Rona would just have to stew. Ben's newscast would be on soon enough.

* * *

Sophia and her team met the Holts along with Ben and his crew in the Bakersfield Marriott's lobby. Bryce and Tricia showed up at the last minute with the motion papers. They were able to take a back route on the Stockdale Highway exiting on P Street and going north until, for no apparent reason, it became Q Street, where the Marriott and the Convention Center were. Ben had paid for and arranged parking for everyone there.

Sophia was keyed up. There were few moments like this in any legal career. None for most trial lawyers.

"So, Ben, we're ready for the big splash at ten?" Sophia was eager to get to the endgame.

"You bet," Ben said. "We're still a magical duo. The rest of my people are already in place outside the courthouse, including Pulitzer and Zohar. They wanted to be here in case we needed anything else when you hit the judge and Sports Gear with your papers."

"Let's go," Paul said. "The demonstrators are multiplying. We don't want to get caught."

Ben agreed. "A real tsunami's coming."

"We don't really understand," Beth said. "But we're excited, aren't we Wallace?"

He just put one foot in front of the other.

Again, thanks to Ben, the Holts and Sophia's team had a police escort through the media clusters and the shouting, chanting, sign-waving, even gun-toting demonstrators. He had made a few wary allies in the Bakersfield Police Department through practiced cultivation and other more concrete gratuities best not mentioned.

\* \* \*

In the courtroom hallway, Sophia was relieved to see Brandon Gallo. He was dressed for his performance in a gray synthetic fiber suit, a gaudy yellow tie, and polished but worn brown loafers.

As Sophia passed him, a woman, obviously his mother, was straightening his tie.

The older man with him—she guessed it was his father—patted him on the shoulder. "You'll do fine, son."

Brandon stood tall and looked confident. Confidence was good. It made him more vulnerable, off his guard, and cocky. It looked as if Sports Gear was calling him as a witness. If not, the Holts would. Either way, the enhanced DVD would bury him.

\* \* \*

That morning, Sandoval met Moschella and Kemper at the office for the drive to the courthouse. Not Jackson. Not after his eviction the previous night.

Because Moschella was local and popular, the Bakersfield police had reserved a parking space for him in the closest lot on L Street adjacent to the courthouse and escorted him, Sandoval, and Kemper through a back entrance after they arrived, away from the media and the demonstrators.

Kemper ignored Jackson, who was in his usual place in the gallery, and conferred with Moschella and Sandoval after they reached the courtroom. They were all comfortable. Gallo would be their last witness. He was ready, actually eager, to testify.

\* \* \*

The Holts and Sophia's team, including Bryce and Tricia with the motion papers, had all taken their seats before ten. Kemper, Moschella, and Sandoval had again gotten there first.

"They almost always get here before us and look so together. How?" Tricia asked.

"They're local, that's how," Bryce said. "That seems to be the answer to most questions here."

"All rise. Kern County Superior Court, the Honorable Robert Ortiz presiding, is now in session."

Judge Ortiz took his seat on the bench, had the jury brought in, and inquired whether the defense had additional witnesses.

"We do, Your Honor." Sandoval stood.

Ortiz and all the men in the courtroom delighted in seeing the lovely Theresa Sandoval in action again. This time their delight was restricted to admiring her face. Her Hugo Boss black Julea pants suit totally covered her other attributes and her shapely legs. Her white silk blouse was buttoned to her neck, her hair smoothed back in a bun with an abalone barrette from Polyvore, revealing her simple oval onyx earrings.

After the incident with French, the last thing she wanted was to encourage the sexual fantasies of any man in the courtroom. It didn't matter. Her natural beauty assured that would happen whatever she was wearing.

"Defendant Sports Gear calls Brandon Gallo to the stand."

Sandoval was all business, utterly professional, and first and foremost an assured and prepared trial lawyer—one who by chance was also a gorgeous woman.

Brandon proceeded up the center aisle. He walked slowly and then hesitated. His head swiveled to find his parents in the second-to-last row. His mother nodded at him, with pride shining in her eyes.

He turned back and moved carefully toward the witness stand, as though walking on thin ice that could crack, sending him down to a cold wet death.

As he made his way past Sophia, he eyed her and then Beth with her oxygen tank.

"Did you see that?" Sophia whispered to Paul.

"I did. What do you think?"

"I think you're going to destroy him," Sophia said. "Hit him with that video first thing, hard."

"I'll use his mother too," Paul said.

"Yes, keep that line of sight open," Sophia said. "He's a mama's boy."

During his deposition, the kid, now nineteen, had shown he was bright, alert, loyal to his employer, and well-coached. Here in a public trial in open court, though, with his parents watching, he was unsteady as he approached the witness stand. Brandon was worried about having lied in his deposition. He knew from the movies they called it perjury in court and it was serious.

He took the witness stand and swore the oath to tell the truth.

\* \* \*

As Gallo began his testimony, across the airwaves and then the Internet, Ben's story, based on Joshua Dreyfus's revelations, exploded exponentially.

But not in the courtroom, where Theresa took Brandon through his paces, ignorant of what was occurring outside and ignorant of the video that would impeach his scripted testimony. The news coverage detailed the unethical, corrupt, and criminal activities of Jackson and the other attorneys in his firm. It went viral on the Internet with no help needed from Dreyfus and just a little covert assistance from Pulitzer and Zohar.

* * *

Theresa continued to guide Brandon confidently through a replay of his deposition. His high school education and his staunch Bakersfield family background. How hunting with his father had led to his interest in guns. How he liked his job at Sports Gear and wanted to become a gun salesman someday.

Just as Moschella and Sandoval had hoped, the jury saw an earnest, boringly normal but likeable guy with an upbringing, life experiences, and job typical of many of them. He was every bit the average Bakersfield youngster, no genius but a hard worker, trying to make an honest living. There was nothing pretentious about him.

Sandoval then had him repeat his deposition testimony about the day Mike Holt bought the fatal shotgun. The bottom line: He had seen little and heard less. His interaction with Mike was brief and inconsequential. Otherwise, he spent the day doing his job, sweeping and restocking the shelves.

Smiling, Sandoval announced, "No further questions, Your Honor."

As she returned to her seat, she saw approving glances from Moschella and Kemper. Then she spotted Jackson near the middle of the gallery, glowering at her. She pointedly turned her back on him and took her seat.

"Any cross-examination?" Judge Ortiz inquired.

"Yes, Your Honor."

Paul stood and made sure his outline was easily readable in front of him. Just as he took a breath to begin his first question, the noise level outside surged with screams and chants. The judge ignored it. Nothing outside his courtroom, short of a bomb, was going to interrupt this trial again. Paul forced himself not to smile. The timing told him it was the demonstrators reacting to Ben's news release.

He had to ignore the commotion outside, forget their decisive motion, and focus on breaking Gallo gently but definitively—getting him to tell the truth about the events of that day, supporting and affirming Wallace's testimony, ensuring that if the case went to the jury solely on damages because of their motion, those damages would be deservedly high. And that if the motions all failed, that the jury would find for the Holts because of the lies the Sports Gear clerks had all told under oath.

* * *

Paul observed Brandon for a moment to get a sense of where he was mentally. Paul read preparation and focus in his eyes. Brandon's jaw was relaxed, but his lips moved almost imperceptibly. He was going through his script, his talking points, his lies. Lies that, but for Paul's impending questioning, would forever remain in the record of this trial—unapologetically announcing that corporate America could and would do whatever it wanted with impunity to any human being in America or the world for that matter.

"Good morning, Mr. Gallo,"

Paul began amiably, to put Brandon at ease. He also smiled at the jury to appear likeable, relaxed, and disarming during his cross-examination. He had dressed down for the Bakersfield crowd in a low-end brown pinstripe suit from the Men's Wearhouse, a nondescript matching tie, and a plain white dress shirt.

"Good morning." Brandon leaned his elbows on the chair arms and shifted in his seat until he was comfortable.

"You remember that I took your deposition, Brandon? Is it okay if I call you Brandon?"

"Yes to both, sir."

"Brandon, you were more than just at the store the day Mike Holt bought his shotgun there, weren't you?"

Brandon was confused and looked at Theresa. "What do you mean?"

"You talked to Mike Holt several times that day, didn't you?"

"Oh, sure. I get it," Brandon relaxed again. "Once, maybe twice. I don't remember exactly."

"Let me read from page thirty-five of your deposition to refresh your memory: 'I talked to him twice.' Is that what you said in your deposition?"

"Objection," Sandoval stood. "That transcript isn't in the court record."

"I filed a certified copy of the deposition with the court this morning, Your Honor. Counsel must not have been informed."

The clerk was embarrassed. "Sorry, Your Honor, everything was a bit hectic."

"Never mind." Ortiz smiled down at her. "The deposition transcript has been properly submitted. Proceed, Mr. Viola."

"Again, is that what you said in your deposition? You talked to Mike Holt twice."

"Yes. I said that there, like you read."

He glanced at his parents.

"How did Mike appear to you?"

"Normal. Like anybody else."

"Do you remember what you told the police?"

"Yes."

Brandon was meticulously prepared. He was answering with a simple 'yes' or 'no' and volunteering nothing unless it was pulled out of him.

"What was that, if you recall?" Paul smiled at Brandon.

"Yes. Ah . . . I asked him if he needed help finding something in the aisle. He didn't. And I didn't sell him that gun."

"Correct. So . . . So you talked to Mike maybe once or twice that day only in the aisle and didn't sell him the gun?"

"Yes."

"Objection," Theresa stood. "Asked and answered. Again."

"Sustained." Judge Ortiz ordered, "Let's move on, Mr. Viola."

"Do you remember seeing the surveillance video that has already been admitted into evidence?"

"What?" Brandon asked.

"The surveillance video. Do you remember it?"

"Yes."

This was Paul's moment to hit Brandon fast and hard with the enhanced video. Paul went straight for the jugular.

"I am going to play parts of the video that . . ."

"Objection. Plaintiffs' counsel has already played that video for Mr. Grimick and Mr. Davis during their testimony, and for their experts too. This is cumulative. What could another viewing possibly add?" Sandoval looked over at Beth and Wallace. "I'm also mindful of the pain it must bring to Mr. and Mrs. Holt each time they see it."

Paul chortled to himself. Sandoval was overplaying her hand. Time to shut her down.

"Your Honor, while it is the same video, unaltered in any way, we have had it transferred to a DVD and enhanced for visual acuity. The copy produced by counsel for Sports Gear, either intentionally or unintentionally, was grainy and unclear. It has taken some time, but we now have a new and much clearer version on DVD for Sports Gear and its counsel, one for the court, and one to use as an exhibit with this witness."

"Objection, Your Honor. We've not seen this before. Lack of foundation, violation of discovery requests, unfair surprise, unfair delay."

Sandoval looked at Moschella, who shrugged. Neither of them knew why Paul was playing part of the video again.

"Some of those aren't even objections, Ms. Sandoval. In view of Mr. Viola's representations, including that the enhancement took time, I'll let him play it. I'll reserve my ruling on admissibility for the time being. But be careful, Mr. Viola. I'm not saying any of this will be allowed into evidence at the end of this testimonial segment."

"Thank you, Your Honor. I only intend to play small portions pertinent to Mr. Gallo and his participation in the events of that day."

"Very well."

For the entire court, Paul played the segment of the DVD showing the short encounter between Brandon and Mike Holt in the aisle. They had actually spoken four times, in sequence, and Brandon affirmed that. Then he played the segment showing the store manager, Arnie Davis, suspecting Mike of shoplifting, and Mike lifting his shirt.

"Now, Brandon, will you agree this is the store surveillance video from that day, just better quality than you have seen before?"

"Um, um, yes, it is."

"It shows what actually took place that day, now that you have watched it, doesn't it?"

"Sure. I mean yes, it does."

"Your Honor, plaintiffs move to have this enhanced video received into evidence as Exhibit 157."

Sandoval and Moschella conferred. They were perturbed but had been caught flatfooted. It obviously was the same video transferred to a DVD. They could think of no valid objection.

"Absent any objection, so ordered." Judge Ortiz was puzzled.

"Where did you go after this incident I just played?"

"To the register to clean up and then back to restocking like I was supposed to."

"That's not true, is it?"

"What do you mean?"

"You didn't go back to restocking, did you?"

"I did. Like I said in my deposition."

"Not immediately, did you? Not until after Mike left and after your manager came back from his break?"

Brandon looked at Sandoval. She looked at Moschella.

"Uh, no. I mean yes."

Paul played the segment showing the sale of the shotgun to Mike Holt and the return of Arnie Davis, the store manager.

"Let's be clear here. You stayed near the cash register and heard every word that anyone said during the shotgun sale to Mike Holt. You did not go back to restocking until after Mike left and after your manager came back from his break."

With alarm in his eyes, Brandon looked toward Sandoval, who was rapidly reviewing the enhanced DVD on her laptop.

"Objection," she yelled before she could stop herself. "Compound. Asked and answered. Badgering the witness."

"Anything else you'd like to throw in before I rule, Ms. Sandoval?"

"No, Your Honor."

Sandoval's and Moschella's minds were racing. They didn't know what Viola was doing. Then with a fast-forward, they both saw it on Sandoval's laptop. Kemper leaned over and did too. It wasn't in every frame, but it was there. It had been imperceptible but was apparent now. A person who appeared to be, and was, Brandon Gallo was right there near the cash register, adjacent to the gun case. The shadow popped in and out of view during the entire sale and the manager's return. It could have been no one else.

"Overruled as to all. Just answer, son."

The court was silent. So was Paul. So were Sandoval and Moschella. The jury waited. The Bakersfield spectators, news reporters, including Ben—who had entered the courtroom a few minutes before—and Tom Jackson all waited.

"No, I didn't go back to restocking until after my manager came back," Brandon mumbled.

"Speak up please, Brandon."

"No, I didn't go back to restocking until after my manager came back," Brandon said loudly. "He told me to."

"In the segment I just played, that is you behind the cash register, isn't it?"

"Yes."

"When did you go back to restocking?"

"After Mike left and the manager came back and caught me."

"Caught you doing what?"

"Eavesdropping by the cash register."

"Eavesdropping?" Paul repeated loudly, looking directly at the jury. "Does that mean you overheard the conversation between Moss Grimick, Joe Spangler, and Mike Holt about the shotgun and, after the sale and Mike left, their conversation with Mr. Davis?"

"I was just trying to learn how to sell guns. That's all. I wanted to be good at my new job. I didn't mean any harm." Brandon looked at his mother, pleading in his eyes.

"Is that a yes?" Paul made sure Brandon had a direct line of sight to his mother.

"Yes."

"What did Mike say to Mr. Grimick and Mr. Spangler, what did they say to Mike during the sale, and afterward what did Mr. Davis and the two salesmen say to each other?"

"Objection." Theresa stood quickly, halting Brandon before he could open his mouth. "Hearsay. Calls for a narrative."

"Your Honor, the statements Brandon will relate in his testimony are not offered for their truth, but for the fact they were made, and that these statements and this conversation during the sale took place between Mike and the salesmen. The question does not call for a narrative, but for concise and accurate testimony as to what Mr. Gallo overheard. In addition, the statements by Mr. Grimick,

Mr. Spangler, and Mr. Davis, as agents of defendant Sports Gear USA, are admissible under the exception to the hearsay rule for admissions against interest."

Though Sandoval's objection had some merit, the judge would not countenance distortions and lies. The issue was close, but he came down in favor of the truth.

"Overruled."

"But Your Honor." Moschella stood to join Sandoval. "We object. We strenuously object."

"On what other grounds? I've ruled on those you asserted."

Neither Sandoval nor Moschella responded. Their options gone, they simply returned to their seats.

"Would the court reporter please repeat Mr. Viola's question."

"What did Mike say to Mr. Grimick and Mr. Spangler, what did they say to Mike during the sale, and afterward what did Mr. Davis and the two salesmen say to each other?"

Brandon gazed into his mother's searching and troubled eyes. Then, he looked at Mrs. Holt breathing from her oxygen tank. He sat up straight and answered a question he had never been asked before in that way or been prepared by the lawyers to answer. He told the truth—this time all of it.

He confirmed that everything Wallace Holt had testified to regarding his conversations with Davis, Spangler, and Grimick was accurate. That he, Brandon, also thought that Mike had acted odd, off, "loony" even. That he had a crazed or strange look in his eyes, like someone who was nuts. That Mike had, at first, tried to buy only one shotgun shell. That he didn't want a case for the shotgun and hadn't asked any questions about how to use the gun, or about any of its safety features.

When Brandon was through, he just hung his head. Davis, Spangler, and Grimick had all lied under oath in this courtroom. Brandon had lied in his own deposition. Everyone knew it—most importantly the jurors. Wallace Holt had told the truth.

Paul decided to ask one more question. It was a fishing expedition, but given what was about to happen, he concluded it wouldn't matter whether he caught anything.

He turned to face a very disturbed, broken Brandon Gallo.

"Brandon, since that day, and outside the presence of any of Sports Gear's attorneys, have you spoken to anyone about this lawsuit?"

"Objection. Irrelevant, violates the attorney-client privilege, more prejudicial than probative. Mr. Viola didn't even ask about this in Mr. Gallo's deposition."

"In view of Mr. Gallo's present testimony, Ms. Sandoval, overruled. But you're on a short leash here, Mr. Viola."

"Thank you, Your Honor. I won't test it."

"Answer the question, please, Brandon."

"Just one person."

"Who?"

"Moss Grimick."

"When was that?"

"After he testified here, the day he found out my friend Joe Spangler was . . . dead."

"Did you approach him or did he approach you?"

"He came to the store. I was workin' that day. He was really teed off . . . excuse me, Your Judgeship . . . mad."

"What did he say to you?"

"Objection. Hearsay, Your Honor, calls for a narrative again."

"Don't bother responding, Mr. Viola. Overruled, Ms. Sandoval."

"Brandon?" Paul proceeded.

"He said he was mad Joe was dead. That he gave him them bottles of whiskey from Mr. Moschella over there. He said he hated Mr. Moschella. He said Mr. Moschella was to blame for Joe being dead."

"Objection, Your Honor, speculation," Sandoval said.

"Not offered for the truth . . ."

"Overruled."

"Did he say anything else to you?"

Brandon looked up at Judge Ortiz. "Do I really have to answer that, sir?"

"You do, son."

"He said he hated . . ." Brandon looked out at his mother. "I don't want to say this, Mom. But that 'damn bitch lawyer for the Holts.' And . . ."

"And?"

Sophia sat proudly—the badge of bitch, as any female litigator knew, meant she had scored, touched a nerve in what had been and still was too often a man's world.

"Answer the question, Mr. Gallo." Judge Ortiz was in for no dithering.

"And . . . he was glad that dead lawyer hit at him with that case thing . . . because . . . because Moss tripped him on purpose and pushed him into that cement planter that day after the depositions."

Brandon looked down and wiped away tears. "I'm sorry. I'm sorry. But that's what he said."

In the courtroom's startled silence, Theresa, who was beyond alert, leaped to her feet.

"Objection and move to strike, Your Honor. That is clearly irrelevant to this case and is unquestionably more prejudicial than probative."

Paul, horrified at this revelation, was battling to keep the truth about Eddie's death—poor Eddie, their volatile but brilliant associate—in this court record.

"Your Honor, it shows bias and prejudice on the part of Mr. Grimick and demonstrates a motive for him to lie on the stand. That clearly goes to his credibility."

"This is a closer call for me, Mr. Viola. But I agree with you. Objections overruled, motion to strike denied."

Chastened, Sandoval sat back down.

"Anything further, Mr. Viola?"

"Just some cleanup questions, Your Honor. Brandon, have you told me everything you can recall about your conversation with Mr. Grimick the day he testified here in the case?"

Looking down, Brandon slowly replied, "Yeah . . . yes."

"Have you spoken to him on any other occasion about anything relating to the case, again, outside the presence of any attorney for Sports Gear USA?"

"No."

"Have you spoken to anyone other than Mr. Grimick about this case, with the same limitation, outside the presence of any attorney for Sports Gear USA?"

"No, I haven't. I haven't. I promise." Tears began to stream down his cheeks.

"No further questions, Your Honor."

Theresa wanted to do a redirect to try to rehabilitate Brandon with the jury. The bombshell about Grimick was bad. It was all bad. She thought of asking Brandon whether he thought Grimick was telling the truth about Eddie Herrera's death, or whether Joe Spangler was just bragging. But she knew two things. First, Viola would object on the grounds she was asking him to speculate, and that objection would be sustained. Second, it would just reinforce that testimony in the minds of the jurors.

She looked at Moschella and, on a legal pad, wrote, "No redirect. More harm than good. Agreed?"

Moschella nodded.

"Counsel for the defense, any redirect?"

"No, Your Honor."

"Very well. Mr. Gallo, you are excused."

Brandon wiped his eyes. He wanted to run out of the courtroom. Instead, he walked out with slumped shoulders, looking at the floor. His parents trailed behind him.

"Will the defense please call its next witness?"

"We have none, Your Honor." The dark expression on Ortiz's face did not escape Moschella's notice. "The defense rests."

"Ms. Christopoulos, do you want to call any witnesses in rebuttal?"

Sophia stood slowly and proudly. "No, Your Honor."

"Very well. It's eleven. We'll take a fifteen-minute recess. When we return, we'll address whether counsel intend to make closing arguments and, if so, their form and duration. I expect to see everyone here promptly at eleven-fifteen. Maybe we can get this case to the jury before we adjourn for the day."

They all stood as the judge passed into his chambers.

"Come on," Sophia said. "Let's get up to the library. Ben's exclusive is out. Those guys won't know what hit them. As if what happened here with Gallo wasn't enough."

"Well, they'll get the next haymaker when we drop our

motions on them." Paul was still reeling from the testimony about Eddie. They would avenge him. He deserved that much.

Beth and Wallace followed them to the elevators.

⌘

# CHAPTER 86

## The Devil Never Takes a Break

*"Audiences like to see the bad guys get their comeuppance."*
-Charles Bronson

Moschella's group started up the stairs for the library. Suddenly, Kemper's cell rang.

"Hold on. It's Wade and Em." Kemper stopped the ascent. "What? Found out what?"

Kemper listened to the president and the general counsel of Sports Gear and then turned accusingly to Moschella and Sandoval. "Did you know that Jackson and his lawyers have engaged in unethical and criminal conduct—attempted murder, witness tampering, bribery—in this case?"

"Wait. What? No," Moschella said. "Of course not. Why . . ."

"What documents?" Kemper cut Moschella off and listened as Wade screamed loudly enough on the phone that all three of them could hear him. "But I helped put them together. So did you, Em. We gave everything to Jackson's firm. Jackson said he produced it all. I didn't withhold any documents they requested. One second."

Moschella and Sandoval looked inquiringly at Kemper.

"Check the Internet . . . the news. It's bad. If it's true, we're in real trouble."

"Hold on." Moschella took out his cellphone, as did Sandoval. They read the damning story as Kemper continued his conversation with Bruckner and Booth.

Moschella paled when he saw the revelations that had apparently originated with a Jackson, Hood & Lee employee, Joshua Dreyfus. Among many other things, he implicated Ambrose Pickett in Spangler's death. Moschella dreaded going back in front of Judge Ortiz.

As Sandoval flipped screens on the Internet, a cold rage infused her. The so-called lawyers who had treated both her and Tony like rubbish, and her like a sex toy to amuse themselves, were essentially criminals. She didn't care about winning the case anymore. She wanted to bring down Jackson and the serfs who did his bidding to make them pay for what they had done to her personally, to their client, to Tony, and even to the poor Holts.

"I agree, Wade . . . Em, I understand." Kemper's face was red and contorted. "I have my marching orders. Let me tell our Bakersfield lawyers. Thank heavens they weren't involved. I'll see if I can get us out of this mess somehow."

He hung up and turned to Moschella and Sandoval.

"This exclusive by this Ben Kowrilsky guy nails Jackson and his firm. Ethical breaches, license-threatening conduct . . . even criminal accusations, all backed up with documentation and verified or verifiable facts. Wade and Emeline are in orbit."

"We saw on the Internet," Moschella replied. "We only have a few minutes until we have to be back in court."

"Jackson and his people have screwed us big-time. We have to distance ourselves from them at all costs. I have full authority over this case now. Wade and Em want to work out a settlement with the Holts before this thing goes to the jury or something worse comes out."

"I agree." Moschella could say little else. "That's the only reasonable course of action."

"Why would the Holts settle if they and their lawyers know about this?" Theresa wanted the case to end as much as anyone, but her keen mind was still working in overdrive.

"I bet they knew last night, if not before," Kemper said.

"What does it matter?" Moschella was as dejected as he had ever been in his life. "They have the upper hand. Gallo killed us with the jury. The Holts may well insist on a jury verdict. Now that I think about it, their lawyers could do something even worse."

Kemper, himself a lawyer, and Sandoval both had a very good idea what he meant.

"They can move for sanctions—including the ultimate one." Moschella was thinking out loud.

"You mean . . ." Theresa didn't want to say it.

"Yes, terminating sanctions, the worst of all possible worlds," Moschella said. "Let's get back to the courtroom. We need to ask the judge for a recess. Perhaps we can find a way out of this nightmare."

"What about Jackson?" Kemper asked. "He and his minions could be on the run by now."

"Jubal, I can try to get the Bakersfield police to keep him from leaving the building, and if he has, to catch up with him and the rest of them at the Padre Hotel."

"Do it."

As they went back down the stairs, Moschella called his contact in the Bakersfield PD, who sprung into action in the courthouse and at the hotel. He had also seen the news reports. Moschella texted a link to Jackson's law firm's website, which would give the police pictures of Jackson and the other Denver lawyers for any manhunt that might occur.

"How much are we going to offer as a settlement?" Theresa asked.

"You mean if Christopoulos gives us the chance," Kemper said. "That woman is a shark. She'll go for terminating sanctions. Just wait and see."

\* \* \*

During the recess, Sophia's team and the Holts took the elevator to the third-floor law library. The tumult outside on the lawns and walkways along Truxtun was filtering inside the courthouse. They spotted Moschella, Sandoval, and Kemper in a desperate, animated confab on the stairs with their consternation and disarray evident.

In the library, Sophia and her team read Ben's exclusive on their cells. They showed the Holts. Ben's bomb had been dropped— dropped all over the Internet and the major mainstream media outlets. It was even bigger than they had been led to believe. Dreyfus had revealed misconduct at Jackson, Hood & Lee going far beyond the Holt case. He had exposed the involvement of their other gun clients in illegal activities, and the active participation of even more lawyers at the Denver firm.

"He nailed them," Paul said.

"Oh, he did way more than that." Sophia almost cackled.

Beth stood listening, this time realizing this was all positive without having to ask. Wallace sat alone, anticipating and planning his impending freedom.

Sophia, Paul, Tricia, and Bryce launched into an intense conversation about strategies and scenarios. They had to plan their moves and countermoves with a real eye to maximizing the monetary outcome now.

Sophia called Derek and Rona to make sure they had watched Ben's broadcast and to briefly update them on what they were filing. Both had indeed seen the news and were obviously gratified but petulantly reiterated that only they could authorize news stories. Sophia let it go. Given Derek's prior betrayal with Chang, that was a nonstarter in her book—ever.

The motion? Derek and Rona conceded it was genius.

* * *

When Kemper, Moschella, and Sandoval arrived at the courtroom, four Bakersfield police officers were posted at the door with jaws set and eyes cold. They nodded at Moschella.

"Jackson's still here?" Sandoval whispered, surprised.

"He sure is," Moschella said.

As the trio entered, they saw Jackson in his seat. He appeared relaxed and was on his cell. Kemper motioned to him to join them, but he didn't move. He considered himself above whatever Kemper might have to say to him.

This time, Sophia's team and the Holts were the first to arrive and seated at the table.

The bulging courtroom was full of excited chatter about the news. The bailiff called it to order and then threatened to empty the gallery if everyone didn't quiet down.

There was silence.

"All rise."

Judge Ortiz took the bench. "Bailiff, can you bring in the . . ."

Moschella spoke. "Your Honor, if it please the court, before the jury returns can we speak to you in chambers along with plaintiffs' counsel about an urgent matter in the case?"

"Certainly, Mr. Moschella." Judge Ortiz's tone was neutral, his visage firm and commanding.

Sophia's group reveled in their new power as they watched the interchange.

Ortiz would have been surprised had Moschella not made his request. His clerk and bailiff had alerted him to the breaking news during the short recess.

Kemper whispered in Moschella's ear.

"One other thing, Your Honor. We would request that you direct Mr. Thomas Jackson, chief outside counsel for Sports Gear USA, to join us. He is sitting in the courtroom and has been the principal attorney supervising the defense of this case."

Jackson stood.

"While the court has no jurisdiction over me, and I have never appeared as counsel of record, I need no direction from the court to do what is in the best interests of my client."

"Come forward then." Ortiz maintained his neutrality with effort. "Bailiff, please ask the jurors to stay in the jury room while the court addresses some administrative matters."

He held up his hand.

"One second. Mr. Moschella, any time estimate for the meeting in chambers?"

"I don't know, Your Honor."

"Then since it's almost lunchtime, bailiff, please tell the jury we're taking an early lunch due to necessary court business, and order them some lunch so that they can remain in the courthouse. We'll resume at one-thirty. Empty the courtroom, too."

The spectators grumbled on the way out, deprived of the drama that they thought they were entitled to witness.

The lawyers for the two sides went into the judge's chambers.

Kemper joined them, but Sophia did not bring the Holts. The chambers session would be heavily legal and technical. Beth, in particular, would be an unnecessary distraction.

⌘

# CHAPTER 87

## This Cat Has Claws

*"The minute you think you've got it made,
disaster is just around the corner."*
-Joe Paterno

"Mr. Moschella, you have the floor. My court reporter will record the proceedings here."

"Thank you, Your Honor. Sports Gear would like to request that the court continue the trial until Monday. Because of certain unanticipated developments, my client wants to explore settlement with plaintiffs and Ms. Christopoulos once more."

"A bit late in the case and early in the day for that, isn't it, Mr. Moschella? We have the whole afternoon yet. I have a full docket with other litigants waiting their turn. Why should these jurors waste more of their lives idling while you pirouette around with plaintiffs' counsel—as charming as she may be?"

Sophia could not resist a smile.

"Haven't you people already tried and failed to settle this case?" Judge Ortiz continued, looking pointedly at Sophia. "And gone through a 'transformative' mediation?"

"We have, Your Honor. But circumstances have changed."

"I'm quite aware of that. Ms. Christopoulos?"

"I don't think a continuance is called for, Your Honor. This is my colleague, Tricia Manning. She has already appeared before you in pretrial motions and has been assisting with this case. And this is our associate, Mr. Bryce McLaughlin, whom you have already seen during the arguments on the motions *in limine* and on the stand."

Tricia handed the three-quarter-inch set of motion papers to the judge and gave a copy each to Kemper, Moschella, Sandoval, and Jackson. They all began to flip through them.

"What is this, Ms. Christopoulos?" Judge Ortiz asked.

"A motion for terminating sanctions, contempt, monetary sanctions and, in the alternative, for a mistrial, Your Honor. The bulk of the papers are supporting exhibits. The points and authorities and accompanying declaration get to the heart of the matter. The declarant, Joshua Dreyfus, and his lawyer are available at his lawyer's office on standby, with a court reporter, if we need to contact them for any reason, including live testimony."

"Well, Mr. Moschella, take this as a lesson in efficiently drafting a succinct motion as compared to your absurd stack of motions *in limine*. I'll have to review this, Ms. Christopoulos, and I suspect Mr. Moschella will need some time to do that as well. But I won't delay the trial. I intend to dispose of this before I charge the jury."

"Your Honor," Sophia said. "If I may be heard briefly. With all due respect, plaintiffs submit that Sports Gear and its counsel have lost any right to present a closing argument or to have the merits of this case decided by a jury. My clients face extreme and unjustified prejudice if you allow that. If you grant terminating sanctions as we request, liability is automatic. Legal authority on point and the reasons for doing so are set out in our memorandum of points and authorities."

"This is very irregular, Ms. Christopoulos. You obviously had these papers ready when Mr. Gallo testified this morning. Why didn't you present them before that?"

"He was a key witness, as Your Honor no doubt gathered, and we needed his testimony on the record as a precaution in the event you don't grant our motion, even though we believe the law mandates that you do. In addition, we are fully cognizant of and sensitive to the fact that Your Honor does not look favorably on delays in your courtroom."

Sophia delivered her last sentence with a straight face. The judge couldn't keep one himself.

"You have me on that one, Ms. Christopoulos. Very well. I'll consider these papers now. I want all of you to wait in my courtroom while I do. I'll call you back into chambers when I'm ready. Oh, and should you need it, one side can use the small conference room adjacent to my courtroom during that time."

"Your Honor, Sports Gear is entitled to submit a written response. We'll object to any decision the court makes otherwise," Moschella argued.

"I understand your position. We'll see. In view of these latest developments, Mr. Moschella, it might indeed behoove you and your client to talk settlement with Ms. Christopoulos and the plaintiffs while I consider what has been given to me here."

Jackson had said nothing during the entire proceeding.

The two groups left the judge's chambers. Sophia and her colleagues returned to their table in the empty courtroom where the Holts were sitting. Kemper, Moschella, Sandoval, and Jackson took the judge up on his offer, and the bailiff showed them to the small conference room where they could talk without being overheard.

\* \* \*

Theresa sat at the table and went over the motion while the cocks postured and fought.

"More settlement talks, Moschella?" Jackson had built his reputation on crushing plaintiffs, not settling with them. "You don't have any settlement authority. Neither does Kemper here."

"That's where you're wrong, Jackson." Kemper kept his voice low, but his tone was threatening, assured, and left no room for doubt. "I have specific authority from Wade and Emeline to take charge of this case, effective immediately. You have no remaining role whatsoever except what I decree. Understood?"

"I don't believe you. You're just a front, the appealing face of Sports Gear I always place at the table for trials."

"Call them, if you actually believe that and if you dare, you smug, lying, unethical pile of manure."

"You want to get your own ass sued, Kemper? Keep it up." Jackson was aggressive to the last.

"Have you seen the news, Jackson?"

"Oh, that? I have. Lies. All lies. Complete fabrications."

Kemper held up the Holt motion papers. "The exhibits to Dreyfus's declaration prove what he says. They came from your firm, where he worked."

"I can't stop him from breaching the confidentiality agreement he signed with us. He's a thief. And because he's a thief, he's a liar. He stole documents from our computer files and altered them. He disclosed confidential attorney work product and attorney-client communications. It's all going to be inadmissible. We'll sue him and get the Denver district attorney to put him behind bars."

"You wish," Moschella said. "That declaration includes evidence of planned future criminal conduct by people in your 'joint' as well. I can't call it a law firm in fairness to *real* law firms. That so-called confidentiality agreement and noises about theft won't stop what's going to come down on your head. They'll bring in the feds. The U.S Attorney is not in anyone's pocket. You're going down, whatever hooks you have in the Denver D.A. office."

"We'll see."

"Stop, please," Sandoval said, barely able to tolerate her physical proximity to Jackson. "I've read their motion papers."

"Do you think we can beat them?" Kemper asked.

"The terminating sanctions maybe, but that's not at all certain given Judge Ortiz's predilections. The other parts of the motion . . . we lose. Not even close."

"What do you mean?" Jackson sneered. "You're a babe in the woods. You think your looks make you some kind of genius? You don't know what you're talking about here. You haven't tried cases before."

"She's a better trial lawyer than you ever were or will be, Jackson," Moschella snapped. "Don't think what happened last night is done and forgotten either."

"What's that?" Kemper started to ask, but Moschella had not finished with Jackson.

"I'll go further than Ms. Sandoval did, Jackson. The terminating sanctions request may be a stretch, but it's a stretch you can bet Judge Ortiz will make. I know him and he hates unethical conduct, let alone all the rest of what's in there. Take your blinders off. He thinks we're dirty. All of us. Sorry, Jubal, but even Sports

Gear and yourself. We're all tarred by what Jackson and his lackeys have done here."

"I am . . ."

"Shut up, Jackson." Kemper silenced Jackson's feigned indignation. "It's my decision now. We're not going to ask to file any opposition unless we have no other option. We're going to settle. Right here. Right now."

"You guys are running scared. Just play the game out. The jury is with us." Jackson was boiling with misplaced indignation, born of the always dangerous combination of arrogance, ignorance, and greed.

Kemper made a quick call to Bruckner and Booth. He motioned Moschella over and told him Sports Gear's starting point and upper limits. They rejoined Sandoval and Jackson.

"Go ahead, Tony, ask Ms. Christopoulos if we can talk to her and the Holts. We have to face reality and fix your clusterfuck, Jackson."

"What you're about to do is the clusterfuck. We're winning with the jury. That's all that counts. Ever. Winning."

"You're an arrogant idiot, Jackson. And one Sports Gear intends to ignore. As far as any 'legal' advice you offer is concerned. But don't worry. We won't ignore you altogether."

"Is that a threat?"

"Oh, no. Not at all. A promise. One you can take to the bank."

Jackson frowned but held his tongue.

\* \* \*

At their counsel table, Sophia's team was animatedly analyzing Sports Gear's likely next move. Beth and Wallace listened but couldn't really follow the discussion. They just hoped it would end and end well—for them.

"Quiet, they're back in the courtroom," Bryce warned.

⌘

# CHAPTER 88

## No Time Like the Present

*"The harder the conflict the more glorious the triumph."*
-Thomas Paine

After Moschella's group returned to the defense table, he walked over to Sophia at the plaintiffs' table.

"Ms. Christopoulos, my client wants to talk settlement."

Sophia looked up at Moschella with a sardonic smile. "That's prudent. If you're serious this time."

From the look on her face, Moschella knew he was in for a tough negotiation. "At my table?"

"Mr. Viola and I will join you there." The Holts were both unpredictable and were better excluded for the time being. "Lead on."

"Let's do this if we can. And may I say, Ms. Christopoulos, along with my client and Ms. Sandoval, I deeply regret what Jackson and his people appear to have done. Regardless of how everything turns out. We lawyers in Bakersfield don't do those things, certainly none I know and certainly not at my firm."

"That may be, Mr. Moschella, but you knew from the Spangler and Grimick testimony that some awfully shady things were going on, if not with your client, then certainly with the handling of the witnesses in this case. And from what I can see, you did whatever Jackson told you to do."

"I had to protect my client." Moschella was embarrassed. "I didn't breach any ethical canons, though."

"We needn't debate that. For the moment." Sophia turned the negotiation screw tighter.

Moschella bridled at the phrase "for the moment" but did not react. He deserved it in some ways—in many ways.

\* \* \*

At the defense table, Jackson was sullen, Kemper grim, and Sandoval quiet with controlled churning anger. Brief greetings and introductions were made again all around. Jackson shook no one's hand. No one offered to shake his either.

"Ms. Christopoulos, Mr. Viola," Kemper said. "As Sports Gear's designated representative here, I have full authority to engage in settlement discussions on its behalf and resolve this matter between us if we can."

"We appreciate that, Mr. Kemper," Paul replied. "From past discussions and in view of these most recent developments, you need to understand that another nuisance offer won't be considered."

"Try that, and we'll press our motion," Sophia emphasized.

"Understood." Moschella stepped in, conscious of the time pressures. "Sports Gear is prepared to offer your clients four million dollars to settle this case. But it has to be now."

Jackson exploded. "That's an outrage. That's what they demanded in their initial letter. That stupid kid isn't worth a cent. Neither are the clueless parents who raised that fool."

Beth and Wallace heard Jackson. She cried. Wallace slowly stood and glared at Jackson across the courtroom, thunder in his eyes. Tricia and Bryce made him sit down and tried to calm them both.

"Shut up, Jackson, you disgusting prick. Look at the Holts. They heard you. That won't help settle this disaster, or rather your disaster." Kemper was not about to take any more nonsense from Jackson. "I'm truly sorry about that outburst. Will you take our offer to your clients, Ms. Christopoulos?"

\* \* \*

As they walked back to their table, Paul whispered to Sophia, "We get to watch that circus and now we have four million dollars to boot."

"When I wrote my initial memo to bring in this case, my anticipated settlement range was between eight hundred thousand to two million. I was being more than optimistic." Sophia was still processing. "I never dreamt of a settlement like this, even though that was our original demand. A jury verdict, maybe, but not a settlement."

"Jackson's little tantrum should be worth another half mil, don't you think?"

"We'd better text Derek and Rona first."

They did. Predictably, Derek and Rona wanted more—needed more. The firm was now deep in the red with the credit line and credit card debt. They had cut their own draws to nothing, had maxed out their own credit cards, and were using Rona's mother as a bank. Collections were slow on the new billable matters. A settlement of four million—after taking care of the firm's current expenses, its past-due expense bills on the Holt case, and reimbursing the Holts for what they had already paid in costs and expert fees—would mean Krause & White's share would barely break a million. That would only give them a few months to get other cases going, with no room for growth. Sophia and Paul understood—they had to squeeze every last cent out of Sports Gear, and get the Holts to hang in there until they did.

Back at their table, all eyes were on them as they sat.

"No one react in any way during this discussion, please," Sophia said. "It's only round one."

"They've given us a high number, but they can do much better, and they will," Paul added. "Don't forget we all have expenses, and there could be tax issues."

"Well, what is it?" Bryce said.

"I'm going to repeat myself. No one react. I want your best poker faces. I mean it," Sophia whispered. "It's four million."

"We're going to accept, aren't we?" Wallace kept his expression bland, but he glowed. He could not take it any longer. He wanted out yesterday.

"We can get more," Beth was dry-eyed and cold. "I see it in your eyes."

Beth spooked Sophia. She was a chameleon, a manipulator, and ferociously avaricious.

"To be honest, yes, we can. Jackson's indefensible and offensive comments are worth a good chunk more, and the motion we filed is very strong. If Judge Ortiz grants it, this case will go straight to a very sympathetic jury on one issue: damages. They could go very high on the portion of the general damages award relating to your emotional distress, in order to punish Sports Gear, even though they aren't supposed to consider that as a factor. Our counter should be substantial."

Wallace was reluctant to take a chance and risk losing the offer they had. Beth wasn't.

"Go for it. I hate all of them. Mike wasn't worthless. He was my life. He was golden. They don't respect him, his memory, or us. What number, do you think?"

Paul took the lead. "That's easy, Beth. Double. Eight million. It's a lot more than we demanded and more than we asked for in general damages in our complaint, but as I said, this jury could return a very big number for you. They're all running scared at that table—except Jackson. He mystifies me."

"Not me." Bryce was sure of himself. "He's a certifiable berserker. He's been lucky up to now. No longer."

"You really think Sports Gear would agree to that, Sophia?" Wallace was focused on the figure Paul had thrown out. He wasn't so eager to quit if that was a realistic target.

"No harm in asking." She wasn't being entirely honest. Sports Gear could reject the counteroffer and withdraw all offers if it found their huge counter insulting.

Wallace looked around the table, turning last to Beth. She nodded. Very slowly, he did the same.

* * *

The discussion had taken all of four minutes. Sophia signaled to Moschella that she and Paul were ready. He waved them over.

"We've discussed your offer with our clients, Mr. Kemper," Sophia said. "Unfortunately, it's too low."

"What?" Moschella couldn't believe it. "I know at least one of your clients seemed eager to settle for a lot less than that a while ago."

"'A while ago' is the operative phrase. Jackson's despicable remarks made things much worse. At this stage, if Judge Ortiz grants our motion, which we believe he will, this case will go to the jury solely on the issue of damages. They'll be outraged at all they have heard."

"Well, they don't know about the news," Moschella rejoined.

"Oh, come on. Are you willing to bet your client's fate on that? We all know they watch the news and talk to their friends. Don't forget what happened with Gallo this morning. This jury could go to town on the emotional distress component, and their award would stand up on appeal. Plus, the judge could easily impose severe monetary sanctions on Sports Gear and its attorneys on top of that, making the number that much larger with your client, you, Jackson, and your firms having to pay."

"Do you have a counter, Ms. Christopoulos? I can't read your mind or your clients' minds after all." Kemper was conciliatory but a bit impatient. They were in no position to let things degenerate further.

"I do. It's a fair number, but more importantly, it's our number. Eight million."

Jackson's face reddened, and he started to speak. Moschella raised his hand to Jackson in warning. Sandoval had astonishment written across her face. Kemper seemed strangely unfazed.

"I'll have to speak with my bosses, Ms. Christopoulos. I have authority, but not that kind."

"Can you reach them? If not, we should just see what Judge Ortiz wants to do with our motion." Sophia was unrelenting. It was no time to soften.

"I can, and I will. They're waiting to hear from me."

"Very well. We'll leave you to it."

Jackson started to object once again, but Kemper drew his hand across his throat—a menacing gesture, universally recognized. Moschella, too, felt he had to offer an objection and was about to do that, but seeing him prepare to speak, Sandoval tapped him lightly on the arm and shook her head. He remained mute.

* * *

Kemper went into the hall and got Bruckner and Booth on a conference call with his cell.

"Okay. I understand. Let's see if this works and then talk about what comes next."

He came back in and signaled to Sophia. It had been a little over five minutes.

"Here goes." Sophia and Paul marched across the courtroom again.

"Well, Mr. Kemper?" Sophia was curious but without any great expectations.

"Sports Gear will pay your clients 7.7 million dollars. We will go no higher. But there are some conditions. We have to enter the settlement on the record, here in court, and before Judge Ortiz does anything with your motion. In addition, that settlement record has to be sealed. Mr. Moschella's firm will be responsible for preparing a very short settlement document. The amount has to be kept confidential, but nothing else."

Sophia and Paul wanted to scream and dance and laugh—but didn't.

"Mr. Kemper," Sophia said. "My clients said eight million, and that's an odd number and below our demand. Do you care to share why you picked it?"

"I do not, Ms. Christopoulos. What I can tell you is that it is in good faith and has some significance to Sports Gear and to me. We believe it is more than generous. It is also our last, best, and final offer."

"Very well. I'll convey your new offer and your conditions to my clients."

\* \* \*

Sophia and Paul sauntered calmly across the courtroom as their minds did cartwheels and their hearts beat out of their chests. As litigation veterans, they knew how the game was played, and they played it very well.

Before saying anything, they sat down. After the ordeal of this case, Sophia felt she was entitled to some fun. She put on her "solemn" face.

"Oh, God." Wallace's face fell.

"Tell us," Beth said.

"Sports Gear didn't withdraw its offer," Sophia said. "They still want to settle, but with some conditions."

"What are they?" Tricia couldn't stand it anymore.

"We have to enter the settlement on the record, here in court . . . now. They want the record sealed, and the settlement amount has to remain confidential."

"So, they'll still give us the four million, nothing else, and only if we agree to the conditions?" Beth was disappointed.

"Sophia, tell them, or I will." Paul couldn't contain himself any longer. "It's not binding until it's on the record. No one react again, okay? Let's bring this one home."

They all nodded.

"Sports Gear will not pay more than . . . 7.7 million dollars," Paul whispered. "That's their offer. There won't be another one."

Wallace and Beth were stunned. Wallace nearly fainted. He was going to gain his freedom from this woman who had abandoned him in the house fire for her son's precious things. Beth was thinking of the wonderful new home she and Wallace would buy somewhere far, far away from Bakersfield.

They looked at Sophia. Beth spoke in a shaky voice. "You have to take it, Sophia. So much money. Wallace?"

"Yes. For God's sake, yes. Tell them we'll take the deal, conditions and all."

Sophia turned to her opponents and gave them an affirmative nod of her head, then turned back to her own tablemates. Sandoval and Moschella stood, stricken and defeated, and Jackson just shook his head, cursing under his breath.

At that moment, about a quarter to one, the bailiff announced, "Judge Ortiz wants all of you back in his chambers, now."

* * *

In chambers, Ortiz sat coldly eyeing the Sports Gear attorneys and Kemper. His court reporter was at the ready sitting next to his desk.

"Mr. Jackson, words cannot convey my reaction to what I have read in these moving papers. And Mr. Moschella, I am very disappointed in you as well. I find it hard to believe you and your firm were unaware of the egregious, unethical, and criminal conduct set forth in these papers."

"Please, Your Honor, believe that we were not aware of any of this. We were representing our client as vigorous advocates, which our Rules of Professional Responsibility require, but my firm and I broke no rules, violated no canon of ethics, and certainly committed no crimes. With your indulgence, can I ask you to wait before going further?"

"What else do you have to say to try to exculpate yourself or Mr. Jackson here, Mr. Moschella? Or to protect your client from its apparent bad choices in attorneys? It had better be good."

"Nothing like that, Your Honor. I wanted to state, on the record, that Sports Gear and Mr. and Mrs. Holt have reached a settlement."

The judge was torn. He had in mind something far more draconian than a settlement. Before him were lawyers who needed to be disciplined and, in the case of Jackson and his co-conspirator colleagues, disbarred and prosecuted. However, those matters, to his great regret, were not before him.

"Am I to know the terms of the settlement, or are you going to draft an agreement outside the court to confirm something you have agreed to verbally here?"

"We want to put the settlement on the record, Your Honor, and plaintiffs and their counsel have agreed that this part of the record may be sealed and the settlement number kept confidential."

"I'm troubled, Mr. Moschella. That deprives the public, and particularly this jury, of information I believe they deserve and have earned the right to know."

"There won't be a settlement otherwise, Your Honor."

"Ms. Christopoulos, I think your clients should join us."

The judge pressed his intercom and asked the bailiff to bring in the Holts.

He did, with Wallace hobbling in pain from his arthritis as he pushed Beth in her wheelchair with her oxygen. The judge saw how spent, how emotionally drained they were from this ordeal—by what had happened to their son and to them. Inwardly, he sighed. It was definitely against his better instincts, but he could not put these poor people through any more pain.

"Mr. and Mrs. Holt, I'm advised that you have agreed to settle your lawsuit with Sports Gear. I want to be sure you fully understand the consequences and that you truly want to do this. You understand the jury will not decide the case, correct?"

"We do, Your Honor," they both replied.

"And that is what you want?"

"Yes, both of us," Wallace replied.

"Mrs. Holt for the record."

"Yes, Your Honor."

"Then let's proceed."

The lawyers for the respective parties put the agreement on the record, and Beth and Wallace both acknowledged their acceptance of it and all of its conditions.

"I hereby direct the court reporter to prepare a transcript of this settlement we have recorded and send copies to Mr. Moschella and Ms. Christopoulos. A copy is also to be filed in the record of this case, but under seal."

"Yes, Your Honor." The court reporter responded.

Sophia looked over at the judge's ornate grandfather clock. The hands were at one, and the clock's single chime was a fitting coda to their long ordeal.

⌘

# CHAPTER 89

## The Heavy Hand

*"Punishment is justice for the unjust."*
-St. Augustine

As they left the courtroom, Kemper confronted Jackson.

"Jackson, you need to come back to Mr. Moschella's offices with us. We have things to discuss."

"I don't think so, *Mr.* Kemper. After all, as you said, you're the man in charge. And this case is done. Badly done."

"Not quite. You're still our chief outside counsel. By written retainer agreement. For now. As your client, I expect you there. In thirty minutes. Don't be late."

\* \* \*

Moschella, Kemper, and Sandoval drove back to the Stockdale Tower together.

"Jubal, where did that settlement number come from?" Tony was more than curious.

"Wade, Emeline, and I wanted to send a message. Not to the Holts, but to Jackson, Hood & Lee. I suspect Jackson received the message. If not, he will soon enough."

"Excuse me?" Theresa was clueless.

"That number is almost exactly the amount we have paid them in legal fees over the past three years."

"Does that mean what I think it does?"

"That we intend to make them pay the settlement, not us? By all means. They're dirty. Their lack of ethics—hell, their crimes—

put us where we are. They broke it, they own it. We'll sue them if they don't. You can be sure we'll be reporting all of this to the Colorado Bar Association and the pertinent governmental authorities there too."

Tony gave a sidelong and relieved glance at Theresa as they parked. There was no mention of going after Moschella or his firm. The three of them went up to their offices.

After getting coffee, they waited in the conference room that had seen too much of this case. It was now empty of every trace of Jackson and his coterie. What they didn't take was boxed and stored.

They wondered whether Jackson would appear. They each doubted it.

* * *

To their surprise, he did and on time.

Kemper looked at him with undisguised contempt. "Jackson, I have two people on the speakerphone here who want a few words with you."

"Jackson, are you there?"

He recognized the voice of Wade Buckner, Sports Gear USA's president, and his close friend and client for years.

"I'm here, Wade."

"That's Mr. Buckner to you now. Ms. Booth is on the phone with me. We'll make this brief."

"Hi, Emeline."

"You know that settlement we reached today?" Wade asked.

"You mean the blackmail you paid . . . that ridiculous amount?"

"Does that number resonate with you at all, Jackson?"

"I sure does. It's highway robbery. That's how it resonates. Moschella's turned you soft. He's a coward and a fool. We had the jury. Even if those terminating sanctions were granted, the jury wouldn't have awarded those dumb old farts damages anywhere close to what you handed them without a fight."

"Ignorant to the end, denying reality to the end," Buckner said. "I should have seen that in you and your firm long ago."

Booth spoke up. "That number, Jackson, is what we've paid your firm in legal fees the last three years . . . give or take a couple of hundred dollars."

Jackson turned ashen, but his expression was unchanged. He wasn't going to show any fear to these cretins. "Interesting. You chose that number because . . . ?"

This time, Buckner answered. "Because Sports Gear isn't paying a cent to the Holts, Jackson. You and your firm are."

"No way in hell."

"If you don't," Emeline said, "we'll file an immediate lawsuit against you for professional malpractice and breaches of your fiduciary duties. We won't be looking at just getting your fees for the last three years disgorged. We'll seek punitive damages. We'll get them, too."

"We're not paying."

"Oh, but you are," Buckner said. "When we hang up, which we're about to do, you're going to call the other two name partners at your firm, Patrick Lee and George Hood. We've already spoken with them. I know the three of you are your firm's executive committee and have total power over its finances. You three will have a signed agreement to pay the settlement to the Holts on behalf of Sports Gear on my desk in an hour, as an email attachment, with a copy to Tony Moschella, and the original to me."

"Lee and Hood will never agree to that."

"For your sake, you'd better be wrong." The connection died.

Moschella could not hide the scorn in his voice. "You can call on your cell in our large conference room. We'll wait."

Jackson stormed out, slamming the door open against the wall.

\* \* \*

"What's your opinion, Jubal? Will they go for it?"

"I'm not sure, given how volatile, uncompromising, and corrupt Jackson is. Hood and Lee were taken by surprise, but they've had time to consider it now. Theresa, what do you think?"

"It's fifty-fifty."

"They would be wise to accept. Wade doesn't bluff. I'm sure he and Emeline already have another Denver law firm drafting a complaint as we sit here."

The three engaged in small talk for a while. Jubal assured Tony that Sports Gear wanted to keep him and the firm on as their local attorneys in Bakersfield for not just litigation but transactional work as well. Tony knew that was just idle talk. What other business would they have in Bakersfield?

"Your only mistake was not being more aggressive about taking control of the case, but that is as much or more my fault and Buckner's and Booth's. Jackson blustered and bullied his way past all of us." Kemper was sincere in those sentiments.

After thirty minutes, there was a loud knock on the door.

"Come in."

A defiant Jackson walked through the door, which he did not shut. Nor did he sit down.

"It's done. Those lily-livered punks back home outvoted me. No guts. None. You'll have the damn agreement in the next thirty minutes. It only takes two signatures of the name partners to be binding. They're signing it. I'm not."

Kemper had a parting gift for Jackson.

"Don't let us keep you. By the way, when you get back to Denver, have all of the files on all of our pending matters boxed up. Our new law firm there will need them."

"Oh, and the things you left here are stored," Moschella said. "You have one day to make arrangements or they are being tossed."

Jackson said nothing. He stalked out of the conference room. He did not look back.

⌘

# EPILOGUE

## Going Somewhere?

*"What separates the winners from the losers is how a person reacts to each new twist of fate."*
-Donald Trump

With the gun trial's hard-earned, life-altering, and life-taking contingency commission, Sophia's firm moved to large offices "uptown" in L.A.'s city center. Sophia furnished her well-deserved new corner office with a custom cherry suite and all the *accoutrements*.

The Ben-induced publicity about the Holt case had given Sophia, Paul, Tricia, and Bryce more than their fifteen minutes of fame and also more clients than they could handle. They were all now "rainmakers" and together held the controlling balance of power in the firm—financial power, the only power that mattered—though they never pulled a Derek, wielding it to intimidate and belittle. They believed in the firm's democratic bylaws and its original mission to help deserving plaintiffs.

Using scalpels forged by rigorous legal acumen, they became incisive slicers-and-dicers of corporate America—whether at home or offshore. They were dedicated to helping worthy people—the hurt and the helpless. The more they succeeded, the more the corporate oligarchy feared them. Justice was their ultimate mission.

They coveted finding a test case to take to the Justice Department that would establish criminal liability and long prison sentences for CEOs since the overreaching, corporation-coopted United States Supreme Court had deemed corporations to be "persons" and money to be "speech." They're still looking.

They also became adept at exposing and getting redress for the medical murders that occurred in hospitals around America every day—proving the old adage that doctors bury their mistakes, literally, in cemeteries.

As a firm, they all swore never to set foot in Bakersfield again. It was the easiest oath any of them had ever taken.

\* \* \*

Derek remained a firm leader focused on profitability and the bottom line. His efforts, now more equalized and less rabid, were appreciated because the survival of the firm meant the survival of its mission.

Bryce became an excellent litigator and soon had his own first-year associate to mentor. Although no one would ever forget Eddie, his untimely death allowed, or rather forced, Bryce to step up and become the incredible lawyer that had always been inside him.

Sophia was proud, but her parents were even prouder. Their daughter's name was in big print, on her business cards—business cards that now read "Krause, White & Christopoulos." They didn't understand the legal world's hierarchy, but they did understand what a name on a business card meant. The only people in their circles who could out-Greek them now were the parents of doctors, *yartrose*, and the parents of judges. Although, from what Sophia had learned about judges in her legal career, that was a questionable pecking order.

\* \* \*

Success, well-earned, deluged Ben Kowrilsky. He was now a national investigative reporter for CBT, with frequent guest anchor appearances on its national network broadcasts. He shared that success with Sophia, snaring her a plum prime-time gig as a nationally syndicated legal analyst every Wednesday night on CBT. The network execs said she had the "look" for the job. She knew what they really meant and didn't care. If her face sold her brain, that was fine with her.

Ben regularly asked Sophia to dinner. Sometimes she even went.

\* \* \*

Jay dumped the bland, generic, living-to-please-him blonde who spent his money and bored him beyond the point of sanity. He missed Tricia's intelligence, wit, sarcasm, loyalty, and incessant surprises—the charming and even, he had to admit, the irritating. He missed Sophia and Paul and their antics, too—and Steve, who was beyond retrieving.

Humbly, Jay again courted Tricia, resigning himself to the nature of her work and its demands. They married with Tricia's student loan almost paid off. Bright woman that she was, Tricia also learned to compromise, and actually managed to spend less time at the office.

Paul, still in love with Sophia, could find no one to equal, much less exceed her. Truthfully, he no longer looked. He couldn't let go but kept his feelings to himself. He was married to their work, which allowed him to be hers and her to be his in his mind. If that was all he could ever have, it would have to be enough.

Derek and Rona groused but yielded to Sophia's exchange of a share of her partner draw for a guaranteed partnership vote for Paul and Tricia the following year. Pounded into her equation for success, she had learned that billings and a client base meant power at small firms too—the only difference was when she gained that power, she used it as fairly as she could.

Peggy stayed on. She loved the firm's new dynamic, and there was no other place she would rather be.

Autumn had been unapologetic when she learned about her ex-boyfriend Stefan and irate that the firm had used her. She left for Willits, Colorado, where marijuana had been legalized and joined her symbiotic friends growing a high-quality herbal product.

Roxy applied to law school and had one acceptance, to the unaccredited California Barristers University in Redding, California—a fly-by-night federal-student-loan-sucking machine feeding on the hopes of the unqualified. Despite warnings from everyone, she earned a useless J.D., racked up lifelong debt, failed the California bar exam to get her license repeatedly, and had no real job prospects. She plans to take the bar again. However, in the mean time, she is working as a waitress at Shameless O'Leery's, a pub in Redding, and struggling to handle her student loan debt.

* * *

Wallace divorced Beth. His hatred of her had hardened, not only for her desertion and betrayal the night of the fire, but also because he now saw her for what she had always really been—an egocentric, grasping, greedy, and Oedipal mother. His love for her and the comforting routine of their home life had blinded him.

With his half of the huge settlement, Wallace put the few personal belongings he cared about in storage in San Francisco and embarked on Crystal Cruise Line's Crystal Serenity for its one-hundred-day Grand Pacific Panorama Cruise. He needed serenity after the nightmare of the previous two years. He booked a penthouse suite with a veranda. The pricey trip was a bargain in his eyes. Such a bargain that he signed up for the following three-month cruise to Rome and beyond in the same cabin. He didn't know whether he would ever stop cruising, but he did know he would never see Bakersfield or Beth again.

Beth, obtuse as ever, was shocked when Wallace announced he was divorcing her. Naturally, she spouted tears, but he was immoveable. She didn't understand because, in truth, she never had and had never tried to understand Wallace, his life, or his needs.

However, Beth did have one last thing in common with Wallace. Bakersfield was dead to her. Even before their home was sold and her divorce was final, she moved to Duluth, Minnesota, to live with her sister, a spinster set in her ways. They had never been close, but Beth's money changed that—they grew close enough for her sister to endure Beth's obsession with floral surroundings in the large elegant home Beth bought for the two of them on East 1st Street overlooking Lake Superior.

Beth fully recovered from the effects of the fire and Beth took to acquiring cats, unconcerned about her sister's allergies. She also acquired an entourage who helped her spend her money. In return they had only to worship Beth's sainted memories of Mike, loudly and often.

\* \* \*

The Holt fire arsonists were never caught. With the Holts gone from Bakersfield, the police made no pretense of investigating further. Nobody cared. Nobody, aside from the Holts, ever had.

Sports Gear USA's troubles multiplied after the Holt case settled. Within a month, it was named as a defendant in a huge class action in Virginia. A customer in its Falls Church store, accompanied by a disturbed friend, made an obvious "straw" purchase of a semi-automatic AR-15 assault rifle with a thousand rounds of ammunition. That disturbed friend went on a rampage in Arlington, Virginia, killing eighteen people and wounding another twenty-three before dying in a hail of police gunfire.

Sports Gear remained a national chain, despite the settlements, lawsuits, and setbacks. It had to close a number of its stores, reducing its payroll by over a thousand employees. Yet it remained stubborn in its refusal to adopt a code or tip sheet with suicide warning signs for its stores or to train its employees to spot potentially unstable or suicidal gun customers. It remained active in and supported the Retail Gun Sellers of America.

Among the stores Sports Gear closed was the one in Bakersfield, because of the negative publicity. Grimick and Davis were unceremoniously let go. However, Jubal Kemper helped Brandon Gallo, who was too young to condemn, get a transfer to the store in Missoula, Montana. Brandon took night classes at the university there but still aspired to sell guns.

Davis left Bakersfield and dropped from sight when Sports Gear closed its doors.

Grimick became a handyman but made his real money from illegal gun sales. One night, when Grimick and his girlfriend, Vera May, were partying at the Arden Vista trailer park in Oildale, the makeshift meth lab in an adjacent trailer blew up. It incinerated its owner and eight surrounding trailers and their occupants. The only evidence that Grimick and Vera May had ever existed was their charred remains. Grimick's landlord called the cops when he took possession of Grimick's grimy apartment to re-rent it. He found a huge cache of firearms, ammunition, and white supremacist and survivalist literature.

\* \* \*

Eddie Herrera's parents filed their own lawsuit in view of the trial testimony. But not against Sophia and her firm. Instead, they hired a two-man Bakersfield firm to sue Grimick, whose fiery death spared him having to answer civilly and criminally for his acts; Sports Gear, Grimick's employer; and the Stockdale Tower owners. They claimed negligence in Eddie's wrongful death and premises liability against the building's owners.

Thanks to the swift intercession of Quarry, Warren & Moschella, there was a quick and confidential settlement. Tony Moschella had set up a brilliant defense, and Theresa Sandoval used her common cultural background with Eddie's parents to keep the case from ballooning out of control. Eddie's parents weren't overjoyed with the settlement, but neither were any of the defendants. That is the norm in most lawsuit settlements, unlike the one in the Holt case.

\* \* \*

Tony Moschella stayed at his firm though his client base declined from all of the negative publicity generated by the Holt case. After Sports Gear closed its Bakersfield store, and despite Kemper's kind words to him, there had been, as Moschella had predicted, no further business for him from Sports Gear either.

Moschella filed a formal complaint with the Colorado State Bar Association against Tom Jackson and the other Denver lawyers who had invaded his law offices and his life. He included a copy of the terminating sanctions motion Sophia had filed with all its exhibits, legal authority, and proof. He honored Sandoval's wishes to keep Samuel French's sexual assault out of it.

Sports Gear joined in Moschella's formal complaint against the Jackson, Hood & Lee lawyers. It added charges of its own. It also quietly told all of the other gun manufacturers and retailers what had happened. In very short order, they all moved their business away from Jackson, Hood & Lee. Without those clients, and facing lawsuits from many other plaintiffs whose cases its lawyers had defeated by unethical and illegal tactics, the firm went under. It declared bankruptcy in an effort to protect itself and its partners from total ruin.

\* \* \*

Rose Boyd and Porter Beauregard received official reprimands from the Colorado State Bar and were each fined five thousand dollars. Boyd went back to the South, where her accent and demeanor were valued, joining a midsize insurance defense firm in Atlanta, Georgia. Beauregard, having had his fill of practicing law and Colorado, became a sales representative for Medtronic, a medical instruments company headquartered in Dublin, Ireland. He is its East Coast representative, working out of Morgantown, West Virginia.

Jackson, French, and Pickett were all disbarred and lost their licenses to practice law. Facing criminal prosecution, Jackson fled the United States before he could be arrested. He had untouchable and untraceable bank accounts in the Cayman Islands and Liechtenstein. He lived without concern in the villa with a private beach he had purchased as a precaution years before near Dubrovnik, Croatia. Croatia has no extradition treaty with the U.S. He remains free and as arrogant as ever, despite diplomatic efforts to bring him back to the U.S. for criminal prosecution.

French and Pickett were both criminally indicted for what they had done in the Holt case and others, including violating numerous federal statutes. They were ultimately convicted of multiple offenses in Colorado's federal district court, receiving ten-year sentences each from the Honorable Jason Booker. Their appeals failed, and they remain incarcerated in the Federal Correctional Institution in Englewood, Colorado.

\* \* \*

After the settlement in the Herrera lawsuit, Theresa Sandoval decided not to pursue claims against Samuel French, Jackson, Hood

& Lee, or her own firm for French's attack. She did not want her mother to know, and she did not want her father or brother to seek revenge via the contacts she knew they still had in the prison population. That would only have made things worse.

More importantly, Theresa no longer saw herself as a defender of corporate polluters, gun companies, and other stalwarts of the ever more rapacious plutocracy in America. With the money Theresa saved, she settled her parents in a new home in a nice gated community east of the Bakersfield city center. It bordered a man-made lake where they enjoyed the ducks and wonderful neighbors. She also left Quarry, Warren & Moschella. Tony Moschella tried everything he could to keep her there, both because he had grown very fond of her and because of her superb legal mind and courtroom abilities. His offer to advance her to a partnership vote in one year and immediately and substantially increase her salary wasn't enough to hold her.

Out of the blue, Theresa called Sophia and told her she wanted to be the kind of lawyer Sophia was and help the type of clients her firm represented. Sophia was surprised but realized what an opportunity she had. Brilliant, effective, attractive, aggressive, Theresa would be a superb addition to their firm. Sophia asked her in for an interview. Everyone who saw her, especially Bryce and Rona, wanted her there—and Theresa was happy to oblige.

\* \* \*

At Krause, White & Christopoulos on a warm mid-May day, Theresa was in a quandary. She did what was starting to become a habit. She walked down the hall to Sophia's office and tapped on the door, looking for advice.

"Yes?"

"Do you have a minute?"

"For you? Anytime. What's up? Everything working out here?"

"It couldn't be better." Theresa sat down. "Here's that methane leak class action complaint you wanted for the Porter Ranch residents. I think they have a good case."

Porter Ranch was a community in the northwest San Fernando Valley. Sophia represented a large group of homeowners there who had suffered from the effects of a massive methane leak from a broken pipe in a Southern California Gas Company storage facility. Sophia hoped that by filing quickly, she would be positioned to be designated lead counsel when the numerous other class action lawsuits were inevitably consolidated before one judge.

"That was quick. I didn't expect it for another week."

"I defended some class actions with Tony, so I know the hoops to jump through to plead a viable complaint."

"Impressive."

"Thanks." Theresa looked down. "I . . . well, I . . ."

"What's wrong?"

"Nothing. I just have a sensitive . . . well . . . maybe sensitive, sort of personal . . ."

"Just say it. That's the easiest way."

"Bryce and I have been . . . um . . . seeing each other. More than that, actually. We were never told about any dating policy here. Is there one?"

Sophia grinned. The relationship between Bryce and Theresa was no secret to anyone in the office.

"Not a problem as long as it doesn't interfere with your work here or cloud your judgment."

"Thanks." Theresa jumped up to go tell Bryce.

Sophia smiled and thought, *Nothing I said would have made any difference anyway.*

\* \* \*

At one o'clock, Sophia decided to take the afternoon off and do some errands. On the way out, she passed Paul in the hallway.

"Heading out, Sophia?"

"Have some things to pick up, maybe getting dinner with my folks. Any restaurant other than Greek. You know my dad only likes my mother's Greek cooking."

"You could do Taix."

"Good idea. We haven't been there in a while. My dad loves French country and bantering with those old waiters. Thanks."

"Want some company?"

"Honestly, I don't think my errands are up your alley. See you tomorrow?"

"Sure thing."

Sophia saw the disappointment in Paul's eyes, but her heart just would not take her there. It hadn't taken her anywhere since Steve was killed. Sophia had moved out of their apartment, and that helped. She bought a condo in the Silver Lake district, north of downtown and bordering East Hollywood and the Los Feliz neighborhood. It was gentrifying but still sketchy. Recently, there had been burglaries—close ones. She was worried, and so were her parents.

She drove from errand to errand, listening to KNX, the 24-hour news radio station. As she put her dry cleaning in the backseat, she debated doing her last errand. She had researched the Internet enough to make a decision but hadn't.

When she pulled away from the dry cleaners, the news reported that a USC law student had killed two armed men who broke into his apartment on South Vermont and fired on him when he woke. The student had bought his gun, an Arsenal AF 2011-A1 Double Barrel .45 ACP 1911 pistol, at a gun show that summer near Pomona with no background check, license, or waiting period required. Some called him a hero—some not. He was out on bail now after being arrested for having an illegally purchased gun.

*At least he's still alive*, Sophia thought.

Conflicted, she headed in the direction of her last planned stop.

She aimlessly circled around Griffith Park, then downtown, wasting too much gas and time as she equivocated. Then she set her GPS and headed for Bell, one of the maze of grimy small cities southwest of central L.A. She drove past her location on Atlantic Avenue once. Then, she hung a U-turn a block down and parked in front of a convenience store. The gutter was littered with discarded beer cans and other nondescript trash. She locked her car and went straight down the sidewalk.

She looked up at the sign reading "Western Firearms." She stepped inside.

* * *

At the counter, a black middle-aged clerk wearing a silver and black Los Angeles Kings jersey was polishing the glass case displaying an array of handguns.

"Can I help you, ma'am?"

Sophia studied the guns in the case.

"I'd like to buy a 9mm Luger, the Kahr CW9, with an extra magazine, and a couple of boxes of ammunition . . . make that three."

"Great choice for a woman. Easy to control. You'll need a license, a certificate showing proper training in gun safety and handling, and there's a waiting period. Sorry, but we have to do a background check, too."

"I understand," Sophia said. "It's the law," I happen to know that all too well."

"Cash or charge?"

* * *

The fate of California's ten-day waiting period for gun purchases is undecided as of this book's publication date.

## *The End*

**Review this book at:** https://www.amazon.com/Trial-Sophia-Christopoulos-Legal-Thriller-ebook/dp/B01AWZFU6G

**More legal thrillers by this author:**

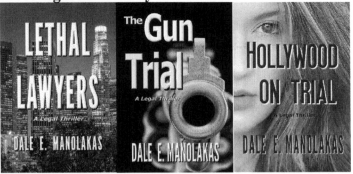

**View Book Trailers and Buy at:** http://www.dalemanolakas.com

**Sample of *LETHAL LAWYERS* follows:**

# PROLOGUE

### Number One With A Gun

The barrel end of a cold gun dug into Frank Cummings' graying temple, which was glazed with sweat.

"Don't. Don't."

Frank's voice echoed through the underground garage.

"Shut up." Jim Henning spit through his clenched teeth into Frank's face.

"I can fix it," Frank bargained.

The two men's eyes locked as they stood beside Frank's black BMW. Suddenly, Jim thrust the gun forward, slamming Frank's head down onto the hood, still warm from his pre-dawn morning commute.

"Like hell you can."

Jim grabbed Frank's suit collar, threw him hard onto the cement, and aimed the gun at Frank's forehead.

Frank gasped in pain.

"Wait."

Frank, a senior litigation partner at Thorne & Chase, looked down the barrel of the gun and then up to Jim's red, contorted face. He searched for the right words, just as he did to win over jurors and manage his law firm. He was a master of manipulation and needed all of his skills right now. He also needed to get that gun from this ex-junior partner, a man who was younger and had the strength of righteous outrage on his side. After all, Frank had destroyed him.

"The Management Committee will listen to me." Frank calculated his odds of grabbing the gun.

"They already did."

Jim lifted his t-shirt to expose a blood crusted bandage and black-bruised flank.

"What? I didn't know! I . . ."

"Don't play dumb. You sent them."

Jim crushed his tennis shoe into Frank's chest. "You're a dead man. You and your friends on the Management Committee."

"Wait. I can get you back into the firm. Wait. Please."

Frank's lie came rolling easily off his tongue. After all, he was a lawyer. But the word "please" caught in his craw despite the circumstances. Pleading was foreign to Frank's every fiber.

"You liar." Jim leaned over and aimed the gun at Frank's heart. "I gave up everything for the great Thorne & Chase and what did I get? Nothing. You ruined my life . . . my marriage . . . my reputation. You stole my clients and kicked me out with nothing."

"You can't do this." Frank changed his strategy with shark-like speed for a Hail Mary pass. "I could . . . but you can't."

Jim hesitated.

Frank had injected just a split-second of doubt. He saw it in Jim's eyes.

Instantaneously, Frank twisted sideways, grabbing Jim's leg and pitching him to the ground.

Frank hurled himself over Jim as he grabbed Jim's hands holding the gun. Locked together face-to-face, the men rolled side to side. When they collided with the tire, the gun went off and a shot resounded through the garage. The bullet plowed into the BMW's quarter panel with a bloodless ping.

The men rebounded off the tire. On top, Frank pressed Jim, full-body, into the cement. Frank sneered into Jim's face.

"Not so old after all, huh?"

Frank, the most powerful person on Thorne & Chase's Management Committee, was in control again. He savored the moment.

Suddenly, Jim twisted, throwing Frank onto the ground.

"Fuck you, old man."

Dethroned from his momentary triumph, Frank kept his grip around Jim's hands and the gun. As Jim whipsawed around on top of Frank, the gun became sandwiched deep into the bellies of the two writhing men.

The gun sounded again. This time muffled. And deadly.

Frank froze as he felt a warm liquid soak into his custom made shirt. Then, he felt Jim's body go limp. As Jim's head fell onto Frank's shoulder, Frank heard Jim's last breath gurgle past his ear.

"Christ." Frank pushed Jim's body off.

The gun lay between the two men covered in Jim's blood. Frank scrambled to his feet and backed away watching the pool of blood grow.

Then from the corner of his eye Frank saw a white cart with a uniformed security guard speed down the ramp towards him.

"Help! Over here." Frank waved at the security guard.

Confidently cloaked in self-defense, Frank gathered his thoughts. He worried only about spinning the incident so as to quell any bad publicity for Thorne & Chase. A gifted tactician and strategist, Frank started formulating sound bites that would fend off the news media. The phrase "deranged ex-junior partner" came to mind, embellished by "planned mass killing." After all, Frank surmised victoriously, who other than a mentally unbalanced person would try to take on Frank Cummings and a Los Angeles powerhouse like Thorne & Chase?

Frank took out his cell phone, found a signal ten feet away, and called his partner Chet Apel, the Management Committee's spin doctor and public face of Thorne & Chase.

"What the hell did you do to Jim Henning last night? He just tried to kill me."

⌘

# Chapter 1

### The Rainmaker

Two years later, Sophia Christopoulos sat across from Frank Cummings in his large corner office at Thorne & Chase. The law firm covered eight sprawling floors of the historic Pacific Coastal Building in downtown Los Angeles. He studied her legal resume, evaluating her for a first-year litigation associate position. Frank was the man who could make her life one of power and wealth or exclude her from that rarefied club called Thorne & Chase.

Frank looked up from Sophia's resume and observed her over his neatly organized stacks of files on his massive desk. He said nothing.

Sophia made the considered decision not to fill the silence. She wanted the first-year associate position more than anything, but was intimidated by the unchecked affluence around her. Sophia knew she could hold her own against any legal mind, but was a neophyte when it came to the highbrow culture of this powerful, international law firm with offices around the world.

She suddenly forgot her carefully prepared questions about the firm and momentarily worried that her blue-collar upbringing left her with no common ground for social discourse. She did not speak.

Frank glanced back down.

"Top ten percent of your class, a moot court finalist, highest grade in five classes, law review. Stellar credentials."

"Thank you, sir."

"I see you were a high school history teacher before law school, Ms. Christopoulos."

"Yes, I was."

"Did you enjoy it?"

Frank smiled for the first time during the interview.

"Yes."

Sophia smiled back.

Sophia was surprised by both his smile and the question. She couldn't see what her enjoyment of teaching had to do with her prowess in law school. She hesitated to disclose that immigrants from male-dominated societies, like her Greek parents, often made teachers of their daughters. It was an acceptable profession prior to marriage, after which raising and taking care of a family became the woman's career.

Sophia didn't know what Frank Cummings wanted to hear. And that was the bottom line in these interviews: tell them what they want to hear.

"I remember my history teachers," Frank recollected before Sophia could decide what to say. "They were nice people."

Frank had tipped his hand. The word "nice" reverberated in Sophia's mind. She discerned that "nice" would not cut it as a litigator in this kind of firm—"shark" would—"vicious" would—"bitch" even would—but not "nice." Sophia knew immediately she had to sever her past teacher-self from her metamorphosed legal-self, the self that clawed its way to the top of her law school's razor-sharp heap.

⌘

# ABOUT THE AUTHOR

*Dale E. Manolakas*

After a lifetime of writing poetry, books, nonfiction, and legal documents, it was author Ray Bradbury's friendship and encouragement that finally inspired Dale E. Manolakas to pursue writing as a career.

Dale E. Manolakas earned her B.A. from the University of California at Los Angeles, and M.A., M.S., Ph.D. and J.D. degrees from the University of Southern California. She is a member of the California Bar, had the privilege of clerking for The Honorable Arthur L. Alarcón at the United States Court of Appeals for the Ninth Circuit, was a litigator in two major Los Angeles law firms, and a senior appellate attorney at the California Court of Appeals, as well as an Administrative Law Judge.

Member of SAG-AFTRA and Actors' Equity Association.

**Author Website:** http://www.dalemanolakas.com. [Sign up for new release notices here.]

**Author YouTube Channel with Book Trailers:**
https://www.youtube.com/channel/UCac1mJynScdPG d2FVz1987A

**Amazon Author Page with Book Trailers:**
https://www.amazon.com/Dale-E.-Manolakas/e/B00H0FMRX6